At the height of his fame Alec Barr walked out on his wife . . . and into a frenetic life of wine, women and war. This is the searing story of a man in desperate trouble with himself. As Alec Barr searches for a purpose to his existence you follow him and his women through the feverish glamour of wartime Washington . . . into blitzed and battered London . . . among Manhattan's jet-set jungles and the real ones of Africa. THE HONEY BADGER reflects all the savage vitality and color of its author, who lived so much of his own story . . . "THE HONEY BADGER couldn't be any more self-revealing than if it came from a diary. Its hero—journalist, best-selling author, big-game hunter—is Bob Ruark . . . the reader will find few more fiercely honest self-appraisals in recent fiction."

—PLAYBOY MAGAZINE

ROBERT RUARK

THE HONEY BADGER

A FAWCETT CREST BOOK

Fawcett Publications, Inc, Greenwich, Conn.
Member of American Book Publishers Council, Inc.

A Fawcett Crest Book reprinted by arrangement with
McGraw-Hill Book Company. This book contains the complete
text of the original hardcover edition.

Three excerpts from this novel originally appeared in
Playboy during 1965.
"September Song," music by Kurt Weill, lyrics by Maxwell Anderson,
Copyright © 1938 by DeSylva, Brown & Henderson, Inc.
Used by permission of the publisher.

Library of Congress Catalog Card Number: 65-23822

PRINTING HISTORY
McGraw-Hill edition published September 29, 1965
First printing, July 27, 1965
Second printing, September 7, 1965
Third printing, October 19, 1965
Fourth printing, November 16, 1965

A Doubleday Dollar Book Club selection

First Fawcett Crest printing, September 1966
Second printing, November 1966
Third printing, January 1967
Fourth printing, March 1967

Published by Fawcett World Library
67 West 44th Street, New York, N.Y. 10036
Printed in the United States of America

This book is for all the nice girls who,
willingly or otherwise,
supplied the vital statistics without which
there would be no book

CONTENTS

THE
HONEY
BADGER

Book I/Amelia

1

It was that hot—steaming, stinking, sewer-vaporous, New York—humid, solid, soul-smiting hot. The penthouse reared seventeen stories above East-Side Manhattan and boasted peach trees on its terraces. No breeze stirred the peach trees, and the terraces were filmed by a fine loose soot. There was no air conditioning in the apartment, which was thick-walled-old-fashioned and ordinarily remarkably cool. Alexander Barr, dressed only in shorts, had just stepped out of a cold shower; two steps away from the bathroom, sweat had already begun to sluice down his face and body.

Alexander Barr's wife Amelia, remaking her mouth in front of her vanity, appeared maddeningly cool. She did not look, as Alec Barr felt, like a person who had just burst in from a world which was entirely too full of anonymous people, all of them obsessed with their petty selfish thoughts. A glass half-filled with what seemed to be gin-and-tonic stood quietly sweating at her elbow. A limp cigarette, its end red-smeared, smoldered sullenly in a lacquered tray beside her. Alec Barr had downed a swift drink as he had come in from the street—furnace-face greasy, sweat-slick, his shirt sticky-sodden—but the drink had only made him hotter. He had ferried his glass out to the sooty terrace, hoping for any small compassionate breath of air, and when he had gazed down over the tree-lined parapet to the streets deep below, he had been almost unbearably depressed by the thought of an unplumbed globe which contained so many tiny ant-people, all hysterically beset by personal problems.

Suddenly the whole wide world seized Alexander Barr's head in its great flat hands, pressed mightily, and squeezed his brain squishing out of his ears. He could feel the sides of his skull collapse, then expand, and where there had been respondent brain there now was only solid cement. He wanted to scream. He wanted to run and hide. He wanted to crouch in a cobwebbed corner and pull a blanket over his concrete-crammed skull. He wanted—he wanted—he did not know what he wanted. But he knew what he did *not* want. He did not want to go to the Hazeltines for dinner.

"No," he said. "No. I won't. I positively absolutely will *not*."

"Will not *what?*" Amelia asked in her standard let's-humor-the-child voice, turning from the mirror where she was drawing herself some new eyes with a paintbrush. "Hurry now, Sweetie; please stop fiddling. We'll be late for dinner with the Hazeltines."

Alec Barr stared at his wife dull-eyed, blankly, as at an only mildly interesting stranger. She was terribly pretty, he thought impersonally. She was sitting in her slip, the sexy black one with the lace top. She was wearing her chestnut hair long this year. She looks so pretty, Alec Barr thought again, but she looks so very like a cocker spaniel with her hair flopping long like that. She had already fixed her hair and done her nails. Her smart black dinner frock—a little Hattie—was carefully laid out on the purple spread of the king-sized bed. As soon as she finished her eyes and remodeled the rest of her face she would sneak the little black Hattie over her head, using a tissue carefully to be sure she got no lipstick on the dress. Then she would give another push to her hair, draw in her lips to spread the lipstick evenly, *smack*, and then she would turn again and say, as Alec Barr knew desperately that she would say:

"Honestly now, darling, we're running late already. Do stop roaming around and finish dressing. You know how the Hazeltines' servants are about sitting you down to dinner on the dot. If there's going to be any time at all for a drink when we get there, you really must hurry."

"No," he said again—had he said it once already, or had

he only thought he said it? "No. I won't. I positively will not."

Amelia finished limning her eyes and looked at him again, this time with annoyance.

"What are you talking about? Positively will not *what?*"

"I positively will not be late for dinner at the Hazeltines."

"But that's what I said." Amelia's voice was as irritably patient as any mother's. She stood now, a tall, oppressively healthy woman in her mid-thirties, the black slip molding pleasantly to fine firm breasts and a sumptuous backside compressed submissively by her girdle. She had a thin, fair skin, dark unseeing blue eyes, and a milkmaid's handsomely featureless face, unless you counted the short straight nose that wrinkled when she smiled, giving her a rather rabbity look. She was not smiling now.

"Please hurry, if you don't want to be late. See, I'm all ready except for the dress."

Alec Barr was not seeing the fine firm breasts and the sumptuous backside. He was not seeing the thin fair skin or the dark blue eyes. He was not seeing a tall, oppressively healthy woman in her thirties. He was seeing a pretty woman drawn by Dali or Artzybasheff.

Alec Barr was seeing a thermometer stuck into a sumptuous backside. He was seeing a chart which logged days and hours between menstrual periods, with red checkmarks against vital dates. He was seeing taxicabs panting at the curb, waiting for the fluid of life (produced by masturbation, trapped by contraceptive, caught after swift withdrawal in a cup) so that the recipient of wishful new life might rush speedily to the gynecologist, who would inject the fluid of life into the cervix, thus avoiding vaginal acids. He was seeing the slow paddle of spermatozoa under a microscope (sufficient, but lazy) and a clear picture of Fallopian tubes being sandblasted in order to determine wherein lay the fault of sterility.

He was seeing himself, Alexander Barr, as a sterile stallion, bought at great price, checked and crosschecked, stuffed on wheat germ until tassels grew from his ears—Alec Barr, stallion at stud who could produce no get from the willing mare. The physical pleasure was still there, if you could forget thermometers and Flit guns for the cervix and waiting taxis and knee-chest positions and sandblasted tubes and red-marked calendars—if you could forget the awkward silliness of old-fashioned Merry Widows, which he hadn't used since college and which aroused momentary merriment and lost erections—yes, the physical pleasure was still to be had. And Amelia was a very pretty woman if you liked composite pictures by Dali or Artzybasheff in which the machinery dominated the flesh.

"I positively will not be late for the Hazeltines, at dinner or otherwise, ever again. This I promise you." The words marched stiffly, like little tin soldiers, from Alec Barr's thin lips. "Because I have no intention of going to the Hazeltines for dinner."

"What *are* you talking about?" Now real annoyance came into Amelia's voice, as she looked at her husband, stuffing his shirt into his trousers with one hand and fumbling in his clothes closet with the other, in blind search of a necktie.

"I am not going to the Hazeltines now—not *now*, not *tomorrow*, not *ever again*, for dinner or anything else." He had captured the tie, a blue one, and was knotting it swiftly, sloppily. He reached for a coat that was hanging on the back of a chair.

"I am going *out*."

Amelia frowned and shook her head. The cocker-spaniel-ears hairdo bounced, hopping, froglike, from her shoulders.

"Going out where? What's the matter with you, anyhow?"

"In answer to both questions, I haven't the faintest bloody idea," Alec Barr said, and lurched into the August night. Nightfall had not helped the day. It was still steaming, fetid with New York's special brand of impossible high humidity. The smell of melted asphalt still hung in the new night air. Alec Barr was in a towering, unreasoning rage, born of an overwhelming combination of things—little worrisome, nettlesome, nerve-pricking things. He wondered as he walked, fuming, what he was so furious about, why he felt so frustrated, why he had made an ass of himself over such a simple thing as dinner at the Hazeltines.

"I'm tired," Alec Barr said to himself. "Tired. I'm sick of it all. The whole damn *schmier*. I'm tired of coping. I don't want to cope any more. I want somebody to do something for me, for a change. There's got to be something more to the whole business than being late for dinner at the Hazeltines."

It seemed now to Alec Barr that there were days when everything went wrong—cumulatively wrong. Things had gone awry before, of course, and he had coped. He had always coped. He was a natural-born coper. He was sick of being a natural-born coper. He wanted, he thought to himself, to have some fun that did not involve coping.

Perhaps the routine, half-apologetic note from a magazine editor had started the reaction. It wasn't an unusual note; Alec had a plump file of such notes. It had merely said "This doesn't quite come off the way I saw it when we talked. Something shaky in the middle. Would you mind running it through the machine again?"

Marc Mantell had attached the usual agent's small-stationery apologetic comment: "Dear Alec, I know it's a bore for you, but this time I think maybe for once Denby has a point. This last really doesn't sound like vintage Barr. It's a little too out for Denby's readers. I think maybe you went a little wrong in the middle bit where you have Steven leave Ellen. There really wasn't provocation enough to justify the breakup of marriage that solid. Not just a simple hot day. Try it again, will you? After all, it is a hundred grand for serial rights. *And please take care of yourself.* Maybe you need another trip to Australia or Africa or somewhere. I think you've been in New York too long. . . ." There was more, involving melting bank balances. In New York in summer, bank balances, like asphalt, always seemed to have a tendency to melt.

Then there was the routine letter from Aunt Sal back home in South Carolina, listing the expenditures of the past quarter. One thing you could say in favor of Aunt Sal: she was meticulous about recording the money she spent unnecessarily for the dubious benefit of Alec's father and mother, and, of course, herself. There would also be a list of downhome outlays from the Mantell agency. Long experience with the income tax-return reviewers had taught Alec Barr to pay everything by check, and as often as practicable via the impeccable accounting facilities of his agent.

The quarterly list from the Mantell agency would record a new and horrifying bill for hospitalization of his parents. Some people's parents collected old china or rare butterflies. Alec's parents collected impossibly exotic diseases of mind and body that called for utilization of equally exotic sanitaria and long-distance emergency ambulances. Anything that happened to them was translated in terms of an emergency. They never wrote; they phoned or wired collect. Alec's brother Martin merely drank; he had not yet achieved the chronic bad-check phase.

"But," Alec said wryly one day to his agent, Marc Mantell, "he's young yet. While there's life there's hope, and I shouldn't want Martin to be a discredit to the family."

Alec wasn't feeling so very wry on this hot Saturday of rejection slips and unwanted dinners. Sore and self-pitying would have been a better definition of his mood. He wasn't feeling properly grateful for Marc Mantell's obviously well-meant request that Alec take care of himself. It seemed to Alec that everybody from Amelia, his wife, to Marc Mantell, his agent, urged self-protection on him. Not, he thought, so much as a person as the purely professional facility which produced the other business commodity which appeared in magazines or between hard covers or was parroted artificially from the greased lips of former carhops who had achieved the title "actress" by freakish fortune and practical availability to producers' nephews. Alec was the primal source of energy which, properly channeled outward from a cluttered desk, wound up neatly on the best-seller lists of *The Times* and the *Herald Tribune*, and in turn produced a certain mild amount of fame and quite frequently a minor fortune.

If it had been Alec's perverse inclination to roam the snows without his rubbers and contract pneumonia fatally; to drink himself purposefully to death; to succumb to cancer or blow his head off in one of the darker moments of desperation which frequently attacked him, he had the unpleasantly uneasy feeling that both Amelia and Marc Mantell, as well as his mother and his father, his tax men and his lawyer, his secretaries and his publisher, would all consider themselves personally cheated, much as if someone had stolen something from them as solidly tangible as a car, a mink coat, or perhaps a movie sale.

It pleased everyone to think of Alec abstractly as indestructible—except Alec himself, who from time to time felt inclined to scream, drop in his tracks, and then quietly sob himself to sleep. But usually he would haul himself together and cope. Now he did not want to cope. This was one of those screaming and falling and sobbing days. Alec decided that it was a nice time of year to go immediately to Tierra del Fuego.

As he walked, streaming sweat in the late dusk, he thought glumly that he had suffered a vague discontent ever since that trip to Chicago. Not guilt; Alec Barr had been unfaithful before, and the little knives of conscience no longer stabbed

him when he occasionally stumbled and fell into a strange
bed. No, surely it wasn't physical guilt; it was morose dissatisfaction, dissatisfaction with Amelia, with their life, sour
dissatisfaction with himself. Chicago had opened a new door
—rather, it had reopened the old one. It was a door that had
slammed shut when the war finished and he came home to
face the gray oatmealy realities of the peace. The old,
secret door had cracked for just a moment, in Chicago, and
had revealed an Alec Barr he had almost forgotten. You
could, perhaps, credit some of the restlessness to Barbara, but
perhaps more than the fragrant brush with Barbara Bayne,
perhaps more than the grim mechanics of baby-building, perhaps more than the *Dear John* note from the editor and the
agent, perhaps more than the dreary bill from dreary Aunt
Sal for his dreary parents' dreary expenses, perhaps more than
the unspeakably hot day and the necessity of hurrying to
dress for an evening of refined torture at the Hazeltines—
perhaps it had mostly been those damned uniforms. Amelia
certainly should have chucked them out. She really shouldn't
have stored them up with all her other resentments in the
attic of the big house in New Jersey.

At forty-two, Alexander Barr was at a precarious age to
be confronted by both a failure at fatherhood and a memento
of a happy vacation from marital responsibility, tripping hotly
as it did on the heels of the recent small adventure in
Chicago with Barbara Bayne. It was a pity that he also, at
this sweaty moment, remembered Sheila. That was another
kind of war.

2

Alec Barr had been rummaging around in an upstairs store-
room of the Jersey house for a long-misplaced fishing jacket
when he saw the uniforms. All of them—dress blues, gabar-
dines, bridgecoat, raincoat, caps (both peaked and fore-and-
aft) and even some of the horrible pauper-gray working
clothes the late Ernie King had sponsored in place of lovely
fadeable khaki. They had been hung behind a secretive cur-

tain, had missed his eyes—and he was an incurable pillager of his own attic—for all the years since the Japs had quit shooting and allowed him to come home.

He smiled when he saw the full commander's cap with the dust-covered gold leaves on its visor.

"By God," Alec Barr said aloud—a habit which was becoming more and more prevalent, and which displeased him when he stopped to think about it—"by God, I really had my aspirations revved up when I ordered that bonnet with all the birdstuff on the bill. It didn't seem likely at the time that the Japs would betray me by folding so quickly."

He settled the full commander's cap on his head, and went downstairs to find a mirror. The full commander's cap looked pretty peculiar with his present working literary uniform of jersey and slacks, so he went back up to the attic and shook out a set of dress blues with two and a half tarnished gold stripes on the sleeves. He slipped on the coat, buttoned his blue wool jersey to the neck like a German submariner, and leered at himself in the mirror, cocking the bedizened cap rakishly over one eye. The coat still fit comfortably.

"By God," he said again, aloud. "I would have made a beautiful scrambled-egg commander. Who knows? If the war'd lasted another couple of years I might even have made rear admiral." Not very bloody likely, he thought. The Navy already owned too many pimply rear admirals since they stopped creating juvenile commodores out of adolescent captains.

He shrugged out of the jacket and resolved to give it to the Salvation Army, or somebody, someday. The full commander's cap he would possibly keep for laughs. It was at least as good a joke item as the crackerjack-prize theater medals he'd accumulated and just about as potent a testimonial to the heroism he never recognized, even when it was forced on him.

He walked back down to his working room and was, as usual, mildly startled not to find Amelia reading, belly-down, on the divan in the little morning room. Amelia never came out to the Jersey house any more. He really hadn't understood that uncomfortable position Amelia affected when she read. But then he had never understood Amelia very well, either, except for one thing: he had understood that she had a positive genius, a dedicated vocation for the ferreting out of small facts which would eventually prove unpleasant, if not downright horrifying, to know. That he had understood. The tracking down of those small defects in his character had mushroomed until he stood finally aghast at the total measure of his sins, of the petty grievances she had magpied over the years. That, he supposed, was what was happening—had happened—to the marriage. That—and he could not repress an uneasy, shamefaced grin—and the fact that he had contributed much more than a normal share of barbs if a girl were in the thorn-collecting business.

"I poisoned a pretty good well," he said aloud now. "But I wonder why she kept these bloody uniforms all these years? A kind of half-happy hair shirt to remind her of the only time I was out of the house without the suspicion of another competing interest or some other woman just over the hill?"

It had been a long time since Alec Barr had really given any serious thought to the war. Other thoughts selfishly occupied him: nagging financial complication, plot troubles, and a fretting over whether he would use a flashback technique on this new one or just try to play it consecutive and risk boring the pants off the reader. When Alec Barr was birthing a new book he was practically useless for anything else, as Amelia would have been the first to tell you. Alec Barr truly *missed* Amelia when he was working; he missed her having always been the first to tell you, out of passionate honesty, for your own best interests. That dedicated preoccupation with his own best interests was what had eventually killed much of the communication between them. Alec Barr was the kind of man who didn't want his own best interests flung in his face, because he hated to admit the stark reality of personal fault. He knew he had them, those fleeting faults, but if he ignored them, perhaps someday they'd go away. It was why he never showed his agent the rough beginnings of a book; he wanted it honed smooth and beveled at the edges before it came up for critical assault. That was why, for years now, he had never talked over his projects with Amelia—possibly, he thought again with hurt self-criticism, that could be why he felt shut out of his work and his life. Funny how a bloke only felt happy when he was either alone and Irish-morose or just about to take off and become Irish-joyous. Maybe that's why he'd felt so fully at ease in that long-past war. A war was just one extended night-before-Christmas-about-to-leave-town-operation, even after you'd already left and were desperately long-gone. Nobody criticized you then for leaving. There were no fights beforehand and no wifely reprisals later. The government underwrote the departure. You could be a dues-paying escapist with the full seal of Mister Roosevelt's official approval.

"I must say, Commander," Alec Barr spoke aloud once more as he looked at the cluttered desk and the half-filled page in the ancient Underwood typewriter which was punching holes with the *o* key again. "I must say that you were never much of a bargain for a lady, particularly for any lady with the odd idea that husbands come home occasionally for meals and might very well discuss the day's doings at the office."

That nonsensical personal reticence about sharing anything had applied even to the war. Through no real aim of his own, quite a lot of exciting things had happened to Alec Barr in the war, and he was seldom able to bring himself to speak of them. Somebody had asked him once: "But what did you do in those four years?" and he had answered, not meaning to be rude: "Nothing very much."

"But where did you go?" if the questioner was determined to persist.

"Oh, places," Alec Barr would say. "North Atlantic. Mediterranean. South Pacific. Islands. England. Australia. Hawaii. Just places. Kept fairly busy packing and unpacking. Sometimes scared out of my wits when I wasn't being bored to death. Not nearly enough whiskey most of the time. But the war gave me something to do with my hands." And dismissed it all with a short, entirely insincere laugh.

The War, Alec Barr often thought when he was thrashing a depressing bathroom combination of bank-deposit inadequacies and plot problems, had been the greatest single boon of a short and very lucky professional life.

The War, finally, totally, irrevocably, Had Gotten Alec Barr Legally Out of The House. It was a pity they didn't make wars like that any more.

The War had reduced Alec Barr to a gloriously unimportant cipher in an undistinguished mass effort. There was no place for a novelist or a playwright or a script doctor in a war. There was not even a place for a personality. Nobody gave a damn about a byline or the man who wrote it. As Lieutenant (jg) Alexander Barr, as Lieutenant Alexander Barr, and finally as Lieutenant Commander Alexander Barr, Alec had minded his manners, arrived at where his orders sent him, performed his duty strictly according to the numbers, and drawn down the same pay as any other naval officer who made lieutenant (junior grade) instead of ensign for a positive brilliance of birth that put him barely on the right side of thirty for a stripe and a half.

Alec Barr had joined the Navy, he said, because blue was his favorite color, and also he did not relish the discomfort of an Army career if fate sent him to a fighting front. Alec had lately been too self-spoiled and purposefully well-tended to deliver himself easily to plebeian mud and lice and cold and hot and sore feet and the GIs. The Navy was such a well-bred branch of the service, and if you did happen to get killed in the practice of playing Navy, the chances were you would be killed cleanly and swiftly and usually all at once. Alec had no intention of allowing himself to be killed; he was marinating several books he wanted to write after the war finished and time allowed. But he felt that he would be cheating himself of experience if he reinvoked his press credentials and allowed himself to look inward from the outside as a foreign correspondent for a big syndicate. Alec practiced only selfishness here. He did not want to cheat the postwar world of his personal effort in a major conflict. He felt he owed his body to the war of today if only to fulfill the promise of a conscientious mind tomorrow.

Quite possibly he could have persuaded the Navy to let him commit some semicivilian reportage in line of duty. All the services were competing with one another for self-applauding documentaries. But Alec Barr did not want to be a reporter any more, and particularly he did not want to be a reporter in a sailor suit. Once Alec had been a real reporter, a very *gung-ho* reporter, and the idea of perpetuating spurious sweaty youth was offensive to him. It seemed to Alec Barr an exercise a trifle undignified for men of age and achievement, rather as if Somerset Maugham were to be apprehended learning the Charleston, or Sir Alexander Fleming were to show up in sick bay with a case of clap.

After some early and rather frightening activity, Alec had quietly and unobtrusively created for himself an aura of Staff. He possessed the looks and bearing for Staff; he was lean and long-faced and handsome in a rather melancholy way, and his motions, although they were actually as precise as the movements of the Rolex he wore on his wrist, almost drawled in their deceptive slowness. Alec Barr was never a man to make another man nervous by ostentatious bustle. He eased through chores, and it always came as a surprise to a superior to find that not only had the tasks been achieved with a minimum of commotion, but also that they had been completed with rather more imaginative energy than the book demanded. Alec Barr had not counted on being sent to such places as Murmansk and Tarawa and Iwo Jima in line of duty. But, once arrived, he signed and took his noisy islands calmly in his slurring stride. Islands, for instance, like England.

3

Alec Barr owned thirty years of age when patriotism claimed him, and already he had achieved a distinguished complement of gray hairs over his neat ears. He was clean-shaven, always—the one mustache he had attempted in college had been a disaster—and for an author who had been successful for the best part of five years he looked remarkably unbookish. He brushed his ash-blond hair at a medium length, since he loathed the false boyishness mellowing men achieved via the crew cut as much as he loathed the idea of being a reporter in a sailor suit. He would never have to worry about his weight. He was reasonably ropy at six feet for the 170 pounds that clad him sparsely, and he owned the kind of long body which made all his clothes, from dinner jacket to uniform blue, fall from his bony frame in a casual attitude of tweed.

Most people, first meeting Alec Barr, were inclined to inquire which university he taught in, or at, and always seemed surprised when he explained that he didn't teach, he just sort of wrote things. Then they replied with remarkable regularity, and usually wide-eyed now:

"Oh, you can't be *that* Alexander Barr," and Alec would answer, with a practiced quirky smile of deprecation, "I'm afraid you'll have to live with the fact that I *am* that Alexander Barr, for whatever it's worth. At least I'm the only Barr I know that takes in writing for a living."

The absence of identifying procedure, repeated with unvarying dullness of certainty through his young-adult civilian life, was one of the major reasons Alec Barr loved the Navy. His wage rate did not compel him either to simper or smirk. The chief petty officers and younger officers who worked under him didn't give a damn about his book or his magazine pieces, or even about the mildly successful first play which was still running when he bought his bridgecoat and rehearsed a few practice salutes before the mirror. And Alec Barr couldn't help it if somebody moved him accidentally to some blighted island. That transaction was out of his agent's hands.

In the Navy Alec Barr had found a home. He was senior enough at the middle and at the end to claim bachelor-officer quarters without roommate. He eventually became vice-president in charge of security for an admiral who knew nothing about writing and presently did not wish to confuse the concept of his own future memoirs. The Admiral was a veined-nose submariner pressed into shore trade by an adverse physical, and his dicky heart lived at the bottom of the ocean, with a wishful periscope about to peep at something large which would shortly explode. The Admiral was happy with Alec Barr; Alec Barr was not always blathering about civilian trivia. The Admiral, sweetly brooding about the time he once sank two Jap destroyers on the same day, more or less by accident, would often ask Alec Barr, as a gesture of politeness: "What'll you do when this is finished, Barr? You're not getting any younger. And that last business in Saipan isn't what I'd call young man's work."

And Alec would answer, with his well-rubbed self-effacing smile:

"The same thing, sir. Write. It's the only trade I know, really, except maybe a little Navy, now."

Then the purpling Admiral would invariably chuff-chuff deep in his throat and say: "Oh, of course. I keep forgetting that you're the writer fellow. Dumb of me, maybe, except you just don't seem like a writer. I always imagined writers to be sort of wild-eyed Communist agitators with a Jew mistress and a permanent whiskey breath. And speaking of whiskey, don't you think the sun's over the yardarm enough for us to splice the mainbrace?"

Alec would always smile inwardly as he moved to the gin cache in the Top Secret files. The Admiral was really a very decent sort, and not at all stupid, but he spoke in naval clichés which he had evidently learned at his mother's breast, the teat tempered by a tot of issue rum. It was inconceivable that he would say "Let's take a drink" or "Let's have a snort." It was forever "splice the mainbrace," just as the Admiral, who was permanently enjoined from sea duty, always "went ashore" when he stepped across the street in Makalapa for a double Old-Fashioned at the Officers' Club.

It was not a popular trend for a great many civilians in a war to cherish the military, but Alec Barr, as an observant writer, was consumed with admiration for the kind of arrested mentality that could function in an approved military manner. He knew people who responded happily to such nicknames as "Thirty Knot" or "Take Her Down" or "Into the Stack" or "Let Her Rip" Jones or Smith or Brown, and they wore their trade names with pride and aplomb. They believed implicitly in their little war games, and the thought never, ever, seemingly occurred to them that the Japs and Germans they were so intent on killing today would tomorrow be their best friends and next-door business neighbors. They were actually furiously angry at the enemy. Alec Barr, being largely incapable of any encompassing anger, admired an honest juvenile anger when he saw one, even if the owner were an adult idiot. He was never angry when childish Navy business took him to a dreadful bloody kindergarten like Tarawa. He left personal sandbox anger to the Admiral. After all, the Navy had stolen most of the Admiral's other playthings when they took him away from the sea on account of his blood pressure. Alec Barr was an expert on other people's playthings, largely because he had enjoyed so few of his own as a young man.

4

There were, Alec Barr thought now—God, had it been more than ten years since the Japs hit Pearl and everybody went shopping for military suits—there were so many lovely aspects to a good clean war that kept the boys out of the saloons and didn't blow up everything in a purely civilian-directed fashion. The pervading *peace* of a good old-fashioned war was unbelievable. There was no hurry about anything. A seamed and sun-fried old Chief P.O., possessed of all the salty requisites of his ancient trade except a tarry pigtail, had once said to an eager-beaverish ensign: "Take it easy, Sonny. There's enough war here for all of us, and when it's over we'll have to go back to work." Alec, at a distance, had echoed "Bravo."

In a war there was no plot trouble. You knew how it was going to come out before it started. There were no real deadlines. If you missed the enemy today, chances are his brother'd be there for you to kill tomorrow, or next month, or next year. You could share a war with other people. A writer implanted himself in the dark womb of a cheerless back room somewhere and found himself assaulting the barren body of the Iron Maiden, a graceless wench sired without love by Underwood out of Remington. No jail was ever so devoid of human contact; no solitary cell ever so desperate in its bleak loneliness as that created by a typewriter, a man, and a sheaf of clean white cheap paper; virginal paper, clamoring to be impregnated with the involuntary spermatozoa of a loveless orgasm. In a war you merely initialed a sterile bucksheet and passed it into oblivion, like taking a casual pee in the back yard. You never had to copyread it later in approved obstetrical fashion, or even peer at the smear in the scope.

In a really righteous people's war there was no trouble with taxes. There was no vulgar competition for financial status. Everybody knew what everybody else was making when the eagle screamed, from the Admiral down to a buck yeoman. Rank had its privileges, and one accepted that a lieutenant (jg) didn't draw as much water or money as a man with silver railroad tracks or a gold leaf on his suntan collar. The estate of being an admiral was inconceivable, so you just didn't worry about it. Promotion mostly came by the numbers, and if you played your cards right, and the war lasted long enough, you might even make full commander and be allowed to sprinkle those scrambled eggs on your visor. If you didn't make the twisted-gold-leaf hat decoration that went with the silver collar badge, then what the hell? You called a lieutenant commander "Commander" just as you called a full commander "Commander." Keep your nose clean and one day they'd give you a discharge. When you got the formal farewell, your civil troubles would begin again, but you didn't have to think about that now. There was still enough war for everybody, even Ernie Pyle.

My Lord, Alec Barr thought. What a richness we owned in a decent old-fashioned war. A state of perpetual suspended animation, and a complete lack of self-determination. No decisions. No sweat. No real straining. Just an "even strain," the one that makes a "taut ship," the Admiral would have said, quite seriously, when he was eating out the troops in his monthly display of awareness that other people lived in the same world he occupied in his austere cell in the ugly barracks of Makalapa. "I don't want any goddam eager beavers," the Admiral would have said, "I don't want any son-of-a-bitch bucking for a medal. Just give me an even strain, and the ship'll stay taut. We don't need any heroes ashore."

I was an eager beaver once, Alec thought. I was the real ring-tailed Yankee-Doodle *Wunderkind*. That was when I had arches in my feet and fire in my eyes and wore the classic trench coat and waved a portable typewriter as a pennon. That was when I could use gin as a substitute for sleep and eat airline food without being hospitalized. That was when there were no mountains too tall, no rivers too wide. That was when I was like Jimmy James, and all the other Jim Jameses. Mostly what happened to them was that they either became famous, fired, useless, or dead. Jimmy James—Alec Barr winced. That had been quite some time ago, and it was so very very wrong that a young man would be a plank-owner in the permanent state of death without really having had a chance to be famous, fired, or become useless and uncertain of all the issues which used to be so starkly delineated in zebra stripes. Jim James—and Alec Barr was forty-two years old.

"Now why, of all days, would I be thinking of Jim James?" Alec Barr asked himself irritably, looking with distaste at a room which invariably roused such comment as "What a perfect place for a writer to work. You must be able to write wonderfully here."

It was a good room—actually, too bloody good a room for solitary confinement. It would have made a much better night club, Alec muttered through the momentary alum in his mouth. Jim James never would have made enough money to afford a room like this. Not even if . . . well, you couldn't tell. If you could be a newspaper reporter you could be a magazine man. If you could write for the magazine you could write a play. If you could write a play you could write a movie. If you had enough professional experience you could write a magazine piece which would sire a novel which would breed a play which would foal a movie. So if you could be a lawyer you could be a judge; could be a Senator; could even be President of the United States. Then you would be rich enough to own a room like this. And possibly hate it for its very richness.

The morning's work lay scattered on a desk big enough to kennel an elephant. There it was—ten typewritten pages. The afternoon's work would be another ten pages. Fudging a little, twenty pages would count seven thousand words. That was the day's output, six days a week, in this rich, rich room for a rich, rich writer. That's what kept the rich writer rich. Six times seven is forty-two, and twice forty-two makes eighty-four, and twice eighty-four makes one hundred and sixty-eight. Thousand, that is. One hundred and sixty-eight thousand. Words. That many words in a four-week month, with a day off each week to dictate correspondence to Luke. Good old Luke. All-Purpose Luke existed around the corner in an office which was much too rich for a mere secretary, but not as rich as the secretary's boss' office. You had to keep proper perspective, or the troops didn't respect the commander.

The workroom was enormous. It had been designed by Amelia for the express purpose of Keeping The Master Happy at His Work. Amelia was very good about things such as Keeping The Master Happy at His Work—or, more bluntly, indulging the small child who lurks in every creative man, and you *know* how creative people are. That's what makes them drink so much, but what can you do?

This was an elaborate playroom for a rich small child. Since the war Alec had investigated some of the more exotic aspects of the robust outdoor life, such as big-game hunting, because there had been a time when any author who did not write at least one double-size book on Africa was unworthy of the hair he wore on his literary chest. Here the trophies stared: tusks and horns, hides and heads, shields and spears, bows and arrows. Tastefully arranged, of course, like the big tiger over the fireplace. Stretched to the ceiling, huge and tawny, and all you need to really make the room, Sweetie, is a copper bowl full of daffodils.

God, I murdered a lot of innocent animals in the name of literature, Alec thought. Greater kudu, lesser kudu. Sable and nyala. Elephant and buffalo. Waterbuck and impala, Grant and gerenuk, Tommy and dik-dik. Warthog coming out of your ears, pig teeth on the beer mugs, and tusks serving as bottle-openers on the bar. Zebra on the floor, leopard over the bed, tiger over the fireplace. Me Tarzan? You Jane? All in the name of literature.

Bookshelves on top of bookshelves. The best leatherbound version of the *Encyclopaedia Britannica. Basic Plots. Extraordinary Delusions and the Madness of Crowds.* Hemingway Maugham Steinbeck Faulkner Wolfe Lewis Kipling Capote Stevenson Poe Conrad Dickens Lamb Boccaccio Du Maurier—name it, we got it, including Dashiell Hammett and Ray Chandler. Books on baseball, books on boxing, books on fornication. Clean books and dirty books, the *Decameron* and Emily Dickinson. Gallico and Galsworthy. Oh, yes! One whole proud file, bound beautifully in deep-stamped-gold-titled leather: *Books by Alexander Barr. Screenplays by Alexander Barr. A whole regiment of scrapbooks of magazine pieces by Alexander Barr. Anthologies in which* guess who *appears.* Jesus please us, Alec Barr thought. When did I ever have time to go to the bathroom? When did I ever have time to make the trips, shoot the animals, drink the booze, chase the dames? Christ on a crutch, when did I have time to go to the post office to send the second carbon? Been a long time since I worried about the second carbon.

The furniture's real nice, Alec Barr thought. The ashtrays are fantastically competent in a basically incompetent world. We perhaps own the biggest ashtrays, and the widest divans, and the most sumptuous chairs that any writer ever bought and paid for with his own little soul, with his own little two fingers. We got deeper-piled rugs, more ice trays, bigger-and-better converted lamps from old fireplugs, and scratchier long-playing records than nearly anybody. We got towels and Kleenex and no razor blades. I forgot to buy the razor blades again. Amelia used to worry about those details. Maybe I'd better saddle them onto Luke. Subject: Razor blades, procurement of; extra-additional duty, the Admiral would have said.

I forgot to buy the talent for the next six books, too, Alec Barr thought, like I must have forgot to buy a talent for loving. That they left out of me as well as the razor blades.

You poor self-pitying bastard, Alec Barr thought. You had it all and it's all your own self-created ashes in your own bitter mouth. Anybody else would have to buy a license to be you, and here you are talking to yourself like some kind of a nut.

What do you want to be, a Jimmy James? Dead before you eat the disillusionment? That's a long time, that dead. And what the hell is disillusionment, that thing you make for yourself, all by yourself, you creep? I don't like you very much today, Alec Barr, said Alec Barr. On you jerkery don't fit, and a jerk is what you are talking yourself into being. You are much, entirely, very much too old to be a jerk. It doesn't fit the distinguished patches of gray in your temples, or your general facial characteristic of Archibald MacLeish. The political poet. That's what I should have been, maybe, a political poet. A forty-two-year-old political poet.

He looked at the typed pages again.

"Perhaps you'd like it better if you still dictated it in cablese," he said aloud again, and headed for the bar for the drink he really didn't want. "Maybe you should have got your dear little self killed in line of duty. All the better ones did. Jim James gets killed, and you just get richer, so you can work in a rich room writing rich pieces for rich readers. Personally, I think you stink, *Mister* Barr," Alec Barr said, and poured a double dollop of gin into the old-fashioned glass. He generally took a drink when he allowed himself to think of youth—of youth and Sheila. He knew without being told for his own good that it was bad for his liver.

5 / Sheila

Sheila. Alec Barr sighed. He had nearly forgotten Sheila. Sheila what? Audrey? No. Aubrey, that was it. With the short-cropped black curls, the milky Irish skin to go with the blue-purple Irish eyes, the good breasts showing firm under the simple sweater. Lovely Sheila.

And that was a very long time ago. Like in 1943—March

1943, if he remembered right. Alec hadn't been an admiral's assistant then. He had been a humble lieutenant (junior grade) in charge of a naval gun crew in a raggedy-seat service called the Armed Guard. The Armed Guard officers and enlisted men were placed aboard the merchant ships which comprised the convoys which lugged America's vast production to dreary places like Murmansk and Calcutta and the Persian Gulf.

"Fish food" was what they called the Armed Guard in the early days of the war, when the Luftwaffe owned the skies and the Nazi submarine wolfpacks were bold enough to hang around American river mouths to blast Allied shipping before the ships actually put out to sea. The Armed Guardsmen were shoved aboard the merchant vessels ostensibly to man the guns, but actually to prevent a wholesale diversion of American merchant marine to Russia if the Russians suddenly signed a separate peace with Germany.

Alec had been arbitrarily ordered into the Armed Guard, like so many other civilian officers with no real mechanical skills—teachers, writers, lawyers—after a brief indoctrination. Four months after he bought his first uniforms Alec found himself shooting at submarines (with a five-inch cannon that certainly was salvaged from a courthouse lawn) on a coastwise trip from Charleston, South Carolina, before he even had a chance to form convoy in New York. For target practice he directed his raw crew to shoot at the masts of sunken ships that stuck up like antennae along the American coastline.

Each convoy—running upwards of a hundred of the slow Liberty ships—had a technical commander with the honorary title of "Commodore" who received the signals from the escorting destroyer escorts and corvettes for relay to the other ships in station. This "Commodore" ship was arbitrarily selected by the Naval Port Director at a convoy conference before the long files of ships formed outside and headed hopefully for Murmansk, shepherded through the angry gray Atlantic by a pitiful complement of American, English, and Canadian corvettes and DEs. Alec's ship was so chosen, on his second run, to herd the thin-skinned sheep, invariably laden with high explosives or high-octane gasoline, through the wolfpacks of *Unterseebooten* that attacked from New York to the North Cape and the Heinkels and Dorniers that filled the skies like angry crows once the de-

pleted convoys rounded North Cape. Murmansk was the
Death Run; the Russians were starving for matériel, and
the Luftwaffe had temporarily eased up in the Battle of Britain to concentrate on Russia and the supply lines that were
victualing Russia. England, almost knocked out in the First
Blitz, was breathing again, and clearing up some of the rubble.

The wolfpacks beat the living hell out of Convoy Fox all
the way from Sandy Hook to the Coast of Scotland. Flares
lit the night into ghoulish noon. Depth charges thumped
shockingly against the fragile bottoms of the eight-knot
merchantmen that plowed through dense fog, scraping bows
against sterns and butting into one another like milling cattle. It was cold beyond belief; the machine guns and Oerlikons were thawed with blowtorches. Beards clotted into icicles—everyone was bearded, because the touch of steel on
skin stripped patches in its path.

There was a twenty-four-hour General Quarters, and there
was one period when Alec never got off his feet for eight
days, snatching catnaps in the wheelhouse occasionally
when he came down from his station on the flying bridge.
Once, when the attack lulled, he took a chance and stripped
off his paper-lined convoy suit to shower his stinking body.
As he soaped himself, the attack alarm sounded and he
hit the freezing deck naked except for a helmet.

No day or night passed that failed to record the massive
display of exploding ammunition ships or the flaming,
greasy-smoking destruction of tankers. Slightly hit ships and
vessels two-blocking the blackball for engine trouble drifted
back and out of convoy and were left sorrowfully to be
picked off at leisure by the submarines. There was no attempt to rescue the survivors of stricken ships. In that ice-
floed water, life expectancy was something under five minutes.

As the crippled convoy hove into Loch Ewe in northern
Scotland, Alec reflected bitterly that he was the last survivor
of a shoreside poker game which had been running in New
York before the trip started, and that three of the four departed participants owed him money.

As commodore, Alec climbed down the accommodation
ladder into a leaping launch run by black-stockinged pink-
cheeked WRENs for a conference on the future of Convoy

Fox. A head count showed 32 ships out of 120 lost—and the worst was yet to come when they rounded the Cape.

The British Naval Officer-In-Charge was very young for a three-ringer. He wore weary red-rimmed blue eyes and a long, curly blond beard.

"You chaps proper bought it this run," he said. "I've been onto Operations and we see little sense in continuing the slaughter. The whole bloody Luftwaffe is waiting for you to round the Cape. London's as peaceful as a parson right now. Been nothing over it for weeks—for which thank God, as I believe we only had about six operable Spits left to throw up."

The NOIC paused for a second and looked at the small cluster of Americans.

"Of course I know this convoy's an all-American show, but you belong to us now. What would you say to a shot at the Estuary? Nothing much around to trouble you but the odd E boat. Nip in and be discharged in a week and off again as bright as buttons."

He looked at Alec, who grinned.

"I say, 'Aye,' and also thank God. There's no Luftwaffe at all over London?"

The NOIC shook his head.

"Pulled out to devote themselves to the Russkies—and anything that's going to old Ivan. I rather imagine the Murmansk thing has about had it. It'll all be going through the Gulf now, and then overland from Abadan. Not that this'll be too easy on you chaps, but at least it'll be warmer. I believe you blokes run a dry Navy. Fancy a tot of rum?"

"I'd fancy a tot of canned heat, if necessary," Alec said. "I'm still frozen."

The pontoons of the antisubmarine nets swept back next morning, and the convoy reformed, with corvettes hooting alongside, to make the quick and dirty run to the mouth of the Thames. They had only the tiniest trouble with E boats, which made swift abortive sorties and withdrew after two were blown out of the water. They sailed tranquilly into the Thames, and Alec's ship tied up at the Royal Albert Docks.

She had been made fast a very short time when another bearded boy—wavy-Navy this time, a lieutenant—came aboard.

"You're to secure your guns and batten down your ammunition lockers," he said. "There'll be *no* repeat *no* fighting your ship if Jerry does pay us a visit. We have our own gunnery control and we don't want any of your eager chaps shooting down our chaps by mistake. You can secure your ship and grant full liberty. We'll put our own people aboard."

He looked keenly at Alec.

"I should smarten up a bit if I were you," he said. "At least trim the beard and break out the Number Ones. You're required at your HQ tomorrow at oh nine hundred. Something to do with Intelligence and also Public Relations—shoot the gen back home to build morale. After that, I rather imagine you'll be free until you sail." He stuck out his hand and smiled. "Have fun. Pay no attention to the shambles. London's still a bright town, even behind the blackout curtains. Any amount of frustrated females milling about, and a sly-grog shop behind every third door. I'm told there's a fine place in Orange Court that serves a marvelous black-market steak. Somebody'll clue you in."

He turned to go, and then swung back.

"I forgot. They'll be sending a motorcar for you at oh eight fifteen. Wouldn't like to have you lost in the bus system, what's left of it."

Alec shook his head as he went back to his tiny quarters with LT. (JG) ALEXANDER BARR, GUNNERY OFFICER stenciled on it. It seemed to him that the British were very casual about their war, which they appeared to be losing by land, by sea, and especially in the air. The Russians were being steadily beaten back; the amateur American mother's-boy Army was being clobbered in North Africa, Rommel was running wild in the Western desert, the supply lines from America—if his baby was any example—were being amputated, and the RAF had been almost totally destroyed over Britain.

He went to the tiny stall shower down the alleyway and scrubbed himself raw. He shaved off the scraggly beard with relief, and decided that the first thing he would do was yell for the Gunner's Mate Third, who had been a barber, and get himself a free haircut. Then he would see to his guns and his ready boxes, batten down the magazine, and take a little stroll ashore to get his land legs back (the old bucket had taken an eighty-degree roll, forty degrees on one side and forty on the other, damned near capsizing her, and he had still kept his footing) and then maybe inquire if there were a pub near the docks where a man might buy a pint of mild and bitter and perhaps a chunk of cheese that didn't taste cabbagy like everything else in the ship's freezebox.

Alec Barr was more than mildly exhilarated as he dressed. The dress blues felt festive on his freshly washed hide, after weeks of smelling his own sealed-in stink in the convoy Teddy-bear suit with its felt face mask.

He had come through twice now, while others had died in the mountainous snow-capped waves of that cruel Atlantic, which was as gray as death, as permanent as forever. Many had died, but he, Alexander Barr, was still alive.

And he had, he thought, done a good job, although he had been frightened out of his skin. Not only frightened at sea, but frightened at the idea of indoctrination school. Alec Barr possessed no mechanical aptitude whatsoever; he could barely switch a typewriter ribbon, and the simple mechanics of changing a tire always managed to bark his knuckles. He had memorized his way through navigation and gunnery and seamanship, and had graduated with the others without cheating.

In actual practice-gunnery, on the shooting ships, he had scored well since at least, as a fair shotgun hand, he understood the axioms of leadoff that appeared to baffle the unsophisticated gun crew he was supposed to be training. He accepted his first ship at Charleston with trepidation but managed to make out a port-and-starboard watch list with the aid of a Regular Navy Gunner's Mate Second who had been banished to the Armed Guard for his considerable shoreside sins.

Now it all seemed pretty easy. He had his crew well in hand. He had learned much of practical value on these last two runs. The Armed Guard complements were generally drawn from the dregs of recruitment—callow farmer lads from Iowa, bullyboys from New Jersey, street fighters from Brooklyn. Destroyers and DEs and cruisers got the cream. The ragtag went to a service nobody wanted, under officers who didn't know port from starboard and who still called bulkheads "walls" and ladders "stairs" and decks "floors."

Alec owned one particularly abrasive character, a squat, beveled boy from New Jersey, a Polish kid named Zabinski. Every ship has its problem child, and Zabinski was Alec's cross. If anybody was drunk and in trouble ashore, it was Zabinski. If anybody was smoking in the magazine while the Baker flag was up for ammunition loading, it was Zabinski. If anybody was smoking on watch, or asleep on watch, or overleave, it always seemed to be Zabinski, whose pock-marked flat face wore a constant air of stupidity combined with sullen arrogance.

Having read *The Bluejacket's Manual* and the Naval Regulations, Alec tried it all, from confinement to ship to extra duty to patient pleading. Zabinski was impervious to it all. He would say "Yah," forgetting the "sir," and lumber sullenly away, his flat hat on wrong, his neckerchief askew, his blouse sloppy.

One day Alec lost patience. He also lost confidence, because it seemed that Zabinski was gradually taking his ship away from him. God knows it was tough enough running a small, underpaid naval complement on a merchant ship in which the Chinese messboy made twice Alec's salary and on which the Armed Guard was bitterly resented as upstarts by the merchant personnel. Discipline was tough enough without Zabinski around to foul it up.

One day Alec, tried beyond endurance, called Zabinski to his small stateroom.

"I've tried to reason with you," Alec said to the sullen Pole. "I've punished you with everything short of a general court. Nothing seems to get through that thick Polack skull of yours. I have come to the conclusion that the only thing you might understand is force. So I propose to peel these bars off my collar and take you out on the hatch, and Zabinski, I'm going to beat hell out of you—beat the bejesus out of you in front of my crew and the merchant crew as well. I've got some boxing gloves; Navy Regs say that they should be used for recreation. We are going to have some recreation."

A slow smile spread over Zabinski's thick lips.

"Dat's okay wid me, Lootenant," he said. "I allus wanted a crack at a goddam officer."

"You got it," Alec said. "Let's go."

They climbed onto number three hatch after Alec had announced the exhibition of skill and science for recreational and morale purposes, and the hatch was surrounded by grinning merchant personnel, whose grins increased when they saw the men stripped to shorts. Alec was lean and ropy, but Zabinski was a beer-keg of lumpy muscle. He shadow-boxed briefly in one corner of the hatch and Alec, who had covered sports, felt his heart sink when he watched Zabinski's footwork. The waddling clumsiness was gone; this man had been in rings before. Zabinski slid his feet the right way; he feinted and ducked and slipped and countered invisible punches in the air.

"The Old Man shoulda asked one of us," one of Alec's men whispered to another. "That dumb Polack was runner-up middleweight in the Jersey Golden Gloves. He's a cinch to cream the boss."

It did not take Lieutenant (jg) Alexander Barr overlong to discover that he was in a nonroped ring with a semipro-fessional. Zabinski toyed with him, using only a snaky left that chewed steadily at Alec's face, an occasional short right that landed in the stomach with controlled force. Alec's arms were longer, and occasionally he got in a punch, and Zabinski did not bother to move his head when the glove landed.

They were fighting two-minute rounds, with the merchant skipper holding the clock, and from the first five seconds of the first round, Alec knew that Zabinski could knock him kicking with a single punch if he wanted to. But Zabinski did not want to; he was toying with his commanding officer, and the snickers grew into laughter from hatchside. Alec could see himself losing his ship as Zabinski smirked and fed him light doses of leather.

In the third round, his face a bloody smear and his middle pounded pink, Alec held up a glove and said "Time!"

"I can't see," he said. "I'm going up to my quarters and fix up a couple of cuts. Take a breather, Zabinski. I'll be right back."

He turned and ran up the ladder to the boat deck and went to his stateroom. In the stateroom was a safe. Among the extra duties allotted to an Armed Guard officer was that of temporary paymaster in foreign ports. Alec dabbed the blood off his face, stuck a piece of adhesive on a split brow, and twirled the dials of his safe. He reached in and drew out a paper-wrapped roll of ten-cent pieces. He inserted this roll of dimes into his glove, flexed his fingers comfortably around the silvered weight, laced the glove tightly, and slid jauntily down the ladder, gloved hands supporting his body on the rails, feet not touching the steps, in the most approved seamanlike manner. He leaped up on the hatch and said: "Okay, let's go!" touched gloves with Zabinski, and bored in.

It had pleased Zabinski to allow Alec to hit him occasionally, in smirking disregard of Alec's punching power, and also because it gave him a beautiful opportunity for a short and painful counterpunch. He would look over his shoulder and laugh at his audience when he took Alec's best punch on the chin.

Now he reprised his act, jabbing lightly at Alec's face, then dropping his hands to give Alec a shot at his chin. Alec saw daylight, with the rock-ribbed chin in front of it, and swung from his heels. The silver-weighted glove crashed into Zabinski's chin, and you could hear the jaw break from Norfolk, Virginia, to Archangel, Russia. It started breaking under one ear and broke all the way round to the other ear.

Zabinski was out, cold, flat on his face. Alec looked briefly at Zabinski and then stared coldly at his own men, then even more coldly at the merchant seamen. He jerked his head. Blood flirted from his face.

"Somebody throw some water on him," he said. "When he comes around take him to the Chief Engineer's cabin. We'll have to fix up some sort of hawsepipe to feed him through, and I am no goddam mechanic." He leaped lightly off the hatch, pushed his way through the gaping crowd of sailors, and went up to his room to clean his cuts and restore the roll of dimes to the safe.

After that Alec Barr had no more personnel trouble aboard ship, and his crews chipped seconds off the time it took to get the guns manned and ready at the bullhorn blare of General Quarters.

Yes, he had his crew in hand and, what was more important, he had come through. If he could make it back and make one more out and back again . . . well, you were due for rotation on this run after six months—if you lived.

And Alec figured to live. He had seen others of his training chums foul with the death smell, the death feel, on them, and they had mostly gone *boom* within two convoys. Alec didn't feel like going *boom*. He felt like getting out of this ammunition-ship business and writing some pieces about it that would sell to the magazines, and then he would graduate to finer things, preferably shore-based in a comfortable billet.

But at least, he thought, *I've done it,* and I'm glad they hit me with a tough one first crack out of the box. My old man tried to go to war in the first big one—he grinned—possibly to get away from my mother, and he wound up with influenza before he got transplanted from the National Guard. He didn't even die of the flu. He didn't even get sick in uniform. He got sick at home, in bed, while Mother was being very big as an amateur nurse with a red cross on her cap. Alec remembered very clearly her coming home in the evenings, full of Florence Nightingale enthusiasm, to a house where everyone lay ill, including Grandpa, Grandma, Daddy, and himself.

6

A putty-colored car driven by an uncommunicative ATS driver, a mousy short-haired female who briefly curtailed his efforts at friendly conversation, conveyed Alec to American naval headquarters.

My God, Alec thought, surveying the shattered East End, the fire-gutted buildings, the vast bomb craters, the old Hun certainly gave this place a working over.

He found the naval people very friendly, not at all so condescending as the Stateside desk jockeys. Intelligence had a brief crack at him after a look at his logbook and then turned him over to the public relations department, which seemed more interested in Alec personally than in the actual fate of the convoy.

"You see," the lieutenant commander PRO said rather apologetically, "you're the first convoy up the Thames since the big blitz started, and as such you're hot news back home. And the fact that you're not exactly unknown makes you even more newsworthy. The Army's been doing a lot of Joe Blow stories from North Africa, and the Marines are getting their whacks from the Pacific, and the Navy's sort of sucking on the hind teat publicitywise Stateside. See if you can tell me how it was and, as a novelist and playwright, exactly what you felt."

"I was just sort of numb, most of the time, during the

attacks," Alec said, thinking: *Barr, my boy, you'll keep most of the how-it-was for yourself for future reference. Give Navy the facts and you keep title to the conjectures. You'll be sure to need them in a book some day.*

"There's really not much to tell," Alec said. "It was cold as charity and we had storms most of the way over and a lot of fog and a great deal of trouble keeping station. I personally was more frightened of some of those merchant-ship farmers we call captains colliding with me than I was of the submarines. We were under attack most all the way to Scotland. I actually saw only one submarine. The DEs depth-charged one up to the surface right in the middle of the convoy and we all turned to on him and blew him to bits."

"You have a hand in it?"

"I don't know. Everybody was shooting, including my boys. Who actually hit him is hard to say. But somebody did."

The PRO lieutenant commander smiled.

"Saving most of it for yourself, eh? You'll need clearance from Censorship in Washington, you know."

"I know." Alec smiled back. "I wasn't planning to do any writing at this very moment. I was more or less planning to get myself a little bit tight and explore the pleasure potential of the town. Remember, we've been a long time at sea. And how about hotels?"

"There're several where we can billet you. But I know the PRO gal at the Savoy pretty well. If you can afford it I can book you in there."

"Book me in there," Alec said. "I used to look at pictures of the Savoy in the papers when I was a kid reporter in Washington and wondered how it would be to live in it. Where's the action otherwise?"

"Friend," the PRO said gravely. "The action is *everywhere*. I would recommend the American Bar at Grosvenor House —downstairs. I would recommend a little club called The Deanery, just across the square from the Dorchester—that's Park Lane—and The Deanery is on Deanery Street. I would recommend any lobby, any bar, any café, any street corner, any park, in London. They tell me it's busy in Washington. Washington is a nunnery compared to London in this year of our Lord. The bombing released a certain amount of British glandular reserve on the distaff side."

"Fair enough," Alec said. "If you'll ring up your friend at

the Savoy I'll just go back to the ship and pick up some clothing. Where's newspaper headquarters, mainly?"

"Savoy again. Quent Reynolds runs a sort of open house for everybody there. Know him?"

"Slightly," Alec said. "Who else is around?"

"Harrison Salisbury. Walter Cronkite. Tom Wolf. Ed Murrow. Red Mueller. Any number. They're Savoy by day and Deanery by night."

"I'll bear it in mind," Alec said. "That all, Commander?"

"I guess so. Write some good pieces and don't forget to clear it with Washington, or they'll have your tripes as well as your stripes."

"When and if I write, I'll clear. Thanks."

"It must be kind of fun to go to sea," the commander said wistfully.

"In a grisly kind of way, it is," Alec said, leaving. "It makes the land seem so steady under your feet."

7

London, charred and scarred and bomb-pitted, blacked-out and hell-dark by night, beset by shortages and austere to the point of starvation, slave to the queue and the ration book, still had an almost violent gaiety. There seemed to be a total absence of fear, and the bravery was not bravado.

London was—well, chirpily cheerful by day and riotous at night. By day the parks, Green and Hyde, were blanketed by home-leave soldiers making love to their girls under newspapers. By night, in the bars and private drinking clubs and sly-groggeries, the roof was an introduction. You walked into the "American" bar in any major hotel, nodded at a lady, and left shortly thereafter for your digs or hers. She might have been a duchess or a tart.

Alec continued to feel the strange exultation of war. America, safe beyond the sea, could know nothing of this feeling. Amelia, whom he had left in Washington, knew nothing of bombs or bombing, of submarines and sinking ships, of the kind of—well, friendship, fellowship—that war engendered.

Polish fliers, RAF types with sweeping mustaches, bearded naval types, WAAFs, WRENs, ATS and ATC girls—girls from Ireland and Scotland and Wales who had come in to work for this ministry or that and who were out on the razzle after working hours—all drank and danced and freely fornicated out of war's peculiar friendship.

There was some resentment of the growing number of enlisted American personnel who crowded the pubs and out-bought the poorly paid local soldiery for the favors of the local lassies, but that was mainly confined to the outlying county towns. In London everyone was nearly on his own, on equal footing, except that the officers kept mainly to their own terrain, while the enlisted men worked the enlisted ranks of the ladies, apart from the tarts around Piccadilly and in the Strand, on Curzon Street and along the Mall.

With such a profusion of femininity, it was unusual that Alec did not meet Sheila Aubrey in The Deanery or at Sandy's or in one of the cocktail lounges.

He met her as he hurriedly ducked into a doorway when the Luftwaffe launched the first massive wave of the Second Blitz, three days after Alec had nursed his convoy up the Estuary.

She was remarkably pretty, Alec thought, black hair crisp and curly, snug to her head, eyes almost purple in their blue-ness, milky skin, and body full in the greatcoat over long slim legs. Irish for sure, he thought as she followed him be-hind the heavy felt curtain.

He took out a package of cigarettes and shook it at her.

"Smoke?" he said. "This ought to be over pretty soon."

"Thank you." She looked at him levelly. "I don't think it'll be over *pretty soon.* Not from the sound of it." She accepted a light. "This sounds like it might well be a big one. I'd almost forgotten what it was like."

"I wouldn't know," Alec said. "It's my first. But I'm afraid it's also partially my fault."

She looked at him through the smoke and raised an eye-brow.

"How could it possibly be your fault?" Another big-mouth Yank. In a minute he'll make a pass at me. Blackout makes the whole world kin.

"Well, I didn't exactly order it from Berlin," Alec shouted over the ack-ack. "But I sort of brought a convoy up the Estuary the other day, and I suppose Jerry got wind of it.

I've been told you've had quite a holiday from our friends upstairs until now. Perhaps this little visit is a gesture of discouragement for future naval activities of my sort."

"They do have quite an intelligence setup," she shouted back, smiling now. "Thank you so much for livening things up for us. I'm afraid we were growing soft—and the weather's been so lovely lately, you'd scarcely know there was a war on if you didn't listen to the BBC."

"My name is Alec"—the rest of his words were drowned as a bomb struck nearby and the building trembled. There was a crash of glass. The drone of motors, uplift by the thunder-rattle of antiaircraft batteries, made him shout—"Barr!"

"How do you—" There was another tremendous explosion on the other side and increased intensity of ground fire. "—do," she shouted. "We're lucky for tonight. They won't drop another in the same neighborhood. I'm Sheila—" Another tremendous explosion rocked the building again. "—Aubrey!"

"Your intelligence is all wet," Alec shouted. "Lightning does strike twice in the same—" Still another explosion. "Somebody up there is looking for us. What did you say the name was?"

"Aubrey. Sheila Aubrey," the girl shouted. "Listen." There was a lessening thrum of motors overhead. "Our chaps have them on the run. They really shouldn't have given us a chance to mend our fences. You'll hear the all-clear in a moment. See? The ack-ack's dying."

In a few minutes the all-clear siren wailed.

"That's all for tonight," the girl said. "Home to beddy-bye for me. I get up early in the morning. The Air Ministry needs me. So nice to have met you, Lieutenant—you said Barr? Even if you did bring this revisitation on our heads."

Alec glanced at his watch.

"It's very early yet. I don't suppose I could interest you in a drink and perhaps a bite of supper? I've done all the damage I'm capable of for one evening." He smiled shyly. "I'm rather short on companionship in this big town. New boy."

The girl looked at him coolly, appraisingly, seemingly conducting a short argument with herself, and then nodded.

"I suppose. You don't really look like that kind of Yank. I don't mean to be rude," she said hurriedly, "but I—"

"I think I know what you mean," Alec said, taking her elbow as they stepped out into the street. "Overfed, over-sexed, and over here. I don't bite. And I'm also a happily married man, if that means anything. We're not too far from a place called The Deanery, where quite a few of my State-side chums hang out—newspaper people, correspondents, radio types, like that. Or we might, a little later, be able to snag a taxi for the Savoy."

"Not tonight we won't be able to snag a taxi for the Savoy," she said. "Look at that. But The Deanery is just fine. I live a few blocks away, in Hill Street. It's walkable."

The Deanery was crowded, smoke-filled, noisy, bar-jammed, tables filled, wild with the hysterical exhilaration which follows air raids in which you don't get killed. Half of London seemed to have used it as an air-raid shelter. All the press corps, it seemed, had been drinking at The Deanery when the first wave of bombers came over.

"This is no good," Alec said. "Perhaps we'd better try the Grosvenor or the Dorchester."

"They won't be any better, not tonight," Sheila Aubrey said. "See here. Working at the Air Ministry entails a few perks. I'm just a hop and a skip away. I've a tiny flat with a few rather illegal things in the frij. If you'd like—only thing is I've no grog, except possibly a little sherry."

"That I can fix with my vulgar American money," Alec said, and fought his way to the bar, where he importuned the bartender. The bartender nodded negatively and then changed the nod to a smile, beckoning to Alec to follow him in the general direction of the WC. A moment later Alec emerged with a slightly bulging jacket.

"Let's go," he said. "Home to Hill Street." He gurgled slightly as he walked.

8

The flat was tiny; one small bedroom, a slightly larger lounge, a gas-ring-cum-refrigerator kitchen in an alcove, and a bath in which one might reach everything from any given position.

But it was bright and cheerfully chintzy behind the heavy blackout drapes, and there were daffodils on a small coffee table in front of a burnt-orange sofa. Alec set a bottle of Scotch on the coffee table.

"It's probably homemade," he said. "But this is the best I could do. At that place. At this hour."

"It's a miracle," she said. "That's the first full bottle of private whisky I've seen since the war started—or almost." She slipped out of her coat, and took it to the bedroom. "It's not very large," she said. "But at least I don't have to share it. There's only room in the bath for one pair of stockings at a time. There should be one tiny ice tray in the frij if you like ice in your whisky, as I'm told most Americans do."

"I can take it or leave it," Alec said. "In this instance I'll take it. You?"

"Just with a spot of soda. I like it warm. I'll be with you in a moment. While you're seeing to the ice, you might check what's in the larder. There should be some cheese and biscuits and possibly some sausage. Or I can make you an egg; yesterday was ration day. Certainly there's Spam, courtesy of your people."

"Sounds like a feast," Alec said. "I'm one of the few members of the military who actually likes Spam. Hell's horns, woman, you're got kippers and sardines as well. You must be running a black market."

"A girl does the best she can," Sheila Aubrey said, coming out of the bedroom. She had done something to the black curls, had freshened her lipstick, and was wearing a simple jersey over a tweed skirt. The jersey showed curves which had been hinted but not verified.

"Tell me about you," Alec said when they sat with their drinks.

"Simple. Born Irish. Raised British. I was orphaned early— father in the IRA business; mother of heartbreak, I should suppose. A sort of renegade aunt sent for me and I grew up in Sussex, hence no Irish accent. Went to school until the war came, and then I went to work. I didn't fancy uniforms very much—I mean I couldn't see being a WREN or a Fannie—so I got a job in the Ministry. That's about it."

"That's all of it?"

"Well, there was a fiancé, sort of." Sheila Aubrey poked a thumb at the sky. "RAF type. Didn't come back one day. Nothing much since but work. I decided early on not to become a member of the officers' mess. Not that it's easy these days, with everybody hurling themselves into bed after one cocktail. . . ."

"It would be difficult to resist the impulse to attempt to hurl you," Alec said, and held up a hand. "Have no fear. I appreciate the hospitality and shall not presume."

"If I thought you might I wouldn't have brought you home," Sheila Aubrey said. "It's the only home I've got. My aunt rather unfortunately got bombed out. What about you?"

"Writing type," Alec said, adopting her clipped phrasing. "Moderately successful. Married. Childless. That's about it."

"What kind of writing?"

"Newspapers first. Then articles for magazines. Then books. Most recently a play. It was still running when I left."

He lit two cigarettes and passed her one.

"Thank you. What is the play called?"

"Not without Laughter. Not a very good play, I'm afraid. But very commercial."

She frowned.

"I've read about the play, and I think I've read a book of yours. If you're *that* Barr, what are you doing in a Navy uniform? Why aren't you a war correspondent? Or, if you're married, why didn't you just stay home? I believe they defer married men over there."

Alec laughed and tipped another inch of Scotch into each glass.

"I didn't want to miss it. I wanted to be the first Barr actually to go to war. Grandpa contrived to get captured by the Yankees early, and my father caught the flu about the time World War I ended. I wanted to be a reluctant hero and see it from the inside."

"You're putting me on," she said. "I can't believe——" and then the alert screamed again outside, and the thrumming was heard again.

"Oh, God, they're back," she shouted above the uproar. "I thought they were gone for good tonight. I don't mind it once, but twice——"

Alec saw her——shaking, and put an arm gently round her shoulders.

"Shush," he said, in a kindly roar. "They'll be gone again soon. And we've had our near misses for tonight. At least this is——" Another bomb drowned his voice.

"——what?"

"A better bomb shelter than that doorway. We've got whisky and lights inside and the percentages with us."

After the all-clear Sheila Aubrey said:

"I don't really mean to be a ninny. But it does get on one's nerves. I mean, after it's happened often enough, and the windows blow out, and the lights go, and there's always a great hole where something familiar has been——" She was still trembling.

"Stop it. I'll have a look outside." He put out the lights, drew back the blackout curtains, and gazed at the night. Half of London seemed ablaze.

"It was pretty bad," he said soberly. "I'll have to wait, I imagine, before I can start beating my way back to the Savoy. Until the streets clear a bit, anyhow, and the fire brigade does its chores."

"You can't go back to the Savoy tonight," Sheila Aubrey said. "It's too far to walk. You'll have to stay here. And anyhow I want you to stay here—I don't want to be alone tonight. And I don't mean what you think I mean. I don't—I mean . . ."

Alec smiled.

"I know what you mean. And I know you don't. Sure, I'll stay, and gratefully. I'll just curl up on the divan and sweat out the dawn. Or we can both sit up and talk until morning."

Sheila turned and kissed him lightly on the cheek. She smiled mistily.

"It's not that I would actually mind so very much, but tonight, I—I just want someone near me without—I want to be held without. . . ."

"I'll hold you, without repeat *without*," Alec Barr said. "On that you can depend."

Alec Barr lay in bed, his left arm cramped by the head that nestled into his shoulder, afraid to move for fear of waking the girl who now was sleeping sweetly. He was wearing shorts and skivvies, the girl was wearing pajamas. She was very soft and fragrant as she breathed evenly beside him.

Alec Barr looked at the ceiling, considered his benumbed arm, and smiled wryly. He had stroked her into slumber as one might gentle a horse or a child. He shook his head slightly.

Of all the women in London you might go to bed with,

he thought, *the sailor fresh from the sea has to wind up
with a platonic roommate.* Here I lie-abed with a beautiful
girl I've not so much as kissed. Amelia would never believe
it. He dozed lightly before he was wakened by a slight touch
on the shoulder.

"There's tea, if you'd like some," Sheila said, coming into
the room in a dressing gown. "Did you sleep at all? And I'm
sorry I was such a mess last night. But thank you, Alec.
Thanks terribly."

Alec scrubbed the back of his hand across his face. His
mouth was dry and gummy.

"Slept like a log," he lied. "And no thanks necessary. You
wouldn't have such a thing as a razor handy, would you? I
hate to walk into the Savoy, if it's still standing, with a green
beard like this one. Navy Regs and all that."

"I would indeed," she said. "And also the egg we didn't eat
last night."

"There were quite a lot of things we didn't do last night,"
Alec said, getting into his pants. "It was sort of an unusual night."

Sheila Aubrey smiled and wrinkled her nose.

"I'm quite free this evening if you have nothing better to
do," she said. "I'm off early. Fiveish."

"I have nothing better to do I wouldn't cancel. Meet me
at the Savoy—in the bar?"

"Love to," she said, and kissed him briefly on the cheek
as he went out the door to search for a cab.

Alec logged in later with naval headquarters and was informed that his ship had taken a hit in last night's bombing.
Nothing really severe, but troublous enough to warrant the
attention of the commanding officer. The number-one stern
gun was loose from its moorings, and a couple of Oerlikons
were past redemption. There was some damage below decks.
It would be appreciated if—

Alec was driven down to the East End by another mousily
anonymous female driver to find a British repair crew already busy with blowtorches and welding apparatus. Four
P.M. still saw him busy. He went ashore and rang up the Air
Ministry, and was eventually put through to a Miss Aubrey
in Coding.

"I'm dreadfully sorry," he said. "But I'm afraid our Savoy
date is off. My old bucket took a little beating from that
business last night, and I'm up to my ears with your country-

men, who seem to want to work around the clock. There's some damage down below that can be repaired at night—damage that'll prevent discharge unless it's fixed fast, and we are aiming for a speedy turnaround. Sorry. Maybe tomorrow?"

"Tomorrow's fine," Sheila Aubrey said. "But I've a better idea. If you finish any time before midnight, why don't you come round to the flat and we'll have another quiet evening. Maybe we won't even have to shout. There's still some of your whisky left."

"Lovely. If I can possibly wind up here, you'll find me knocking on your door."

Alec got out of his working khaki at 8 P.M. and whistled while he shaved carefully again and flicked a quick brush over his blues. You had to hand it to the Limeys, he thought. They had accomplished in a day what it would take a week to do in Hampton Roads back in the States. The battered old bucket had been welded back as good as—or possibly better than—new. Maybe the Blitz had taught the Limeys how to turn to and get things done in a hurry—the air-raid wardens, the fire-brigade boys, the bomb-disposal squads. He whistled. Here it was only just past eight and with luck he'd be back in the West End by nine. If he were just lucky enough to find a taxi. . . .

The evening promised much. What a lovely girl, this Sheila, whom he'd met in the doorway—what a beautiful girl, what a nice girl, what a sweet girl—and after his exemplary behavior of last night, what a gorgeous promise of things, more serious things, to come. He whistled and silently applauded himself for taking no advantage of proximity last night. When the moment came it would come, with full eagerness on both sides, because time was short and she knew time was short, that he'd be shipping out again in a week or less.

Sheila was no tart, no military mattressback, like the easy ones he'd seen in the hotels and bars and clubs. But at the same time she was all woman—she'd been engaged and semi-widowed in wartime, and she knew the briefness of time in war. There was no thought of Amelia, of infidelity, here. This was wartime in London. There were submarines beneath the sea and aircraft overhead. Time was short, and time was also sweet. And tonight Sheila would come as sweetly into his arms, and not merely for comfort, like a child in the dark.

God smiled. Alec walked off the docks and beheld a taxi. The cabbie was agreeable, he was going back to the West End anyhow.

"Took a proper pounding, we did, last night," the hacker said almost with pride. "Where to, Guv?"

"Hill Street," Alec said. "And step on it as much as you can. I've got a lovely lady waiting."

"Too right, Guv," the hacker said and winked. "Nuffink like a war for lovely lydies, eh?"

"Too right," Alec said shortly, and settled back in the corner of the cab to meditate on fate and blackouts and air raids and doorways and lovely girls named Sheila.

They were coming into Grosvenor Square when the air-raid siren went.

"Cor," the driver said. " 'E's back agyne. I can just get you to Grosvenor 'Ouse, unless you want a shelter?"

"Make it Grosvenor House," Alec said. "Damn it to hell. In another five minutes I'd have been at Sheila's. Well, I can beat it over there after the all-clear."

"Wot was that?" the driver asked, as the thrumming grew and the antiaircraft began to bark in the distance.

"Nothing," Alec said. "Step on it."

The driver drew up in front of Grosvenor House. Alec paid him and dashed inside. The lobby was jammed, and so was the American Bar downstairs, but he managed to wriggle through to the bar and extract a large Scotch from the bartender.

Jerry was over in force tonight, and he seemed to have abandoned the dock area for a repeat run on the West End. The crump of big bombs rattled the windows. Once the hotel appeared to have been straddled—how close, it was difficult to say. The ack-ack batteries in Hyde and Green parks rattled your teeth as well as the windows, and you could hear the scream of the Spitfires over the steady thrumming of the big bombers. After half an hour the thrumming died again, as on the night before, and the ack-ack faded as the Nazi striking force headed back to Holland.

"Nasty one, that," the man next to Alec said. "I don't mind it so long as they concentrate on the docks. It's when they plonk one straight down the Café de Paris that a bloke feels uncomfortable. Bastards have no class consciousness. That's the trouble with the Hun."

When the all-clear sounded Alec stepped out into the

night again, and once more found London stabbed and ringed round with fire. Ambulances screamed, and the rescue-and-fire teams were already at work.

He picked his way through rubble in the general direction of Hill Street, uncertain still of London topography, and after several blocks concluded that he was lost. But no—the fires were bright enough for him to pick out a sign, HILL STREET. He recognized the corner.

His feet carried him numbly in the direction they'd taken last night, in the dark, and suddenly his stomach twisted.

There was no bell to ring.

There was no door for him to knock on.

There was no house behind the door.

There was no girl in the house that was not behind the door which had no bell for him to ring.

There was no girl. There would never be a girl—not *that* girl.

Alec Barr awoke next morning, his mouth brassy and foul from whisky. The girl, some loose-lipped painted wench he had collected somewhere, was gone. His pillow was still wet with what, he supposed, were tears.

---

9 / Barbara

He had embarked on a lecture tour starting in Chicago, just after the birth of a new book, had got himself drunk because he hated what he was doing, and he was wearing such a crashing hangover on the plane that it was an hour before he noticed his seatmate, who had settled in a sort of blonde mist beside him.

"They don't seem to serve any booze on this flight," a soft, clearly enunciated voice roused him from his drowsing limbo. "I just happen to be the sort of old-fashioned girl who packs a flask in her handbag. I think you ought either to be revived or else be put entirely out of your misery, Mr. Barr. Which will it be?"

"You know me?" Alec asked foolishly, blinking. The light hurt his scratchy eyes. "Have we met?"

"I know you. You're not entirely unknown. I haven't actually met you, but they put you on jackets of books and also in newspapers. As a matter of fact, we're on the same TV panel show after you do your little rope trick for your publishers. I'm called Barbara Bayne. I am a professional bad actress."

Alec blinked again, this time slightly less stupidly, and accepted the half-pint hammered-silver flask. His eyes focused painfully.

"Of course I know you. I've seen dozens of your movies. But you were brunette then. And that last play, the one that—"

"Folded after five performances? You saw that, too, did you, and you're still willing to drink my whisky?" Barbara Bayne's voice was very cheerful for a morning flight to a grimy wind-nagged city Alec hadn't wanted to visit until this moment.

"Actually I didn't think the play was all that bad. And I thought you were—"

"*Adequate,* the critics said. That's about all they ever see in me, that nasty word—adequacy. But the truth is that I do direct easily and rarely feud with the other, better actors. That makes me constantly hireable. You want some water with that Scotch?"

"Nunh-uh." Alec shook his head, then bowed slightly at Barbara Bayne. "I intended to take this one straight. I need the transfusion. You not having any?"

"Not until you take me to lunch in Chicago," Barbara Bayne said sweetly. "I've been waiting for this moment for years. And I did think your last book, that *Total Loss,* was magnificent. Must have been hauled straight out of your guts."

Alec Barr took a deep pull at the flask and shuddered.

"It did. Come out of my guts, I mean. But it's the last intestinal gesture. Anyhow it's a very nice compliment, and I would love to take you to lunch. And I would also love to take you to dinner, and I would also—"

Barbara Bayne smiled, the dimple deepening.

"No. That'll have to come much later."

Alec could feel himself blush. He groped for cigarettes and offered her one, using the motion as an excuse for closer inspection. Barbara Bayne had a clear cameo face and that one very deep dimple.

"I meant to say there's a fair fight on tonight which I thought might amuse you, if you like fights." He made conversation.

"I like fights," said Barbara Bayne, "of all kinds. I'd love to see a prize fight for real."

"You look larger on the stage," he said through the cigarette. "And older. You look very wicked and worldly in the movies. But I suppose that's because you were brunette. I suppose you'll hate me for saying that close-up you look both younger and prettier. And vastly more innocent."

Barbara Bayne dipped her shining blonde head and produced a fair imitation of bridling.

"It's my hairdresser's fault," she said. "I really don't know what the pansies are plotting from day to day. I'm told the fluffy-duckling bit goes very well with my special kind of beady brown eyes."

"I'd like you if your eyes were pink. And crossed. That's my first compliment from your whisky, and so I think I shall invade the flask again and appear at some later stage resembling normal. Then I make compliments on my own time."

He drank again, and handed back the flask.

"Is your name really Barbara Bayne?"

"The Barbara is square enough. But it didn't go very well with O'Shaughnessy, which is what I was born, and the first agent I ever had decided in favor of Bayne. I think he actually meant *bane*, which is precisely what I must have been to his existence at the time. My married name is Emory. You know—*that* particular Emory, with the noble nose and the superb lack of acting ability. We're in process of final disenchantment, legally. I find that two bad actors never made a summer."

"It's a refreshing view to take," Alec said. "All the actors and actresses I ever met, onstage and off, seem to have the idea that Duse constituted a personal affront to their individual talent, and that Bernhardt was barely making it in summer stock."

"It's a common failing in the trade, and I don't honestly find much difference between actors and writers. But I must say you don't look like a writer. You look more like a reasonably successful stockbroker. Do you act like a writer?"

"No. Thank you." Alec Barr shook his head again. "Most people say I look like a reasonably successful professor. And I have very little hair on my chest, and practically no colorful peculiarities."

"You're much too tidy for a professor. Not tweedy enough. Where's your pipe, if you're a real author? Where's the thing you rub against your nose to improve the publisher's grain?"

"Ungot. Hate 'em. Bulge your clothes and stink up ashtrays. Air of spurious manliness. Air of false intellectuality. Love cigarettes. Cinch for lung cancer by age fifty. Filthy habit, but I'd rather give up food, whisky, or sex than nicotine."

"In which order?" Barbara Bayne murmured. By God, she wasn't just a pretty face. There was cleanness and good strength in the bone structure.

"Well, food and whiskey, anyhow," Alec smiled. "I say, you are a lovely lady, now the alcohol's at work. Maybe even without it. You've a nice early-morning face."

"Thank you, kind sir. That's a pretty turn of phrase. I might say the same for you. Even with that hangover you're wearing instead of a pipe. And you really don't strike me as the mysterious sort of public kind of writer with something very important to say that nobody really understands but you."

"I am really only a professional writer who makes a decent living writing. If anything important slips out it's largely accidental. I'm afraid I don't qualify for the Faulkner-Hemingway school of offstage eccentricity. I just sort of write, dull-like, daily, and hope my agent doesn't grimace too much when he gets the copy. He's been known to. He's got the face for it."

"No pride of authorship? No reassessment of the priceless pearls that spill from your fingers? No hammer-and-tongs warfare with your employers over a delicate, if possibly moot, point of craftsmanship?"

"Very little. Practically none." Alec Barr grinned uneasily. "I don't like to sound smug, but I've been a pro for such a long time. I'm like a good, sturdy whore. I can handle any number of sailors on any given night."

"You sound like a publisher's dream author," Barbara Bayne said. "Any other noble aspects of character? Not even a touch of ordinary artistic temperament? Wife-beater? Dog-

kicker? Child-hater? I know you have a wife, of course.
I've seen her quite often at '21.' She's very pretty."

"Thank you. She *is* very pretty, and she's also a very nice
woman. She has one basic fault. I've a feeling she understands me too well. That's to say I think she knows I'm a
rotten husband. I think she hates the mistress I keep in the
back room."

There was no intentionally coy blankness on Barbara
Bayne's face.

"That lousy typewriter?"

"That lousy typewriter. The unfortunate thing is that I
don't know any other way to make a living. And, equally
unfortunately, when you're being director, production manager, producer, scripter, and all of the actors, young and old,
male and female, black and white, you're so bloody tired at
the end of a day in the embrace of the Iron Maiden that
you've lost your own identity. All you want to do is sink a
couple of fast martinis and fall in bed with your book on
your subconscious back, so you can get up and tackle the
whole dreary mess again tomorrow. Eventually you may have
a book but you've mostly canceled out yourself as a human
being in the dismal process of building it."

Barbara Bayne burlesqued a shiver.

"If I'm not being too personal, what does your wife actually
do when you're pregnant with a new literary baby?"

"I really don't know," Alec Barr answered seriously. "The
usual things, I guess. House. Hairdresser. Clothes. Theater.
She reads a lot, too. Some charity nonsense, I suppose. The
usual. We don't have any kids."

"Gracious," Barbara Bayne said. "I don't think I'd want
you permanently for a house pet. Don't you ever have any
fun?"

"Not when I'm working. I'm generally much too tired.
Once in a while I used to take off and go looking for what
you might call fun, but I find I don't care much for
carousing any more. I have vicious hangovers and I'm sort of
shy about sleeping with people I don't know very well."

"It's my personal opinion that your chromosomes have
seized, friend," Barbara Bayne said. "I think your genes have
frozen, or something. Your psyche needs a little shaking up.
Shall we attempt it tonight after the work's done? After the
fight's over?"

"Consider me shook," Alec Barr said. "Well, here's Chi-

cago. You made it a very short trip. Thanks. Now if only we
don't crash coming into this lovely inefficient airport."

"We'd only be following the current fashion if we did,"
Barbara Bayne said. "Now I'm hungry and terribly thirsty
and I haven't been to the Pump Room in a coon's. I warn
you, I'm expensive to victual. I'm a very strong girl, and I
need my steady rations."

"I brought some money with me and have beautiful credit
cards as well," Alec Barr said. The plane landed with a bump.
"Well, we made it alive again. Come on, let's go produce a
taxi and hasten to the Pump. Not to insult the handy flask,
which saved my life, but I'm mostly a martini man at midday."

"You bought yourself a boy," Barbara Bayne said. "Let's
go. I hope you don't object to holding hands in public. It's
a lousy sentimental habit of mine."

"In your case I'll break a long-established rule against
public handholding," Alec Barr said. "I might even grow to
like it."

"You know something, Barr?"

They were walking off the airstrip now, heading for the
terminal.

"What?"

"I don't think you've got a chance," Barbara Bayne said.

10

"I don't know if this thing is going to be worth our effort,"
Alec said.

"It seems to me there's more bums around than when I
was a boy. Last really good one I saw was the first Louis–
Conn, just after the war, when Conn had old Joe loopy until
Conn got cocky and Joe cooled him."

They were having a quick dinner before the fight, which
was supposed to be for the honor of meeting the middleweight
champion of the world at some future date to be decided
by the television sponsors.

"I have never heard of either one of these guys, but then I

don't follow fights much any more. I know some names like Sugar Ray and Marciano and Graziano, sure, but there aren't any Barney Rosses around—no Henry Armstrongs, no Lou Amberses, not to mention the Baer boys and Ceferino Garcia and, God help us all, Tony Galento. I saw most of the good ones—I should say all the real good ones—before the war. After the war I switched from prize fights to bullfights. At least the bull is honest."

Barbara took a bite of her steak.

"I love 'em, bums or not," she said. "I watch them on TV all the time. But I never saw one in the flesh before."

Alec shook his head.

"It's the TV—and prosperity—that's ruined the racket. Television killed all the little clubs where kids really learned how to fight before they got tossed in against real opposition. And prosperity ruined the burning urge. Who wants a busted nose and a lumpy ear any more when he can make a hundred bucks a week as an office boy, and three hundred as a plumber? A growling belly made the good fighters. It was the only way they could struggle up from the streets."

He looked at his watch and called for the check.

"About time we got moving if we're going to see Tiger Taggert demolish Bolo Bermudez. It's an unusual fight for these times. The Tiger is actually white. I thought we'd about run out of white fighters."

They pushed their way down the aisle to the third row.

"Why, you've got working-press seats," Barbara said, impressed.

"Hell's delight, honey, anything for a hundred rows back is called 'working press' these days. It's a status symbol. And some of the boys still remember me from the good old days of Jacobs' Beach, when I covered these things."

A gnomish, almost-albino man turned from a corner of the ring, caught Alec's eye, and waved.

"Hi, Whitey," Alec yelled through the smoke. "That's Whitey Bimstein—probably the greatest and most imperishable handler of all time. See Whitey with a couple of swabs in his mouth and you know nobody's gonna call the fight on account of blood. He and Ray Arcel were the best."

An owl-eyed Italian waved from the other side of the ring.

"Chris Dundee. He's promoting his own stuff now. I knew him when he was a manager and strictly from hunger. I suppose I knew 'em all. Lou Diamond. We called him 'The

Honest Brakeman' because he never stole a boxcar. Al Weill
—who had Ambers and retired him when Lou didn't have it
any more. Fat Eddie Mead and his Indian princess. I guess
I knew them all when I was young and eager to learn about
everything."

"You like remembering it, don't you?"

"I suppose. I like remembering the night that Galento, full
of beer, caught a prime Louis with a surprise left hook
and damned near chilled him. And I remember a night in
Washington when Buddy Baer, who wasn't much fighter,
started a right hand in Bethesda and hit Joe on the chin and
knocked him clean out of the ring and into my lap. You
could have scraped my eyes off with spoons. But Joe always
came back and demolished the people who got lucky with
him—that is, until his legs went and Marciano persuaded him
to retire. With a lot of right hands."

The announcer was introducing the fighters.

The white boy, Tiger Taggert, was lean and freckled and
tow-headed and looked mean. He also looked durable. The
colored boy, Bolo Bermudez, was compact, with no rough
edges, no corners.

"He's a Cuban," Alec said. "There's one country that's still
hungry enough to produce good fighters from the canefields.
They get a lot of practice swinging that *machete* for ten cents
a day. I will bet you two to one—ten bucks to five—on the
Cubano."

"You've seen the odds?"

"There aren't really any important odds on a fight like
this. Six to five and take your pick. You want it the other
way round, I'll give you two to one and take the white boy."

"I'll go with the Tiger," Barbara said. "He looks like a
hitter. Lots of leverage in those long arms."

"Well, we'll see," Alec said. "Here's the bell."

The Tiger was a shuffler. He moved flatfooted toward the
center of the ring, hands low, and as the compact Cuban
roared in, swinging, the freckled white boy lifted a long left
and stuck it into the Cuban's nose. There seemed little effort
—not much more than a push—but blood jumped from Bermudez' nostrils. The Tiger moved in, still flatfooted, and sank
a right into the Cuban's stomach, doubling him over. Stepping back, the Tiger hooked his left sharply to the Cuban's
jaw, and you could see his head snap.

"Looks like a short night," Alec muttered as the Bolo wrestled into a clinch. "You want me to pay you now?"

"Not this very moment," Barbara said huskily. "Look at *that*."

Bolo Bermudez was biting the Tiger on the neck, and in the clinch he was pumping furious short punches at the white boy's lean, muscle-ribbed belly. When the referee pushed them apart, the Cuban took a solid shot at the white boy's jaw, staggering him, and the referee held the Cuban off, cautioning him against hitting on the break. There was blood on the Tiger's shoulder, from Bermudez' bleeding nose, but there was also an angry area of pink on the white boy's belly—pink which had come from the infighting.

"Maybe my lad's tougher than we thought," Alec murmured. "Now look at *that*."

Bermudez roared in, took another straight left in the mouth, ignored it, and hit the Tiger a solid hook to the jaw, followed by a straight right to the chin. The Tiger's mouthpiece flew out in a spray of spittle, and the Bolo was on him, crowding him into the ropes, driving piston punches to the belly.

Taggert catapulted himself off the ropes, led with a left that looked low, and crossed with a right that put the black boy down on one knee. He took the count of eight and was up when the bell rang.

"Well, my lad loses that one on points as well as that foul from hitting going out of the clinch," Alec said. "But we ain't home yet. Here's round two coming up."

Both fighters roared into the middle of the ring, slugging flatfooted, firmly planted. Alec looked at Barbara Bayne, whose breath was coming in short hisses from white-pinched nostrils. Her lips were bitten together in a straight line, and her breasts heaved every time one of the men connected solidly.

There was no finesse to the fight. The men swung as Tony Zale used to swing, Alec thought, when he was indestructible; as Henry Armstrong punched when he was a flailing windmill of leather. The Bolo's right eye was completely closed, with a deep cut in the brow that gushed blood. The referee was making small effort toward separation as both fighters heeled and butted and punched as they voluntarily broke themselves. Alec was reminded briefly of the story of how a wild animal named Ace Hudkins once broke Ruby Goldstein's heart, body, and spirit by literally eating him alive after the classy little Jewish boy had the match in his pocket on points. Gallico had written that one very well.

The white boy, Tiger, was painted with the Cuban's blood. He himself was not cut, but both eyes were swollen into slits, and his belly was almost as red as his shoulders from the savage inside pounding he was taking. The crowd had risen, screaming, and Alec was astounded at the savage shrillness of the voice belonging to the pretty blonde girl beside him.

"Kill him, Tiger! Now, now, the right, the right!" Barbara Bayne was screeching, and Alec could see the white showing above her pupils, like the eyes of a crazy horse.

The bell rang as the men stood toe to toe, and they kept slugging until the referee pulled them violently apart.

"My mistake," Alec said mildly to Barbara. "We seem to have run onto quite a massacre here."

Barbara did not appear to hear him. She was leaning forward, breathing heavily, her eye intent on the white boy's corner, where the seconds were working frantically to give him his breath back.

The bell for Round Three banged and both men rushed out again, with no attempt at feint or parry. Both swung right hands from the deck, and each connected on the point of the other's jaw. Both went down like axed beeves—the white boy on his face, the black boy on his back. The crowd was standing, a solid animal roar filling the arena, and again Alec was startled, and not a little shocked, to hear a keening, almost a crooning coming from the mouth of Barbara Bayne. Her lips now were drawn back over her teeth.

Quite obviously the referee had never been confronted with a similar situation. He stood, finally, equidistant between the two men, and began his count. At seven Bolo Bermudez got up on one knee. He was on his feet at nine. He staggered over to the neutral corner and clung gasping to the ropes. At the count of ten the white boy hadn't stirred. The referee walked over to the neutral corner, beckoned to Bolo Bermudez, and the black Cuban staggered out. The referee raised his hand. When he released it, the Cuban sank to the floor again, out as cold as his opponent.

Elbowing through the crowd, Alec said:

"I'll be damned if I saw anything like that in all the fights I covered—two guys knocking each other stiff on the same punch. You live and you learn. Hey, what's the matter with you?"

Barbara was deathly pale.

"I—I can't get my breath. I need some air—some air and maybe a drink. And to sit down. I guess I got carried away. Was I very noisy?"

"Noisy enough," Alec grinned. "I was afraid once that you were going into the ring with a shoe in your hand to help your boy. How come you never saw a real prize fight before?"

"Nobody ever asked me," Barbara Bayne said. "But it was marvelous. I've never been so excited in my life."

"I better keep you away from bullfights," Alec murmured, "if the sight of blood affects you this way. The bullfighters have a saying, if a lady is emotionally affected by a *corrida*, '*Qué mantenga el taxi corriendo.*' "

"Which means?"

"Keep the taxi running during the last bull so you can get the lady home quick before she cools off."

"Do you have a taxi running?" asked Barbara Bayne. Her eyes were open very wide.

"There are lots of idle taxis in Chicago," said Alexander Barr.

11

"I was told it could happen this way," Alec said. "I did not believe it could happen this way. I still don't believe it can happen this way. Not so soon—not so swiftly. It almost did, once, in London, a long time ago, in similar circumstances involving blood and excitement. But I was putting off for tomorrow what should have been done at the time, whether either one of us knew it or not."

Barbara Bayne was unashamedly naked as she walked across the room to find cigarettes.

"I suppose you think me wanton," she said. "I'm not, really. I don't— I really don't—"

"It is a very familiar line," Alec said. "Last heard in London."

"And what was London?"

Alec's voice was bitter.

"I was put in the position of being rather indirectly responsible for killing a girl with whom I was about to be in love. It's a long story and will wait. We should have succumbed to impulse, as you and I did tonight, but—" he shook his head. "I didn't know then that you were supposed to seize happiness in your hand at the moment of offer. I returned next night to collect my love and found a flattened house. The Germans beat me to my date. Enough of that."

"I'm terribly sorry," Barbara Bayne said. "But I'm not sorry about our precipitous rush into bed. And don't blame it on the fights, either. I'd have had you sooner or later, although"—she chuckled—"I must say that ready taxi was a fine idea. Now," she said briskly. "It's early. I suggest we sling on some clothes and go out to inspect the village. There's a lot of night left."

Alec got out of bed and Barbara slapped him lightly on the backside.

"I think you could use another shave," she said. "You're just a little bristly. There's a razor in my dressing kit."

Alec winced. There was entirely too much Sheila in the room tonight. His mind raced as he showered and then scraped at his midnight beard. These things didn't happen to stodgy, professorial, married authors. Not to meet in the morning and to bed before eleven. It was too fast—much too fast. But there it was. It wasn't cheap and it wasn't awkward and it was altogether—lovely. Barbara Bayne. Famous actress. Three bloody rounds of prize fight and straight off to bed. He shook his head again, like a groggy boxer. All of a sudden he felt lightheaded and strangely purified and young and—and wonderful!

"You can't stay in there all night," her voice said. "Give a girl a chance at that shower, will you?"

"All yours," Alec said, and came out with a towel wrapped round his loins. Barbara kissed him in passing, and patted him lightly again.

"Mmmm," she said. "What a clean, sweet-smelling, lovely man. I'll be out in a minute. My flask is at your disposal."

"I don't need a drink," Alec said. "I'm drunk already. Leave the door open and I'll tell you a parable about the time

I saw a dead bullfighter get up, kick a bull in the face, and then kill him with a sword, and then the bullfighter and the bull lay down and died together. Nobody knew whose ears to award to whom—more or less like in the fights tonight."

"I can't hear a word you say," she said, over the rush of the shower. "Get yourself dressed. I'm in a festive mood."

"You're a very strange man," Barbara said hours later. "Somewhere along the line you must have been stultified by something or, more likely, clobbered by somebody. Mother complex?"

They were sitting in a place called Le Bœuf, listening to a tremulous piano being played by a girl named Jeri, who sang in a hesitant voice and dipped frequently into a brandy, double, in a water tumbler. There were red-plush walls against which a dying fire set the shadows scampering. Barbara Bayne had just reached out and touched Alec Barr tenderly on the cheeks with her fingertips and, rising in her seat, had kissed him lightly on the lips.

"Wasn't anybody ever nice to you before?" Barbara Bayne asked. "Nobody ever patted you on the fanny because she felt like it?"

"I really don't know," Alec said. "Maybe I never thought about it much. I have, it seems to me, been so very terribly busy ever since I can remember. Maybe I haven't had time for anybody to be what you call 'nice' to me. Maybe I haven't allowed it."

"You are a fool, you know," Barbara Bayne said. She was looking beautiful in the firelight, which did dramatic things to her cheekbones and the fine straight nose, digging a deeper smoky hole into her dimple. She was wearing a simple black frock with a pearl choker and pearl earrings, and just a touch of eye make-up with no lip rouge.

"You're a fool," she repeated. "Because you have an unrealized talent for fun. I watched you in that horrible place on Rush Street where the strippers wore the tassels hanging out of their G strings. It was crude and vulgar and you laughed like a hyena. You were happy today at lunch in the Pump, and you were sincerely pleased—maybe even a little flattered—when Phil remembered you and Kup came over to have a drink. You were happy to be recognized at the fights. You've a nice way with people; I watched you with the waiters and the cabbies. You're great in—pardon the expression—bed. But don't you ever, ever, really let loose and howl?"

"I'm afraid howling doesn't run much in my family, with the possible exception of one uncle who used to get drunk and curse God as incompetent. He was quite an uncle. He also hated Santa Claus."

"Do you ever get drunk? I mean really. Fallin'-down-stinkin'. Ugly. Noisy. Furniture-breaking sort of drunk?"

"Not that I can remember," Alec Barr said. "I am what you might call a well-contained load. That's to say I generally know enough to go to bed before somebody advises it. Truth is, I get sleepy."

"By God, you're contained, all right," Barbara Bayne said. "I don't know if I'd want to be around when you spill over the millrace. You'd probably fire the barn and shoot the constable before you raped the Duchess."

"I've very little experience with Duchesses," Alec said. "I knew a rather nice Viscountess once, though, on shipboard."

"You tell the damnedest anecdotes," Barbara said. "Then what?"

"Nothing very much. I haven't got the facility for personal color. Everybody does something unusual in a war, even if it's only a command that changes the world. In my case my best command came when a gun broke down in an unlikely manner, and immediate counsel was sought."

"What'd you say? 'Damn the torpedoes'? 'Full speed ahead'?"

"No," Alec replied. "I just said to the gunner's mate on the battlephones: 'Fix it.' The story gained considerable currency as time wore on."

"You're a complete phony about your war, aren't you?"

"I didn't know it showed so clearly. Actually I was scared to death."

"And still are?"

"Not really. Well, yes, maybe. Some of the time. I frequently have the feeling that whatever I've got somebody will surely come and take it away from me someday—when they see through me, I mean. I don't really believe I was ever in a war. I don't really believe I've written all the things I've written. Every time I sign a check I think maybe the cops will slap me into jail for forgery. I don't believe I ever shot an elephant or kissed a pretty woman, or went satisfactorily to bed with one."

"I have, as they say, news for you, friend. Maybe you've never been in a war. Maybe you never wrote a novel. Maybe you never shot an elephant. Maybe somebody will come and take everything away from you someday. But you know something else?"

"I think so," Alec Barr dipped his head. "Yes, that I believe."

"You better believe it," Barbara Bayne said, and leaned across the table to kiss him. This time her lips were warm and soft and lingering.

"It's an old joke," Alec Barr said. "But I'll make it again. My room or yours?"

"Don't argue," replied Barbara Bayne, snatching up her handbag.

12

Red eyes of two cigarettes winked in the dark. Barbara lay warm-close with her head cradled in the hollow of Alec's naked shoulder. Presently Alec sat up and snapped on the bedside lamp.

"I don't want to waste you in the dark," he said. "You're much too lovely to be wasted in the dark. I want to see exactly what I have here. I know almost nothing about what I have here." He reached backward and plumped a pillow behind her head. The blonde hair was moistly tousled, making damp babyish tendrils around the hollows of her throat and shoulders. The bright brown eyes looked steadily at Alec Barr, and the full, sharply cut lips were slightly parted.

"You have a very happy woman here," Barbara Bayne said. "I just don't remember running into it before—two strangers, electricity, *pow!* Straight into each other's arms and off to bed. Lovely, wonderful, marvelous bed."

"I'm still a touch shook myself," Alec said, sitting up and throwing his legs over the bedside. "I think perhaps a drink might unshake me. I'm rather unaccustomed to miracles. You?"

"I suppose. I really don't care. I'm sort of floating in

outer space at the moment, and a drink one way or the other doesn't seem to be very important right now. I suppose I was intuitively right about you, Mister Barr. Don't you ever dare to leave me for long."

Alec got up. He poured two drinks from a bottle of Scotch on the bureau, lit two more cigarettes, and carried one drink and a cigarette over to Barbara. He sat on the edge of the bed and let one hand rest on the cool sheeted curve of her thigh.

"I said earlier I wasn't much good at sleeping with strangers," he said. "Maybe I ought to know a little bit more about you if this is going to take on an aspect of steady habit, Barbara Bayne. At the moment I feel like something out of a fairy tale. Who *are* you, anyhow?"

Barbara smiled at him slowly, and let her eyelids droop.

"I told you. I'm a professional bad actress. A product of the system. An *ersatz* commodity. I was born in a test tube, professionally. I am not really me. I am an assembly-line creation, compounded equally of press-agency activity, Hollywood caste systems, producers, producers' nephews, charity benefits, saloon society, assistant directors first and full directors second, actors of course, and finally a little personal curiosity which earned me a college education on my own spare time. I am the original Galatea, pre-World War II-fashion. All that I have left of the original me you have just made very much free of."

"And will again, I hope and trust." Alec smiled, kissed the end of his finger, and touched her on the nose. "And soon. Who were you really before Pygmalion took you in hand?"

"Believe it or not I was once a little freckled girl named Barbara O'Shaughnessy, who had the usual pigtail and a spotted pony. I was never much for dolls. I also matured quite early. Girls grow their sweater bumps very early in Kilgore, Texas, where I was conceived, born, and raised by not-so-poor and very honest parents. Physically I was precocious. I was so precocious my mother and I conned Dad into letting me enter a beauty contest. It was in connection with a rodeo. And Pygmalion entered my life with a bald head and a cute little potbelly. His name was Shelley Waxman—a talent scout bucking for the agency bit. Want to hear, really?"

"I want to hear, really. I know the little O'Shaughnessy girl. Now tell me about the creation."

"Give me another cigarette," Barbara said. "And lend me your shirt. I talk much better sitting up, and right now I feel very, very naked, much more than before. The whole thing started with the contest, which sent me to Houston after I became Miss Kilgore, Texas, 1936. . . ."

13

Barbara Bayne laughed, and her voice was low and rich and accentless. She looked very French-postcard-fetching, clad only in Alec Barr's shirt.

"To answer your question, Mister Barr," she said. "That is how a girl from east Texas becomes a moving-picture actress. Or at least that's the first step. There are several other steps. I learned a great many things in Hollywood, including a variety of wrestling holds. One of the first wrestling holds I learned was to ward off Miss Plum—that really was her name, Miss Primula Plum—my English teacher. She was a leathery old dyke who taught me pear-shaped words and voice modulation and breath control while missing very few opportunities to touch me in passing. She wore wool stockings, even in that climate, and looked like a character part, but she was a determined old doll, and under her lumpy corsets beat the heart of an Errol Flynn. It was from Miss Plum I first learned that ladies had better lock the door of the john—something they had neglected to teach me in east Texas. But in time I learned to speak English as she is spoke. Miss Plum ironed out the hills at the end of my declarative sentences, and she sandblasted my nasal passages and she peppered my long flat expanses with sharps. We didn't do the 'haow naow braown caow' bit, but at the end of two years you couldn't tell where I came from unless I got stinking mad and lapsed into that old Taixus twang."

"Sounds like a hell of a lot of work," Alec said. "Rather like my own apprenticeship. Sometimes I thought I'd bust a gut because I knew enough to do a man's job and nobody would let me do it."

"The speech wasn't all of it," Barbara said. "I had to go to high school—special classes for movie brats, and of course I took singing. They made me go to dancing classes, and walking classes, and posture classes. I really don't know why they took so much trouble, because as it turned out I never did set the place aflame. I had a lot of class in my ass, you should pardon the expression, but not much talent otherwise."

"When did you work? I mean actually work?"

"When I wasn't going to school. It all seems sort of hazy now. I wasn't old enough to date—they were very careful about that, because they still remembered Fatty Arbuckle out there—but I wasn't too young to show off all my goodies for the cheesecake cameras a couple of days a week. That sort of obliquely paid for the lessons. Sid Polman, my agent, made nothing off me during the apprenticeship. I was just a sort of dirty post card working for free. My legs were almost as well known as Grable's, and my bo-zooms were as much in the public domain as Elsie the Cow's.

"I was Miss Everything: Miss Baked Potato, Miss Eat More Yoghurt—anything that the Chambers of Commerce declared a week for. I had my picture in the paper oftener than Hitler did. I was in more movie magazines than Crawford or Davis. I did everything but act. Eventually I got to be eighteen years old—safe enough for dating without a statutory-rape hazard.

"Then I went on The List. Be Kind to the Visiting Fireman List. The Press List. The Visiting Relative from Chicago List. The He's a Barrel of Laughs List. That's when I learned *all* the wrestling holds. And by some miracle, mostly Mama, I hung onto my priceless jewel until I was a red-hot nineteen and about to bust with repressed vitality. Then I got married—pure Hollywood, fast courtship, elopement to Vegas—to an assistant director who figured that was the only way he'd ever get me in the sack. The marriage didn't last long but he did find me a couple of feet in a pretty good picture, a small part in one of the better Bogarts, and all of a sudden I had it made in Hollywood. I was legitimately deflowered, owned a few column-notices to paste in the scrapbook, and now Sid was asking real money for me."

Alec Barr walked over to the window, towel flapping round his loins.

"Dawn's early light," he said. "I must say we've made an evening out of it. I see no point in trying to sleep now. Let's have another drink, and then I'll ring down for some breakfast. What ever happened to the poor little man who found you in Galveston?"

Barbara shrugged. "Nothing very much. It happens like that out there. Sid unloaded him after a while. I guess I was the only thing that Shelley ever found. Sid kept him in the office until my education was finished—I suppose nursemaiding me was all he ever really did—and then bounced him. I think the poor little man was in love with me, although he never said so. As a matter of fact I got him a pretty good job later—one of the assistant chiefs of publicity on the Falcon lot. I doubt he'll ever make chief. We still have dinner together once in a while when I'm on the coast. He's married to a nice little strudel of a girl and has two kids, one of whom is named Barbara."

"And Polman? Did he go villain on you?"

Barbara shrugged again, spreading her hands.

"No worse than most, better than a lot. He got me work and he never cooked the books, so far as I know. His office kept me out of tax trouble and held me to a pretty rigid allowance in the first days of fairly fat money. My dad came out, by the way, wearing his six-gun, but he couldn't find anything wrong enough to shoot anybody for. Ma hung on, looking richer all the time—about the first big thing I bought was a mink for Ma—until I was that square nineteen and married. Then she went back to Kilgore to brag about her daughter in the moompitchers. They're still in Kilgore, in what passes for a rose-covered cottage. They're nice people, really."

"I wish I could say the same for mine," Alec muttered. "So?"

"The whole deal was so simple it's almost corny. I never had a real beef against either Shelley or Sid. They spent quite a lot of early money and they did invest a lot of faith in me. Sid stuck up for me pretty well in the clinches—I probably made only half as many dogs as the average Grade-B actress, and I never had to screw my way into a part, and I never got into any real switches with messy studio fights. But then I was never top talent. Poor old Sid grew himself a bad heart fighting for his more exotic clients. It killed him just after Pearl Harbor. I didn't look for another highly personalized agent. I just hooked on with MCA and let them worry about the whole shebang."

"I remember seeing a lot of your pictures during the war," Alec said. "When movies eventually reached wherever I was at the time. Looking back, it seems to me you must have turned out about one a month. You must have had eight million men in frantic love with you. I know I was. So were the Japs. They used to sit up in the hills in places like Peleliu and watch the movies through binoculars. If they didn't like the actress, they'd turn loose a few salvos of gunfire and pepper the screens. They never ventilated your screens."

"We made a lot of boy-girl junk for fast distribution," Barbara said. "The poor guys overseas would take anything, I guess. I got tired of it in 1944, and joined up with a USO outfit. You didn't have to do anything special. Just sing a song, shake a hip, crack a joke. Merely seeing a girl with standard equipment was all the poor guys wanted. It kind of slowed my movie career down, though. After the war there was a fresh crop of young beauty abroad, and I wasn't—am not—quite young enough to compete with the new beauty or good enough an actress to be anything sensational on the character side. I do much better on the stage, where I have some little texture. Sure, a movie now and then, but I'll never be a Jean Harlow for solid buyable sex or last as long as Bette Davis for acting."

"Debatable. You hungry now?"

"I don't think so. Look, Sweetie, why don't you have yourself a little nap? I'll go up to my room and throw myself together, then come down and wake you, and we can eat then. Okay?"

Alec yawned.

"Fine. All of a sudden I am very very sleepy. Forty winks won't do me any harm. Be sure and wake me, now. It was a wonderful night—and day—Barbara. See you in a few min—"

Barbara smiled at the slight whuffle of snore as she gathered her things and tiptoed to the bath. Dressed, she sat down at the desk, searched for paper, found a pen in Alec's coat, and scribbled a note.

14 / Amelia

Amelia Barr sat at her vanity and inspected herself in the mirror. The eyes were fine, but the lipstick was the tiniest bit crooked. She remedied the error with a wisp of Kleenex and looked over at the little black Hattie lying on the bed. She shook her head irritably, went over to the bed, sat down on the purple spread, and picked up the bedside telephone. She dialed a number rapidly, using the pencil from the note-pad.

"Mizziz Hazeltine, please," she said and lit a cigarette, tapping her foot as she waited. Then:

"Hello, Ruth? Amelia." Pause for station identification.

"I *know* we're running late. And it looks very much as if we won't be there at all. No—now wait a minute." *Goddammit* implied.

Then:

"But I can't help it. It's Alec. He's having some sort of tizzy. Marched out of the house and off into the night. No, we didn't fight or anything like that. He just said suddenly he wasn't going to dinner; he didn't know where he was going but it wasn't to dinner and he sort of lurched out of the house . . .

"No, he was *not* drunk. Not even a little bit tight. He just sort of had a wild kind of look in his eyes . . . sort of dazed.

"No, I do not know where he is, and I do *not* think it's another woman."

Long pause while the telephone hummed.

"But I don't want to spoil your table setting. Seven's awk-ward. Just take off the two plates and make it for six."

More humming on the other end.

"Well, I suppose he would if he's free. But I wish you wouldn't keep calling him my 'house pansy.' He's a very charming, important man in his own business. Oh, all right, all *right*. I'll ring him up—he's usually home at this time."

Buzzbuzzbuzz. Amelia blew a cloud of smoke into the phone.

"Well, darling, I really can't help it if I haven't got a lover on tap like some people. I'm fortunate to have Francis, even if he is a little . . . delicate. All right. But you'd better hold the dinner an extra fifteen minutes to give the poor dear boy a chance to change his after-shave lotion. I'll be right over now. 'Bye."

Amelia rang off and dialed another number.

". . . . and hurry," she said.

Amelia pulled the little black Hattie over her head and went back to the mirror to give her hair a final pat. She looked at the long bob, shook the hair irritably, and remembered a few acid remarks Alec had made about cocker-spaniel hairdos and the fact that she hadn't the face for so much hair on both sides of it, even if all the girls were wearing it this way this year.

"God *damn* him," she said, and yanked viciously at the long hair. She swept it up and over her ears, hauling it high on the back of her head, jabbing viciously with hairpins to hold the knot in place. Her ears and nape now were bare. She searched her jewel box frantically for the right pair of hoop earrings, found them, screwed them into her ears, then tethered a few stray tendrils into the upswept hairdo. She dabbed perfume onto the naked nape, touched her ears with perfumed fingers, patted the over-all effect, and smoothed her black dress around her hips.

"God *damn* him," she said again, and went off to the bar for one quickie before she rang down for the doorman to call a cab.

Settled back in the taxi, glossy nyloned plump knees crossed and a fresh cigarette held carefully in gloved fingers, Amelia reflected that she was lucky to have Francis on tap. Of course he was as queer as a coot, but he no longer was quite so vicious with his gossip and no longer so mean with his money. And he *was* a man—at least he wore pants—and he was still quite handsome even at middle age, not like a lot of fairies who sort of faded and folded. He was bright and witty and—well, available. No matter if Alec had made jokes about Francis' picking up sailors and the crack that Francis would murder his own mother for a free martini, a girl had to have some sort of escort who wouldn't rouse a lot of gossip and who could be depended on in this kind of crisis. And if you were married to an Alec Barr, there was always some kind of crisis.

Writers, she thought, *God damn them all.* A girl was a fool to be married to a writer. Her family had warned her. Her gynecologist had warned her. Her best friends had warned her. And, she sighed, how very, very right they were. Even when a writer was physically home he was mentally absent.

She let her mind flick back to the earlier newspaper days, and recalled all the nights she had sat alone when Alec was off on some story. Or later, when he left newspapers and went to magazines, off on assignment God knows where—that submarine story—for days or even weeks at a time. Then he'd come home full of what he'd seen and bury himself in the back room until he had squeezed the juices of his information out of his brain and onto paper.

And then books, my God, and plays, out-of-town rehearsals, my God, and the war, my God—the war the worst, four whole long dreary years of it, with cigarette shortages and ration cards and no man in the house except the very, *very* occasional deskborne hero or visiting military firemen she'd let into her bar and occasionally her bed, out of boredom and frustration—my God, she couldn't even remember their faces, let alone their names. She didn't count that as infidelity—there was a war on, and everybody was leaping into bed with everybody else.

15

The War in Washington was quite fun for a while, after you accepted the changes of living accommodation—after you got used to Cuban cane spirits and Canadian "Scotch" and California brandy and ration coupons and meatless days and black market and having several men in your bed instead of just one.

And after you got over your anger at your husband for running off to play sailor when he didn't really have to go at all.

Amelia was furious with Alec—Alec who qualified exempt as a man married before the Selective Service Act;

Alec who could have as easily been a correspondent; Alec who might as easily have sought and received a desk job in Washington, in public relations or intelligence; Alec who might as easily have claimed a physical 4F but waived some physical defects to qualify for full sea duty.

"Why do you *have* to? Why do you have to go play hero when you don't even have a real draft status? Why don't you wait your turn? When they need you they'll call you," Amelia's voice had rasped.

Alec had smiled maddeningly.

"I don't want to wait to be called. I don't want to *have* to go to war. I don't want to wait until all the shine's rubbed off it, and it's full of farmers and deferred husbands. It's the only big adventure I'm ever likely to see, and I want to be part of it."

Amelia nearly wailed.

"Then why don't you be a foreign correspondent, a war correspondent? At least you'll live pretty well and maybe get home every so often!"

Alec lit a cigarette and blew a cool ring.

"I don't want to be a correspondent. I don't want to see a war from outside *in*. I want to see a war from inside *out*. I want to be part of it. And when it's over I don't want to be huddled in the wrong end of a room at a cocktail party explaining to a few, a very few, civilians why it was more practical to stay out than go in. Perhaps if we had children . . ." His voice hung.

"It's not my fault we haven't any children! I haven't used anything since the first six months! If we haven't any children it's—"

"I know. It's *my* fault." Alec's voice drawled in a way that always infuriated Amelia. "Perhaps that's why I want to go to war . . ."

Now she raged.

"You want to go to war like you want to go to spring training! You want to go to war like you always want to go to New York to cover prize fights and the World Series! You want to go to war like you want to cover out-of-town assignments! You want to go to war because you just want to get out of the house!" Amelia covered her face with her hands, then glared at him through tears. "Then go to your goddamned war and get your head blown off!"

Alec said smoothly:

"I'm delighted you didn't attribute my warlike desire to anything so simple as patriotism, and that the words 'Pearl Harbor' and 'Nazi' and 'Jap' did not intrude. Also that there's no hint of 'Mom' or 'apple pie' or 'the American way of life' to confuse the issue. Actually, war is just one big picnic, and I don't want to miss the three-legged race. In any case, it's too late to change my mind. The commission came through today." He handed her a sheaf of papers. "Here are the orders. You may address me as Lieutenant from now on . . ."

Amelia looked at the mimeographed pages blindly, through tears.

"When do you leave?"

"Two weeks. But not immediately to die. There's a matter of eight weeks of indoctrination at Dartmouth to teach me how to tie knots and talk salty. And then, with my luck, I'll probably get stationed right back in Washington, and you'll have me on your hands for the duration. Now, let's have a drink to Lieutenant (junior grade) Alexander Barr, USNR, the scourge of the Japs and the nemesis of the Nazis."

The sneaky son-of-a-bitch probably volunteered for the toughest thing they had, Amelia thought bitterly some weeks later, when her husband informed her that he was ordered to a mysterious duty called Armed Guard, which involved the constant blowing up of ammunition ships en route to Murmansk. My boy Barr, she thought, always trying to prove something, like when he slugged the ballplayer and got his nose rearranged.

But as a practical woman, Amelia realized that there was nothing at all to be done about the war, or about Alec Barr, or about the kind of duty for which he had been selected. She rented the house for a walloping sum to a reactivated bird colonel who was a cinch to stay on in Washington for the duration and moved to an apartment which she shared with two other girls, Norma and Betty—both young-married and both temporarily widowed by the Army and the Marine Corps.

Norma was blonde and very pretty. Betty was brunette and very pretty. Amelia was brownette and very pretty. They all had allotments from their husbands. They all had jobs of one sort or another. And the only meal they really had to buy was breakfast.

The *thème pathétique* of wartime Washington was the excessive trappings of femininity which afflicted the dwellings of women suddenly deprived of the rasp of beard and the musky man-smell to which they had all been accustomed. Amelia's apartment was a thicket of feminine harness—underpants and bras and stockings drying in the bathroom; perpetual borrowing of each others' stockings ("Damn! There goes my last good pair of nylons!")—and the pots and jugs and boxes of creams and powders and lotions and nail polish.

The kitchen was really the ironing room; the icebox held more cosmetics than food; the refrigerator shelves contained peanut butter and personal bottles of milk. There is no more savagely lonely jungle than a forest of femininity, with its female smells and half-naked or wrappered women in hair curlers, borrowing each other's clothes and sanitary napkins and, quite frequently, men. (That's *my* bottle of milk!)

After a considerable stretch in this nunnery of frustration, when Tom, Dick, or Harry's V-mail was later than usual and the loving memory dwindled, the girls took a hitch in their girdles and began to look alive. Slips no longer hung on hangers in the kitchen. Drying lingerie disappeared at nightfall. The handy aids to beauty were shoved into drawers; the implements of feminine hygiene no longer hung unashamedly behind the bathroom door, and the girls began to blandish the supermarket manager for bargains in superior brands of alcohol in order to have something rather better than Cuban gin as a nightcap enticement for gentlemen friends.

And the apartment, from 6 P.M. onward, witnessed a Big Parade of uniforms—all officers, of course, Army, Marine, and Navy, mostly young men on temporary duty, passers-through on their way to war. Each of the girls had a steady, more or less—generally stodgy, usually balding, quite often stout and more often scrawny—who was permanently posted to Washington in some sort of desk job. These men had names to match—names like Jeb and Josh and Horace and Elmer—while the young birds of passage all seemed to be named Don and Tom and Tony and Mike. They were invariably crew-cut and blue-eyed blond, or mustachioed and oily-eyed brunet. They all seemed to be married, too, to some nice girl in Wichita or Boston or Chicago or San Francisco. They carried pictures of wives and, if any, children.

The Washington war widow, if she happened to be young and attractive, had really two simple choices. She did or she didn't. If she did, there was action; drinks and gaiety and uncouponed steaks at Fan and Bill's. If she didn't, she went to movies, Luxed her undies, and read books, because Don and Tom and Tony and Mike were all in a hurry to rush off and die in places with unpronounceable names and one date was enough to waste on a dud. Washington courtship became so formalized that it was almost understood, over the first probing cocktail as the Mayflower or the Willard, whether the date would be worth the price of dinner.

For a while Amelia drifted into the easy-dating stream with the rest of the girls. But the presence of only two bedrooms in the apartment, and the necessity of the odd-girl-out using the living-room divan, eventually disgusted her with the almost sterile promiscuity of The Game. Amelia was not a prude, but she was preoccupied with the idea of at least semipermanence, and the game of musical beds did not amuse her. Each morning found a fresh hangover and a new male face shaving in the bathroom. At times it became difficult to tell who belonged to the various service pants slung over chairs and hooked onto doors. Amelia dated but she did not share her bed, and thus had very little repeat business.

Amelia rebelled. She stopped "dating" and spent her leisure hours flat-hunting. She finally found a small studio apartment at a reasonable rental and, risking loneliness, moved into its blessed privacy—where, she reckoned, any man she found in bed there would at least be identifiable as hers without having to check the dogtags, and the bath was not forever festooned with drying stockings.

She continued to go to cocktail parties, but she parried the stark advances of the ensigns and second lieutenants and quite frequently went home alone until Francis Hopkins entered the party. And her life.

Amelia made her days reasonably monastic, in a girlish sort of way, now that she had a friend and confidant in Francis Hopkins, a delicate gentleman who constituted no menace to navigation and who was fun to chat, and drink, and occasionally, to dine with. Francis was down from New York on some defense project or other and was a welcome relief from the breast-seizers.

During her stay with the girls in the big apartment, she

had been the square one—the non-sleeper-about, the apartment cleaner, the shopper. She had been the girl who took the couch of nights when Norma or Betty were entertaining past midnight in the bedrooms. She was determined not to fall into the rut of nightly mate change. Now that she had her own flat, the easy Washington infidelities would have been facile and private, but something vague held her back.

She had no communication with Alec and could only assume he was at sea. So long as her man was at sea Amelia found it easy to blunt her frustrations with museums and zoos and movies and occasional theater dates with Francis. She relegated sex firmly to the back of her mind, to be filed for future use, and worked herself to exhaustion in the store.

She saw one other man apart from Francis; a Washington newspaperman who had been on assignment in London and who was back doing a duty dance in Washington while awaiting assignment to the Near East or Russia or whichever front appeared bloodiest in the eyes of his employers. He was a comfortable fellow, Timothy, in his late thirties, divorced and the father of two. He had been a friend of Alec's in a mild sort of way, and they had infrequently dined and drunk together before Alec went off to the wars.

Amelia was happy to have Tim drop around. It was a link with Alec and with the old days, when people covered stories which did not involve landings and explosions and crashed aircraft. Tim evidently liked dropping around. He usually brought a bottle with him—Godsend!—and quite frequently a steak. He was handy in the kitchen, and they had cosy evenings, with Tim generally leaving early.

Tim Jason seemed more a solid citizen than a man who would be wearing a war correspondent's patch on whichever uniform of whichever unit he might be accredited to in whatever part of the world. He looked like a civilian: heavyset, rather florid, with a deep voice and rough features. He was an amusing man who held his liquor well, and he had a seemingly inexhaustible fund of stories. Tim had been warcorresponding since the Germans went into Poland; he had been a foreign correspondent before that.

He was a very attractive man, Amelia thought, and she wondered idly, if a trifle perversely, why he never made a grab at her, in a town where an introduction constituted freedom of the grope. But she was content to sit, curled in a chair, and listen to Tim in between news broadcasts.

This night it was Ed Murrow with his "This . . . is London." Murrow was discoursing drily, and colorfully, as usual on the carnage attendant on the fifth straight night of the Second Blitz, in which the Nazis were over in force, and London once again was roaringly ablaze.

"It's not so bad as it sounds," Tim Jason said. "They drop a lot of bombs, and blow up a lot of buildings, but it's amazing how few people they actually do kill, and even more amazing how ordinary life goes on. It's almost as if the bombing woke up the British to the fact that they had blood in their veins. Particularly the women . . ."

He chuckled.

"I have seen a lot of overheated gals in my time, and a lot of easy socializing, but London today makes Washington look like a nunnery. You can't step between the squirming bodies in the parks, and my God! When the warning siren goes, the nearest woman falls flat under the nearest man. The God of War is not Mars. In England, at least, he flies his flag in Piccadilly Circus, and his name is Eros."

". . . The resumption of the Blitz," Murrow was saying, "is believed to have been started by the first diversion of Atlantic convoys up the Thames Estuary, drawing most of the Luftwaffe forces from Russia, where they had been harassing the convoys to Murmansk . . ."

"For everyone who's killed, a hundred thousand will be bred," Tim Jason said. "All stops are out in dear old Blighty, because the boys aren't home for very long, on short leave, and the entire island's in heat. Well, I better push off now."

At the door he said: "Heard any more news at all of Alec?"

"None," Amelia said. "I keep waiting for that awful four-P.M. Western Union message, but it hasn't come, so I can only presume he's all right. Good night, Tim." She lifted her face and kissed his cheek. "Thanks for the steak—and the bottle."

"I'll come by tomorrow and drink the other half, if I may," Tim Jason said. "If you're not doing anything better?"

"Nothing better, and delighted, too," Amelia said. "Good night."

The next morning Amelia got her first V-mail. It bore a naval censor's stamp. It said:

Amelia darling:

I'm censoring my own stuff, but I'm allowed to say I'm in London, since we're in the clear, the Germans know we're here, judging from the noise over the last few nights. Also public relations is planning to exploit the fact that we made it up the river, and also that the RAF is more than completely operable again. Public relations is making a big deal out of this one, and I wouldn't be surprised if you see my picture in the paper, seeing as how I kind of led the flock up to the dock. We got hell beat out of us on the way, but we're doing better and better with the antisub stuff.

Can't say where I'm going or when, but I should be around for a few days or even weeks yet. London's pounded to bits, as Ed Murrow is undoubtedly telling you, or you're undoubtedly reading if you see Reynolds in Collier's. *He's cabling his stuff and working on a weekly deadline.*

But it's a great, gay town, despite the battering it's taken, and I think the Jerries are beginning to get a little bit discouraged. I've met some very nice people, and the beer is drinkable, if warm. I don't mind anything that's warm, not after that last cold trip across that nasty old gray ocean.

Very little more that I can say except that you can buy a steak, if you know where to look, and whisky is not altogether impossible. These people are very brave and, oddly, apparently unafraid. I'll write what I can when I can. But can you believe it? In the midst of all this shooting, I'm about to go to a cocktail party at the Savoy. Must be terribly discouraging to the Hun.

Write and don't worry if you don't hear from me.

> *All my love,*
> *Alec*

Amelia tapped the V-mail letter with her nails. The first joy that Alec was safe again ebbed slightly at the mention of the cocktail party. What *kind* of cocktail party? With whom, in light of what Tim Jason had told her last night, was he going to a cocktail party? What was Tim's line? "When the warning siren sounds, the nearest woman falls under the nearest man." Discouraging to the Hun, my foot, she thought. He's at the Savoy, and I'm sitting on my virtue in a town where everybody else is in bed with somebody else's husband.

Amelia Barr's mind strayed far and wide as she went about her sales chores at the department store. It was marvelous that Alec was safe. Of course it was marvelous that he was in London, and that London was gay despite the bombing—marvelous that there were steaks and whisky and —girls, too. Any man who had crossed the Atlantic in convoy deserved a little fun on the other end, even if—what she didn't know wouldn't hurt her, certainly, but her brain continued to paint pictures.

Amelia Barr had lived with two girls, and she knew what was happening in wartime Washington, even without bombs to activate the gonads. If the District of Columbia could be changed into one huge mattress by a bloodless war on this side of the Atlantic, what in the name of God must London be like if every moment might well be your last? Amelia Barr was a woman; she certainly knew a little of the urgencies that even a football game might engender on a crisp autumn afternoon, a planting to be harvested under a harvest moon with the aid of a little whisky and soft music. What then did bombs and the beat of airplane motors do? Especially to a woman who might be just a day away from losing her man?

Alec Barr was human, and home was a far piece away in terms of time, space, and probability of return. How could you blame him if—she put the thought irritably out of her head.

She was almost angry at Tim Jason when he met her at the corner at six o'clock. He looked different—of course he looked different. He was wearing a uniform again, instead of the civvies he had affected since he returned from his last assignment. He noted the surprised look, and grinned.

"You're right," he said. "I'm off and away—thank God! Here, taxi!"

"But where, *where?*" she said when they settled into the taxi and headed toward Connecticut Avenue.

"Can't say," Tim said, grinning happily. "Big military secret. But it sounds like fun."

"But when?"

"Can't say. I would think tomorrow. In any case"—he pointed at a bulky brown-paper parcel—"I got us the fixin's for a farewell party. There's a steak that never saw a ration coupon. There's a bottle that never knew a tie-in sale. There's a carton of real Chesterfields. I aim for us to celebrate."

"Of course you know I've grown terribly fond of you during these last few weeks," Tim Jason said. He was lounging, half-sprawled, at one end of the divan, nursing a post-dinner brandy. "I'm going to miss you dreadfully. This is going to be a very long one—maybe for the duration, certainly until the tide changes one way or the other. I wish. I wish—"

"What do you wish, Tim?" Amelia, soft with cocktails and wine, touched him gently on the thigh. "Tell me what you wish."

"I think I'm very much in love with you, and this is the last of it! I waited too long, goddam it! Now it's too late to—"

Suddenly they were kissing each other fiercely, and it was Amelia who reached backward and snapped off the light.

"I suppose I really ought to feel like a bastard with Alec away," Tim Jason said, much later, as he sipped a nightcap. Amelia, in a slight silk robe, was lying on the divan, Tim sitting on the floor beside her. "But I don't feel like a bastard at all. I just feel sad that I have to leave now that we've—now that . . ."

Amelia stopped his lips with a forefinger.

"I don't feel like a bitch or a betrayer, either," she said. "Nor, I imagine, does Alec, whatever he's doing right now in London. And," she said rather too brightly, "I'm sure he's doing something. It's going to be a very long war, even if we all live through it. Come on now, Tim darling, you must go home and let me get some sleep. I'm a working girl, not a war correspondent. Kiss me good night, and call me before you leave tomorrow."

Tim Jason pulled himself to his feet and reached for his jacket. He bent over and kissed her lightly.

"I'll call," he said. "And thank you, lovely Amelia."

His call came just before noon the next day. The voice was chipper.

"I've had a change of plans," he said. "For me, good news, very good news. Army's delayed my orders for at least a week. Happy?"

"Very happy," Amelia said. "Look, I've got a customer. Come out for dinner tonight. There's a key under the mat."

When Tim Jason came for dinner that night he brought another steak and his suitcase. He didn't leave Washington for ten days, and he generally had dinner half-prepared when Amelia arrived home from work. When he did depart, finally, destination still unannounced, Amelia had become accustomed once more to having a man around the house.

As the months passed she still depended heavily on Francis Hopkins for steady company, but when Francis' society waned, she did not find it difficult to invite an occasional attractive man up to her apartment for a nightcap. If her conscience occasionally smote her in the small hours, with a strange head on the pillow beside her, she reflected that the Allies were in Italy now, that Alec was undoubtedly there, and that the Italian girls were notoriously loose-moraled as well as attractive. She felt rather sorry for Tim Jason, however. She heard from him less and less frequently, from Moscow, and she had heard that the Russians watched their women very closely and that decent food and drink were very hard to come by.

Washington began to bore her, as the war dragged on, and at the repeated urgings of Francis Hopkins she decided to move to New York. If she wanted to work, Francis said, he could easily find her a good job in his own store. Francis was always very considerate in matters of that sort, as Francis was considerate in most things. If only Francis hadn't been so definitely queer.

Francis Hopkins was 4F for the rather obvious reason that the forces already owned enough unostentatious homosexuals to take on such an obvious deviate as Francis, whose eyes lighted with a *smörgasbord* gleam when he marched through the ranks of naked men at the physical-examination center. Francis had been declared safe from the enemy for the duration. He had come to Washington from New York, he said, to "do some war work," but was delighted to return to New York.

He was tall, slender, graceful. He stood very erect, but arranged to ooze himself into any position, like melting sherbet. He didn't bounce when he moved across a room, but rather slunk. His graying hair was crew-cut, and he had a dark olive skin which made his almost purple eyes striking, with their hedge of thick black lashes. He dressed beautifully in grays and blues and blacks, and he didn't really twitter or fling his hands about or switch his hips. But the purse of his mouth and the shark cut of his lower jaw, and the pouting use of obscenities, mouthed frequently with girlish emphasis, stamped him immediately, even if you hadn't noticed that when he crossed his legs, he tucked one instep under his ankle. He also had the habit of lingering overlong on his consonants, especially the *s*s and *c*s, and his clichés were all girl—"to die over," for instance, and "divine." Funny about Francis. If he had been a man he would have been beautiful. As a fairy you really couldn't remember the shape of his face.

Francis had become a frequent caller at the flat. He cooked divinely and was very good about washing up in the absence of help. In wartime they had a thing about unescorted women in bars and restaurants, so Francis became a built-in beau when the walls closed in on Amelia and she felt she was going stir-crazy if she didn't put on a pretty frock and go out to one of the restaurants that served real meat, and later to a night club which was offering real Scotch. In the Washington beginning, Amelia nearly always shared the check on these expeditions, and Francis always drank her whiskey when he came to the apartment. But he *was* a man . . . he wore pants—and he was devoted to her. And he didn't mind going to concerts and the other time-killers. He loved the theater. He was entranced to escort her to the few fashion shows that the war allowed and was positively uncanny in choosing the right clothes and hats for her type.

This superb taste in clothes was no more than natural for Francis, since he had spent a great deal of time in his earliest youth playing dress-up in his mother's frocks. He was the only child of a strong-minded widowed seamstress who did not mind—indeed, found it rather entertaining, when Francis stole her perfume and occasionally appeared dramatically at bridge parties with fresh feathers added to one of her old hats.

"Such an adorable child," the other ladies said. "So well behaved." And were completely unaware that the cat shunned him and the dog shied from his touch.

16

Amelia, paying the taxi, and heading up the lift to the Hazeltines', thanked God for Francis, now and previously. Alec Barr, breeding a book, was hopeless. He wandered about the house in a daze, his head full of characters and plot, his physical self a million miles away in space. He was useless in bed at that time as well, because he was always so beat at the end of the day. He took his characters to sleep with him and worked subconsciously on plot. The few times that Amelia attempted to break through the barrier she had the definite feeling that she was sharing the couch with at least a dozen other people, and that Alec Barr had caused his erection to be delivered by Reuben's delicatessen service.

Nearly everybody liked Francis, because, they said, he wasn't really very bitchy except where his ex-friends were concerned. They went on to say that he was clever, too; he was terribly discreet about his private life. He didn't say "Get *you,* girl" to both sexes. To the best of everybody's knowledge he did not openly cruise, and if there were one or two favorite bars on Third Avenue or in Greenwich Village they were not exclusively devoted to young gentlemen of similar persuasion. Francis was *persona grata* at "21," the Stork Club, and the Oak Bar at the Plaza. He scorned the Fire Island set as raving queens, and if he took casual lovers he took them quietly and kept them well hidden from view.

Francis was very sympathetic to his lady friends, and offered a ready ear to their problems of husband, lover, maid and landlord, decoration and clothing. He had spent much time traveling for Mandell's Stores during his apprenticeship, and owned a wide acquaintance in Dallas and San Francisco, Boston and Detroit, Chicago and Cleveland. Consequently, many of his professional lady friends, making their annual visits to New York for the fashion shows or a session of theater, preferred to spend a week end with Francis rather than waste their money in a hotel. Francis was so amusing, and his flat in the East Sixties was sheer fun. And, at home, Francis poured a generous martini. He gave little parties for his lady guests and regaled them long into the night with the freshest and juiciest gossip on recent abortions and other aberrational behavior among the rich and famous.

Francis was a person a girl could talk to, and achieve both the male and female reaction to the dilemma. Francis Hopkins gave Amelia no sexual solace, but he did listen attentively to her plaints, and he did think up amusing things to divert her—such as a trip to Jamaica or Europe— and sometimes even managed to find time to accompany her, no matter how busy he was at the store. It was tacitly understood of course that Amelia would foot the basic expenses, although Francis was very good about paying for little luxuries.

They always came back from these jaunts in high spirits. Francis was a relentless driver of bargains. He was an authority on foreign furniture and a passable critic of art. They haunted the back streets and flea markets and generally returned with a trove of cut-rate antiques and absolutely startling examples of nonfamous artists who somehow had been overlooked by the collectors. He knew the couturiers on a first-name basis, as well, and Amelia's wardrobe was generally much enhanced when she returned to inquire how Alec was doing with the book.

Indeed, Francis was a treasure, if only because he was always there when a girl needed him—if not for such a simple thing as a last-minute fill-in for a dinner, then for the post-dinner rehash they were conducting now in Amelia's apartment. They had not tarried long after the coffee and brandy; this party had been a particular bore, even for the Hazeltines. There had been some sort of explorer, with a leather-faced wife, who talked endlessly of the breeding habits of penguins—in which, it appeared, the male penguin fetched his lady fair a small stone and dropped it at her feet to attest his love. There was a foreign correspondent who had evidently burned down the Reichstag personally, or who at least knew the inside story of who struck the first match, and a couple of other people whose contribution to the evening was a repeated "Really?"

"Jesus," Amelia said, flopping down on a divan in the living room and kicking off her shoes, "*what* an evening. In a way I don't blame Alec for defecting to the East, or wherever he went. Be a darling, Francis, and fetch me a Scotch—a double, dark-browny one, with a lot of ice."

When Francis returned with the drinks, Amelia had taken the pins out of her hair and was shaking her head violently to restore scalp circulation. She took a long pull at her drink, and smiled.

"Bless you, Francis," she said. "You are indeed a tower of strength in time of need."

Francis buried his face in his drink and looked at Amelia with warm purple eyes.

"I was going to ask you about that hair. What got into you? They haven't been wearing it like that since Pearl Harbor."

Amelia shook her head again, irritably, and again the long locks swirled.

"I don't know. Alec always liked it like that. I think he hates it flopping. When he walked out on me, I suppose I had some sort of reversion to childhood. I had been naughty and wanted to make amends after the spanking. Something like that—silly little-girl stuff."

"Who is she?" Francis fired the question. "Do you know her name? Anybody we know?"

"Who is *who?*" Amelia's eyes rounded.

"The woman. There has to be a woman. Alec Barr isn't the kind of man who'd walk out if there wasn't a woman."

"Oh, no. There isn't any woman. I'd know if there was. He's been working hard, and he's tired, and . . ."

"Don't give me that innocent crap," Francis said nastily. "There has to be a woman. There's got to be a woman. There always is a woman. He wouldn't have shot out like that if something wasn't on his mind, and that something ain't a book, Sweetie."

Amelia pulled at her chin.

"I can't think of any. He's stuck awfully close to home lately. I've practically had to chase him out for a drink at Toots' or Tim's, and he either doesn't go or is back in an hour. No. I don't think it's a woman."

Francis Hopkins lit two cigarettes, handed Amelia one, and crossed his ankles. He bounced one big foot rhythmically up and down.

"When was he out of town last?" Now his voice crawled, slow and furry like a caterpillar. "And where'd he go?"

Amelia sat up with a start, spilling some of her drink. Her mouth made an O.

"But of course. Three weeks, maybe a month ago. I'd forgotten. He was only gone a day and a night, though. Chicago. Some sort of autograph thing with a lecture and a TV appearance. He said he went to a boxing match, too. But he was only gone a night and part of two days."

Francis narrowed his eyes and watched the smoke plume upward.

"They say Rome wasn't built in a day. But many a baby's been made in a minute. A night and a day is enough to create a bother. Airplanes, you know. Hotels. The lion of the hour. The flocks of adoring females. . . . The handsome author."

"I don't believe it," Amelia said sharply. "Alec's not that sort."

"They're all that sort, lovey," Francis replied, drawling again. "There aren't any other sort. And to paraphrase Noël Coward or somebody, a sucker's born every minute, with two to take him. Alec Barr is a handsome man, and a big shot on the literary campus. He was away in the war a long time; he could have formed the habit. There's an awful lot of grown-up coeds in them hick-town hills, girl."

"You are a bastard," Amelia said. "You really are."

"I'm not a bastard. I'm a realist. Gentlemen grow weary of wives. It's the same old trade, day in and day out. It lacks mystery. And anyhow you're too fat."

"I am not too—*am* I too fat?" Amelia's voice changed in midstream.

"I wouldn't say fat, exactly. I was teasing. But you are beginning to heavy up a little in the upper arms and thighs, Amelia. I noticed at the last fitting. Once that sort of weight gets a grip on you it's dreadfully hard to lose. And you're a big girl, you know. Once it grabs you it's got you."

Amelia felt herself on arm and thigh. She touched her chin.

"Just a suspicion of double, nothing to worry about," Francis said. "But they're hard to shake, too. Have you been eating a lot lately?"

"I suppose. I've been pretty unhappy. Yes. Nibbles—trips to the icebox. You know. Odd cravings. Chocolate, for instance."

"Oh, my God, I'd rather see you eating rat poison. And don't tell me Cokes, too?"

Amelia's voice was sheepish.

"Well, yes. Cuba libres. I've been having the morning shakes some, and a Cuba libre in the morning sort of steadies me down."

"How many Cuba libres in the morning?" Now Francis' voice was stern, the voice of the family doctor.

"Two—three, maybe, while I dress for lunch."

"And how many martinis for lunch?"

"Two. Well, once in a long while, three. Depending on who I'm lunching with."

"Good God. And I suppose three more before dinner, and wine, and a little brandy after, and then some Scotch, and then a nightcap, and you can't sleep and have another nightcap, and then take one to bed with you?"

Amelia looked over his shoulder and took another drink before she answered.

"Yes. Yes, I suppose so. I know I've been drinking too much. But there doesn't seem to be much else to do."

"I'll tell you what else to do." Francis' voice rose. "I'll tell you exactly what else to do!"

"What? I feel such a mess . . ."

"Exactly. My dear girl, spend some money! Spend lots of money! You deserve it. Buy yourself a new body and a new head and a whole flock of new clothes. Take a trip to Europe. Buy a new mink. Shake him up. He needs it. He's taken you for granted too long."

"I don't know," Amelia shook her head slowly. "We spend an awful lot of money. Taxes and his people and just living here—" she waved a hand around the room. "Not to mention the Jersey house."

"He didn't mind spending a fortune on that Jersey monstrosity—that hunting lodge—you never use," Francis' voice spat. "He doesn't mind spending a year's pay on one of those safaris he's always taking with the other hairy he-men. His taxidermy bill alone. . . . And right now"—he let his voice drip into a purr—"right now I don't imagine he's counting the money he's spending on that other dame."

Amelia sat straight up in her chair, knocking her drink off the side table.

"Don't fret, Sweetie, I'll clean up the mess and get you

another drink," Francis said. "Just hang on a minute while I get a bar towel."

He came back with the drink.

"Of course," he said, "we don't know there's another woman. But when a man can't stand ordinary pressures there's generally something weighing on his conscience. Why else would he just launch off like that? You haven't been fighting lately, have you?"

"Fighting? *Fighting?*" Amelia's voice was bitter. "Christ, we haven't even been talking. We haven't been doing anything. He sees his agent. He shuts himself up in the office here or goes out to Jersey for weeks at a time. The place gives me the creeps. There's nothing to do out there but read or look at the television. All the neighbors are either farmers or you know—"

"What else?"

"You know. Togetherness people. Cookout people. Two-boys-and-two-girls kind of people. Everybody so damned hearty you want to throw up. It wouldn't be so bad if Alec ever talked to me any more, or—"

"Or?"

"Or made love to me as if he meant it—as if I didn't have a pistol poked in his back or something. But when that man is buried in a new book he might as well be dead so far as being any use to anybody else."

"Well," Francis spoke deliberately. "There are exactly three avenues of egress, girl."

"What sort of avenues? And skip the egress."

"Take a lover or get a divorce. Or do what I said. Make yourself into a new woman and shake him up a little. The money'll shake him, anyhow."

"I don't want a lover. And I certainly don't want a divorce. I like the way I live—if—if only I could get my husband out of the stratosphere. Lovers and divorces are so damned messy. I'm about the only woman I know who hasn't had one or the other or both."

Francis curled his voice in a stretching sneer, like a cat before a fire.

"I should hate to see you cheated, Sweetie. Maybe after you've pulled off a pound or two and bought yourself some new hair, you'll change your mind about one or both. Now," briskly, "I see you as blonde, fairly shortish, more or less a

halo. I detect the beginnings of gray, and we might as well
cut that off at the draw."

"I like my hair this color," Amelia spoke defensively. "I
don't want to be a blonde. And I'd look like hell in a halo."

"Two will get you six that the other one's a blonde,"
Francis said gently. "They always are—the first serious ones,
I mean."

"But we don't know, damn it, we don't . . ."

Francis held up his hand and uncoiled his ankles. He rose
to his feet.

"Wait and see, precious, wait and see. Now, I'm off and
away. I've got a bitch of a day tomorrow, and I'm still
weary from the explorer's wife. Not to mention your friend
Mrs. Hazeltine. I must dash. Don't get up, Sweetie. Just sit
there and hope for the best and think about what I've said
about the new you."

"Is there any place for a general remodel job that isn't
Arden's?"

Francis chuckled.

"Oddly enough there is. At least as good. It's in Colorado.
Marvelous climate, they say. It's called El Rancho Nuyu.
'New you,' get it? Frightfully expensive, though. About a
thousand a week—not counting tips. Well—night, lovey.
Dream sweet."

And Mr. Francis Hopkins slithered out, leaving Amelia
Barr staring into her drink. After a while she drank it off in
a gulp and walked in her stockinged feet to the bar to mix
another.

17

The girls were seated at the center table in the front room of
the bar at "21." They were on the second Bloody Mary. They
had all been to the hairdresser that morning, and the hairdos
were nearly identical, give or take a zebra stripe or two.
Glorious hats smashed atop the new hairdos, and none of the
jewelry was junk. Some was just larger than others', and the
pearls were all real.

"I think she's gone off in looks over the last year or so. I liked her better when she was a brunette. She looks so hard as a blonde," Ruth Hazeltine said.

"Whom are we knocking?" Amelia asked. "Anybody I know?"

"Oh, I think so. Barbara Bayne. Have you seen her lately?"

"Only in the movies. Once in a while on TV. And in that last play." Amelia laughed shortly. "I think it was the last time I was able to get Alec out of the house. I think she's beautiful."

"Oh, I thought you knew her," Mary Ferris said, and turned to the captain. "I'll have the tossed salad with lemon, and the hamburger rare, please, Vincent. But let's have one more Bloody Mary first. All right, girls?"

"I shouldn't, but all right," the girls said with one voice. "And I'll have the salad and the hamburger too, Vincent. Rare please."

"With just a little spinach, Madame?"

"I suppose so. But it still reminds me of baby food," Dolly Norton said. "But the other drink before I face any food, please."

"Very good, ladies. Shall I send the sommelier?"

"God, no," the ladies cried, again as one. "Black coffee, with."

"Thank you, ladies," the captain said, tucking his menus under his arm, and the girls settled back into the comfortable gloom.

"Why would I know her?" Amelia Barr asked.

"Who?"

"Barbara Bayne."

"Oh," Mary Ferris answered. "I sort of thought she was a friend of the family. Did a play with Alec or something like that. Maybe they're working on a new one? Talking it out together?"

"Not that I know of." Amelia's lips felt suddenly stiff. "Why would you think that?"

"No reason at all, Sweetie. I stopped in at the Plaza bar yesterday afternoon and saw them with their heads together in a corner. I just assumed they were working on a play. I didn't mean—I mean, the Oak Bar *is* rather public, isn't it?"

Amelia set down her drink very carefully. Her face had paled. She lit a cigarette and her hand trembled only slightly. Then her voice came, false and bright and brittle.

"The heat must have taken hold," she said. "I'm losing my tiny mind. Of course. There's some talk of reviving that old one of Alec's—*Not without Laughter;* remember, before the war? They're thinking of making it into a musical, and they want a straight singing—almost a talking part to bounce off Merman or whoever takes most of the music. That's what that would be about. But as for the lady, I never met her in my life."

The waiter arrived with the fresh Bloody Marys and Amelia drank half hers in a gulp.

"God, it's thirsty out today," she said. "I think perhaps I'll drink most of my lunch. Make it a martini this time, please," she said to the waiter. "I've had enough tomato juice. Health food bores me."

Amelia made it through the salad, but pushed back her hamburger after shredding it with her fork. She looked ostentatiously at her watch.

"Damn, it's later than I thought," she said. "I've a dentist thing at two. If you'll excuse me, I must run. Vincent! Put my share on the tab, please. I'll sign next trip." She smiled brightly at the girls. "See you again soon—call me," and hurried through the lobby and up the steps. She made it into a taxicab before the tears came.

"That was darling of you," Ruth Hazeltine said to Mary Ferris. *"Sweet."*

"Don't raise your hackles at me, Sweetie. What'd I do bad?"

"I suppose you didn't know Alec Barr walked out on Amelia last week? In this town, this big blabbermouth town, nobody told you?"

Mary Ferris held up her hands, palms out.

"Don't hit me," she said. "I wasn't being a bitch. I just got in from the Cape yesterday morning. What's this all about?"

"Mr. Alexander Barr, the well-known author-playwright, walked out on his wife on the eve of my dinner party last week," Ruth Hazeltine replied. "It was assumed first that it was a nervous breakdown, due to hot weather. When nothing was reported from Bellevue, it was assumed that he was shacked up with some broad. You have now brought his loving wife the tidings that the broad is none other than Barbara Bayne, the well-known barracuda. You have done an excellent day's work for a country girl, dear heart."

"Jesus, I'm sorry. Didn't any of you private eyes ferret out the facts?"

"Until yesterday Mr. Barr has been underground with his love, holding hands in dim places unfrequented by the better element," Ruth Hazeltine said. "Yesterday was the first time he surfaced, or one of us would have known about it. Check, Vincent!"

"Would anybody go along with just a teensy-weensy dessert?" Dolly Morton asked. "The pastry looks delish."

"Not today," Ruth Hazeltine said. "I haven't the figure for it." She looked appraisingly at Dolly Norton. "And neither, my girl, have you. Check!"

Back at the apartment, Amelia Barr rummaged through back issues of *Life* until she came to a cover which bore the photograph of Barbara Bayne. Presently she tore the cover in two, went back to the bedroom, and attacked a large picture of her husband with the spike heel of a shoe, shattering the glass. Then she fell on the bed and sobbed.

Presently she pulled herself up, went to the bathroom, and washed her tear-flushed face in cold water. Then she went to the bar, fixed herself a stout Scotch, and picked up the bar phone. She dialed a familiar number.

"Let me speak to Mister Hopkins, please," she said. "Mrs. Barr calling."

She sipped her drink, eyes narrowed, foot tapping. Then:

"Francis? Amelia. You were dead right. What did you say the name of that goddam health farm was?"

18 / Alec

It had been very pleasant, that Chicago interlude, but Alec was a busy man in New York, and Amelia was being fairly difficult, and babies were hard to build, and it was hot, flaming hot; as well there was a necessity to make quite a lot of money in a hurry, and it was the kind of year that all the editors had the red-ass about all copy, none of which seemed to quite come off. So Alec hadn't rung up his new friend from the Chicago trip, not really wanting to hide in any corners and not wanting to flaunt himself publicly in the more pleasantly familiar pubs where anything other than a crass business acquaintance would sponsor a raised eyebrow from the help—that apart from the chance of Amelia barging in with Betty or Tess or one of the accepted faggot friends who seemed always to be part and parcel to any well-run household these days.

Barbara Bayne had left a scrawled note on the night table when she had departed Alec's Chicago hotel room early in order to take an earlier plane: "You were sleeping so sweetly I hadn't the heart to wake you. Call me sometime when you're back in New York and feeling lonely. I'll have my own domestic problems sorted out. I wish you nothing but the best in yours. And last night—all of it—was lovely. Cheers, chum, B." The "all of it" had been underlined in lipstick.

Now Alec had lunged blindly, like a rutting bull, out of the apartment, with an avowed intention of going—where? When his temper settled and he was in the taxi heading uptown, the question nagged him. Where? A little boy running away from home, he thought, all charged up and ready to disappear over the horizon—*that'll* teach 'em a lesson—but quite at a loss as to which direction the horizon lay.

Alec Barr snapped his fingers. There was a hotel he remembered from his early days in New York, a shabby-genteel little hotel in the Fifties, popular with English expatriates. It had had a jolly red-leather fumed-oak approximation of an old country pub, and he wasn't apt to see anybody he knew there.

"I haven't any clothes with me," he said as he approached the reception. "I'll possibly send for some tomorrow. Meantime I'd like to pay in advance."

The clerk smiled an ancient, cynical, conspiratorially comradely smile which revealed roquefort teeth better left unrevealed, and preened a minuscule blond mustache. Suddenly there was the smell of cabbage—perhaps Brussels sprouts—in the faded lobby.

Alec wrote in a large clear hand *Alexander Barr, 30 Rockefeller Plaza* and shoved the pad back to the clerk. The clerk leered.

The clerk bared all his green-veined teeth. "What accommodation would you like, Mister Barr?"

"A double room." He put a bill on the desk. "That should

hold me for a couple of days. When my clothes arrive I may change to a suite."

"You understand I don't make the rules," the clerk said, "but without baggage—"

"I understand. Forget it. Now give me a receipt for the money and hand me my key."

Alec ascended in the rickety lift. The smell of cabbage was still strong in his nostrils. The room was not too bad, with timeworn chintzy curtains and a puffy but use-frayed yellow satin spread on each of the twin beds. He opened the door to the bathroom and noticed that it was at least clean, if cramped.

He washed his face, which was greasy-slick with sweat, and wished he had a change of clothes. Melancholia assailed him. He thought of ringing down for a drink, and decided he couldn't drink in this sleazy, shabby, stranger-tarnished room. He went back down and slung his thief-proof-weighted key on the desk.

"Room all right?" the clerk asked.

"All right," Alec answered sharply and headed for Shor's. It was drinking time. Shor's would be air-conditioned and would dry the rivulets of perspiration which pasted his shirt to his back and was shrinking the knot of his necktie. There would be somebody to talk to in Shor's. There always was somebody to talk to in Shor's, even on a Saturday night in late August in the abandoned city of New York.

19

Alec woke with the sun hurting-bright in his eyes, his throat parched sore, a horrid taste of verdigris in his mouth. Pain gouged his eyeballs, and his head pounded in time to a racing heart. He was still wearing his shorts. He kicked off the underwear and sought the bathroom.

He looked at himself in the streaky mirror over the clothes cabinet and winced again. Somehow a naked man always looked a great deal nakeder than a naked woman. The shower had plastered his graying hair to his skull. His beard showed greenish-gray against a sick and pallid skin. His eyes were streaked and bloodshot, his eyelids grained and puffed. But his trousers were hung neatly on a hanger.

His coat was wrinkled in the elbows, from perspiration, but it also was neatly draped on another hanger. The shirt, too, was stretched over a cheap wire frame, but its collar had melted from sweat and its odor was stale. The necktie, sweat-stained, was draped over a chair, and the socks were laid atop his shoes.

"Somebody must have put me to bed," he muttered. "God knows I wouldn't have hung anything up—not in the shape I was in. Somebody—oh, God. It couldn't have been anybody else but Dinah—unless? No, Jesus. I remember, it was Di."

He retrieved more from memory as he dressed, shaking fingers fumbling over buttons and wrestling awkwardly with the still-damp necktie. Bending over to tie his shoelaces started the pains stabbing inside his skull again. He felt weak, queasy-sick, and the green taste of bile rose rankly high in his throat. Alec Barr rarely got very drunk, and almost never had a drink in the morning except in he-manly good fellowship on hunting or fishing trips. He looked at his watch: only twelve noon, and the saloons didn't open on Sunday until one o'clock. Right then Alec Barr, afflicted by conscience and monstrously overhung, would have given nearly anything in the world for a double Bloody Mary, a double whisky sour, or a long cold orange juice reinforced with gin. He rang room service and was informed that the hotel bar did not open until one. A whole hour before the bar opened.

Feeling crummy as any Bowery bum in his cigarette-smoke-stale clothes, Alec looked around the room. He felt in his pockets—no money. But there it was, stacked neatly on the bedside table, and with it, too, was a note, hastily scrawled.

Author: I tried to get you to come home with me, but you were most violently stubborn. So the best I could do was to convoy you here and tuck you in. Sometime, when you're in a little more lucid mood, ring me at the office and we'll give l'amour *another whirl. Last night wasn't my night for romance, especially as you kept calling me Amelia. Take care of yourself. It isn't as bad as all that.*

The note was signed simply:
Dinah.

Alec winced again. It had all come back loud and very clear, from the first lonely drink at Shor's, kidding falsely with Ziggie, until Dinah Lawrence had walked into the bar.

"Hi there, Book Author," she said. "What's our mostest and firstest literary light doing all alone in New York town on Saturday night? I thought all you hard-cover fellows went up to the Hamptons every week end."

"Hi, scrivener," Alec said, almost hysterically glad to see Dinah Lawrence. "Come and have a drink. Or are you meeting somebody?"

"Meeting nobody. I'm one of those Saturday-night-is-the-loneliest-night-in-town-type girls. Got bored looking at the TV and pondering the hopelessness of my barren future and decided to come downtown and try to pick up a sailor or something. This seemed a likely place to start."

"In The Great War," Alec said, "I was an old sailor once myself. Come aboard, mate, and grant me solace. What'll it be?"

"Gin. Large, lavish amounts of it. Tonic first and then I graduate. What really brings you out to mingle with the sporting set?"

Alec was feeling better. He gazed with almost-happy approval at Dinah Lawrence. She was looking very pretty, he thought, even if she was getting a little long in the tooth.

Di Lawrence was what they used to call, back in the war, "a good Joe." That was her major problem as a desirable woman, being a good Joe. Men loved to be with the good Joes, but they generally seemed to marry the sweet-Alice types. She was damned pretty—curly black of hair, smoky blue of eye, going more than a little gray and not bothering to dye it. She would have been latish thirties, maybe even cracking forty. She was a highly respected, veteran newspaperman in the town—nobody would ever have called her a newspaperwoman—and Alec had known her ever since the early days in Washington. She was not girlside; she wrote straight news and features, drew a top salary, and scorned the obvious assignments which used to be called sob-sister stuff. She was as tough on a fast-breaking murder yarn as the best; she had seen more than her fair share of flood and blood and earthquake and general disaster.

She had been married once, to some vague fellow who had disappeared in another general disaster and whose only reminder was a very pretty teen-age daughter to whom Di had devoted a lot of time raising. The daughter was in school somewhere now—God, Alec thought, she's probably in college. How the time does fly. Kid must be nearly twenty; of course she's in college. And to think I used to baby-sit her when I had to get out of the house to save my earlier sanity. Well, her mother's still a dish. Maybe a little overblown on the curves, but the legs still good, the hips still trim, even if you could see the rampart of girdle-ridge.

"How's my favorite child?" Alec asked, ignoring the question of what brought him out into the world of New York Saturday night. "Where's my pretty Penny?"

"Good God," Di Lawrence said. "Your pretty Penny is a junior, at, of all places, Northwestern. I could be a grandmother any minute now, heaven forfend. You didn't answer my question."

Alec looked again, more appraisingly this time, at Dinah Lawrence. She was wearing a plain gray worsted suit, severely cut, over a turtleneck sweater, with only a lapel brooch to relieve the severity. She did not, he decided, even vaguely resemble the average newshen.

"That's a hell of an outfit to pick up sailors in," Alec said. "It's much too ladylike. I'm glad you found a friend. A friend in need, I might say. I just left Amelia. The walls caved in on me. I took off in what I stand in. Combination of circumstances. Combination too bruising to bear."

"You've been leaving Amelia for years," Dinah Lawrence said. "So now you finally went and done it, huh? She come at you with an axe?"

"I finally went and done it and, as Tim Costello would say, me heart is black and me spirit sick and sore, and she did not come at me with an axe. I was planning to get plastered. Care to join me?"

"Why not? It won't be the first time I've seen you through the awful-awfuls. Remember that convention in Philadelphia?"

"Do I not. I remember the aftermath, too."

Dinah Lawrence looked at her drink and colored slightly. "Don't be a bloody cad, amigo. We were both ministering to each other's needs. I don't usually run to romance on assignment. It must have been Truman's give-'em-hell speech that spurred my girlish glands to unwonted action."

"It was a nice night," Alec said. "I've often wondered why we haven't reprised it."

"I don't poach other people's property on their own premises," Di Lawrence said. "There was always Amelia. I was happy just to have you drop by for a cup of coffee. You know, Penny adores you still, and her a grown girl and all?"

"I had a very happy time baby-sitting Penny. She was a swell kid. Very pretty now? I haven't seen her in, oh my God, ages."

"She's damned pretty. Black like me, but going to be less Mack-truckish in build. Here. There's a snapshot." Dinah Lawrence opened her purse and took out a wallet. She produced a color photo from under the isinglass card-cover, and passed it to Alec. He saw a smiling girl with great blue eyes, standing spraddled in shorts and jersey. She had curves already, and the promise of lovely legs after a little baby fat melted off the thighs. Her hair was cut short, and was dark, curling naturally around her ears.

"How old now? She's really lovely."

"Rising twenty. Damned smart. I think you must have baby-sat her very well. Postnatal influence. She's bookish. Passed her college boards with top marks. Getting straight As at school. Wants to be a doctor, I think. Or an atomic scientist. Or a missionary. Or a journalist, perish forbid. Or a ballet dancer. You know. Remarkable lack of interest in getting married early so far, thank God. But that'll change."

Alec signaled the bartender for another round. The gin was establishing a nice firm stand in his stomach. Quite a lot of the earlier, shocked-by-what-I've-done blues were leaving him. Dinah Lawrence always made him feel easy. God knows she was feminine enough; that all-night session in Philadelphia had been tumultuous. But she also had that wonderful we're-boys-together, don't give-me-no-bloody-quarter-because-I-catch-the-curse sort of approach to men when she had her working clothes on. Alec felt soothed, as he always felt soothed—as he had felt his ragged ganglia massaged when from time to time he used to drop around to Dinah's book-filled flat and drink coffee and play with the baby and spill his indecisions to a sympathetically receptive ear. *Maybe I should have married her* he thought briefly, and shook his head.

Dinah noticed the headshake.

"What, bugs?"

"I just had a fleeting thought. Maybe I should have married you. But then, two writers in one family . . ."

"No good, Jack. Two writers? Forget it, Charlie. You made a great babysitter, and once"—she smiled—"once an exceptional lover. But husband? Hoo-ha! Leprosy I'd rather be having already."

"You know, I forgot you were Jewish?" Alec said. "What was the Lawrence? I never met him."

"I married a *goy*. Mama said it would be murder. Mama was right. Such a business. Such a husband."

"I remember now. Vaguely. He never did anything at all about Penny—support, I mean?"

"I didn't want it. I didn't need it. Penny was mine. And I had a nice free babysitter." She smiled. "Quit ducking. What happened with the Amelia bit?"

"Not much. Certainly not her fault. I had the goddamnedest feeling all of a sudden that I was choking to death—smothering. Life-passing-me-by sort of thing. Menopausic, I suppose. And it was one of those days when nothing works. Suddenly I thought I would go tearing mad if I didn't get out. I don't suppose it's original with me."

"It's not." Dinah Lawrence patted his hand. "Sounds more like rejection slips and hot weather and Mother-knows-best. How right am I?"

"Right enough so we don't have to belabor it any more. Let's drink some more drinks and eat an enormous meal and be briefly polite to the Great Man and then let's plunge out into the night and show ourselves around the Village. That's if there's anything open in New York on Saturday night in August."

"You've got a deal. I start out looking for a sailor and pick up a lieutenant commander. The kid's still got class. Maybe it's my nice legs and imperturbable digestion."

Alec twirled the olive in his martini on its toothpick.

"Tell me something," he said. "Why does everybody in this bloody town always have to talk so sharp, so slick, so brittle? How come somebody can't say, once in a while: 'I love you' or 'Get lost, you jerk' or 'No, I'm not glad to see you; I hate your guts' instead of always pitching in the darlings and the gags and the funnies? Why is everybody so goddam cute?"

Dinah hummed the first two bars of "Manhattan."

"It's a state of mind, sired by Hollywood out of Madison Avenue. All the men call each other 'honey,' and everybody calls everybody else 'sweetie.' If you got an emotion, you're supposed to bury it, then go to the psychiatrist to spend a fortune to find out why you're frigid or something. The biggest ram I know in this town claims he can't sleep with his wife because he married a wishful whore and woke up in bed with his mother."

"You would not," Alec Barr said, "by any chance be referring to me?"

"Let's go and eat some of the Great Man's prime ribs," Dinah Lawrence said. "And I was not referring to you."

"Maybe you didn't know it, but in point of fact you were," said Alec Barr. "Send us another round to the table, Zig."

As the headwaiter seated them, Alec grinned and said:

"Remember when we conquered the City of Washington, D.C., without firing a shot?"

"That I do. Sometimes I still say thank God for H. L. Mencken."

20

There were women on newspapers in those days, but mostly they kept to the inside specialties—society, clubs, homemaking, music, drama, and occasionally the offbeat feature that wanted a woman's-eye view for shock effect. Generally you didn't find the ladies on the beats, the police run, the courts, the District Building, except when something special demanded a distaff angle.

Young Alec Barr was swinging, in those lusty prewar days before television poked its inquisitive snout into the news business. John Barry, the managing editor, was trying young Barr at everything—a stretch with sports, a siege on the copy desk, a semester on the drama desk, a solid sentence at police court, and now a steady assignment at the District Building (which in unemancipated, voteless Washington, comprised City Hall). Next would come District Court, then Capitol Hill, and finally top general assignment.

Alec walked into a closed shop in the District Building. The *Star* was firmly implanted with a grizzled veteran; so were the *Times*, the *Post*, and the *Herald*. It was a day in newspapering when a beat-man, once he mastered his run and sewed up his contacts, was kept permanently in the same job —except, possibly, on the *News*, the fifth-running paper, shorthanded, brash, and prone to turn the staff upside down once or twice a year.

Alec, dashing in a fuzzy fedora and plaid sports coat, walked into the pressroom and made himself known. His presence created slight interest. The boys looked up from a four-handed stud game and grunted. They looked like beatmen; shabby, ash-strewn, alcohol-battered creatures of habit who generally phoned their notes to the desk and left the writing to the rewrite bank. Occasionally they groaned over an overnighter or a command think-piece for the editorial page, but typewriters were anathema. Harry Barrett, bald and slight, from the *Times*, would take a nip out of the bottle in his desk and say to Mike O'Creary, of the *Herald:* "Hey, it's your turn to go see what old Blatherguts [the District Commissioner] has on his mind this morning. Tell the old windbag to keep it short, whatever it is." And the endless poker game would resume until smudge-mustached O'Creary would return with a few scribbled notes and the news that there was going to be some Congressional action on the new highway extension or the water bill or whatever occupied the honorary mayor of a town which had Congress for its city council.

They regarded Alec Barr bleakly and with animosity, first, because he was young; from the wild-eyed *News*, second; and apt to be eager, third, which would mean more work for all hands. So they immediately set out to discipline the intruder. Routine newsbreaks were withheld. Small exclusives were shared among the veterans. No day passed that the desk didn't ring Alec and say: "Where the hell were you on this?" when the first city editions of the afternoon papers hit the streets. Alec wore his arches flat pounding the halls in search of news, but the city fathers had few answers, because Alec had few questions to ask on a strange beat, and when any story of prominence arose, the afternoon *Times* and *Star* rubbed Alec's nose in it, and the *Post* and *Herald* confirmed the beat the following morning. Alec felt roughly as if he were being chewed to bits by piranha fish. Perhaps John Barry was understanding, but Tom Freeland, the city editor, was not. The *News* was getting murdered, and the desk was raising hell.

The *Post* man, Peter Shotton, had been kind since he was not in a competing medium, and from time to time offered Alec a helping hand against the afternoon opposition. But there was an iron rule that newsbreaks would be revolved, turn and turn about, between morning and afternoon releases, so the best that Alec was able to achieve was a sorry rewrite of the *Post*'s and *Herald*'s morning stories for the first edition of his afternoon paper, after which the story was killed as the afternoon competition drove it off the pages with fresh information.

One day Shotton, on whom whiskey and boredom had made a deep imprint, dropped dead in the pressroom of a heart attack. One moment he was pecking at his rickety old Remington, the next he was slumped over the machine, one outflung arm knocking a pint of rye to the floor. Alec was the only man in the shack at the moment, so he called the *Post* and suggested that they send both the meat wagon and a new boy.

Alec was not prepared for the replacement, having grown used to sallow old men in mussy clothes; scruffy old men with burst veins in their cheeks and noses and orange nicotine stains on their forefingers.

"I'm the new boy from the *Post*," a voice said, and Alec looked up from his machine, because the new boy's voice was not that of a boy.

The new boy was approximately twenty-one years old, with smoky blue eyes and black wavy hair. The new boy's sweater was filled with most unboyish curves, and the new boy was wearing an oatmeal tweed skirt which showed most unboyish hips.

"I'm Dinah Frankel," the new "boy" said. "I'm sitting in for poor old Pete Shotton. Did he go easy?"

"Like that," Alec said, snapping his fingers. "With the boots on."

"Pity," Dinah Frankel said. "But it gives me a job of work to do, anyhow. I've written enough club news and woman's-page guff to gag a goat. We're shorthanded at the moment—another one of the upheavals—and somebody, God bless him, remembered that I used to be a newspaperman in Ohio before I became a newspaper*woman* in Washington, D.C. Can you show me a few of the ropes, or do I get it from the old sweats? By the way, what's your name?"

"Alec. Alec Barr. And you'd better ask one of the old

sweats to show you the ropes. I've only just succeeded in locating the men's room. This beat is a real closed shop. The old boys don't want to spoil it for themselves by any undue work."

"Hmmm." Dinah Frankel looked appraisingly at Alec. "I know the practice. We had pretty tight job security in Columbus. Took me a whole year and a lot of running to convince the boys I wasn't really a girl, but a reporter instead. Let us see what we can do about loosening up this journalistic monopoly."

One by one the other beat-men came in, and jaws dropped when they saw Shotton's replacement. A brash kid from a young newspaper had been sufficient affront to their kingdom, but now, Holy Christ! A woman in the press room! No more swearing, no more tobacco juice on the floor, and very possibly flowers on the *Post* desk. What was the business coming to? There was protracted grumbling to various city desks, and even formal protests to managing editors; dames were all right on the women's page, but on a *beat* . . . Jesus!

Dinah Frankel, on sex alone, was luckier than Alec. She switched a saucy hip past resentful secretaries, wore tighter sweaters, and managed quite a neat number of small exclusives by sheer weight of female blandishment directed at the hacks who had been posted by Congress to run the District's affairs, but she was still being monotonously murdered by her opposition, the morning *Herald* gentleman, who seemed more misogynistic than any other of the men in the press room.

As underdogs, both young and one female, Dinah and Alec banded together and started pooling their own small very seldom triumphs, so that occasionally they could hear a snarl: "And where the hell were you on this one?" filtering through the opposition telephones.

"But it's not good enough," Dinah Frankel said. "We're still getting clobbered on the major stuff. This is a joke beat, anyhow, and neither one of us will be on it very long. But I'd like to kick those old mossbacks into some kind of line before I quit."

"I couldn't agree more," Alec said. "Want another beer before we eat?" They had formed an inflexible habit of lunching together at the Ceres across Pennsylvania Avenue, and when business closed for the day they as inflexibly walked a block to the Café of All Nations on Fifteenth Street for a cocktail or two before Alec went off to collect Amelia and Dinah went off to whatever newspaper girls went off to in Washington. Alec suspected a steady beau—they rarely mentioned either Alec's wife or Dinah's boy friends. As the days passed, they had worked almost into a husband-wife relationship—Alec pleased, but not excited, to pass a working day with a pretty and very intelligent young woman, and Dinah not at all disappointed that the newly married rather handsome young Alec Barr wasn't trying to make a sneaky liaison for after hours.

One day, over twilight drinks on Fifteenth Street, Alec whipped a magazine out of his pocket. "Read this," he said. "It's by H. L. Mencken. Evidently he had the same trouble we're having when he was a young reporter in Baltimore."

Dinah scanned the article rapidly, and her eyes lighted.

"That's the answer. This is the ever-loving answer," she said. "We'll murder them."

Plucking a leaf physically from Mencken's book, Alec and Dinah began to *invent* stories. It could not be a one-man job; it needed corroboration from another newspaper to prevent its being knocked down by the scoopees.

Alec would write a story about an outbreak of rabies in southeast Washington for the afternoon late editions, and Dinah would confirm it for the early editions of her paper. They would both descend on the city stepfathers to demand what the Board of Public Health was doing about it, while the opposition floundered, trying to run down incidents of actual bitings. Dinah would invent a public housing scandal for her paper, and Alec would confirm it with a follow for his paper, and again they would descend on the harassed commissioners while the opposition continued to flap. If Alec invented a smallpox scare, Dinah confirmed it. If Dinah invented a new plan to raze a residential block to make room for a freeway, Alec confirmed it.

At the end of a month the other three papers came pleading, typewriters figuratively in hand. The senior officer present, the *Star* man, said simply:

"We're licked. We know what you people have been doing, and we've tried to explain it to the desk. The desk don't listen. The desk just says we're goofing off, sitting on our fat duffs while the young people are out digging up the news. We quit. We want to sign a peace treaty. From now on, we pool all the newsbreaks, nobody scoops nobody, and you kids can quit writing fiction. Okay?"

"Okay," said Dinah and Alec, shaking hands.

"But tell me," the *Star* asked wistfully, "was there really a rabies outbreak in Southeast?"

"Of course," Dinah said. "You don't really think we'd invent stories, do you?"

Shortly thereafter, with news fairly apportioned and handled on an equable basis, Alec was recalled for general assignment, and Dinah followed him as the star byliner for her paper. They covered everything from murders to trials to floods to rape to Congress, and always leaned on each other in the pinches. Dinah worked one side of the street, Alec the other, and when they met at the end of a grueling day, whether at a murder trial in Hagerstown, Maryland, or a World Series in New York, they pooled resources. The wonder was that it took them until the 1948 elections in Philadelphia to fall into bed, by which time Dinah had married somebody named Lawrence and had borne a child and Alec had been to war, written three books, two plays, innumerable magazine articles, and was in the process of falling out of love with his wife.

"And that, my boy, was sheerest accident," Dinah was saying now as they ate. "I just wish it had happened earlier, and on purpose."

"Me too," Alec said. "Hey, do you remember the murder we solved when we weren't happy with the District cops?"

"Do I not," Dinah said, her mouth full of steak. She laughed and almost choked. "Do I damn well not remember! I thought we'd both go to jail."

Just before the war there had been a particularly revolting murder in Washington, in which a lady of no particular principle had been hacked to death and stray portions of her dismembered body found stuffed in a culvert in the vicinity of Bowie racetrack.

The cops fumbled and bumbled and the papers wrote editorials damning police inefficiency, as the murder had obviously been committed in Washington and the body transported in a trunk to Maryland.

"It looks like war any minute," Alec Barr had said to Dinah over their ceremonial drink. "It seems to me I ought to do at least one thing for our police chums before patriotism grabs me. They say they got no clues; let's make 'em some clues."

"What'dyou have in mind?"

"I'd rather you didn't know the exact details," Alec said. "However, your paper will find the first clue, which I will substantiate for the afternoon field. You will then allow me to find the second, which you in turn will dignify with your byline. After three days, the editorial-page boys will take it out of our hands—"

Alec made a variety of purchases—a small, black-haired goat in Virginia, some gunny sacks, a rusty-bladed axe from a junk dealer, an old, jagged-blade butcher knife, and a small pick and shovel. He reread *Huckleberry Finn*—the first part, in which Huck simulates a murder in order to escape Pap— and went to work.

He slew the goat, wincing, with the pick, cut its throat, and then proceeded to make a laborious drag of its bleeding body through bushes near the final disposition of the disso- ciated human remains. He smeared the axeblade with blood and black goat hair, and buried it. He made another drag and buried the butcher knife. He then removed the sacrificial goat from the gunny sack, half-burned the sack, which was soaked with blood, and then scattered unidentifiable pieces of goat around the countryside.

He then wrote a small but powerful piece to the effect that if the combined forces of District and Maryland police could not solve this murder, it was the duty of the newspapers to take up the job. (A small but intense reference to *Timberline*, the story of Bonfils and Tammen by Gene Fowler, came in handy here.)

If managing editor John Barry knew what was in the wind, he ignored it, but Dinah, prodding her own paper, achieved a piece of similar cooperation from the executive end, and the two amateur sleuths set out to solve the murder.

Dinah followed the bloody trail of the bagged goat for the first clue, and a banner headline resulted. The police joined up like a pack of well-trained fox hounds, and suspect after suspect was dragged into custody. Next day, Alec dug up the bloody, hair-smeared axe, and the view halloo increased, with the other papers joining in the screaming headlines.

It was a fine story, worthy of Charles MacArthur or Ben Hecht in the hairier Chicago days. Everybody got into the act. The opposition papers started finding their own clues; the District police quarreled bitterly with the Maryland police, and both facets of law and order were furious at the press. Ringing editorials were written, demanding the resignation of police officials, and in Washington, a Congressional investigation of the District Commission was threatened.

Alec and Dinah, after the story got out of hand, merely covered the coverage, until one day the frenetic activity of the goosed police dug up a small, rather wilted Filipino who confessed, during a shortage of heroin, that he had carved up his lady love, and led the cops to the real murder weapons and to some rather nondescript vestigial remains of the lady which roughly fitted the jigsawed contents of the culvert.

Alec and Dinah toasted each other gravely, as befitted two civic benefactors who had committed a public service.

There had been considerable hanky-panky of this youthful persuasion, including one instance at the Maryland seashore when Dinah had overdone her lip rouge and eyeshadow, lowering her decolletage and showing rather more leg than necessary, in the entrapment of a sticky-fingered politician whose tactility extended to flesh as well as money. Alec had played the other half of the ancient badger game, hiding behind the curtains of a cabin, while Dinah fed the politician whiskey and temptation. The politician loosened his tongue at approximately the same time Dinah ostensibly was to loosen her stays, and Alec touched off a flash camera which showed all of the politician and a great deal of Dinah's person with the exception of her face. There had been an exceptional cleanup of the political situation in Montgomery County shortly thereafter.

Then Dinah moved on to New York and Alec to war. He had heard vaguely she was married to somebody named Lawrence, and later, that she had had a baby. He didn't cut her trail again until the 1948 Convention in Philadelphia, in which they fell happily into their old habits of sharing the story—and, at very long last, a bed.

21

Immersed in reminiscence they had drunk copious wine with dinner, and the Great Man had stopped off and had bought several rounds of brandy. They visited a variety of other places, including a West-Side Mexican joint for the *mariachi* music, and Alec remembered making a noisy point of drinking tequila. They went to the Blue Angel to see somebody or other, and Alec remembered they had sat in the outer bar with the press agent and drunk Scotch. They went down to the Village and saw something fuzzy in the way of flamenco dancing and drank more whiskey. The last stop Alec remembered was a slow-piano joint on Second Avenue, where an old prewar friend insisted that all the drinks were on the house, and then the world went away in a whirl, with one bright eye in the hurricane: Alec remembered making drunken, inept, fumbling motions and blurred protestations of love to Dinah in public and almost violent approaches to her person in some private place, at some time—

"Christ, it must have been here," Alec Barr said through stiffened lips and swollen tongue as he looked at his hotel room in The Bishop with a hangover that might be measured in furlongs. "She brought me home and I tried to make her. I must have been a beautiful baby, last night. What that girl must think of me."

I ought to call her, he thought. But not in my condition, not as the mess I am. I'll haul myself together and maybe ring her later on today. No, not today. I'll give her a few days to get over being out with a maudlin monster. I suppose I really ought to call Amelia, too, but I can't. I just can't. I've made the break, and I haven't got guts enough to call now. It's no good making the break if you go running right back the next day, reeking of penitence and alcoholic remorse.

What I want most right now, Alec Barr thought, *is a drink . . .*

He looked at his watch again. Twelve thirty-five. Another twenty-five minutes before the room-service bar opened. At

109

least, he thought, anybody but an idiot would have ordered
a bottle yesterday, against future need. Not me. Idiot Barr.
The little boy running away from home and forgetting his
knapsack. I can't ask that jerk on the desk to break any
rules, and I will not debase myself any more by ringing up
any friends. Not at Sunday midday.

"Well, Barr," he said aloud. "You got some heavy thinking
to do. Walking is good for the thought processes. Fresh air
is good for a hangover. And maybe there's a baseball game
on today. When in doubt, go to the ballgame. At the ballgame they will have, at least, a beer to soothe your croak-
ing throat. And at a ballgame they will not mind that you are
wearing yesterday's shirt."

He closed his door and rode down to the lobby, conscious of his stubble of beard, his bleary eyes, his rumpled
clothing. There was a new clerk at the desk—a clerk who
looked at him as if he were a species of rare insect.

"There a ballgame today?" he said.

"I think so," the new clerk said. "It'll be in the papers;
there's a *News* left."

Alec put a coin on the counter and retired to a corner behind a dusty rubber plant. He flipped rapidly to the sports
page and saw the billing: YANKEES VERSUS RED SOX, DOUBLE-
HEADER, 2 P.M. Then there was a story about Joe Di Maggio's hitless streak extending to seventeen games.

"Well, at least I'll shave and buy myself a toothbrush,"
Alec said to himself. "I'll shave, even if I have to use both
hands," and set off in search of a Sunday-open drugstore.

The shave, in which he only cut himself once, improved
his physical state a little, but the butterflies still battled in
his belly, and the orange juice and coffee he had consumed
in the drugstore rudely deserted him as soon as he returned
to the hotel.

For the lack of anything better—there was no place to go,
no bar to lean against, the idea of the Sunday *Times* re-
pulsive even if he could lift it in this condition—Alec Barr
set out to walk a hundred blocks to Yankee Stadium.

The walking soothed him somewhat, but his mind was a
raging misery of guilt. Amelia, he thought, how can I do
this to Amelia? I'm all Amelia's got, he thought. Amelia without me will be lost. You conceited bastard, Barr, he thought.
You selfish, conceited bastard. When the ship was about to
blow up in the war, your whole life didn't race past you like

they say in the books. All you could think of was that there were a lot of quail unshot, a lot of books unwritten, a lot of steaks uneaten, a lot of girls unscrewed—and that Amelia would have a hard time finding another fellow that she could get along with. Always the *I*. Always the *me*, Barr. Self-centered, stupid, selfish sonofabitchbastardbarr.

As he strode the Sunday sidewalks, an agony of conscience whetted the hangover. He thought of the early, hungry days, when he was making thirty a week and had gall enough to get married. He thought of Amelia working in the department store for the extra twenty bucks a week that allowed them the one bottle of cut-rate whiskey and an occasional night out. He thought of the successive raises which culminated in the first little house; he groaned mentally as he remembered the nights he and Amelia had sat in the little study, he writing the magazine pieces that wouldn't sell, the novel that wouldn't sell, the play that wouldn't sell. He wallowed in self-abasement when he remembered the first time that a magazine bought and actually paid four hundred dollars for a piece—he remembered exactly what the piece was about, although the subsequent hundreds blurred in his brain. The four hundred dollars was two months' pay, and he and Amelia had blown a good bit of it on a really wild night on the town. That was the week end after he met Marc Mantell, who had given him the magic key.

He remembered the brave Amelia, smiling him off as he left for the war, saving the tears for after he had gone, quite handsome, extra-jaunty, and tremendously exhilarated in his blue suit with the stripe and a half on the sleeve. He remembered the week end Amelia came up to Dartmouth at the halfway mark of his indoctrination; he remembered Amelia camp-following, as Navy training shifted him to such unlikely places as Biloxi, Mississippi, where they lived in a literal whorehouse because there was no other place for temporary gentlemen and their wives and children to live. The whores had been kind, baby-sitting the officers' children and even lending the officers money when Navy got its payroll fouled and the eagle forgot to scream; that had been a good time, a funny time, as Boston and New Orleans had been good and funny and sad, everyone young and terribly brave, and wildly excited about going off to die. Alec had no ideas about dying. He had told himself he wasn't the type. Remorse gouged him again as he remembered his first serious infidelities—in Washington, out of spite; in London, because the bombs were falling, and you mightn't see tomorrow. In San Francisco, because you were shipping out for the last assignment of the war, and you knew you would either live or die but you wouldn't get back until they wrapped up the Japs. In Melbourne and Sydney, because you were accustomed to it by now, and after four years your conscience no longer gnawed you when you met a pretty girl and took her to bed, allowing yourself to be briefly, semi-in-love, or at least fond of the fondness, susceptible to the liking.

And the postwar, the postwar, when the stuff you had written to kill the boredom of the war had miraculously changed you from Alec Barr, Lt. Cmdr. USNR, to Alexander Barr, author, and the papers were full of reviews and interviews, and magazines came round to do pieces on *you*, and all of a sudden the Mantell office was flooded with offers for Barr to write this and Barr to write that, Barr to go on *Information Please* and Barr to take the lecture circuits, and Barr to go on TV, and Amelia helpless before the circumstances which had transformed her mild man into a strange, monstrous figure, the property of everyone and of no one at all.

Then, God pity me, Alec thought, there was the first Book of the Month, the first movie sale, the first magazine cover, and the first big money with all of the problems that go with big money. And the parents. Always the goddam parents with their problems and the bloody brother with his problems, and Amelia with her problems—or, in frankness, he thought—one problem. Me. Alec Barr. Alec Barr the book author. The literary figure. The chaser, the wencher, the stander-at-stud. Alecbarrsonofabitchbastardauthorbarr.

Alec was walking steadily through Harlem now, minding his own business, paying no attention to the Spanish curses flung at him by the Puerto Rican sidewalk loungers. ("Look at the white whoreson," one café-au-lait zoot-suiter with sideburns was saying to his carbon copy. "Dirty the milk, a white man walks alone in Harlem, perhaps in pursuit of a black woman or a fresh supply of pot?")

I was wed to stay married, Alec thought. We get married for keeps where I come from. I better go back; I will, by God, go back. I owe it to Amelia. None of it's her fault; nobody could have tried harder. It's all my fault. I don't know what the hell's wrong with me, except that I want everything all at once. Don't blame it on the war, Commander, he thought. The war didn't give you anything but a long vacation and a lot of time to think. God bless the war. Just blame yourself, Commander. Write it on your own fitness report.

All of a sudden Alec Barr began to feel better. He would be noble; he would go back to Amelia. He could feel his hangover lifting, and suddenly he had lost the craving for a drink, although he could see the saloons opening along Lenox Avenue. He felt suddenly fine. Nobility was the great thing. Be noble. He'd go to the ballgame and then go back to Amelia. He hailed a taxi. He had walked far enough.

Alec Barr bought a seat behind third base, a front-line box. Frankie Crosetti, lean and whippy as always, turned to smile from the coaching box. Crosetti was portion to Alec's past, which had begun in newspapers about the time Tony Lazzeri was bowing out at shortstop. Now it was Rizzuto at short—stubby little Phil, who had come up that season so long ago from Kansas City with Gerry Priddy; the year Ted Williams beamed in with the Bostons; the year Di Maggio was already establishing himself as immortal. Crosetti was finished as a player; Di Mag, little Phil, and Williams were very much around, very vibrant. Except Di Maggio, who had been hitless in seventeen straight games.

The sun was warm and friendly. The stadium was less than a quarter filled, for August was still exhausting the Sunday citizens on the beaches and in the mountains. Alec waved at a vendor and bought a beer. It was warm, too, but settled happily in his stomach, and the next time the hotdog purveyor passed, Alec ordered a couple of franks. The flag stirred only briefly in the breeze. The infield was baked iron-hard, and the grass had yellowed from the long summer suns.

Di Maggio was batting cleanup, and when he came to the plate with Rizzuto on and two away, in the first, the crowd greeted him with a mighty boo. The boos increased as he waited out two strikes and, wide-legged, imperturbable, stretched the count to three and two. Alec could see the Boston pitcher curse at the last call. The umpires were in on the act, too; Di Mag, out of respected seniority, was getting a little the best of a low outside curve that bit a tiny corner off the plate before it fell away.

The Boston boy was sore. He made no motion to hold

Rizzuto at first, and little Phil danced away, halfway to second base. The Boston boy reared back and plowed one straight down the middle. Di Maggio swung his incomparably level swing, and at the sound his brother Dominic, in center field for the Red Sox, turned his back and ran. The ball traveled on a rising line into deep left center, with Dom Di Maggio coursing it like a hound. He plucked it off the turf and unleashed the unbelievable strength of a small man's throwing arm. Ted Williams, standing flatfooted in left, watched the operation as if he had paid admission.

Dominic's throw-in came on a string to third base, and his brother hooked a slide under the throw. Rizzuto, off and running at the sound of the bat, was already back to the dugout when Joe Di Maggio hit the ground in a puff of dust. The umpire's hands spread flat. Di Maggio got up off the ground and beat the dust from his flannels. He took a long look at his brother in center field, raised a thumb in a sign which could have been "Okay, kid" in Air Force language, or which could just as easily have been "Up yours, brother" in Italian. Crosetti, the other San Francisco Wop, walked out of the box and said something which made Di Maggio laugh. Then Di Maggio turned in the direction of Alec Barr's box seat and winked; a long, slow, deliberate wink.

Alec Barr winked back, and toasted Di Maggio with the beer bottle. All of a sudden Alec Barr felt much better. The bad day was over; the screaming conscience had departed. It was a funny Sunday in New York. Di Maggio had snapped his slump. The Yankees were ahead, 1–0.

"The hell with her," Alec Barr said aloud. "She's had as much good out of me as I've had out of her. The hell with her. I'm never going home again."

22

Di Maggio got three for five that day, including a towering home run into the left-field bleachers. Rizzuto homered inside the park, and lost his cap rounding third under a full head of steam. Williams went sulkily oh-for-four. Alec Barr drank three beers. The Yankees won by an overwhelming margin, and Alec Barr decided not to stay for the second game.

A sudden lassitude struck him, the same small-feverish, bone-weary, emotion-drained feeling he had sometimes experienced at bullfights, when the *faena* was authentic and the matador and the bull were working very well together, anticipating each other's needs. He felt spent; used, satiated. Di Maggio's triple had pulled a plug in his feelings.

He went back to the hotel, ordered a bottle of Scotch from room service, and went to sleep with the first glass standing half-full by his bedside. He slept the night through, and no nightmares galloped his bed.

He rose at noon the next day and dressed, once more, in his abused garments. He had thought to call Dinah, but sleep had robbed him of politeness. He tossed the key on the desk before the clerk with the roquefort teeth and asked for his bill. He had shaved again, but the suit, the shirt, the tie, were definitely crummy.

"Leaving us so soon?" the clerk said, showing his deplorable fangs. "I thought perhaps by now"—he looked Alec up and down—"I thought perhaps by now your fresh clothes might have arrived."

Alec looked at his bill, accepted the change from his deposit, and threw the bill, together with a five-dollar note at the clerk.

"If I were you," Alec Barr said, "I really would shave off that mustache."

He turned and walked to the door, leaving the clerk with his mouth still open to reveal the green-veined yellow teeth.

He headed west, crossing Park, and decided to stroll. It was still hot, very hot, but somehow the pressure seemed to be lifting, the humidity lightening. There was, or perhaps he imagined it, the faint beginnings of a crisp feel of autumn just around the corner. He began to hum a favorite song, whose words he did not know, except the first few. It was "Autumn in New York."

"The thrill of first-nighting," Alec Barr sang, causing a nice old lady to stare at him, "Is often mingled with pain." That was the wrong verse sequence, actually, but remembering some of the stage productions he had been involved in, he laughed aloud, this time invoking a solid stare of rebuke from a solid gentleman in a solid bowler hat.

"It's so nice to have a man around the house," Alec Barr then sang. "Even though he turns out to be a louse. And I'm out, out, out! Do you hear me, Barr? Out! And I think I shall just go to the Ritz. It'll be nice to have a floor waiter and some buttons to press again, and a valet looking in to see if all's well with your nonexistent wardrobe. And I will bet you that there will be no cheap cracks at Reception, not after all the money I've spent watching the ducklings in the Promenade. . . .

"Ducklings? Ducklings! Of course ducklings!" The smile sweetened from its sour start. "That's what she called the hair-shade, 'fluffy duckling to go with the beady brown eyes.' Now let's see how your luck runs, Barr. We will check into the biggest suite in Mr. Ritz's Carlton, and we will go downstairs to the Little Bar, and we will order a double martini, and then we will sort out various things for phone numbers, and see if Miss Barbara Bayne, *née* O'Shaughnessy, is still encumbering the village, and if she's gotten rid of that dreadful actor yet."

Alec walked into the weathered old Ritz and wished he had a stick to swing. The Ritz always hit him that way; no matter how he was dressed, he longed for a gray flannel suit, reverse-calf shoes, a carnation in his buttonhole, a Trilby hat, and a stick to swing. There weren't many places like the Ritz left in New York, with all these new real estate changes, and it would be only a matter of time before it toppled to make room for some horrid tomb of micaed stone and staring glass frontage.

"Oh, Mr. Barr," the desk clerk said. "How are you? How terribly nice to see you. Looking for someone? I haven't seen any of your editors disappearing into the Black Hole below as yet. But I suppose most of them are up on the Cape. I'm told that's where all good editors go in a summer as hot as this one."

"How terribly nice to see you—Can—it's Cantrell, isn't it?"

"Almost." The clerk smiled. "You're very good. Actually it's Cantwell. May I serve you?"

"You may indeed," Alec Barr said. "I want a suite. I want a very big suite. And I want to be semi-incognito for a few days. I haven't a stitch with me, so I want your best valet to go to Brooks and pick me up half a dozen shirts, two pairs of pajamas, a half-dozen pairs of black socks, the same number of shorts, and two or three plain black neckties.

I'll also require some shaving tackle, toothpaste, toothbrushes —hard—deodorant—you know, the complete drill. I'll ring up Mr. Florian at Brooks and tell him your man's coming, and settle a couple of other details. They have all my measurements."

"Fire in your home?" The clerk pushed the registration pad at Alec and permitted himself the luxury of a familiarity between almost equals.

"You might say," Alec Barr said. "You might just say. I suppose you'll want me to pay in advance, as I've no luggage."

"Mister Barr!" The clerk made a face of incredible horror. "Not even in a joke. You're at home here."

"It's nice to feel wanted," Alec replied. "I'll just jaunt down to the Little 'un and have a drink and make a phone call whilst your man is out picking up my things. And oh, yes. Would you do me the favor of ringing room service and saying I'll require two bottles each of Scotch, bourbon, gin, and brandy—Chivas, Jack Daniel, Beefeater, Otard— and the fixings? I may be having a little business company."

"But of course, Mr. Barr," the clerk said, reaching for the desk phone. "But immediately."

"Thank God," Alec murmured, walking down to the Little Bar. "Thank God they still make Ritzes. I don't know why I didn't come straight here. Shock, I guess."

Her voice spilled swiftly and coolly onto the phone on the third ring.

"Thank God again for all His graces," said Alec Barr. "This seems to be my day for thanking God. I had some awful idea you'd be in Canada salmon-fishing or, at the very least, in Paris. This is an old friend of a friend from Chicago. I have a note from you, with old lipstick on it. May we talk?"

"We may talk. I am a free woman in her own almost-freeheld house. How very nice to hear from you, Alec. I'd rather expected you to call earlier. Can *you* talk?"

"I can talk. I'm a free man in somebody else's hotel, specifically the dear old Ritz. I'm having a drink in the downstairs Little Bar. I am registered into this pub with no clothes. I wonder if you would care to eat a pound of Mr. Romanoff's best caviar with a man who has no luggage, and then investigate the night life of a town I've never been allowed to cavort in? You see I've just left my wife, and I rather imagine it's mostly your fault."

"Well," said Barbara Bayne, "you know what they say about the Chinese. If you pull one out of the water and save his life, you own him forever. Now the point is this, friend: Who owns whom?"

"I'd venture that the responsibility for me is distinctly yours," Alec said. "And I don't want to be a cad, but—"

"I love you as a cad. You're a charming cad. You should have taken it up ages ago. It fits some people. Gauguin, for instance."

"I must remember to mind my manners. One, I didn't really identify myself on the phone. So: This is Alec Barr, Mrs. Emory. It's a dull Monday in late August and I'm bored to distraction and I'm registered incognito under my own name at the Ritz and I believe—although lunch is quite distant, such as tomorrow—that one is able to feed charmingly in the Promenade in which swim fluffy ducklings who reminded me of your hair so I am asking what you are doing at this very moment and would you come over and eat about a pound of Beluga?"

"You sound a trifle mad, and in sore need of aid. Would half an hour be too early for Your Worship? I'm about two thirds clad anyhow."

"I pant. I languish. I swoon. Try and make it twenty minutes. I don't know what suite I'm in, but it'll be big enough to be respectable. Gin or vodka or what with the caviar?"

"Aquavit," Barbara said. "Buried in ice. And champagne to chase the aquavit with. It's Saturday night, ain't it?"

"As a matter of fact it's Monday. It just feels like Saturday."

"I think I'm going to be dreadfully in love with you, you silly, serious, foolish man."

"Hurry. It's contagious," Alec said.

"You look very happy, Mr. Barr," the waiter said when he brought the check.

"I am reborn," said Alec Barr. "I am born again in another body. And I think also I'm a little drunk. Also I'm in love."

"I'm very happy for you, Mr. Barr," the waiter said. "About being reborn, I mean."

"Keep the change," Alec said.

"But, Mr. Barr, it's change from a twenty and you only had two—"

"Keep the change, like I said. See you in heaven. Just ask for Alec. Somebody will let you in."

"I am *very* happy for you, Mr. Barr," the waiter said, and rolled his eyes back as Alec strode out whistling "Autumn in New York." "Two martinis, twenty bucks, he says keep the change," the waiter said to his colleague. "I know most authors are screwy, we see enough of 'em here, but this one must be some kind of a real nut."

"Count your blessings and don't forget we pool the tips in this joint," the colleague said. "Thank *you*, chum."

It was still quite early, and Alec looked at his watch. He spoke to the valet who was unboxing his new, emergency clothes.

"Look—what's your name? I'll be here for some time."

"Albert, sir. My colleague is called Sidney."

"Fine. Look, Albert. I'm expecting a lady shortly, rather a special visit. Would you please be so kind as to ring for the room waiter again, and ask him to bring me two one-pound tins of Romanoff caviar, all the fixings, and a little later, some blinis and sour cream when I ring? He's been here with the basic booze, but I'll be needing two bottles of aquavit—here, do you want to write it down?"

"No need, sir," the valet's voice carried a mild reproof. "But two one-pound tins of the Beluga?"

"That's right. I feel festive and foolish, and I never knew how much caviar I could eat until tonight."

"I quite understand, sir. And the champagne?"

"Leave it up to the waiter. Mumms was a true friend of the family, but I'll accept the recommendation of your other colleagues. All I want is that the champagne starts immediately in the ice bucket, and have him plant the aquavit in crushed ice the way the Danes do. Right?"

"Indeed, sir."

"Fine. I want a shower, fast, and by that time you'll be back with my shoes, right?"

"Right, sir. Asking your pardon, sir, are you an American?"

"I was," Alec Barr said. "At the moment I wouldn't say I was very much of anything special, except happy. Off with you now, you've a lot of work to do."

"Thank you, sir," the valet said, and went to press the

button for the room waiter, who obviously lived in a kennel outside the door.

Well, now, Alec Barr mused in the shower—the old-fashioned kind, with a dozen delectable knobs to twist and all sorts of surprising streams of water striking you in unlikely places. Well, now. Are you an American, Mr. Barr, begging your pardon, of course? Have I come that far away from the home folks, I wonder? I suppose perhaps I have. You come hungry out of a place like Kingtown, South Carolina, and somebody asks if you're an American just because you spent quite a lot of time with the English language and with English people, and know how to talk to room servants, and have your emergency measurements on file at a dozen places in a dozen cities.

I don't suppose you really are an American any more, Mr. Barr, Alec thought. The aircraft changed all that. Any time you can cross half the world in a day you're apt to lose your insularity. The steamer-trunk people must be having hell's own trouble in the sales department. Gone with the buggy whips.

"Hey, Barr," Alec said aloud as he toweled himself, and reached for the razor which had been laid out with his other toilet gear. "Hey there, Barr! I think you're happy. I think you've been bringing this to a head for quite a long time. And Barr"—he stared at himself sternly as he plumped his face in lather—"Please do be careful, Barr. You're fairly new at this love business, and for an awful, dreadful, horrifying long time you've wanted to be in love. You can get yourself bit real good, Barr, and that ain't no English euphemism for murder."

The new shirts felt lovely and caressing on his skin, as good unwashed shirts always feel, and he noticed that the valet had slung a swift press into his only suit while he dawdled in the shower. The new shoes were there and unboxed—the only shoes he ever bought were from Church in New York or Peal in London, when he had time to have them made to order—sleek black calf with shining pinkish soles like the skin of a Negro's palm.

He could make it tonight with clean underpants, clean shirt, fresh necktie, pressed suit, and new shoes and socks. Tomorrow he'd have three emergency suits sent over from dear Mr. Florian at Brooks, and then he would see about

sending round for some of his own clothes at the flat.
That might depend on Amelia's mood.

Right now he didn't want to think about Amelia or her
mood. He wanted to think about Barbara Bayne, with her
fluffy-duckling hair, and what they would do this night as
free folk. As he slid his feet into his new shoes, savoring
the clasp of the lovely-smelling leather on fresh silk socks,
he thought impatiently:

"Christ, I wish she'd hurry. For the first time in my life
I feel like a groom."

At this precise moment the door-gong sounded, and he
rushed to open it. It was only the waiter with the caviar
and champagne. Alec Barr's face expressed extreme disappointment.

"Oh, sir, I shouldn't really look like that if I were you,"
the room waiter said cheerfully. "There's a lovely lady just
behind me in the hall. Where would you like me to put the
caviar?"

"Anywhere at all," Alec Barr said, and rushed past the
waiter to take Barbara Bayne almost brutally in his arms.
"Excuse me," he said over his shoulder to the waiter, and
then kissed Barbara soundly, overlong, careless of make-up,
holding her closely.

"I thought you'd never get here," he said. "It seemed like
years."

Barbara Bayne looked at her watch. "It's been exactly
thirty-seven minutes since I hung up the phone."

"I don't believe I can afford that much time of my life
without you," Alec Barr said. "Would you like some caviar?"

"Not," replied Barbara Bayne, "at this precise moment."

23 / Amelia

Amelia Barr was acutely, hauntedly miserable. She was, as
her friends happily reported, driving herself up the wall.
There was no word from Alec, but daily communiqués
drifted in from the intelligence corps of the hairdresser–
girl-lunch–dressmaker–cocktail espionage system. Alec had

been seen lunching at the Brussels with Barbara Bayne. Alec had been seen dancing at the Persian Room with Barbara Bayne. Alec had been seen in Greenwich Village, in Harlem, on Third Avenue, in the Ritz, at the Marguery, at the Penthouse Club—and always with Barbara Bayne.

Amelia assiduously searched Alec's clothes and papers for any letter, any clue, leading to a previous association with Barbara Bayne, and found none. She found nothing concerning any other women, either, but her imagination painted grotesquely vivid pictures of fleshly misconduct with a variety of glamorous women on every occasion that Alec had been even momentarily out of her sight since their marriage.

Her girl friends were vocally sympathetic, demonstratively comforting when they dropped by at teatime for three or four martinis, but Amelia had the feeling that the sympathy was fraudulent, and that her companions of the luncheon table and the charity balls were secretly gleeful at the addition of a new member to a miserable company. Most of Amelia's women friends were victims of previous matrimonial catastrophe; all, in one way or the other, had experienced "trouble with" Bill or Dick or Jim. Some of it had been secretarial trouble—one friend, more waspish than the rest, had been the secretary who caused the trouble and was twice as suspicious of her husband now because she remembered how she snared him. Some had just been routine, out-of-town-business-trip trouble, or pretty-neighbor trouble, or any other kind of trouble likely to time-tired marriage. There was an almost perceptible gloating over Amelia's induction into the sad sorority.

Amelia Barr inspected herself long and searchingly in the mirror, and saw a handsome blue-eyed brown-haired woman in her mid-thirties—good breasts, good skin, good hips, good legs (and she was forced to admit, a stout but unquenched libido) and wondered miserably what she had done wrong. She had always, she thought, been an understanding and loving wife. She looked at her home and saw taste and comfort. She looked at her wardrobe and saw expensively conservative frocks and fine shoes and superb lingerie. She looked at her kitchen and found it neat; she looked at her servants and found them competent. The fireplace did not smoke; the elevator did not creak overmuch. There were plenty of ice trays in the refrigerator. The stock in the bamboo bar was adequate, always, and the pantry reserve abundant. She spent a lot of time in that bar. She looked again in the mirror and saw that she was spending too much time in that bar. The clear skin was beginning slightly to mud, the blue eyes beginning to streak, and the pads of flesh beneath the blue eyes more than starting to puff.

She found that she derived very little aid or comfort from her female associates, and reflected that in all these years of New York she had acquired perhaps one—at the outside, two women friends. The rest were longtime acquaintances, the same acquaintances you kissed on the cheek at cocktail parties and lunched with and saw at the hairdresser's and sat next to at dinner and ran into in Paris and London and Rome. Amelia Barr was a generous, bountiful woman. There were no children to occupy her time. She desperately wanted to give, and in New York there was nobody to give to. Nobody, perhaps, except Francis Hopkins.

Alec Barr, in one of his ruder moods with the cutting edge of his tongue whetted to epigrammatic edge, had remarked after Francis left the house: "A good trustworthy house pansy is as necessary to a modern New York marriage as the license and preacher." Hurt, Amelia was now beginning to believe it.

She was afraid—not afraid, perhaps, but reluctant—to go out to the accustomed spas, for fear of running into Alec and this Barbara woman, who by all accounts were quite shamelessly appearing in public; holding hands and nibbling at each other and drowning in each other's eyes. Drinking and eating by herself gave her the screeching fantods, so she became daily more dependent on Francis Hopkins. Francis was a pillar of strength. He invited her over to his flat for dinner. He took her out to dine in dim places which, he said, "Alec and that girl couldn't possibly know." After the maid left for the day, he would whip up a batch of scrambled eggs or prepare one of his special salads in Amelia's apartment. But mostly he listened patiently, and let her weep at will. He agreed with her when she stormed over what bastards all men were, and Barr the worst of the lot, but was himself intelligent enough not to point an accusing finger at Alec. This was an accrued wisdom; he had seen Amelia charge like a tigress at people who had dared suggest that Alec Barr wasn't the best writer in the world and the paragon of all male humanity.

Exactly two weeks after Alec had fled the roost and most of the better bars were buzzing deliciously with the town's newest and hottest romance (it hadn't made the papers yet because all those married writing bastards stick together) Francis handed Amelia her fifth post-dinner Scotch and arranged his features into their best Dutch-uncle mold.

"You've got to stop this foolishness," Francis said. "You're drinking like a fish, driving yourself crazy, and quite frankly you're beginning to look like the wrath of God. You're a mess, Sweetie, and you're getting messier. I told you what to do the night Alec walked out, and you haven't done *any* of it. You haven't done anything about that Nuyu health farm, I'll bet you. You haven't bought any new clothes. All you've done is sit around feeling sorry for yourself. Alec isn't worth it. No husband is."

Amelia's eyes were pink-puffy from the most recent freshet of tears.

"I honestly meant to get in touch with the health farm thing, but I kept sort of expecting Alec to come back—like it was a bad dream that would go away—and I hate the idea of shutting myself up like some kind of criminal with a lot of fat women, doing silly exercises and drinking raw carrot juice."

Francis got up and yawned. He looked at his watch.

"It's three A.M.," he said. "Perhaps I'm willing to let you kill yourself, but I'm not going to let you kill *me*. Now see here." He made his voice stern. "I'm going to get in touch with the Nuyu people early tomorrow, and I'm going to book you a plane for Denver. Pack all your best clothes—to hell with the excess baggage—those women dress to the teeth for dinner out there. At least they do at Arden's. And I'm going to sling you on that plane if I have to handcuff you."

"But I don't want to go," Amelia said stubbornly, jutting her jaw. "I'm all right. I'll be all right." She drummed her fingers.

"The hell you'll be all right," Francis said irritably. "Where you'll be is Bellevue, and I'll be in the cell next to you. No more monkeyshines, now, girl. Drink your drink and take a pill and go to sleep and get yourself packed tomorrow and I'll be by with a car and put you on the plane myself. I'll see about hotel reservations for tomorrow night in Denver, and you can go out to the ranch the next day. Hear me?"

Amelia collapsed in tears again, burying her face in Francis' collar. Francis shrugged purposefully away from the contact.

"Enough of that, now," he said, more kindly. "Put on your nightie and I'll tuck you in. Come on, now, or I'll paddle your bottom."

Amelia sniffled, and managed a smile.

"You're terribly kind to me, Francis," she said. "I don't know what I'd do without you."

"Neither do I," Francis muttered, staring at the ceiling. "Neither, by God, do I."

24

Amelia was quite drunk when Francis shoved her onto the plane, enlisting the assistance of an airlines public relations man who reacted disgustingly swiftly to the name of Alexander Barr. Despite the heat, she was carrying one mink—full-length—and two stoles, since Colorado promised to be chill and the order of the day, Francis said, was big *big* dressup for dinner. Her knees wobbled only slightly, and she managed a smile as Francis stood waving good-by under a NO SMOKING sign.

A week later Francis received the first bulletin. It said:

"Dear Svengali:

"Out of solitary and one of the wardens lent me a pen and some paper. I don't know if you really realize what goes on in these places, for a thousand a week, so for lack of anything better to do, I'll tell you. First off, you'll never recognize me. They have jacked up the old chassis and run a new car underneath it. Or so it feels.

"Before you so blithely advise another friend to take the cure the hard way, you had better know something about what goes on inside these walls so I'll give you the play-by-play. 'Tain't funny, McGee.

"To go alone is very *déclassé*. It appears I am very *déclassé*. I should have brought you.

"It *is* expensive. Maybe $1000 a week. Haven't got to the tips yet. Everybody too well-bred to mention money. We live in little groups of houses around the main building which is the central station. At least I'm not lonesome.

"First they check your own doctor's papers and give you a physical exam. Next they establish a sort of regime for you. If you're here to lose weight, and who ain't, it goes more or less like this:

"They get us up at dawn. They issue us darling little peach-colored shifts which are very short and belted loosely so that you betray very damn little of your basic girth. Everybody wears same outfit like in girls' school. Run around in sandals which are also GI. Seems if you're a good little girl you get to keep these. Goody-two-shoes-five-hundred-bucks apiece!

"Breakfast consists of 'simply delicious' fruits and juices and black coffee or tea. The fruits are all fresh and clean and lovely and homegrown on the premises. The gardener wears a surgeon's mask to keep them pure. It is a very filling breakfast. If you like breakfast. As you know, I *hate* breakfast.

"Next we have an exercise period—big group deal. Everybody lies down on spotless mats (peach again) while music plays and a lovely, skinny female (*hate* her) gives directions for rolling for the hips, and sit-ups for flattening the tummy. We do this a little longer each day, but basically, it *never* gets any better.

"The mid-morning break comes in the form of grass tea. It mostly replenishes the lost liquids.

"Everything we eat is lightly salted, and there is no sodium chloride on the table. Outwardly, we are losing weight like mad but mostly it is just stored water. Football players can lose up to 10 lbs. of this excess water in one game, they tell us. But we are not football players.

"Now we have a mid-morning break for refreshments. This is either tomato juice or various teas made of old gumshoes or possibly even imported, exotic seaweed, depending upon what *PARTICULAR* kick our all-knowing doctor is on. The seaweed tea has great snob value. It tastes like castor oil.

"After the juice-cum-tea break, we go swimming, but under strict supervision. Miss La Roache takes us to the big, overheated pool where we thoughtfully do so many breast strokes to build up our flabby pectoral muscles, etc. We wear caps. We look *awful*. We wear issue swim suits which are sloppily pleated and Neo-Grecian in derivation, and which do not betray our figures unless we are absolutely soaked. In this case, we cannily observe one another from the corners of the eyes, but we refrain from comment. We are in *NO* position to criticize. We are all in this mess together.

"We do the swim thing the easy hard way. Sometimes we just flutter-kick fifty times slowly, so as not to exhaust us, while we hang onto the side of the pool. Drowning is frowned on by the management.

"After the swim we might have a brief game of badminton, but this is optional, like cancer. Most of us choose the shower and change into our peachy shifts (short and Grecian, with peach ballet tights beneath) but leisurely. About this time I would *maim* for a martini; *KILL* for a Bloody Mary.

"Oh *boy!* Now comes lunch. Vegetables, demi-cooked, or revoltingly raw with a low-calory, health-giving dressing based largely on tomato juice, spices, and mineral oil.

"For your information, Sweetie, mineral oil has wonderful laxative qualities, but it also has a tendency to *leak* when least expected.

"We have next a free period in which we can take a nature walk, just lie in bed and gossip about *WHO IS HERE NOW*. This is very important. It is dreadful to be here the week *AFTER* the Duchess of Windsor and the week *BEFORE* Mamie Eisenhower. It is like Russian roulette to hit the right week.

"Next there is the treatment, or therapy session. It varies. The resort urges you take the mud bath for *YOUR PARTICULAR PROBLEM*. Treatments are fairly grim. For one thing, a maiden lady might just get a male *masseuse*. It is true that he uncovers only one area at a time, and (honest!) never gets what you would call *fresh*. But it is mostly the idea of having a male rub you the wrong way that really rubs you the wrong way.

"There are all sorts of possibilities in this therapy racket, but mostly it is pretty damn dull. Goes like this:

"1. *The steam cabinet or mud pack.*

In either event, it is hotter than the human flesh can stand and we sweat off absolutely *POUNDS* of *FAT,* darling! (Or is it that goddam accumulated water?)

"2. *The massage*.
   This is where you get pummeled by a Swiss or Swede who speaks hardly a word of English so that it will be embarrassing later to go home to your husband covered head to toe with bruises because the goddam masseuse couldn't comprehend when I said, 'Goddamit, you're breaking my back.'

"3. *The rest period*.
   It makes us nervous to lie in the booth with the curtain only, and no lock. The table is hard and it doesn't quite fit, no matter which way we turn because in spite of our natural overstuffing, the bones have a way of digging into the thinly padded leather table, or vice versa. At some point we doze off.

"4. *The shower*.
   Brisk and cold. We dry. We put on our peachy, short shifts, and then pad back to our cottages in time to change for cocktails and dinner.

"Cocktails and dinner are full-dress, and done properly by candlelight which softens the wrinkles. Now—for reducers, there might be choices of sauerkraut juice, tomato, orange (grape is too high-cal), or any combination of fruits and vegetables blended and strained. There is even something called The Elimination Cocktail. I can only assume it has a prune-juice base.

"We drink the cocktails from the cocktail-looking glasses. You can have them straight like a martini, or on the rocks, or with water or soda. We stand around sipping and chatting elegantly. We are wearing full evening regalia, and all our *genuine* diamonds and pearls. No men are involved, except possibly Doctor God up there who is the Physician of us all, and who is *SUCH* a charmer. He told me this morning that he was *TERRIBLY* pleased with my progress with my *INNER THIGH PROBLEM*.

"Now, Sweetie, we stroll into the dinner room at the proper time when the chimes *chime*. In twos and threes we stroll. Leisurely. Trailing trains, flaunting plumes. We case one another, which is to say: How much money can you wear at one time and still maintain good taste? Also we are very keen to track down the designers of each others' gowns. We sort of show off, like so:

" '*Chanel* said it was perfect for me, but I never felt at home in it.'

" 'I hate to confess it is three years old, but of course Charles James did it and He is timeless.'

" 'You are *SO* sweet to say so, but Trigère's one great fault is that you *MUST* hold your tummy *in*.'

" 'Yes, it's a Rentner, but it hasn't fit right since the last baby—you just don't know what it's *like* to have a menopause baby . . . not that we don't just *adore* little Afterthought.'

"Dinner is formal. We are seated in groups according to our diets. Our reducers' group has lean meat, cooked vegetables (mostly stalks and leaves, because the roots have more carbohydrate), and salads. Sometimes we have fish. Always the sauces are excellent in a loathsome sort of way. They use a lot of herbs, lemon juice, and vinegar.

"That's about the shape of it. I'll probably come out of here looking like Betty Grable—or at least like Betty Grable's mother. If there's any news, like maybe Alec just divorced me in Mexico, please drop me a line. And please look in on the apartment to see if the maid's watering the plants. You know where the bar is.

"Love,

"Trilby, *née* Amelia, Barr."

Three days later, Francis found another bulletin from the fighting fronts. It said:

"Dear Pygmalion:

"One would not recognize us girls by now. We are not women—we are *creations!* By now we have been completely created by the famous M. de Quatrefages himself who, lest you forget, absolutely eclipses Antoine, Michel, and Mr. Kenneth when it comes to hairstyles, skin care, beauty, and general inspiration.

"Some of us pronounced Monsieur de Quatrefages correctly right from the beginning, but there is a certain element here that still fluffs the lines when it has to pronounce him. Quatrefages sounds very funny with a Houston accent.

"He is not much to look at. He is dapper and brisk. The reason he is brisk is because he damn well *better* be brisk. He is highly paid to give *PERSONAL* attention to a number of us, and there are *QUITE* a number of us.

"First there is the personal analysis, which is a pip. You are ushered into his private office, which is so austere you expect to be sterilized before sitting down—sprayed, maybe, like they used to do in airplanes. He sits behind a stern desk. He wears a black business suit to match his mustache and eyes. (And heart.) By contrast, you feel absolutely naked in your skimpy little peach shift. I keep tugging at the hem of mine.

"A battery of lights like in the gangster movies is aimed at your face. *He* sits hidden in the gloom to study *you*. You are aware that his walls are covered with framed certificates, but God only knows what these are for—you never get a chance to read them. Probably vivisections.

"'Do *not* speak,' he says, holding up one finger, while he studies you. You immediately feel guilty, and a couple of little muscles around the mouth get absolutely taut and begin to hurt. My right eyelid develops a tic.

"'Ah, Madame Barr,' he says finally, 'you really have a *lovely* bone structure, and marvelously *malleable* features, but you haven't been taking *care* of yourself, now *have* you?' He shakes his head in a slow, meaningful negative, like a gynecologist pronouncing the loathsome truth.

"You shake your head in shameful, childlike guilt. He is The Truth and The Light and can see *right* through *you*.

"'It is very fortunate that we met before it's too *late*. We will put you *back on the track*. We will *reveal* your *hidden beauty*.' And you know, all of a sudden, he's *right*. You got beauty you didn't know you had.

"And so he begins to sketch, but you can't see *what* he is sketching. We suddenly realize the reason for Mona Lisa's smile—her mouth is twitching from sheer nervous exhaustion and cannot quite be captured.

"'*Voici!*' cries M. Quatrefages, turning his sketch pad over so that we can see. (I jumped a foot.) But it is really an expert likeness of my face, but totally *without* hair. It is the very *ESSENCE OF ME* in a glorified sort of way, but *without any hair at all!*

"I defied Jovian wrath and mumbled: 'A maybe sort of golden halo, please?'

"He says, tut-tutting and shaking that goddam finger,

"'Ah, but Madame, *you* are *here* for *ME* to *decide*.'

"He hid the drawing from me again while he designed the new hair for Our Particular Type of Undisclosed Beauty. We strain to peer over the top of the pad, but he conceals it until he is finished.

"'*Voici!*' he cries, and this time I only jumped six inches. He shows me the completed sketch with the new hairstyle. It is large, a full face from the front. Two smaller sketches near the bottom show the profile and rear view.

"In my particular case it *is* a golden halo sort of thing. Hurray! *Olé!* It occurs to Very Damn Few of us that his every hairstyle is the EXACT OPPOSITE for our current style. It gives us HOPE.

"He now writes my name under it like a title and signs his own just like an artist.

"He then takes out my Personal Skin Care and Beauty Analysis Chart. And for the first time he really speaks— first of skin care, then of cosmetics. Studying me like some sort of bug, he puts checks on this chart, item by item, while he explains our Problem in terms of Fat Flattery that would be outrageous if We weren't in such dire need of it. (Goddam that *We!*)

"Wrinkles on the forehead are mere 'worry lines.' Whaddaya know? All the time I thought it was sun.

" 'Ah, Madame, life has not always been easy for you,' he murmurs sympathetically. (He can say *THAT* again!) 'But I can tell from the laugh-lines about your eyes that always you have tried to keep the sense of humor—it is a part of your charming nature—' That sort of horseshit. *Laughlines?* It is but to *weep*.

"From the number of marks he makes on the chart, I'm going to need a ton of creams and cosmetics, but what the hell, kid, what the hell.

"He even discusses Our Fingernail Polish Plight with a keen sense of deep understanding. Not to mention *compassion*. I actually was sorry when it all had to end. I felt like I'd been to *communion*.

"He rings a bell to summon his first assistant in charge of all *salons*. Mlle. Lorette appears like a genie from a jar. They don't start to keep you waiting until after you've bought all the crap.

"The Maestro indicates the sketches and the chart of new products. Mlle. Lorette regards these as if it is the first time ever she has seen anything so admirable. She then regards *me*, still floodlit, like a species of snake. She hardly can restrain her enthusiasm, but she manages.

"He waves his hand in godlike dismissal. She leads us out into the main salon. I am still numb and half blind from the floodlights. I would confess to *anything*.

"The salon is upholstered like the inside of a womb, to

the best of my recollection of what wombs are like inside. It is peach-colored throughout, except for the actual fixtures they need for the hair. Even the fluorescent lights are peach-colored. We don't learn until *MUCH* later that an old survey (circa 1846) showed peach to be the most flattering of all colors to the human skin. Sometimes the wardens around here blab such secrets to the prisoners.

"A maid ties us into a peach-colored smock while Mlle. Lorette waits (at what they must pay *HER* an hour!) to introduce us to M. Paul, our hair boy.

"With the help of about twenty other people M. Paul converts us into a *natural* blonde with a proper halo. His haircut is radical, but nothing like so bad as a hysterectomy. I'm pitifully pleased that he does the haircut, roll-up and comb-out himself. Sometimes he turns clients over to an intern for these critical stages of the operation. Then *EVERY-BODY* in the salon notices, and the client loses face, whoever she be.

"Under the dryer, someone hands me a magazine to read. It is an elegant glossy affair called *Connaissance*. It is entirely in French.

They *ASSUME* that we read *le* French. The only French I know is *bidet,* but I was afraid to ask for *Field & Stream.* I read *Connaissance*.

"At the Grand Finale, M. Paul selects Our Particular Type of hair spray and lacquers the new hairdo into the hardness of a turtleshell over my suffering skull.

"At this golden moment of completion, M. Paul hands us a looking glass, and suddenly M. Quatrefages, Mlle. Lorette, and all the other imps magically materialize for a moment of prayer over the absolute Miracle of It All.

"From the corner of my eye I note that M. Q. gives a little bow to Our Newfound Beauty.

"It is the same in the skin care and make-up parlor where M. R. Donald (U.S. citizen, whaddaya know) takes me in hand. Carefully following M. Quatrefages' chart, he shows us our proper ritual for night and day. It will leave very little time for anything unimportant like sleeping and eating. He cleans the skin until the pores spout blood. Then he beautifies *US*. At the last he applies the new false eyelashes. They *itch*.

"Again, at the finale, the entire staff pops out of the magic lantern. At this point I felt that M. Quatrefages is absolutely inflamed by Our Newfound Beauty, and might just rape me behind the cosmetics counter. *He didn't.* Chicken.

"(I wonder what Alec would think of all this, assuming he hasn't run off to Tahiti with that slut.)

"It is the same with the skin care and make-up *salon.* It seems *we* need special face-muscle exercises to tighten up the lovely clean line of *Our* jaw so that *We* more nearly can approach the lean Katharine Hepburn type we really were destined to be until Something Went Wrong. We also must have *Our* daily facial to 'tone' our tissues.

"Although we have had abiding faith in Chanel No. 5 for years, M. Quatrefages has unsold us on it. It might just louse up the Total Effect of the Nu-*Us.*

"In short, we have a new *parfum,* too. For our Particular New Type.

"Stand back! Cleopatra's coming home!

"Love,

"Galatea Barr"

25 / Alec

Alec Barr entered suddenly into a way of life as foreign to him as if he had achieved sanctuary in a Tibetan lamasery or—possibly more accurately, he thought—as if he had been transported to the Left Bank of Paris in the Twenties, when Fitzgerald's favorite parlor trick was reciting while standing on his head, and Hemingway was being noisily abashed for the sin of allowing himself to be knocked stiff by Morley Callaghan. Nobody was doing much work in those days; drinking and talking about work occupied a great deal of time, and Alec kept feeling that any minute Sylvia Beach was going to ring up to tell him that James Joyce wasn't home to *anyone* except Sylvia Beach.

The typewriter to Alec Barr had always been a sort of shrine, something to be visited and prayed over daily, or else God would wreak a terrible vengeance, and a dark angel would come and steal Alec's testicles. Alec, even with a hangover or a miserable cold, felt a great sense of guilt on his nonwriting days. Even if he wasn't torturing the typewriter, he read a-purpose. He read everything from newspapers to Plato to *Vogue* with an idea of learning something, anything, that might come in useful some day.

Amelia had charged, in a half-joking fashion, that Alec was an old maid about writing things down in neat notebooks, in hiving up useless clippings, and amassing mountainous collections of dull books he had no intention of reading. She also complained that he never really let himself go on a party or even on a trip abroad; that he didn't know how to play, but always stood bleakly outside as a spectator, refusing to fit himself into the herd.

"You're not a man," Amelia had said more than once. "You're a goddam filing cabinet. You don't care what people do; all you care about is your thoughts about why they do what they do. For Christ's sake, can't you accept the fact that once in a while somebody gets constipated, laid or stony-assed drunk without an analysis of the motive?"

"Sweetie, I spent a long time poor," Alec would invariably answer. "My manhood is all tangled up in that keyboard. As long as they make cheap yellow paper and carbons I'm a man."

Amelia would shake her head.

"I never married a man. I married a contrivance—one half pencil, the other half typewriter. I own stock in the woodpulp business instead of a husband."

"You signed on for the writer," Alec had said. "A sailor goes to sea. A salesman travels. I write for a living, and if I don't write there isn't any living. And if there isn't any living . . ."

"I know. No mink. Your brother doesn't go to college. My old mother sells matches in the snow. Father has to work again. Your mother runs out of nerve juice. Your father has to buy his own whiskey. I heard it all before."

Amelia burst into tears. Amelia was not attractive when she wept. Weeping women, attractive or not, made Alec acutely nervous, and instead of arousing sympathy achieved the opposite effect of anger.

"There's really nothing to cry about," Alec said crossly. "For Christ's sake, why do women always cry as a reflex to a lost argument?"

Amelia stopped crying immediately.

"That's my boy. Any other man in the world would either

hit me in the chin or just say: 'For Christ's sake, will you for Christ's sake stop your blubbering.' But not *my* boy, the writer. He says coldly, analytically: 'Why do women always cry as a reflex to a lost argument?' I love you, but sometimes you make me sick. Today you make me real sick."

"Thanks," Alec said. "It's nice to know I have a capacity for inducing nausea. Perhaps I might bottle it and sell it, and then I wouldn't have to write any more, and you wouldn't be sick, but you'd be bloody hungry if it didn't sell."

"Oh, stop writing dialogue," Amelia said. "Save it for the typewriter. You know something, Baby?"

"What?" Alec said, without interest. "Baby."

"On the rare occasions when we make love—I have a feeling that you're not only counting your own strokes, but that you're tabulating any new movement on my part. It really makes a girl afraid to wiggle with any honest enthusiasm."

"You're having a very good day today for a girl who's sick," Alec said. "Maybe *you* ought to be the writer in the family. Meanwhile, I suggest you do something rather immediately about your hair. You haven't the face for the shaggy-dog arrangement. See you later. Perhaps."

"Oh, damn you, damn you, damn you!" Amelia had cried, as Alec went softly, straightbacked out the door. He was always careful never to slam it.

26 / Barbara

It had all changed now, miraculously, in this dying month of August. Alec hadn't touched a tap on a typewriter for a week. He hadn't even thought about a typewriter for a week. There was a half-finished novel and a couple of rough drafts of magaziners in the study at what he tried not to think of as "home," and Alec had forgotten the characters and their interwoven problems. Possibly this had come about when he kicked over the ashcan, the first night he and Barbara hit the town.

"That was quite a lot of caviar," Barbara said. "That was the most caviar I ever saw, let alone ate. Do you always ply your women with so much caviar?"

"Only the ones I love, and they have to go to bed with me first," Alec said. "You qualified on both counts. It's the first time, really, I ever had an *hors d'oeuvre* before I had an *hors d'oeuvre*."

"Oh, what a very funny man you are, except possibly in bed. In bed you seem quite serious."

"In bed with you, lover, I *am* quite serious. I can't imagine any man not being."

"It's rather hot for it, in August, but all told I think we acquitted ourselves very well," Barbara said. "But damn me if it isn't the first time I ever sold myself for a pound of caviar."

"Live and learn," Alec said. "Now I suggest we go out into the night and do something outrageous before I assault you again. There's still another pound of caviar left to buy your physical favors with."

"I hope I never see another kernel of caviar for the rest of my life. You can have my physical favors, as you so nicely put it, for free. But I'm not in a mood for dinner. Let's go hear some music or something. Piaf's in town. You like her?"

"She's the only thing ever came out of Paris that I do like. Where's she?"

"The Versailles."

"It has an advantage of being close, but it's early yet. I don't suppose you'd consider——"

"Absolutely *not*. There's an old joke about a girl who ate too much caviar before she got assaulted. I don't intend to prove it."

"Okay. So get yourself decent again. You look rather vulgar in the top half of those new pajamas. You didn't even bother to take off the price tag."

"You're pretty silly for a lover, friend. Lovers are supposed to go about with long faces and an air of doleful pre-occupation."

"That's all behind me," Alec said. "Lineally, my face may pertain to the horse, but my soul is that of Cupid, hot in pursuit of Psyche."

"I will get dressed," Barbara said. "You ain't safe to hang around half-naked with."

"Prude," Alec Barr said, and reflected that in all his life he had never said so many silly things as he had just uttered in the last half hour. "Actually the reason I sound so silly is that I am very much in love and haven't had very much practice describing it to the victim."

"That I will buy," Barbara said. *"Darling."*

Piaf was simply great. There was something special about the little Parisian sparrow, a sweet sadness, that seemed especially tailored for lovers. She looked so much like a butcher's bride, in her little, badly-shaped black dress, but all the bittersweetness of lost French loves came out of her great eyes and surprisingly robust voice. She was, Barbara said, a great gal to hold hands to. She offered no opposition to the girl who was holding hands with her man.

"Unlike, I might say, Lena Horne," Barbara said. "I won't go and see her with any man I like, ever. I get the distinct feeling that when a man hears Lena, and sees Lena, my fellow wishes I would go away and leave him alone with Lena."

"You're roughly right. A guy I know once wrote that her voice reminded you of the crisp rustle of clean sheets and the sound of lights snapping off," Alec said.

"You really are a sex maniac," Barbara said. "Like that Russian."

"We seem to know all the same jokes," Alec said. "And I agree with the Russian. Tonight, everything reminds me of you-know-what."

"I know what. We'll get around to it again in good time. Meanwhile, I suggest we go to the Lantern, have a slight slap of Wiener schnitzel, to keep our strength up, of course, and listen to some of that lovely, lousy fiddle-playing. I'm fresh out of *la vie Parisienne* mood now. I vant some *Weltschmerz* like 'Wien, Wien.' "

"Well, leave us press on for some *Weltschmerz*. But does it have to be Wiener schnitzel?"

"I'll settle for a potato pancake if it'll make you happy," Barbara said. "Haven't you really ever been out on the New York town before?"

"I got dragged into the Stork Club once," Alec said. "But we just sat in the Cub Room and looked at Morton Downey. I didn't feel very uplifted by the Cub Room. And I was never able to get put on the right side of the dance floor in El Morocco. Also Chauncey Gray failed to move me. I'm a Piaf man, and a fiddle *aficionado*. Fair?"

"A girl couldn't ask for a fairer," Barbara said. "But you must remember one thing before we get past the hand-holding stage. I am engaged to marry Joe E. Lewis, even if it means going to the Copa every night."

"That's a lie," Alec said. *"I'm* engaged to marry Joe E. Lewis. He has been my only vice for years. I'm a secret Copa-sneaker. And later, let's go kick over an ashcan."

27

The ashcan rolled, clanking, and shivered to a stop in Macdougal Street. It was the first of a succession of trash cans to feel the freed foot of Alec Barr since he and Barbara had flown out of Eddie Condon's, with Wild Bill Davison's trumpet and Joe Sullivan's piano reboiling the alcohol in their blood. It seemed great fun, this can-kicking. At this time of morning, at 2 A.M., Alec Barr thought that he had wasted a great deal of his life by not kicking cans in Greenwich Village, with a pretty blonde girl swinging arms, kid-fashion, as they ran through the streets holding hands. But now there was this cop. He had suddenly appeared from shadows and was standing under the street light.

Alec Barr looked at the cop. The cop looked at Alec Barr. The cop had a fighter's face, long nose many times flattened into considerable improvement of its original dimension; a scar running through a light-blond brow, foxy red hair showing in the sideburns under the cap, light blue eyes narrowed in a fighter's squint. It might well have been an Irish face, but not the fruity kind which made you think immediately of unfrocked priests, shifty-eyed jockeys, and underdone sirloin. More likely it was a Jewish face, re-shaped by fists from an original sensitivity—a red-haired, blue-eyed Jewish face which had fought the Irish gangs on the lower East Side as a kid and had then protected its right to self-determination by winning the middleweight championship of the Golden Gloves before electing to go on the cops. This was a face which would never make the Vice Squad, be shortly promoted to detective and retire, more than mildly rich, to a semidetached home in Queens. The hair, undoubtedly, would whiten, but the face would never empurple.

The cop looked first at Alec Barr, and then at Alec Barr's female companion. They did not appear, the cop thought, the kind of people who would be apt to kick over ashcans in a dirty Greenwich Village street at two of a Tuesday morning. They were both fried to the teeth, that was obvious, but the guy looked like a James Thurber character gone AWOL—the cop was a devoted reader of *The New Yorker* —and he was damned sure he had seen the broad somewhere before. She had to be some kind of an actress—of *course* she was an actress, her name was Barbara Bayne, and he had seen a million of her pictures during the war when he was pulling island duty in the Pacific. It did not figure that a Barbara Bayne would be running around kicking over ashcans with a scholarly lush, but the cop had seen some very peculiar things since he joined the force after the war.

"So what exactly do you think you're doing, bud?" the cop asked. He had rung in; it was otherwise a quiet night and he had been walking, killing time. He was two hours off duty, anyhow, and finally was headed home to read himself to sleep with a law book. If O'Dwyer could make mayor off the cops, then Nathan Shapiro could make mayor off the cops. It was high time they had a Jew in Gracie Mansion, anyhow. The Wops and the Irish had monopolized the job too long.

"So what is with the can-kicking?" Patrolman Nathan Shapiro asked again, taking note that Alec Barr's long, gentle, rather horsy face did not belong to the kind of creep who busted windows when he took on his load.

"Why, officer," replied Alec Barr, mildly. "I'd think that what I was doing was rather obvious. The lady and I were kicking over ashcans. The road to hell is paved with un-kicked-over ashcans, and we are rectifying the matter. You may book the lady if you like. She has no fixed address, no obvious means of support, and besides, as they say in the Bible, the woman tempted me."

"That is a filthy, rotten perversion of truth, officer. I never tempted a man in my life," the lady said. "We are in this thing together. We have devoted a great many years and a great deal of money to the art of kicking over ashcans," the blonde, dimpled lady who looked like Barbara Bayne said. "Not just anybody was sufficiently talented to kick over an ashcan with real *élan*. Not to mention *éclat*."

"You heard the lady, officer," Alec Barr said. "We have been in the *élan* and *éclat* business for years. Sometimes even chocolate *éclat*."

"Oh, brother," the cop said. "What have you people been using, laughing gas?"

"Only alcohol, officer, only alcohol. There are some people who say that if you begin with aquavit, liberally mixed with caviar, subsequent infusions of champagne, brandy, Scotch whisky, and Edith Piaf are not really injurious. It breeds only a certain carefree, not to say contemptuous, attitude toward the permanence of ashcans as a social structure."

The cop pushed his cap back and scratched his head.

"I see a lot of strange sights, and hear a lot of strange things on this beat," he said. "Maybe I should write a book."

"Pray don't," Alec Barr said. "It is an exquisite form of torture. You are talking directly to the horse."

"Now I got it," the cop said. "You're Alexander Barr, the book-writer. So that makes it possible for the lady to be Miss Barbara Bayne, the actress. How wrong am I?"

Alec bowed low, as Barbara dropped a sweeping curtsy. A starved Village cat prowled the edge of the lamplight, scavenging early breakfast.

"It is indeed we, if that is a sentence," said Alec Barr. "And you cannot mug us in the same classification as ordinary stoplight-runners-through, or even makers of public nuisances on city sidewalks."

"That last is really a dirty, filthy, rotten lie!" the lady cried. "A true queen of the silver squeen—I mean squilver scene, the hell with it, moving pictures—never made a wet on a sidewalk in her entire life. And I am indeed a screw tween of the twilver squeen. Behind rhododendrons, possibly. Perhaps even petunias. But *sidewalks?* Never! I've never been so insulted in all my life. Officer, I demand that you arrest this man!"

"I think you're both nuts," Patrolman Shapiro said. "Whatever it is you been drinking, I wish I had some."

"Don't you dare evade your duty on grounds of sobriety,"

the blonde lady said in a deadly chill voice. "Look at him now, kicking that poor defenseless can!"

Alec had just aimed a loving foot at the can, which emitted a loud clang and rattled loudly for a few yards, coming wearily to rest against the curb.

"I'll have you know this is a respectable neighborhood, officer," the lady continued her high moral tone. "If everybody kicked cans in it, what would happen to the parochial schools? What would happen to the United Nations? What would happen to Carmine De Sapio? How about Adam Clayton Powell? Does he let Hazel Scott kick the gong around? And Cardinal Spellman? Does *he* kick cans?"

"Black coffee," said Patrolman Shapiro. "Is indicated. Before some dedicated lawman comes along and runs you in for abusing the peace. Me, I ain't working. I am just about to go home and make myself some Irish coffee, which is a bad habit I picked up from the Hibernian element on Third Avenue. I have a suggestion, Miss Bayne and Mr. Barr. I live just around the corner. I am a lonely bachelor and do not sleep well of nights. I invite you now to my modest pad for an Irish coffee. It smoothes the rough edges without diminishing the beautiful glow. Howsabout?"

"Flank speed," said Alec Barr. "Let us proceed at flank speed. Your name, sir?"

"Nate Shapiro. Unsuccessful pugilist. Former gunner's mate second, USNR, Pacific, no medals. Current occupation police work. Future aspiration, the law. With a face like mine I can pass for Irish. Pleased to make your acquaintance, Miss Bayne, Mr. Barr. That flank speed business tells me you were Navy, too."

"Forty-Knot Barr, they called me in the Pentagon, more in envy than in accuracy. Light commander. Desk forces, Pacific. No medals. Miss Bayne was a camp follower. I was an admiral's house pet."

"I wish she had followed *my* camp," Officer Shapiro said wistfully. "Come on folks, let's get off the streets before we all get arrested."

"It's a pleasure to do business with you, Mr. Shapiro," Barbara said, tucking one hand in the crook of the policeman's arm. "Pardon the silly dialog. We just felt a little lightheaded, due to being suddenly in love, I guess. It'll pass. The lightheadedness, I mean."

"It figured," Shapiro said. "The flat's just over there under the light. "Tain't much, but then I don't need much. Not at these prices, anyhow. Here we are; second floor, no elevator. Up we go."

Patrolman Shapiro flipped a light switch. The small living room exhibited a bachelor's neatness. A record player sat atop a chest in one corner, next a neat stack of records in their jackets. There was a green leather contour chair in front of a fireplace that appeared to be functional. Three walls were lined with bookcases. One case was devoted almost exclusively to law books and manila-covered briefs. Some fresh carnations occupied a vase in the middle of a long coffee table of some dark wood, ranging in front of a green-and-red-figured chintz-slipcovered broad divan. A corner table held a small array of bottles. The lamps which had sprung into life were amply watted. It was a clean, bright room, and it looked happily used.

"Not much," Shapiro said again. "But I got unlocked from matrimony during the war and haven't taken it up again. I've got a little kitchen and a bath and a bedroom back there." He swept an arm toward a door. "And I manage to make out. Excuse me while I get out of this harness, and then I'll produce some coffee. You get the habit in the Navy, Commander?"

"That I did, Guns," Alec said. "That I did. The coffee habit was about all I got out of the Navy. I'll be rude and look at your books, if I may. Oho. I spot two of mine. A book-buyer, Barbara. Imagine, a book-buyer in these dreary televised days."

"Go ahead and prowl." Shapiro took off his coat and unbuckled his gunbelt, hooking the belt and gun over one shoulder as he headed for his bedroom. His blue shirt was sweated dark under the arms. "If you want a drink, there's the mixings. Ice in a bucket at the bottom. I'm going to wash the face and slip into a sports shirt before I activate the Silex."

"We'll wait for the Irish coffee," Barbara said. "You've got a fine place here, Mr. Shapiro. It was nice of you to ask us in after all that silly talk."

"Sometimes you meet nice folks," Shapiro said, disappearing. "Comes as a contant surprise, after a steady diet of pimps and pushers and bums and JD's and gang-fighters and muggers and creeps and queers and lushes and all the other charming people I encounter in this interesting profession. Back in a minute."

Alec sat down on the divan, pulling Barbara down beside him. He pecked a swift kiss, and reached for his cigarettes.

"Nice fellow, this new friend of ours," he said. "Wonder why he asked us home? We were acting pretty damned far out for two adults."

"I imagine he smelled the basic love factor in the over-all silliness. He seems like a perceptive fellow. *And* lonely. Strange a man like that would wind up as a policeman."

"Not so strange," Alec said, looking at the law books. "I could write him now. Fought his way out of a slum as a scrawny Jewish kid in an Irish neighborhood. Tried the amateurs, got his face busted, and decided he couldn't make it in the pros. War embraced him and he married little Sarah Cohen around the corner. Little Sarah Cohen *Dear John*ed him for a 4F dentist. Ex-Gunner's Mate Shapiro comes home to a lot of civilian confusion, after having been sequestered on enough ships and islands to allow his active Jewish brain to exercise itself. Ex-Gunner's Mate Shapiro decides that he has muscles enough to get a job on the cops—a job that won't tax his brain too much, and will keep him in Irish whisky and cigarettes and law books while he puts that sharp brain to work after hours in the study of law. And some fine day, he will pass little Sarah Cohen on the street, with her ex-4F dentist, and Nate Shapiro will look at Sarah Cohen's dentist and sneer a quiet little sneer, for Nate Shapiro will suddenly be 'my son, the lawyer' in the hierarchy, and later, no doubt, 'my son, the Senator.' And with that battered red-headed puss of his, it is not entirely unlikely that he'll wind up in Gracie Mansion. That would be my summation of Patrolman Ex-Gunner's Mate Nate Shapiro."

"Pretty good summation, at that," Shapiro walked into the room. "We got thin walls here. I was eavesdropping. Apart from a couple of minor points, you're dead right, bang-on, Commander."

Shapiro had washed, they saw, and his damp red head bore the toothmarks of a comb. He was wearing an outrageously flowered Hawaiian sports shirt and had changed into khaki walking shorts. He wore Mexican *huaraches* on his bare feet.

"I like to slip into something loose," he grinned. "The coffee's making. I'll just slide the booze into some glasses." He walked over to the table with the bottles. "For a guy who was kicking over ashcans a few moments ago, you're a pretty snappy summarizer, Commander."

"I like 'Alec' better than 'Commander,' " Alec said. "Fast summarizing is my trade. You stopped a lot of punches with that face, Nathan."

"It was a point of pride. When I had a long nose like my grandfather, the rabbi, everybody called me Ikey. Now they settle for Nate. Nothing like a busted face to give you dignity in an Irish neighborhood, or even in a war. After a while you don't have to fight any more. And I tell you, I spent more time fighting Southern hillbillies in the late nastiness than I did Japs. Them there tobacco-chewers just plain don't like Jews. But what I don't understand is you, Comman—Alec. How come you and Miss Bayne are so loose at the plate? The can-kicking bit, I mean. You don't strike me as very violent."

"I am, without doubt, the quietest, gentlest, sweetest, most considerate coward in the world," said Alec Barr. "But the other day I just didn't want to have dinner with some people named Hazeltine. Also the middle part of a piece didn't quite come off."

"I suppose you know what he's talking about, Miss Bayne?" Shapiro turned to Barbara.

"Barbara, please. Only vaguely. He seems to be in a darkly rebellious mood, and is trying to commit suicide by the caviar route. Apart from kicking over garbage cans."

"It just goes to show you how a woman never knows anything really basic about the man she loves, worships, adores, the man who buys her minks, gives her fleets of children, cozens her with Cadillacs, weighs her down with rubies and emeralds, and occasionally even comes home to dinner without being reminded. This woman—this cop-baiter—doesn't even know that I flung some rocks at an admiral once."

"Does he always talk like this?" Shapiro turned to Barbara Bayne. "Or does he use maybe a little, like musicians? Or maybe too many mushrooms?"

"I think he's merely a case of arrested development suddenly come in full rapid flower. What's all this about throwing rocks at the admiral?"

"Matter of simple, provable fact. It was the only way

I could get into his office. Not important. The Japs betrayed me, and stopped the war, making it necessary for me to consider the distasteful idea of work. Ergo—I love that word ergo—ergo. I decided to forego the warrior trade and get myself home and out of the beautiful blues before, you should pardon the expression, fourteen million people like our friend here came home and snaffled up all the jobs. So I rather illegally wrote some orders packing me home from Australia, which had been most pleasant but was now stagnant. I forgot, almost, that when I arranged my transportation, I bumped a buck general off the flight, but he was only infantry and useless in the space age. The Admiral's aide wouldn't let me in, so I threw rocks at his window."

"The aide must have been some kind of a nut," Patrolman Shapiro said. "Imagine not letting a deserter in to see an admiral. Tsk."

"Precisely what I thought. So I went back out into Constitution Avenue and collected a handful of rocks and started throwing them at the Admiral's window. This was somewhat more difficult than it sounds. There was nobody in Washington then beneath the rank of four-striper, and so frequently I had to pause in my rock-throwing to salute the senior passers-by."

"They didn't think it odd for a lieutenant commander to be throwing rocks at an admiral's window?" Barbara asked with no change of expression.

"Of course not. This was Washington. It had been a long war. They probably thought I was a double spy from the Air Force and the rocks were bombs." Alec kept his face equally expressionless. "Where was I again?"

"Saluting between fusillades," Barbara said. "What next, Boy on the Burning Deck?"

"Well, just as I was about to run out of ammunition, the Admiral's face appeared at the window. He appeared perturbed. Perhaps *annoyed* would be a better word. I couldn't hear what he was saying, but his lips moved, and appeared to be saying something like "You dirty such-and-such of a so-and-so, you're supposed to be with the British in Australia. What the this-and-that sort of unprintable bloody hell are you doing in Washington?"

"Logical point of view," Barbara said. "So why didn't they shoot you?"

"Yeah," said Patrolman Shapiro. "Why didn't they shoot you? They sure as hell woulda shot *me*."

"Matter of simple practicality. The Admiral beckoned me to come aboard, and this time his Marine snotnose let me in. I must say that the war was so freshly over that I was the only officer processed back to peace out of Washington, D.C., that day."

"And how have you found the peace, so far?" ex-Gunner's Mate Patrolman Shapiro asked.

"It stinks," Alec Barr said. "It has too many civilians in it."

"You got a point," replied Shapiro. "You certainly got a point."

They left Patrolman Shapiro at dawn, sober now, peacefully happy, with the assurance that their new friend would dine with them on his first free evening. The sun was sneaking up over the East River, and the morning was deliciously cool, with a slow breeze stirring the trees. They decided it was much too nice a morning to take a cab.

"Quite a boy, our policeman," Barbara said. "I didn't know they made them like that any more."

"He seems to have a lap full of horse, all right. It *is* pleasant to run into somebody who knows where he's going. I often wish I did."

Barbara stopped and kissed Alec briefly on the cheek.

"*I* know where you're going," she said. "You're going home to bed. And you know something else? I'm going with you. It's been a lovely evening, Alec. I hope we have a lot more of them, if a little less frenetic."

"You bought yourself a boy," Alec said. "I use that quite a lot now, don't I? Come, here's a taxi. After that last indelicate suggestion, I don't want to walk any more."

"That's my good fellow," Barbara said. "Save your strength for the really worthwhile things."

28

There came then the blessed days, the glittering days of sweet September, the golden, shining days of early autumn in New York, all a revelation for Alec Barr. He met no more cops, kicked no more cans, but as he said a great many years later to Barbara Bayne, they held more hands in front of more headwaiters than any single pair in the recorded history of love.

Barbara was making the first half of a film in New York; Alec went unwillingly back to work on the long-neglected magazine articles (he had a summer rate at the Ritz but caviar and sheaves of new recordings and great shaggy bouquets of chrysanthemums wanted a certain amount of currency, and Amelia's immediate retirement to the matron's nunnery, Rancho Nuyu, also demanded money in the bank).

But there was a magic to being in love. Strangers smiled at them. Ordinarily surly waiters were smilingly attentive. They exhibited the incandescence of honeymooners, and the sun shone warmly bright, the stars glittered crisply in the sky. The only trouble was Alec couldn't seem to get any work done.

"I suppose it's really the suit," Alec said to Barbara one day, in some dim cave of a restaurant. "No lady ever bought me a suit before."

"It's a handsome suit," Barbara said. "I absolutely refuse to allow you to wear most of your other stuff. I am a gray-flannel girl for autumn, and you are a gray-flannel-type author. The pleasure was all mine."

Alec Barr was still a mite shocked at the transaction. He had asked Barbara to meet him at his tailor's, just around the corner from her flat. He wanted some feminine judgment on a new batch of suits he was choosing. (Barbara had already begun buying him neckties from Sulka and Bronzini.)

She shuddered at the swatches the tailor set forth and which Alec seemed to like.

"No," she said. "Great God no! You're not a Broadway columnist. You're not a Hollywood-and-Vine type. You're a *writer*, a real writer. You've got to dress like a banker if you're a real writer. And this also means not ever, ever growing a beard. Here; we'll take this and this, and this," slapping aside bolts of sober blue, pin-stripe gray, and a muted though sporty check. "That's enough. Now let's go to the zoo."

When Alec went back for first fittings, he was surprised when the tailor produced the skeletons of a fourth and fifth suit, both of gray flannel, one charcoal, one medium.

"I didn't order these," he said. "You've made a mistake."

"No, Mr. Barr, there's no mistake. Your lady rang up and ordered them for you as a present. They're to be billed to her."

"But she can't buy clothes for me," Alec said.

"She said that you'd say exactly that," the tailor said. "And she told me to say it was no good arguing, that her mind was made up. She seemed quite determined, Mr. Barr."

"Well, it's a nice cloth," Alec said. "Make 'em and I'll sort it out with her later."

When the suits were finished, somehow it seemed that no suits had ever draped so caressingly on his rangy frame. He was not surprised to find himself buying a carnation for his buttonhole and even toyed with the idea of purchasing a cane. He did buy the Trilby hat, however; Barbara went with him to Cavanagh's to choose a couple; a pearl-gray and a midnight blue. She then took him to Sulka's for some silk shirts.

"You're really quite a festive fellow at heart," Barbara said. "You're *my* festive fellow. We must look festive as well as feel festive."

Alec Barr had never been a night prowler in the city. Mostly he had worked at night, when the phone quit and the traffic noises subsided. He would work until two or three in the morning, then stun himself to slumber with a deep-brown Scotch. To Alec, the city by night was largely unexplored jungle.

Now he found himself trying to work mornings, generally skipping lunch and working fruitlessly with nervous impatience against the fall of dusk, when the phone would ring and the clerk would say: "Mrs. Riley is on her way up." He was working, but he wasn't getting anything done.

Riley had seemed a nice name, a good and private name for them both. When they went off occasionally to the Cape for a week end they registered shamelessly as Mr. and Mrs. Riley. They had slipped swiftly into the kind of sexual casualness which allowed silly pet names, and the "dearest Mrs. Riley" or "darling Mr. Riley" was reserved for the almost hurtful peace that followed a screaming climax.

Any room, any room at all, brightened when one or the other entered it. Surprisingly, they sought public places, not to be seen but to be surrounded. They haunted the darker cocktail dens, always searching for an unobtrusive piano;

they investigated dives in the Village and pansy joints on Third Avenue and jive dens in Harlem. Barbara seemed to know everybody on "darling" terms—musicians, black and white, queer and unqueer, and most of the headwaiters everywhere. Alec, naturally shy, hesitated to trade on his name as a writer, had previously limited himself to a few restaurants where he was certain of welcome. Now he found fat black female swing-singers calling him Alec, far-out trumpet-players saying "Here comes old Barrsie-boy, let's slip him a riff," and the headwaiters suddenly providing him special tables, inevitably reserved for him and Barbara.

They drank far, far too much, of course. Barbara had a limitless capacity for alcohol, and even more limitless knowledge of off-beat, off-track bars where she seemed to be a prime favorite with the bartender-host and the trio in the smoky corner. Alec suddenly discovered that six hours' sleep was more than enough for capable function, if not as a writer, certainly as a lover. He regretted all the thousands of hours he had spent, in the past, merely sleeping in bed.

29

During his years with Amelia, Alec Barr had fought sporadically—usually about trivia common to most young marriages. They had bickered about money, or the lack of it; about extravagance on both sides, whether it was clothes for Amelia or a completely unnecessary shotgun for Alec. They had battled horribly about Alec's absences when he was a young reporter. Amelia considered each out-of-town assignment, each late-night story, a plot, carefully contrived by the office to steal her man away and offer him to the predatory potential of other women.

Alec had protested feebly that really, he did not leap upon the first woman he saw the first minute he was out of the house.

"I'm not all that good, Sweetie," he had said, over and over. "Really I'm not." But he was met with black moods for days before departures, and sly probings for days after his return. He had no real problem with mail, because he received his personal correspondence at the office, but occasionally he would stick a letter from some out-of-town friend carelessly in a pocket, and when it was not in his jacket when next he sought it, he would assume that he'd lost it. Weeks, sometimes months later, he would be suddenly confronted with a soft but loaded question such as: "Do you ever hear from Pamela Moore any more?"

And Alec, working late over a magazine piece that wouldn't sell, would stare blankly and say: "Who? Pamela Moore? Who the hell is Pamela Moore?"

Then the cold, accusing stare, and something like "Oh, you have so many girl friends you can't remember the names? Pamela Moore from Dayton, Ohio."

"Oh." Weakly. "Sure. That Pamela Moore. Dayton. *Sure.* Babe on the paper out there—you remember, when I was covering that murder trial. Nice gal. Filled me in on some local background. Took her to dinner one night with some of the other reporters. How would you know about Pamela Moore?"

Then the withering look.

"Really darling. If you *will* leave letters from your lady friends in your clothes, I can hardly be blamed for seeing them when I turn out the pockets to send the clothes to the cleaners. She sounded as if you had a lot of fun together." Then, like a shot, "Did you see a lot of her?"

The answer always sounded defensive, even guilty.

"No. Not really. Just around the trial. Grab a sandwich or a cup of coffee together. You know how it is . . ."

"Yes." Sharp and snappish. "I certainly *do* know how it is. Was she pretty?"

"Not very. Sort of. Well, maybe you could call her pretty if you liked the type. Pleasant, mainly."

Then, deep into the filing system of Amelia's mind would go the name of Pamela Moore, never to be forgotten, to enrich and simmer and seethe with time so that at some future date, when Alec might be holding forth on his newspaper days, when he mentioned a murder trial Amelia would interject sweetly: "Do tell them about the gory one in Dayton, darling. When you were scampering around with that pretty Pamela Whatsername—Moore, wasn't it?" And, with a light and false laugh in the sweeping direction of the audience: "Alec had *such* a good time when he was a reporter. It was so good for him to get out of the house, and he always seemed to meet such pleasant people on assignments, even on murder trials." And, with a completely spurious chuckle: "Do tell about the lady city editor, or was it the *Time* magazine girl, at the convention, darling? You know, the one who came knocking at your room in her bra and panties?"

The suspicion had burgeoned after Alec had found an agent and had begun to sell magazine pieces with such regularity that he could afford to quit the paper and work, mostly on assignment, as a full-time free lance. Now the assignments were more exotic: a trip to Hollywood to do a series on certain film stars; a week in New York to discuss projects with various editors. Amelia had her own selling job in a department store, so it was rarely practical for her to accompany him. Sometimes Alec would be on the Coast for as much as a month, and although he called Amelia two or three times a week and wrote her frequent notes, he could never quite squeeze the nonexistent guilt out of his voice on the phone or from the typewritten lines on the notepaper. He was gun-shy of admitting that he was having any fun at all and was wary of dropping many names, particularly if he were interviewing any of the female stars. On his return Amelia would question him relentlessly, searching for any tiny discrepancy of detail, and sometimes months later coming up with: "But you never told me she had you out to her house in Palm Springs, Sweetie. Were you there very long?"

Any chance meeting, in later years, with early acquaintances outside Amelia's cognizance generally produced a frigid, stiff-lipped politeness on the part of Amelia and a scathing sweep of eye that amounted to a visual frisking of the friend in question. Amelia had built a rigid wall of demarcation: Anyone they met together, in unimpeachable circumstances, was a candidate for friendship. Anyone whose acquaintance with Alec predated her introduction was immediately suspect. If the person happened to be a woman, and attractive, it was assumed that Alec had laid her. If it were a man, it was assumed that he and Alec had shared bawdy revels together; or, occasionally, that the man was queer and actually in pursuit of Alec.

In this line of reasoning Amelia had never forgiven Alec for his participation in the war. She had been quite content when he was starkly scared at sea or isolated on dreary islands, but when he moved to Staff and started roving around with the brass in such women-fraught places as London and Australia, her attitude toward personal patriotism abruptly changed. She had borne with admirable courage the six months in which Alec was erroneously reported missing in action, but she never forgave him for winding up the war in Sydney and Melbourne. Vestiges of his past from the London and Australian days jetsamed into their lives in the postwar, and Amelia looked with horrid suspicion at them all as shady conspirators in a secret life she would never know and of which Alec was loath to talk.

And so they quarreled. But they bickered more than they fought, and only occasionally did Amelia's black anger cause her to throw her glass at Alec or to storm weeping off to bed, door slamming hard behind her.

The mark of Amelia was on Alec, and on the houses she made for him. The mark was the cause, possibly, of the first big fight between Alec and Barbara. It had started innocently enough. Alec had wanted to drop by the penthouse to pick up some research material and some extra clothing. They had both been scrupulously set against making love either in Alec's apartment or in Barbara's slim brownstone bowfront town house, still technically the property of her actor husband, pending the divorce settlement.

"Want to see where I lived when I was a family man?" Alec said one day at lunch. "I got to go ho— I got to go to the apartment and pick up some notes and a few odd items of clothing. Won't take long. I'll buy you a brandy in my bar while I collect my clagger, and we can take off."

"Sure. Why not?" It had been a lovely lunch, quiet, with not many of the summer vacationers back in town, and most of the homosexuals still on Fire Island. Alec and Barbara were full of food and empathy when they hailed a taxi to head uptown to the penthouse.

They stepped off the lift, into the foyer, and Barbara walked into the living room. It was a huge room, with a wood-burning fireplace at one end, with huge gold-framed Federal mirror, oval, topped by a fierce-visaged eagle. A widely curved white sofa faced the fireplace and was flanked by two lofty-backed wing chairs of brass-studded yellow leather. A low, round coffee table with enormous space for magazines and ashtrays as big as basins intruded between the fireplace and the sofa. Two low daises of leopardskin nudged each other beneath a square Italian mirror that occupied the best part of a whole wall, and a gleaming black Steinway squatted obliquely in one corner. The acre of rug was apricot Indian chenille. The walls were sparsely hung with primitives, Haitian, and neo-primitives, African. Barbara caught sight of a Sheraton dining-room table in the next room, through a square doorway, its shining surface an island in a sea of expensively restored companion chairs.

"You could hold a football game in here," Barbara said. "But I must say the lady knows her stuff. What's that other mirror?"

"Came out of a Neapolitan cathouse, I think," Alec said. "I don't know anything about this stuff. I leave it to Amelia."

"It's a nice room, a very nice room," Barbara said, walking over to the double French doors which opened on a terrace in which small trees bloomed seventeen stories above the city, and flowers still grew in low boxes. "Christ, what a terrace! How long is it?"

"Exactly seventy-four yards. There's another, on the Madison side, off my study. And another in back"—he jerked his head toward the foyer—"for the poor people."

"Show me where you work."

Alec led her back into the foyer, down a narrow passageway, and into a huge converted bedroom which fronted on the long terrace, with side doors giving onto another, broader, shorter terrace. Here too there was a companion fireplace to the one in the living room; cabinet-shelves stretching halfway up the walls were lined with books, some few bright-jacketed, most handrubbed with use. The rug was furry black; in front of a black-leather easy chair a leopardskin sprawled.

Alec walked over to one of the cabinets snugged beneath the books and touched a button. A door swung out, unmasking a bar, which also included a small icebox.

"Buy you a drink? Brandy? Scotch?"

"Brandy. That way you don't have to wrestle with the ice. I must say, my lad, you know how to live. Any music?"

"Sure." Alec walked over to the companion cabinet, touched another button, revealing a combination hi-fi-record player-cum-radio-cum-TV unit. He swiftly sorted out a few records from another cabinet, and presently "Autumn in New York" drifted into the room.

"Man of distinction, not to say taste," Barbara murmured,

her nose in the brandy snifter. "And that monster in the corner, that obscenely big black desk, that's where the great man writes his great prose when he's home?"

"That's where he writes it. It's a good desk. Somebody, I forget who, gave it to me as a present. Some one of the plastics people. Got a lot of knee room. I find when I punch that machine for long stretches it's not my mind or my back that hurts, it's my bloody legs."

"With this big place—and I haven't seen the bedrooms, or the kitchen, nor do I wish to," Barbara said, "with all the solid comfort you've got here, what do you need with that hacienda in New Jersey? This is heaven."

Alec paced before the fireplace.

"I'm a country kid," he said. "I got to have my country. This is fine. This is lush living—mid-Seventies, fashionable East Side, all that nonsense—but from time to time I have to see a real tree that doesn't have a mugger hidden behind it. I have to breathe air that isn't full of the flatulence of buses. I like to see the ducks beam in, and the deer come down in the evening to drink. In less than one hour by car I can achieve all that in a place with the unlovely name of Wykcoff, New Jersey, just across the line from Suffern. If I need savages we always have the Jackson whites. They're just as inbred as anything they've got in Tennessee."

"But you can't spend a lot of time there. Not with this, and the travel—"

"I spend more than you'd think. Once I'm really stuck into a book I need space. I can set fire to a birch log as long as a canoe, look through the plate glass at my little lake, and make myself younger by the tick. I feel good; I look at the trophy heads on the wall; the tiger over the fireplace, and something in me loosens up. I don't know. When I work in New York I always feel like I wish I was finished. When I work in Jersey I am actually sorry when fatigue makes me quit."

"Does Amelia spend much time there?" The question was carefully gentle, and suddenly Alec was reminded of the way Amelia would suddenly say: "And who is Marilyn Thompson?" out of the blue.

"Not much. She calls it my cloister. She likes the city. I spend most of my time—working time, I mean—out there on my own. It's basic home. I keep most of the treasured stuff there, and the best part of the library." He swept a hand at the bright array of books. "A great deal of this stuff is duplicates, just for convenience. How many people do you know with two sets of the *Encyclopaedia Britannica?*"

"Why doesn't Amelia like it in the country? It sounds lovely."

Alec scratched his chin.

"I don't know. Maybe because it doesn't *include* her very much. Maybe because it's sort of all mine, like a hunting lodge, like a tree house, like a small boy's cave. I'm afraid I'm pretty primitive, Sweetie. Give me the gift of fire and water and I ask not alms of any man. Would you like to drive out some day and see *my* house?"

Barbara said very quietly: "No. I don't think so. I think perhaps I am beginning to understand Amelia a little better. Come on, sport; scratch up your belongings, and let's head for the downtown. Somehow I don't feel easy in another woman's house—not, at least, in her absence."

"All right. I won't be a minute. Another short brandy?"

"No. But I would like the sanitary facilities."

Alec gestured to the door. "The hall. Sharp right, and right again."

Barbara picked up her purse and turned right, and then turned in the gestured direction. This, then, she thought, is where they sleep—slept. It was dark, and she flicked on a light. Her first glance lit on the bed—an enormous structure with a dark-purple coverlet. Her glance switched then to the dressing table, and to the huge blown-up photograph of Alec Barr which had been framed and hung behind the vanity lights. Alec was smiling unevenly—a smile made more uneven by the fact that the glass which covered the photograph was shattered in the middle and the face itself attacked by what very likely had been the sharp heel of a shoe.

Barbara fled to the bathroom, and when she came out Alec was still puttering in his files.

"I just remembered," Barbara said. "I have a date—an important date with a producer. You take your time, darling. I don't want to rush you, and I'll meet you back at the hotel at six. All right?"

"All right, Mrs. Riley," Alec said absently, peering into a manila folder. "The doorman will get you a cab. There *are* a few more things I should do here; things I'd forgotten. Be my good girl, now."

"I'll be your good girl, now," Barbara said tightly. "I'll be a very good girl now."

30

Suddenly, for no real reason, except it was possibly triggered by the descent of a fleet of screeching, fluttering fairies who kissed Barbara extensively and carved the air with their flying hands, calling each other, Barbara, and even Alec "girl," Alec achieved extreme nervousness, and with it both stifling boredom and unreasonable anger. They had been sitting in a Third Avenue den, talking happily and holding quiet hands when the pansies descended, ruining the mood and filling the room with shrillness.

"Let's go," Alec said, getting up abruptly. "It's stuffy in here."

"It's stuffy in here, all right," Barbara said. "And I know what's causing it. Sit down; I want to talk to my friends."

"Get him, girl," one of the fairies said, cocking an arch eyebrow. "Your new boy friend doesn't dig us. I thought you said he was a sensitive artist, Barbara."

"I'm not a sensitive artist," Alec growled. "I'm an insensitive man who greatly dislikes faggots. All faggots, but you in particular." He pressed one hand on the chest of the nearest pansy, and pushed. The fellow stumbled backward and fell over a chair. "Get the hell out of my way," Alec said, and turned to Barbara. "You coming, or not?"

"No, I'm not coming!" Barbara's voice lifted. "And I won't have you talking to my friends this way!" Alec noticed again that there was a terrifying tinniness in Barbara's voice when it rose.

"Right." Alec tossed a ten-dollar bill on the table. "That'll pay for the drinks. If you get bored with the girls here I'll be back at the hotel." Without waiting for an answer he turned abruptly and walked out of the café.

"Well, Barr," he said half-aloud as he strode the sidewalk,

heels clacking angrily. "That was certainly childish of you. But why, *why* does she always have to surround herself with all these people? Why are we always being pawed over by pansies and ganged by lesbians and black musicians and half-smart actors and those dreary people she knew in summer stock and Hollywood and the Cape? Why the hell does she have to know so many *people?*"

You're being very unfair, Barr, he thought, riding up the lift to his suite. You know damned well that you've thought the last weeks were wonderful. You know damned well that you've been living a life that you were hungry for—a life that you kicked over the traces and left Amelia for—you've been having fun. You've been living it up. You've been alive. For the first time, maybe, you've been *alive*—in love, and alive.

Alec unlocked his door, turned on the lights, and went over to the drink tray and mixed himself a stout Scotch.

"But maybe you don't like being alive," he said. "Maybe you're basically a very dull dog and you miss the leash. Maybe it's too bloody much trouble to be in love."

31

That, some several hours later, as they sat furious, more than a bit drunk, was what Barbara was saying.

"You don't know how to be yourself! You don't want to learn! You don't want to be happy—you don't want to cut loose and let yourself go and have fun and live!" It *was* true; Barbara angry had a very different voice. It was harsh now, metallic, screechy. It bore no resemblance to the lovely low timbre of her ordinary speech.

"You miss Amelia, admit it! You want to go back and chain yourself to a typewriter and whimper and be bored so you can run away again and then come trotting home to your mama. You don't want a real woman, Alec, my boy. You want a mother to spank you when you're bad and kiss you to make it well and button your little pants and wipe your little runny nose. You're afraid to take on a real woman permanently. You're not big enough for a woman! What you want is a nurse!"

"I don't see as there's any real need for hysteria," Alec said *ersatz*-mildly. "I don't see where my not liking to be always surrounded by a fleet of faggots and creepy second-rate actors and boozed-up musicians makes me a candidate for an Oedipus complex. I don't see where my wanting to stay home or sit quietly with you in a restaurant without having to kiss a dozen people I don't know and don't want to know makes me odd."

"You make me sick! You really *do* make me ill." Barbara lowered her voice now. "At first I thought you were just a fellow who'd never had the opportunity to be let off the leash. Now I wonder; I wonder very much. I began to wonder when we first talked politics. I wondered some more when I saw you with my friends. I don't think you like Jews. I think you hate Negroes. I don't think you like being around creative people. I think—I think you're jealous of *real* people, honest people, people who aren't afraid to be honest and say and do what they believe in. I think—"

"I think you're talking a lot of balls," Alec said. "And let's for God's sake try to keep Mrs. Roosevelt and Adlai Stevenson and the National Association for the Advancement of Colored People out of this dialog. I don't like lesbians, black or white, Jewish or Gentile. I don't like faggots of any color or persuasion. And I certainly don't like third-rate actors who scream and wave their arms, or dirty comedians who need a fix between their funny filths. I don't like—"

"I don't give a damn what you don't like. But I don't think you really like *me*. You don't like my friends; you surely *can't* like me. You seemed to like them well enough at first, though. In your ashcan-kicking stage." Barbara's voice tore at him. "When we first began sleeping together, I mean. *That* was all right, wasn't it? My friends were all right *then*, weren't they?" Her voice was like fingernails on a slate, scratching at his nerves.

"Let's not fight any more, please, Barbara. I suppose I'm basically a very dull fellow who can't play seven days a week. I have to have a little dull routine, if only to think. I'm sorry about being rude to your friends. But I've got to temper myself down a little and get back to working hours.

I have to find a flat, I think. This hotel business is beginning to get on my back. It was fun at first, but—"

"I get it. I understand perfectly, darling." Barbara spoke harshly, falsely, monotonously, sarcastically. "'Twere a far, far better thing I do.' *This* . . . is good-by. Thank you, *Ed* Murrow. I-could-not-love-thee-less-loved-I-not-Amelia-more sort of crap. I know when I'm being eased out. I ease out real easy. Okay, so I'll leave you to the muse. Go back to your precious Amelia and bore yourself to death."

"But I'm not going back to Amelia."

"Yes, my dear, you're going back to Amelia. Whether you know it yet or not, you'll go back to Amelia, even if it's by way of Pago Pago. You've got an acute case of arrested marital conscience. Baby ran away, but Baby got scared of the dark, and Baby will go whining back to Mama. Baby don't like it out there in the dark, alone in a world full of wicked strangers."

Alec got up and paced, fingers laced behind his back.

"I said I don't want to fight. But you're not being fair. I don't want to leave you. I love you. And I don't want to change you. But I can't make me over into a perpetual night-hawk, either. Come on now, darling. I'm sorry I was a bastard, let's go to bed. It's late, and I have *got* to get some proofs finished tomorrow."

"You go to bed so you can finish your precious proofs. I'm going to sit up and have another drink and read the papers. I'm too mad to go to bed."

She turned her back and walked over to the drink tray. Alec shrugged, sighed, and headed for the bedroom. He looked back at the doorway, but Barbara was still standing stiffly over the drink tray without pouring a drink.

Alec shrugged again and began to take off his clothes. When he had finished cleaning his teeth, he peeped back into the living room. Barbara was now standing in front of the window. The papers were still unopened on the floor. Alec was weary, from the argument as much as anything else. He snapped off the light and in a few moments was asleep.

He woke to the presence of a warm body beside him. He put a hand on her bare hip.

"I didn't mean to wake you," she said softly. "I thought I could sneak in quietly. Go back to sleep, darling."

"What time is it?"

"Nearly four. Oh, Alec, I'm sorry I was so bitchy. I wasn't being fair. I've a nasty tongue on me when my Irish rises."

Alec turned and drew her close. He felt tears still wet on her cheeks.

"Maybe it was the martinis," he said. "Maybe we should give up martinis altogether."

He could feel her smile now.

"*And* some of my more exotic friends. I do love you, Alec Barr, square as you be," she said, and sought his mouth.

In the soft blackness of bed, plastically molded to the firm hot globes of Barbara's body, Alec rid himself momentarily of anger and recrimination. The urgent knowing thrust of Barbara's hips and warm bond of arms, the hard pressure of breast and soft prison of thigh took him out of time and high, high into space, then plunged him into shuddering brief eternity. After, when Barbara had tenderly cleansed him, he fell deeply, gratefully asleep, tucked spoon-fashion into the soft curve of buttocks and thigh, one hand babyishly grasping her breast, as a child clutches a favorite toy for comfort when he enters the frightening realm of dream.

When he woke next morning she was gone, and Alec looked at his freshly roused body with distaste; not only distaste, but also fear. The bed was still warm and fragrant from her presence. Alec missed her deeply, wanted her again terribly, and was, for the moment, terribly, terribly afraid because he wanted her so terribly again.

32

Ben Lea was possibly Alec Barr's best friend, with the exception of Marc Mantell, his agent. He had a latish luncheon date with Marc and Alec was dreading it. He was dreading it because he knew exactly what Marc Mantell was going to say to him, and he didn't want to hear it, because he knew it was true. So Alec had rung up Ben Lea for earlier fortification.

It was noon and they were sitting now in the Marguery courtyard, over a first gin-and-tonic. Ben Lea was fat, splotchy-freckled, and merry-blue-eyed. He wore a stiff pink stand of hair in a ridiculously short crew cut. He was vice-president of a large advertising agency, but he had run the gantlet of the writing table—newspapers, magazines, radio, high-powered press-agentry, and now had settled for a long contract, a fat expense account, and a bushel of stock options in one of the larger agencies. He never worked regular hours. He cultivated a long list of friends for his daily gin.

Ben Lea was pushing sixty, and he fought a friendly fight with the bottle. He had also fought a friendly, happy war as an over-age Marine. He had been married five times, and now, even with the ravages of war and matrimony and wine becoming more apparent, still was regarded around Manhattan as an exceptional lover.

But with men Ben Lea invariably combined salty wit and sagacity. His friends ranged a wide field. He went to baseball games with Toots Shor and George Jean Nathan; he talked poetry (he wrote some, as well) with Robert Frost; he went bullfighting and talked bulls with Rex Smith; with Alec Barr he talked writing and women and bulls and baseball and poetry and the theater. Right now he was talking women.

"You very frankly look like hell, Alec," he was saying. "You're frazzled. You look jumpy and itchy and off your feed. Don't gimme any talk about plot trouble. Love is your plot trouble, lad. You're not cut out for a lover. You better go back home to Amelia and get yourself grooved again."

Alec's voice was irritable.

"Everybody tells me to go home to Amelia. I don't want to go home to Amelia. I've never been happier in my life. I am *not* frazzled. I feel fine."

Ben Lea signaled the waiter for another drink. He sighed.

"My God. Amateur Casanovas. There ought to be a law. Friend, you started too late to be a lover. Lovers are basically born, and early developed. Now me—I am a proper, pure lover. To be a lover is a full-time job. That is why I never stuck to any one line of work very long."

Alec smiled.

"Five wives and you're a lover?"

"I kid you not. They never left me. I left *them*. A lover always leaves, and he stays left. A lover is also a very moral sort of chap. He marries them as he goes along, until he passes fifty. A lover is not some short-order Lothario who preys on shopgirls and hat-chicks. He aims high, and collects big. But the man who cultivates actresses and ballerinas and torch-singers cannot expect to stay married long. You plan to wed this Barbara female that's put all the bags under your eyes?

Alec gazed moodily at the tip of his cigarette.

"I don't know, Ben. Quite frankly I don't know. There's never been anything like it for me before—you know, the guns going off and the ceilings falling down and the floor-pacing until the phone rings and all that sort of kid-stuff. But I feel it's sort of closing in on me."

"Like how?"

"Well, it seems to me that every day we drink eighteen martinis and then have a fight about something and then we make up and then we go to bed and it's dawn before we get to sleep, because you can't climb into the same bed with Barbara Bayne and go immediately to sleep. Quite frankly, I am not used to living up to a reputation *every* night. What writing I do I seem to do when Barbara's got the old unspeakables. I don't suppose I'm the lover type, after all."

"You're right. You're a cornpone kid, not a poontang kid. You need your rest. You need to be bored into creative activity. And you are definitely not like me. I would rather die than eat a home-cooked meal. You're a homebody, my friend, whether you like it or not."

"So everybody tells me. You tell me. Barbara tells me. In half an hour, Marc will tell me. For my own good. God-dammit, I am sick and tired of being told things for my own good. But"—Alec smiled sheepishly— "I have to admit that this hectic night-life business is wearing pretty thin. God Almighty, do you realize that the other evening I found myself in both the Stork Club *and* El Morocco? I'm becoming the headwaiters' pinup boy. Horrible." Alec shuddered.

Ben Lea laughed hollowly.

"My poor friend. Alec Barr, the quiet writer's writer. The sober recluse. Thralled to love and a three-A.M. night-cap at P. J. Clarke's. *How* my boy has come on! Frankly, I never suspected you had it in you. How'd all this first come about, anyhow?"

Alec shook his head.

"I don't quite know, really. I met Barbara innocently enough. We bumped into each other on a plane. And one day, a couple of months ago, I couldn't stand it at home any longer. I was working on about five projects at once. Copy paper was coming out of my ears. I was ass-deep in proofs. It was hot. I had a couple of rejects. The plot jammed. It was *hot*. Amelia was on one of her more persistent accusatory kicks. We were supposed to go to dinner with the Hazeltines. I stalked out of the house in a real tizzy, like my head had closed down tight and there were too many people in the elevator. I checked into the Ritz. Then I called Barbara. We got drunk on the town and I kicked over an ashcan, and wound up drinking Irish coffee with a Jewish cop. We fell into the sack, and I haven't been up for air since."

Ben Lea rubbed his bristly pink crew cut. He clucked.

"I cannot believe it. Not my boy, the quiet Barr. Kicked over an ashcan? Waiter, bring me a double pink gin."

Alec grinned with a small shamed face once more.

"All of a sudden I felt I was living. I was doing things I'd never done. I was meeting a lot of the kind of people you know, but I don't. Actors. Musicians. Crazy people. Stay-up-all-nighters. Singers. Sleep-out Louies. Headstanders. Negro piano players. Pill-takers. For a while, it was fun. Now," he sighed, "I sort of miss the old dull routine. I guess I miss Amelia, as well."

"Where is she? Amelia, I mean?"

"Went to Europe. Spain or Italy, I think. I've had no messages."

"Take my advice, boy. Find out where she is and join her for a spell. Then come home and get back to work. I like this Barbara broad of yours, what I've seen of her, but she carries too much voltage for your wiring. You'll wind up as another one of these drunken talking-writers, your chin on somebody's bar all day. The saloons are full of them. Pack it in, friend. You're too old to start being a gay dog."

"What the hell's wrong with me, Ben?" Alec sounded patient. "I'm a normal guy. I would like to be happy. But I'm miserable if I'm home, with the collar on me, and when I shake the collar and show my ass all over the town, I feel just as shackled by the freedom as I did by the prison. Christ, Barbara's getting to be more of a wife than Amelia.

I feel like apologizing every time I need a night off to catch a little sleep or do a little work. What the hell's wrong with me?"

"Son, you're a writer," Ben Lea said. "There ain't no such animal as a happy writer. A writer is really only happy when he's miserable—when he's shut up in the back room with a typewriter and a hunk of paper with no words on it. Then he bitches and growls and screams about being tortured, but he's really happy. He's a *writer*. Writers are not as normal as men."

"May be. Maybe so. But sometimes I wish I had taken up another line of work."

"That's a lot of crap. You'd be miserable doing anything else. You know what a writer is? He's the worst ham that God ever made. He says he hates writing, but look what it lets him be. When he sits down at that machine, he is Superman in the best Nietzschean sense. He is both father and mother. He is God Almighty because he gives life. He is all-supreme, and his balls are wrapped up in the space bar."

Alec called for the bill.

"My check," he said. "Now I got to go let my agent tell me the same thing. But for that I'll stick *him* for lunch. I expect you're right, Ben. I hear the stripers are running at Montauk. Want to go fishing this week end?"

"To hell I'd go for you, *amigo*. The shirt off my back you can have. My bank account is at your disposal. Over broken bottles, for you, I will crawl. But I wouldn't go fishing with Jesus Christ Himself, even if it meant rewriting that loaves-and-fishes bit in the Good Book. Thank you, no. Instead, let's go to New Orleans and get laid."

Alec Barr shuddered. He held up his hand.

"Please," he said. "Not that word. Thank God the Series starts next week. Baseball at least will take my mind off *l'amour*."

"Call me when you get steady work," Ben Lea said. "Come on. I'll walk you over to Rockefeller Plaza and you can collect your conscientious reflection in the water, the great Mister Mantell."

"I'd rather be walking the last mile to the chair," Alec said. "Come on. Guillotine, here I come."

Book II/Alec

33

Perhaps the only person Alec Barr had ever really thoroughly hated was his mother, and this ancient feud made the rest of his war with the world—including the war he actually served in—seem tepid. He could not bring himself to hate his wife. Somehow it seemed a waste of time.

Even now the thought of his mother never failed to disturb Alec Barr. She had been a big, hearty woman who prided herself on the fact that she rode astride when proper ladies rode sidesaddle. She worked when proper ladies did not work. She boasted of "understanding" children, of being a "pal" to children, of "getting along well" with the friends of her child.

This unwanted togetherness was a source of considerable embarrassment to Alec, especially as he approached puberty, and some of his schoolmates came to play baseball in the huge front yard of the rambling big brick two-storied bungalow on the wooded hill, or to pretend to be cowboys and Injuns in the series of interlocking caves the boys had dug in the back lot. Emma Barr was forever intruding into the games, wanting to take her turn at bat, questioning his friends in a bird-bright, spuriously interested way about their families or confiding household secrets that made Alec writhe in embarrassment. Emma Barr was one of the reasons Alec took little interest in formal athletics or other mass gatherings of the young.

He did not desire, at any conscious age, an equal for a parent. He wanted parents like other boys had—parents who were not colorful, who did not intrude on their children, and who occupied a proper gray background of respectability in a house which was run on regular hours, with a stated time for meals. He wished that Emma Barr—he seldom thought of her as "mother"—would devote more time to his father and less effort to making a companion of Alec Barr, less time trying to appear perpetually young before his friends.

Perhaps Alec did not actively hate his mother for her arrogant disrespect of his father, her strident overrulings of any opinions he might offer, and her shaming of James Barr and his son Alec—by adopting pants and coming to fish, uninvited and unwanted, among men who wished no women to share their masculine escape. But he was ever ashamed in her presence. When, as a child, he was occasionally invited on a coon hunt or a deer drive by the adults of the the area, he was never quite sure Emma Barr would not appear, making much loud display of hail-fellowship, with a gun she handled so carelessly as to make the hairiest tobacco-chewing sportsman cringe.

Perhaps James Barr tried at first to keep his wife in womanly submission at home. But James Barr was a frustrated, ineffectual, slender man, blond like Alec, diffident to the point of self-effacement, and possessed of a stammer, with the habit of clearing his throat and biting his nails when he was nervous. Emma Barr, strapping and importunate, nagged him constantly and reduced any mild expression of dissent from her stated plan to the futile whining of a child. Emma outweighed her husband by forty pounds physically, and by forty tons in authority.

James Barr was a fox-faced man with thinning hair, an obtrusive Adam's apple, and muscle-lumps at the corners of his sensitive mouth. People said that Alec Barr was the spit of his father, and, like his father, would be another quiet one.

Alec's father had assumed adult responsibility very swiftly. James' father Angus had complained of poor health, and retired early from all toil. James had achieved four years of grammar school before he shouldered the burden of his mother, younger brother, and two sisters. Another elder brother, Joseph, had prematurely flown the nest. The elder sister, Annie, had married a visiting Yankee schoolteacher and had migrated North with her husband.

James had gotten a job as office boy with a wholesale grocery house at the age of fourteen and had gradually, through midnight study on correspondence courses, learned the basics of costs accounting. Secretly he wrote poetry and drew quite remarkable pictures, which he was ashamed to show anyone.

Jessie Barr, James Barr's mother, took in boarders, and James Barr's earliest memories were of strangers at table, strangers in the little living room, strangers always to be deferred to even in the quality of food at table. She quarreled bitterly at her husband Angus, a veteran of the Confederate Army, who complained that his wounds deviled him and he couldn't do any heavy work on account of his back.

Son James brought his pay packet intact to his mother, who counted him out fifty cents a week at first, and later, when he had advanced his earnings to ten dollars a week, increased his personal allowance to a dollar, complaining that "she didn't know what he did with all that money."

With his thick mop of blond, waving hair, a bony frame on which even shabby clothes rode smoothly, and a good baritone singing voice, James Barr might have been popular with the girls, but Miss Jessie, as James Barr's mother was called, generally managed to discourage any serious romances by a constant disparagement of the girl as soon as she heard that her son was "dolling up of nights and stepping out."

Unkind people said that James Barr had been chosen by Emma Davis because nobody else would have such a bull-necked, stiff-chinned, driving woman. They said that poor Jamie Barr didn't have any choice, once Emma raised her topknot against the idea of spinsterhood, because she was twenty-five years old and not getting any younger. Some hinted that Emma had gotten herself pregnant by another man, and had lumbered Jamie with the child—a patent libel, because Alec Barr was not born until a year after the marriage. In any case they were married, and Jamie's mother, Miss Jessie, retired to her room and refused to come out for a week. Father Angus Barr got drunk at the wedding and stayed drunk until Jessie Barr recovered from her nervous attack sufficiently to emerge from her quarters and sober Angus up with a combination of hot coffee, hot gruel, and the razor edge of her tongue.

Business was good. James Barr was studying law on the side now, and sitting for a certified public accountant's license. His salary had been raised to seventy-five dollars a week, and he had started to draw plans to build a big new brick house. Everyone said he was lucky to be married to such a fine woman as Emma, who had injected some spirit into him. "Without Emma, Jamie wouldn't have spunk enough to say boo to a goose," they said. "She's got backbone aplenty for both of them, and enough left over to keep 'til Christmas."

When America came into the war, there was no chance of James Barr being called up. There had been an influenza epidemic, killing both his younger brother, Dan, and the younger sister, Gertrude, and leaving James Barr with a permanently weakened chest. Emma Barr had nursed them all and spent her lavish extra energies outside as well, relishing her work and reveling in her white nurse's cap with the red cross on it. Labor on the new house was suspended until after the Armistice, but shortly thereafter they raised the new brick house on the outskirts of town, and the family of Jessie and Angus Barr, James and Emma Barr, and young Alec Barr moved in. This more or less confounded the other unkind people who had said that James Barr married Emma Davis just to get out from under the wing of Jessie Barr. More unkind people had said that in swapping Mother Jessie for Emma Davis, James Barr was merely exchanging wardens. Still other people said that the only reason Jamie asked her was that he couldn't tell the difference between Emma and Jessie so far as domination ran. James Barr had betrayed them; he wound up with both Mother and Wife in what people said later could only be labeled a hoorah's nest. It was an assumption in the town that when James Barr married Emma Davis at the age of twenty-four, he came to her couch a virgin, since none of the bucks could ever remember his sitting up seriously with any other girl, tomcatting around back of town with tarnished belles, or patronizing any of the local whorehouses. "Why," said one friend, Alexander Leslie by name and for whom Alec Barr was named, "why, Jamie never even sampled a nigger wench, far as I know." Alexander Leslie stood up at the wedding for James Barr, and they remained firm friends for a great many years, until James Barr's borrowing habits finally ended the friendship on a note of legal disharmony.

That defect of character, the compulsive borrowing without repayment, was to afflict James Barr all his life. His intentions were good, everybody said, but he never quite got around to finishing anything he started. If he bought a car, the car was likely to be repossessed. A time-payment shotgun was taken back by Sears, Roebuck, and at one time someone even reclaimed a partially paid-for bird-dog. James Barr borrowed in good faith, but once the money was in his pocket, some mysterious alchemy took place and the money became his, with no further obligation to pay.

It was inevitable that James' mother Jessie should hate James' wife Emma. For as long as Jessie Barr lived she and her daughter-in-law made the various homes into a series of battlegrounds. Young Alec Barr grew up in an atmosphere of constant bicker and shouted recrimination of snarled charges and countercharges, with no meal free of agitation. The Barr men said little: James Barr stammered when he asked for the biscuits, and his father, Angus, silently dribbled food into his untidy beard. Young Alec sat nervously indrawn, gobbling his meal in order to excuse himself and leave the table.

Alec merely disliked his grandmother, for her whining reproaches of his grandfather and her perpetual battle for the chatelaine's keys with Alec's mother. But young Alec actively hated Emma Barr for her constant usurpation of his father's authority as head of the house. He hated her disparaging comparison of James Barr's puny achievements with those of other men, her unceasing reminders of her own stout strength in a family of spineless men. In later years Alec would often wonder how the regular accouchements, invariably ending in stillborn children, were accomplished in such a turbulence of sexual antagonism.

The hatred—or perhaps cold dislike—had begun roughly at the age of three or four, when Alec first became conscious that his mother, for all her self-professed competence, all her hearty activity in the life of the town, really despised her husband; that she disliked the idea of motherhood, was jealous of her brother, envious of her father, and owned a positive talent for meddling in the lives of everyone around her while her own dishes went unwashed, her own beds went unmade. Once, in a fit of misguided generosity, she had given all of Alec's clothes away to a mendicant milltown family. Her passion for good works kept her physical motors racing eighteen hours a day, and her passion for describing her passion for good works kept her tongue racing for twenty hours a day.

Her brother was a doctor; Emma Barr yearned for scalpel and lancet. At one time she decided to be a nurse, self-deluded in preparation for an internship. She was forever collecting funds for some hospital activity, and quite as frequently mishandling the funds she collected. She inflicted Alec at a minute age with unwanted medical knowledge; horrid glossy photographs of breech presentations, flowering chancres, awful areas of sores and ulcers and rashes and cancers from her quite extensive library of pseudo-official medical books.

Her delight in all illnesses, both personal and public, ran second only to her pride in herself as a mental and social nonconformist. She would summon a doctor or an ambulance at the drop of a symptom; at the same time she read poetry she did not understand and quoted philosophy she understood less. Also at the same time, the cook would invariably quit for some unreasonable (to Emma) reason, such as the nonfurnishing of basic raw material for meals or very possibly a long delinquency of salary.

For his first few years of human consciousness, Alec was helpless before his mother's unbridled energy, aimless activity, and unleashed garrulousness. He was a small reed of a child, with a limp lock of blond hair forever in his eyes, defeated before his mother, mountainous, supercapable, intimidating.

When he was somewhat less than twelve a magnificent thing happened to Alec Barr. His father, consciously delicate in the lungs, contrived a possible pneumonia which turned into a debatable tuberculosis which developed into an argumentatively necessary internment in a lunger's refuge in Asheville, North Carolina. Jessie Barr involuntarily succumbed, either from asthma, morphine, or shame at having a tubercular son, and shortly thereafter Grandfather Angus fell fatally under the influence of his cancer and the homehewn whiskey with which he assuaged it.

Emma Barr had to go to work. There was, as yet, no Brother Martin to be considered logistically. Thoughtlessly,

Martin would be a footnote to Alec's father's graduation from the hawking-and-spitting academy in Asheville. There was only young Alec to be considered, as Mother Emma was forced to channel her boundless energies into the demeaning salaried chores of a saleslady, and there was a vastly bosomed sloven Negress named Lil to run the house. Lil was an economy; the going wage for servants then was two dollars a week and totin' privileges, if they didn't tote too much. And in Alec Barr's house there was not a great deal left over to tote, because the credit was very skinny in the local Piggly-Wiggly, a sketchy foreshadow of the supermarket.

Lil owned a little girl, last of an innumerable crew of snotnosed children, named Puddin'. Puddin' occupied a great deal of Lil's time, as did Buster, her gonorrheal husband, who was known to drink moonshine on purpose and occasionally carve a companion with a large, old-fashioned cutthroat razor.

This fortunate combination of social circumstances left Alec Barr alone, for the most part, in his formative years, and he reveled in the loneliness. He went daily to school, where he was largely regarded as a teacher's pet, since his omnivorous reading had equipped him with an outrageous arsenal of adult knowledge. When he rode his bicycle home from school, there was nobody in the house, usually. Lil would likely be occupied with Puddin', or possibly bailing Buster out of jail for his newest extralegal incision, and Mother was trapped in the shop until six P.M. This left Alec largely on his own during daylight hours.

After Alec's paternal grandparents died, when Alec was about twelve years old, his mother rented the now-vacant upstairs rooms to four school-teachers—coarsely pretty, rather chapped country wenches, each of whom appeared to own a ceaseless supply of slack-lipped boy friends. Mostly the boy friends seemed to Alec too old for the girls, who were in their early twenties. The boy friends arrived by night, and often screams of laughter from the teachers and the heavier basso voices of men were heard through the thin beaverboard partition which now separated the hallway connecting the upstairs with the downstairs. The men always came by a backyard driveway, parking their cars behind the house. They invariably carried bulky paper packages which clinked and gurgled. Alec was discouraged by his parents from going around to the back of the house after dark, but occasionally he would slip upstairs in the afternoon to puff at a forbidden cigarette. He was deeply drawn to the atmosphere of tousled femininity; the slips and stockings flung helter-skelter, the smell of powder and perfume and, from the kitchen, the not-infrequent odor of raw corn whiskey.

He was just achieving puberty. The girls fascinated him and raised strange unformed emotions. They dressed and undressed casually in front of him, walking around in brassières and knickers, laughing and chattering and smoking and occasionally teasing him with a swift kiss or rough tickle. One, Hazel, a tall, dark country girl who spoke in backwoods accents and taught in elementary school, was his particular favorite. She was very pretty, Alec thought, and she was long-legged and full-bosomed. She kissed him oftener than the others, and poked fun at him about his girl friends, and rumpled him in embarrassingly intimate places. She would slip him a cigarette, and once let him taste a concoction made of Coca-Cola and some raw spirit which made his eyes water, although he manfully restrained a cough. She would cuddle him in her lap, ruffle his hair, and tell the other girls that Alec was her special fellow and she was saving him for when he grew up a little more. Alec liked the physical contact; the smell of warm flesh, the slightly musky odor of woman, the overlay of powder that clung to Hazel roused delicious feelings. She would pull his head back against her full breasts, or nibble at his ears, and Alec would experience the strangest sensation of heat in his loins and an embarrassing muscular reaction in his nether parts. This would cause him to blush and rush downstairs with his hands in his pockets, and the other girls would roar with laughter.

"He's goin' to be a devil with the girls when he grows up," Hazel would say. "Give him a couple more years and we'll have to be careful about lettin' him come up here. His mother would skin us alive."

"We better start bein' careful now, Haze," one of the other girls, Clara, said one day, to Alec's acute discomfort as he fled downstairs. "The little bugger had as good a hard on as ever I saw."

"You ought to be a pretty good judge by now," Hazel said drily, as the other girls roared with laughter. "You've sure had enough practice."

As approaching manhood lent Alec frightening ideas and

produced even more frightening sensations as he lay in bed on the sleeping porch, he imagined himself in love with Hazel and entertained thoughts of marrying her some day. He was in a Sir Walter Scott stage at the time, and thought seriously of flinging her across the withers of a noble steed and galloping off into the horizon. He even thought of talking to her about it, but, deliciously, memorably conscious of her half-naked body when she stroked and petted him, he lacked the courage to face reality.

One night, when his father was ill in Asheville and his mother was out of the house on some aimless merciful errand, Alec sneaked upstairs. Hazel was home alone, he knew; the other girls had trooped out laughing with assorted heavy-faced blue-shaven men. Alec screwed up his courage, went around to the back door, and stepped softly up the stairs. The house was silent, and only one light shone—the light in Hazel's bedroom. Alec walked along the hall, making an effort to conceal his presence. He was lonely and he wanted to flutter in the light of his love. Suddenly he heard low laughter and the rumble of a man's voice, then the man saying: "You're first up, baby, you bring the drinks."

Alec stood rooted, as Hazel, stark naked, came laughing through the door. Alec gasped. He had never seen a living naked woman before, although he had been thoroughly indoctrinated on feminine physiology in the family's medical library.

He gasped, unable to restrain himself, and Hazel lunged at him like a tigress. She seized him fiercely, shaking him, her naked breasts jouncing as she shook. There was a rank odor about her he had never smelled before.

"What are you doin' sneakin' round up here, you little devil?" She shook him again, and he stared fascinated at the bobbing bulbs of her breasts. "What do you mean comin' up here and sneakin' around!"

The man's voice said "What's the trouble, baby?" and there was a rustle of bedclothes. Equally naked, the man came through the door. Alec switched his stare to the man, a huge, hairy fellow. He was a county deputy sheriff named Tom Something, and Alec knew him vaguely by sight.

Hazel slapped Alec with a full swing of her arm.

"Get out of here! Get out of here, and if you tell your mother, I'll kill you!" she cried. "Now get out and don't you never come sneakin' up here again!"

Alec fled in horror and disillusionment.

"You shouldn't have slapped him, honey," the big man was rumbling as Alec plunged down the steps. "I'd of give him a dollar to shut him up. Now he'll tell his Ma, sure."

Alec heard no more. He rushed out into the yard, flung himself on the grass, and wept bitterly. It did not occur to him to tell his mother anything. He wept not from the swinging slap, which still stung his face, but for the loss of his first fresh love in a horrid tableau of naked flesh.

He never went upstairs any more. He hated all the girls now, but he hated Hazel worst of all. Once in a while he might see her entering or leaving, but he never spoke to her again.

A year later, now fully emancipated from boyhood, he answered a midnight ring at the front door. Flicking on the porch light, he saw the faces of four men.

"What do you want?" he asked. "There's nobody home but me."

"Good God Almighty!" one of the men said, and Alec recognized him. It was the new barber, recently come to town from Charleston. "It's little Alec Barr! I cut his hair jest last week. There must be some mistake. We got the wrong house, son. Sorry to bother you."

"There can't be no mistake," one of the men was saying. "That manicurist gal down at the hotel said there was four—"

"Shut up, you fool," the barber said. "We must of come in on the wrong side of the house. Now let's get the hell out of here." He dropped his voice. "That boy comes from respectable people. It ain't likely they'd be running a cat-house."

"All I know is what the manicurist told me. She even wrote it down on a card. Here."

He flashed a pocket lamp and drew something from his pocket.

"See," he said, "it's the right house, all right."

"Well, right or wrong house," the man who had recognized Alec said. "We're gettin' the hell out of here. That poor little feller . . . what the hell do you think of people like that?"

There was a roar of motor as the car swerved around the circular drive. This time Alec didn't weep. And suddenly, also, he knew how those white rubber elliptical balloons, which reared upward like huge asparagus in the bubbling septic tank down among the tiger lilies, had gotten there. No boy from the age of six onward in that community had not giggled evilly and experimented with pouring water or blowing air into what were called Merry Widows and which came three to the little round tin box labeled "Agnes, Mabel, and Becky."

Disappointed in love, distrustful of and now abominating all women, hating his family for permitting what he knew was evil and ugly and a trespass on his home, Alec Barr gave up the society of humankind and concentrated on God's outdoors and dead men's books. He wandered lonely in the wood, and he read until his eyes puffed red and scratchy.

The Barr library was more than adequate, since Grandfather Angus Barr had preferred reading and whiskey to work or conversation with the wife. Alec streaked through the library in a kind of panic, as if someone might steal the unread books before he got to them. When he had finished the supply at home, he became a steady customer at the public library and tottered home under great stacks of books.

The Barr house snugged along a green hill in an undeveloped part of town, which made field and forest available to the boy. He was too slight for the organized rough sport of the older kids who encumbered his class in school, and he owned no boats or dogs or guns or other hearty, hairy paraphernalia of the lusty young. But he loved the towering trees of the back lot, where Grandpa Barr had once kept an incompetent milch-cow; he loved the millpond with its disappearing die-dapper grebes; and he loved the rioting birds: the swearing bluejays, the red-shouldered blackbirds, the bright scarlet slashes of tanager and golden glints of oriole. He would go to the woods with a book and hate it when the diminishing sun died behind the blue woods and he had to trudge home to meet Emma for the badly prepared supper that Lil, depending on the various plights of Puddin' and Buster, might or might not have prepared.

Emma Barr was a handsome dark woman in the fashion of the late nineenth century, which is to say she was forty pounds overweight, the pallid meat smoothly troweled on, and she assaulted a room with excessive vigor. She was in fact a pathetic product of her time; a great many years later Alec realized that if lesbianism had been recognized as a fairly normal female condition, his mother would have made an excellent lesbian.

Alec's mother was unchanneled, misdirected, unfulfilled, and hateful. She owned a positive genius for the invasion of personal privacy, and would follow Alec into the bathroom to press home a pointless point. She disapproved of his heavy reading, and forbade him to read at night in bed. Alec solved this frustration with a flashlight that he was forced to steal because of a shortage of pocket money. He read clandestinely under the blankets of his bed on the sleeping porch of the bungalow.

A great many things puzzled Alec Barr about his mother. He could not understand why she was always being confined with stillborn children when her scorn for the feeble father James was starkly apparent, and her dislike for the maternal estate noisily obvious. It is impossible that Alec Barr could have recognized the symptom at the time, but Emma seemingly aborted out of whim, bearing yet another dead baby as a reproof to her husband. Cats, she said, terrified her; Alec plumped a kitten on her shoulder one day and years later she accused him of murdering a brother.

When James Barr's mother died of asthma, Emma immediately acquired asthma. Asthma, at this time, in a loosely coordinated pharmaceutical area, was treated by narcotic, and it was not really necessary for a doctor to write a prescription. And Emma Barr, because of her famous brother, the surgeon, and her famous fund-raising activities for the hospitals, and her frequent presence in the hospitals, and her proneness to send all her dependents to hospitals, and her wide acquaintance among doctors, seldom needed a prescription to cure her of her cyanosed plagiarism of her mother-in-law's favorite disease. She merely went to the drugstore, and came home with a little paper packet which she would certainly need when her breath came whistling short and her fingernails turned blue.

It was during Alec's last year in high school when she approached him on a hearty man-to-man basis and said:

"How would you like God to send you a little brother?"

"I don't think God sends little brothers," Alec said. "And if he does, will this one be a dope-fiend, too?"

Emma Barr looked around for something to strike her son with. Finding nothing, she burst into tears and shortly was brought to bed with Martin, who was from the start a candy-box baby, with cheeks like painted peaches, moist golden ringlets, and a predisposition to cry on any and all occasions.

Well before the advent of Brother Martin, Father Barr had emerged from Asheville, with the report that he had never had tuberculosis at all and that it was all a mistake of the miserable medical profession. Emma was enraged at this infringement of her superdiagnostic powers, and her pride was only soothed when James Barr presented her with a nervous breakdown as a palliative replacement for the tuberculosis. James Barr's nervous breakdown occurred roughly at the time of the birth of Martin Barr, thereby reaffirming his wife's belief that men were at best unstable.

The occasion of the nervous breakdown allowed Emma Barr to revert to her own family, in terms of daughterly blackmail, and persuade her father, a rather stupid but competent hardware merchant, to mortgage his tiny home in the coastal hamlet in which he had lived since his wife had died of a stroke. Emma was furious at her father at the time. Father Edmund Davis had been keeping company with a bleached-blonde widow-woman of uncertain morals, and Emma felt that this was an insult to the memory of the pharmacopoeia which still dwelt in her mother's bathroom.

When pressed, Emma Barr was an overpowering woman, and so she celebrated Martin's birth with a full-grown narcotics addiction of her own, a foreclosed mortgage of her father's home, complete poverty on the part of her nervously afflicted husband, fresh plaster on the big bungalow in the country, an international depression, the failure of all local banks, and the accusation of complicity in the embezzlement of hospital funds which she had collected, and for which other pillars of the city went to jail.

That was the year that Alec Barr graduated with the highest honors in his class, and was proved by test to own the highest intelligence quotient in the state. The year was 1929.

34

Every time Alec Barr dropped in to select a fresh clutch of suits from Brioni in Rome or Caruso in New York; every time he realized that an order for silk shirts or hand-carved shoes would be filled without question from his permanently filed measurements; every time he was greeted effusively by a headwaiter in New York or Nairobi or London; every time he ate less than half his steak or was brought a postdinner liqueur by the management of the various expensive restaurants in which he did most of his extrawriting business, Alec Barr thought of college. He thought of college in the same way one remembers a bad dream, hoping to put it out of his head.

Most old grads, grown boozily sentimental, might remember the university days as the good old days, the fine brave days of fraternity dances and crisp golden autumn afternoons of football; of yielding fragrant female flesh in rumble seats and under rugs in stadia or tenderly trembling on divans to the music of Hal Kemp's records and the smell of jasmine on spring nights. Or possibly, the greasier grinds, grown hatchet-faced and myopic from peering into cultures or legal briefs, might recreate the triumphs of the delivery of the Phi Beta Kappa key, the *summa cum laude* citation, the triumphant awakenings of knowledge in laboratories or the special favor of a certain professor in a certain classroom.

For the athlete, now waxed fat and selling insurance, the ears of memory might ring with the roars of an autumn crowd, the rolling thunder of a stadium. Memory would recall the knifing block that cleared the path for the vital touchdown or the marvelous thudding impact of a long pass taken over the shoulder on the dead run, with nothing ahead but the chalklines of the goal. The athlete would remember the great block numeral on the cable-stitched sweater; the golden football for the watch-chain; the noisy adulation of the drunken old grads in the fraternity house after the Big Game—or, perhaps, the less exuberant but more sincerely demonstrable admiration of the girls in their pleated skirts and swollen sweaters, with their smooth brown legs twinkling over saddle-shoes and thick white bobby sox. The athlete might also recall, in an occasional bitingly honest appraisal of himself, that he was given certain illegal sums for purely academic chores in the dormitory sweetshop, or in the campus tailor shop, and that he was bid to his fraternity on a jawbone basis. He might remember that a jockstrap scholarship, provided by a rich alumnus, paid his tuition and that another alumnus picked up the tab for his room and board. But he would not forget the feel of the girls in their dancing dresses, their white shoulders and breasts soft against the starched shirt and the hug of the dinner jacket's broadcloth, even if the boiled shirt and the dinner jacket had been supplied free by The College Shoppe. Triumph on the playing field the athlete supplied for himself; sex on the campus after training broke was something no alumnus could buy for the hero.

The Big Man On Campus, now serving as a junior representative in the state legislature after two or three unsuccessful shots at Congress, might salve his painful consciousness of a shiny-seated law practice and the nagging of an overburdened wife with preslumber memory of being named editor of the yearbook, of being elected president of the student body, of writing the column on world affairs for the college paper, of being nominated Most Likely to Succeed in his senior year, when his picture in the yearbook carried a fat six inches of italic statistic listing of his achievements.

Alec Barr owned none of these healing memories. Every time Alec Barr thought of college he cringed, and put the thought swiftly out of his mind. College to Alec Barr was now a blur, mercifully finished and best forgotten. He had gone off to school in the depression's nadir; the depression was still dingily manifest when he finished college.

There was no money at all forthcoming from home. His father, now more or less recovered from the supposed tuberculosis and the actual nervous breakdown, was trying to sell insurance, and nobody was buying any insurance. The schoolteachers above stairs had been supplanted by nurses. The house, still occupied by the Barrs despite a lapsed mortgage—nobody had enough money to buy up any mortgages after the bank failures—had been turned into a nursing home. At least there was a big sign in the front yard which said CONVALESCENT HOME, although few patients could afford to be sick outside their own houses these days, and customers who came to recover from a drunk or to rest after an operation grew pitifully few to the hill.

Alec rarely went home, and never took any classmates with him. The memory of the schoolteachers haunted him, and he wondered whether the nurses were not providing specialized aid and comfort to the patients. He had come home once, on a Christmas vacation, and blanched at the vulgar sign planted in the front yard profaning the area in which he had played baseball.

He had worked in a parking lot the summer before he went to university, and had managed to save nearly all his salary for three months. The salary had been ten dollars a week, and so Alec Barr had nearly a hundred dollars in his pocket when he presented himself at the Dean's office, thence being directed to the office of the Student Loan Fund. He could not as yet qualify for a scholarship, but the hundred would buy his books and pay his matriculation fees, and he would worry about eating and tuition later. Thereafter he worked in the summertime—once as a lifeguard, another summer in the parking lot, another as a drugstore soda jerk. The small cash he accumulated allowed him to squeeze back into school, now with scholarships to aid him, and part-time jobs around campus to keep him fed and clothed after a fashion.

He had almost no money; his hands were wrinkled and greasy from washing dishes in the Student Union, and his pride ached from the necessity of each fresh pleading with the Loan Fund. He had been bid to a fraternity, true, but he paid his dues then by keeping the fraternity's books, and then he paid for his food in the fraternity house by waiting table for his brothers of the secret handclasp and sacred pin. His clothing was minimal; the one good suit rubbed shiny with use, the sweaters frayed and leather-patched at the elbows, the shoes resoled until the uppers cracked and collapsed.

He had not been able to afford the big dance week ends or to invite girls down for the big houseparties. He had bummed more cigarettes than he liked to remember, even now, and he winced again at the dishonesty which made a friendly soda jerk allow him to walk out of the drugstore without paying for his milkshake or package of cigarettes. Once he had desperately needed an alarm clock and, being completely without money, had stolen it from the same drugstore.

Alec was not a big man on campus. He was not even a little man on campus. He was nobody on the campus. He was generally too busy scrounging bare necessities to make a pass at campus activity. As a less-than-indifferent athlete in a school which imported its massive meat and muscles from Pennsylvania coal mines, he was not candidate for any athletic endeavor. So far as he knew he had no talent for the highbrow area of campus life, and worked on none of the publications. His strictured funds kept him out of the ten-cent poker game and Saturday boozing bouts and trips to the whorehouses in nearby Durham. Movies cost money and so did soda pop; Alec Barr dated infrequently—girls were in extremely short supply on the campus.

Thus Alec Barr studied, chiefly because play was disallowed. Moonlight was unimportant to him, because when it shone sweetly on the Arboretum, Alec Barr would not be in the bushes with a girl. He would be in the campus library, most likely, because there was no other interesting place in the town that was free. He did not think of himself as a bookish fellow; he thought of himself more as a prisoner of war. Some day the war would be over, and then he would be free. Meanwhile, it was necessary to trudge daily through the paces, because even as a very young man Alec Barr had realized that pants were unimportant if you owned some, but very, very important indeed if you did not. This, he felt, applied equally to a college education, because in the commercial life to come, the man without the degree would stand trouserless in the halls of commerce.

So he read everything he could find, growing ever hungrier as he eyed the vast stacks in the college library. Sometimes he felt a tremendous futility, knowing that it would never be possible to absorb all the massed knowledge that man had wrung from his brain to place between covers. But he set out doggedly to dig a dent in it, and so proceeded shabbily, mostly unhappily, when he wasn't reading or studying, into the spring quarter of his senior year.

But in this spring quarter, a rowdy March being replaced

by a soft Southern April and a sweet-smelling May gone riotously mad with flower and birdsong, Alec Barr's grades fell off alarmingly.

Her name was Fran.

35

At the time, Alec Barr was regarded as handsome, even "cute," by some of the coeds who sat in his classes. His face had formed into an adult mold; a face rather horsey in fact, but the girls said he looked like Leslie Howard, with his ash-blond hair and lean, controlled features. There was a certain easy style to the way he wore shabby corduroy slacks and threadbare sweaters; he spoke softly and precisely, almost elegantly, in a land where shorthand is practiced in vocal self-expression and every third word is "you know" or "whatsisname." He was tall, touching six feet, and diffident in his classroom display of knowledge. His erudition had become a campus joke, even among the professors, especially the few who, knowing Alec's famine of sociability, occasionally invited him to their homes for coffee and cookies or, more important, a proper meal. On particularly knotty questions in economics or philosophy, the professor might quiz a third of the class, then shrug wearily and say:

"I suppose we'll have to get Mister Barr to tell us again. Would you kindly oblige us, *Mister* Barr?"

Alec would rise and deliver the short, necessary lecture, and the professor might bow gravely and say: "Thank you, Mister Barr." Then, to the class: "You see, it isn't impossible after all." One day, after a particularly precise rendition of something inverted attributed to Kant or Hegel, the professor had headed for the door.

"Mister Barr," he said, "will conduct the class for the rest of the day. I have spring fever, and suddenly I am overcome with awe that this state has been able to breed any child with the potential of understanding what he is told to read."

Alec had not made the mistake of taking the professor seriously. He said swiftly: "I've got spring fever, too, so I declare this court adjourned until tomorrow." He followed the professor swiftly out of the door, and was striding loose-jointedly down the graveled path, under the ancient oaks, when a girl's voice said: "Hey, Professor, wait for me."

She was a small, secret girl, with Indian-black hair and eyes. She was wearing a yellow cashmere sweater and a nubby-wool green skirt. Her legs were bare and brown, over the inevitable saddle-shoes and short athlete's wool socks. Alec had seen her around, of course, but today had been the first time she had appeared in any class of his. He knew—everybody knew everything about everybody else on that small campus—that she was Pi Phi, that she was a junior, that she was a working member of the college dramatic club, and that she was studying journalism.

Her cool, brown Indian skin was stained scarlet by health on the high cheekbones, her mouth painted even brighter by lipstick. The cheekbones rose too high in her face, lending a curiously babyish pouched look to the bright black eyes.

"Hi," Alec Barr said. "What got you into old Van Gelder's lair? I thought you were learning how to be a sob-sister on the other side of the campus."

"If I played it smart I could say it was because I wanted to meet you," the girl said. "Since I don't know how to play it smart, my dean said it wouldn't be a bad idea to sit in on Van Gelder once in a while and find out how the intellectuals live. By the same token he's got me sitting in on Merriwether in ancient history and Maxwell in archeology, and with nary a credit to be had. I know your name; mine's Fran—Fran Mayfield. Would you like to buy us a cup of coffee at the Greek's? We've got a full three quarters of an hour to kill before next class."

Alec colored, pushing both hands in his pockets.

"Golly, I'd like to," he said. "But I switched pants this morning and forgot to change my money from one to the other. It's a bad habit of mine."

"Then maybe I can buy you a cup of coffee?" she smiled, showing strong white teeth against the slash of scarlet lip. "That's one nice thing about being a girl. You generally have to carry a purse to include all the gunk girls seem to need all the time."

"I'll say yes only on condition that you let me take you

to the movies tonight," Alec said. "They're rerunning that last Jean Harlow. Seen it?"

"As a matter of fact I haven't, and I'd love to," the girl said. "Come on. I overslept this morning and missed my breakfast. I think I might be able to handle a jelly doughnut, too."

They sat in a corner booth at the Greek's and drank coffee, and Alec wondered where he would find the necessary dollar to buy two movie tickets, with enough left over for a milkshake at the end of it. Never mind, he said to himself, I'll find it. I'll find it if I have to kill somebody.

"Where do you come from?" he asked.

"Up where they grow Injuns," she replied. "Waynesville. I'm sort of a half-breed. Actually not quite. Maybe a quarter Cherokee. My grandmother was a full-blood. I might say she was kind of a princess, and there was a lot of trouble in the tribe when she ran off with my white grandfather. They thought she was taking a backward step socially, and they could be right. How about you?"

"South Carolina. On the border. Kingtown. One-horse town with a paper mill surrounded by millionaires and quail. After a while you get used to the stink of the paper mill. I never smelt any of the millionaires yet."

"I know about that smell. We've got a mill outside of Waynesville. We also got a lot of millionaires scattered around, but the trouble is most of them have tuberculosis. They come there for the climate."

"I know. My old man was in Asheville for a spell," the boy said. "Turned out it wasn't too serious. Or, more likely, he ran out of money."

They sat silent, and Alec thanked God he had a pack of cigarettes. Lighting them, and smoking them, and having the Greek refill the coffee cups occupied the awkward lapse of conversation.

"You know," the girl said, "you must be awful smart. But you don't look like the professional sort of campus smarties —you know what I mean, the ones with the greasy hair and the hornrims. You look like—oh, I don't know—a kind of nice friendly *young* professor. You going to teach?"

"Great God no," Alec said. "I can't stand the idea of starting out in some backwoods high school and coming to summer school for the next ten years to get a master's, and then hoping they start hiring instructors instead of firing professors. I want something faster, and with more future—something that I won't have to wear out my eyes on, grading papers. Only trouble is I don't know *what*."

"How about law? You'd make a wonderful lawyer, I bet."

"It takes time, and it takes money, and I haven't got any money. I've managed to scratch by for the last four years, and when I get out this summer I'm going to have to get a job—a real job, a job that pays real money, even if it's swinging a pick somewhere. I'm tired of trying to study with one side of my brain and earn a living with the other half. And it's only a half living, in a college town."

"You'll find something," the girl said. She looked at her wrist watch. "I have to gallop. I've got a class coming up at eleven. Journalism Four. Where you going?"

"Nowhere, actually, except maybe back to the house. I've got a twelve-o'clock, and don't laugh. It's Music Appreciation. A nice one to sleep through, and no exams. I sort of doubled up last year, and I've got more credits than I need, and I'm kind of loafing this spring."

"Well, then," the girl Fran said with disarming honesty. "I don't see why you can't take a little simple journalism to round out your education. We could meet for coffee"—her high color deepened—"we could meet for coffee and talk at Chapel period and then you could walk me over to the journalism school and I bet you'd love old Prof. Henry. He calls everybody by their first name and cusses right out loud in class."

"I can't see any reason against it," Alec Barr said. "Except I got to be frank with you, Fran. There will be mornings in the Greek's when you will have to buy the coffee again. I'm *that* broke."

"I know you're that broke. I watched you blush and I heard you lie when you felt in your pockets. And just where do you think you'll get the money for a movie tonight?"

"I have a secret hoard for emergencies," Alec replied, smiling. "Don't worry. I'll show up with my hair combed and a tie on and money in my one decent suit."

"Well," Fran said. "If it's not putting too much of a strain on your one decent suit, we're having a tea dance Friday at the Pi Phi house, and I haven't asked anybody yet. I'd like to ask you now to come as my date."

"I'd love to," Alec Barr said. "I haven't gotten out and around very much because of—" he shrugged. "You know."

"I know," Fran Mayfield said, and frankly took his hand as they walked through the campus toward the journalism building. "I know. And I don't give a damn. Come on now and I'll introduce you to Prof. When you get to know him better you call him Skipper, but not before he's insulted you a few times first."

"Tell me one thing," Alec Barr said, as they walked up the broad, lichened gray-stone steps of the journalism building. "Quite obviously you know that I'm nobody, and I've only got a couple months left at school here, while you've still got another year to go. Why this sudden interest in me?"

"My woman's intuition tells me you've got a future," Fran Mayfield said. "And you never can tell whether or not I'm planning to be included in it."

It may be noted that, at the time, 1933, aged twenty-one, Alec Barr was still a virgin, unused to the society of young women, good or bad. For the second time that morning he blushed.

36

Professor Henry, called Skipper by the people he liked well enough to insult, looked like a benevolent old sea-turtle, up to and including the barnacles. His eyes hooded behind glasses that clung precariously to the end of a hooked nose. The smell of home-cooked corn liquor clothed him, for Skipper Henry believed that the best thing to clear a man's sinuses in the morning was a stout slug of whiskey, and he also believed that a man's lunch tasted better after two or three stout slugs of whiskey, and that man did his best thinking in an easy chair of nights over three or four or five stout slugs of whiskey.

Skipper Henry was somewhere in his sixties, and he had been a newspaperman most of his life, beginning as printer's devil when he was fourteen years old. He had never made the big time; never made the slick magazines, never worked New York or Washington or Chicago. He had never written a book. But as a working newspaperman he had found time to accumulate enough credits for a college degree, mostly achieved at night school and via correspondence courses, and he had also found time, in Raleigh and Norfolk and Greensboro and Charlotte, to uncover a variety of political bodies which had made him the coroner of political corpses for two states—corpses of which the odor might occasionally be smelled as far north as Washington.

He had come to the University because he liked the climate, because he did not want to work very hard any more, and because the University was the fountainhead of the political life of that portion of the South. Raleigh had the State House; Greensboro had the tobacco millions; Charlotte had the textiles; Wilmington had the culture; but Chapel Hill flexed the political muscle. Chapel Hill owned the tradition, and its alumni sat in legislative halls, became governors and senators, and influenced the backroom caucuses which made the governors and the senators who passed laws that made textile barons and tobacco millionaires.

The Skipper still wrote a column which was carried in half a dozen influential papers, state dailies, as well as innumerable weeklies and semiweeklies. It was called "Grits and Chitlin's," and the backwoods simplicity of its title was deceptive. It did not really deal with the intestines of hogs and of a meal called hominy; it pointed enlightening fingers at various dark closets, spoke in parables which were closely studied in the State House, and from time to time elected or ruined a politician. He sat, corn-likker-smelling, rumpled, turtle-faced, as a full professor in the School of Journalism, and every time he two-fingered a few sticks of type for "Grits and Chitlin's" on his rickety Oliver, seismic tremors were felt in the state, and occasionally a temblor buried a scheme in the legislative backstreets of Washington.

He was, indeed, a dedicated man, with a laugh like the rasp of a crosscut saw. He was a fat, sloppy, ash-sprinkled, egg-speckled, tie-askewed, stringy-haired, liver-spotted old Buddha. He was a Delphic oracle to whom politicians came for campaign advice, to whom lobbyists kowtowed, and on whom, finally, the publishers of newspapers large and small came to depend as a bureau for the provision of young talent. At graduation time each year, editors petitioned Professor Henry for first crack at his favorites.

"Skip," Fran Mayfield said. "This is a new friend of mine.

As of today. He's got an hour to kill this quarter and he wants to sit in on the class."

"Why? He looks like a goddam intellectual," Skipper Henry said. "What's he want wasting his time with me?" He swung his veiled turtle's cold eyes toward Alec.

"It's a handy location if I want to buy Fran a coffee at Chapel period," Alec said. "I won't have to walk so far. Excuse me, Sir," suddenly remembering his manners. "I didn't mean to be rude. I guess that one just slipped out."

Skipper Henry threw back his massively jowled head and roared with laughter.

"By God and by Jesus, I feel like Diogenes! After all these years I've found an honest man! You're accepted," he said suddenly, seriously, keenly inspecting Alec Barr. "You want to work or just sit and look at Frannie's legs?"

"I wouldn't mind a little work," Alec said. "If it won't bother you too much. And doesn't interfere with Frannie's legs. I don't know anything except what I've read in the papers. Or books. But I got an *A* in English literature out of Professor Jamieson. If that's any recommendation."

"You got an *A* out of that old mossback? I've known him forty years and I never knew him to give better than a *B* to anybody, including the present Governor."

"Yessir," Alec said. "It's in the record."

Skipper Henry looked more keenly at Alec Barr.

"You major in what?"

"Economics, mostly."

"What do you mean *mostly?*"

"Well, I kind of like the English language. So I started off with an English minor, but I took enough extra elective, so you might say I got an English major, too."

"*Hmmm.*" The old professor lit a cigarette and stuck about half of it in his mouth, spitting out a fine cloud of tobacco shreds.

"What you figger on doin' when you get your skin this June?"

"I don't know, Sir," Alec said. "I really don't know."

"There ain't a whole hell of a lot of jobs running around yelling for wet-eared economists and juvenile experts in English literature," Professor Henry said. "The Law, maybe?"

"No money, Sir. Chronic absence of money. Law's one

thing you really can't work your way through and do justice to the books, any more than you can with medicine."

"Teach?"

Alec laughed. "Too long a road. Not enough money at the end of it. Begging your pardon, Sir."

Skipper Henry blew upward in the general direction of his cigarette, spraying ash and sparks.

"Tell you what," he said. "We don't get much talent—excuse me, Fran, you're pretty enough not to take offense—but we really don't get much talent in here. Most of the kids take the course because I'm supposed to be a vulgar, cussin' old coot who tells dirty jokes and don't hold any final exams. But once in a long while we get some talent, and once in a long while I can smell it."

He paused to spit the mangled cigarette in the direction of an old-fashioned spittoon.

"You ever think of the newspaper business?" The shuttered eyes squeezed into slits.

"Not really. No, Sir."

"You got the look. Maybe you got the feel. Tell you what. You know the old Bible thing about Abraham and Isaac?"

"Yessir. Roughly."

"You know the one about Esau and the birthright and the selling of it for a mess of pottage?"

"Yessir. I believe so."

"Right." The old man looked at the door. "Here come the faithful, in search of knowledge. What's your name again?"

"Barr, Sir. Alec Barr."

"Get the hell out of here, Alec Barr, and write me two pieces. Write me a color piece about Abraham and Isaac and the burning bush, like it happened today—like it was a crime story that didn't quite come off because the preachers got mixed up in it. Write me a sad piece, if you can, about Esau and the birthright. You use a typewriter?"

"No, sir. Never owned one."

"You better start, then. You can use the one in my office. The hunt-and-peck is as good a system as any. Write the first pieces in longhand—I'll sweat through 'em this once—but come in tomorrow and see if they don't write better on the machine even if it's slow at first. I like your fellow, Injun," he said to Fran. "Glad you brought him aboard."

Alec Barr looked at the blowsy old man, and a sudden chill contracted his nipples, pimpled his flesh. Suddenly he knew exactly what he would write about Abraham and Isaac, about Esau and the birthright. He could see it forming as a story, modern story, in pathetic terms of Southern superstition, in terms of the Depression which rode the land.

"Thank you, Sir," he said. "You'll have the stories tomorrow."

The old man dropped an eyelid in what could only have been a wink.

"Don't try to improve too much on The Good Book," he said. "Them old Jew boys knew the value of a good hard verb, even if they did get a little muddled up on the facts. See you tomorrow." He waggled his head slowly. "Alec Barr. It's a nice name for a writer."

37

There was no real reason for Skipper Henry to take a special fancy to Alec Barr, who was not enrolled in the School of Journalism, was not even officially registered in the class. But the mussy old man, profane and blunt, seemed to find something special in Alec that was not present in other members of the class. Professor Henry sent his students on regular assignments, to the police courts and to the State House, to sports events and on special-feature trips to insane asylums and prisons. He did not lecture, as lectures went, but made them write reports on the various assignments and then chose Friday to pull the stories to pieces; to dissect them, quite often cruelly.

Occasionally some offering, generally a feature, was selected for praise, and after a little time, Alec Barr's efforts were more and more frequently singled for the old man's approval. Alec had gotten off to a fast foot with his first attempt at rewriting the biblical incidents. He had been youthfully cynical about Abraham and Isaac; he had been rather heavy-handedly sociological about Esau and his birthright.

"You got a nice touch," Skipper Henry said. "You write fast—like a sheep slippin' on shingles. Maybe you got too much imagination for straight reporting. Maybe you ought to go into the advertising business or write short stories or even books. You ever try any fiction?"

"Some. Themes, kind of. I wrote a kind of parody on *Sanctuary* for a lit course. When I was a freshman, and real smart-aleck, I wrote a short story about spending Christmas in a whorehouse."

"You ever been in a whorehouse?"

"No. Can't afford it."

"You still got the themes? Anything else?"

"Yessir. There was one theme I wrote about my Cousin Tom who just got married, after a pretty wild life as a seaman. I had been reading a lot of Somerset Maugham at the time, and I guess I was being little-boy cynical about the eagle with the clipped wings. And then there was one more —a sort of short story for my own amusement. About the effect of an accident, causing the loss of hands, on a killer, a painter, a violinist, and a surgeon. I guess I sort of stole the idea for that from a Peter B. Kyne story in *Cosmopolitan* about four fugitives who came to the same accidental end they'd have met if they'd faced justice in their own countries. You know—the Mexican got shot in the back, the Spaniard got garroted by a posse, the Frenchman had his head guillotined in an elevator shaft—like that."

"Bring 'em to me," Skipper Henry said. "And come around to the house this evenin' for a drink, so we can talk. You drink?"

"Been known to take one. Not much. Can't afford to buy it myself, and don't want to sponge on the other fellows in the house."

"It's a nice habit not to start, if you got any idea of being a serious writer. A newspaper bum, if he's got zinc innards, can last for a while, but a serious writer has trouble enough without soaking his head in booze. Come over anyhow; I'll give you some home brew I just run off. Beats the hell out of this three-point-two slop."

"Thank you," Alec said. "Only one thing. I had a kind of a date with Fran. I can postpone it."

"Don't. Bring her. I like her. Bring her if you don't mind taking a chance on what I'll have to say about the pieces. I don't soften up what I think when it comes to criticizing stuff. Some people in this business need chasin' out of it before they get in it. Be better off selling shoes."

38

The old man was sitting on the front porch of his elm-shaded paint-peeling gray bungalow, shoes off, feet tilted onto another chair, gross body thrown back into a tattered, kapok-dripping brown-leather easy chair. The glasses had worked all the way down to the end of the hooked nose. He had a jar of corn whiskey and a half-filled glass beside him.

"There's some brew cold in the icebox," he said. "Nigger wench has disappeared somewhere. Fran, the kitchen's straight back. You like to go pour a couple of brews for you and Alec?"

Fran Mayfield disappeared into the kitchen. The old man fumbled a cigarette into his mouth and looked at Alec. He took his glasses off, laid them down on the table by the whiskey. He took a long pull at his glass, coughed, and wiped off his mouth with the back of his hand. He waited until Fran returned before he spoke. She handed Alec a glass of foaming home brew and sat down on the steps, pulling her blue flannel skirt down and tucking it under her knees.

Skipper Henry gestured at the stack of papers on the floor by the chair.

"I'll tell you straight," he said. "You got something. You ain't got a diarrhea of words like Tom Wolfe had, but you got enough words. You got something better than Tom Wolfe had. You got some natural discipline, a sense of form. You couldn't have learned it. Some people just get born with it. You got imagination and you got—you got *feel*."

Fran Mayfield looked at Alec Barr, and her black eyes shone.

"I don't know what to say except thanks," Alec said simply. "Thanks. Thanks a lot."

"No thanks. It ain't often you run into unsuspected talent, like a diamond in a dungheap. Only see it once or twice in a lifetime. But the point is you don't know a damned thing about professional writing, and practically nobody at all starts out at the top. You just can't sit down and call yourself a novelist or a short-story writer until you've lived some, had some experiences, learned to work under pressure, learned the tricks and shortcuts. And the fastest way is to break in on a newspaper. This way you eat while you learn; you got shoes on your feet and a coat on your back while you edge up your tools."

Alec said nothing for a moment.

"This is nineteen thirty-three, Skipper," he said. "I don't expect the papers are taking on as many as they lay off these days. Particularly green hands."

The old man took another drink and reached in his coat pocket for an envelope. He shook a crisp yellow check out of the envelope and waved it in front of Alec's nose.

"You're a professional already," Skipper Henry said. "This here's a check for twenty dollars. You know that piece I liked about the new treatments in the insane asylum? I sent it over to an old friend of mine who runs the features for *The Observer*. He paid twenty bucks for it. Here." He handed the check to Alec, and watched Fran Mayfield get up and kiss him. Then Fran Mayfield kissed Skipper Henry, and her eyes had brightened through a film of tears.

Alec Barr looked at the check as if it were a snake. He shook his head.

"I don't feel right taking it," he said. "This is really the only unexpected cash money I've seen in the last four years."

"Hell, you wrote the piece, you earned the money," the old man said. "Now listen to what I have to say. My friend on *The Observer* says that ordinarily they'd take a chance on hiring you as a cub, but that they got a new economy order from on high and they're laying off seasoned hands, and there's a thirty-seven per cent cut in force in the payroll. He says maybe if things get better he'll take you on, but things don't look like gettin' better any time soon, even with Roosevelt in and Prohibition off and all that New Deal crap supposed to prime the pump.

"But I don't think I'd let you take a job in Raleigh even if they offered you one. You get stuck in Raleigh or Durham or Greensboro on one of them one-horse dailies, you don't learn much that'll do you a lot of good later. And the chances are you get married and have a baby or so and you're trapped, making thirty-five or forty dollars a week and afraid to take chances. Nothin' kills a young talent quicker."

"What do you suggest, then? It looks like a dead end before it even starts."

"Fran, go fetch you and the boy another glass of beer," Skipper Henry said. When she had left, he said softly: "She's a damned nice girl and will make into a woman that won't fade or sag on you. You got serious intents?"

"Golly, I guess I might have if I had any prospects," Alec said. "But she's got another year of school and I still don't know how I'm going to eat. You can't start a family on twenty bucks."

"Some have, and lived to regret it. Now listen to me some more, Alec. I got connections on nearly any paper in North Carolina and Virginia. Most of my people are just about good enough for those papers.

"But I got other plans for you. There's a half-assed job in a half-assed little railroad town called Center City, in the Piedmont, on a half-assed little country weekly. It's run by a mean, shifty-eyed son-of-a-bitch named Roy Ketchum. He don't wash much or change his shirt but once a week and you can smell him a mile. He'd strangle his mother to save a dollar. He's so all-fired mean he can't keep a hand more'n about six months, and the pay's nothing that a nigger'd grab at, let alone a white man. I can get you maybe twelve, maybe even fifteen bucks a week, but no more. That's the bottom *and* the top."

"You said you could get *me* twelve or fifteen dollars a week?" Alec's voice was incredulous.

"I said *you*. It's such an awful job I wouldn't wish it off on nobody else, but I think maybe you could cut it for as long as it's useful. You'll cover the news—all of it—write the stories—all of them—you'll sell advertising and probably subscriptions. Ketchum don't know anything about journalism, or care. He'll leave you alone as long as you get the paper out once a week and don't insult any of the advertisers or write any editorials favoring the bus people over the Seaboard Railway.

"But you'll learn. There ain't any better all-round experience than what you get on a country weekly. You'll learn about boilerplate—mats and canned editorial matter and such. You'll learn how to cover any story that happens in a small town, and believe me, Bud, there are just as many ripe stories in a small town as there are in a big one. You'll write captions for pictures and you'll work with engravers and typesetters and stereotype men. You'll write church picnics and murders, rapes and lynchings, robberies and weddings. But you'll learn a hell of a lot more than you write. You'll hush up abortions and ignore early births in hurry-up weddings. You'll cover fires—hell, you'll probably be a member of the volunteer fire department—and you'll even have to go to church, if only to see how poison-pious a bunch of sanctimonious bastards can be on the Seventh Day, after they've spent the rest of the week stealing, snapping garters, drinking whiskey on the sly, and talking dirty-mean about their neighbors."

"I've seen some back home," Alec said. "But not much. I spent most of the time in the woods with a hound."

"There are small towns and small towns," Skipper Henry said. "Now where Fran comes from, there ain't so much concentrated nastiness."

"Mostly square-dancers, drunken Indians, and summer people," Fran smiled. "Some of my relatives cut up real dandy when they slide off the reservation for a few days spreeing. About the worst thing we do, I guess, is make moonshine and drink it up and occasionally take a shot at each other with a squirrel rifle."

"This Center City," the old man continued, "is a kind of little Sodom, a sort of solid concentration of small-bore evil. It ain't got much of anything but peaches in the sandhills and the railroad running through, but one or two big toads own the entire puddle, from the Coca-Cola factory to the railroad yards, and when they crack the whip everybody jumps. They choose the police chief and elect the sheriff and handpick the legislators. They fix the taxes and set the electrical rates. You'll learn a lot about human nastiness in Center City, son, and that is a necessary thing in your business.

"When you can't stand it any more, then I suggest you up stakes and go to a big town. New York's a little too major-league to bull your way into right off, but Washington has a lot of newspapers. What's more, it's got a mess of new faces, a new government, a new President, what appears to be a new set of social rules and regulations—a whole new idea of government, in this New Deal thing. It'll be a powerful interesting town to work in for further seasoning. In a way I wish I'd done it myself." The old man sighed and poured himself another drink. "I wish I'd done a lot of things different when I was a young un."

"I can't tell you again how thankful I am for all you're doing," Alec said. "But the thought strikes me suddenly that country-weekly experience ain't exactly the greatest recommendation in the world for a job on a big-city daily."

"There's ways," Skipper Henry said. "Ways, and means. Pull is good, of course, but I don't draw no real water in the big cities, and a Congressman ain't no good as a recommender. But big papers got slave jobs you mostly don't have on smaller papers—copy boys, kids, mostly college graduates, that hustle coffee and Cokes and mix paste and rush copy from the city room to the composing room. If you're willing to scuffle, and keep your eyes open and your ears unplugged, you can learn a lot. There'll always be somebody with time to teach you. And one day . . ." he let his voice trail.

"And one day?" Fran and Alec spoke together.

"One day somebody'll get drunk or sick or a big story'll break when the staff's short and you'll find yourself covering it and writing it, because by then, if you're smart, you'll know *how.* And when you wake up the next day you'll find out that they've hired a new copy boy and you're all of a sudden a reporter. After you've been a reporter there ain't no place you can't go—city to city, paper to paper, learnin' all the time. And if you're smart, once you've ironed the wrinkles out of your belly and are doing a man's job, you'll branch out. You'll study the magazines and try to write articles and short stories. You'll read everything you can lay hand to and try to learn how the best professionals do it. And someday, when you've seen enough, and hurt enough, and been hurt enough, you'll sit down and write yourself a book and all of a sudden you'll be on the back of a dust jacket and if whiskey ain't killed me, I'll be a very proud old man. I'm gettin' a little drunk, and a little sleepy. Go spend some of that twenty bucks."

"I don't know what to say," Alec said, rising from the step and holding out his hand to Fran. "So I guess I just won't say it. Thanks, Skipper."

The old man held up a deprecating hand.

"Shush. But one thing more. There ain't but a few rules to this racket. Don't write what you don't know. Don't start out to write it until it's clear in your head and *you* know what you're writing. Don't listen to anything off the record; it only confuses you. Don't rat on your sources. Don't take no cheap little gifts from *nobody.* Lot of people think they can buy a pressman for a jug of cheap Christmas whiskey. Take it easy on the booze, and kiss no man's ass, however big he is. That's about all. You already know how to spell."

That night, after the movies and a soda, Alec walked Fran slowly home, stopping to kiss in the scent-filled greenery of the Arboretum. The air was soft with spring, heavy with jasmine. Frail moonlight filtered through the flowering bushes, and for once the Arboretum was not filled with frenetically necking couples.

"I'm so proud of you," Fran murmured. "You can do anything. I know it. I love you, Alec. I'll wait for you, if you want—wait as long as you want."

They kissed again, and suddenly Fran's tongue darted sharp and hot into his mouth, forcing his lips apart. Her body strained at him and she caught his hand to her breast.

"I love you," she breathed again, and Alec Barr could taste her want, acrid on the softly opened lips, feverish in the sharply probing tongue. Fran Mayfield suddenly let her body go slack, and sank softly onto the springy clovered turf, bringing Alec's body down on hers. Her lips bit at him now, and she had opened the front of her dress, her small breasts showing white and black-pointed in the moonlight. He buried his head between the breasts, and she made soft moaning noises while she did something to his trousers.

"I want you," she said. "I love you. I want you, want you, want you!"

As in a dream he felt himself enter her, probing the warm, the wet, the sweet and the hot, until his whole body burst and lost itself inside her. Her arms now were tight around his neck, and she was making little mewing, whimpering noises, her body quivering as he pressed heavily upon her.

"I love you, Fran," he said, when his heavy breathing had slowed. "I want to marry you as soon as I can."

"I'll wait forever, my darling," she said. "Come now, we'd better hurry, or I'll be locked out of the house. Fix yourself." She did brisk things to her frock. They were silent on the short walk to the Pi Phi house, kissed once, long and closely, and then she ran up the stairs and into the house.

Alec Barr walked slowly back to the fraternity house, his head in the stars, his thoughts striding wildly in the direction of Washington. There would be a plot to assassinate Franklin D. Roosevelt, and he would discover it and break the story. Or, perhaps, the President would be assassinated and Alec would be first to find the body—exclusively. He would be rich and famous. He would marry Fran and write wonderful books and make a million dollars. They would travel the world and have beautiful children and never, ever grow bored or weary of each other's minds or bodies. He would win a Pulitzer Prize first, then the Nobel Prize and then. . . .

They saw each other nearly every night until the term ended, making love in odd, uncomfortable places—in the darkened stadium, in the Arboretum, by the lake, occasionally in a borrowed car.

When she had watched him graduate and he left that very night for his new job in Center City, they had vowed to write daily, and he had promised to come and see her in Waynesville as soon as he had solidified the job enough to steal a week end.

They wrote: passionate, repetitive, trite declarations of undying love. Then for two weeks no letters came, and Alec invested a portion of his small savings in a long-distance phone call.

An adult woman's voice answered the phone, harsh with mountain twang.

"This is Alec Barr," he said. "Please, might I talk to Fran?"

"Frances ain't here. Neither is none of the rest of the family. I'm the house girl."

"Tell me, is Fran all right?" A horrid picture of Fran in an automobile accident, Fran drowning in a mountain lake, Fran in the hospital burnt into the brain. "She's all right? There's nothing wrong, I mean?"

The woman cackled.

"She's all right, all right," she said nasally. "Right enough to run off and get herself married. Her folks is off to Asheville straightenin' it out with *his* folks, now. I'll tell her you called when she comes back home for her clothes."

It did not fully dawn on Alec Barr, until he received a short letter a week later, that he had truly been the virgin on the first encounter, and that Fran Mayfield had seemed awfully knowing in her skillful manipulations.

The letter was brief.

My dear Alec:
I can't blame you for hating me for this, but I hope you will try to understand. What we had last spring was lovely

and dear, and I do love you. But it would have been such a long time before we could have married, and suddenly I couldn't stand the idea of going back to school for another year, and then waiting around until I was an old maid. John's a dear—much older than me—and I'm sure you'd like him. His people own one of the pulp mills, and they live in Asheville. I do hope you'll try to forgive me, but it just sort of happened. I wish you all success, and hope you'll find another girl, not like me, who'll make you very happy. If you get up this way, do come and see us. I've told John a lot about you— except some things, *of course.*

> *Love always,*
> *Fran*
> *(Mrs. John Dalrymple, Jr. We're in the book.)*

When Alec Barr came off a monumental drunk, his first, he counted his money and found that he did not have enough for a fare to Washington if he wished to eat when he looked for a job. He could not, in fairness, demand his week's wages from his employer, who was understandably furious when Alec, pale, sweating, trembling, informed him that he was quitting his job as soon as he put the paper to bed.

Alec Barr packed his scant belongings and hoisted his thumb, aiming for the general direction of Washington, D.C. He wound up eventually in Hamburg, Germany, on a freighter, but he later reflected, as he drank with the painted woman in the Grosse Freiheit, in the company of two Russian female sailors and a Negro mess cook, that in one way he was following Skipper Henry's advice. He was seeing life, and if you were going to be a writer, life was something you had to see. Some months later, when he paid off in Norfolk, Virginia, he actually made it to Washington.

39

Amelia Macmillan had noticed with amazement that Alec Barr's mouth trembled almost pitifully when first he kissed her. Amelia Macmillan had surely been kissed before—on porches, in rumble seats, on beaches, in sorority houses, and she had almost yielded her virginity to a basketball player in an empty gymnasium at College Park, Maryland. But she had never been kissed before by a young man whose feelings evidently were so fragile that his lips trembled when he kissed her the first time, losing the false arrogance which had marked their first relationship.

But then Amelia Macmillan was a Washington girl, District-born and District-bred, and her family had almost always owned two title-free automobiles. Her father paid his bills promptly and belonged to several secret societies which endowed their members with diamond-studded lapel pins and allowed them peculiar hats on feast days. Her mother was as solidly planted as a plinth in the church; by churchly comparison, Amelia's mother considered her bounden duty to the PTA almost sort of an architrave. But tremulous kissers were foreign to Amelia's experience as a member of the Chi Omega sorority in the coeducationally concrete campus of George Washington University. The boys Amelia had met recently in the Chi O house were more apt to seize a breast before granting the boon of a polite peck on the mouth.

Washington had a way of spoiling the boys. The government cellular structure was cancerous with pretty female clerks from unmapped hamlets in prehistoric Mississippi and remotest South Dakota. They lived a sterile life of unwilling spinsterish loneliness, an existence compounded of cafeteria meals, triply shared rooms in molding mansions on K and Sixteenth streets—formerly genteel houses whose sagging floors and unplumbed walls had been beaverboarded into chaste dungeons for Uncle Sam's children. In Washington, a refugee from Yemassee, Georgia, or Butte, Montana, was very likely to open her legs before she opened her heart, if only as an escape from the shrill female pincurled world of perpetually drying stockings and damp underclothes in bathrooms whose tubs always exhibited the pubic hairs of earlier seekers after Hygeia. No, Washington surely spoiled its young men—the sharply dressed bucks who worked as Congressional assistants by day to time-purchase their Hecht Co. clothes and the Joe Cherner Ford coupés, and who attended classes at George Washington and Georgetown by night in a dogged moonlit search for a law degree or a career post in foreign service. Mostly the young men lived in converted stables and always meticulously split their meal-and-bar checks.

Alec Barr, then, came freshly, shockingly as a surprise to Amelia Macmillan, the dutiful only child of Walker and Betsy Macmillan. Amelia had been born in the pleasant fieldstone house in Chevy Chase, an English half-timbered house with deeply green Virginia-creepered walls and a designated playroom well before the playroom's time of general popularity. Walker Macmillan was in the real estate business, with a general insurance agency bolstering him to the side, and had achieved a high state of talcumed Babbittry in the only big city in the world which had not been grievously gnawed by the Depression. Walker Macmillan belonged to the Lions and the Elks and the Optimists and the Shrine. He was a big, florid, hearty man with a booming baritone voice, its timbre cultivated by infinite business lunches into an operatic tone of perpetual congratulation. He played no golf, but belonged to three country clubs for the contacts they gave him in business. He refused to attend church, but Betsy Macmillan sang a slightly off-key soprano in the church choir and was a basic ingredient in the church supper—and also, in a less cynically direct fashion, a patient scaffold to her husband's career of contact with the contacts. Betsy Macmillan was the kind of Elizabeth who would never be called Betty or Lisa or Liz or Beth. She was a predetermined Betsy from the day she first cooed at her father—clear-eyed, clear-skinned, clear-voiced, with a brain equally clear of any confusing thought process which might lead to complication of her daily social, sexual, religious, and maternal pattern. If she had been born of her mother's time, she would surely have conceived children under a nightgown, and called her husband Mister, even in a transport of unadmitted delight which she would carefully conceal as "not nice." In her early forties,

Amelia's mother still mentally described her own lunar cycle as a state of being "unwell."

But Amelia's parents were a kind of couple, a well-upholstered, well-dressed, well-behaved couple, with rosy cheeks and a comfortable marital resemblance. They were born to be a couple; it was inconceivable that they had ever been unmarried to each other, and one always saw them as sharing the same bathroom. One never referred to them, *in absentia*, as Walker or Betsy. One said "the Macmillans," using the plural meaningfully in its singular sense. They of course adored Amelia, who had always been a very good little girl, and now was a good big girl—a good big girl who did not stay out overlate of nights, and whose boy friends were always well shaved and shone, with the mark of the most recent shower still fresh on their invariably close-clipped hair and polite assembly-line faces which bore no trace of either beard or intellect.

The boy friends were offered no drink by Walker Macmillan when they came to call for Walker's daughter Amelia, but being painfully well-bred they always bored themselves and Walker Macmillan with a half-hour's polite topical conversation in order to convey the idea that their intent was not to plunge a hand immediately down Amelia's bodice. In return for this amenity Amelia was allowed to neck in automobiles for an exact half-hour after she returned from an evening of movies or dancing—allowed to neck, that is, if the boy's car were parked directly in front of the house, within easy screaming distance of the familied dark bedroom. It was in such a parked car that Amelia had first allowed a boy to touch her intimately, and allowed herself to touch him in return. Both had been dismayed at the result, which had spoiled her tulle party frock to such a point that she had gone to the kitchen for coffee to spill as camouflage and also as an excuse for immediate noisy washing activity in the bathroom. The boy whose blurting ejaculation had wrecked her dress never called for another date, possibly from shame at his lack of control, even more possibly from a dark old-fashioned suspicion that if Amelia actually manipulated him pleasurably by hand she had been to the well before, and thus constituted no serious candidate for marriage.

Amelia was her mother's spittin' image, everyone said—the same clear brow and finely textured skin, the same tawny-browny hair with the blonde lights in it, the same generous full-lipped mouth, short, cute-wrinkly nose, good upstanding breasts and useful hips over long and plump-thighed legs. She was a big girl, as her mother was a big woman, but fat would never blur her basic line, and no computable number of children would sag the large firm bosom. Amelia's mother was placid; so likewise was Amelia placid. Amelia's mother coped well; Amelia was a coper, too, as witness the swift reaction of the purposeful coffee-spilling.

Amelia was mother-wise; she made mostly *A*s in all classes, and had been rigidly schooled by Betsy Macmillan in the refinements of homemaking. Amelia could play a jolly rigadoon and sew a fine seam; she could bake a cherry pie, Billy boy, Billy boy, and hospital-corner a bed. Her own chaste room was a miracle of daily neatness; her body glistened with Lifebuoy cleanliness; her teeth were startlingly bright from Ipana and two trips to the dentist every year; her menstrual period kept time as precisely as the high-school-graduation-present Patek watch she wore—except that whereas Betsy Macmillan chose to think of her Eveish indisposition as a state of nonwellness, her daughter would say outrightly that she couldn't go swimming because she was "off the roof." Amelia's hair was brushed nightly with the ninety-nine harsh strokes and her nails, both finger and toe, were polished to a high sheen. Her suspendered stockings went unrun and her shoes unworn at heel; her underwear was immaculate in the event of an accident, and her outer clothing impeccable. Amelia, at the time she met Alec Barr, was a young thing who was more than very well prepared to leave her mother.

Having been more or less weaned on the brush-haired open-faced tweed coats, having teethed on the serious young FBI types, having been groped by the Senatorial assistants—having seen her share of other people's smirkingly loaned apartments on rainy Sunday afternoons—Amelia was sharply taken aback by this young Alec Barr. Alec Barr had no convertible, no crew cut, no family, no country club, no Sunday-afternoon friends with apartments, and a very flimsy future in a most uncertain business.

Alec Barr pathetically referred to himself as a newspaperman, but Amelia knew that the difference between a real newspaperman and what Alec Barr was in actuality was oceans-vast indeed. But she had no stomach for reminding Alec Barr that he was only a copy boy on a paper that never advanced copy boys to staff jobs, even to the debasing coverage of police courts or second-run movies. Alec Barr was a college-graduated office boy. He mixed paste and ran errands and fetched coffee and helped photographers with their flash equipment at night football games. He trudged by dawn from his paper to the morning papers to collect the bull-dog editions for the early city editor's perusal and later rewrite. Before he had been a copy boy, Alec had been that lowest of all life-forms in a newspaper—he had been a detail boy.

If minus-nothing were to be perpetually multiplied by ten, the sum still would not adequately connote the position of a detail boy on a large metropolitan newspaper. A janitor, perhaps, has dignity, and so has the muscle editor who runs the race wire and collects two-dollar bets on the side. Even a copy boy has a certain professional chic which comes of association with the second floor, where the reporters and editors toil. But a detail boy is a downstairs chattel for the advertising echelon. He works at the front counter on the ground floor, accepting death notices and classified advertisements by telephone and hand-writ copy; he lugs advertising layouts on hurtive foot to department stores and the makers of home-ground coffee; he sells papers across the counter and, at this time in this epoch, made the wage of fourteen dollars for working twelve hours a day on a seven-day week. Alec Barr had taken a two-dollar cut to forswear the apprenticeship to a richer, fuller life of advertising salesmanship. He had signed on at twelve bucks for the close association with boozy literary deep-thinkers that a job of copy boy would give him.

There was really small doubt in Alec Barr's mind that someday he would scale the wall of achievement and realize the goal of twenty-five whole dollars every week. He raised his sights no higher at the moment; his dream of frustrating the death plot for the President had dwindled considerably, and he husbanded no literarily lecherous ideas of either Pulitzer or Nobel prizes. He wanted to make Staff, even if it involved the coverage of the activities of the Citizens' Association in Seat Pleasant, Maryland.

In the meantime he was sorely pressed to stay clean, fed, housed, and alive. He had been infested by the most unpurgeable of parasitic worms, book hunger, and a matched set of Somerset Maugham had cost him a year of lunchless days. The economics of existence were bare indeed. A street-car pass required a dollar and a quarter a week. His half share of a furnished room cost three-fifty. Out of an income which dipped dizzily downward from fourteen dollars to twelve, the opportunity to maintain racing stables or fleets of chorus girls was somewhat less than nil. Somewhere, some-how, by avoiding breakfast as well as lunch, he had amassed sufficient capital to buy a dictionary, secondhand, and to make a down payment on a library card. A half-gallon of muscatel demanded fifty cents, and so Alec Barr spent most of his leisure time wining off the California grape and dining on rented books. He reined himself with a harsh hand; when he did not know the etymology of a word, he reached for the blowsy dictionary and memorized its tiny type. On fine days he visited the zoo.

Alec Barr, now twenty-two years old, was breasting a period of enormous frustration. He looked about him in the paper's city room and saw hacks—drunken hacks, sober hacks, young hacks, old hacks. He carefully read the copy they wrote on his way to the composing room; the copy looked no better on rough raw yellow copy paper than it would look tomor-row in the actual newspaper after the linotypists and stereo-typers had blessed it with an immortality of exactly one day. Alec Barr itched. Alec Barr fretted. He itched and he burned with a passionate, groin-aching yearning for access to a timely topic and a private typewriter and a professional status which would allow him to raise his head from the machine and bellow "Boy!" without wincing when he heard the word.

Of nights, eyes granulated from reading, he sometimes re-played the last advice Skipper Henry had given him. He doubted, now, that Skipper Henry knew what he was talking about in terms of big-town papers. So far as Alec Barr could see, the plumed knights of two newspapers had evinced no tiny intent of advancing their panting squire to the estate of apprentice-toiler in the heraldic trade.

Alec made weekly, dutiful rounds of the other papers, and Washington had many papers. Mostly managing editors were too busy to see him. One, a Swede of uncertain alcoholic choler, had Alec bodily thrown out of the town's most flamboyant morning journal. He tried sports; the field was closed to a newcomer. He tried drama, he tried cityside news, he tried copyreading, he tried everything but the woman's page. And always, always—except for the hungover

Swede—he got a kindly but deadly shake of the head. *No.* Come back next week. But right now—shake of head—nothing doing.

In the midst of the frustration Alec met Amelia. He met Amelia via a roommate who arrived in Washington from the high Carolina Hills, was working for the government for the splendid sum of sixteen hundred and twenty dollars a year, or roughly thirty-five dollars a week, and who owned a belted-back coat from Kaufman's and an unpaid-for gray Ford coupé with a rumble seat. The friend was spending his money freely, as the economic royalist he was, on women. Jimmy James was studying law on the side, at night school, because an overpreoccupation with a girl had busted him out of the law school at Carolina, to the great displeasure of a craggy modern-primitive father who also happened to be a circuit-riding salty judge.

Conscience toiled well in the fields of the errant barrister's mind. In a very short time he had wearied of his governmental career and had amassed enough night-school credits to allow him to return, if not in triumph to his father's land, at least with sufficient dignity to resume his perusal of Blackstone's best at the university which had ejected him. He announced his decision with sorrow to his roommate, Alec Barr, explaining that full-time education had seduced him once again, and that he was heading home to the hills for further cultivation of the tort crop.

"You never met Amelia, did you?" Jimmy James asked his impoverished roomie, Alec Barr, as he was slinging his more-than-one suit into a liberally stickered traveling bag.

"Who?" Alec Barr was reading in a meager single bed that occupied nearly half of the narrow room. He looked up absently, marking his place with a thumb. The dictionary lay spraddled open on a chair between the beds, and Alec Barr had penciled a passage that described flotsam as opposed to jetsam. "Met who?"

Jimmy James shook his handsome, young, about-to-become-a-lawyer's blond head in amiable exasperation.

"Amelia. Mele Mac. Macmillan. You know, at least one of us occasionally goes out of nights into the wide world which extends beyond Sixteenth and U Street."

"Oh sure." Alec slapped closed his book and stacked it atop the sprawled dictionary. "That's the big sort of kind-of-blonde-but-not-quite girl you been wearing the lipstick of. I saw her waiting in the car out front one day when you came up for a pack of condoms."

Jimmy James shook his head, wagging it slowly back and forth in a legally leonine gesture of reproof. He walked over to the bottle of Four Roses on the bad-pine bureau and took a drink straight out of the neck.

"You're hopeless, roomie, hopeless. Amelia would kill you for that description, and anyhow, I didn't come up here for any rubbers. Amelia ain't that kind of a girl. She's marrying material."

"They all screw," Alec Barr said. "Sooner or later, for better or worse, they all screw."

"A cynic I got for an almost ex-roommate," Jimmy James said. "Some do, Author. Some don't. This is one of the ones that don't. But the hell with that; all I had in mind was that she's a nice dame. I might even come back and marry her someday myself when I pass the bar and the old man takes me into his practice. I was only planning to do you a temporary favor."

Alex Barr yawned. "The Mexicans got a good saying," he said. "I learned it out of my Spanish book."

"Okay, I bite. What kind of good saying have the Mexicans got?"

"No me ayudes, por favor."

"Meaning what, Brain Boy?"

"Meaning, 'Don't do me no favors. I got trouble enough.'" Alec picked up his book again. "Finish packing, why don't you? You make me nervous."

Jimmy James plumped down on the bed and plucked the book from Alec's hands.

"Life is passing you by, Junior," he said. "You got to get out and get under the moon. Now listen to your Uncle James James. I'm older than you. You're driving yourself crazy with this newspaper foolishness. You're about ready to crack the nut. Shut up"—Alec had raised a hand. "Shut up. I know you ain't got any money. But there's no reason for you to be a goddamned hermit. And Amelia's the answer to your problems."

"I got no problems a staff job and a raise wouldn't cure," Alec Barr said. "I am tired of being a coolie, waiting for the big break. 'Come back next week.' For God's sake. And you want to wish a dame onto me, at my wages?"

Jimmy James' voice was elaborately patient.

"I am merely trying to tell you, Knothead," he said. "I am merely trying to tell you that this is a good girl for you. She has a fairly rich family. The icebox is full of beer and delicious cold cuts. They also let her use her mother's Mercury. They have a playroom and a phonograph and a radio. They are swell people. They belong to country clubs. And Amelia is a damned nice girl. If it'll help you any, she even reads for fun. She is always quoting Dorothy Parker."

" 'Enough Rope' or 'Sunset Gun'?"

"Huh?"

"Skip it," Alec said. "Go back to the classic M'Naghten on murderous derangement. Only man I ever knew that slipped on the wrong Peel. Excuse me. I made a legal joke which you ain't far enough along yet to understand."

Jimmy James shook his head again.

"I really don't know about you. I don't know what will happen to you. But I will bet you one thing. It sure as hell won't be ordinary."

"That's a very pretty compliment, for a nonqueer almost-ex-roomie," Alec said. "Now let's get rid of this Amelia topic, Counselor. What exactly have you in mind?"

The sigh from Jimmy James was pure exasperation.

"Oh, brother," he said. "Nothing. Forget it. I just offer to introduce you to a nice babe with a bulging icebox and a housebroken family and ample necking room downstairs and also on the porch. Skip it. I'll bequeath her to somebody else."

Alec Barr sat up in bed, then swung his feet over the side.

"You're going to make a lousy lawyer if you haven't got sense enough to realize that a man like me won't take anybody's castoffs—doesn't want any favors done for him, and won't, will not, repeat *not*, expose himself to anybody's kindness until he can pay it back double. You had an *allowance* in college. It makes a difference in personal outlook."

"Don't get your ass on your shoulders, little man," Jimmy James said. "You ain't too poor to accept a sock in the puss."

Alec smiled tinily, slightly shamefaced.

"Ah begs yo' pardon, Boss Man," he said. "Ah was out of line. Please don't y'all hit po' ol' Mose. He don't mean no harm."

Jimmy James clapped Alec Barr on the back, then ploughed his hair, pushing it forward into Alec's face.

"Look, stupid. You probably ain't going to have a better friend than me, ever." He roughly smoothed the hair back again. "You're having a hard time, Alec. You're dead right about me having an allowance in college. But rich wastrel or not, boy, I got a word for you. Don't you be bitter about how slow it is while you're still this young. One day you'll hit it; one day you'll bust it wide open, and that one day you'll look at old Judge James and wonder how you were ever able to put up with him as a roommate when you were busted-ass-broke in Wash, DeeCee. Just don't go sour on me now. Okay?"

"I stand reproved," said Alec Barr. "Let's us go meet this delectable doll of yours. On the condition that we plainly state my position of poverty. I ain't what my old man would have called a finale-hopper. Right?"

"This is my buddy," Jimmy James said that night to Amelia, when they stopped off to collect Alec Barr. "He's the genius of the group. Untested, but rapidly on the rise. That's my necktie he's wearing. He's a little short on neckwear at the moment, but long on gall. Take care of him, Mele. He's also short in the temper, terribly poor, terribly proud, and most often terribly hungry. For food, I mean. The hunger for general acclaim is already built in."

Amelia Macmillan looked at Alec Barr and smiled, wrinkling the short straight nose, squeezing her eyes into happy slits.

"It'll be a rare fine pleasure," she said. "My real pleasure."

"Fine," replied Jimmy James. "Leave us now go and get plastered on my last evening before I return to the salt mines. Fortunately I have some money with me."

"Unfortunately, I don't," Alec Barr said. "It's a condition that you'll grow used to, Amelia. With me it's chronic."

"Shut up," Jimmy James said. "I am tired of your noble poverty, and I predict it will shortly end. But for Christ's sake, for the now, leave it lay."

Alec Barr did not enjoy the drinks at the Hamilton. He did not enjoy Papa Livera's antipasti, Papa Livera's buttered mushrooms, Papa Livera's spaghetti *al dente*, Papa Livera's steak and garlicky salad and rum cake and sour red vino and inch-thick coffee. He looked steadily at Amelia Macmillan, and saw a figure beyond touch. He saw a girl who had never known family shame; a girl who had never pleaded with the Dean of Admissions about a loan; he saw a girl who selected a sorority from a choice of several and had never known the correct spelling of blackball. He saw a girl whose family signed automatically at the country club in the solid responsibility of paying. He saw a girl who could charge a dress at Garfinckel's or Woodward and Lothrop; a girl who was never short of cab fare.

"If I can steal some streetcar tokens from the city desk I'd like to come and see you after the lawyer's gone back to his books," said Alec Barr. "How far out in Chevy Chase do you live?"

"One stolen token will do it if you don't mind walking a few blocks," Amelia said. "And if you don't want to take up a life of crime, I'll lend you the token and you can pay me back when you're rich and famous. Next week's Thanksgiving. Can we count on you for dinner—I mean it's lunch really, but it's the main meal. My mother's wonderful with a turkey, and Pa might even buy us just one drink to celebrate the season."

"I'd love it if we aren't working," Alec Barr said. "But you know how it is. The news waits for no man."

"Of course I understand," Amelia said. "A fast-breaking story."

"That's right," Alec Barr replied. "Sometimes they need everybody to pitch in." And then wondered miserably if this healthy, richly glowing girl knew that his exact chores consisted of the mixing of paste, the running of errands, and the waiting in a bullpen until some brass-voiced vassal yelled "Boy!" with the intent of conveying the idea that the assistant editor in charge of editorial-page poetry craved a fresh batch of dogfood for his pet fox terrier.

Amelia looked closely at Alec Barr. She saw a haggard young man who badly needed a haircut and who wore a soiled trench coat as if he were daring the world to challenge his right to wear it. She saw a frayed shirt and a roommate's necktie, a sensitive mouth and deeply bitten fingernails. She saw, she thought, a young man on the verge of exploding, and wondered, more than idly, what it would be like to share the explosion.

40

Alec Barr did not make it to the Macmillan household for the celebration of the Pilgrims' arrival. His mind watered at the thought of the turkey, for his gut growled steady obbligato, despite an economic arrangement whereby a fellow with a clear title to twenty-five cents might dine sumptuously off hard baked beans, strawy frankfurter (1), lumpy mashed potato, sleazy slaw, nutrient-free bread and transparent coffee at a one-armed joint called Thompson's. Alec Barr lost his nerve at the last moment, when he inspected a clean but frayed-collared shirt, a suit which seemingly had been broken in spirit, some rather mushy-looking shoes and a cash estate of seventy cents to feed him over the week end. He waited for a washroom-visiting moment in the city room, and then, harshening his voice to pretend that he was an executive, swindled the switchboard into giving him an outside line. He was burlesque brusque-and-businesslike when he informed Amelia Macmillan that the paper was sending him out of town on assignment over Thanksgiving, inventing an outrageous lie about covering a murder trial in a town safely distant from investigation for verity. Thereafter he put Amelia Macmillan firmly out of his mind and renewed his assault on the executive desks of every paper in town except the one which employed him.

Apart from the whiskey-nerved Scandinavian who had caused him to be slung out of the office for the sin of asking for a reporter's job, Alec had been treated generally kindly and courteously by most of the graying men with raddled faces who sat behind desks labeled CITY EDITOR and MANAGING EDITOR by the presence of copy spikes and sheaves of embalmed writing in yellow envelopes. One in particular, on the town's smallest afternoon paper, had been signally nice. Perhaps it was a similarity in names—this fellow, a sort of *pro-tem* managing editor—was named John Barry, only one consonant away from Alec. John Barry had a close-cropped bullet head, a good-humored broad freckled face, hairy freckled hands, and what Alec thought to be a sincerely sympathetic smile. Alec came to visit the man at his desk under the big clock punctually at 4 P.M. every Thursday, since he was on the early shift at the *Star* and the shift knocked off at two. Each Thursday Alec came and quirked an inquiring brow; each Thursday John Barry would lift his eyes from a sheaf of papers, smile, and shake his head. But the smile continued warm, and the nod was staticly friendly. Alec felt no dread of the weekly visits that ran into months. John Barry had told him that when there was a vacancy on the copy-boy staff, the job was Alec's. Hope replaced food as a fuel for Alec Barr; he knew that the *News* was a young, understaffed paper, with an amazingly high turnover of talent and no deadwood at all.

It was a dismally gray, rain-soaked Christmas Eve, with the dingy remnants of formerly festive snow still crusted on the slushy streets when Alec made his round to the *News'* offices. It had been a miserable season. The furnished room had seemed insupportable, and for once, Alec had been unable to drown himself in a book. It seemed to Alec Barr that everybody in town had gone home for the holidays and that he was the only person left alive in Washington.

As Alec entered the squat red-brick *News* building, walking up the stairs in the direction of the clicking-clacking sounds that came from the composing room, he wondered bitterly why he was taking the trouble. There wasn't any Santa Claus; there was no Bob Cratchitt for Alec's Tiny Tim. John Barry was a nice freckle-faced man, but he was never going to hire Alec Barr. Nobody was ever going to hire Alec Barr. He paused at the door of the city room, almost decided to turn back.

"Ah, the hell with it," he said to himself. "I'll give it just one more whirl." He walked past the abandoned morgue, past the empty sports desks and the rows of unemployed typewriters to an almost-empty room. John Barry was sitting in a corner, plodding through a stack of copy, and one of the women reporters, an angular sallow old maid with a pencil thrust through the bun of her skinned-back hair, was touching a typewriter dispiritedly in a corner. She looked as if she might be in the office on Christmas Eve only because there was no other place for her to go. The paper's only discernible activity clattered from the composing room.

Alec moved slowly toward John Barry's desk. At the soft

sound of footsteps, John Barry looked up, and the freckled
face under the cropped bullet head creased to a broad smile.
He nodded strongly. But this time the head-shake was different. It was up and down instead of from side to side.

"I was just about to phone you," John Barry said. "You
got yourself a job. We had some fresh firing going on and
I've just upped a couple of copy boys to staff. There's a
lobster-trick night copy-boy job open if you want it—midnight to eight—and the pay's fifteen a week. Still want it?"

Alec hesitated for one brief moment and decided to take
the chance.

"No," he said. "I don't want it if it's just another copy-boy
job. If there's a staff job in it any time soon I'll take the
copy trick and love it, and anyhow it's three bucks more a
week than the *Star* pays. That's nearly my room rent. But
not without a pretty fast future, Mr. Barry. I'm sick of hus-
tling coffee and Cokes."

John Barry looked at the gangling young man in the shabby trench coat, gaze flickering down from the thin face to
the sodden, winter-ruined shoes.

"Could you come to work tonight?" he asked.

"I could come to work tonight. But I have to give the *Star*
two weeks' notice. If I could leave just before eight in the
morning I could make it over to the *Star* in time for the day
shift. But not unless I feel like I've got a chance to do something *real* here pretty soon."

"Can you write a news story? Do a feature? Copyread?"

"I can write a news story. I can write a feature. I can copyread. I can write headlines and I think I know how to handle art. What I don't know I can learn."

John Barry smiled at the young man again.

"I think you're lying in your teeth," he said with great
good humor. "But I got my first job here more or less the
same way. On bluff. Except I was a cab driver at the time,
because nobody thought I was any good as a piano player.
I admire a resourceful liar. Okay, young fellow—what's
your first name again?"

"Alec, sir. I reckon you remember my last name, it's so
close to yours."

"I do. And——" long pause, and smile again. "I think I
always will. We'll probably always be mixing up each other's
mail. You're on the payroll. You really won't have to serve
your sentence with the *Star*. Your M.E.'s a friend of mine.

I'll phone him now and he'll strike off your shackles—not, mind you, that I don't approve of your willingness to work out a contract. And you've got the first vacancy on the staff, even if it's night clubs or woman's page. Right enough?"

"Right enough. What does your night copy boy actually do? Routine, I mean?"

"Mixes paste. Then he learns how to get along with old Fitz, the nightside copyreader. If you can make it with Fitz I'll try you dayside with Riley. If you can make it with Riley *and* Fitz, you're an automatic candidate for my job. So long, youngster. See you tomorrow morning."

"I'll be here on—" The phone jangled on John Barry's desk. John Barry held up a quieting hand and listened. "Oh, Jesus," he said into the phone. "I've got to hold the shop down. We closed the Blue Streak early, and there's nobody here but Abigail and"—he looked rather wildly at Alec Barr —"Hold it." He dropped the phone on his desk and looked at Alec Barr.

"You ever cover a really big fire?" he asked.

"Nossir. Small ones, yes."

"Well, a big one is only a small one that's easier to cover. Half of Southwest Washington just touched itself alight. It'll be tomorrow's big story and there's nobody in the shop but you and me and Abigail—and Abigail isn't a big-story reporter. You want to be a reporter, fast?"

Alec Barr didn't answer. He merely nodded tersely. John Barry spoke again into the phone.

"I got it fixed. I'm sending a man. Get out there yourself when you can dig up anybody sober enough to handle the shack. I'll start sifting the bars for a photog. I'm sending the new boy now." There was a pause, and John Barry spoke again. "*Barr*. Alec *Barr*. I just hired him. Right. Call in, and I'll handle what I have to for the Redline replate if the Barr kid moves fast enough."

He cradled the receiver. He looked again at Alec and barked.

"Move," he said. "Jump! Get out to Four and a Half Street and look for where's the most smoke. You got any money?"

"Not much," Alec said. "I got a streetcar pass—"

"If we make a line for the final, which is about ready to go, don't monkey with a streetcar. Here's five bucks. Get on it, fast, and call me back as soon as you get an estimate on the deaths and damages and cause and effect. Jump!"

Alec Barr snatched the bill and darted for the door. When he came back through the door again, smoke-grimed, eyebrows singed, six hours later, John Barry was still at his desk.

The Managing Editor looked up at his new copy boy.

"Damned good work, kid," he said. "We made a fast replate for the final. You dictate pretty good. At least Abigail understood it. How's the story for an overnight?"

"It was quite a story," Alec said, and sat down on a corner of the nearest desk. "Some drunk evidently fell into a Christmas tree and set a whole block of tenements afire. It spread. It was pretty awful. The smell, I mean. It was like a kitchen in a big restaurant with the cook drunk. And what really got to me was the dead kids and dead turkeys and the dead dolls."

"What do you mean, the dead kids and dead turkeys and the dead dolls?" John Barry pushed his chair back, crossed his arms over his chest, and looked at Alec Barr.

"It really hit me. It was so—well, the little dead kids were laid out in a row, alongside the little cindered turkeys and the little melted dolls. All in a line. A kid, a turkey, a doll. Line after line—stretched out on the fire-charred little pathetic lawns."

"Can you write it like that?" John Barry asked.

"I can write it like that," Alec Barr said. "Which typewriter can I use?"

"Write it like that," John Barry said. "Write it just like that, and you can use any typewriter in the joint. Let it run and write what it takes to tell it." He reached into his desk drawer, and produced a pint of rye. "You look a touch peaked. Have a drink?"

Alec Barr looked at his new employer. He smiled. Some color was coming back into his face, and the roasting flesh was not quite so strong in his nostrils.

"Not until after I've finished the piece, Boss," he said. "And then I'll be delighted."

Alec Barr sat down and pounded out his story, writing savagely, swiftly with two fingers on somebody else's Underwood. He fed the copy to John Barry, a page at a time. When he had written *endit* on the last page, it was a quarter to midnight.

He stretched himself, scratched his back, yawned, and walked over to John Barry's desk. John Barry looked at the last page, and reached once more into his desk drawer.

"I highly disapprove of copy boys drinking on duty," he said, handing the bottle to Alec Barr. "But as you've only got one night on the job, I don't mind. Here; drink hearty, because come eight A.M. tomorrow you're fired." He smiled again, the broad warm smile that made his freckles stretch and glow. "You've got a new job."

Alec did not choke when he took a long slug of raw cheap rye out of the bottle's neck. He handed the bottle back, and said briefly, "Thanks. Where's the stuff for the paste?"

"My *reporters* don't have to mix paste," John Barry said, and stuck out his broad, hairy, freckled hand. "We leave that to the copy boys. That photog show up in time to get anything?"

"I think so," Alec Barr said. "I told him what to shoot. We were losing light fast. We wouldn't have got much but it ought to be good if your guy knows anything about his Speed Graphic. At the end I popped a couple of bulbs for him. He's developing early for the first run."

Next day Alec Barr's story occupied the entire front page, with only minor changes. The bulbs he had popped had served well; both Alec Barr and the photographer won awards that year for their little dead babies and little dead dolls and little dead turkeys.

41 / Amelia

The first really significant thing Alec Barr did with his new riches—the jump from twelve dollars a week to fifteen for one night's work as a copy boy on the *News* and then the ten-dollar raise to the munificence of twenty-five was staggering in its inference of affluence—was to buy a car.

The car was a secondhand Ford coupé, rumbleseated, described in the classifieds as "clean, repossessed," newly repainted and smooth of gear and braking mechanism. It would cost Alec thirty dollars a month in time payment for exactly eighteen months. The burden on the budget was unoppressive. Armed as he was with the buckler and cuirass of staff reporter, Alec swiftly acquired a job writing publicity for one small hotel and a night club, boosting his immediate wage to a staggering fifty dollars a week. The leap from twelve to fifty was breathless in its possibilities. Suddenly his clothing credit was firm at Kaufman's and Hecht's. Suddenly there was more than one pair of shoes in the closet of the small furnished two-room apartment on Wisconsin Avenue that he rented to occupy, gloriously, alone. Suddenly there was the shaped weight of new, fresh-milled wool on his back, the stroke of unworn broadcloth soft on his skin. He clung to the battered trench coat, as a badge of craft, but he balanced it with a furry fedora pinched into the exact rakehell block of John Barry's hat. His neckties were new; there was money in his pocket.

Spurs rattling, armor shining, sword clanking, lance couched at the ready, Alec Barr a-courting rode. He flew his byline as a pennon, and his steed was lively with high-test gasoline, its coat shining with wax. Two years after graduation from the University, incorporating all the dreary frustration of apprenticeship at debasingly menial chores, Alec Barr was finally a man, working at a man's job for a man's wage. The wrinkles were gone, at least momentarily, both from belly and from brow. Alec Barr was a reporter with a byline on a metropolitan newspaper, even if it was the smallest and poorest paper in town.

Amelia Macmillan was sitting on the side porch, reading in the shade of a canopied glider, when Sir Alexander Barr, knight-errant, arrived in a flourish of trumpets with his shiny new secondhand, black-repainted charger. Sir Alexander Barr arranged his bony limbs inside his new suit of cheviot armor and strolled up the flagged pathway to greet his damsel fair. He had his newspaper with him, and he appeared to have been invented for the purpose of starring in a Grade-B newspaper movie.

"Brought you the latest edition," he said. "Had to write a fast piece for the Blueline. We're a little short of news today. They stuck it on the front page." He dropped the paper front-page-up on the glider seat.

"It's awfully nice to see you again, Alec," Amelia said. "I thought you'd left town or died or something. You promised me last fall that you'd call, but you never did." She did not look at the sprawled ink-damp paper.

"Busy, terribly busy," Alec said. "We run a very short-handed shop."

"Oh," Amelia said. "I thought the *Star* had lots of reporters." She still had not glanced at the newspaper, at the three-column ruled box at the bottom of the front page which bore the byline of "Alexander Barr, Staff Reporter."

"I switched to the *News*," Alec said. "It moves faster. No family to clutter up the progress."

"We don't take the *News*," Amelia said. "Daddy won't have it in the house. That's why I guess I didn't know what you were doing." Now she looked down at the paper. "Oh, there's your name! How divine! You have to be something pretty special to get your name on a story, don't you? And on the front page, too."

"Not so special. Just lucky, I guess."

She looked now swiftly at the automobile.

"What a pretty car," she said. "Could I have a ride in it?"

"Sure," Alec said. "Let's go over to the Hot Shoppe and have a milkshake or something. I bought the car the other day and was just driving past when I remembered you said you lived on this street and thought I'd say hello. You hear anything from Jimmy?"

She got up from the glider, smoothed the front of her dress, and then picked up the newspaper.

"I'll just tell Mother I'm going for a drive," she said. "You can meet her when we come back. No, I don't hear anything from Jimmy. I guess he's found a new girl at Carolina. I guess he must be pretty busy learning to be a lawyer."

"I'm glad all that studying is behind me," Alec said. "I really don't understand how a grown man has the patience to keep on going to school with kids."

Amelia arched an eyebrow and walked into the house.

"I'll be back in a jiff," she said.

It was warm early spring in Washington, with the cherry blossoms already out in Potomac Park, the dogwood snowy in Rock Creek. Amelia was wearing a brown linen skirt with a blue silk shirtwaist that nearly matched her eyes. Her bare legs were already slightly tanned. The motion of her hips under the brown lines was smooth and easy as she walked long-striding in brown-and-white pumps.

Alec watched her disappear, and looked about him at the house and yard. It was not a staggeringly opulent property, but it had a look—*the* valid, solid, look—for which Alec Barr had hungered as a child and even more as a young man. It looked purposefully completely tended—the lawn neat-clipped, the jonquils butter-fresh and perky, the flagged footpath closely barbered, even the fieldstones of the house itself looking scrubbed as they appeared through the glossy green fretwork of creeper.

So, fresh, scrubbed and perky too, appeared the maid who slid swiftly onto the side porch to collect an iced-tea glass, a plate with the fragments of sandwiches from an earlier snack, two books, and a magazine. She nodded politely to Alec Barr, who noted the neat submissive face and trim figure in its black, white-aproned uniform, approving the snowy lace cap on the primly coifed head. Alec had never seen a *white* servant at close hand before; his only connection with servants had been the blowsy pillow-bosomed black Lil of his boyhood and a fleeting observation of cinema butlers as played by Arthur Treacher.

Amelia appeared at the door.

"Mother would like to meet you," she said. "Daddy's taking a nap, but he'll be awake by the time we get back. Let's go now and try your new car."

"It isn't really new, you know," Alec said. "I'm not quite up to the new level yet."

"Well, it looks new," Amelia said, getting into the car with a brief exposure of thigh. "It even *smells* new. I think it's a lovely car, Alec, and aren't you the smart one to be able to buy such a nice car on your first real job?"

At that moment, Sir Alexander Barr would have cheerfully gone up against any dragon of any dimension with his bare hands. Instead, he eased in the clutch, and remarked casually that in *his* business, a man had to look a little shaggy, because the public expected it and anyone foolish enough to aspire to Cadillac status would be drummed out of the Press Club. He was conscious as he spoke of the glossy elegant newness of his clothing.

They drove, chattering aimlessly of the loveliness of early-evening spring in Rock Creek Park and of the likelihood that Amelia would be graduating from George Washington University in June. There was no further reference to Jim James by Amelia until Alec mentioned that he planned to visit the University for the June dances—it would be nice to see old Jim again—and "My fraternity is having a house-party. I don't know how you people do it up here"—long pause to emphasize the inverted snobbishness that would go well with a rakehelly hat and a purposefully shabby trench coat—"but down there we kick all the fellows out of the house—my fraternity house, I mean—and the girls move in. The housemother rides herd on the ladies, and all the fellows den up with the Dekes or the KA's or the Kappa Sigs or SAE's across the street. It's a lot of fun."

It sure as hell would be fun, Alec Barr said to himself, maneuvering his shining iron stallion into the Hot Shoppe's striped parking lanes. It sure as hell would be fun to hit the old Delt house again in my very own car, with maybe the prettiest girl from maybe one of the best families from a big town like Washington, D.C., with a brand-new tuxedo and some money in my pocket—real money in my pocket and a half-dozen bottles of good hooch locked in the rumble. "Well, here's good old Brother Barr," his mind recited. "How are you, Brother Barr? What's all this I hear about you being Washington's star reporter, on the front page every day?" Alec licked his mental chops.

He said then mildly, with just a touch of labeled mock humility:

"It will be nice to go back to the old school now I've got something better than an office boy's job to talk about. Particularly to see old Skipper Henry again. He's the guy who got me my first job on a country weekly, you know. I was pretty proud of getting that job even if the job itself wasn't much. I wasn't even a regular journalism student and old Prof Henry gave me the first lousy job that bobbed up. But I just couldn't stick it in that dreary hick town, so I quit and hopped a ship and went to Europe." Alec's tone intimated that deeper reasons, such as personal liability in a bastardy case, underlay his departure.

Amelia looked at Alec with a kindled interest.

"I didn't know—Jimmy never told me you'd been to Europe. That's very exciting," she said. The carhop approached. Amelia raised her eyebrows at Alec. "What are we having?"

"Trust me," he said. "I got a discovery. Two double limes, with a lot of ice," he said to the pretty waitress. He winked at Amelia. "I don't think it's too early in the day for a drink," he said, and reached into the glove compartment. "I just happened to have a bottle of gin with me. Your family let you drink?"

"We don't generally serve it. But after I got to be a sophomore they haven't said anything about me taking a small one now and then on a date. Except one night." Amelia laughed. "I went to a dance and came home a little bit high. I managed to lock myself in a closet while I was undressing and Mother had to let me out. She gave me real hell that night."

"You really got to drink some in my business," Alec said drawling, almost heavy-lidded. "I mean, we're not covering Sunday schools, exactly, and there's a lot of waiting time on the average story. Somehow—thank God Roosevelt repealed Prohibition, because I cut my milk teeth on corn whiskey—we manage to spend that spare time in the handiest saloon. America's still pretty uncivilized about drinking, though. They take drinking for granted in London and Hamburg and Rotterdam and Antwerp and Paris and places like that." The drawl now had achieved the status of smirk. "In Washington you can't even stand at a bar."

"You've really been to all those places?" Amelia's voice was pleasingly wide-eyed.

"Not exactly first class. But at least I've *been.* Some people have rich parents who give them the Grand Tour. Other people shovel sheep manure and stand eight-hour wheel watches. I shoveled sheep manure and stood eight-hour wheel watches. But I guess the girls are all the same, no matter how you get there." Alec had difficulty controlling a lewd wink and something as extra-asinine as "You know how girls are the wide world over." Fortunately he let his sentence hang, almost secure in a knowledge that Amelia would say:

"And how *are* the girls in Germany and England and France?"

"Oh, you know how girls are the wide world over," Alec said, now unable to resist the phrase. "Some pretty. Some ugly. Some—" he shrugged. "An ordinary seaman on a tramp ship doesn't get to meet many debutantes." Oh, boy, Alec's mind exulted. How *about* me?

"It must have been a marvelous experience. If I don't maybe get married I'm going to try to persuade my folks into sending me over this summer—if the grades are all right and I graduate with my *cum laude.* I've got sort of a leg up—just squeezed by enough to make Phi Beta Kappa."

"That's pretty nice squeezing," Alec said. "I squoze the same old squeeze. It ain't easy."

The waitress came now with the iced lime-drinks. Alec paid and thanked her, and waited until her trim yellow-

uniformed backside disappeared into the Hot Shoppe's Laby-
rinth, to vanish forever as sacrifice to the Minotaur who
demanded a yearly tithe of maidens who had unsuccessfully
assaulted the halls of Government. Then Alec swiftly spilled
a measure of gin into the two green iced drinks, and stirred
rapidly with the thick Hot Shoppe straws.

"This'll put hair on your chest," he grinned, and then said:
"Excuse me. Nothing personal. Now how about this getting
married?"

"Nobody really handy at the moment. It was just a figure
of speech." Amelia grinned back, looking upward under her
lashes as she sipped her drink. "My, this *is* good. And if I
wanted any hair on my chest"—the word assumed the
pointed proportion of *breasts*—"if I *wanted* any hair on my
chest, I'm sure this would provide it. It's just that we mustn't
tell my mother." They grinned again, conspirators, and Alec
had a sudden smug feeling that he had just placed his hand
under the brown linen skirt, on the firm tanned thigh, and
had not been repulsed.

"Somehow we got sidetracked between the Europe and
the hair on your chest," he said, and now there was rakish
assurance in his voice. "Do you think your parents would
mind your going to the June dances with a disreputable
newspaperman? As a sort of feeler toward Europe, I mean?
See America First sort of thing?"

Amelia sipped her drink and smiled again, mouth buried
in the green liquid, gazing upward through her lashes, which
Alec now was prepared to swear were gold-tipped.

"I guess maybe they won't mind. I'm a big girl now. Twenty-one in May. There's nothing very much you can do about
a girl who's free, white, twenty-one and—"

"Ready to be kissed?" Alec finished.

"I think that's how the line goes," Amelia blushed slightly. "I think I meant to say that I've already been kissed but
now there's no legal way to keep me from more of it. Or
something."

"We shall see, we shall see," Sir Alexander said firmly,
brashly. "We shall certainly see."

"Just so I'll know when they ask, you're not a Catholic,
are you?"

"No," said Alec Barr. "I'm an atheist."

42

Walker Macmillan, standing spraddlelegged in front of his cold fireplace, seemed approximately ten feet tall to Alec Barr when he came into the living room of Amelia's house. Walker Macmillan matched the room's double-storied oak-beamed ceilings in massive accomplishment, as Betsy Macmillan matched the antimacassars on the overstuffed mahogany furniture. The Kirmanshah rug on the highly polished blond parquet flooring was no richer in texture than Amelia's father's complexion; the white tulle curtains no more delicate than the skin of Amelia's mother's cheeks. Walker Macmillan wore a Shrine crescent in his buttonhole; Betsy Macmillan wore a froth of lace at her only-slightly-crêpy throat.

"The wife tells me you're one of the newspaper boys," Walker Macmillan boomed, as if establishing an indisputable point before the annual conclave of the Optimists' Club. "I've found them to be a bunch of pretty good fellows as a rule. Anyhow they've always treated me real nice when they reported anything I was connected with. Maybe a little inaccurate—but I'd say some of my best friends are the newspaper boys."

Alec Barr suppressed a desire to scream, thinking of some of the citizens' association meetings and hail-fellow club breakfasts he had covered, as sidebar necessity to a copy boy's wage, when he worked for Washington's official mother-in-law, the *Star*. Any minute now Walker Macmillan would say:

"I reckon the newspaper boys are kind of underpaid, not like the advertising fellows. I always remember to send a couple jugs around at Christmas. What sort of news do you —uh—cover?" Walker Macmillan smiled in self-congratulation. He had lit as unerringly onto the apt word as one Shriner smells another Shriner in a strange town.

"General assignments, sir," Alec Barr said. "Anything from fires to"—he rapidly rejected "rape" and "Optimist Club" as alternates—"Congressional hearings."

223

"That's all very interesting," Walker Macmillan boomed. "I bet you meet all sorts of interesting people." He winked, and gazed at his wife with heavy humor. "I reckon it isn't too early to buy The Press a drink, is it, Mother?"

"Oh, *you*," Betsy Macmillan said. "I declare to goodness." Alec suddenly knew where Amelia had learned the upswept glance through the fringe of eyelashes. "I suppose it won't hurt—just this once—Mr. Barr being a real newspaper reporter and all." Alec felt his stature heightening. He was a real newspaper reporter and all and could be offered a drink in a house which did not drink daily but which was making an exception because he was a real newspaper reporter and all. A dashing, dissolute fellow—and all.

"Oh, you men," Betsy Macmillan said, and Alec's brain supplied the words "dimpled" and "bridled," rejecting "simpered." "I think I might just have a little teeny one myself so long as you don't put too much liquor in it and if Sister has one with me."

The air of congenial conspiracy was complete. Father Macmillan fetched the drinks, heavy bourbons light on the soda side, except for Mother's and Daughter's, which were light bourbons heavy on the soda side.

"I think the ladies do better when they drink it heavy on the soda side," Walker Macmillan said. "Well, here's mud in your eye."

"Mud," Alec Barr said, downing a quarter of his drink in order to pursue the masquerade. "That's real good whiskey."

"Sippin' whiskey," Amelia's father said. "An old one I remember before Prohibition. Sour mash. Called Jack Dawson. I never drink anything else. It's the mixed drinks that kill you."

"I quite agree," Alec Barr said, wondering if anybody ever sat down in this house. Amelia caught the idea.

"Come and sit by me, Alec," she said. "Daddy, Mom, Alec's asked me to a houseparty at the University of North Carolina when school's out. You remember Jimmy James? We'll be seeing him—and his girl"—she bore down heavily on *girl*—"and Alec tells me it's a wonderful set of dances."

"Where would you stay?" Mrs. Macmillan moved in with a dreadnought's delicacy. "At *night,* I mean. Certainly not in a *hotel?*"

"Oh, sorry," Alec said. "Amelia didn't tell you. My fraternity house, of course."

"Alec's a Delta Psi," Amelia said swiftly. "It's one of the best."

Walker Macmillan started to draw his tufted eyebrows down over the crease at the top of his nose. Alec cut him off at the draw.

"Oh," he said, and smiled in a manner he thought to be winning. "It's all very prim and proper. What we do is we give the house to the ladies, and the housemother throws all the fellows out into the street. Not really in the street—but we sort of sharecrop on the other people's lodges. And nobody's allowed upstairs in our house until all the girls are out, of *my* house, I mean—and of course the housemother's on tap all the time. Her name's MacPhail," he said hurriedly. "*Mrs.* MacPhail. She's a widow."

Walker Macmillan's face lightened at the Scots name.

"I reckon any frat house with a housemother named Mac-Phail couldn't be a den of iniquity, eh, Mother?" he winked at his wife. "We've got some MacPhails among the other monkeys in our own family tree." He laughed at his own rich wit. "I must remember that one, other monkeys in own tree. I know just where I can use it."

Now his heavy, highly polished dewlaps dropped into seriousness.

"We've only got one little girl, Alec," he said heavily. "We have to look out for her. But I don't see why she couldn't go to the dances, do you, Mother?"

"Not if you say so, Father," Betsy Macmillan said. "You know best about these things."

"Well then, now, that's settled," Walker Macmillan said. He gazed at Alec Barr with narrowed eyes. "I don't suppose another little drinkie would do us any harm, hey?"

"Oh, we wouldn't want *another*," Mother and Daughter said in chorus.

"A very light tap for me, sir," Alec said. "I got to be on deck real early tomorrow; I can drink or I can work, but I can't work *and* drink."

"By George, that's good," Walker Macmillan said. "I must remember that one, too. Work *or* drink but can't *and*." He touched Alec lightly on the shoulder. "It's a kind of shorthand I use to remember things before I write them down."

"I can really go to the dances then, Mom?" Walker Macmillan had gone back to the kitchen to replenish the drinks. "Really?"

"If your father says so," Betsy Macmillan replied. She looked at Alec and spread her hands. "I never worry about my little girl. But fathers? You know how they are when they only have the one chickabiddy."

"Of course." This was the time for hearty humor. "If I had a little girl as pretty as Amelia I'd mount a machine gun on the front porch and mow the boys down in droves."

"I guess a shotgun is enough for just one daughter," Walker Macmillan said, returning. "Now then, young fellow, how long has it been since you've had a real old-fashioned home-cooked meal?"

"Too long," Alec said truthfully. "Entirely too long." Christ, he thought, I doubt if I ever had what you would call a real home-cooked meal, not if you count the dismal home-fried provender my mother and old Lil managed to scare up between them.

"In that case," Walker Macmillan said, "I reckon you'd better stay and have supper with us. Alec looks like he could stand a little feeding-up, doesn't he, Mother? I guess they work you pretty hard on the paper—irregular hours and all?"

"Yes sir. We do work pretty hard, and the hours are pretty irregular. I'm up by five-thirty, usually—we lock up the first edition at eight-thirty—and sometimes the assignments take me past midnight. Not often, though. Mostly I'm finished by four in the afternoon." He looked then at Amelia, seeking aid.

"About supper—I—I—maybe Amelia has something she wants to do, a date or something?"

"I *do* have a date," Amelia said. "But it's not until eight-thirty, and we eat at seven. I'd love to have you stay for dinner"—she stressed *dinner*—" if you don't mind too much if I run away afterward. Sorry, but I've had this date for a week."

Alec stared at his fists.

"I'd love to stay—Mrs. Macmillan, Mister Macmillan—if you're quite sure I'm not imposing. I didn't intend to—"

Walker Macmillan held up a brilliantly manicured hand with a big diamond winking on its third finger.

"Of course you're not intruding. We don't have much chance to really meet any of Amelia's friends, and there's always enough for one more. We're Virginia folks originally, and we still set an old-fashioned country table. Both Mother and I come from families where you're likely to have another six cousins drop in for supper." He clapped Alec heartily on the shoulder. "I'll just show you the washroom," he said. As they walked away, he winked. "And if we don't mention it to the women we can stop off in the kitchen and have a little dividend before we sit down."

The white maid was even more immaculate now in her crisp black-and-white, and the table was beautifully laid, with a silver bowl of roses in the centerpiece. Iced tea was the beverage, apart from water. There was red-sauced shrimp cocktail as the first course, followed by a roast of beef with tiny new brown freckled potatoes, and various dishes of beets, string beans, watermelon pickles, and some sort of relish made of pickled corn. Alec raised an eyebrow in surprise at the beans and beets, since it was very early in the year for any fresh garden vegetable.

Betsy Macmillan noted the look.

"I still put them up in Mason jars for the winter," she said, half ashamedly. "I guess it's an old country habit I can't break."

"I hope you never do," Alec said devoutly, before he popped another quarter-sized hot biscuit, soaking with butter, into his mouth. The beans and beets were equally bathed in butter, and the roast beef was overdone for his taste.

"These watermelon pickles are the best I ever tasted in my life," Alec said. "You put them up yourself, Mrs. Macmillan?"

"I'm afraid so," she said. "I'm afraid I spend too much time in the kitchen."

"We can't keep her out of the kitchen," Walker Macmillan boomed. "We've got a maid *and* a cook, but Mother reckons they can't make out without her assistance. Maybe she's right; I've quit trying to reform her. Mother's very strong-minded about some things, including stag poker parties." Walker Macmillan's laugh boomed, and his wife slapped him lightly, coyly, on the shoulder.

Amelia said very little during the meal, but picked at her food, shoving the potatoes relentlessly around her plate, eating chiefly from a salad of cole slaw and tomatoes.

"You're not hardly touching a thing, Sister," her father said sharply. "Not feeling good?"

"Oh, I feel all right. I guess I've got the spring tizzies, or something. Don't pay any attention to me."

"Well, I'm eating enough for all of us," Alec said, attempting to divert the critical parental attention from Amelia. "I hope you don't mind if I make a pig of myself. But this is the best meal I've had in six years, at least. On the kind of money I've made since I got out of college—until just recently—you kind of get used to the thirty-cent blue-plate in the drugstore across the street. And when I was going to sea—well, excuse me for repeating it at the table, but we had to sort of knock the cockroaches out of the biscuits."

"How horrible, you poor boy," Betsy Macmillan said, ringing for the maid to pass the roast beef again. "It must have been awful. How did you happen to go to sea?"

Alec smiled his best practiced rueful smile.

"Not very much choice. I was flat broke down South and a ship came along and I was lucky and got a job on it. The work was terrible and the food was worse but it took me to a lot of strange places I wouldn't have been able to see otherwise."

Amelia spoke now, relieved to have the family attention centered on Alec:

"Alec's been just *every*where," she said. "He was telling me this afternoon. Places like London and Antwerp and Hamburg and all like that."

"Well, now, I suppose seeing the world is all right in its place," Walker Macmillan said. "But there's a lot of little old America that Mother and I haven't seen yet. We're going to California for the Shrine convention this summer—see Yosemite and all those other places. The redwoods and all. Last winter we did Florida. I sure was glad to get home. I kind of like my winters cold. Seems unnatural to see people going around in sports shirts in February with their shirttails flapping outside their pants. Maybe we'll get to Europe some day, but I'll bet Amelia beats us to it, eh, Sister?"

"That's my plot and plan," Amelia said, falsely brightly. "Maybe Alec can tell you that little girls don't get sold into slavery in Paris and London."

"Not any that I saw," Alec said swiftly, reflecting rapidly that he never met any girls farther distant from the docks than the nearest waterfront saloon. "But I really don't see how a person can afford *not* to go to Europe if they can afford it —financially afford it, I mean. Before the war breaks out, I mean."

"There's not going to *be* any war," Walker Macmillan said, as if that finally settled it. "I think that fellow Hitler is good for the Germans. They needed a kick to get them started again after the last war. If it hadn't of been for Hitler the

Communists and the Jews would of had Germany by now. I was reading only the other day—"

"Oh, Father, let's not talk politics at the table," Betsy Macmillan said. "You know it's very bad for your digestion."

"Like to have a talk with you about it all the same sometime, Alec, with no ladies present," Walker Macmillan said, with his fourth wink of the evening. "You can tell me all about the Frenchy girls and things like that." He grinned wickedly and accepted a slab of apple pie topped with whipped cream from the trim-rumped maid.

"Seriously, Alec, what did you think of Germany?" Amelia asked. "I've always wanted to go there—more even than France or England, I think."

"Well, it certainly is a neat, well-run country," Alec said, thinking of a fight in the North Star Bar in Hamburg, a boozy battle in which he found himself under an upturned table, flailing at passing ankles with a broken chair-leg, with bottles smashing and curses of the whores shrilling as they tore at each other's faces with hooked fingers. Big Joe, the Negro mess cook, had started that one in an argument with a white fellow off another ship over the favors of a buxom Rhinemaiden with two long flaxen braids hanging ropy over her watermelon breasts. . . .

"Yes, it's a neat country, all right, and seems to be very prosperous. Everybody's got a job of some sort. The food is wonderful and the streets are clean and the shops have plenty to sell. You see a lot of uniforms, of course, and everybody marches everywhere. You understand I didn't get to visit much of the interior. We never docked long in one place. It was a quick-turn-around ship."

Great God, Alec thought, what a bombshell I could drop if I told them about the night I was drunk in Two-Mark Allee in Saint Pauli, saw the pretty dame sitting in the window, staggered inside and they switched an old hag on me in the dark, and me not realizing it until after I shot my wad. Suppose I told them how I sweated out the clap for a week, and then worried about the Big Casino for another two. . . .

"But the trip from Hamburg to Bremerhaven was very interesting. I went into a sort of bar that was run by Max Schmeling's sister." And what a bag *she* was, if she really was his sister, Alec thought. You can have the kind of German woman I saw. All tits and hips and cow faces.

"Well, one thing you can say," Walker Macmillan said.

"Hitler's sure got the Jews on the run. About time, too. We could use a lot more of that over here."

Alec gritted his mental teeth, and was proud of Amelia when she said:

"Daddy, I just won't sit here and listen to that kind of talk. I've told you and told you I—"

"All right, well all right, don't make a ruckus in front of our guest," Walker Macmillan said. "You know very well some of my very best friends are Jews. Especially in the Shriners. It's just that when you get too many of them concentrated they try to take over and run things to suit themselves and a white man hasn't got a chance. All right, all *right*—" he held up the furbished pink fingernails. "I promise. Have another piece of pie, Alec."

"Thank you," Alec said, and devoured his second slab with his eyes fixed on his plate.

They drank hot, rather watery coffee at the table, and then Amelia excused herself, saying she had to dress for her date. Alec heard her heels softly thudding on the carpeted staircase. Walker Macmillan said:

"It's warm enough outside still. Let's go out on the porch and smoke a cigar. Mother doesn't like me to smoke them in the house. You like cigars?"

Alec smiled winningly, he thought, frankly.

"I don't really know, sir. I really never was able to afford them. A pack of cigarettes a day was about all I've been able to manage until just recently."

Walker Macmillan offered him a cigar from a fancifully carved Moroccan leather case.

"Try this. Real pure-leaf Havana. I smoke one after every meal. Fine for the digestion."

He watched Alec light the cigar, and then said:

"You know, there's a thing I like about you, young fellow. You don't put on any airs. You're poor—you've *been* poor—and you're not ashamed to admit it. You don't make any bones about it like so many of these fancy young squirts that come courting Amelia. Like this—this *Catholic* fellow that's coming around tonight. You'd think his uncle was the Pope, or something, from the airs he puts on, and I'm damned afraid Amelia is serious about him."

Alec opened his mouth, but Walker Macmillan stopped him.

"Wait a minute, now, hold on. I know you think it's pretty

strange for me to talk like this about my own daughter to a boy I've just known for a few hours. But I'm a man of quick decisions—that's how I got to where I am"—he paused to smile insincerely deprecatingly—"I'm a man that makes a fast judgment, and I *like* you. I think you've got your head screwed on right. And I know you're not a Catholic because I asked Amelia."

He blew a plume of smoke into the soft spring night.

"We liked your friend Jim James a lot. He was a nice boy, but a little wild. Drank a little bit too much. We kind of hoped maybe there was an understanding between him and Amelia. But now he's gone back to law school, as you know, and well . . ." Walker Macmillan shrugged. "You know how young girls are. Two or three years is a long time to wait."

"But Mr. Macmillan, I—you don't know me from Adam," Alec said, embarrassed. The cigar tasted foul. Alec yearned for a cigarette.

"I don't need to know you from Adam." Walker Macmillan spat out a shred of moist tobacco, and his sleek jowls quivered. "I know a steady head when I see one. You like my daughter, don't you?"

"Yes sir. You know I do."

"Well, then, if you like our Amelia, we want to see a lot of you around here. I know a lot of people say newspaper reporters are wild as buck rabbits and drink too much, but you don't look wild and I like the way you handle your liquor. I wouldn't trust a man who didn't drink as far as I could throw a horse. Something wrong with a man don't drink. He's hiding a weakness. We want to see a lot of you: you come to dinner next Sunday."

Alec felt a little overpowered by the command.

"I'd love to, but—but I don't know if Amelia . . ."

"Amelia will be glad to see you. We *never* ask any boy to Sunday dinner. It's purely a family affair. You'll come?"

"Yes sir. I'll be delighted to, if you're sure—"

"I'm sure. How do you like your cigar?"

"I'm not quite sure. I think I like it. There's an awful lot of it, though, isn't there?"

Walker Macmillan laughed, and clapped Alec on the back.

"That's pretty good. You're all right, Alec. I'm pretty certain we're going to be friends. Come on." He flipped his half-smoked cigar onto the grass in a small shower of sparks. "Let's go join the ladies."

They walked back into the house, just as Amelia, dressed in a powder-blue gabardine spring suit with a white blouse-collar flaunting a Windsor bow of darker blue, came down the stairs. She was wearing high heels and sheer stockings, and had dragged her hair tight over the ears and piled it high on her head. She looked lovely, flower-faced, Alec thought, hating the boy who was taking her out into the night, to do—to do *what*?

"Young Alec's coming to Sunday dinner," Walker Macmillan stated flatly. Alec looked at Amelia with something close to pleading. It isn't my idea, his eyes said.

"Why, that's just fine," she said, surprisingly happily. "And maybe we can go for a long drive or to the movies or something in the afternoon; all right, Alec?"

Alec's desperation vanished. Sunday was only three days away. He decided not to crowd his luck; the three-day interval was best. Then he swiftly changed his mind. Better move in right now.

He grinned, a sincerely boyish, honest grin.

"I don't want you-all to get sick and tired of me before I even start," he said. "And I know you're bound to be busy on Saturday night. But if you weren't, Amelia—" he directed his question over her shoulder to her father—"if you weren't, I'd love to take you out. There's a very good show at the Coconut Grove, or maybe we could go out to Maryland to Beverly Farms. There's a swell band out there . . ." He let the sentence die.

"I've got a sort of date," Amelia said. "But I think I can wiggle out of it. Yes, I'd love to go out, Alec. If it's all right with—" she turned to her parents.

"Of course," Walker Macmillan boomed. "And there's no such thing as seeing too much of people we really like, is there, Mother?"

"Of course not, dear. And you will come for Sunday dinner, Alec? We have it at one o'clock."

"Gives us time for anyhow one mint julep after church," Walker Macmillan said. "You go to church, Alec?"

Alec thought hurriedly.

"When I can," he said. "Whenever I get the opportunity."

"Good boy. A little church never hurt anybody, even if you don't believe everything the preacher says. We'll see you Sunday, then, and don't you be too late Saturday night. I don't want my little girl showing up at church with a hangover." He winked again, ponderously.

Alec fidgeted.

"Thank you," he said. "Thank you for a wonderful supper. I'll run along now. Thank you all. Good night."

"Good night," the parents said together. "Come again soon," as if they had not already confirmed the other invitation.

Amelia escorted Alec to the front door, switched on the porch light, closed the door behind her, took one of Alec's hands, and giggled.

"What in the name of God did you do to Daddy?" she whispered. "I never saw him take to one of my boy friends like this before in my life. Mostly he isn't even polite to them."

"I'm damned if I know," Alec said. "Look, Amelia, I don't want to—"

"Don't be such a silly," she said, and brushed his cheek lightly with her lips, squeezing his hand. "And don't pay too much attention to Daddy, one way or the other. He's not as bad as he sounds—that Jew business and all. It's something they teach them at the Rotary or something."

The dark low shape of a long car eased up to the curb.

"Oh," she said. "Here's my date. What time then Saturday?"

"About eight be all right?"

"Delish. See you then. 'Night." She squeezed his hand again and ran back into the house.

Alec walked slowly down the winding flagged path. He passed the dark figure of a young man as he reached the sidewalk, headed toward his own car.

"Evening," the young man said briefly.

"Evening," Alec said, and proceeded to his own Ford, which suddenly seemed very small and shabby by contrast with the sleek Buick convertible parked just behind him. He slid into the Ford, then looked through the darkness to where the young man stood impatiently waiting in the bright light, ringing the bell.

The young man was tall, broad in the shoulders, slim in the hips. Even at that distance Alec could see the easy drape of the blazer over what seemed lighter flannel slacks. Even the back of the young man's neck looked arrogant, and his hair snugged sleek, like fur, to his head.

"I'll fix the slick-headed Catholic son-of-a-bitch," Alec

Barr said, easing in his clutch as he flicked on his headlights. "I'll fix him before he knows what's hit him."

He thought of Amelia as he drove through the fragrance of the Washington spring; thought ripely, tangibly, touching her mentally here and there. He could smell her, he thought, the female smell of her, and certainly he knew what she would feel like, soft and springy under his hands. He thought it rather odd that her father should make such a sudden naked pitch, almost eagerly suing for Alec's favor, as if Amelia were some homely duckling daughter to be hawked to the first bidder. Then he dismissed the thought of Amelia's father, and let his fancy travel backward to the conversation he'd had with Jimmy James.

Jimmy had been dead right about one thing. Amelia Macmillan's people certainly set a fine table, and he hadn't even gotten round to the beer and the cold cuts in the icebox yet.

43

Spring resolved into one long holy procession of Sunday dinners. The Sunday dinners consisted of rib roast, pot roast, roast beef, chicken fricassee with dumplings, roast chicken, and broiled chicken. The Sunday dinners consisted of butterbeans, string beans, green peas, creamed carrots, creamed cauliflower, buttered beets, candied yams, mashed potatoes, roast potatoes, baked potatoes, boiled potatoes, predigested spinach, zucchini, beefsteak tomatoes, cole slaw, lettuce-and-grated-carrot salad, apple-and-nut-and-raisin salad. The Sunday dinners consisted of pale-pink watermelon pickles, rosy crabapple pickles, jaundiced peach pickles, liverish plum pickles, and pallid pear pickles. The Sunday dinners consisted of cornbread, corn sticks, hot biscuits, and hot rolls. The Sunday dinners consisted of apple pie and apple cobbler; peach pie and peach cobbler; blackberry pie and blackberry cobbler; strawberry shortcake and strawberry cobbler; rhubarb pie and rhubarb cobbler; cherry pie and cherry cobbler. The Sunday dinners consisted of vanilla, chocolate, peach, cherry, coffee, walnut, butter-pecan, lemon, orange, and peppermint-stick ice cream. The coffee was always hot and always thin.

The Sunday dinners consisted of Aunt Hattie and Uncle Fenwick, Cousin Randolph and Cousin Emily, Uncle Jasper and Aunt Naomi, Cousin Wilbur and Cousin Sally, Uncle Joseph and Aunt Olivia, Cousin Norman and Cousin Debbie, Aunt Cynthia and Uncle Raymond, Cousin Tess and Cousin Cass.

The Sunday dinners consisted of Alexander Barr, a stag at bay as he fed before the family.

The Sunday dinners consisted of Alec Barr's dread of the Sunday dinners, Alec Barr's enslavement to the Sunday dinners, Alec Barr's first futile efforts to avoid the Sunday dinners, Alec Barr's ultimate resignation to the Sunday dinners, and finally, when May flowered hotly into June, Alec Barr's escape from the Sunday dinners to a blessed week end in Chapel Hill, North Carolina, for the Spring Finals, where the Sunday dinner consisted of milk punches in the Zeta Psi House.

44

Alec and Amelia had progressed normally to necking in the car, parked with parental permission outside the house, near enough to headquarters to avoid the menace of night-prowling rapists and murderers, close enough to allow Amelia to scream for help if Alec's spring-fed fumblings constituted serious assault on Amelia's virtue.

Alec did not, in fact, importune. Some memory of his collegiate conjunction with Fran Mayfield checked him from an actual consummation with Amelia, though the necking had increased swiftly to petting and the petting frantically to everything short of penetration. Amelia was more than willing, when the musky moments became almost unbearable, and Alec was deliciously shocked at the knowing sinuous clutch of fingers which brought him relief into a hurriedly produced handkerchief. They were tacitly engaged; Alec's handsome, seal-haired rival, the Walker Macmillan-hated Catholic, had long since disappeared. Amelia dated nobody else. But Alec, with a restlessness he could neither justify nor quite understand, took an occasional night off from true love to seek the purging release of purest debasing lust.

Profane love was provided in the front seat of his car or on a blanket in Rock Creek Park or, very occasionally, in his own rooms, by the person of a wiry, dark, bird-faced nymphomaniac government secretary named Harriet, who quivered like a plucked lute-string to the briefest touch, and whose breath came harshly swift even at the sound of a faintly suggestive lyric. Harriet moaned and writhed and bit and clawed, saying *"ayiee!"* if Alec touched her here, and *"oyyee"* if he touched her there. Harriet demanded neither movies nor presents nor alcohol nor dancing nor formal dating, even, in return for access to her fevered body. Her skill at fitting herself into the strangest corners, for utmost convenience, would have credited a professional contortionist, and her shrieking orgasms were as sharply defined and as steadily rhythmic as the pound of a bass drum. Nor rain nor snow nor curse deflected Harriet from her appointed rounds, the basic aim. She did not confine her attention to Alec; she was any man's woman under any conditions. She was merely pleased to hear Alec's voice on the phone, and generally managed to arrive at his beck, quick-step, girdle at half-mast.

Alec felt a delicious sense of iniquity in his double life—not real guilt, but rather a devilish feeling of near-nobility in the subjugation of his basic beast outside the technical spoliation of Amelia. He had read a phrase somewhere in an eighteenth-century English novel—"she is for marriage"—and that is exactly how he felt about Amelia. Amelia would be for marriage, even though he knew by now that Amelia was no virgin.

This fact Amelia had confessed in honesty one night while they parked after a moving picture and had reached a taut testicle-aching pinnacle of passion in Alec, with the copper-penny taste of want in Amelia's opened mouth. They had touched each other hotly, wetly, and their bodies arched yearningly toward each other. Alec's trousers were unbuttoned; Amelia's skirts were flung backward to her slowly, unconsciously undulating hips. Her blouse was unbuttoned to the waist, brassière unsnapped, breasts showing whitely in the dark.

"You can if you want, Alec darling," she murmured. "I want you to. Please, please, I want you to."

"No. *No.*" Alec snatched his hands abruptly away from her body. "I won't. I will *not*—not until we're married. I don't want to start out with a memory of a lot of car seats and furnished rooms."

"I—I have before. This wouldn't be the first time. It wouldn't make—it wouldn't be hurting any—I love you, Alec, I don't *want* to wait until we're married." Amelia's voice pleaded huskily.

Alec sat straight behind the wheel of his car and began to button his pants. He flipped Amelia's skirt tersely down over her white gleaming thighs, and lit two cigarettes. She smoked, the cigarette drooping from her lips, while she swiftly re-snapped her bra and buttoned her blouse.

Alec consciously smoked, staring straight ahead over the wheel.

"Who? Jimmy?"

"Yes." Amelia's voice was very low. "Jimmy."

"Others?"

"No. Not really. One other then."

"The other fellow? The guy your father hated? The Catholic?"

"No. Not him. An older fellow. You don't know him. I thought I was very much in love with him. I—I wanted to marry him. We—we went all the way for nearly a year. I found out finally that he was just stringing me a line. He—his name was Harry—"

"I don't want to know his Goddamned name," Alec said. "But I'd like to kill him, the son-of-a-bitch."

"He—kind of made a collection of girls around the campus. I—I found out that it was a sort of joke, how many girls he was making. I heard some of the fellows laughing about it one time when we went to the apartment of one of his friends . . ."

"So a lot of other people knew about it? A lot of other people were in on the act?"

"I suppose so. We—we *did* double-date a lot—we went to a lot of places together . . ."

"What kind of places?"

Amelia shook her head. Even in the dark Alec could see the glisten of tears.

"His apartment. His best friend's apartment. Once—after a football game in Baltimore—a hotel. A motel, really."

Alec gnawed his lip. He threw away his cigarette and lit another. He did not light another for Amelia.

"And you wanted to marry him?"

"I loved him very much—I thought at least I loved him very much. Also I thought I was—I thought I was pregnant. I told him." Amelia's voice came swiftly, tear-choked now. "I told him I was pregnant, I asked him if we could get married—he had a good job—and then he laughed. . . . He—he—"

"He *what?*"

"He laughed and asked me how I could be sure he was the father, that he knew I was sleeping around with half the fellows on the campus, and that—that anyhow he had no intention of marrying anybody."

"Son-of-a-bitch. Dirty son-of-a-bitch."

"I was going to kill myself. I bought a lot of pills. I thought about drowning myself. I was going to run the car over a cliff. I was going to cut my wrists. I"—then Amelia giggled, half-hysterically—"I couldn't make up my mind *how* I was going to kill myself, so I didn't kill myself for a little while and then—then I came around. I was all right again. Maybe I'd been pregnant, or maybe I just missed a month out of imagination or worry or something. Anyhow I wasn't pregnant and I was awfully glad I didn't kill myself."

"You ever see him again?"

"Yes. A few times."

"You—you let him touch you again? You . . . ?"

Amelia's voice was very low.

"Y-yes. I did. I couldn't seem to help it. But after the one other time it all seemed so awful and sordid and rotten. And then I met Jimmy."

"And immediately went to bed with Jimmy?"

"No. Not immediately. We had a lot of fun. He—Jimmy sort of erased some of the hurt from Harry. We went to football games and dances and movies and picnics and things and of course when he wanted to kiss me I let him. And—you know how it is—"

"Yes," Alec said savagely. "I certainly do know how it is."

"Well, when he wanted to I let him. I didn't love him but I liked him and when he wanted to, well, I let him. Because I liked him—and—you might as well know it," Amelia blurted now. "I liked *it*. I liked doing it. I *like* doing it. I would love doing it with you. But I don't suppose you want me any more now I've told you all this. Boys—boys don't like honesty in girls, I guess. They want to be fooled even if they know they're being fooled."

Alec lit another cigarette, and handed it to her. He patted her gently on the knee, drew her close, and kissed her on the flushed cheek. He could taste the salt.

"I love you, Amelia," he said. "I do love you, and I still— I want to marry you. I don't mind about the other one—the first one, really. That can happen to any girl. But it kind of hurts to think that my friend—that Jim would just sort of pass you on, like a—"

"A what?" Now Amelia's voice edged. "Pass me on like a *what?*"

Lamely, Alec said:

"Like a sort of meal ticket. A good thing. Free board and screwing. I didn't really mean that last crack—but it cheapens you, and it cheapens me."

Hardness chill-tempered Amelia's voice.

"Perhaps you haven't taken full advantage of the screwing privilege. But I haven't seen you turning down the free board."

"I deserved that, I guess." He put hurt in his mouth.

"No, you really didn't. I'm being a bitch. And I *have* sort of hurled myself at you. And the whole damned family has hurled me at you. Daddy'd have done anything to get rid of Timothy. He has some sort of built-in hatred for Catholics. Worse than the Jews. No, you've been truly wonderful, and I'm sorry I threw all this at you at once. But I love you, Alec. I really do love you—as a woman, not as a silly girl, and I think you ought to know all about me before we go any farther. Or let's just shake hands now and quit friends. At least you and I haven't any cause to be bitter about each other."

"I don't want to shake hands now and quit friends. I don't want to be bitter about each other. I want to go on loving you. I want to love you all my life. I don't really give a damn about the others." Alec laughed shortly. "I really don't know why people make such a fuss about purity in women and think it's smart for a fellow to sow his oats. I wouldn't call me any rose geranium if you want the truth."

Amelia held up her mouth softly to be kissed. She slid quickly out of the car and smoothed down her creased skirt, adjusted her rumpled blouse, slicked back the wild ends of her hair. Alec got out and put his arm around her as they walked up the flagged pathway.

"I'll talk to your father tomorrow night," he said slowly. "We'll be married sometime this fall—after we've gone to Chapel Hill for the dances—after I've got my next raise. Maybe even earlier if I can swing it. I'm glad you told me all the things you did, baby. I like knowing what I know *now*. I want us to start off everything neat; fresh, clean, but mostly, *neat*. I've had a lot of ugly disorder in my life."

Amelia turned and kissed him, pressing the whole length of her body close, as they stood on the darkened porch. Her lips still tasted brassy. Then she flicked on the light and unlocked the door.

"I didn't know there would ever be anybody like you," she said. "Good night—darling."

"Good night." Alec turned and walked swiftly, heels clacking on the flags, toward his car. His mouth tasted of aroused woman. His updrawn testicles ached. A strange sense of perverted exultation filled his head. He felt light and free and a little drunk. He felt like a *man*. He felt like an experienced man of the world—a man to whom bourgeois convention was nothing. He had flaunted convention. He was going to marry a soiled woman, but he himself would not soil her further.

He drew his car into the Hot Shoppe and went to a telephone booth.

"Hello," he said. "Harriet?" A sleepy voice muttered an answer.

"I'm sorry I woke you. But it's not very late, and I thought maybe—?"

Sleep had left the voice quickening on the other end of the line.

"Right. I'll pick you up in front of your place in ten minutes." A smile downcurved his lips. "Don't bother putting on too many clothes. You'll only be taking them off again."

He hung up, and again, felt his spirits soar. He was committing no sin against anyone. He was not being unfaithful. He was not betraying a trust. Suddenly he felt hungry. There would be just enough time for a barbecue sandwich and a beer before he collected Harriet, waiting trustfully in the shadows in front of her apartment. Damn that roommate. He'd have to smuggle Harriet into his own place, he supposed. There was too much reeking memory of Amelia's excited body left in the front seat of his car for any sort of extra-emotional comfort. And besides, he was terribly weary of front-seat sex.

45

The slight kiss of spring still quivered at Chapel Hill, although heavy-bodied June had come and school was out. Alec felt marvelous when he pulled up in front of the Delt house in his shiny car—he had stopped outside of town at a filling station and had flicked the dust from the paint while Amelia visited the ladies' room. He was wearing a new gabardine suit with a half-belted back and bellowsed sleeves (everybody was wearing gabardine that year) and locked in the rumble seat was a white-jacketed dinner suit, a plaid sports coat with complementing gray flannels, a blue blazer and a pair of white gabardine slacks. He had brought half a case of assorted liquors with him. He had money in his pocket, and the prettiest girl who would be at the prom got out from the seat beside him. She was wearing lime-green linen—she had taken her suitcase into the ladies' room and had changed swiftly from traveling sweater-and-skirt—and in her brown-and-white pumps with the toast-colored stockings on the long beautiful legs Amelia roused a covey of whistles from the creepered veranda of the fraternity house. Jimmy James set his glass down on a broad banister and lounged down the walk to greet him. He was as blond, as tall, as easy as ever.

"Hi, Mele. Got a kiss for a simple student of the law?"

Alec felt very strange as Jimmy James casually kissed Amelia Macmillan on the mouth—lightly, but still on the mouth. It was not jealousy, but a swift surge of possessiveness that caused him to slide one arm around Amelia's shoulders as he shook hands with Jimmy James.

"Hello, Jim," he said—and thought he said it coolly. He also thought he saw a swift darting look of comprehension in his former roommate's eyes. "It's nice to see you—nice to be back. Got any idea of where Amelia's staying? She'll want to take her things upstairs."

"I've stuck her in with Liz." Jimmy James smiled his big blond smile. "You haven't seen Liz yet. Another Pi Phi. I can't seem to break the habit." He picked up a suitcase which Alec had taken from the rumble seat. "I'll just chuck this inside, and the housemother'll square you away, Amelia. Liz is taking a bath or a nap or something. You'll recognize her by the"—he made a vast cupping gesture—"spectacular."

"Where am I?" Alec felt the old inferiority as Jimmy James tucked one hand under Amelia's elbow and steered her toward the door, carrying the suitcase with the free hand.

" 'Cross the street. Zeta Zips. Stan Roberts isn't staying on for the bloodletting. Very kindly gave up his room. On a clear day we can watch all the girls dressing from our window. Gimme a minute to settle our gal down."

They disappeared through the door, and Alec stood sourly on the curb, feeling left out and lonely despite his new clothes, his almost-new car, his cargo of whisky and the money hot in his pocket. There had been such an air of old proprietorship about Jimmy's immediate possession of Amelia. Alec heard the familiar voice shouting: "Missus Mac!" and then a murmur of female talk. Jim James came back out of the door, beaming.

"By God, it's good to see you, Author," he said. "And that Amelia gets prettier by the minute. I told you she was the girl for you, didn't I? And I was right, wasn't I? Come on, kid, let's dump the junk in Stan's room, and then we'll go down to our bar and have a snort. I tell you, son, I'm proud of you. You look rich—and well, sort of like you're about to be famous. Come on. Good whiskey waits for no man, and your gal says she wants to take a long time getting herself clean and gussied up."

Alec felt the earlier rese.tment melting. There was so much hearty, almost puppyish good fellowship about this big blond friend of his. It was difficult, as they sat moments later in the cool malt-smelling bar of the fraternity house—the bar in which he had spent so little time as a student, because of the abject poverty of his undergraduate condition and his overdeveloped pride—to recreate the self-torturing image of a naked Amelia twisting in the arms of a naked Jimmy; his friend Jimmy, who had given him Amelia in the first place. Given him Amelia, he thought with fleeting bitterness, as he might have left behind a pair of used golf-shoes or an old but cherished tennis racket.

But it was changing; it was certainly changing, and the thing that was changing it was he, himself, Alec Barr. The change came from the inside out; confidence glowed in him now like a pilot light. He looked at the handsome, debonair ex-roommate with the big allowance and the later good government job, with the gray coupé and the sharp clothes, and saw a student—an apprentice, still unfledged in a profession. That was it, exactly; Amelia had been briefly to bed with a college *boy*—she had not been to bed with a man.

Amelia's man was *here;* he had just opened a bottle of good Scotch whiskey from Washington, D.C., and was saying to his old rich roommate: "How much soda?" on the bar which had been made from the ancient country-store counter stolen from Carrboro—the bar with the mock-Doctor Seuss drawings of hungover dragons on the wall behind. He had a right to be in the bar now; he had his own whisky with him and his suit had not come from the Hecht Company. The suit had come from Lewis and Thomas Saltz on F Street in Washington, D.C., a town Alec Barr shared with Franklin D. Roosevelt.

"We want you to be the first to know," Alec said. "Amelia and I are going to get married later on this summer or in the early fall." He looked keenly at his friend's face, expecting he knew not what, and was almost disappointed to see only genuinely pleased astonishment. Somehow Alec had felt—almost hoped—that Jimmy James would be crushed by the announcement. Instead the happy extroverted face split in a broad grin, and a mighty slap on the back nearly dislocated Alec's spine. The expected triumph was stillborn.

"By God, that's really wonderful!" Jimmy James roared. "It couldn't happen to a couple of finer people! I demand only one thing, to be best man, because it's all my fault in the first place!" Yes, you cheerful son-of-a-bitch, Alec thought, it's nice all right. You spent my wedding night for me. But I got the girl. None of this "I may come back and marry her myself some day" shit that you were talking when you took us all out big-dealing to dinner. That last supper.

"Why sure, James," Alec said mildly. "Don't break my back or there won't be any wedding. I wouldn't consider anybody but you as best man." Did he accent the *best,* and was that a tiny frown on Jimmy's forehead? No. It was dark in the malt-smelling bar of the Delt House.

Jimmy James sounded serious now.

"You must be doing better than I thought if you're thinking marriage so soon. You couldn't ask for a finer girl—I *told* you that—but can you afford to get married on newspaper pay? I mean, Jesus, it's only been six months since you made staff on the *News*. Last I heard they fire everybody on the first of January, *every* first of January. That's a big step, marriage, and you're still awful young, son."

"I'm not too young to know what I want," Alec Barr said. "I'm not too young to know what I can do. And I'm not too young to know that if anybody gets fired it won't be me."

"You sound a little sore. What're you sore at? Surely you're not worried about anything that happened between Amelia and me, because nothing did. We just ran around and had a lot of fun."

"I'm not sore. And I'm not worried about anything that Amelia might have done before me. Nobody's perfect anyhow. I just want to get myself settled down so I can go to work. Not newspapers, not forever. I got some plans, Jimmy, and they won't work if I'm running around drinking up all the whiskey they serve the boys from the press to keep the boys from the press happy. I want some real action out of my typewriter."

Jimmy James got up and walked over to the bar. He turned, rested his palms flatly on its top, and hoisted himself easily to a sitting position. He looked directly at Alec Barr. He frowned, and scratched his ear.

"I wouldn't have believed it," he said. "I really wouldn't have believed it. I left a bewildered little boy in Washington and here, by God, we got a tough grown man. A real tough man—with one exception. I still think there's a bit of little-boy jealousness about Amelia and me. Forget it, son. I told you: *nothin'*. Nothin' at all."

"I never gave it a thought," Alec said. "You're the heavy." He flipped his empty glass suddenly at Jimmy James.

"Fix us another drink," he said. "My ass is achin' from the drive down, and in a minute I got to go get cleaned up so I can take *my* girl over to say hello to old Skipper Henry."

"Return of the prodigal, hey? Home with the bugles blowing? Damned good." Jimmy James slid off the bar and poured a stout three fingers into the glass. He was elaborate in the mixture of ice and soda. He handed the drink to Alec and said swiftly:

"Are you gonna be all right now that you've come back with your car and your girl and your new suit to tell 'em all to go to hell?"

Alec looked at him steadily.

"I was all right before I left," he said. "You just have to come back to know it. I won't come back again. If I need anything from down here I'll send for it."

46

The whole idea of marriage was perversely fascinating to Alec Barr—fascinating in its entire connotation of legal fornication, pride of possession, the position of ostentatiously appearing before the world, including Amelia's mother and father, with a sandwich-sign saying: "I am bedding with this high-class woman who is my wife and my whore." Having been raised in an atmosphere of furtive sex, the spread-legged-sprawling-sweaty voluptuousness of legal marriage had an appeal vastly more erotically exciting to the young Alec Barr than any number of shadowy doorway liaisons or rumble-seat romances. Alec Barr craved no beach-blanket bed; he wanted a double-mattressed-locked-door-bathroom-adjacent-towel-handy romance or he wanted no romance at all. Omar Khayyám did not figure in his marital plans; pine needles were apt to be scratchy.

There had perhaps been slight temptation that week end of dances at Chapel Hill. Hal Kemp had played a particularly brilliant set of dances, for Kemp too was returning in triumph to an Alma Mater. Kemp played two specialties which bore his special copyright, and which were guaranteed to melt the starch in the trousers of the most obdurate virgin. Both were sung by Skinnay Ennis: One was "Heart of Stone" and the other "I've Got a Date with an Angel." It was an era in which one listened rather than danced to the big name bands. One held one's ladylove closely and swayed in front of the bandstand. Dancing to Hal Kemp, with his special crew of Ennis, Maxine Grey, John Scott Trotter, Earl Geiger, and Saxy Dowell, would have been regarded as pure sacrilege—as sacrilegious as dancing while Glen Gray's Kenny Sargent sang "Under a Blanket of Blue" or hit the stratospheric falsetto on "For You."

The impoverished Thirties wallowed in tenderly realized *Weltschmerz*. Every Rogers-and-Astaire movie and every Crosby film spawned a clutch of enduring ballads, for the Gershwins, Arlens, Porters, Mercers, Burkes, Yagers, Yellens, and Van Heusens were writing the durable stuff that Sinatra would still be singing thirty years later. The name band occupied a position of positive godhead; Kemp, Artie Shaw, Ellington, Gray, Nichols, Weems, Lombardo, Ray Noble, the Dorseys were all conjurable names; high prophets, even, and Chicago's Blackhawk was the principal mosque for the broadcast wails of the muezzins. Female defenses crumbled before Al Bowlly's delivery of Noble's "The Very Thought of You," and anybody at all singing "Stormy Weather" or "Body and Soul" caused a distinct tautening of brassières as breaths expanded crisp young bosoms. It was the time of the crooner; the age of listening music, and calisthenics had not yet invaded the dance floor.

Alec Barr was abstractly conscious of the permanence of the evocative art form as he held Amelia by her tender flesh and swayed, stiffly starched in his white dinner jacket, pleasantly flushed by the drinks they gulped outside the Tin Can at intermission, headily elated by his reception by his old friend, Prof Henry, almost giddily proud of having dragged the prettiest girl on the dance floor. Boys, younger fraternity brothers and strangers alike, eagerly cut in on Amelia when they danced at all, so mostly they did not dance, but only swayed and listened.

The week end compounded all of the university life that Alec Barr had missed as a college man. All the triumphs for which he had yearned, all the little half-formed wantings, all the missed camaraderie, came flooding home for one week end during which Alec Barr was a kind of Joe College emeritus. There had been a piece written about the return of the native in the local weekly; Skipper Henry had devoted half a column of his "Grits and Chitlin's" to his successful protégé; even the Raleigh morning paper had carried a piece about the hometown boy who had made good with a byline in the big city. It was a time of meat and drink and milk and honey and roses and moonlight for Alec Barr, who was feeling a youth he had never experienced as a youth.

They had drunk steadily without getting drunk—milk punches in the morning as they pub-crawled from fraternity house to fraternity house; solid slaps of bourbon whiskey with old Skipper Henry, who beamed at Amelia and bragged to anyone who would listen how he had spotted Alec Barr's talent the moment he saw him with that pretty little Injun girl that run off and got married (Amelia looked inquiringly at Alec, who shrugged with an actor's insouciance). There were successions of straight shots as the night climbed higher and the boys produced flasks outside the gymnasium, the boys taking it neat out of the neck and girls downing their smaller portions from Dixie cups which also contained Coca-Cola. Clothes were changed frantically; a few of the girls got sick and had to have their heads held; a whore, imported as a joke by one of the more raffish brethren, became overwhelmed by the collegiate atmosphere, appointed herself housemother to the fresh young fowl from Peace and St. Mary's, and stoutly refused to sleep with her escort the whole week end.

The change of clothing produced a profound effect on Alec Barr, who had gone through the University on one shabby suit, a couple of pairs of slacks, and some elbow-darned sweaters. It was sheer animal luxury to dress modishly in sports jacket and flannels for the morning rounds, changing again for the tea dance to blue-flannel coat and white trousers, switching again after supper to white tuxedo jacket and black pants, with the starched front of the boiled shirt pleasantly harsh over a skin that glowed with soap from a third shower of the day, the coat snugging well to the shoulders and the glittering patent-leather pumps as light as kid gloves on the feet.

The plump bare shoulders of the girls flowered from their tulles and (occasionally) satins—Jimmy James' girl wore satin, and her creamy curves thrusting upward from the deep V of the bodice of the wine-red satin invoked the aspect of an ice-cream soda. The pervasive odor was of gardenia corsage and perfume and lightly sweating clean young woman, while the boys smelled skeptically of soap, astringently of shaving lotion, and ripely of whiskey. No one needed sleep —the fraternity-house lounges were fireflied by glowing cigarette ends until dawn, until someone decided to organize a swimming party at Sparrow's Pond and a later milk-punch breakfast. There literally was no time for fornication. Fornication was for weekdays—this was The Weekend.

Alec Barr would not have been able to explain, at the time, that he had searched for, and was finally discovering, the prim and proper romance for which he had hungered and thirsted in his threadbare shiny-seated student days. This was how the other people had always lived, and Amelia was a very vital portion to it. Alec's short romance and brief confused sexual experience with Fran Mayfield had been conducted on a budget basis; it had not included automobiles and whiskey and spending money and good clothes and easy conviviality with the more fortunate. Alec had remained the social ascetic to the end. He had been the non-greasy grind who had been fortunate enough to attract a handsome young woman of decidedly nymphic tendencies during his final few weeks of undergraduate life. Fran Mayfield had tossed scornful alms to a beggar.

It had been nothing at all like the soaring triumph, the exultation of *belonging*, that Alec Barr was now experiencing. His actual career as a college man had begun on Friday and would end of Sunday afternoon, when he started the long drive back to Washington, eyes beginning to itch from lack of sleep and the hangover from two days of steady drinking beginning to scratch at his nerves and dig into his stomach.

He had managed to preserve the illusion of undergraduate innocence even after the last dance on Saturday night—when, after hot pastrami sandwiches and beer at the Greek's, Jimmy James had suggested they take a jug and drive out to Sparrow's for a dip in the moonlight. It was assumed that the dip would be taken in the nude; at least, no coy question about bathing costume was advanced by either Amelia or Jimmy's lush Liz, whose conversation seemed largely limited to giggles.

The moon was bright, a vast pitcher spilling a huge pool of milk into Sparrow's pond. Cars were parked here and there; there were shouts and screams and giggles and splashes from the pond. Other people had evidently conceived the same idea; as they drove up, Alec's headlights caught the white blur of a female body cutting like a deer across his path.

Amelia and Liz retired to one end of the car for their disrobing. Alec and Jimmy shucked their clothes behind a tree. Both girls had brought towels, which they draped modestly over bosom and thigh until they reached the water's edge, and then Alec saw Amelia naked—stark in the gas-flare of moonlight—for the first time. He was acutely conscious of the jouncing of breasts, the dark triangle of pubic patch, and the vivid flash of thigh as the girls ran squealing into the water, but the nudity roused no sensuality in him. Eroticism roused naturally in the warm waters of the pond, when he swam close and took Amelia naked in his arms. She opened her legs while treading water and he placed himself carefully between her thighs from behind, cupping her breasts with both hands. She turned her head and kissed him briefly, then freed herself and swam away in a high-kicking flurry of moon-silvered water.

They dressed, shivering slightly, and had a drink out of the car-bottle before they drove back into town. The moon had died and the sun was pinkening the sky when they reached the fraternity house, and already a group had gathered on the porch for the early milk-punch session. It seemed silly to go to bed, and equally silly to remain in last night's evening dresses. The girls went upstairs to change to sweaters and skirts, but the boys remained on the porch, drinking and listening to the records, adolescently vain of their melted shirt fronts and lipsticked collars.

Alec and Amelia went later for an early brunch with Professor Henry. Jimmy and his pneumatic Liz had not been invited. Skipper Henry had asked, instead, some of his cronies from the faculty—Van Gelder of Philosophy and Maxwell of Archeology and Carson of Economics and Merriweather of Ancient History—shaggy, rumpled, baggy men all, with age-tufted eyebrows, thickets of nostril hair, and ragged salted mustaches. Amelia was the only girl present, and felt herself signally honored at the respect with which the older men, full professors, treated her young fiancé. The deference was difficult for Amelia to understand; Alec was, after all, only an apprentice reporter on the smallest paper in Washington, with nothing much more tangible to show for his efforts than a small byline which occasionally crept onto the front pages. Amelia knew Alec worked, worked hard, and she knew he wrote, but she was mystified as to why that should be considered so important by these stained, seamy old men who all bore the title of doctor.

"Will you go to the war?" was one of the first questions Skipper Henry asked Alec, as if he were inquiring as to whether he would like another tot of the sour-mash bourbon the old man served his guests.

"Not as a writer," Alec said. Amelia looked from one to the other in surprise. There *wasn't* any war to go to, except some sort of nonsense about the Chinese and the Japs on the other side of the world.

"I think you're right," Van Gelder, the philosophy professor, said. "It is much too big an experience to be estimated from outside. A war must be seen from within. It is not a spectacle for casual strangers to view from afar. War is more intimate than marriage."

Amelia said timidly:

"But there *isn't* any war. Pardon me, sir, but you talk as if there was one and America was already in it."

Old Skipper Henry smiled his turtle-lidded, hook-nosed smile.

"But of course there is a war," he said. "Our friend Van Gelder could explain it to you from a standpoint of absolutes and intangibles in the best Grecian confusion, but I won't ask him to. We have been at war since Hitler quit paintin' houses. It's just a matter of when we make the formal announcement."

"When do you think?" Alec asked. "The announcement, I mean?"

The old man shrugged.

"Not for two or three or five years. The madness of crowds ain't quite revved up to it yet. We're still in the extraordinary-delusion stage—listening to Peter the Hermit but not yet ready for a Crusade. When this one comes it'll be a big 'un. I'm only sorry I'm so old I'll have to miss it. But remember a thing, Alec: no writer can afford to miss a war. Particularly if he plans to write books. It's the most basic research."

"Henry tells me you're going to be married." This was Merriweather of Ancient History, turning to Amelia. Alec answered for her.

"It'll take a little more affording first, Dr. Merriweather. Amelia's just out of school—graduated the other day—and I'm still on my first leg up on the paper."

"It's a good thing, I think, marriage, for a writer," Dr. Merriweather said. "Steadies him. Nothing like a wife and a couple of kids to keep the old quill to the papyrus. Trouble with writers is they mostly never develop any steady habits

unless they load themselves with crass responsibility. And—
I'm sure my friend Henry will tell you the same—writing is
not a thing of adjustable mood. Nor is any creation, including art." He turned to Maxwell, the archeologist. "Would
you say the Greeks dabbled, Chick?"

"I would not," the archeologist said. "Any more than I'd
accuse the Egyptians of sloth when they were gluing the
Pyramids together. Manny a mickle maks' a muckle sort of
thing."

Alec felt vaguely uneasy—almost trapped. The clichés
flew thickly, and the burden of most was that there was nothing like the love of a good woman to settle a man into potency of production. What made him uneasiest was that most of
him yearned for the steadiness, the respectability, the quiet
order of matrimony, the eight-hour sleep and the regular,
uncomplicated sex, the good meals, the sobriety, the evenings around the fire, but the unquiet portion of him yearned
for this war they discussed so calmly—this unborn war
which would whisk him off and away from the very things
he craved.

The Weekend, he knew, was over. He had capsuled his
collegiate career from Friday afternoon to midday Sunday.
He felt Amelia tugging gently at his sleeve. The men were
talking all at once about the coming war, the Japs, the Germans, the English appeasers, and the frailties of the French.
Mr. Roosevelt and the New Deal had not once been mentioned, although the year was 1935.

"We'd better leave pretty soon," Amelia whispered. "I
told Mother we'd try to make it home before dark. You
know how she is; she'll save supper for us."

"I suppose," Alec said. "It's been a long week end, and I
owe the office a day."

They said good-by, and the old journalism professor
hugged Alec with a fatherly affection.

"I told you you were going to make it," he said. "You're
headed right. Come back and see us when you can."

"I will," Alec said. "I will, when I can." And he knew as
he said it that it was very likely he would never pass this
way again. Not even suddenly, he knew he had finally graduated from school.

47

They were married in October. Alec had received another raise—to thirty-five dollars a week, which made him affluent enough to quit his publicity work, and Amelia had found a sales job at Garfinckel's. Her twenty dollars a week made them mildly rich for the time—rich enough to afford a sixty-dollar-a-month apartment—and there was no need to buy much except basic furniture. It had been a full-dress wedding, and the family's friends had come down handsomely with presents. There had been five waffle irons, six electric toasters, and an assortment of other electrical hardware which, referred back to their shops of origin, provided ample capital for such homely necessities as extra lamps, ashtrays, and frying pans.

It was a more-than-adequate flat in a not-quite-fashionable neighborhood, far enough out from town to allow parking, hard by a supermarket, reasonably close to a neighborhood theater, and near enough the Maryland line to allow the purchase of a drink on a dry-District-of-Columbia Sunday. It was furnished tastefully—Amelia had devoted most of the summer haunting sales, "antiquing," she called it—and had even provided a quiet corner for Alec to describe as a study. The corner contained a cheap yellow-pine desk, a dictionary, a thesaurus, a reconditioned Underwood standard typewriter, and a stack of red-penciled magazines. Alec was attempting to memorize the form of a salable article and short story, and was finding the process difficult if not impossible.

Both the wedding and the honeymoon had been unspectacular. They had gone to Atlantic City for a week—they originally had planned two weeks—but a staff crisis on the chronically shorthanded newspaper had recalled Alec to harness, and he was almost glad to return. There had been no trouble about nuptial sex; they had gone easily and naturally to bed, with an alarming lack of rapturous expectation on both sides, and had functioned competently with a minimum of embarrassment.

Perhaps Alec had exhausted his expectation with the first tremulous kiss. Perhaps Alec had imagined a galaxy of shooting stars and the sound of cannon fire. He received instead an almost bovine acceptance of his thrusting internal presence. Her motions were skillful and a bit, it seemed to Alec, too practiced for a bride, even an informally deflowered bride. But she was eager and loving and willing, and not at all coy about the mechanics of rearousing his abated desire. They had decided to have no immediate family; Amelia had been fitted for a diaphragm before the ceremony, and she wore it nightly as a matter of routine. The surfeit of sex stopped when she reported a minor bridal ailment, a vaginal trichomoniasis, and Alec was ashamed to be relieved. What did not relieve him, however, was the fact that his thoughts occasionally flitted to the animalistic Harriet, whose faculty for excitement far exceeded, in retrospect, Amelia's peaches-and-cream quiescence, however hearty in practice and lubricious in performance.

They settled into early uxorious boredom. Monday night was now inflexibly devoted to supper with the family, and Alec developed an active case of acute, if psychosomatic, indigestion at the idea of a lifetime of meals which had been switched from Sunday midday dinner to Monday seven-sharp supper. This life would contain the simple components so far missing from Sunday dinner. Eternity would consist of pork chops, breaded veal cutlets, lamb stew, meatloaf, spaghetti and meatballs, macaroni and cheese, fried chicken and fried ham, hash from Sunday's beef, corned-beef hash with an egg atop, and endless oceans of spinach, wax beans, and sheared corn kernels. For dessert, there was Brown Betty and occasionally tapioca pudding.

The rigidity of the Monday rendezvous frustrated Alec and was the cause of their first real squabble.

"Why the hell does it always have to be *Monday* night?" Alec was finally furious. "I love your folks—you know that —but why can't we come on Tuesday or on Wednesday or maybe skip a week and not come at all? Why have I got to look forward to nothing but a lifetime of Monday night suppers and Lowell Thomas? Why the hell do we have to live by routine—*their* routine?"

"Don't get yourself in an uproar," Amelia said with maddening calm. "It's an easy night for them. Daddy has his club meetings and such on Tuesday and Thursday and Mom has her church thing on Wednesday and some sort of circle on Friday and I know you like to keep the week ends free so what the hell is so wrong about Monday if we have to see the family *some* time? You have to admit that they're wonderful about not dropping in or meddling with our lives and you also have to admit that we never leave there without a basket of something from Pop's garden or a few jars of something from Mom's canning. Also it's a meal *I* don't have to cook. It's a meal we don't have to buy, either."

Alec could find no answer, but the resentment mounted illogically until he began to experience heartburn even before he sat down at the sparkling table and listened to a steady recitation of doings in the Church, the Shrine, the Optimists, the Church again, the real estate business, the insurance business, and the Parent-Teacher Association, interlarded with country-club gossip and the condemnation of Catholics in direct relationship to the carryings-on of "that Jew, Rosenfeld" in the White House. Occasionally he would volunteer for an evening assignment if it fell on a Monday but the ruse wore thin. Amelia invariably saw through the excuse and was either noisily angry or tearfully hurt.

The other plodding aspect of routine was equally galling to Alec although he himself realized the unreasonableness of his attitude. Amelia finished work at 6 P.M.; it was Alec's domestic assignment, come flood or famine, to collect her on the corner at six-ten. The stated time of ten past six graved itself on his brain. It pimpled into a kindred pustule with Monday-night supper at his parents-in-law's home. No matter where he was, no matter what he was doing in line of duty, the red-flashed warning at *6:10* would begin to blink, on and off, like an annoying beacon on a dwindling gasoline tank, and he was incorrigibly uneasy until he saw Amelia's tapping foot on the corner, observed the swift impatient look at her wrist watch as he pulled out of the traffic line and into the curb. On a few occasions he was unavoidably late; a puncture once, a traffic jam on the Baltimore turnpike another time, and Amelia was coldly furious. She stood on her feet all day, she said, and the least he could do——

But mainly, there was an even pleasant boring tenor to their lives. Living was cheap. A five-dollar bill bought two heaping bagsful of groceries, with a carton of Chesterfields sticking out of the top of one bag and a quart of $1.69 Golden Wedding poking its head out of the other. Both were exhausted at the end of the day—Alec, because he had risen at five-thirty, and was lucky if he could fold in a nap before meeting Amelia (fires and kindred catastrophes always seemed to develop about closing time for the day shift) and Amelia because she was on her feet from nine to six, selling whatever it was she sold as the store revolved her from one department to another. Quite often they stopped at a cheap restaurant or tearoom on the way home for an early unwanted meal. More frequently Amelia would open a can of spaghetti and toss a couple of meatballs into the skillet. They rarely drank during the week, but saved the festivity for Saturday night and Sunday morning. Mostly the gang came round to their apartment, and it was a tacit rule that the gang would bring its own booze. None of Amelia's college contemporaries had married yet, and the Barrs' marital status placed them admirably as candidate for casual chaperonage, especially on such week ends as they contrived to borrow the family's beach house. The beach house descended rapidly in status to house of assignation for their mutual friends, with Alec and Amelia bearing the madam's stamp of respectability.

Meals improved at the Barr apartment when Amelia (who cheerfully contributed her weekly paycheck to the common fund) suggested brightly that seeing as how Alec generally had a lot of free time at midday or in latish afternoon, it would be real nice if he did the shopping. Without knowing exactly how he slid into the routine, Alec found himself prowling the supermarkets and butcher shops with a shopping bag. He did, indeed, get to know the butcher and greengrocers well and was rewarded with superior cuts of meat at inferior prices. He fell then into the habit of actually preparing the meal in the waste space of an afternoon— trimming the steak, washing and chilling the salad ingredients, frying the chicken and laying the table. It seemed easier than before. All they had to do was come home, allow Amelia to kick off her shoes, and supper was ready except for the final fire under the meat. Everyone said that Alec Barr was the most considerate husband they ever heard of.

After the first year of marriage they began the habit of the one drink before the evening meal. Alec had been raised to

fifty dollars and they had moved to a large apartment on
Wisconsin Avenue. They had no cook but a maid came five
times a week to wash and dust and superficially clean for a
couple of hours a day. The one drink drifted into two drinks,
and then proceeded normally to a nightcap, and then to a
prenightcap, and finally into a ritual as they sat quietly
after supper, each going silently about his own business.
Alec's business was writing magazine pieces that stubbornly refused to sell; Amelia's business was the clipping and
filing of any and all magazine articles dealing with interior
decoration, architecture, furnishing, or fabrics. She had succeeded to a steady job as saleswoman in the furniture department, and had her eye firmly fixed on an eventual career
in interior decoration. By 10 P.M. yawns collapsed Alec,
and he went dazedly to bed. The disparate hours of arisal
vexed them both; Alec was up and gone in the black dawn, in
order to be at the office by six for the preparation of the
first city edition; Amelia was able to sleep until seven-thirty
and still easily make the store by a quarter to nine.

Their sex life had deteriorated almost immediately, much
to Amelia's annoyance at the omission, and Alec's annoyance at her importuning insistence on an uninspired activity.
Alec was deadly tired at the end of a day. His brain bulged
with fires and murders and rapes and trials and the vagaries
of crackpots, left over from the office, and from the monotonous futility of trying to write, by night, magazine articles
and short stories that nobody would buy. Amelia, healthy
and ebulliently resilient as any farmgirl, recovered her spirits and revived her libido as soon as her feet stopped hurting. At ten Amelia was ready for the exotic aspects of bed,
and Alec, with a gaping yawn, was suddenly asleep before
she could insert the pessary.

Tragically, Alec would awake in the early morning with
a replenished carcass and a stout erection, his body yearning toward the fragrant presence of Amelia as she lay curled
in her nest at his side. But then the coin reversed, and Alec's
attempts at arousing interest in early-morning sex evoked a
sleepy snarl and a grunt from Amelia, with her back rigidly
presented as a bastion and her breasts firmly flattened to the
mattress, aloof from his seeking hands. After a few feeble
attempts at early-morning indoctrination, Alec gave up and
submerged his woken lust in batting out a rough three thou-

sand words of pre-first-edition copy, his earlier desires quenched by a quart of cardboard-contained coffee.

Their incompatibility of hours finally became a grim joke.

"Saturday looms," Alec would say, mock-brightly. "F-Day. Tomorrow is All-Fucks Day. Sunday is F-Day too. Five days shalt thou labor and on the sixth and seventh thou shalt screw, unless the lady has the curse or is sore at the husband for having been out too late covering—"

"Harriet?" Amelia said one day, eyes slitted accusingly. "Covering Harriet?"

"Harriet? What Harriet?" Alec managed not to gasp, but his face made him a miserably poor actor. Amelia's eyes nailed him to the wall, a butterfly pinned to the board.

This Harriet." She waved a piece of paper at him. "This very same Harriet who wrote you the note and said: 'Are you mad at me? Why don't you ever call me any more? I know you're married, but you're not dead, and neither am I. You can't have forgotten so soon. Let me hear. Love much —Harriet.' " Amelia almost spat. *"That* Harriet, and lying won't get you out of it."

Alec shrugged hopelessly. He had forgotten that damned note. It had reached him at the office, and he had stupidly crammed it in his pocket with a sheaf of other notes, meaning to destroy it later. But something had come up—a three-alarm fire or a nude body stuffed in a culvert or something equally diverting—and he had forgotten all about it.

Amelia was saying: "And don't try to wiggle out of it by accusing me of going through your pockets. I wasn't looking for anything. I was just turning out a suit for the cleaner and this was in the pocket. Now just who the hell is this Harriet? Have you been seeing her since we got married? Were you sleeping with her before we got married? Is that why you were so goddam noble about not screwing me?"

Now Amelia burst into tears. Alec patted her awkwardly. Tears defeated him. Always, instead of arousing pity or remorse, female tears irritated, even actively angered him. His mind raced.

"Now, Sweetie, there's nothing to cry about. I haven't seen the damned woman since a long time before we were married. She's just a girl I knew—and I did go to bed with her a couple of times. But that was a long time ago—while you were still dating Jimmy. She lived in the same rooming-house, and she was lonesome too."

Amelia stopped weeping abruptly.

"Was she pretty?"

Alec heaved a mental sigh of relief.

"No. She was ugly as a homemade sin. But she had very hot pants, and she was real handy. She didn't know anybody in Washington—she comes from some tank town in Indiana—and I didn't have any money to go out on or know anybody very much either. We fell into bed out of sheer loneliness and boredom—and, I suppose you could say, desperation. But there was nothing more to it than casual."

Amelia's face had cleared, but her voice sharpened angrily.

"Maybe for you it was nothing more than casual. But this note"—she snapped the paper between her fingers—"this letter tells me it was a good deal more than casual for *her*. You're going to do something right now about this woman, Alec. You're going to pick up that phone and call her up and tell her that I know all about her and I'm going to be listening to you when you say it."

"Oh, for Christ's sake, Mele, that's not necessary. There's no sense making a mountain out of a molehill. Harriet's gone and forgotten. She was probably still lonely, and maybe a little drunk, when she wrote that silly note."

"You'll call her or I'm leaving you," Amelia said flatly. "You'll call right now."

"I am not going to like you too much for making a point out of this. I'll do it, but I won't like it. If I didn't love you—and if I didn't want to keep you, and didn't want to make a row out of something silly—I think I'd tell you to go straight to hell."

"Just you call her. That's all. Just you call her. Have you her number written down?"

"If I had I threw it away a long time ago. Maybe she's in the book."

"The book won't be necessary," Amelia said. "I didn't read you the P.S., although I expect you remember well enough. In case it's slipped your mind, it's this:" Amelia made her voice mince sarcastically. "I've finally gotten a little apartment of my own out on Georgia Avenue, the number is 1908. New phone, too: Decatur 7763. Please ring me when you have a moment. I'm usually home by five."

"Now isn't that sweet," Amelia said. "She's usually home by five. Well, you've got time now, buddy. Ring her."

Alec bit his lip and reached for the phone.

It needed only two rings before the answer.

"Hello, Harriet? Alec Barr. No, it's *not* my wonderful idea to call you." Alec made his voice brutal. "It's Amelia's wonderful idea. She's here now. She came across that note you wrote me. I *know*. I'm sorry too. I just want to say that I won't be seeing you, and please don't write me or call me any more. Sorry—" Amelia snatched the phone out of his hand. Her voice rose to a fishwife screech: "And keep your goddam hands off my husband, you whore!"

"That was very pretty," Alec said. "So ladylike and refined. Well, satisfied?"

Amelia turned her back and walked into the bedroom. Alec went over to a side table, picked up the car keys, and went into the bedroom for his coat. Amelia was lying belly-down on the bed, her face buried in a pillow. Alec put on his coat, and said:

"See you after a while."

Amelia raised a tear-flushed face. Her voice was still harsh. "Where are you going?"

"Out," Alec Barr said, and slammed the door. Ten minutes later he pulled up in front of a red-brick apartment house which bore a brass plaque numbered 1908. He went into the lobby and looked for a phone booth.

"Harriet?" he said. "This is Alec again. I hope you understand I had a gun in my back. No, I'm *not* home. I'm downstairs in the lobby. No—I don't think I'd better come up. Your phone's sure to start ringing. The car's out front. You come down and we'll go find a motel. Fine—two minutes it is."

Alec Barr was still coldly angry as he waited. He was angry at himself for the lies he had told, and he was angrier at Amelia for making it necessary for him to tell the lies. But basically he was furious at Amelia for forcing him to telephone Harriet, like a naughty boy being made to apologize for rudeness in front of the entire class.

"Okay," Alec Barr said half-aloud, as he waited for Harriet to come down. "If she thinks I'm cheating, I might as well be hung for a sheep. So she gets home at five, does she? Well, from now on I'll have something better to do with my afternoons than hang around a frigging supermarket shopping supper for Mummy Dear."

Harriet was coming out now, trim tight backside switching in her compressed nymphomaniac's walk. She looked just great, Alec thought—wide red slash of hungry mouth that hid the flickering, pointed tongue; small tiptilted breasts, deep unsatisfied dark eyes.

She slid into the car, and Alec put a hand briefly on her inner thigh. She immediately relaxed her legs, opening them to his touch, and her breath hissed as she exhaled.

"It's been much too long," she said in a thick voice.

"Yes," Alec Barr said, pulling away from the curb and heading for Maryland. "It's been very much, entirely too much, much much too long."

48

Amelia Macmillan Barr sometimes looked at this strange man, her husband, with great wonder and amazement. She did not understand Alec; her parents certainly did not understand Alec. She loved him, and her parents were fond of him; of that she was entirely sure. But even at the age of twenty-four, a year after their marriage, he had been an indrawn, secretive person, chary with confidence, wary of intimacy. The change from the shy, uncertain boy she had met and fallen in love with—the frightened boy whose lips had trembled when he first kissed her—had been replaced by a rather frightening young man. If inside himself Alec was really a mass of troubled complexes, outwardly he was very much the self-possessed career man on his swift way up.

He had leaped ahead on the newspaper. It was a volatile journal—twice a year its editor took the paper by the heels and shook it, with the result that yesterday's news editor suddenly found himself on the sports desk, while the drama critic became city editor and the city editor was shunted off to Capitol Hill. Out of each upheaval, Alec Barr emerged in an ever stronger position.

At twenty-four he was the paper's top reporter. He had learned to cover anything, and was highly valued as a swing man if the District Building boy took drunk or the White House man decided on an unscheduled vacation with a blonde. In addition, Alec wrote a brief daily column of notes and comment which found favor with the town, particularly with the government workers. Alec called the column "Uncle Sam's Stepchildren," and circulation soared as one saw the *News* opened to page three by the side of every cafeteria tray in Washington's Federal compound.

At twenty-four, Alec Barr was making the unprecedented sum of seventy-five dollars a week—twenty-five dollars more than the city editor. Seventy-five a week was riches, and added to the twenty-five dollars Amelia was now earning, it put them in the Buick-and-Cape-Cod class. That was what everybody was building, and that was what they built —a neat white-brick Cape Codder with a screened side porch, wall-to-wall carpeting, one bedroom converted into a workroom for them both, a playroom with bar in the basement, two fireplaces and a quarter-acre of maple-shaded land in one of the less expensive suburbs of Maryland. The garage was two-car, and the mortgage was computed in both first and second phases. The status-symbol Buick, light blue, stood in front of the small, neat-clipped lawn, and a brass knocker gleamed against the white front door.

Alec was laboring at the short stories and the articles which almost but never quite came off. The rejection slips were tempered with praise, but always interlarded with *buts* and *ifs* and *try it agains*.

Finally—after having attempted a piece which bore the "Uncle Sam's Stepchildren" title of his column in an effort to describe the loneliness and isolation of the immigrants from the provinces who had come to seek federal employment under the New Deal's mushrooming but limited-budget temporary agencies, Alec received a letter from one of the subeditors of *Collier's* magazine. Its tone was friendly.

Dear Mr. Barr:
I have been watching with interest the general improvement in the stuff you have been sending us, and, indeed, I have twice suggested that we buy the pieces, but have been overruled because my seniors feel that you haven't mastered completely the techniques of either short fiction or the article field. There is, as you must know if you are as perceptive as your copy indicates, an almost cliché form for material which is generally acceptable to slick-paper publications. You have been battling in the dark.

If you can steal a day—week ends would be all right, because I live in Manhattan—and come to see me in New York, I think I can straighten you out. My interest is purely selfish. It is no secret here on Collier's *that I am leaving the magazine to enter the literary agency business. I am not starting cold; a great many good writers whose work I have edited are coming into my stable. But they are mostly all established pros, of largely restricted fields, and frankly I must build for the future with new talent and new material.*

I am interested in the kind of man you might be, and in what we might be able to do together. You know the office telephone; my home phone is listed under the Christopher Street address. I hope to have the pleasure of meeting you soon—and be sure to bring the manuscript of "Uncle Sam's Stepchildren" with you. I think I can show you at first hand in a very short time what you have been doing wrong.

    All very best,
    Marc Mantell

Alec showed the letter to Amelia with great excitement. She did not share the excitement.

"There's got to be a catch in it somewhere," she said. "What does an agent get out of a writer? And if he's willing —and so able—to teach you how to write so it will sell, why doesn't he just keep his mouth shut and sell stuff for himself? I bet he'll steal your ideas, and that'll be the last you'll hear from this Mr. Marc Whatisit."

"Oh, for Christ's sake, Mele," Alec said. "You'd throw cold water on a miracle. Can't you understand that this may be just the break I'm waiting for? Can't you understand that there are real professional tricks in this business and that nobody's offered to show me any until now? Can't you—"

"I understand that you're making very good money on the paper, and that you're so tired when you come home you're half dead. I understand that tired as you are, you still sit up writing things nobody wants to buy until you can hardly find the bedroom. I understand that any time we go to bed *together* is the signal practically for a national celebration. And I think this Mr. Mantell, or whatever his name is, is a phony or he wouldn't be out beating the bushes for unknown writers. If he was going to be a good agent the writers would be knocking on *his* door."

"Well," Alec said bitterly, "having taken most of the enthusiastic wind out of my sails, do you want to come to New York with me or not? We can afford a week end. I can get a due-bill from the advertising department for a hotel, and we can drive up. It won't cost a fortune and the change will do us both good."

"Oh, I'd like to come, all right. I'll be glad to get out of this town for a little while. Do you know, we haven't been *anywhere* since the honeymoon? And I haven't been in New York in five years."

"I haven't ever been in New York, strange as that sounds," Alec said. "I'm looking forward to it very much."

"At least we can see a show and go to a night club," Amelia said. "You used to take me out a lot before you started writing the Great American Novel five nights a week. Now we never even go to a movie—you're too tired."

"Oh, come off it, Mele," Alec said, kissing her on the back of the neck. She shrugged irritably. "One day I'll hit, and when I hit I'll quit this goddam newspapering, work only two hours a day, and we can get drunk every night. *And* live in New York. That's the next stop. It's where the big money grows."

"I like it here—here in this town, in this house. Or would, if I had a husband I saw once in a while when he wasn't buried in a book or pounding at a typewriter. New York's too big, money or not."

"So far as I'm concerned," Alec Barr said, "nothing is too big. It's just a matter of learning how high to jump."

49

Marc Mantell's quarters were not impressive. Alec did not respond enthusiastically to Greenwich Village; he found the sleazy, littered streets, the starved mangy prowling cats, the sodden doorway bums and the unbarbered bohemians in Washington Square depressing. Alec had somehow formed the idea that everyone in New York dwelt in a penthouse; he was vaguely disappointed to find that Mantell lived in a high-ceilinged studio apartment on the ground floor, with a tiny garden behind. The huge room was almost bare of ornament except for some bold modern paintings on the wall, a gleaming Steinway grand piano, and some basic bachelor furniture of tufted black leather. There was, however, an alcove which contained a vast desk stacked high with manuscript. The walls were bright with hundreds of books, and the functional fireplace was enormous. A door evidently led to bedroom, bath, and possibly kitchen.

Alec had left Amelia at the hotel. She was going shopping, and Marc Mantell had suggested that Alec first come down to the Village, and then they might go uptown for lunch. Mantell had suggested 11 A.M., and Alec made a double point of promptness. It was a bright sunny Saturday in November, with a cidery nip in the air, and Alec was quite comfortable without topcoat.

"Don't you sign anything," Amelia had said as he left the hotel. "Don't you dare sign anything!"

If Alec found Marc Mantell's living quarters a bit disappointing, he found the man himself somewhat more than rewarding. Marc Mantell was in his early forties. His hair had gone bone-white, except for heavy black eyebrows. He was lean to the point of emaciation, and his features were sharp as a blade. He had piercing black eyes behind massively rimmed spectacles, and the net effect of his face was of a modern painting of the cubist school—straight slash for nose, transverse slash for mouth; cheeks, jawline, and forehead cut square and sharp in a series of angled planes. He was wearing, this morning, an old cardigan over a flannel shirt, with corduroy trousers and plaited sandals. Suddenly Alec felt overdressed in his best Sunday serge.

"Come in, come in," Marc Mantell said. "Don't worry about my work clothes," he said, and a smile eased the angles of his harsh-cut face. "I'll put on some proper duds before I expose you to food in public places. Would you like a drink now?"

"Thanks, no," Alec said. "I don't use it much in the daytime."

"Well, I live off coffee, and I've just brewed a fresh pot."

"That I'd like," Alec said. "Thank you very much."

Mantell, moving with easy grace, poured the coffee, nudged a cigarette box in Alec's direction, and sat facing him with his arms crossed over his chest. Looking upward under the heavy

brows, through the heavy glasses, he resembled a hungry
hawk.

"You brought that piece I mentioned—the 'Stepchildren'
one?"

"Of course. Here." Alec handed him a large manila envelope.

"Good. I'm going to show you some tricks with a pencil—
carve up your story a bit, after I've drawn you a graph of
what a magazine piece is supposed to look like. It has just as
much of an architectural form as a building or any other
precise structure. It's what editors buy—and unless you're
Hemingway or Faulkner it's the *only* kind of piece they'll
buy. Short-story form is different, but we'll get into that later.
Actually this particular piece would be a better short story
than article, but since you've written it as an article we'll
dissect it as nonfiction."

Marc Mantell went over to his desk and came back with a
soft black pencil and a pad of notepaper. He sketched rapidly,
drawing a series of triangles, squares, rectangles, and thick
oblongs, studded with circles and crosses and checkmarks.
The finished sketch looked rather like two spangled Christmas
trees attached to each other by their bases.

"This is the anatomy of a magazine article—say, of the
approximate length of yours, five thousand words. The top
square is your opening anecdote; it's supposed to set the
scene and the mood and be most indicative of the character
of the piece, whether the piece is about a person or a
thing. The bottom square is a matching anecdote; it complements your opening, and gets you out of the piece in the same
mood. I'll show you in a minute what I mean.

"Now this next, this thin, upended rectangle that I've
crosshatched, is your customer-grabber. It comes in just behind your opening anecdote, and is your sales pitch to the
reader. Here is where you seize the son-of-a-bitch by the
lapels and rub his nose in your story. Here is where you demand that he read the piece; here is your personal guarantee
of why he must waste an hour reading the piece. The sentences should be short, punchy, and indisputably true."

"I think I got it," Alec said. "Let's just see if I have. I
write an anecdote about, say, me—how I came to Washington, flat-busted, no credit, couldn't get a job, haunted the
papers, wound up selling apples, considered suicide, but one
day I helped a kind old lady out of the gutter and she

turned out to be the sole owner of the Washington *Star*. That's the anecdote.

"Then I switch to the justification. It reads something like: 'Today, five years later, Alec Barr is editor-in-chief of the *Star*, just won a Pulitzer Prize, married the President's daughter, raises blooded race horses, has a blonde mistress, and two billion dollars in the bank.' Then I suppose, having grabbed the reader, sold him my net worth, I go on to tell how all this came about?"

"You've got it, kid. What you do then is expand, first, your reader-grabber, at considerably more length. This is written in time the present, and describes what you actually do—what you actually did—to arrive at your present vulgar condition of affluence. That's this big fat rectangle. The circles in this thing are anecdotes—illustrative anecdotes. The crosses are factual substantiations. Every time you make a flat statement, you've got to bolster it with either a short anecdote or at least a statistic. If you say a man's a good horse trainer, you have to come in behind with the statement that his nags had ten firsts, twenty seconds, and thirty thirds out of sixty-five starts last year—like that. Fact or fiction, your reader's got to *believe* you."

Alec was excited. His mind went back to stories over which he had slaved, becoming more and more confused, and he could see exactly where form had eluded him and the story had sagged out of shape. He had been attempting to adapt the what-where-when technique of newspapers to a different medium, and had succeeded in creating a sad picture of his own—a heavy-headed monster dwindling down to a thin tail-tip. He had always owned the flesh, but he had surely lacked the bones.

"I'm with you, Mister Mantell," he said. "Please go on."

An hour later Alec Barr took his rejected piece.

"May I have your pencil, please?" he asked. "And excuse me for five minutes?"

"Sure. I'll go put on some street clothes," Marc Mantell said. "Take your time."

Alec went over to the light in the working alcove and started carving up his article. He circled and slashed and drew arrows and moved certain paragraphs forward, other paragraphs back. He marked certain sections REWRITE and chopped chunks out of others. He scribbled a hasty opening anecdote from an incident he suddenly remembered, and moved a segment from the middle down to the end of the article. He had just finished when Marc Mantell appeared again, attired splendidly in the uniform with which Alec forever after identified him; cross-barred shirt, white hard collar, pale satin necktie, and severe suit of bankerish gray. Elegance cloaked him, and he radiated sincerity. Alec now felt shabby by comparison. His Sunday serge had developed a shine.

"Here," Alec said, handing him the article. "It's rough, but I think I've just fixed the piece. All it'll need to conform to your terms is one smooth rewrite—I think."

Marc Mantell took the article, sat down, and flipped the pages rapidly, nodding his head. He slapped the manuscript on a table, and nodded.

"You've got it, all right. I'll guarantee a sale. If not to us, certainly to one of the other slick magazines. Don't ever forget that little graph I drew you. It's the signpost to success. And I've got another one for when you tackle fiction. Now, I'd say let's go uptown and eat some fine rich food and we can continue our talk on a little less technical plane."

"May I have the graph you drew, and will you sign it?" Alec asked as they rose.

"Sure. What are you going to do with it?"

"Frame it," said Alec Barr.

Book III/Barbara

50

They were sitting now, nearly fifteen years later, in Marc Mantell's private corner in the English Grill, which Marc Mantell used as an extension to his Rockefeller Plaza offices. Marc Mantell now was regarded as one of the last of the classic agents; not a peddler of flesh in the Hollywood sense, not a once-over-lightly quick-sale vendor but a man who prized his own reputation as an agent equally with the reputations of his writers. When the manuscript went out from the office in the tawny fiber folder with the deep-cut green letters MARC MANTELL, you could be sure there were no typographical errors in the offering. You could also be sure that it had been read keenly by Marc Mantell and had found his basic approval. Else it would not have been offered for sale.

Editors did not resist Marc Mantell. Rather, they invited him. Marc Mantell had been a good editor, both for a syndicate and a magazine, before he went into the agency business. He looked more like a lawyer than the popular concept of a man whose life was bound to theater and moving picture and publishing house. And indeed his contracts, finally approved, contained a lawyer's tight protection. The various executives who paid his clients an average five million dollars a year for their goods and services complained about his toughness, but they complained with wry humor, for Marc Mantell refused to ride a present popularity by allowing a follow-up sale of shoddy product. A handshake with Marc Mantell was regarded as better than another man's contract, and he had probably made, in the last fifteen years, at least fifty million dollars' worth of deals over the long-distance telephone.

Moreover, as he sat now, tall, frosty, white-haired, hawk-faced, white-mustached, austere in his unchanged uniform of banker's gray with the hard white collar on the cross-barred shirt. he represented Alec Barr's aching conscience.

"The last batch of stuff you sent me from the new book was but awful," Marc Mantell said. "It sounded like you were writing it for one of the women's magazines. You always had discipline. I passed the last magazine stuff against my better judgment: here, here's a note from Carl Hendricks."

Alec took the note and read. It was from the editor of one of the most important mass-circulation magazines.

Dear Marc [the note said,] *I'm sorry to have to kick back the last Barr serial. I thought he'd catch it on the re-do but I'm surprised at you for letting this effort out of the house. We love Alec, and we love you, here at* Globe, *but this isn't up to Barr standards, and certainly not up to Mantell agency standards. What the hell's happened to Barr, anyhow? Menopause, love, or has he taken to the bottle? Tell him to run it through again, and I suggest you remind him that we are a sophisticated magazine here. He is not writing a happy-ever-after for* Woman's Weekly. *Give my best to Alec, and let's have a long drunk lunch one of these days.*
Best,

    Carl

Alec looked up and shrugged.

"I guess I can't win 'em all," he said. "One says I'm too far out. The other says I'm writing for the housewife. I can't write any better than I can write, or I'd do it. It's the same writer that they've been buying for a great many years, Marc."

Marc Mantell's deep-set shiny black eyes slitted behind his glasses. He was wearing his hungry-hawk look.

"You're young, pal," Marc Mantell said. "I'm shoving hard

on the sixties, and you're not even forty yet. You got a lot of writing in you. But the word's getting around that you've slipped. You know that cover *Time* was planning to coincide with the new book? I got another letter here, from the *Time* boys." He fumbled again in his brief case.

Alec held up his hand.

"I don't want to see it," he said. "I know what's in it." He made his voice mince. " 'We have decided to shelve the Barr cover until we see how the next book is received. We thought he had a permanent status; lately his magazine stuff seems to have slipped, and we hear talk that he's having an awful time with the new novel. We'll wait until we see the galleys before we reschedule the cover piece.' That about it?"

"That *is* it," Marc Mantell said. "Give or take a word or two, that's it."

"So? Now I'm ready for the fatherly advice. Tell me, Maestro. For my own good."

"Look, chum. We've been together since you were a wet-eared reporter writing hopeful magazine pieces that wouldn't sell. You're one of the few that's got it, and should keep it. I don't want you to lose it. Quit this adolescent nonsense that's making all the cheap columns. You're not some stupid Broadway playboy, for Christ's sake. You're Alec Barr."

"What the hell, Marc. I haven't really been so very bad. Sure, I left Amelia. Sure, I've been going out with another girl. Sure, I've been seen in public a lot. I guess I have made quite a lot of the garbage columns. But Jesus, Father, I'm a man. I'm not a goddamned machine. I'm having a little fun. I'm entitled to some fun."

"You're wrong, friend. You're *not* having fun. You're just kidding yourself. You're running around like a bloody sophomore sniffing after his first piece of tail. You're trying to drink all the booze in New York, and you're screwing yourself silly. And you're spending money. *Here*." He reached into his brief case again. "Here's the last quarterly account, chum. I pay the bills you sign. You're living like the Aga Khan. And, as they say, everything's going out and precious little's coming in. I'm beginning to get some chits back from Amelia for Europe, too, kid. She ain't economizing. She's mad, and she's spending, and I don't blame her."

"Put that thing away," Alec said, shuddering. "The last thing I want to see is an itemized rendering of my own wrongdoings. We have got *some* money in the account?"

"Some. Not a hell of a lot. That last tax installment didn't make us any richer. And there's always the folks back home. Your father's been in the hospital again."

Alec Barr smacked himself in the head with the heel of his hand.

"I don't know, Marc, I just don't know," he said. "I made how much last year? One fifty? Two hundred grand?"

"Counting an installment on the last movie sale, about that. But the tax boys got a big chunk of it. And face it, kid, that big penthouse you run and those trips abroad eat money. Not to mention your country estate. I don't have to tell you where it goes."

"I don't *know*," Alec said again. "If anybody ever told me, ten years ago, that I'd make two hundred thousand dollars in ten years I'd have thought he was nuts. I've made the best part of a million dollars since the war, and I always seem to be flat broke. There doesn't seem to be any daylight."

"You didn't really *have* to buy that place in Jersey," Marc Mantell said. "You remember it wasn't only me that vetoed it. The bank didn't like it, either, with the load you were carrying."

"I wanted it," Alec said, defensively. "I liked it. I work well in it. It's got that lake, and it's quiet, and—"

"And it costs money, and half the time you don't live in it. You're off on an Africa kick or chasing around the Far East or taking slow boats to Australia or something."

"I wanted a place to hang my trophies," Alec Barr said stubbornly. "And you can't quarrel with my Africa kicks, as you call them. We've had our money back from those trips a hundred times over. I went to Africa to shoot, and I stayed to learn. And the place in Jersey is a better deal than a farm in Kenya, which is what I wanted to buy in the first place."

"That I don't deny," Marc Mantell said. "With the world political situation the way it is, all we need for complete ruination is a sisal plantation in far-off Whatisit. But we're beggaring a point. The point is, my friend, when are you going to grow up and get back to work? Quit all this horsing around and straighten yourself out with Amelia and become Alec Barr, the writer, again, instead of Alec Barr, lover, *bon vivant,* and jerk."

"I suppose I'll take that from you," Alec said. "I already had some from Ben. He and you seem to have been writing each other's copy. Come on now, tell me Amelia is a steadying influence and I can't write a good line without her. Is that what you were going to say?"

"Not precisely." Marc Mantell smiled thinly. "But almost. Nearly. You've got to admit she does create an atmosphere of calm, and you work well in an atmosphere of calm. For very goddam sure you don't work well out of a hotel suite or a night club or Toots Shor's or one of those Greenwich Village dives. Some people may work well in bed, but they work in bed without a woman in the bed with them. Fornication may create people, but it sure as hell doesn't create words."

"Your advice then is that I get in touch with Amelia, plead forgiveness, embark on a second honeymoon—if we've got that much money—and then come home and lock myself into the dungeon again?"

"Exactly. You have a great deal of talent, Alec, but this is a very delicate field you operate in, and you can't afford even one bad book. Look at that last crap Lewis wrote, when he was trying to chase the young stuff and drink the world dry. Christ, he didn't have a book—a real book—after *Arrowsmith*. Hemingway hasn't been heard from since *Bell*. Where is Dos Passos? Down on a farm in Maryland somewhere? This is a forgetful business in a forgetful town, kid. Saroyan? Where the hell is Saroyan?"

Marc Mantell paused and crooked a finger at the waiter.

"We'll have the menu," he said, and then turned again to Alec Barr. "You've got strong competition coming up. Young people. It's a new writing age. Jones wrote a hell of a book in *Eternity*. Mailer has a lot of flash. Wouk won a Pulitzer with *Caine Mutiny*. Guthrie did a fantastic fine job on *Big Sky*. There are snot-nosed kids around who will be chewing at your heels pretty soon, because the old gray mare, she ain't what she used to be, and we don't want any objects of scorn or pity in the stable, do we? In this racket of ours we got to kill ourselves just to stay even."

"I'm glad you said 'we,'" Alec Barr said bitterly. "Okay, boss, you make a point. I accept it. I went dead dry with Amelia, and I tried to fan a little spark back into my swirling ashes. I guess I just accumulated a few more ashes. *Right*. I shall return. I shall harness myself to the Iron Maiden and give it of my best. I shall eschew the fleshpots and adopt monkish garb once more. I shall—oh, the hell with it. I shall have another martini."

The waiter was standing over them now, waving the menu. "What do you feel like eating?" Marc Mantell asked. "The mixed grill's good."

"Nothing." Alec Barr's voice was bitter. *"Nothing.* Suddenly I ain't hungry."

51

Alec Barr had to admit it; he did miss her terribly. Life had been very sweet and almost serene with Barbara after the first catfight, and now she was gone—suddenly rushed off to Spain to finish the picture in Andalusia. Alec tried working in the hotel, and then, in desperation, in his office in the barren apartment. Neither was any good; he acquired claustrophobia in the hotel, and there always seemed an endless clutter of strayed papers. The apartment was too big, too empty, and there was too much Amelia alive in it. The imprint of Amelia was everywhere. The house in New Jersey had always been a specific for most of his blockages—now, it seemed suddenly too far away from the city haunts he had grown accustomed to visit with Barbara. He went to bed—alone—with Barbara and he woke up—still alone—with Barbara. He could not, try as he would, settle himself to a steady writing routine and what he did manage to write seemed, to him, to have been composed entirely by thumb.

He finally gave up. He cabled Barbara in Seville to book him into a hotel, and rang up TWA to ticket him to Madrid and arrange a connection to Seville. Feeling more like a hound dog than a man, he called Marc Mantell and told a bare-boned lie—that he was a little off his feed and thought he'd take a long week hunting deer with some friends in Texas.

It had been a number of years since Alec had been in Spain, but the shambling airport in Barajas had not changed, and neither had the little, white-gleaming, flower-twined, orange-treed airport outside Seville. Nor had the dark brooding Arab faces of Andalusia changed, despite the growing influx of tourist money and the beginnings of a moving-picture industry. Alec was not looking for picturesque Spaniards or giving much thought to economics. He was disappointed that Barbara was not at the airport to meet him, although logic told him that she was making a movie, that this was a working day and she couldn't hold up shooting just to pull a lover off a plane. Nevertheless he brooded on the long dusty ride into town. He was feeling seedy and prickly-bearded and rumpled and plane-stained and he had a panicked feeling as he approached Recepción in the cool cave of the Alfonso Trece that the clerk would say he never heard of him, and throw him out into the steaming, dusty streets.

His mood improved immediately when the clerk greeted him with politeness, handed him a note from Barbara, and rang for the porter to take his bags. Alec read the note on the way to his suite.

Darling: We're shooting a good way out of town, in Carmona. I won't be back until about eight. Why don't you have a nap and be all rested for me when I come back? Hope your rooms are all right. I had them put you next door to me. So wonderful to have you here. All my love. B.

Alec felt much better. He rang down for ice and limes and a bottle of gin and some *agua tonica,* peeled off his travel-staled clothes, and spent half an hour in the shower. He lay in the cool shuttered darkness of his bedroom, refreshed by the gin, listening to the street sounds, but he was too excited to sleep. He looked at his watch, and it was only 4 P.M. He rose, dressed, and went downstairs to hail a horse-carriage to prowl the streets and savor the smells of dust and cooking oil and horse manure that distinguish any Arab town, and felt considerably uplifted when he saw the sluggish filthy Guadalquivir, passed the big bullring with its golden sands, and clip-clopped down the narrow cobbled streets and into urine-smelling alleys outside brass-studded Moorish doors that barred the world from bougainvilleaed walls that hid secret patios and God knows how many centuries of blood and lust and intrigue.

The afternoon sun smote him painfully, so he asked the driver to take him to a hat-shop, where he purchased the flat-brimmed black Cordobés sombrero of the area. With the hat slanted across his face, he felt less like a tourist and was suddenly hungry. They passed a likely-looking sidewalk café, and Alec halted the cab again. They were in the Triana, now, the gypsy *barrio*. Alec dismissed the hack and took a seat at a shaded table. He tipped his hat over his eyes, ordered a pitcher of beer and a plate of *cigalas*—the big prawns—some shriveled green olives, and a plate of hard Serrano ham. He ate hungrily, the beer tasting delicious, until he had cleared his table and the beads of moisture had disappeared from the pitcher. Then he ordered coffee and an *anis*, and sent the waiter for a cigar. With his coffee and *anis* in front of him, his Cordobés flat hat shielding his eyes, his *puro* in his mouth, Alec watched the crowd and suddenly felt very *flamenco* indeed. He dozed, leaning back against the brilliant white wall, and when he awoke his cigar was dead in the ashtray and it was nearly seven-thirty. He hailed another horse-coach and clattered his way back to the stately entrance to the Alfonso Trece. To his relief, the clerk said that the Señorita Bah-een had not yet returned from the *shutín* but could be expected momentarily. Alec went upstairs and took another bath, reflecting that the Bayne in Spain required lots of rein, and laughed at his own corniness.

He was padding restlessly around the room, loins wrapped in a towel, when his phone rang:

"I'm back," the well-remembered voice said. "But I'm damned if I'll expose myself to your *americano* eyes until I've washed a half-ton of Andalusian topsoil off me and have gotten rid of quite a lot of pancake and eye gunk. *Bienvenido* to Seville, my love. Good trip?"

"Not bad. Blew myself to a berth and slept some, anyhow. Wanted to be fresh and lovely for you."

"Well, while I'm getting myself fresh and lovely for you, why don't you just go down to the bar and stare at the pretty *señoritas*? I'll join you in half an hour. *Bueno?*"

"Right," Alec said a little sourly. I come halfway across the world to see a dame and she says meet me in the bar; and then, he thought, you're being a damned fool, Barr. No sensitive person is ever quite at ease for the first hours after a separation, even a short one, and it's downright gauche of me to imagine that she'd throw herself on the bed in the form of a cross the second she gets back from a hard day's work. I need a little adjusting myself.

He dressed and went down to the bar, sitting in a quiet corner and listening to a farrago of Spanish in which occasional words like *shutín*, which he assumed meant "shooting," and "set" and "two shot" and "pan" were mingled with the machine-gun fire of half-swallowed Andaluz. All the men, Alec noticed, had mustaches trimmed to unbelievable mathematic precision, and the teeth against the swart faces were unbelievably white. All haircuts achieved perfection, and there was no suit that bagged, sagged, or appeared to have been on its owner's body for more than one minute, at most.

He was reflecting moodily that when *he* got a haircut, they either skinned him or left shelves and ridges and shaggy patches. He was staring through the smoke at nothing in particular—the *señoritas* hadn't started to come in yet, evidently—when cool lips touched his cheek and there was Barbara.

He lurched to his feet and they clung, briefly, without kissing, and then he pushed her away to take inventory. She was wearing a white dress, simple and sleeveless, and she was toast-colored from the Andalusian sun. She was wearing a vivid red lipstick, a single red rose in the blonde hair, and the contrast of brown skin and brilliant red lips and rose against the white of the dress was staggering.

"Welcome to our little pueblo," she said. "It's got some strange smells in it, but we call it home. It's wonderful you could come, darling," clinging to his hands and swinging away from him. "Here, sit me down and tell me all. But first buy me something long and cold. I'm scorched, inside and out."

"You look like something straight out of Bizet," he said. "No red shoes and ruffles?"

"Don't think I haven't. And a dress with red spots. And I can do the damnedest *flamenco* since Carmen Amaya was the local Shirley Temple. There's no point in my asking what brings you to sunny Spain. But it *was* sort of sudden."

"Only a cliché'll answer that one," Alec said. "I missed you terribly. I couldn't think; I couldn't write; I couldn't even read. So I sent a cable and hopped a plane. I love you. That's what brought me to sunny Spain."

"Oh, darling," she said, and squeezed one hand with both

of hers. "I've missed you too, but they've worked us so hard
—that director's a real bastard—on this low-budget dog that
I haven't had time to miss you as much as I'd like. We're
up at the crack of dawn, and we don't get to bed much
before we get up. Nobody eats in this town until after midnight, and then somebody suggests a fresh *flamenco* joint
in some new alley, and by that time you've had enough *vino*
to make it sound very interesting and . . ." she let her voice
die.

"I was afraid I'd find you with a rose in your teeth, a
tortoise comb in your hair, and castanets on your fingers,
dancing on tabletops 'til dawn to the throb of gypsy guitars."
He grinned. "I guess you haven't changed much, New York
or Seville. Still find it hard to get to bed o' nights, do
you?"

Barbara looked at him levelly.

"I told you. Nobody ever eats until midnight here, and
it's only just past nine. If you'd buy me just one more of
these nice limey things I'm open to almost any suggestion to
kill a little time before midnight."

Alec snapped his fingers at the waiter and smiled.

"I thought we might go out and sit at a sidewalk café, but
I did that this afternoon and it's too dark for sightseeing. I
guess there's only one alternative."

"I guess you're right," she said, and rubbed a cheek
against his shoulder. "There's so little, really, to do in
Spain . . ."

"This will be my third shower since I got here," Alec said.
"And will be the third time I've changed clothes. We could
have saved time, you know. I wasn't dressed when you first
rang me."

"Put it down to girlish shyness," Barbara said. "Not to
lack of inclination."

She sat up in bed and yawned. "I dropped off, didn't I?
After . . ."

"You almost dropped off right in the middle," Alec
smiled. "I decided to grant you an hour's rest, to make you
all bright and fresh for the *flamenco* joints."

Barbara yawned again, and stretched out her arms.

"Come here," she said. "Lots of people don't eat dinner
until *one* A.M."

52

They managed three different *flamenco* caves after dinner, which finished at two-thirty. In each of the side-street cafés faces lit when they entered, and the gypsies invariably said "*¡Hola! Señorita Barbara!*" Or simply: "*Olé! Barbara!*" The *guitaristas* came immediately to the table to play what seemed carbon copies of her favorite songs in each of the places they visited. The singers, corded necks swelling like frog's throats, yelled what also seemed to be her favorite songs. Twice, on loud demand, she got up to perform what appeared to Alec a very creditable *flamenco*, with loud hand-clappings and frequent *Olés* and "*¡Ay, que tia!*" from the performers as well as from the few dark men who rested against the bar and drank manzanilla. At the table, whole armies of bottles of manzanilla disappeared as the *flamenco* singers and guitarists produced private performances for Barbara, with glares of rebuke from the head *cholo* if a rival group started a song for another table in another part of the room.

It was five o'clock when Alec's yawns almost eclipsed the woody clack of the castanets.

"I done come a long way in the last twenty-four hours," he said finally. "I think we've had enough clicking and clacking for one night, wouldn't you say?"

Barbara looked at her wrist watch.

"My God! And I've got to be up at six! Well, there's no point in my going to bed now. You can buy me breakfast in another place I know, and then I'll just bathe and slip into my working duds. You want to go out on the set with me tomorrow—I mean this morning?"

"Great God, no," Alec yawned again. "All I want is to sling these creaky old bones into bed."

"*My* bed?"

Alec shook his head emphatically.

"Great God, no, again. What with the flying and the love-

279

making and the food and the *flamenco,* I am what you might call 4F at the moment. Take me back to the Trece, lead me to my room, and I will bolt the door from *my* side. I aim to sleep twelve hours straight."

"You always did lack stamina," Barbara said. "Come on. We'll skip the breakfast. I'll have some tea and toast sent up to my room, and eat it while I dress."

"For this small boon I am indeed deeply grateful," Alec said. "I can take guitars with most meals, but not with breakfast."

Alec made one trip out to the set and swore off. It was the same old Hollywood mumbo-jumbo that he knew so well, except that it was being done under a copper sun and was supposed to be an oil-well picture shot in the Middle East. But it was easier to use the local camels and rig the Andalusians up in burnooses, which made some sense. The gypsies were all Moors, anyhow; the camels came from a nearby game preserve; the mock-up oil-rig was convincing, and there was always the Spanish Army for extras. The noise was the same. Take and retake and retake—the same smack of the take-slate, the same harassed script girl, the same ill-tempered director, and the same distractive cough into the sound track. Once in a while an aircraft would zoom low and wreck the take, or a jeep would get mixed up with the camels, but then that was picture-making anywhere: a bloody dull way to make a living, Alec thought dourly, as he announced that in future he would sleep late of mornings, to prepare himself for the *flamenco* ordeal of nights, and possibly go sightseeing in the afternoon. Barbara was amiable about the whole thing.

"I do quite understand, Sweetie," she said. "It must be terribly dull for you, just standing around while we do the close-ups and matching shots and middle shots and long shots and insurance shots and all the rest of this vital trivia. But I have some happy news for you. The week end's free: Svengali over there has wrapped up my sequence, and he's going to torture somebody else from Friday to Monday. We can do exactly what we want. Isn't that splendid?"

"It is indeed. The trip can now be described as worth the effort. In light of that wonderful news, do you suppose we might give the clickers-and-clackers a little rest tonight, and perhaps flout the local customs by eating in our rooms and going to bed early?"

"Poor, poor Alec," Barbara said, and smoothed his hair. "How you do suffer."

"I don't mind some aspects of it," Alec said. "But it's enough to sit up all night with a bunch of gypsies without being sneered at all day by a bunch of camels."

53

They strolled the streets, buying things—Alec bought some gorgeous evil-smelling carved-leather chaps he didn't need, and a wicked-looking hunting knife he didn't need, and was measured for some boots he didn't need, and fought off the inclination to buy some *trajes cortos* he certainly didn't need.

"But you'd look wonderful in them," Barbara said. "I've got some to wear to the *tientas*—" She clapped a hand to her mouth. "I forgot, clean forgot. We're invited out to Juan Mendoza's *finca*—*ganadería*, actually, for Sunday's *tientas*. A *ganadería* is a bull-raising ranch, and a *tienta* is . . ."

Alec tweaked her nose.

"I know what is a *ganadería*. And a *tienta* is where they test the young cows for bravery because the fighting spirit of the *casta* comes from the mother's side. I'm the bull expert in this family, remember? You've sure gone real *flamenco* for a girl who's only been in Spain for a couple of weeks. Why don't you try talking to me in English? I understand that, too."

"My Boy Barr, the supercilious son-of-a-bitch, is back," Barbara said without rancor. "Why do you always try to steal my toys?"

Alex shook his head.

"I don't want to steal your toys. But I am a little amused at how thoroughly ladies become Hispanofied after two weeks in the bull country, or Italianated when they've been seven days in Rome and spent a dirty week end in Capri. I'll bet Amelia is speaking nothing but purest Roman when she eventually gets back to the States."

"She's in Italy, then? You've heard?"

"I haven't heard. But the last batch of bills were sent from Florence, which I am sure she will call Fiorenze forever."

"What'll you do about her, eventually?"

"I don't know. That'll depend largely on you."

Barbara shook her head.

"Let's don't talk about her. We're in Spain, and we're having fun, and to hell with her. I don't want to think about her. Do you want to go to this calf-testing or not? It's fun, I'm told. Big fiesta—lots of pretty people and big booze and fine food."

"Sure." Alec smiled at the childish excitement in her eyes. "I haven't been to one in ages. Not since Mexico with Ben Lea."

They sat now at a café table and ordered manzanilla and *tapas*—*cigalas* and olives and anchovies and fried squid and ham and cheese.

"There's so much I haven't seen," Barbara said wistfully, chewing around a big prawn. "I suppose that's why I kind of show off when I run into something new. I haven't even seen a bullfight, let alone a *tienta*. Exactly what is the purpose, anyhow, apart from fun and games?"

"It's mostly an excuse to get drunk," Alec said. "A big houseparty. But the basic idea is you test the two-year-old *becerros* for bravery. You put the calves, male and female, up against a *picador* on a horse to see how many *pics* they'll take. The brave heifers, who keep charging the horse despite the pain of that iron pike, are set aside to be bred to the stud bulls. The nervous Nellies become veal for the market."

"How about the little-boy bulls?"

"They get a shot at the pike, too. The difference is that while you cape the cows, for fun, after the *picador* bit, you don't cape the bull calves. They're not supposed to see a cape until the celebrated moment of truth—the day they die when they're four years old, and go to their death as virgins. The brave chargers go back to the pastures to prepare for death. The cowards become beef, immediately."

"It all sounds very intricate. How do you know that the courage passes through the mother?"

"*I* don't know it. I only know what I've been told. And Spain is a very intricate country. Where is this *ganadería*?"

"Not far. About thirty minutes outside. I forget the name

of the place. But Juanillo is sending his car for us about noon Sunday, if it's all right with you."

"It's fine with me," Alec said. "How do you know this Juanillo?"

"Just around. He's nice. Met him with some people at a *flamenco*. He took me to dinner a couple of times."

"What did he do with his wife when he took you to dinner?"

"Wife?" Barbara's reaction was honestly blank.

"*Wife*. They all have wives. But I don't expect you'll meet her Sunday. Wives don't get asked to *tientas* as a rule. Only pretty *Americanas* and *Francesas* and *Inglesas* and other visiting firemen, like writers and movie actors, get asked to *tientas*. Spain is a very intricate country, like I said."

"He never mentioned any wife," Barbara said thoughtfully.

"He wouldn't. It's an old Arab habit that rubbed off after about eight centuries of Moorish occupation. This Andaluz country ain't Europe, Sweetie-pie. It's Africa. Europe stops at the Pyrenees. A lot of people still don't realize that Spain is still Moorish. Anything that starts with *el* or *al*, from *algebra* to *alfalfa* to *Alhambra,* is Arabic. That nice dirty river, where the Bobadillas grow the caviar, is not really Guadalquivir. It's Wadi al Kebir, bastardized."

"You make me so damned mad sometimes," Barbara said, with no indication of anger. "You're a smart-ass, you know that? You make me feel so stupid."

"I'm not a wishful smart-ass," Alec said. "I'm a writer. Just like you're a ham. We're both hams. You adopt the protective coloration of a country or a situation or a group just as a chameleon changes his color. Yours is surface—Smithfield ham. I soak up my contact with situation, and store it away. That makes me a Serrano ham. I'm cured in the snows, after I've been cut off the pig, before I'm fit for consumption. But we're both hams, in the end. And I could have as easily said *por fin* or *au fond,* if I was swanking it up."

Barbara stuck out her tongue at him.

"Let's go back to the hotel and stop being smart-asses," she said. "I don't want any lunch. These *tapas* are too much. What I want is a nap in a cool dark room."

"Your aim is noble, if exactly not in the mind," Alec said, and clapped his hands for the check.

54

A fat Jaguar was waiting in front of the hotel when Alec and Barbara came down. The whipcorded chauffeur touched his cap.

"*Buenos días, Señorita,*" he said. "*Señor,*" as an afterthought to Alec. "*Don Juan envía su complimentos pero no era posible encontrarles personalmente. La finca es cumplida con invitados desde anoche.*"

I'll bet a pretty, Alec thought, that even if the house is full of guests, that Don Juan would have found it *posible* to encounter the señorita *personalmente* if the word hadn't spread that the señorita had a Yankee boy friend in town. I do love the Spaniards, particularly the Southern Spaniards. Everything from bathroom to breakfast to bed is *muy torero* —*molinetes* with the eggs, *veronicas* with the bacon.

"Nice car," Alec said. "Must have cost a fortune to get it into the country." He patted the red leather upholstery. "I'm only surprised it wasn't a Mercedes or a Rolls."

"He keeps those for Franco," Barbara said. "Now you be nice and uncynical and, for Christ's sake, speak English. Juan is very proud of his English. Don't go hitting him with any Spanish slang, just to impress him because you're wearing a tweed coat instead of the *trajes cortos*. Snobbery gets you nowhere, even when it's inverse."

"Why," Alec said mildly, "I am only wearing tweeds because I don't have any *trajes cortos*. I do not intend to fight any cows today, with the rest of the tourists. And speaking of *trajes cortos,* may I say you look very fetching in yours?"

She was, indeed, looking very sharp in the *ranchero,* the country costume. A flat gray Cordobés hat was tilted over the blonde hair, which she had twisted tight and swept up in a knot. The shirt collar was stiff and prim and almost little-girly. The narrow tie was black and proper over the frilled front of her shirt, and the bolero jacket was dove-gray.

A black cummerbund confined the slim waist of her highly braced trousers, which were circumspectly striped with black-on-gray, in the manner of bankers' costume. They were short, split at the bottom, meeting her flat-heeled rawhide *botas* just below the calf.

"When did you order this outfit?" Alec asked.

"The second day I got here," she said. "You never know when some nice man will ask you to a *tienta*. I didn't want to accept the invitation wearing *tweeds*. Anyhow, Juanillo says he wants to teach me bullfighting, and you can't do it in a skirt."

"*Olé* for the mother of the Virgén de Macarena," Alec said, and reaped a response from the chauffeur. Alec concluded immediately that the chauffeur didn't care much for his presence.

The trip through the flat fields of wheat and rice was uninspiring, as well as dusty. Andalusia is only an extension of North Africa, and its hills like camels and long flats are equally uninspiring. Camel country, Alec thought. Camels and goats and bulls. Sun and rocks. Small trees and short water. Good bull country—make 'em walk over the rocks to water—and always an oasis in the middle.

The oasis was spectacular. A sudden island of greenery blurted at them as the chauffeur turned off the dusty main road into a dustier small winding road. He stopped the car to open a gate, drove the car through, and then got out to close the gate again. Black blobs of bulls appeared on the long sweeps of pasture. The excess of verdure came closer, and now the road was lined with flowers in huge pots— geraniums—and as they neared the house, great beds of *cresta de gallo*—coxcombs with blossoms as large and solid as loaves of bread, as red as the insides of the pomegranates which grew from glossy green-leaved trees interspersed with the golden globes of oranges.

The *casa grande* was white plaster, strangled in red and purple bougainvillaea. It was classic Spanish-Moorish, sprawling over an expanse of watered green, red-tiled; approachable through an archway, pillared and porticoed inside the arch. A swimming pool winked blue-eyed to the left—trees shaded the big house. A vast patio surrounded the many doors, all cut in arches. White pigeons wheeled and carved small jet streams over the red rooftiles. The curving driveway was packed with Cadillacs and Jags and Bentleys and Mercedes-Benzes. There seemed to be a solid acre of roses, and another acre of orange and lemon and olive.

"*Ya está,*" the chauffeur said, pulling up the Jaguar as if it were a horse. *"Creo que el dueño está en el otro patio. Es la hora de cokteles."*

Cheeky bastard, Alec thought. Even I know it's martini time, bull ranch or no bull ranch. And the *dueño* is bound to be in the other patio, because that's where the shade is and it is exactly 1 P.M., Andalusian Standard time.

"Gracias para sus bondades," Alec said, as they got out. *"Donde está la ruta para los cokteles?"*

"Este lado," the chauffeur said, touching his cap. *"A sus ordenes, Señorita."* Pause. *"Señor."*

"And what was all that?" Barbara asked.

"Nothing very much. I just thanked him for his kindness, and asked him which way was the booze. I've a feeling he disapproves of me. I ain't wearing country bullfight clothes, and I seem to be cutting in on the boss's girl friend."

"Now you just stop it," Barbara said. "Just stop it right now. Stop being cynical and superior. We're guests here, and you're an added starter."

"I know it," Alec said. "And I feel like an added starter. No matter. I'll be good and speak only English and perhaps maybe a little pidgin Spanish to show I'm a tourist. I wish I'd worn my Cordobés hat, except it clashes so with Irish tweeds, don't you think?"

"You—" Barbara stopped as a tall brown man came down the flagged, flower-hedged path to meet them, both hands outstretched.

"Barbará!" he said. "So very enchanted you could come and bring your friend." He took both her hands, then bowed and kissed her right hand, planting the kiss on his own thumb. He turned to Alec, bowed, and then extended his masculine hand.

The grip was firm. The eyes were the blue-green of the South, clear in the baked brown face. The mustache was a charcoal line over the red lips, and the teeth were dazzling. The body was wearing *trajes cortos* but as host, Juan Mendoza had allowed himself a red necktie. It went well with the ruffled shirt and the gray short-jacket.

"Alec Barr, *a su disposición,"* Alec said, without thinking. *"Encantado, y muchísimas gracias para su bondad de incluirme."*

One finely drawn black eyebrow arched.

"It is your house," the owner said. "You speak Spanish well, Señor Barr. So few Americans do; it is always surprising. It is an honor to meet you, Mr. Barr. Barbara has told me much about you. Tell me, *guapa,* how is the picture going?" he transferred his attention. "No, tell me later, first we must go and meet our other friends and have a drink and then you must tell me everything. This way please, to where you can hear the noise."

Barbara cut her eyes dangerously at Alec as they walked toward where the noise was. *You promised to be nice,* the slitted eyes said. *You promised to be nice and not be a smart-ass about bulls or Spain or anything else.*

Alec nodded, and they walked into a seething mass of people. A bar had been set up on the other patio, which was flanked again by big clay jars of geraniums and bordered in vast beds of wide-eyed pansies and the loaflike coxcombs, with roses crawling up the trees. This patio stood hard by the swimming pool, and the bar was sheltered with a kind of Polynesian-thatched-roof hut of palm fronds and cane.

"First we get a drink, and then I introduce," the host said. "There are so many people and I am so bad at introduction. Some you know, Barbara—Pepe and Chelo and Teresa and Ramón and Ygnacio and Blanca and Abundio and Paco and Linda and Pilarín, from the last party. The others are mostly Ingleses and of course your director. Maybe one or two from Madrid—an artist and a good writer of plays, I think, and two bullfighters taking a holiday. One is not bad. The other—" he shrugged. "But *simpático.* And what do you wish to drink?"

"Martini, please, with vodka," Barbara said. "If you have some?"

"Of course we have some. And you, sir?"

"I don't suppose you'd have a pink gin?" Alec could have kicked himself for being rude again, but something about Don Juan's mustache and teeth annoyed him. His clothes fit too well, in any case.

"Of course we would have a pink gin. I went to school in England," said Don Juan. "Would you like to swirl the bitters yourself? Although Eladio here"—gesturing at the bartender—"is reasonably expert."

Touché, Alec thought. It takes one to know one.

He inclined his head respectfully in the direction of the bartender. Again he spoke in Spanish, but at the bartender.

"I should be delighted," he said, using the subjunctive, "to place myself in the capable hands of your *peón de confianza.*"

"*Un* martini *drry* on the *rrocks*," the host said, "and *un peenk geen, à la Inglesa*."

Eladio the bartender smiled a tiny smile at Alec as he twirled the glass to spread the Angostura evenly. I don't think his bartender likes the son-of-a-bitch either, Alec thought, and then thought again: Why do I think of him as a son-of-a-bitch? Jealous of a man who has done me no harm, or just out of my depth with a lot of Spanish aristocracy? People who fight calves on Sunday for gags? People who never did a lick of work in their lives? Quit being a *boy*, boy. You've been through this before, in college.

Alec raised his glass.

"Health," he said, this time in English. "Chin-chin." He tasted his drink, and raised the glass again at the bartender.

"Perfectly constructed," he said in Spanish. "You must have an English grandmother."

The bartender's tiny smile split into a grin.

"*Irlandesa*," he said. "Irish, Señor."

"Now we go and see all the lovely people," Juan Mendoza said. He took Barbara by the elbow. "I don't think you have encountered my brother Tomás yet, nor my cousin Carolina."

There was nothing really wrong with it, Alec thought—nothing at all. But I never feel really *in* it. I know who I am, and what I do. I know what I got and how I make it and who respects me for what I do and what I got. There are bulls' heads with no ears in this lovely cool adobe house with the black beams against the white plaster and the red flowers in the jugs. There are the moth-bit heads of deer and the heads of ibex and the heads of pigs in the long hallways, and I got better tigers and lions and elephants and leopards. They call hunting the *caza grande* here, and feel like they've had a big day if they shoot some poor *ciervo* with a horn on his head. They get their rocks off by watching some beardless boy in tight pants kill a bull—thirty thousand people in a *plaza de toros* dying vicariously while a kid in a gold jacket and tight pants waves a red flag at a bull and accepts the possibility that he might lose his manhood. If he had any to lose, which is doubtful.

And now we are all gathered together over this interminable lunch—my God, *gazpacho, gambas, zarzuela, pollo, judias, filete, ensalada, patatas, pan, flan,* the whole bloody lot, with three kinds of wine in pottery mugs, before we get to the *anis del mono*—in order to work up another kind of appetite to go out to the private bullring to watch a guy on a horse shove a lance into a calf. Then a bunch of drunks who should be having a siesta will get down at the ring and the host will take one end of a *capote* and the prettiest girl will take the other end and they will play bullfights with the calves.

Only the female calves, of course. They don't cape the little bulls, and they only give the little bulls three shots with the *varas,* because they don't want to discourage their hatred for men on horseback—men on horseback whom they will meet two years hence when they are playing for keeps and the little bull calf, having been adjudged brave, will go out in that nice arena to be rendered into steak. Possibly for the poor, or possibly to be sold in the butcher shops as *carne de toro*—bull meat—instead of just plain old *carne.*

"You know about the bulls?" the host was being polite. "You have seen some *corridas,* Mr. Barr?"

"A little. I've seen some few *corridas.*"

"Do you like them?"

"Very much. When the man doesn't ruin the bull. And the horns aren't shaved. And not too much laxative administered before the bull comes out of the *toril.*" *Now why did I say that?* Alec asked himself.

Here came the arched eyebrows again.

"Whom have you seen?"

"The last Belmonte. Manolete. The early Arruza, Dominguin—Luís Miguel—after the war. The earliest Ordoñez. I never knew his father except as a manager. Niño de la Palma was a little ahead of me. Some others I knew in Mexico. Like Silverio."

Olé for you, father of the showoffs, el rey de los adornos.

"You have written perhaps about bulls?"

"No."

"But why? You seem to know about them?"

"I can't stand the thing about the horses." Alec was making a feeble joke for the Englishwoman on his right.

The eyebrow again. No sense of humor here.

"But you know we pad them now?"

"That's just it." *Oh, damn me, I can't help it,* Alec thought. He's putting me on.

"The fact is that I hate horses, and when they stopped getting it in the guts, I kind of gave up the *afición* business. Also when they started cutting the vocal cords so the tourists couldn't hear them scream, it put me off my stroke."

Ooooh. Small squeak from the British lunch partner.

Don Juan laughed a hearty host's laugh.

"For a moment I thought you were serious. Now I see you make a joke. We call it in Spanish a *'chiste inglés'*—English humor. Truly, why have you not written about the bulls?"

Alec shrugged.

"Truly, everything worth writing about bulls has been written—Hemingway, Tom Lea, Barnaby Conrad, some woman, I forget who, a couple of Mexicans, at least a thousand Spaniards, and finally an American, a friend of mine named Rex Smith, who did a biography of all the bulls and bull people. It seems to me the subject has been tapped out—exhausted. Bulls have now become a property for the tourists."

Don Juan Mendoza the host was leaning on the lance now, burling it.

"The bulls don't move you any more, then?"

"No. They don't move me any more. Neither do the bullfighters. Not since Manolete."

"And Manolete moved you. Why?"

"Because both the man and the bulls were honest. The man worked his *corrida* day by day, without looking to the winter bookings in Mexico or Venezuela. And the bull had strong legs and unclipped horns."

"You have been to *tientas* before, Mr. Barr?"

"Several. Many." Here it comes again. Up goes the eyebrow.

"Have you ever tested the calves? Have you ever known what it feels like to be in a ring with a wild animal—even a two-year-old calf?"

Alec shook his head, and lit a cigarette.

"No, sir."

"Would you like to try your hand with the cape this afternoon? We could easily arrange a more suitable costume."

Alec shook his head.

"No sir. I'm basically frightened of cows. I got butted once when I was a kid."

The table exploded into laughter, with three exceptions.

The exceptions were Alec, the host, and Barbara Bayne.

Alec turned to his British neighbor.

"I didn't really mean that about the horses," he said. "I love horses, really. I've often hunted with them."

"Oh," the squeaky voice asked, restored to faith. "Foxes? Wild boar?"

"No." Alec raised his voice a little. "When I hunt from horseback it's mostly African elephant and, once in a while, lion."

That'll hold the bastard, he thought, and attacked his *flan*.

The host was not yet finished.

"You hunt elephant and lion from horseback?"

"Yes. And sometimes rhino."

"But you are afraid of cows?"

"Exactly. I understand elephant and lion and rhino. I do not find myself fascinated by cows. A twelve-inch horn up your backside is just as long as the best horn on a four-year-old Miura. The prospect fails to amuse me."

"But elephants move you." This came as a statement.

Alec laughed.

"Often. I have probably run from more elephant than Rafael El Gallo ever ran from bulls. Except when you deal with elephant you have no servant of confidence to take the elephant off you with a cape, and no *callejon* to jump over. I generally use big trees to hide behind."

Again laughter, with the exception of three.

"It is a pity," the host said. "I would like to see a man who hunts elephant from horseback throw a cape at one of my calves."

"Sorry to disappoint you, Don Juan," Alec said. "But I am basically an *aficionado* of the spectator sports. I will sit, with your permission, in the judge's box and drink brandy and award ears for the best performance. Ever since a leopard had me I have developed a distinct distaste for close contact with animals."

"A leopard had you? " Now both eyebrows moved up another floor.

I'm bored with all this *mierda*, Alec thought. Let's kill it now.

"Would you like to see the scars?" He pulled up the cuff of his jacket, and rolled back a shirtsleeve. The left arm was ridged and pitted by old wounds that went all the way through. He made a gesture at unbuttoning his coat, and then laughed.

"Ladies present," he said. "But I've got some very interesting landmarks on my chest and tummy."

"I think we will have coffee on the patio," the host said, and stood up. Barbara Bayne looked at Alec Barr with the same expression she had employed when he had dismissed the fleet of screeching pansies. It was a look Alec might have described to define him as socially unacceptable.

55

Alec Barr sat lonely in the *dueño*'s seats of the private bull ring. Nearly everyone had had a crack at the *becerros*. The two professional bullfighters—one fair, one nothing—had performed some flashy capework in taking the two-year-old heifers away from the man on the horse. The host, Don Juan, had strapped on his leather chaps and had produced some more flashy capework in the *quites,* performing acceptable *reboleras* and *chiqueliñas,* wrapping the cape around him in a flash of magenta and yellow. The brother, Tomás, was playing the part of *picador,* maneuvering the horses well, leaning stoutly on the *vara*, laying the iron into the shoulders of the calves without unduly brutalizing them.

There are some damned good embryo bulls down there on that yellow sand, Alec thought, blinking against the slanting sun of the late afternoon, sitting off to himself in the white plaster of the little private ring. That last one took sixteen before she quit. She will be put to the seed bulls and yield some mighty calves for the brave festival.

I wonder, he thought, what makes me so bloody ornery? I led that poor bastard, Juan, into a *cul de sac* at the lunch table. I was unforgivably rude. I guess it's merely insecurity in strange places, but I would love to see one of these big mouths with the amateur capes and the country clothes go up against a really nasty elephant in thick bush, or a leopard suddenly in the lap. He massaged his welted wrist as he remembered the screeching fury he had peeled off himself, so many years ago, choking it finally to death with the barrels of a shotgun.

I got books to write, he thought. *I got bills to pay. I don't need no horn up my ass.* Not, as he thought, unless I can sell the product via Marc Mantell. This business of the drunk socialites playing with half-grown bulls is like playing chicken with cars, where the first one to swerve is a coward. You remember that actress that got kicked in the face with a horse, in this same Spain, when she was learning how to bullfight from horseback? It took a lot of plastic surgery to get that dimple straightened out again, and she still does her closeups from the left side of her face on account of the lip don't turn up on the right side of her face when she smiles.

The hell with it, he said, and took a sip of the brandy. Now we got the star turn. Little Miss Twitchett, the Barbará Bah-een from Hollywood, is going to fight a bull. *Qué tengas la suerte,* he whispered. *That you should have luck.*

Barbara looked marvelous out there on the golden sands of the arena. (Golden sands of the arena? What kind of writing is that? Arena *means* sand in Spanish, unless you are in Cataluña, where it's spelled *arenys.* Smart-ass.)

She had her Cordobés sombrero tipped at exactly the right angle, a little forward. Her backside was tight and trim in the striped pants. Her shoulders were braced well back, and those fantastic breasts pushed the frilled shirt forward, with the vest-cut jacket swinging free as she raised the cape to cite the little cow. (Little cow? Enough horns there to unzip her from navel to neck.)

"*Olé Barbará! Olé la señorita Americana! Olé la actriz brava!*" The voices swelled, all twenty of them, as Barbara planted her feet, one–two, as brave as Manolete, who is dead, and cited the *becerra.* (Barbara had the actor's gift of magnificent mimicry. At the moment she was playing *Blood and Sand*—second version, Tyrone Power—with himself, Alec Barr, playing critic by courtesy of the late Laird Cregar.)

"*Huh! Huh! Huh! O hey, toro!*" He heard that trained actress voice saying the words just like something out of Hemingway. "*Eh hah! HohohohoHah! Toro!*"

Perfect take. *Cut.*

Now here came the brave cow. (Horns a good fourteen

inches long, and sharp as needles. Weight four hundred pounds, and full of *plomo*.)

Barbara (Belmonte) Bayne swung the cape with nice slow gypsy wrists, taking the cape low, sculpturing, head bowed, looking at the feet, as the calf came roaring, blood from its *pic*ing streaming thickly from its shoulder. *Ay, qué torera!*

The calf passed her and took the cape with her as she went. Then the calf shook the cape irritably from the horn and looked again for an enemy. She found the enemy. It was wearing beautifully cut *trajes cortos*—tight pants, fine bolero jacket, correct Cordobés hat, bosoms swelling under frilled shirt. Standing alone and uncertain.

"Huh!" This time it was the calf who cited, and charged. The host and his brother ran into the ring with capes, but not soon enough. Barbara ran for the *burladero*—the joke-maker, the little pantry in which bullfighters sometimes find it necessary to hide—with the calf goosing her all the way.

Barbara tripped and fell just as she achieved the entrance to the *burladero*. The cow lowered her head (she's left-handed, bad left hook, Alec noted) and unzipped Barbara's tight pants as she crawled to safety behind the *burladero*.

The host and his brother caped the calf away, and Barbara emerged from the *burladero*.

Her backside shone white in the Sevillan sun. She had lost her hat. Her pants were down around her ankles. She had badly torn the front of her blouse, and her nose was scraped by sand. Her face was ashen, and she had begun to cry.

The host, Juan, ran up and wrapped her in a fighting cape.

Alec shuddered. He decided, if somebody could find her a pair of pants or something fairly decent to wear until she got back to the hotel, that this was going to be no night to spend on a late dinner with *flamenco* until dawn.

It is not, he muttered, the hasty ascent up the thorn tree when you are being chased by a rhino that hurts so much. It is that long trip down. It was going to be a long trip back to the Alfonso Trece, and a smart man would be well advised to keep his mouth shut.

56

Smoke from the cigarette plumed acridly from the ashtray, fueled by ignition to the cork butt on another, blended sulphurously into the varnish of the tray, and then sucked straight into Alec Barr's nostrils. It smelled like a smoldering boot on a burning ash heap, and it made Alec Barr's throat itch, which made him cough, which made him sneeze.

He sneezed seventeen straight times. Barbara entered the living room of the darkened suite.

"What's the matter? Hay fever?"

"That." Alec pointed at the smoking cigarette. *"That."* He blew his nose and mopped his streaming eyes—"I wanted to see how long you'd let it burn. For the love of God, why must *all* women leave their cigarettes stinking in ashtrays? If you're going to smoke the goddamned thing, smoke it. You've been out of the room five minutes, with that bonfire going all the time. I can trace your progress around the joint by discarded cigarette butts that've burnt a hole in the window sills. Apart from the fire hazard, it's lousy manners."

"You're some paragon of perfection, I suppose?"

"We're not talking about people who light cigarettes and then put them into ashtrays to smolder and stink and blow fumes in other people's faces. We're talking about people who have sloppy habits and who are inconsiderate of other people."

"So I am sloppy, am I? And inconsiderate?"

"If you're referring to cigarettes, yes, you're sloppy. Very damned sloppy." Alec made his voice flat. *"And* inconsiderate."

Now Barbara lifted hers, in a kindling rage.

"And you're an intolerant, biased son-of-a-bitch! Nothing's right except the way you see it! You've got a head full of little slots and pigeonholes, and anything that doesn't fit those cramped little personal spaces is rejected!"

"Oh, God." Alec shook his head. "I merely mention three or four hundred times that it would be a nice idea if you either smoked your cigarette or put the damned thing out, and now I'm intolerant, with slots in my head. At least the slots are in my *head*. At least I don't have any ovaries to think with."

Barbara glared at him.

"Here we go again—old Doc Barr's favorite thesis about women thinking through their reproductive equipment, while noble man is a cerebrator. Tell me some more, Professor."

"I don't want to fight about such a little thing as a cigarette. Everything we fight about is silly, anyhow. We never seem to fight about anything worthwhile. We fight about Mrs. Roosevelt and crooks and bullfights and faggots and Paul Robeson and Charlie Chaplin and Frank Sinatra and Adlai Stevenson. Christ, it's getting so I'm afraid to open my mouth for fear you'll throw a joe."

"Me throw a fit? *Me?* You're the joe-thrower, my lad, not me."

"I know," Alec's voice wearied elaborately, annoyingly. "Boys is bad, girls is good. Girls is right, boys is wrong. Of such stuff is moonbeam made. *Balls.*"

"And balls right back to you, friend. You know how to hurt me. You *like* to hurt me. So I'm a slob. So I believe that there are maybe one or two nice things in life, and people are pretty nice. You and that literary cynicism of yours, picking everything to pieces, looking under all the beds, questioning any simple, honest, decent—" Barbara began to weep.

"Yes, Amelia. Of course, Amelia." Alec's voice was cruel. "Just as you say, Amelia . . . weep on, Amelia. *Olé,* Amelia!"

"And don't call me Amelia!" Barbara stopped her crying and shouted the words. "Don't you dare call me Amelia!"

"There's quite a remarkable similarity, you know," Alec drawled. "Except Amelia hasn't had as much practice at being a ham. She's not so skillful at dramatizing herself."

"Ham? Just because I—"

"Exactly. Just because you—and I can fill in the gaps, if you'd like," Alec cut in. "If you're prepared to listen a minute I can give you some fine recent examples of hamming it up. You hit a complete technicolor production the other night over what started out to be a mild observation about crooks being crooks, whether they were gamblers or night-club owners or any other brand of hood with haircut. This, you recall, was at dinner, and you left the table in a torrent of tears and stale Sarah Bernhardt. For that I was also marked intolerant, opinionated, and arrogant."

"And I still mean it about the gamblers. I got screwed plenty on my second divorce, and the only people who were nice to me were a few 'hoodlums,' as you call them, that I'd known around the edges of show business. My fine friends from Palm Springs and Acapulco didn't show any consideration for me when that bastard of an ex framed a lot of lousy, lying evidence and got my little girl away from me—turned her away from me, made her believe all the filth . . ."

"Which ex was that?" Alec's voice was calculatedly cruel. "I have a little difficulty keeping up with all of your formers without a scorecard."

"You know well enough which ex it was, you sarcastic bastard. We've talked about him often enough. Josh. Josh Lewis. *The* Josh Lewis."

"Oh, yes. The producer. Let me see. First we had an assistant director who didn't understand us, and then we had *the* kind of producer, who didn't understand us, and now we have an actor, currently in process of getting lost, who didn't understand us—"

"And now are in process of falling out of love with a supercilious son-of-a-bitch of a writer who doesn't understand *me,* or any other woman!" Barbara's voice rose brassily. In a moment it would be tinny, and for some curious reason Alec wondered how much more baiting would be necessary to lift her from cultivated chest tone to Texas shrill nasality.

"So in any case we made a federal case out of a flat statement from me that I don't care for the society of crooks, even when they run the most respectable casino in Las Vegas, and so we wreck the evening."

"Crooks or not, they've got heart. They're common people, kind people, not like—"

"Yeah, they're good common, heartful, kind people. I agree. With actors, everybody's got heart. I agree that they've got heart up to the point where you owe them a little money and they send some hired thug around to break your legs or mark up your kids. Then they aren't such heartful, kind, common, lovely, simple children of nature any more. They're hoods. Manicured bums. Polished lice. Tailored crooks. And I don't care how many hotels they own or how much they pay a singer to work their rooms, they're still hoodlums."

Barbara got up and swung up and down the room, clasping and reclasping her fingers.

"Okay, Bette Davis," Alec said, nastily again. "I know the walk. *Cut.*"

Barbara turned in fury, her eyes slitted, her mouth spitting words.

"By God I don't know what I saw in you! Narrow, spiteful, devious, arrogant, middle-class, nasty *little* man!"

"I confess to it." Alec managed a yawn. "I am nonreclaimable. And I confess I bore easily when confronted with a constant display of painfully acquired fireworks. It is really a pity to educate actors in the Method system of histrionics. It breeds a tendency to self-belief, a fatal fascination for staying *on*. Whatever the topic. I mention calf-testing *tientas* as an example in point . . ."

Barbara was in tears once more. She moved blindly over to the tabouret and poured herself a drink, slopping the whisky into the glass, draining half of it in a gulp.

"Now that's very helpful," Alec drawled. "When in doubt, always feed the Irish another slice of hooch . . ."

Barbara threw the remainder of the contents of the glass at him. Alec got up, wiped his face, and took the glass out of her hand. He slapped her lightly, mock-playfully, on the wrist.

"Naughty," he said. "Mustn't waste good whisky. Not when it'll feed the dramatic flame. It isn't proper *flamenco.*"

"At least I *tried*. At least I got down in the ring and tried. I didn't sit up in the stands drinking brandy and pouring cold water on other people's fun. And I wasn't bloody rude to a host who was only trying to show us a good time. And that business at the table, about fighting elephants on horseback, lions on horseback—at least I'm not always trying to cut people down to midget size in front of other people—"

"I'm not trying to cut people down to midget size in front of other people." Alec made his voice weary. "I merely object to the wholesale presentation of horseshit. And I resent being baited by some slick Spick who's trying to get into your pants through the process of making me lose mine."

"Maybe he's already been into my pants, as you so sweetly put it! Maybe that's why he was having you on! Maybe he was jealous—or just disappointed that I go around with squares who won't enter into the life of the country, won't have any fun doing what other people do!"

"All this because I see no point in getting goosed by a cow. If I'm going to get trod on I'd at least hope it was an elephant that did it, not some bloody heifer."

"You and your damned elephants! You and your lions and tigers! Well, I'm no white hunter. After the other day, I don't even know if you shot the stuff yourself. And I'm no expert on anything. You and that patronizing business about bullfighting at the man's own table—you and that nasty crack about his wife. I wish I *had* let him—"

"It's not too late, at all. A short telephone call. And anyhow, I only said—"

"Yes, I know what you said, you bloody expert. You're the authority on everything. You and Hemingway. The how-it-is brothers. The boys with the self-cultivated hair on their literary chests. Why didn't you pick somebody else to imitate? Why content yourself with just being a pale shadow of the *real* tough writer?"

Alec Barr went pale, and curled his fingers into fists. He stared past Barbara's shoulder, and the muscles knotted in his jaw.

"I really ought to smack you for that," he said. "Unfortunately I don't hold to the Noël Coward school of woman-and-gongs. But consider I just slapped your face for some extremely dirty pool."

"Don't do me any favors, Author. If you want to slap, slap. It won't be the first time I was pushed around by a big brave man who couldn't talk his way out of a truth. Come on, hit me if it'll make you feel better. It's all in keeping with the tradition. 'How it feels to strike a woman, by Alexander Barr.' . . ."

"You know—you really *are*," Alec said. "I wouldn't have believed it, I can't believe it, but you really are."

"I really am what?" Barbara's voice was as rough and rasping as a hostile stranger's. "Really am *what?*"

"Like the rest. There doesn't seem to be any exception anywhere." The weariness came back again into Alec's voice. "It's all ovarian. First the good-fellow fun and girly sparkle. Then the serious game. Then the bruised look of love. Then the haunted-eyed penance for the love. Then the extreme sensitivity because of the love. Then the tears. Finally the fights. Then the cold hatred. Then the noisy finish. All centered in the female reproductive organs. I admit it; I do *not* understand women. And I doubt very much if women understand women, either."

For a moment, a brief twinkle of almost-amusement came to Barbara's eyes.

"On that last I just might admit you have a little right on your side. But you've got to admit that you like to fight. You love the sound of your own cool, logical voice piling up point after point. And you like somebody to needle, so they'll fight back and give you that heady sense of masculine superiority. Well, I've got news for you, friend. I'd rather go to bed with a simple truck driver, if he was kind. I'd rather be married to a dockwalloper, if he had any grain of understanding of what a woman's like."

"I've no doubt about it," Alec murmured. "None at all."

"And right there, goddam it, is what I mean." The momentary bid for truce flickered, died, and Barbara's voice reached once more toward fishwifery. "That's exactly what I mean! You don't talk, you don't really fight, you don't really care! You just read your bloody lines! *Me* a ham! Man, I couldn't carry your jockstrap as a ham! There never was an actor could touch a writer as a ham!"

"I'm inclined to argue that point," Alec said drily. "Mix you a drink?" Without waiting for an answer, he poured Scotch and water into two glasses. "There is no living woman who is not an accomplished liar, cheat, and evader of self-hurting reality from the day she first bullies her father into a second ice-cream cone until she appears, weeping tastefully, at the coffinside in the best black frock she can afford," Alec Barr said, as if talking to himself. "The whole career of femininity is built on purposeful sham, which refuses the recognition of truth if truth is personally offensive, and which is always able to end the unpleasantness with shouts of personal recrimination on long-stored resentments and a final purging freshet of tears."

"Which book is that from? Or are you just writing a new set of lines to store up for some future dull day in the dialog business?"

"No book. No lines. Just ugly truth. From crib to first confinement, from dolls to defloration, from diaper to death, it's all one great act designed to make up for the fact that men and women are made differently, that the winds blow up

a skirt and create lonely cold, that the woman is an unwilling receptacle for the lust of man. The resentment is
not so much that the wench is caught with child, but more
that she cannot pee easily on a picnic. The headshrinkers
call it penis envy. I call it the greatest example of Method
acting since Eve conned Adam with that bloody pomegranate,
or whatever it was."

Barbara laughed loudly, falsely. She clapped her hands in
mock applause.

"Keep going, Professor," she said. "You're off and winging. You really hate us, don't you? I'll admit you're great in
the hay, but come on, be honest for once, confess. You
really *do* hate us, don't you? Because you can't understand
us, you hate us."

"No." Alec's voice was slow and very serious. "No, I
don't hate you. I just dislike some things about women—
mostly the deception you practice in your personal war against
mankind and the world. Some of it amuses me. Some of
it just annoys me. The rest of it infuriates me, because man
has no defense against a practiced harlotry that starts on the
sandpile and continues until papa's planted and the will's
read."

"That's a sweeping statement," Barbara said sarcastically.
"I thought that all little girls were made of sugar and spice,
et cetera."

"That's the part that annoys me most. And all boys are
not created exclusively of nails, snails, or puppydog tails.
It's the assumption that irritates me—the smug assumption
that is drummed into your groin—you notice I did not mention either heart or brain—into your groin from the time
you learn to toddle until you first fall into a man's bed.
It's all feminine fraud, handed down from mother to daughter."

"I wonder you spend so much time with us if we're as
horrible as all that. Give us some more of that fraud bit,
that harlotry jazz, Professor. I am learning about life. I
am all ears."

"You're all ovaries," Alec said. "There is no such animal
as a listening woman. You hear through your crotch. You
tug down your skirts against the flirting wind, but wrap your
naked legs around the neck of the man who pleases you.
You cross your knees carefully in the drawing room, and
sit sprawled on the beach in a bikini with the vaginal crease

you are sworn to protect until such time as you can sell it for fancied love or real money."

"My, my, our boy is really bitter tonight." Barbara arranged her voice artificially light and brittle. "Our boy is really writing us some beautiful rhetoric. You sound like a rather mussy carbon of Philip Wylie. Play, Phil, and I will listen with my crotch, as you so delicately put it."

"Okay, so sneer," Alec said. "But I think that deep down, somewhere in that intricate coil of life-producing machinery, you know I'm right. You will faint at a mouse but kill an elephant with your bare hands if the elephant represents a threat to your female security. You will practice a coy shyness until some poor devil is bemused by withheld sex, when you're wondering when the stupid clot will actually get around to putting his hand up your frock. You'll fake a virginity when half the town has been up you, and you'll wiggle with a false enthusiasm that is exceeded only by the mechanical swindle of a non-felt orgasm in order to keep the poor boob secure in his splendid male superiority. And when all else fails—the cute little dirty tricks that you allow him to think *he* taught *you*, the wicked fellow. When all else fails, there are always tantrums followed by the deluge of tears. No man is stout enough to withstand tantrum, tears, the fainting spell, the melting to the floor in the liquid swoon. All false. All sham. All inherent. No woman needs to go to school to learn to act. She's been an accomplished actress since the first day she butted at her mother's breast and screamed for more milk."

Barbara yawned now, an elaborate, mouth-patting yawn.

"I'm only surprised you bother with us at all, if you hold us in such low esteem. I'm surprised you don't simply turn faggot and give us up altogether. There must be some other substitute for the pathetically small aid and comfort we afford you."

Alec grinned crookedly, smally, sheepishly.

"Unfortunately there's not. You have a corner on a certain market, and when you take the trouble to skip the tricks and forget the dramatics, a certain sweetness that is irreplaceable. When you're honest you're marvelous. When you're hyping yourself with your phony attitudes, you're abominable."

"You really wouldn't like us honest," Barbara replied darkly. "You'd hate us if we were truly honest. In a way—a sour sort of way—I have to agree with you. There never was a man alive who could face a woman's honest opinion of him. You're all spoiled brats, and you won't play unless we keep telling you how marvelous you are"—she flipped her lashes rapidly—"you great big old strong brilliant hand-some wonderful man, you. Ah sweah, honey, Ah don't know how y'll do it, Ah sweah Ah don't. Crap. All crap. You wouldn't like it if we told you exactly what we think of your struttings and posturings and pathetic efforts to convince the little woman that she's happy in bed. *Happy?*" Her laugh was a bark. "No wonder we have to pretend to like it. No wonder we have to fake our orgasms. *Happy? That's to die over.*"

Alec pursed his lips. He nodded.

"Right. I expected that one. It comes in the logical se-quence to the earlier dialog—the I-love-to-feel-you-inside-me bit—and the back-rolled eyes and the soft moans and wet-crumpled sheets of love. Right. It's all a delusion, and you're only in the business to be accommodating."

"Oh, I didn't mean you. I meant all the other fellers. Of course." Barbara made great circles of her eyes. "Never *you*. It's all the other fellers—all you old ex-husbands and old boy friends and old one-night stands in Chicago." She lashed the last line at him. "They're the lousy ones, the fumbling ones, the inept ones, the rabbity ones. Not you, my love." She wagged her head violently from side to side, making her hair swish back and forth across her face. "Never, ever *you*."

Alec lit another cigarette and noticed that his hands were steady.

"You dirty bastard!" Barbara threw the glass this time, and Alec ducked. The glass smashed against the wall. "You rotten bastard! I feel filthy, just from having known you! I never want to see you again!"

She raged to her feet and stormed into the hall, slamming the door. Alec rubbed his jaw reflectively and methodically began to pick up the shards of glass. He could hear the harsh sound of her heels, going away, for what seemed a terribly long time.

"I guess that's the end of that," he said aloud, and went to mix himself another drink. "I guess that's the finish of old Alexander Barr, unlikely lover." He raised his glass in a bitter toast to himself. "Hail, unblithe spirit. Loverboy thou never wert—at least not for very long. It's entirely too much trouble."

He dropped into a chair and exhaled a long breath. He felt suddenly free again—as free as the day he had walked out on Amelia in an unreasoning rage. A load had lifted. He didn't have to play house any more. He didn't have to teach any new dogs any old tricks. He could get back to work, and quit pretending he was a sophomore—what had Marc Mantell said?—a sophomore, sniffing after his first piece of tail.

All of a sudden he felt hungry. Room service? No. He wanted to get out of this room. He looked at his watch. For Seville, early yet—only a little after one. He glanced out the window and saw to his satisfaction that the night was clear and crisp, a half moon riding high.

"You impossible bastard, Barr," he said aloud again, and went over to the desk where he kept a notebook. He sat down and scribbled rapidly, filling two pages with notes.

"You never can tell when you'll need the scene," he said to himself. "That's the trouble with most boy-girl stuff. The fight scenes never quite come off. Nobody ever quite gets them right—the ping-ponging back and forth that finally winds up with the hurled glass and the bitter tears; the careful, almost gleeful goading of each other."

He put the notebook away and rested his hand briefly on the portable typewriter. Tomorrow, he thought, I'll get to work again. I'll go home where I belong—back to America, out to Jersey, back to my house—and I'll get to work again. I'm free, and I feel just fine.

57 / Jill

He went down in the elevator and nodded negatively at a cab. He would walk over to Third Avenue; he felt like walking tonight. He took a deep breath, plunged his hands into his pockets, and strode strongly into the dark city, his heels snapping staccato on the sidewalk. He had missed his work; missed his full work, complete work—not bloody part-time

work between the act of standing at stud and waiting for
telephones to ring and flying off to Spain like a lovesick
calf. That's for boys, he thought. Not for men. Especially
not for writing men. And now I am a man again. I'll ring
up Dinah Lawrence tomorrow, and maybe she can come out
to the house for the week end. That's a fine girl, Di—a
comfortable, easy girl. You don't have to be on parade
every moment with Di, and she doesn't always think with
her glands.

He felt a little sad, as he walked, that his brief spate of
bliss with Barbara had ended so sharply, so unpleasantly—
cheaply, he supposed, was the word. Cheaply, with glasses
flying and shrillnesses and countercharges and vulgarities
and deliberate intent on both sides to inflict hurt. But that
was a thing he knew about women; when they fought they
fought to maim. Some went for the jugular, but most went
invariably for the balls.

"We're both—men and women alike—sort of weak in that
area," he murmured, as he turned left on Third Avenue toward the comforting late-night lights of Paddy Clarke's
shebeen. "I suppose, really, I could ring this up as an experience. Certainly it's an experience in my lack of competence for concentrated romance. I guess Amelia was right.
I guess Barbara was right."

Alec Barr winced.

After Barbara Bayne had slammed the door at the Alfonso Trece, she had flung a final hurtful handful of words
over her shoulder.

"You fool, you fool," she had said, wresting open the
door. "You don't know what you're throwing away!" Her eyes
were bright with tears, and her mascara was running into
little streaks on her cheeks. "There's no woman in the
world big enough to stand between you and that goddam
typewriter!" That was when she had not reslammed the door,
and he could hear the angry click of her heels as she half-
ran down the corridor.

He walked through the doors of Clarke's, into the smoke
haze, and was happy to see Ben Lea brooding into a drink
with both elbows planted firmly on the bar. Ben was alone.
His pink hair was hedgehoggy on his head, and when he
turned at Alec's greeting, Alec could see that he was well
along on his load.

"Well, well," Ben Lea said. "Here's old lover boy, all alone and loose again in the wicked city. What happened? The new mama give you a night off from the feathers?"

"Shut up and buy me a drink," Alec said. "Also I'm hungry. Let's have a hamburger. I've been in Spain. The idyll died there over a *tienta,* of all unlikely reasons."

"Never, ever eat when you drink," Ben Lea said. "Tommy, two more whiskies, large ones. Eating while you drink is a shameful waste of booze."

He squinted at his friend with the bleared blue eyes. "Hey, buddy, there's a change in you from the last time. You don't look as completely moonstruck any more. What *did* actually happen? You look like you just been let out of school. I didn't even know you'd been to Spain. Tell all."

Alec picked up his drink and walked over to a table. Ben Lea followed him and they both sat down.

"Cheeseburger," Alec said to the waiter. "And a cup of coffee." He turned back to Ben Lea. "I have, in a manner of speaking, been let out of school. We sort of wrapped it up. I guess you were right that time at the Marguery, Ben. I'm not cut out to be a lover. And she got goosed by a calf while I was being superior, and rude also to her host."

"Like I said. You're a writer. Writing is a full-time job. So go write, and leave the lovemaking to the old pros, like me." Ben Lea nodded drunkenly, sadly, mock-wisely.

"I intend to," Alec said, raising his glass. "Immediately. I'm moving out to the Jersey house to whip the living hell out of this new book."

Ben Lea narrowed his eyes into blue slits. The eyes weren't so bleary now. He nodded to himself.

"You look better for it, though," he said after a moment. "You look nice and loose. I think that Barbara babe was good for you. Unbuttoned you a little. You were entirely too tense for too long. Did you care very much about her?"

Alec blew a smoke ring and poked a hole in it with his finger.

"I suppose so, yes. *Yes.* It was a new thing for me, like I told you that day. I haven't had any experience at big emotions. This one was too big for me. *She* said that." He shrugged. "I'm inclined to agree with her, even if it hurts. Yes, I care for her a lot. But not enough to fight all day and make up all night and hurl myself completely out of the only field I'm secure in. I'm a dull dog basically,

Benjamin. I am really too old for the new tricks. I can't always keep running off to Spain or Greece or Hollywood or Greenwich Village."

"Well, it's nice you know it. No substitute for learning it for yourself. You—oh, hi there, darling! Come and have a drink and improve your mind!" He was waving at a girl who had just come through the door ahead of quite a mob of people. Alec turned to look in the direction of the wave. The woman was tall, with abnormally broad shoulders showing bare above a mink stole. She had bright, almost carroty red hair, crinkly eyes that seemed, at that distance, to be green, and a broad humorous mouth that turned up at the corners like a clown's paint-lines when she smiled and waved back at Ben Lea. The teeth in the smile were dazzling.

"Can't—I'm with a mob," she said over the crowd noise. "Call me tomorrow and take me to lunch?"

"If I live," Ben Lea called back.

"Tomorrow," she said, and was rushed along into the other room.

"Who's that?" Alec asked. "She's a smasher."

"That is not for you. She's not for anybody at the moment. English lady. Lives in London. I knew her during the war. She flew for the ATC. Very stylish sort of broad. Last husband just died. Some sort of Georgian prince. She's been here settling the estate. I gather he left her quite a packet. He was in some facet of the export-import business. Old China hand. Tangier type. You know the breed. She'd left him before he died, but I guess he forgot to change the will."

"What's her name?"

"Jill. She uses her maiden name now—Richard. Husband was one of those long Russian things from the old Czarist aristocracy, Aghmashvani or some such. Very noble family. He was rather a charming crook, and good at his job. I believe he was very much in love with her."

"I can understand it. I haven't seen that much style on a dame in ages. What else about her?"

Ben Lea took a long pull at his drink and looked upward at Alec under tangled pink eyebrows. He frowned.

"What is all this? I thought you were sick of heart and just cut loose from a tragic love?"

"Nothing. I just thought she was damned attractive. A

very happy face. I love the upcurled mouth. She looks like Emmett Kelly."

"I doubt she'd be very pleased to have herself likened to a clown, even if you meant it as a compliment. She's had a hell of a life. Married quite young to some British actor who was full of complexes. Made her recite the cricket scores to him while they made love, or something equally unusual. Went quite hairless from an accident in the war. Then she fell in with a RAF type—this after she divorced the hairless cricket-fancier—and saw her own true love shot down in flames over London. Met the noble Georgian later—he was flying with one of those Polish squadrons—at a mess at some airfield or other, and eventually married him. Nobody surpriseder than she when he actually buckled down and made some money, after the war. They lived all over the world. I met her in Hong Kong three or four years ago. Very stylish broad."

"She's got gorgeous legs, in any case," Alec said. "Where're you taking her to lunch tomorrow?"

"I don't know. Twenty-One, I suppose. Maybe Laurent. Why?"

"I might just join you, if you asked me nicely. Well, now I think I'll roll home and hit the hay. Tomorrow—very possibly after lunch—I have *got* to tackle the old Underwood. I've damned near forgotten how to play it." Alec tossed a five-dollar bill on the table. "Pay for my sandwich, will you? I'll allow you to buy me lunch tomorrow. Good night, pal."

He swung jauntily out of the door, looking back over his shoulder at the table where Jill Richard was laughing with a group of exceedingly handsome men and women.

Ben Lea stared at Alec Barr's back, then gazed up at the ceiling.

"I think the kid's in heat," he said to nobody at all, and signaled the waiter for another drink.

58

When she entered, Alec was seated alone at the bar—Ben Lea was not late; Alec had come early—he again noticed the breadth and swagger of shoulder, the high but not opulent breasts, and a waist so small the hips were almost square as they flared from waistline. She looked at Alec with recognition and smiled. Alec hoped at this moment that his friend Ben Lea might break his leg on the way to lunch.

Alec rose and walked over to meet her as she gazed coolly and inquiringly around the red-plush, dark-paneled room.

"I'm Alec Barr," he said. "I was with Ben last night at Clarke's. He very kindly invited me to join you—after, of course, I subjected him to some exquisite Chinese tortures." He hoped that wasn't too brash; evidently it wasn't. She smiled again.

"Perhaps in that case you'll buy me a pink gin while we wait for the good man," she said, and let Alec guide her to Ben Lea's table.

Now they were seated in a warm corner of the Laurent, safely away from the martini-gulping business conferees.

"It's so nice you could join us," Jill Richard said. "I recognized you last night from your book-review pictures. I've read all your books, I expect, mostly in the English version. Do they change them much?"

"Not much. *Jail* becomes *gaol*. *Curb* is *kerb*. *Windbreaker* is *windcheater*. That sort of thing. and once in a while some slight excision to comply with your rather archaic postal laws. Nothing of any importance. Doing anything special here in America?"

"Settling a few straggling details from my late husband's estate. He did a great deal of business in America. We used to keep a house here. There's a few odd bits of old furniture that I'm shipping back to England. Been seeing some theater and drinking far too much."

She smiled, blinding Alec with a dazzle of teeth. The bright red-gold of her hair gleamed like a casque, and the eyes were emerald against white skin. Alec noticed a slight scatter of freckles across the almost snubby nose. The corners of her mouth *did* turn up like a clown painting when she smiled. She was wearing a severely tailored, almost mannish, moss-green suit with a froth of white lace at the throat.

Alec felt schoolboyish in her presence. He wished he could say something brilliant—something very witty—that would keep her eyes crinkled and her mouth upturned. All he could think of was the banal:

"Have you known Ben very long?" He already knew the answer.

"About three years. He had some doings with my late husband in Hong Kong. We painted up the little town somewhat. I adore Ben. He's fun. Very old chum of yours, I suppose?"

"Forever. At least since I came to New York before the war. One of the first—and I must say most useful—people I met. Knew a power of important folk, apart from all the headwaiters in town. I was feeling pretty shy and gawky and country-boyish, and Ben steered me into city-slickerism."

This was better. He signaled the waiter and ordered two more pink gins.

"I can't imagine you being shy and gawky and countrified, not from reading your books." The smile was smaller now, but still blinding. "You sounded to me like a very self-possessed, assured, and rather cynical young man."

Alec waved a dismissing hand and promptly knocked the freshly arriving drinks off the waiter's tray. He apologized to the waiter and turned to Jill Richard.

"See what I mean? I'm still gawky and country-boyish, and even shyer than when I came."

"Success hasn't spoiled you, then. It's nice to know that."

"Absolutely unspoiled." Alec decided to see if he could make her laugh. "As Ben says, 'Success hasn't changed Alec Barr. He's still the same stupid SOB he was when I first adopted him.'"

She did laugh then, not loudly, but in a warm controlled voice. It was a laugh completely unlike Barbara Bayne's. Barbara would throw back her head and guffaw when something tickled her. It was amusing in private, but slightly disquieting in a room full of strangers. Alec decided he could live a long time with Jill Richard's laugh.

The waiter was attaching a phone to the table.

"It's for you, Miss Richard," he said. "Mr. Ben Lea."

"Excuse me," she said to Alec, and took the phone.

"Oh, I *am* frightfully sorry," she said. "Of course I mind being stood up, seeing it's you who's doing the standing. But you couldn't have offered a nicer substitute. *Certainly* I'm having fun." She squeezed her eyes at Alec over the phone. "No, I'm afraid not. I'm off to England tonight. I'm furious at you, of course, but I'll forgive you if you come and stay with me instead of at the Savoy next time you're in London. Yes, I'll surely tell him. Have a good trip, darling, 'Bye."

She hung up, and Alec beckoned the waiter to take the phone away. He raised an eyebrow at Jill Richard.

"That, as you may have gathered, was your friend and mine, Mr. Benjamin Lea," she said. "Seems I'm abandoned, and you're stuck with me for lunch. I hope you don't mind too much."

"Mind? Before you came in, I was hoping he would break his leg. But I also hope I wasn't too prescient. What's wrong with Ben?"

"Got himself caught up by some crisis in Los Angeles just as he was leaving the office. Said he had barely time to catch the plane, that the crisis—whatever it was—was something that only he could handle and that he couldn't do it by phone. Didn't specify."

"It must have been of considerable magnitude. I can only count my blessings. But what's all this about you leaving for England? I was planning on trying to monopolize you indefinitely."

Jill Richard took a sip of her drink, and fitted a cigarette into a holder, waiting for the flick of Alec's lighter before she answered.

"I'm most flattered, I'm sure, but Ben isn't the only person with crises that want personal handling. I *must* be in London tomorrow; I've put off the trip far too long as it is."

Alec infused burlesque horror into his voice.

"Not getting *married?* I couldn't bear it."

Jill blew a cloud of smoke and laughed.

"Nothing so exciting, I'm afraid. It's just that I'm trying to run the remnants of my husband's business—export-import is always in a mess that can only be untangled personally —and there are several contractual knots that have to be unsnarled. There are short-time people from long-distance places like Hong Kong and Tokyo in London at the moment, and the lawyers are sitting around gnawing at their nails."

Alec heaved an exaggerated sigh of relief and took a big gulp of his drink.

"I think we can stand one more while we look at the menu," he said, crooking a finger at the waiter. "The same, and the card, please." Then to Jill Richard. "I was horribly afraid that you were dashing back to the arms of some handsome young fellow who was panting at the airport with a preacher chained to his wrist."

She shook her head.

"I imagine Ben may have mentioned some of my previous emotional and marital complications. I'm getting on for being quite an old lady, and I think I shall avoid the risk of fresh matrimony for the quiet calm of widowhood." Then she giggled for the first time, a little girl's giggle. "And besides, nobody's *asked* me. The invitations well-ripened widows and chronic divorcees get these days are only propositions to leap immediately into bed."

"I wish there were time for me to add another scalp to your collection," Alec said. "But it does seem to me you're a touch cramped for time for the effective prosecution of romance."

Jill Richard smiled again.

"It does seem a pity, but I'm a bit old for what you Americans call a quickie. In my rapidly dwindling thirties, I'm more the deckchair-and-long-voyage type. Also I rather like to know something about the people to whom I might conceivably grant my favors, such as they are. A little more than one lunch, let us say, with packing yet to be done and airplanes to catch."

"Reluctantly I'll have to agree," Alec replied, taking the menus from the waiter. "Although, at the risk of seeming overeager, I was wondering if I might take you to dinner and then drive you to the airport?"

He thought her voice sounded sincere, tinged with real regret.

"I'm afraid it's quite impossible," she said. "Some very old friends—those people you saw me with last night—are having a cocktail buffet and then taking me out to Idlewild *en masse*. However"—Alec could have sworn her voice brightened—"it's very informal, with lots of people, and I'm certain Tess and Bill would love it if you dropped in for a drink and a short good-by. They all know who you are, of course, and I'm sure they'd be flattered if you called in."

"It would be marvelous, even though I'm usually not much of a party-crasher," Alec said. "But I'd crash it with a Sherman tank if it allowed me one more look at you. Is that terribly forward of me?"

"I wouldn't say so." Jill Richard looked at him levelly. "No, I wouldn't say so. As I said I've always liked your books, and now I think I like the man who wrote them."

Alec dipped his head.

"I'm also pretty poor at accepting compliments and, in this town, quite unused to very much in the way of sincerity. And on the strength of three pink gins I might say that in future, with your permission, I plan to see a great deal more of you than is permitted by the smoked trout we are about to order and one farewell drink at somebody else's buffet. Permission granted?"

"Permission granted. Do you get to London very often?"

"Not too often in the past. But I think that very shortly I shall have some absolutely vital business that must be transacted personally with my British publishers—something that cannot possibly be handled by the transatlantic telephone." He grinned.

"I like it when you smile," Jill Richard said. "You don't smile very often. It changes your face entirely. As for me, I'm always baring my teeth. With a mouth as wide as mine about the only thing you can do is grin like a Cheshire cat. Keeping it shut merely calls attention to its size."

"I think we make a very complementary, not to say handsome and distinguished pair. Now, what do you say to some of this trout? I'm told Eisenhower personally catches it."

59

Alec handed Jill Richard into a cab, and decided to stroll back to his hotel. He wanted to think, and he thought better on his feet.

It was absolutely immature of him, he thought, to be at-

tracted to another woman so swiftly after his fling with Barbara—very immature and more than a little vulgar. Not to
mention impractical, with the girl living in London and he
and his work headquartering in New York. And no doubt
about it, the work *was* shot to hell. All this tomcatting
around had practically ruined his old regular habits. And the
way Amelia was spending money in Europe, he had to get
himself grooved again pretty soon.

Amelia. Something had to be done, one way or the other,
about Amelia. She couldn't stay in Europe forever, and he
couldn't live on in hotels indefinitely, fighting shaky portables,
deprived of his old laboring comforts. He missed his secretary, whom he had sent off on a long leave when the Bayne
business started—and, it came with a shock, he missed Amelia.

I suppose you have to face it, Barr, he thought. You're
a selfish bastard and you miss your comforts and Amelia was
comfortable to have around. It was nice having someone
in the house who was not overdemanding; someone who
did not try to make a lover out of you when you were lost
in a book and who truly tried to fend off a lot of petty
nuisances when the brain was beamed in on the work.

Meantime, what a woman this Jill looked to be! The late
thirties were a wonderful age for a woman who had kept
her brain and body trim. The body was marvelous, from all
indication, and probably hadn't changed a pound since it
lost its baby fat. The skin was young and clear, and the
face, cheerful, was not the shapeless spoiled dough-mass of
so many American women. It kept all the marks of maturity
with few of the wrinkles. The generous comic mouth laughed
easily, but there was a lot of living and some pain printed
in the eyes. She was no eyelash-flapping flirt. She had darted
to the basic point of a possible relationship as swiftly as
swallow to nest. There was no doubt in Alec Barr's mind
that given another week of pursuit, another week of learning
about each other, she would also have come happily to his
bed.

Well, she was leaving for England tonight. He would stop
for just one drink at this Bill and Tess address he had in
his pocket, impress himself a little more deeply on her
mind, and give her a ring next time he went to London.
Perhaps it was just as well she was leaving tonight. There
were a lot of unwritten words sulking in that old typewriter.

60 / Dinah

Alec hailed a taxi and decided to go home to the deserted flat. There were no servants about; they left early, and they had been working half-shift flourishing unnecessary dustrags and watering the plants, anyhow, since Amelia left. He would ring the hotel and tell them to pack and send over his clothes tomorrow.

The flat was depressing, and Alec paced around turning on lights. The rooms smelled empty, with that particularly funereal fragrance of homes abandoned by love and bereft of the smell of activity. There were no papers eviscerated alongside the wing chair, no *New Yorkers* or *Lifes* or *Times* flung carelessly on the big coffee table. And there were no fresh flowers in the vases. When Amelia was home there were always fresh flowers.

He walked to his office, flicking on lights. The doorman had summed it up when he touched his cap and said "Good evening, Mr. Barr. You've been away a long time. Much too long a time."

The office neat, of course, and all his treasures intact. But it looked barren, as the long unused body of a woman might look barren. It seemed to have shrunk, somehow, and the idea of working in it depressed him acutely. He walked here and there, touching books. He took the cover off his typewriter and put it back, opened his little bar to take a drink and decided that he didn't want to get the ice out of the trays and anyhow he didn't want to drink alone in the gloomy, empty apartment. When his clothes came back and he had sorted out some bills and mail and other unpleasantnesses he would telegraph Luke and tell him that his long holiday was over; to haul his ass back to Jersey because they were in the book business again. Alec didn't mind being lonely in the Jersey house. It was all his, as this place, with the exception of his office, was all Amelia.

It would be very good to work again, and Monday he

would get in touch with his agent, maybe for lunch, and they could review the unfinished projects.

But tonight he didn't want to be alone—not until bedtime and a pill made his whereabouts indifferent to him. And he didn't want to go back to the hotel; there was too much smell and memory of Barbara Bayne in those rooms. Suddenly he snapped his fingers, and reached into his desk for the big address book.

"Hello, Dinah? It's Alec here. How *are* you?"

"Fine. Peachy. Dandy. I've been hearing lots of things about you, my lad. And you've certainly been making yourself absent about town."

"Yes, I suppose so," Alec said. "But I've been pretty busy." Dinah Lawrence chuckled.

"I heard about what kind of busy. Oh, boy! Some busy."

"Never mind. What I rang about was, I'm lonely and sad, and I wondered if you'd have a drink and dinner with me. I promise you I'll be better-contained than the last time. Did I really try to rape you?"

"If you'd been capable I'd have probably let you," Dinah Lawrence said. "But in your shape, sonny, you couldn't have overpowered a Singer midget. As to this drink and dinner, ordinarily I'd love to, but my child just rolled in for the week end, and we're having cocktails and dinner here at the apartment."

"Oh. I could take you both out." Now his voice brightened. "I'd love to see my pretty Penny again."

There was a pause while another voice was dimly heard. Then Dinah Lawrence said:

"That was your pretty Penny in person. She insists that you come over here and have dinner with the girls. Come right now; I'm just whipping up a batch of martinis. You won't find us at all dress-up; we're in slacks and haircurlers. If you can risk the sight, you're welcome."

"I can stand the sight, thank you very much. Keep me a mart cold, I'm coming over as fast as cab can drive."

Alec took a hurried shower, shaved, and changed his suit. He stopped at the first florist and bought an armful of red roses.

Oddly eager, he rapped on the door of the downstairs flat in the remodeled brownstone, and was totally unprepared for the girl who answered his knock.

61

Alec Barr only actually recalled the child. He had recently seen the snapshot of Penny Lawrence. But somehow the child image had persisted—the fat-legged little girl who had crawled over his lap and clung to his knees, and who called him Unca Alec.

This new girl was a tall girl, with a hull like a racing yacht, clustered coal-black curls, enormous black-lashed blue eyes, and a high curve to her cheekbones that reminded him of the young Hepburn. The mouth was gently full-lipped and soft. She was still quite tanned, and the eyes against the tan were startling in their lightness.

"Come in, Unca Alec," she smiled, and kissed him lightly on the cheek. "What gorgeous roses! It's been a long, long time."

"Great God," said Alec Barr, entering the room. "This can't be *my* Penny—not the Penny whose backside I paddled and took to the Zoo. Not the Penny I took to the Aquarium. Not the Penny I read the stories to. . . . Great God."

"It's been a lot more than ten years," the girl said. "People are apt to change. You haven't changed much, though. A little grayer—maybe better looking. Hey, Ma! The man's here with a whole graveyard full of roses."

Alec let his eyes rove the room. He'd nearly forgotten the two walls of books, the small fireplace, the light-green walls, the comfy-shabby furnishings. Dinah's tastes still ran to greens and yellows. The easy chair was yellow; the rug a warm orange, but the leather sofa newly upholstered in black. It was a room that had soothed him in past; the old footstool was still there, still comfortably dented. The wood of the furniture looked oiled and well-rubbed; the chartreuse curtains were new and crisp. A modern silver jug—a lovely thing of one flowing sensuous curve—he remembered the vase as well as the two Chinese ivory dancers he hadn't been able to resist when he was Sunday-strolling. The sideboard, he remembered, contained the hi-fi and the radio.

Dinah Lawrence came into the room with a silver tray of martinis, which she placed on the sideboard before she walked over to take Alec Barr by both hands. He pulled himself to his feet, grasped her by the shoulders, and kissed her on both cheeks.

"Where are the curlers?" he asked. "And how are you *really*, Di? And where did you get such a daughter?"

"Have a drink first. You're looking well, Alec, but a little tired."

"You're looking marvelous, and *not* a little tired at all. You look beautiful."

Dinah Lawrence did look well. The hair was all silver now, smoothly waved to fall over one eyebrow. The eyes were smoky-blue and clear, and the complete gray had made her appear startlingly young.

Alec Barr reached out and touched her hair.

"Oh, that. I was pretty streaky. I got pretty tired of the streaks and I couldn't see going all black again. Like?"

"Love it. Takes years off you, if that's a polite thing to say to a lady. As a matter of fact if you had done it all black, you and Penny could pass for twins." He looked her up and down, noting the clean line of body in a hip-hugging, blue-taffeta housecoat. He thumped her on the hip.

"You've been up to something else," he said. "You lost yourself a pound or two here and there."

"Long hot summer. Lots of swimming. Few discreet trips to the masseuse. Flop, rest your bones, and tell all."

"Not a hell of a lot to tell. Amelia's in Europe, and I hear by the cocktail grapevine that she may go on to the Far East. I haven't heard a word from her. I've been doing up the town pretty well—"

"So I heard." Dinah's voice was dry.

". . . any case, I've got to go back to work—hard work. I've got a book that I've forgotten all about, and a couple of serials, you know." Alec spread his hands. "There was the barest start of a play. . . . I can't work in that empty apartment. So I think I'll run out to the Jersey place tomorrow, sort of tidy up, and prepare for toil. Tell you what." He held up a finger.

"Why don't you and the kid run out with me tomorrow after an early brunch? You've never seen the place, and it's lovely at this time of the year. Leaves turning and the nights beginning to feel frosty. No servants in the house—but there's plenty of stuff in the deep-freeze and plenty of booze in the locker. We could come back Sunday in easy time for Penny to catch her plane."

"Sounds like great fun. But I'll have to ask Penny."

"Sounds like great fun to Penny, too," Penny said, re-entering the room. "Cook here, cook there, it's all the same to me. The salad's done, Ma, and the rest of the fixin's. All we have to do is slap the steak on."

Alec looked at the girl again. The kitchen heat had brought a flush to her cheekbones, and the blue eyes were very bright. She was wearing a tight pair of high-waisted blue slacks, and he had been right about thinking that when she had lost her baby fat—she had certainly lost her baby fat.

"I'd love to see how a real live author works," Penny said. "Especially now I've got one in the family."

"What's all this about 'author in the family'?" Alec raised an eyebrow.

Dinah regarded her daughter with some annoyance.

"You and your flappy lip," she said. "I wasn't going to mention it until I was far enough along to really believe I have a book instead of an idea. But long as Miss Big Mouth here has let the book out of the bag, I've taken a six-month leave from the paper to see if I can't find out what all newspaper hacks believe—that somewhere in the reportorial body lies buried a book."

Alec passed her a cigarette and offered the pack to Penny. The girl shook her head.

"No thank you. I'm a member of the Cancer Scare generation. Go on, Ma. Tell about the book."

"Well, it's nothing like the things you write, Alec. I wouldn't dare attempt that at my age, after all these years of short-order assignments. But your agent thinks the idea is sound."

"I know it's sound if Mantell likes it. So what's it all about?"

"A kind of female *Front Page*—*Eve among a Million Adams* idea. We haven't settled on the title yet, but Mister Mantell thinks there's a play in it, too, after we shake the book down. I rather like *My Life in the Men's Room*, but Mister Mantell thinks that's a little too earthy. If it turns out to be more fiction than fact we'll think up something cute like *Kitty Foyle, Esquire*—something like that."

"How much of it done?"

"Not a whole lot. I'm just starting the sabbatical. I'm afraid to talk much about it until I see how it runs. Mind?"

"Not at all. It's all right to talk books with somebody who's having his own miseries—parts of books, that is—because sometimes you can save yourself a lot of trouble just free-associating the problem out loud with a good listener. You'll find Mantell helpful, and if there's anything I can do all you have to do is yell. Come to think of it, I remember chewing at your ears with plot problems of my own."

"I vaguely remember a few. I suppose you're way past that point now."

Alec shook his head.

"Don't you believe it. The longer I go, the knottier it seems to get. At last count, I had one editor saying I was too far out, and another saying I was too far *in*. Seems like when I was a kid I used to sell stuff straight out of the typewriter. Now, a few million words later, somebody always seems to want a revise."

"Well, I won't bother you—much, anyhow," Di Lawrence said. "Penny, fix Alec another drink and keep him amused while I finish off the dinner."

"You know, I love my Ma," Penny said. "I love her because she makes nearly everything sound like a joke. I happen to know that this Mister Mantell thinks she has a darned good book going; she showed me a letter from him. You'd think she was just tossing off another feature story. But she was the same way about raising me. She'd kid a little, and suddenly I'd find myself doing exactly what she wanted me to do without a whole lot of parental hoo-hah involved."

"Have you had any spiritual aid and guidance from Di on what you might want to do with your life? You're a junior at college now, right?"

"That's right. I've flirted with a lot of ideas and Ma hasn't tried to steer me in any particular way. I went through most of the phases, I suppose, the world-wide do-gooder bit, get a job with the United Nations, travel abroad and save the heathen from himself—"

"God forbid," Alec murmured.

"But I got rid of that pretty snappy. In the first year of college, I had some idea of being a lawyer, then becoming the first lady President—"

"Double God forbid."

"Then it was the doctor stage—you know, discover the

cancer cure—but that doctor jazz is a long haul and most lady doctors I know seem awfully antiseptic and kind of over-hornrimmed. I thought some more about following in Ma's footsteps and trying to write, but quite frankly I don't think I have the talent. From what Ma tells me, being a good writer is tough enough, and being a bad writer is like but very awful."

"Your Ma is a wise woman as well as a good writer. What do you think of the stage? You're certainly pretty enough. Ever try any acting, college theater, things like that?"

"Little bit. Not much. I don't think I'd be any good at that either. I'm not intense enough. I don't burn with that crazy flame. I'm lazy. And I think I'd hate the kind of phony dreariness that goes with being a constant somebody else, night after night on the stage, day after day before the cameras."

Alec nodded and lit a cigarette. His glass was empty, and Penny walked away to fill it. Alec noticed the fluid swing of her hips in the tight toreador pants and thought irritably: For Christ's sake, Barr, are you so far gone you think of everything in terms of flesh, even children?

"Thanks, sweetie," he said. "You sound like a very intelligent young woman. But you've got to do *something*. What?"

"You'll probably think I'm some kind of jerk, Alec," Penny said, grinning. "But I think I'd like to make somebody a pretty good wife—a smart wife. Of course I'd need a good man, too—somebody I could respect as the raw material in this project. I wouldn't care particularly what he did or where he did it. That sound funny?"

"I'm amazed. It doesn't sound funny at all. But before you run into this fine fellow, unless you marry a college boy, what then?"

"I've decided to major in science, general, with some side courses in business administration. This way I can get a job when I finish—in a lab, in a factory, in a law office, in a department store, and make myself at least a fair living to take me off Ma's hands."

Alec smiled at the girl.

"I think it's terribly bright of you. Half the world wants to do something it doesn't know how to do, and the ones that know generally do it badly. Have you worked at all in college—part-time jobs, I mean?"

Penny shook her head, and the black curls bobbed.

"No. Ma put her foot down. She said colleges were for

studying and fun, that the work would start soon enough and would last the rest of your life. So I haven't worked, although there are plenty of jobs—waiting tables, librarian, that sort of stuff—I've studied and I've dated and gone to dances and that's all."

Alec nodded, violently approvingly.

"Your mother is, indeed, a rare woman. Sometime I'll tell you about what it means to go to school without going to school. It happened to me. I scrabbled so hard for beans and bread that the actual university life passed me by. I might just as well have taken a correspondence course."

Dinah Lawrence came into the living room.

"What are you two jibbering about?"

"Life," Alec said. "And steak. I can smell it, and I can use it."

They sat at a small table with a silver bowl containing some of Alec's roses. It was a meal that Alec favored, a simple succession of shrimp cocktail, salad with roquefort, steak with baked Idaho, a sound red wine, and after, coffee.

"My God," Alec said. "It's the first real meal I've had in months. I've been on the furry-menu-with-sauce-on-everything kick. I'm fuller than a tick." He rubbed his stomach luxuriously. "I think I feel the beginnings of a paunch. This was marvelous, Di. Thank you both for taking me in out of the snow."

"It's so nice to have a man around the house," mother and daughter sang more or less together. "You must come oftener, Alec, like you did in the old days."

"But I won't have anybody to baby-sit," Alec said, smiling at Penny. "She's too big now to fit my lap."

"I wouldn't say that, exactly," Penny's mother said. "And in the absence of Penny you can baby-sit *me*."

"You can start right now." Penny yawned. "I was up before dawn in Chicago, and that plane trip takes it out of you after a full day of classes. Night, all."

She bent and kissed her mother, then dabbed Alec swiftly on the cheek.

"I feel like I've been horning in," Alec said. "Was I?"

"Not at all. One of the nicer things about Penny is she and I haven't indulged in a lot of mother-knows-best since the earliest explanations. About the only thing I ever tried to instill in her was a basic sense of politeness and responsibility. If they're what they call 'making out' with the boys when they're fifteen there's very little to be done about it."

"You've done a hell of a job, Di. She's a swell kid, and I think a level-headed one. She doesn't seem as flitbrained as most of these adolescent experts on the state of the world. I think I'd rather have a little backseat tramp in the family than a chronic hornrim with six degrees in political science and a sidebar course in Swahili."

Dinah yawned and patted her mouth.

"Looks as if we're all going to sack in early if we're to make this safari into darkest New Jersey. What do we wear —after lunch, I mean. Pants?"

"Pants and sweaters. Suppose I meet you both at Twenty-One at twelve-thirty. We can grab a reasonably hasty, sober-sided lunch and be in the country before the sun quits lighting up the trees. I'd like you to see the place by daylight. You haven't before."

"Do we have to be very lofty for the Numerical Place tomorrow?"

"Oh, hell no. Something tweedy. Saturday's non-pearl day in Twenty-One. I'm wearing a sports coat and flannels. Tell Penny to wear something she can travel in. We can drop her off at the airport on the way home."

"Sounds fine. Now scram, lover boy. You may be an all-night kid, but your Aunt Dinah has been killing herself for the past week, trying to emulate an author."

She led him to the door and kissed him coolly, lightly, on the cheek. Alec walked out on the street, searching for the toplight of a taxi. He grinned wryly, tapping a foot on the corner.

"Seems to be your night for early dismissals, Barr," he said aloud as the cab drew up. "I suppose I could stop off at Toots' or at The Blue for a last blast. The hell with it; you drink too much, Barr."

The cab stopped, and Alec opened the door. "Uptown, corner of Park," he said. "You'll recognize the place by the no lights in the window."

"Huh?" the driver said. "What was that again, Mister?"

"Sorry," Alec said. "I was thinking out loud. Park, corner of Seventy-ninth will do. And let's see if we can pass a newsstand on the way."

Back to bed with the bulldog editions, Alec thought. That is the kind of life a happy bachelor leads in New York.

Thank God for the *Daily News* and the *Mirror*. At least I've got Winchell to keep me warm.

As he alighted he checked the sky. The night was crisp and the stars cold and glittery. It looked as if tomorrow would be a nice day for the country.

62

Alec Barr, wearing an ancient chamois-patched houndstooth hacking jacket, gray flannel slacks, and reverse-calf jodhpur boots, got out of his taxi just as the cab bearing his guests drew up behind him. He noticed mother and daughter with approval; Dinah trim in gray tweeds, Penny dressed for travel in blue-gray gabardine suit.

"Hang onto the bags for me, please, Red," he said to the doorman. "I'm having my car sent around at two." Then, to the women: "My, but don't we look tweedy-country-week-endy, and what a lovely day for it."

"We took you at your word, Squire," Dinah Lawrence said. "You said nothing fancy. I hope we don't run into a mess of mink inside. I feel like something straight out of an English pub."

"You were never lovelier," Alec said. "And Miss Penny looks like a *Vogue* ad. Come, let us enter the lair of the expense account and tie on the nosebag."

He steered the women down the steps, past the little iron jockeys, and the heavy door swung open. A tall saturnine man and a small, plump, cheerful man occupied the reception desk. The dark saturnine man's face lit, and the small cheerful man broke into a broad smile as they entered.

"Welcome home, Mr. Barr. Good afternoon, ladies," the tall man said. "Your usual table, Mr. Barr?" the small cheerful man said. "You've been avoiding us lately."

"Hello, Monte. Hi, Jimmy. Yes, thanks. Nice to see you again. I haven't really been avoiding you. Some work; more travel. How's the family?"

"Fine," both men said. "Right this way, ladies."

"Thanks," Alec said, and allowed a tall young man to

lead them into the cool dark cavern, the first of three rooms whose ceilings were strung with model aircraft and whose walls were hung with old Peter Arno cartoons and, in recesses, studded with ancient tankards.

Alec nodded and smiled at half a dozen employees, all of whom said invariably, "Welcome back, Mr. Barr." A tall, tanned, freckled man met them as they entered the bar. "Hi, Alec," he said, "you're a real stranger. Don't you love us any more?"

"Hi, Pete," Alex said. "I still love you. I'm sure you know Mrs. Lawrence. I doubt if you know *Miss* Lawrence. This is Pete Kriendler, one of the five thousand relatives in the joint. How's everybody?"

Peter Kriendler was seating them at a small center table in the front room.

"Not much change. Mac's in Europe buying booze. Bob's off on some Marine maneuver. Charlie and Jerry are around. Sheldon and I are doing all the work. You buried in another book?"

"More or less. Hope to exhume myself pretty soon." He looked around. "Nice crowd for so early in the day."

"Most of the steady folks are back from Europe and the Hamptons," Pete Kriendler said. "Vincent, buy these nice people a drink for me, please. Very nice to have met you, ladies. Alec, let's shoot a duck or something later on this year."

In the first lull Dinah Lawrence said.

"How long since you've been in here?"

"About two months," Alec said.

"Jesus," said Dinah, "I would have thought at least two years."

"Did it ever occur to you," Dinah Lawrence said when the drinks had come, "that there really is no such thing as a wagon in Manhattan? Everything you do or say, any business deal you make, any story you cover, any plane you catch, is all done in the vicinity of a saloon? You don't need an intellect to succeed; what you need is a cast-iron liver and a zinc-lined stomach."

"Well, being possessed of neither, I have the unpleasant prospect of putting myself on the old cart until the work's done. I just can't do it any more—drink *and* work, I mean."

"When does this ordeal start? I might just take up sobriety with you. I know damned well I drink too much, and I'm new at this book-writing business." Dinah sounded serious.

"Tuesday, I'd say. I have to meet Mantell on Monday, and that's never successful over ice water. And I probably have to see a couple of editors for lunch or cocktails with Mantell. But as of Tuesday I am a very good boy, shaky but noble. And I'm dreading it."

"You two sound like a couple of candidates for Alcoholics Anonymous," her daughter said. "A drink now and then doesn't bother *me* any."

Alec and Dinah looked at each other.

"There are times when I positively hate the very young," Alec said.

"Especially in the morning," Dinah said. "Well, here comes the crab, and the winebucket. Let us put off the sacrifice until next week, and get on with the wassail."

The meal was served with the usual precision which justified the prices, and from time to time some one of the customers stopped off at the table to nod and enquire about how the next book was coming. Alec rose to kiss a few pretty ladies on the cheek—most of them actresses or members of the kindred arts, singers, lady editors and such— and his introduction to his guests seemed to Penny almost a cross section of the famed from television, moving picture, and stage. The gentlemen were different, mostly large-faced smooth-jowled men in either the fomal city blue with the gray silk tie or else in something rather obvious in Saturday tweeds. They answered to the tag of corporation, production, manufacture, or advertising. It seemed to Penny that her Unca Alec knew everybody of any importance in New York, and that they were all delighted to see him and to meet his friends.

"Damn, it's difficult to eat in this trap," Dinah said. "I thought you mentioned something about table-hopping?"

"I think it's all wonderful," Penny sighed. "When I go out at school we usually wind up in a dogwagon or a chow-mein joint, and half the time we go Dutch. It's so nice not to see a lot of crew cuts for a change. I'd almost forgotten that men wear neckties."

"Don't let it spoil you for the intellectual life," her mother said. "Come on, dear, let's visit the loo before we embark on our journey."

"It's to your left around the corner," Alec said absently.

"*I* know it's to the left around the corner," Di said sharply.

"It's Penny, not *me*, who hasn't been to Twenty-One before."

Alec walked over to the bar to talk baseball with Henry and Emil, the bartenders, and allowed himself to be persuaded into a quick cognac by the cluster of men who gathered in the corner. It was good, he thought, to be back in his own territory again. He had purposefully eluded the old haunts which he only visited in the company of Amelia. No mystery about the effusiveness of the greetings; it occurred to him that he hadn't been in "21" since he had met Barbara Bayne.

63

Now, spinning down the highway with the top down—it was still warm enough in the early afternoon—and two pretty women snuggled in the broad red-leather front seat beside him, he was conscious of a feeling of intense well-being. He was going home, and he was going home to *work*. The nagging conscience was eased, and the lush lunch was still warm in his stomach.

The women were silent, listening to the whish of the tires and to the radio playing softly from WPAT in Paterson.

"Penny," Di Lawrence said suddenly.

"Yes, Ma?" Penny's voice was sleepy.

"Not you, baby. I was offering Mr. Barr your namesake for his thoughts. What's on that keen authorial mind, Alec, this bright autumnal afternoon?"

"Nothing. Everything. I was just ruminating. College. Youth. Uncertainty. How fast it all moves. Mainly I was wondering when Luke gets back. I wired him this morning."

"Who's Luke?" Penny's voice was fully awake now.

"Luke? He's the other half of my hermitage. Luke is Luca Germani, ex-chief yeoman, USNR, second-generation Italian, hero of a thousand battles with Navy red tape, and for a long time the man who brings some semblance of order into my working existence. Luke runs my life when I am out here in Jersey, and he runs Jersey when I am off to the wars of Manhattan, Africa, or darkest Elsewhere. In short, Luke is my chief cook-and-bottlewasher-cum-secretary-foreman-slave."

"Explain. I don't think I ever heard you mention him before." This was Dinah.

"Not much to explain. Luke and I were in the Great War together. He was attached to my admiral's staff, and he was sort of allocated to me as personal secretary in charge of such heroic things as filing, cutting orders, fouling up personnel records. Skinny Wop—smart as hell—do anything you needed doing in the office. Made fine coffee. I didn't hear from him until well after the war, about the time I built the house in Jersey. It was like some sort of miracle. I had scarcely moved in and was having a lot of domestic trouble —the town servants hated moving back and forth, and there's not a lot of help forthcoming from the local Jackson Whites; I needed my gal secretary in town, and Amelia loathed the idea of the hearty outdoor life on a Jersey lake. She also hated cooking.

"Well, I got a letter from Luke saying he was tired of the kind of jobs ex-yeomen were offered. He said he'd read a couple of my hairier-chested books, and did I have anything for him that would combine stenography with fishing and hunting and fresh-air. I told him to come see me."

Alec swerved to avoid a head-on collision with a hotrod, and lit a cigarette from the dash lighter.

"It turned out fine all round. Luke had been dear-Johned in the war, and evidently none of the local *ragazze* around Scranton, Pennsylvania, took his postwar fancy. I guess maybe he was sour on women, and very possibly sour on the peace. A chief yeoman on a ship or shore station had a lot of authority, and being a chief clerk ashore wouldn't appeal to a man who had run the inner workings of a carrier.

"So Luke lives here in Jersey with me most of the time. He's still a fast typist, even though his dictation is shaky. But he likes to chop wood and build fires and fish in the lake and, most important, he doesn't want to be an author. He can't cook very well, but you can live on spaghetti and meatballs if you have to, and I'm a pretty fair chef myself in a simple sort of way, like steaks and scrambled eggs. I hope to God he brings home a couple of new recipes, say like a good scallopine, from Momma and five sisters. But mainly between frozen foods and the canned stuff—God bless Chef Boy-Ar-Dee—we eat pretty good Wop fare."

"Seems a strange combination, a secretary-handyman-cook," Dinah said.

"Not so strange. Most Italians are raised in the kitchen. They don't see anything degrading about taking a turn at the skillet. They've been watching Momma back of the stove for most of their formative years."

"Well, I hope your paragon fetches you a fresh batch of recipes instead of bringing back a wife," Dinah said. "I'd hate to see any female intrusion into this All-Boy paradise."

"No fear," Alec Barr said, turning off the main highway. "No bloody fear. If a wife comes in, out goes Luke, and Luke knows it."

"That's narrow of you," Dinah said. "Horrid old misanthrope."

"Golly, the country's lovely now," Penny said. "Look at those gorgeous trees. They're just turning."

They had come into a second-class road now, and it was closely rimmed with the crisping gold-and-red leaves of maple and beech against the deep backdrop of evergreen. Silver shafts of birch stood like bright palings among black-greenery, topped by the color-splotched canvas of the autumnal change. The air was growing colder, and the sun was painting the sky as it started to slide behind the swelling blue hills in the distance. In a few short minutes the change from grimy factory town and car-maggoty highway had been startling.

"That's why I love it," Alec said. "Two turns and you might as well be in Kenya. We'll be home in a few minutes."

"I hope so," Dinah said. "My old bones are beginning to chill."

He swerved the car into a graveled road. The road curved among the silver-glowing birch and a tumble of briared underbrush, with big pines and firs forming a canopy over the track. He squealed his tires as he achieved the summit, and drew up the Cadillac with a flourish behind a fieldstone house. The birch forest came almost into the graveled back yard.

"Home," he said, and went back to the trunk to retrieve the bags. "We go in the back way, like proper country folks. Enter through the kitchen, I always say, and see what kind of people live in the main house."

He unlocked a door and pressed a light switch. The

kitchen seemed enormous, full of gleaming enameled dinosaurs.

"It's a do-it-yourself kitchen, all right," he said. "There's enough cubic feet in that deep freeze to store a couple of steers. Even an adult can cook on the stove, and we barbecue nearly everything outside, anyway. Come on into the headquarters. There'd better be a fire laid, or I'll skin me an Italian."

He plopped the bags at the side of a broad hall that led into what at first appeared to be pure space overlooking a lake. But the space had a flagged floor, and a stone fireplace to the right, and constituted infinite space confined by two huge sheets of glass. The view was straight into the side of, and over, a mountain, with the sun-dyed blue sheen of a lake between. The drop from glass terrace to lake was sheer. A drained swimming pool lay level with the flagstones on the left, and the whole was confined again by the silver birch.

"My God!" Dinah said. "I thought I was going to step right out into the stratosphere! You've got yourself quite a view here, boy. How do you get down to the lake? Dive?"

Alec was stooping lighting the birch fire. He looked over his shoulder.

"Easy enough. You can't see it from this particular promontory, but the slope to the right is really very gentle, and the view less stark from the other rooms. Except of course upstairs. I built this place kind of on a tilt."

He straightened up as the curled parchment bark of the logs began to crackle.

"That'll fry us in a moment. I got a thermostat for real winter, but I hate that kind of heat when I can get enough warmth out of a fireplace. We eat out here a lot. It collects an awful lot of sun in the wintertime. Now, the bar."

He turned his back on the view and walked over to a long oaken slab, mounted on a cabinet which occupied half the walled end of the room. One game head, a black-maned animal with an arched neck and long back-curved horns, looked arrogantly out at a corner of the lake.

"What's that thing?" Dinah asked. "A moose?"

"No, it's not a moose. It's a sable."

"Oh," Penny said. "That's what they make those lovely coats out of!"

"I'm afraid not," Alec smiled. He had been subjected to that assumption several hundred times. "What they make those lovely coats out of is a kind of black weasel that runs around loose in Russia. This is an African sable antelope, and it's called sable only because it's black."

He was behind the bar now, standing in front of a bright array of bottles and glassware on shelves behind him.

"What'll it be for two cold girls?"

"Anything with gin," Dinah said. "A Gibson be too much trouble?"

"Not if you can wait a second for the ice," Alec said, and disappeared into the kitchen. He returned with a bleeding finger and a zinc airlines bucket, which he plumped into a hole in the bartop. He sucked at the bleeding finger.

"Been a long time since anybody defrosted anything around here," he said. "Luke *told* that idiot in the village to look in once a week. I guess he's drunk."

"You want a Band-aid for that finger? I suppose you've got them under the bar too." Dinah tasted her drink. "You make a powerful Gibson, man. Cheers." She walked over to the fire and lifted the back of her skirt against the blaze, which was now beginning to leap. "I don't know why a girl always gets colder back there than anywhere else, but it's a matter of scientific fact."

"When you've thawed out a bit, I'll show you the rest of the joint, and also your quarters," Alec said. "Meanwhile, look!" He pointed a finger at the far shore of the lake. Five deer, three does and a couple of yearlings, were tiptoeing daintily down to drink. Simultaneously, an echelon of black ducks flighted in and splashed hard as their undercarriages hit the water.

"That's what I mean about this place," he said. "It's still real country."

"Doesn't shooting them scare them off?" Penny asked.

"We don't shoot around this lake. There's plenty of deer —too damned many—within a mile or so, and we only shoot the transient ducks off the ponds back there."

"I must say it's beautiful," Dinah said. "You'd think you were a million miles away from Times Square."

The ceiling in the next room was lofty, the room's dimensions vast. An enormous desk occupied one corner of the room, which elled off to still another room.

"My God, is this where all the old elephants come to die?" Dinah said. "Penny, we're lost in a zoo."

Alec looked a little rueful.

"I'm sort of fond of my pets," he said. "That lion was a personal friend of mine. That elephant"—he pointed to two enormous ivory curves to the left of the fireplace—"that elephant I spent the best part of two months chasing. And that tiger"—he jerked a thumb at the monstrous striped beast over the fireplace—"just about cost me my neck. But they sort of soothe me. At least they don't remind me of editors and agents and traffic jams."

"Did you really shoot all these animals yourself?" Penny's voice was a little awed. "Like those great big black ugly things on the other wall? Weren't you scared to death?"

"I suppose I was, at the time, particularly with those great big black things. They're called Cape buffalo. But mostly you're excited first and frightened afterward. I remember after I shot that lion I threw up behind a bush."

"I'd have thrown up *before* I shot that lion," Dinah muttered. "Can you really live comfortably with all these things you've—shall we say deprived of freedom and the pursuit of happiness?"

"You'd be surprised how comfortably I can live with them. They grow on you. And if it's any consolation, most of them would have been dead pretty soon, anyhow. They're all old males, well past breeding, kicked out of the tribe, and subject to all the ills old people contract for." His voice had suddenly become a little impatient.

"I suppose that does make a difference," Penny said. "If you're old and sick and dying and lonely, I mean."

"I don't mean to be presumptuous," her mother said. "But do I detect a touch of Mister Hemingway's influence here?"

Alec swept them to a seat on a circular green sofa before the fire and sat across the circular coffee table, a brass-studded wooden Arab brazier. He placed his drink on the edge.

"I suppose so," he said. "I've been accused of it. We both write. We both hunt. We both scuffle in the commercial end of the trade. They make lousy movies out of what we both are lucky enough to sell, and we're grateful for the money. We both like the outdoors. Anyhow, he's an old friend of mine."

"Oho, sister, I think I touched a nerve," Dinah said lightly. "Excuse please. Didn't mean to be rude. Could I have a little more of this deelicious gin, please, and then could I see the rest of your castle?"

"You're forgiven," Alec said, heading out to the bar. He jerked his head over one shoulder, pointing with his chin.

"The girls' room is there, but I'm afraid you'll find a wart-hog glaring at you if you use that one. If you're sensitive to warthogs there's another john just off the next hall, to your right. No warthogs."

Mother looked at daughter.

"I think we also stepped on a corn," she said.

"I think you were pretty horrid," Penny said. "He's so proud of his house—and I think, lonely in it, in spite of all that talk about this Luke person."

"We'll try to make it up to him," Dinah said.

64

No wonder Amelia stays in town, Dinah thought, as Alec led her to the double-bedded guestroom, which supported still another spotted creature—a jaguar—snarling from the wall. *I'll have nightmares all night.*

"Does Lassie up there bite?" she asked, indicating the big cat. "Does a gun go with the bedside paraphernalia?"

"All right, kid me," Alec was goodnatured about it. "So I'm not but fourteen years old. But the point is, I like it, and can work in it. The fireplaces draw and the ashtrays are big enough. It's my kind of house—not that fancy-schmancy Park Avenue stuff."

"I think it's a wonderful house," Penny said with startling vehemence. "I think it's a *marvelous* house," causing her mother to stare at her quizzically.

"Of course it's a marvelous house," Dinah said. "But I've known Alec so long he'd think it was very strange if I suddenly drowned him in flattery."

"Correct," Alec said. "Now if you ladies want to tidy up a bit, I'll go down and cope with the steaks. Charcoal takes a little time. Don't hurry; there's a hi-fi arrangement in that Arab chest in the big room, and you know the way to the bar, now. Make yourself easy until I yell."

"Couldn't I set a table or something?" Penny asked.

"That would be nice. We'll eat off the big table in the patio room. The stars look pretty through the glass. You'll find all the necessities in the big cupboard in the kitchen."

Alec went whistling downstairs to see to his charcoal. Dinah Lawrence looked curiously at her daughter again.

"What are you doing, chum, bucking for Luke's job or something?"

"I'm not bucking for Luke's job. I just don't think you ought to tease him so much. He loves this place, and you're making fun of it. I'll bet—I'll bet—"

"You'll bet what, honey?"

"I'll bet that his wife spoiled it for him and that's why he left her."

"What do you know about Alec leaving his wife?" Dinah's voice sharpened. "I never mentioned it. She's just in Europe, far as I know."

"I heard it in the ladies' room in Twenty-One. Somebody saying—just as you left—something like 'Well, I see old Alec's cutting up high and handsome since he walked out on Amelia. First it was that Bayne broad and now he's got two summer replacements, mother *and* daughter.'"

Dinah Lawrence prodded her daughter's shoulder.

"Look, Junior," she said. "Whatever the reason for Alec Barr's leaving Amelia, it didn't have anything to do with her lack of appreciation for this hunting-camp retreat. And don't pay too much attention to the things you hear in ladies' rooms. Mostly they're a flock of lies."

"It didn't sound to *me* like a flock of lies. It sounded like a flock of truth. And you're in love with Alec, aren't you? You always have been, haven't you? And he's always cheated on his wife, hasn't he? And you've slept together, *haven't*—"

Dinah Lawrence slapped her daughter, hard.

Penny Lawrence pressed her hand against her cheek, and her eyes were huge and hurt.

"You shouldn't have done that," she said after a moment. "I won't forget it. You really shouldn't have. I'm a woman, not a child."

"You're not too much of a woman to get smacked for being rude and childish and way out of line." Dinah Lawrence made her voice flat and cold. "You've got half a crush on a man old enough to be your father, and you're stumbling around like a puppy. What I feel for Alec Barr is nobody's business. Particularly it's none of *your* business, and I'll thank you to mind what few manners I've taught you. That clear?"

"That is very clear. And it only confirms what I was saying."

Penny's voice was equally flat and cold. Her eyes were very bright, and free of tears. "And don't you *ever* slap me again, do you hear?"

Dinah shook her head and ran fingers through her hair.

"I'm sorry, baby," she said. "Really sorry. There are some things . . ."

"All right," her daughter said. "We'll forget it. But don't call me 'baby'."

65

The dinner had not been a total disaster. Alec had exhumed some frozen corncobs, which he had managed to roast without charring too much, and with the help of a few more packets of quick-frozen garden products had contrived a meal of which he was quite proud. The steak was only a little bit scorched on the outside, and only a touch blue and mildly clammy in the middle.

They drowsed from the fire and the keen country air, and went early off to bed, sleeping late into the morning. When Dinah and Penny came downstairs, Alec was bustling, whistling happily. He had already laid the table for breakfast.

"Look at that day!" he said, indicating a flawless autumn sky and a vulgar excess of golden sunshine. The light had flooded the closed patio, and he had opened one door leading out to the flagged terrace. "How'd you sleep?"

"Died," Dinah Lawrence said. "And Lassie didn't bite me even once. I must say there's something to be said for gin and that gorgeous red wine. What is our host preparing for breakfast, might I ask?"

"First, a covey of Scotch sours, if that pleases you, and then waffles and hard ham from Virginia. There are some English muffins and some fine, fresh canned fruit. That's about the best I can do at the moment."

"Lead us to those sours," Dinah said. "Do you think we're making a drunkard out of Penny?"

"Hell, I was drinking corn likker out of Dixie cups when I was fifteen," Alec said. "And it never stunted my growth any. And we'll all be on the wagon tomorrow—or at least Tuesday. How do they taste?"

"You have unforeseen talents, Barr," Dinah said. "I never knew you were a housewife before. I do believe you actually adore this Boy-Scouting."

"I must confess to it. Give me a good piece of meat to ruin and blow some smoke in my eyes, drop a lot of sand in the soup, and I'm as merry as a bird. Come on now, Di, it's about time to activate the waffle iron. Penny, you're in charge of the coffee detail, and I shall fry the ham."

After breakfast, over a third cup of coffee, Alec said:

"While I was stirring around among the papers, waiting for you two slugs-abed to arise, a thought hit me. Penny, seeing as how your mother and I are both writing books, a dreary business at best, why don't you persuade your Ma to move out here with me? We're amply chaperoned, for Luke'll be back tomorrow or next day. No, wait a minute—" Dinah Lawrence had started to speak.

"Hear me out. It makes sense. No noise, no telephones, a hell of a reference library—we'll set up your mill *in* the reference library, Di—a built-in secretary for the recopying, and somebody to talk to when the day's work's done. Also somebody to try out ideas on. It's lonesome as hell working in a city apartment, and always tempting to drop into Tim's or P.J.'s for a drink when you should be pounding that machine. What do you think, Pen?"

"I think it's a simply marvelous idea," Penny's voice was cold as she turned to her mother. "After all, it's your first book, Mother, and Alec's had so much experience and it's so quiet and I'm sure Luke is a lot better cook than Alec said."

Dinah Lawrence raised her hand.

"Whoa," she said. "Whoa right up. Just a minute. Apart from the dubious propriety of my moving into the country with a married man, there never was a house big enough for two writers. I think we've been over that route before. You write your book and I'll write mine—both in our own quiet corners. We've been friends a long time, Alec. I'd like to keep it that way."

"But Mother, Alec only wants to help you."

"Forget it. I know what I'm talking about. We'd be at each other's throats in three days, if not less." Dinah fixed her daughter with a stare.

Alec shrugged, looking disappointed.

"It was just an idea. I thought . . ."

"It was a fine and generous and entirely impractical idea but no dice. Penny, you've more to pack than me. Why don't you throw your things into the bag, so we won't have to rush for that airplane?"

"Yes, Mother," Penny said in a small voice.

"What's wrong between you and Penny?" Alec asked, after Penny disappeared.

"Nothing very much. Slight mother-daughter tiff. It'll pass. Ignore it."

Alec shrugged. "Women," he said, "of all ages."

They drove slowly through the burnished autumn afternoon to Newark Airport, subdued as people are when the week end is over and one is to leave the others behind. Alec flicked on the radio again, with the crack that "now is the time to hear an announcement about another Pearl Harbor" and was withered by both women. He chopped off the station and drove in silence.

Am I going to ask Amelia for a divorce? His mind roved. It's a hell of a lot of trouble, and damned expensive as well. She's done nothing really to deserve it. I'm the bastard in the basement. If I do divorce her, what do I find that's better? There's the work to be done, and you sure as hell can't work when you're separating the silver and dividing up the books.

If only I were actually desperately acutely in love with someone. Dinah's wonderful, but Dinah sees me all too clearly. There's no use building a new trap that I'll only be running away from, cheating—lousy word, *cheating*—as soon as I get bored and fiddlefooted. He sighed deeply.

"What's the matter?" Dinah Lawrence asked. "That one really came out of your boots."

"Nothing. Not really. I'm just feeling despondent about tomorrow. Work and wagon and harsh reality. The honeymoon's over."

"Honeymoon, how?" Penny asked him. Her voice was still very small.

"Not exactly a honeymoon, Sweetie," Alec said. "Say a

vacation from responsibility. The time has come for nose and grindstone to merge, and it makes me sad. For a little while this summer I thought I was young. It's a mistake all of us old fellows make. When are you coming home again?" He spoke suddenly, brightly.

"Thanksgiving, I guess."

"Well, unless your Ma's so deep in her book as to be impossible, let's all get gussied up and misbehave outrageously one night. By Thanksgiving I'll need a break. We'll eat some caviar and hear some jazz and kick over an ashc— and paint the town bright red."

"It sounds wonderful, if Mother isn't too busy. And thanks for a lovely week end, Alec. I truly love your house, and hope you'll let me come back."

"Thanks, Pen. Incidentally, have you read that last book of mine, that *Total Loss* thing?"

"No, I'm ashamed to say I haven't—"

"Figured. If you'll reach into the glove compartment, you'll find one. It'll give you something to read on the plane. It's hand-writ in, but don't show your Ma. Wait until you get on the plane before you flip to the flyleaf."

"Golly, thanks, Alec. And I won't show my mother. She'd only be jealous."

"I doubt if a simple signature can stir the modern female to jealousy," Alec smiled. "Anyhow, it was fun playing with you. I'll just let your mother see you off." He drew up to the unloading stand, and beckoned a porter. "Bye, Sweetie, and thanks."

Penny got out of the car, came round to the driver's side, and kissed Alec on the cheek. She whispered:

"If you'd made me the same offer you made my mother I'd have taken you up on it."

66

"Sunday is really the day for long sad silences, isn't it?" Dinah Lawrence had slid over in the seat and was resting one hand lightly on Alec's knee. "It starts out so beautiful bright in the morning, so full of sunny festivity and noisy birds, and always lapses into nocturnal sadness. I'll bet more people get drunk on Sunday nights than ever got waffled on Saturday."

Alec nodded. He was watching the traffic, and there didn't seem to be much of an answer. His head was full of tomorrow's book now, the tight, about-to-explode feeling that always presaged the prison-pent burst of energy.

"I suppose you know I love you," Dinah continued amicably, conversationally. "I suppose you know that I've never been capable of really falling in love with anybody else since we first started knocking around together on stories, oh, so very long ago. I only let myself go once— that night in Philadelphia—and then I could have kicked myself in the pants." She seemed to be talking to herself.

"In your early days when you were having a lot of trouble—I suppose, with Amelia, as well as with the editors—I used to wait for you to call and ask to drop by. You always used that favorite phrase of yours, 'to preserve my sanity.' I suppose maybe I helped. But it didn't do much for mine. Would it surprise you to know that I haven't been to bed with another man since Philadelphia?"

Alec was embarrassed. This wasn't the Dinah he knew, the flip, hard-cracking Dinah who could hold her own in any bar and on any story with any of the fellows. This was suddenly a soft and vulnerable woman he didn't know at all. That Philadelphia caper had been a product of too much booze and too easy proximity. He had barely remembered it next day—the details—but for the fact that there was a head-print on the pillow and a warm fragrant nest on the other side of the bed. Dinah hadn't even left a note.

"I really don't know what to say, darling." The word tasted awkward on his lips. Dinah was no darling; she was "chum" or "Toots" or "mate" or "Sweetie," but never "darling." "I knew of course we were friends, and that I loved you in a special private kind of way, but it never occurred—"

"It wasn't meant to occur. I kept both feet planted hard on it to keep it from occurring. I wasn't going to hand out a heart for laughs. I could have slept with you on the side for as long as we played it straight, but not with pieces of me breaking off and you not even noticing."

"Amelia—"

"*Damn* Amelia. It wasn't Amelia I was worried about. It

was *me* I was worried about. Amelia didn't have anything to lose, because she had long since lost anything to give. At least to you, the way you wanted it. If you fell into bed that easily with me in Philadelphia, it had become a habit by that time, and I wasn't having any. I wanted some to-morrows, or else nothing. For a sophisticated writer-fellow you're a pretty blind boy, Alec Barr."

Alec lifted his hands helplessly from the wheel for a split second. His knuckles whitened when he replaced the hands.

"You know," he said levelly after a moment. "I get the feeling that I have never done anything right in my life. Not with Amelia, not with you, not—well, you know all about my fling—not even with Barbara Bayne. I am a babe in a wood full of women. I wanted—I *want*—I reach out for love and I draw back a nub. When love is there I don't know about it. I lack a vital part somewhere. What's wrong with me?"

Dinah lit two cigarettes and handed him one.

"I guess you never had time to be in love," she said, and Alec, eyes pinned to the road, couldn't see the tears dew suddenly on her lashes. "I guess you just never had time."

"All right, so I never had time." The muscle jumped and knotted in his jaw. "Supposing I do ask Amelia for a divorce? Supposing I realize—like they won't buy in fiction any more —supposing I realize suddenly that I have loved you all the time? That used to be plot justification enough for the slicks. Would you marry me?"

"No," said Dinah Lawrence. "I wouldn't marry you if you were the last man on earth, not in your current condition."

"And if by some chance I repaired my current condition, at some future date? If I became a human being instead of an extension to a bloody typewriter? Would you marry me then?"

"You wouldn't even have to marry me then. I'd crawl on broken bottles to live with you and be your love." Dinah fished for a handkerchief and blew her nose. "This is a pretty damned silly conversation for two old pros," she said. "Excuse me for going all-girl on you. It's not a thing I generally indulge in."

Alec shook his head.

"I do believe my education in the female sex has been sadly neglected," he said. "At the ancient age of forty plus

I find I know nothing, nothing at all, despite all the smart-ass books and crappy dialog I've written. It makes me a little groggy." He shook his head again. "I think I'll start writing outdoor books for boys."

They had crossed the bridge and were turning off the West Side Highway, heading into Manhattan.

"You suggest any cure?" he said after a bit, edging the car through the double-parked sidestreets. "Or am I completely hopeless?"

"You're not hopeless, not completely hopeless at all. All you have to do is find somebody to give yourself to—all of you, against all the business practicalities, over all the city sophistries, against all the social necessities. And don't tell me that sounds like something out of the Brontë sisters. It's the only cure for what ails you, Alec Barr."

He drew the car up in front of her brownstone and let the motor idle. He walked around to the trunk and got out her overnight bag, carried it to the steps, and then said:

"If you'll give me one minute to find a parking space, I'd love to come in for a drink, and pursue this a little further."

Dinah Lawrence put both hands on his cheeks, drew his face down, and kissed him lightly, gently, on the lips.

"Not tonight, my love," she said. "I don't think my daughter would approve. My daughter's in love with you too."

"I still don't understand women," Alec said helplessly. "Was that what was wrong with you and Penny all day?"

"That was what was wrong with me and Penny all day. She accused me of being in love with you, and of sleeping with you, as if she had a right to you. I slapped her, hard, for the first time in many a year. I regret the slap; I think I did it out of fear of growing older. Jealousy, if you like."

"Good night," said Alec Barr. "I'll call soon."

"Jesus," he murmured as he slid the car into gear and headed home.

67

There is only one time more starkly subject to the awful-awfuls than Sunday night in New York, after a week end in the country, and that is a winter Sunday morning in the deserted caverns of Wall Streets, when the wind hurls yesterday's newspapers like maniac tumbleweeds through the vacant corridors of commerce. Invariably it rains on Sunday night in New York, but even if the night is clear and the stars bright, there is still an intimation of rain. Few restaurants are open; moving pictures and Chinese restaurants provide the *unital bomas* against the vultures that peck at the eyes of the spirit.

Alec considered a movie and decided against it. He did not want to talk baseball with the loaded loners at Toots'; he did not want to stop off at The Embers and hear the Sunday replacement piano. He certainly did not want to investigate the Village. So he settled for a dispirited dinner at The House of Chan, and not even the owner was there to amuse him with his fractured English. Alec poked at his spareribs and egg roll and clammy Chinese vegetables and decided to go home, although the night was very young. He felt a belly-emptiness, a weakness in the knee, a shakiness of finger, as if he were recovering from a protracted drunk.

The apartment was just as empty, just as depressing—perhaps a little more so because of Sunday night. He went into his bedroom, took off the country clothes, put on a pair of pajamas and a robe, and sat down with the early morning papers. He kept reading the same headlines over and over again, until in desperation he went to the bar and mixed himself a very brown drink. It tasted vile. He felt old and ugly. But he had looked at himself in the mirror as he undressed, and nothing in particular had happened to his face. It was still long, still horsy, and the hair seemed no whiter over the ears.

He thought of the week end. He had lost Barbara on Thursday night—that was forever, that was a relieved loss—

and he had met Jill Richard on Friday. He had lost Jill
Richard on the same Friday . . . quite probably forever. He
had met an entirely new Dinah Lawrence on Saturday and
Sunday—Sunday was still today—and had seen the arrowed
passage of his own life targeted in the woman's face of a
child he had once taken to the Zoo. It was Penny, he supposed, who really caused him to feel handled and used and
rejected—hollow—*hollow* was the only word. He had chased
Amelia away; even that comfortably irritating presence was
denied him. He was unable to concentrate on a newspaper.
Books were beyond him. The thought of television was abhor-
rent. And Dinah Lawrence was in a bitch-fight with her own
daughter.

Well, Barr, he thought, there's the work. There's always
the bloody work. Tomorrow's another day, and we've always got the work. Back to the ranch, after Marc gives me
some more hell; back to Jersey and Luke and dull routine
and the old sweat shirts and no more dames. No more dames
—at least for a long time. Put 'em in books if you will, but
stay the hell out of their beds.

Bed. Bed alone. Bed alone is no cure for the dreadful-
dreadfuls, that sad admixture of overdue conscience and future fear. Man shall not live by bed alone. Alec grinned
sadly at the terrible pun, took a double-dip of soda bicarb
and collapsed onto his lonely couch. Sleep touched him fit-
fully, then mockingly skipped away. His brain squirmed with
fragments of plots and sleazy scraps of dialog. He reviewed
his banking position. What if I get too sick to finish this book?
Suppose I get hepatitis and can't work for a year? Suppose
I go blind? What happens to everybody if I crumble and
fall? Literary styles always changing. Mantell says so. That's
gospel. Lots of competition in the space age. Remember
Peter B. Kyne. Peter had it made until the styles changed
on him. Remember Jack London. What do I know about
science fiction? Poor old FPA. The hottest column of them
all, once, that "Conning Tower," and then that last pathetic
begging letter asking for bottom-of-the-trunk stuff for an an-
thology, the last starving resort of has-been writers. I
couldn't stand being poor now, not at my age.

Alec squirmed, sweating lightly. The sheets clamped wrestling holds onto his limbs, strangled him in mummy-wrappings. The pillows gouged his eye, and prickles attacked his
body, inch by inch, as if ants were crawling his frame. The

connection of heavy smoking with lung cancer, of cirrhosis with drinking, of softening of the brain with cirrhosis occurred briefly in connection with rejection slips and the death of so many magazines. What happens when there are no more markets for my kind of stuff? Suicide? Better men have done it. His scalp began to itch unbearably now, and all the words he had ever written seemed flat slugs devoid of life or meaning. *How could I have fooled them for so long,* he thought, *when none of it was ever any good?*

I wonder where Amelia might be at this moment? I suppose she drops post cards to the luncheon girls, the cackling sorority. I suppose the Hazeltines would know, but I can't see me ringing up the Hazeltines on a Sunday night to ask if they know where my wife is. Alec's spirit writhed in embarrassment. What an ass I've been making of myself the last two months, carrying on like a goddam sophomore. Second childhood. Male menopause. Last Gasp Barr. *Jerk.* But I would like to know where she is, what her plans are. Who else would know—who would have her itinerary? Francis Hopkins? Very likely. But I'll be goddamned if I'll call that bloody faggot to find out.

Alec lurched out of bed, went to the bathroom, and took a couple of sleeping pills. He went back to bed, straightened the wrinkled sheets, and tried to compose his head. Thoughts still devil-danced in dark ballet. Now it was his parents, stark in black-and-white clown suits. He'd had no bulletins from that front lately; he supposed Mantell was still sending the money. Those people were way past him now. Funny how the act of love that created you could finally resolve into a sterile description like *those people.* And young brother Martin. Jail? Possibly. Suppose Amelia was sick somewhere in Europe? Would anybody let him know? Suppose she died alone, hating him? Suppose she became despondent and killed herself? He'd never be able to write another line, never be able to forgive himself. *Never be able to write another line.* Selfish bastard, Barr. Alec squirmed, and the mummy-wrappings choked him. Sweat was sluicing now, prickling under his chin, creeping down the backs of his ears, seeping down his neck. Hairs had drifted onto the pillow and were itching in unreachable places on his shoulders.

He flopped over and tried sleeping on his face. He tried thinking of pleasant things; of very early sunrise in the Rift Valley; a pride of jovial lions tumbling in the high yellow grasses of the Masai; first firelight, and that first fine drink with his African friends over the exaggerated retelling of the day's adventures. There had been that big salmon on the Resti gouche, in Canada, and the big, big elephant, whose tusks lived now in New Jersey. Suddenly Alec felt very sad over all the animals—even the fish—he had killed. He wished he had never taken any life at all, since his own life was doomed to such pitiful shortness. He could see the rapidly glazing eyes, the horrid still-life of bloody evisceration, the encompassing fat blue flies and the vultures always hovering, circling. He too would end that way, one last sad day, with one blurting seminal ejaculation while his bowels finally spilled. He shuddered, snapped on the light, and got up.

He put on his robe and went back to the bar, and mixed himself another stiff drink. There wasn't going to be any sleep tonight, not while the devils rode him. If he only knew where Amelia was. If he only knew what her plans were.

Alec Barr went to the telephone, and thumbed through the address book until he came to the *H*s. He grimaced and dialed a number. After three rings there was an answer.

"Hello, Francis? Alec Barr. Forgive me for ringing at this hour of the night."

The voice dripped smoothly, sirupy from the other end.

"No bother at all, Alec. I was just sitting here trying to read myself to sleep. *The New Yorker* these days is better than any pill. What do you hear from Amelia?"

"As a matter of fact, nothing." Alec swallowed pride for bluntness. "Nothing at all. That's why I rang you. I thought perhaps you . . ."

Francis laughed lightly.

"I do believe I have some sort of schedule. Of course I haven't seen her for about six weeks. I went over with her as far as Paris, and we caught a few cathedrals. But I had to come back—work, you know how it is. I left her in Rome. Just hold on a moment, Alec, while I rummage."

Alec lit a cigarette during the pause, and frowned. So she took her house pet with her, did she? And very possibly *I* paid the passage. Now Francis Hopkins was back, voice spuriously triumphant.

"By some miracle I *did* happen to find her rough itinerary. By all accounts, they—I suppose you know she joined up with Nancy Patton after I left her in Rome—ought to be in Tokyo this week, and then on to Hong Kong for a week, then back through Singapore and Hawaii. She went out to Tokyo via Beirut, that way. All of this subject to change, of course. Two attractive women on the loose; *you* know . . ."

Blast him, Alec thought, making his voice polite.

"I don't suppose you'd know the name of the booking agency, if she's using one?"

"As a matter of fact, yes. It's the Moffat Agency. London Headquarters. There's a New York office on Madison at Forty-Fifth. They'd probably have some sort of net on her."

"Thank you very much, Francis. Again, my apologies for ringing at this hour, but I was beginning to worry . . ."

"Any time at all, any time at all. And if you're bored and want to look in for a drink, please do. I hope you can persuade Amelia to come home. The town's so *dull* without her. Good night, Alec. Pleasant dreams."

Perhaps Francis Hopkins was not laughing as he rang off, but Alec knew he had heard laughter, and that the laughter had come from a second party in Francis' room.

Alec Barr cursed, drained his drink in one gulp, turned off the lights, and went back to bed. At least she wasn't dead, but how about that crack about "two attractive women on the loose"? Ah, well, I can always find her through the agency, he thought, and buried his face in the soggy pillow. This time the pills took hold, and presently Alec Barr began to snore.

68

Marc Mantell hadn't given him more than a reasonable amount of hell, for his own good, of course.

"I'm glad to see that you've got rid of whatever it was you may have had in your system, Alec. I suppose rampant biology happens to all of us one time or another. Skipping biology, we are very nearly broke, boy. Your balance in the office is deep in the red, and that last batch of checks from Europe—" Mantell whistled. "I covered the overdraft. It's a matter now of you either finishing the serials and getting on with the new book or we'll just have to sell some stock. Let the play slide until we get some more dough in the bank. How do you feel, really?"

"Lousy," Alec said. "Just lousy enough to go back to work. My conscience kills me and I've been drinking much too much. So I ought to be able to work. Let's have just one more martini. I'm cold turkey tomorrow."

"Good man," Marc Mantell said. "Let me know when you've got enough to show me and I'll come out for the night and we can kick it around."

Alec drove out to Jersey in the late afternoon and was gratified to see smoke drifting from the chimneys, lights glowing pleasantly inside. Luke was back. At least he'd have somebody to talk Navy with, after the work was done, somebody to take a drink with—no, that part was over, beginning tomorrow. It was never any fun, that abrupt cessation of all alcohol, but it was easier than stretching it out.

Luke opened the door as he heard the car approach. He came out into the yard, a lean dark Italian of about forty. He had a beaky nose but no hairline mustache, and his hair was entirely gray. He was wearing a plaid Pendleton lumber jacket and old green corduroy pants. There was honest welcome in the brown Italian eyes.

"Nice to have us home again, Boss," he said, and extended a bony hand. "What do you hear from the Missus?"

"Still in Europe," Alec said shortly. "I gather you didn't get married again this time?"

"Nope. Lotsa chicks, but no wife material. But my old lady checked me out again on chicken *cacciatore*. I was glad to leave, if you want to know the truth. I got too many sisters. Seems like I couldn't turn around in the bathroom without strangling myself on a stocking. How you been keeping?"

"Well enough. You look fine."

Alec walked ahead of Luke through the kitchen. He gazed around.

"Ah, good. I see you got some fresh vegetables. We'll make a checklist after dinner and you can run in tomorrow and stock up for a month or so. We got a lot of work to do, starting bright and early in the morning."

"Wagon?"

"Tomorrow."

"Oh, oh." Luke rolled his eyes. "I'll stay out of the way for the first three or four days."

Alec smiled.

"It won't be that bad. I think what we do now is build us a farewell drink or so, and then see what you can wrestle up for an early dinner. Hamburgers, spaghetti out of the can, anything. Then I want to see all the folders on the new book and the top copy on the serial—you know, the one for *Globe*. They want a rewrite in the middle, God knows why, but they buy and I sell."

"Did you have a good time here over the week end?" Luke asked. "The weather must of been nice."

"Sure, I had a good—I suppose we didn't clean up too well, considering I was coming back today. Old lady friend and her daughter. Very old friends."

"There never was a woman could make a really tight bed," Luke said. "And there's always a hairpin in the bathroom."

"Quit playing private eye and start thinking about dinner," Alec said. "And change the ribbons on the typewriters."

"I already changed 'em," Luke said. "And we ain't going to have hamburgers for supper. I took an hour off and snagged us a couple of bass this afternoon. How does a little fresh fish sound?"

"Fine," Alec replied, shuddering inwardly. "Just dandy."

He walked to the bar and mixed a pitcher of martinis, pouring two. He handed one to Luke and raised his own in a toast.

"Welcome, aboard, mate," he said, and firmly corked the bottle of gin.

69

After the first few days of chronic craving for a sundown drink—a ceremonial observance more than of actual need for alcohol—Alec began to feel wonderful. He rose at seven, shaved and showered, went for a walk around the lake or down to the dam, and was ravenous by eight. He consumed enormous breakfasts of bacon and eggs, hotcakes and ham, and drank quarts of coffee.

He was seated at the typewriter before nine and worked

steadily until one, by which time Luke would be back from town with the papers. He read newspapers until two, ate a light lunch, and went back for the other half of the day's chore. Alec Barr always shot for twenty pages a day, when he was writing long fiction, and was satisfied with less when short story or specialized magazine work called for tighter construction. He supped simply with Luke at nightfall, and was back at work with the pencil by 8 P.M. Two hours of carving and reorganizing tired him sufficiently to drive him into bed by ten thirty.

Alec told himself he was happy now, and certainly fit. He chopped wood for half an hour some mornings, and always walked a mile or so. He had an appetite like an anaconda. He only cheated on the work when the World Series was in progress, that first shaky week on the wagon, when he switched on the TV for a couple of hours. He watched no television thereafter except for the seven o'clock news. He generally took a book—some old, well-tried friend who needed no analysis—to bed with him, and it invariably dropped out of his hand after a couple of pages.

Luca Germani had a most un-Italianate gift for silence, so conversation was limited almost entirely to essentials involving typing or household chores. Luke had a way of disappearing, when the work was done, with a fishpole or an ax, and the house on the tall hill was a house of peace interrupted only by the clack of typewriter.

There was only one trouble with this house of peace, where the birds sang by day, the loons called on the lake, and the owls hooted by night. Alec's fingers marched bravely up and down the keyboard, and the pencil carved and recarved in front of the fire. Yards of Scotch tape stuck inserts on top of inserts—and nothing happened. Luke's clean-copying did nothing to improve the quality of the prose. Already-wooden characters turned to stone. Desperate strivings for plot twists led Alec into dead ends—dead ends preceded by thousands of words of . . . *words*. The words were mere assemblies of letters. They not only lacked fury; they lacked sound as well.

In the working life of a professional author, when he is lucky, the fictional characters take over and become fleshly people, with solid dimensions and minds of their own. They do things the author never intended. They say things the author never dreamed of. The happy author is thus reduced to the minor role of coachman, using no whip, driving only slightly with a very slack rein.

Now Alec Barr, sober, fit, eager to work, found himself in the role of galley master, attempting to scourge slaves at their benches—cursing, lashing, hoping for a responsive beat to the cadence. The galley slaves toiled, in response to Alec's whip, but only in sullen submission, and the galley wallowed heavy in the water.

He had reworked the serial three times, finding it increasingly leaden. He had abandoned the novel again, as its characters changed from pasteboard cutouts to slips of tissue paper and its plot structure strangled in quicksand. He finally called Marc Mantell in desperation.

"Don't come in," Marc Mantell said. "I'll come out. Maybe you're still stale. It happens to everybody."

Mantell arrived for the week end, looking out-of-place in his city clothes. He spent all Friday night and all day Saturday reading Alec's copy, making notes on the long yellow pad that Alec once had named the "hate book."

Just at dusk, Marc Mantell mixed a short Scotch and settled himself in front of the fire.

"I don't know what it is you want me to tell you, exactly," he said, his eyes enormous behind their spectacles.

"You can tell me the truth," Alec said, pouring himself another cup of coffee. "Have I lost it, Marc? Is it all gone? This"—he pointed at the stacks of manuscript—"is purest horseshit. And every time I rework it, it gets worse. This is worse crap than I wrote when I first started. Nothing bites. Nothing takes hold. Nothing sounds real. I don't believe anybody in it, or anything anybody says."

"That is the criticism I would make. It seems to me you have written sort of an elaborate skeletal outline, blocked in as a treatment, of something you might really write once you sit down to it."

"But I *have* been sitting down to it," Alec's voice rose. "I never worked so goddamned hard in my goddamned life! And it all comes out crap!"

Marc Mantell rubbed his forehead and took another sip of his drink. His voice was dreamy as he spoke over Alec's shoulder.

"A writer," he said, "is a delicate, mysterious organism. Nobody ever knows quite what makes a writer. Pain and poverty may forge one, and might as easily ruin another.

Some write best in seclusion; others can't write a line away from the clatter of Times Square. Riches spoil some and improve others. Some need deadlines—some need limitless time. Some need Spain or a South Sea island; others are miserable outside a grimy hotel room or a cold-water attic."

"And where do I fall?" Alec asked grimly. "I've been poor and I've been rich. I have written in city rooms and on boats and off boxes and in penthouses and the best thing I ever did I wrote in this room. This room—where right now I can't even write the word *hello* without making it sound stilted. Where would you say I fall, Maestro?"

Marc Mantell's voice continued to dream on.

"Another thing about writers, I have noticed to my pain after forty years in their company, is that they are very sensitive to personal criticism. I would not accuse you of this fault, Alec. I merely mention it. Writers are all egoists—ham actors, if you will—or they wouldn't *be* writers. Very few have the guts to face a simple truth, if it runs against their ego."

Alec's face paled slightly. He got up and walked over to the bar.

"I think a month of this spartan existence hasn't helped me any—hasn't unbound any mental muscles. I think I will just join you in a slug of that Scotch."

Marc Mantell nodded. "You can carry clean living too far."

Alec poured the drinks, took a deep swig of his, and then said:

"Shoot. Give me the worst."

"You are a strange and rather extra delicate mechanism, Alec. You need a conscience; one of your own, and another in someone else's body. You need a hair shirt to prick you into production.

"You've been running away from home all your life, Alec. It's chronic with you. *But you can't run away unless you've got somebody or something to run away from.* Without the nag, without the hair shirt, without the weight around your neck, you don't have the balance to goose you into top production. It is, I suppose, a form of literary masochism. You only produce at top form when you feel you're being abused. You revel in what you consider millstones around your neck, and you're triumphant when you consider you've done your job well *despite.*"

"Go on," Alec said. "I can take it. I like your 'despite.' I must be a real can of worms."

"You *are* a real can of worms," Marc Mantell said. "All writers are nuts of a sort. I'll cut it short. You need someone to run *from,* and you need someone to run back to."

Marc Mantell paused.

"I don't have to draw you a picture, do I? You need Amelia!"

Alec opened his mouth to protest, and as abruptly shut it. His shoulders sagged as he exhaled sharply. His hands shook slightly as he set his glass carefully on the coffee table.

"I know it," he said miserably. "God help me, I know it. I guess I've known it all along and didn't like to admit it."

"Well then," Marc Mantell said, "for Christ's sake get her back. You're not the first guy that ever went over the hill. About the easiest thing a woman does is forgive, even if, like the elephant, she never forgets, and never forgets to remind you that she hasn't forgotten."

Alec sighed and the color was back in his face. He took another drink, and sighed again with satisfaction.

"Damn, that tastes good. I'd almost forgotten how good it does taste. What do you suggest?"

"Do you know where she is at the moment?"

"Yes. I think so. Approximately, anyhow."

"Well," Marc Mantell said, rising. "For Christ's sake grab the first plane and fetch her home. You've still got an Air Travel Card. And get out of those silly lumberjack clothes and come on back with me to New York. We can have dinner at the Stork Club and let you breathe a few healthy cigarette fumes."

Alec rested his hand briefly on Marc Mantell's shoulder.

"Amelia always asked me what a successful writer really needed with an agent," he said. "I have always found it rather hard to explain."

"Ten per cent covers a multitude of services," Marc Mantell said grumpily. "Hurry. This country air is getting me down."

70

Alec's aim had been painfully sincere. Marc Mantell had said for Christ's sake, go fetch her, and Alec had fully intended to go fetch her. But a certain Scots caution took him first to the tourist agency. There Amelia was located as currently in Singapore, staying at the Raffles. Whereupon, not wishing to embark on the wildest of wife chases, Alec cabled MISS YOU TERRIBLY STOP LIKE JOIN IF OKAY REPLY URGENTEST LOVE ALEC. He had received the answer UNNECESSARY JOIN AS EYE UP FED TRAVEL INTEND FLYING STRAIGHT HOME STOP SUGGEST WAIT NEW YORK CABLING FLIGHT NUMBER LOVE AMELIA.

That, Alec thought with a visible sigh of relief, was that. Air Travel card or no Air Travel card, he was suffering a sharp financial pinch, and right now the idea of colorful coolies and gilded pagodas and romantic beachbows interested him about as much as a conducted tour of a leper colony.

He was much more than visibly relieved at the idea of not having to indulge in a uxorious sparring match on strange terrain, pretending to be on happy holiday while really eating a certain amount of domestic crow.

The meeting was going to be grisly enough in any case, no matter where they staged it; it would be less grim if conducted on home territory, without benefit of gongs, rickshaws, or singsong girls.

Amelia's second cable informed him that American Airlines would deliver her from San Francisco within a week's time, and as the days lessened, Alec's panic rose. What did you say to a wife you'd walked out on? What did you say to a wife who knew well and truly that you had been off on a flaming affair? What did you say to a wife who, for once, had pulled the switch on you—who had herself become the world traveler while you warmed the home hearth? Alec didn't know. Not knowing, he picked up the phone and invited himself around for a drink at the brownstone apartment of Mrs. Dinah Lawrence. It did not occur to Alec that after Dinah's flat declaration of long-standing love it was perfectly ridiculous for him to seek advice from her. He had to talk to a woman, *some* woman, and Dinah Lawrence was the only woman he knew who would be apt to give him a straight answer. He discounted Barbara Bayne as a likely source of unbiased counsel.

Alec entered sheepishly, small-boyishly, figuratively twisting his cap in his hands. It was cocktail time, but Dinah had not bothered to dress for the visit. She was wearing faded blue jeans and scuffed sandals. A scarf hid possible pincurlers, and her unmade face was shiny. Horn-rimmed spectacles were pushed high on her forehead.

She extended a cheek for the comradely kiss, beckoned Alec inside, waved him to a chair.

"You'll have to excuse the beatnik appearance," she said. "But I'm up to my elbows in this damn book"—she gestured at loose stacks of typescript scattered on table and floor, at a typewriter with a half-finished page still on the roller—"and I don't seem to have time to prettify me very much. You sounded urgent on the phone. Don't tell me you're in love again?"

Alec brushed a negating hand in front of his face.

"It's not all that urgent. And I'm not, as you so coarsely put it, in love again. But first, tell me, how's the book going?"

Dinah shrugged.

"Who knows? I write a certain amount each day, and it sounds awful. I put a pencil on it and it looks worse. Then I rewrite the penciled mess and it looks a little better. I've got maybe a hundred pages now that don't actually nauseate me. But Jesus, Alec, why didn't you tell me that bookwriting was real work? How are *you* faring over the last month? All wrapped up and ready for another one?"

Alec sat down and gestured feebly, shrugging his shoulders.

"You're a writer, all right. You've already learned to moan like one. Since I saw you, five weeks ago, I have worked like six galley slaves. I have been stony sober; I have gone to bed early; I have rewritten until all the sentences march backward and down, like Chinese. And I haven't got a single page I'd feed a self-respecting goat. I don't know, Di. My head is full of cotton, and everything I ever knew I've forgotten."

Dinah made a sympathetic clucking sound.

"You still on the wagon? Want a drink? A cup of coffee? I've been living on the stuff."

"Drink, I think. Mantell rescued me from the wagon the other day. Scotch, please. Marc's one of the reasons I'm here. I'm stuck. I need counsel. I need tender loving counsel —smart talk from a smart dame."

"You done come to the wrong house, Bud," Dinah said. "But the drink I can furnish. I'll even join you, much against my working principles."

She went to the sideboard, mixed a couple of Scotches, and then sat down on the footrest, hugging her knees. Her drink stood untasted on a side table.

"So, what is bothering our boy? Tell your old Auntie Dinah, who never had a solution for a personal problem in her entire put-together."

Alec sipped his drink and spoke slowly.

"This. Mantell was out to the ranch the other day, heeding my piercing cry for help. He took a look at a mile of copy and threw up his hands. We had a long soul-searcher, and the upshot was a kind of psychoanalysis. Net result: It seems I can't work without Amelia. I need a hair shirt. I need a conscience. I need a mother figure to run away *from,* and back *to.*" Alec bit his sentences brutally. "How about *that?*"

Dinah nodded slowly.

"Could be he's right. I think I might have told you the same thing, except I don't think I see you taking it from me. So what else, and how do I fit?"

Alec looked into his drink, twirling the glass in his hands. "Amelia's flying in from the Coast tomorrow afternoon— straight through, Singapore—Honolulu—San Francisco— New York."

"Then what's your problem? Looks like all's forgiven, and you can play house again."

"That's just it! What the hell do I say to her?" Alec's voice burst its fetters. "What in the name of God do I do with a woman who's bound to be coming home with her eyes full of daggers and a heart full of accumulated hate!"

Dinah held up a hand.

"Stop. Quit talking like a writer. 'Eyes full of daggers,' yet. What you do is really pretty simple. *Cool it.* You fill the apartment with flowers. You hire a Carey and meet her at the airport. You tell her you're glad to see her. You tell her you've missed her. You kiss her casually. You ask a lot of polite questions about the trip on the way home. You take her home for a rest and a change, and then you take her *out* to dinner—Twenty-One, I should imagine, but any place, any place at *all* where you never took Barbara Bayne. You stuff her with caviar and drown her in champagne, and then you take her home. Then—"

"Then?"

Dinah's lips tightened.

"You take her to bed. You take her to bed with enthusiasm, with sweaty lust, rowdy roughness, but absolutely with *no* new tricks you might have learned from—you might have learned recently. And if she has any *you* don't remember, ignore them. This is very important."

Alec looked at Dinah with amazement.

"You can say this, say it *that* flatly, with what you said last time, with me knowing how you feel—"

Dinah's voice was harsh.

"You came here for womanly advice, Sonny. I am a woman. I am giving you advice. There is only one way to get back into a woman's graces—a spurned woman's graces—and that is to crawl back into her bed. Perhaps she's had her little fling. *Fine.* All the better. She'll have some guilt on her back, too. If she's been rigidly faithful, and you are sufficiently ardent, she'll still be pleased because she'll feel superior . . . superior to this—this *lecher*—who has finally seen the light and chosen her above his other purely carnal love. That was only flesh, a passing fancy, and you know how men *are* . . ." Dinah let her voice die sarcastically.

"But—"

"*But* nothing. She's already won her battle. She's *wanted.* You made her feel wanted with the cable about joining her. The other broad's in the ashcan. Mama's back. Mama's back among her personal things, her own possessions, including you. Mama's in complete charge. Mama don't want to hear any lurid confessions or any play-by-play on Papa's neck-arching. And another thing Mama don't want—"

"What?" Alec had abandoned conversation for monosyllables.

"Mama don't want to know *why* you sent for Mama. Mama don't want to ever, *ever*, learn that Papa can't work without Mama's inspirational presence. If you ever get drunk enough to confess that you only sent for her because you can't work without her, I hope she shoots you. And if she doesn't, *I* will. That clear, my semirepentant Prodigal Son?"

"The words are clear. Women are *not* clear," Alec said, shaking his head. "You mean to say that we will pick up old threads just as if nothing has happened? I didn't walk out? I didn't show my ass all over town for two months? There never was any Barbara Bayne?"

"That's right, little boy. It was a long hot summer. Daddy had a slight aberration induced by heat, eyestrain, and overwork. Mama was just a touch nervy herself, so she decided to take a trip to clear the air and let Daddy get his balance back. Now it's lovely November in New York, the hot weather's all gone, Daddy's himself again, and the chrysanthemums are in full flower. There's a whole mess of new shows—I suggest you conquer your dislike for the theater and take Mama out to all the new ones—and make no reference to finances *whatsoever*. Not if she spent the mint. Sell some stock, stick up a bank, but *no* money talk. And keep on bundling her off to bed. It's the only sure way to shut a woman's mouth *and* mind. I've told you a lot of trade secrets, chum, because I love you."

Alec got up and paced before the fireplace, clasping and unclasping linked fingers behind his back.

"I can't believe it'll be all that simple, Di," he said at length. "I can't believe she spent the last two months without a lot of soul-corroding mental pictures of what I was up to in New York. She's bound to secrete a lot of grudge. Maybe Amelia loves me, but I did do an unforgiveable thing—"

Dinah's voice was cross now, exasperated.

"There you go, thinking like a goddam writer again. Females have an infinite capacity for pretense. Their life is basically built on pretense. If Amelia pretends it didn't happen—*so long as she's got you and the other broad hasn't got you*. Just don't go twisting any old knives by any leering confessions of guilt, as if you were half proud of being a naughty boy. *Forget* it, Charlie," she said, going back to her favorite throwaway line. *"Forget* it. And all will be well— until . . ." Dinah pursed her lips.

"Until *what?*"

"Someone—some kind friend, male or female, will make a crack, and pry the scab off the old sore. Or you'll get mad or bored and open the subject yourself. Or you'll have a money fight and it'll simmer down to how much *she* spent in Europe and how much *you* spent in the Ritz and on the town. Or someone you met in her absence will greet you as a long-loster, or someone—possibly attractive—that she met will show up one day and hint at unknown intimacies that she hasn't bothered to mention. You know, like: 'You can't imagine what a marvelous time Amelia and I had in Bangkok. We *never* got to bed,' intimating that they never got *out* of bed. Then hell'll pop all over again, and you'll be looking for a new exit."

Alec sighed.

"It scarcely seems worth the effort." He held out his glass beseechingly. "You wouldn't buy the condemned man another drink, would you?"

"I would indeed, but a lecture goes with that, too. Gin is not a sound basis for a domestic discussion, when both parties are trying to avoid certain issues best left buried. I would recommend a regimen of late-night sobriety, because gin leads first to confession, then to accusation, and finally to total war, even if nobody listens to the enemy. I should confine my drinking with Amelia to the pre-dinner cocktail bit as much as possible. And I should work hard, very hard, in full view of the lady, for quite a spell. None of this sneaking off to play Injun with your Man Friday in the boondocks."

Alec accepted his drink, and scratched an ear. Both eyebrows now were raised, his forehead wrinkled.

"I ask a simple question, I get a whole course in marital relations. You know so much, how come you ain't still married?"

Dinah Lawrence slapped him, hard, and burst into tears.

"Now that, God damn you, is exactly what I've been driving at! One nasty, snotty, sardonic crack like that and the whole house falls down! Marriage is nothing but a series of elaborate deceptions and compensations anyhow, mostly based on good manners and no bloody sarcasm. And to answer your stinking question, the reason I got a divorce was that I was married to a jerk like you and didn't have sense enough then to know how to humor him! Satisfied?" Dinah Lawrence glared at Alec, and swung away.

Alec dropped a hand on her shoulder.

"I'm sorry," he said. "Truly. I didn't mean it that way. It's this nasty bloody tongue of mine. You pack quite a punch for a mere slip of a girl." He rubbed his jaw and grinned.

Dinah Lawrence swung to face him, and there was still a

haze of tears in the smoky blue eyes. She smiled slightly.

"I guess this marriage-counsel business is more of a strain on a girl than I thought. I'd forgotten Mister Lawrence pretty thoroughly until just now. Sorry about slapping you. I seem to be slapping everybody I love lately. Forgive me. Pure reflex. Wasn't meant . . . it was more a self-inflicted wound. Let's talk about something else."

"Fine." Alec slipped an arm around her waist, walked her over to the big chair, plumped her down, fetched her drink, and then sat down on the hassock, his bony knees reaching to his chin. "Let's talk about your book, for example."

Now Dinah gestured helplessly at the strewn papers.

"I get so confused. I run around in circles. I feel like I'm in a tunnel with both ends blocked. I wallow in paper, I sweat print, and all the clear thoughts I originally had get all swirled up in a kind of Fourth-of-July sparkler arrangement—all glitter and no form."

"But you say you've got a hundred pages that you're not sore at. That's thirty thousand words—a damned good month's work. Has Marc seen any of it?"

"Yes. The first hundred pages. He didn't tell you?"

"No. I guess we were too preoccupied with my own problems. And then there's a marvelous thing about Marc Mantell. He never—at least very rarely—ever discusses one writer's work when another writer is working. He figures a reputable agent is sort of like a good doctor or lawyer or banker—he oughtn't to mouth his clients' business around."

"I'd hoped he might have told you. I was sort of waiting to hear from you that he had. When you called today I thought that was it."

"Do we know what we're talking about?"

Dinah's face widened and lit. Her face became almost childlike.

"I wasn't going to tell you, because I knew you had a lot of troubles of your own. But oh, Alec, it's so wonderful! Marc's sold the serial rights to *McCall's,* on the strength of the first hundred pages, and he's sold the book to McDonald-Enright, and there's some movie talk already, and I can't believe a word of it except he says it's so!" Dinah flung both arms around Alec's neck and hugged him. "I can't believe it's happening to me, after all my newspaper masterpieces you wrap fish in!"

Alec Barr got up, pulled Dinah to her feet, and held her briefly close. He kissed her lightly on the lips.

"By God," he said, hoping his voice sounded as hearty as he sincerely meant it to be. "By God and by Jesus, that's wonderful! Now I tell you exactly what we are going to do. You are going to go to the bathroom, get out of those ratty dungarees, take the pincurlers out of your hair, put a lot of gunk on your eyes, break out your best dress, and we are going out and eat all the caviar in the city. And don't argue. I've got one free night left in New York and I intend to spend it with a howling success." He gave her a push and a pat on the backside. "Off with you now, and give me a carbon to read so I can see what makes Mantell and the rest of the world think you're so special."

"You're a real sweet guy, Barr," Dinah Lawrence said. "Among other things a sport, Sport." She handed him a sheaf of clipped carbons. "Here's the first milestone to fame and fortune. You don't really *have* to read it."

"Go on with you now. I *want* to read it." Alec settled himself in the chair. "Scram. You bother me."

Dinah left with a childishly grateful smile. Alec leaned back in the chair and looked unseeingly at the ceiling. He reached blindly out until his fingers found his drink on the side table. He lifted the drink in an idle toast.

"It couldn't happen to a greater gal, and I'm as happy for her as I said I was," he said to himself. "I'm delighted it happened, even if I can't write a line that would make the old *American Boy*. But why, why, did it have to happen to *me* today?"

He reached into an inner pocket and got out his reading glasses. The first page, he thought after a moment, reads like cream. It reads like my stuff used to read, but that was a long, long time ago.

71

Alec Barr slept until nearly noon, being awakened by the first delivery of flowers for the flat. The night out to celebrate Dinah Lawrence's fresh success had been strenuous indeed. A very very expensive dinner at Pavillon had led to a variety of noisy, smoky places, including El Morocco (which Alec detested on principle), finally finishing in the Village at Eddie Condon's jazz house, in which Alec's scalp lifted half a foot every time Wild Bill Davison reared back and blew a blast. The same scalp was still lifting slightly now, as he fed himself a couple of aspirin and then padded out to the kitchen in search of tomato juice with a suspicion of gin to leaven its health-giving qualities. The Bloody Mary coupled with half an hour in the multiple-nozzled shower restored a mild portion of necessary courage to face the day.

The plane was due at four thirty in the afternoon.

Alec shaved very carefully and chose his clothes with great deliberation. There was a soft blue cashmere that Amelia particularly liked, and with it went a Sulka cream silk shirt and a subdued maroon tie. He had acquired a fresh haircut earlier in the week, and he was not, he decided, checking himself out in the mirror, looking too badly for a roisterer who had tottered home at approximately 4 A.M.

He looked around the apartment. Carl and Elsa, the butler-cook couple, had been hurriedly dragooned back to full-time service. Carl, a popeyed, stout German-Swiss with offensively yellow hair, confronted Alec in the living room and demanded that he approve the flower arrangements. Evidently Elsa, whose face was permanently flushed (not from the heat of the kitchen so much as from high blood pressure) had spent most of her formative years in Basel learning flower arrangements in order to prepare for this particular *Tag*. Elsa, who had disapproved with downdrawn mouth when Alec sought the makings of a Bloody Mary in the kitchen, now melted when Alec remarked that the Japanese were clumsy amateurs at flower arrangement when compared to Basel-born Swiss.

"You vant some breakfast, Mister?" Elsa said. (Alec had long since despaired of expunging the "Mister" from her direct address.)

"No," said Alec. "I have a luncheon appointment. I'll just settle for some brunch." He grinned in what he hoped was a genial fashion. "Be sure and see that everything's right for Madame's return," he said. Husband and wife stared at him with righteous disapproval.

"Everyt'ing is always cowwect ven ve vork *full time,*" said Carl.

"*Ja,*" said Elsa, sketching endless orgies in her mental air.

He ducked into the clanking elevator run by a slack-lipped pimpled youth who could only be a sexual degenerate in his spare time.

Alec noticed that the doorman was not at the door, but was possibly off placing horse bets, so he hailed a taxi himself and decided that a quiet corner at the Laurent would be apt to keep him out of any undue trouble with the kind of friends he might be likely to encounter at either Shor's or "21." This was *one* plane he wasn't going to be late for, and you never knew about that traffic. If you took the Triboro somebody was apt to be wrecked in the middle, with the traffic stacked up on either end. If you took the Midtown Tunnel it would be worse. He decided on the longer route via the Triboro and told one of the brothers at the Laurent to check with Carey and instruct the limousine to collect him at 3 P.M. An hour and a half, he thought, should get me to Philadelphia, and Idlewild isn't quite that far.

He permitted himself another Bloody Mary before eating, and ostentatiously read the early afternoon editions to stave off comradeship. He spied Marc Mantell in a far corner with a couple of clients, and waved without walking over to say hello. Mantell knew that this was A-Day; Alec had telephoned him when he received Amelia's first and second cables.

The ride out was easy. The driver was nontalkative, and Alec finished all three afternoon papers leisurely, shuddering slightly when he checked the stock tables. He was early; there was nearly an hour to kill before plane time. He sent the driver off to the parking lot, armed himself with a *Time* and a *Newsweek,* and went into the bar to sweat out the arrival. The clerk at the desk had pronounced the West Coast plane on time.

Alec sipped slowly at a long weak Scotch-and-water and tried to read *Time,* but today its jerked-English sentence structure failed to enrage him. He flipped the pages, turning first to the book section and observing that as usual the critics didn't like books of any sort. He went on to Stage and Moving Pictures and counted twenty-seven puns on two pages. Whereupon he gazed moodily into his drink and wished heartily that he were somewhere in the vicinity of Marsabit, on the Northern Frontier of Kenya, or even in Garissa, which was still further out of touch with civilized humanity.

The idea of the first meeting with Amelia terrified him. Guilt rode him with harsh bit and heavy hands. Uncertainty stripped him of his blue cashmere. Amelia would not beat him up, and he did not think she would divorce him, but the idea of the first few awkward hours appalled him. He ordered another drink, on the rocks this time, and shortly felt a tiny touch brighter.

After several centuries the loudspeaker blared the announcement of the arrival of Amelia's flight, and he went to the arrival area. The momentary flush of false courage was rapidly paling again, and he felt frail, very, very tiny. He paced, and smoked, and finally the door opened, and there, indeed, she was, coming up the ramp. She was obviously looking for him, and he waved, almost succumbing to the temptation to yell "Yoo hoo!" remembering barely in time that people didn't say "Yoo hoo!" any more.

Yes indeed, there she was. She was brilliant *blonde*—that came as a decided shock—as blonde or blonder than Barbara Bayne. She was unduly slim in her neat beige gabardine traveling suit. She was wearing two fur coats over her right arm, the long new leopard and the old honey-brown mink. In her other hand she was carrying a handbag the size of a suitcase.

She saw him, waved, smiled, and yes—she wrinkled her nose in the rabbity way she had. She looked marvelous, tanned (of course, she had decided to break the long trip in Honolulu) and not at all travel-scarred.

She doesn't look sore, Alec thought. She looks glad to see me. And by God, I am glad to see her. But at closer range there seemed to be some strain, some petulance that was not discernible at first.

Oh, God, Alec thought, I wonder. Maybe she is still burning and is saving the explosion for when we get home, so we can have a real heart-to-hearter. I hope to Christ Di was right in her prognosis. What I do *not* want is a real heart-to-hearter. I always lose heart-to-hearters, as well as man-to-maners, and this-is-for-your-own-gooders. At least she won't start any serious war until we're out of the car and home. Do I kiss her on the mouth, or just peck her on the cheek? Do I fold her in my arms, or merely stand politely aloof and offer to carry the coats? I wish I'd brought Marc or Ben or somebody with me, except I'm damned sure that would have made her furious.

He stood, slightly spraddle-legged, braced for conflict, in front of the gateway. And now, he thought, the moment of truth. Here comes the bull out of the *toril.*

She came out, smiling, and did not quicken her pace. He walked hurriedly toward her, and said, for lack of anything better:

"Well, hello. Welcome home, darling."

"It's so good to be back, darling," she said, and offered her cheek coolly for his kiss.

"Let me look at you," he said, stepping back a pace. "You look simply marvelous—including the new hair. That gave me considerable shock at first."

"I'm glad you think so—I'm so glad you like the hair. I got tired of the old color. You look well, too, perhaps a little thinner. Perhaps you'd better send for the bags. Here are my checks. We *do* have a car?"

"Of course," he said. "Here, give me those coats. The car's just in front."

Thank God, he thought, that was easy enough. Now if we can just make it home without any histrionics. If I had the sense God gave a crabapple I'd have brought a flask in the car.

The trip in was a *succès fou* of conscious inanity on both sides. Amelia watched Alec appraisingly, searching, it seemed to him, for the mark of Cain, or at least a *fleur de lys,* to appear suddenly on his brow.

"Where-all did you go?" he said finally, in desperation, almost adding "And why didn't you drop me a card?" but biting his tongue in time.

"Oh, most of Europe," Amelia replied. "We—Francis Hopkins came over for a couple of weeks—we did the châteaux-cathedral country in France, Paris of course, and then I haunted a lot of churches in Italy. Francis went home about that time, and I ran into Nancy Patton—you remember Nancy, she used to be married to Charlie Lyons before the war—Nancy and I went to Spain for a while and saw some bullfights and the Prado and some *flamenco.* Nancy knew a man who raises bulls and we had a very interesting week end on a bull ranch."

"It sounds very interesting," Alec said politely, shifting in his seat and thinking, Damned lucky we didn't know the same bull-raisers. "How did you get out East?"

"Nancy knew some people in Beirut so we went out to Beirut and decided to go East from there. Japan was pretty dreary, I thought. Maybe it's all right for *men*—the women are certainly pretty enough, and *submissive* enough—but the Japanese men are horrible. They don't even look like they belong to the same race as the women, dark and hairy and terribly rude in spite of all you hear about Japanese politeness."

"And you went from there to Hong Kong?"

"That's right. I loved Hong Kong. It's the world's best for shopping. Everything is terribly cheap. I'm afraid I spent a lot of money in Hong Kong." Amelia looked at him challengingly.

"That's nice," Alec said foolishly. "How did you find the food?"

"It was too rich in France, nothing but sauces and *Guide Michelin*. It's too fattening in Italy, nothing but *pasta* and more *pasta*. It was terrible in Spain. Nancy and I both got the trots—seafood, I guess. I always heard about hot Spanish food but it isn't so. It's insipid. They even put mayonnaise on the rice. The food in Japan is wonderful but only because I found a marvelous Chinese restaurant in Tokyo and after that I never had another spoonful of Jap food. The Chinese food in Hong Kong is wonderful, of course. If I was writing a travel book I would recommend that travelers in strange places eat nothing *but* Chinese food."

"And Bangkok? Singapore? Any fun?"

"Bangkok was nothing but canals and temples and heat. My God, it was hot. The people are pretty but the canals smell worse than Venice. The Raffles Hotel in Singapore is real olde worlde in the colonial sense, dark and dull. I don't know what I expected, but Singapore seems to be more like what I imagine mainland China would be than a part of Malaya. Godowns and coolies and rickshas and of course the Britishers sitting around drinking pink gin and talking about what things were like before the Japs took over. It seems to me that half the male adult British population of Singapore spent the war interned at the race course that they had built with their very own hands."

They were rounding the high curve of the Triboro now, headed for the homestretch, thank heaven, Alec thought, as he offered Amelia a cigarette and lighted it. (God! That had been close! He had almost, automatically, lighted two cigarettes!)

"You sure covered a lot of ground for a little over two months," Alec said, after a silence.

"We didn't stay long in most places," Amelia replied. "A week is generally enough. The cocktail parties are mostly pretty much the same everywhere you go. I was lucky to bump into Nancy. She seemed to have letters to *everybody*. After a while they all get to look exactly alike. And you get real tired of packing and unpacking. Your clothes get to where they smell stale, no matter how much you have them washed and dry cleaned. I tried buying some new stuff along the way, but in the end it all smells the same."

Christ, Alec thought, the cultural advantages of travel in the age of the aircraft. All the cocktail parties the same; the people look exactly alike, and in the end, all the clothes smell stale. And for this you get diarrhea and sometimes dysentery, at a cost of about a dollar a mile.

". . . I was gone?" she was saying now.

Alec started.

"Huh? Oh, sorry. I was woolgathering a little. Plot trouble again. What did you ask me?"

"I asked you if you had any fun while I was gone, or were you working most of the time?"

"Working, I guess, most of the time. The only trouble was that nothing much seemed to come of it. I spent a month in the country, just Luke and me, and hammered the hell out of the machine, but it came out tasting mostly like sawdust. The apartment was too lonesome to work in. It gave me the creeps." Now he smiled. "I'm afraid I need you in it to make a house a home. Somebody to shift the furniture around."

Amelia did not rise to the feeble attempt at flattery.

"I must say I'm delighted to be back. New York looks marvelous. It'll be wonderful to wear some clothes again I haven't had on twenty-five times in fifty days. How are the shows? Anything good?"

"Sweetie, I don't really know," Alec said. "I haven't been reading the reviews, and I thought I'd sort of wait until you got back and let you catch up on them."

"All right. *Who did you see while I was gone?*" She fired the last question at him.

"See? Oh. Nobody much. Nobody at all when I was out in Jersey. In town, the usual Toots-Twenty-One bunch. Marc, of course. Couple of editors here and there. Went to some ballgames with Ben. Down to Condon's a couple of times. Nothing—nobody much. It was a pretty dull September, and I worked all of October."

"Didn't you have any parties or anything at the apartment?"

Alec shook his head.

"No. No parties. No guests. As a matter of fact, I only moved back about ten days ago. I was out in Jersey, like I said, and when you went to Europe, the apartment was pretty grim, so I stayed at the Ritz for a while."

"That must have cost a pretty penny," Amelia said waspishly, and Alec's nerves tautened at the words "pretty penny."

"Not so bad," he said mildly. "It was off season and they gave me a very decent rate. And it was only for about a month." *We'll forget my little side-trip to Spain.*

"More like *two* months," Amelia said.

"I suppose so. Here"—Alec pressed the button and the glass partition slid down—"here, driver, turn right and come around from Fifth. Well," he said to Amelia, "Welcome home. We is done arrived."

Amelia compressed her lips and said nothing.

The doorman was on duty now.

"Take care of the bags, Mike," Alec said, paying the driver.

"Welcome home, Mrs. Barr," the doorman said, touching his cap.

"Thank you," Amelia said without enthusiasm, walking into the lobby. They rode up the elevator in silence. The operator pressed their private bell-button, and when the door slid back, opening directly into the foyer, Carl and Elsa were waiting in the lobby, polished to a high sheen.

"Velcome home, Madame," Carl said, bowing.

"Velcome, Missis," Elsa said, with a mockery of a curtsey.

They both looked at Alec then with a *let's see if you can talk yourself out of this one, chum* look peculiar to domestics.

Amelia walked ahead of Alec and gazed about her in the living room, which was banked wtth flowers.

"How nice everything looks," she said, with no great enthusiasm. "The flowers are lovely. That was very thoughtful of you, Alec. I love *these*—" pointing to three dozen yellow hothouse roses in a silver vase atop the Steinway. "My all-time favorites."

"But I didn't—yes, they *are* lovely," Alec said, noticing a card propped alongside the vase. "But I'm afraid they came from another admirer. There's the card."

Amelia dropped her coats over the corner of the divan and walked to the piano. She opened the envelope and read the card.

"How absolutely darling of him," she said. "They're from Francis. Here." She shoved the card at him. It read: "Don't you dare ever to stay away again so long. The village is absolutely *barren and desolate* without you. Welcome to the open city. Love, *Francis.*"

"Very sweet of him," Alec said, returning the card. "Very thoughtful. But I wonder how he'd know you were coming back today?"

"Oh, I dropped him a note when I decided to leave, and I suppose he checked the airlines. Francis is awfully clever at things like that," Amelia said lightly. "I wonder if you'd be a sweetie and mix me a large whisky and water, Alec? I'm parched."

"Scotch or bourbon?" Alec said, stupidly.

Amelia's laugh had a false tinkle.

"Oh, forgive me. I've been with the British too much lately. Maybe you've forgotten, but whiskey is only one thing —Scotch—to the British."

"Pardon me for being such a bloody colonial," Alec muttered, heading for the bar. "I keep forgetting that we've switched roles; you do the traveling and I keep the home fires burning. Back in a jiff with your *whisky,* ma'am."

72

Not on his wedding night, not on any of his extramarital excursions had Alec Barr approached the couch of love with such panicked hesitancy. Things had eased in the early evening. A few drinks had unstarched the tension; Amelia had left him for a short nap and then a bath and fresh clothing.

They had gone to dinner at "21," and everyone, from management to a considerable clutch of friends, had performed masterfully in the charade. One might have thought that Amelia Barr had been on a short visit to her parents, or at most a week end in Bermuda. Innumerable people stopped by the table to kiss her hello and welcome her home. All were kindly casual and even hearty toward Alec. There was no perceptible innuendo, no slightest hint that all was not well, no suggestion that Alec Barr had walked out on his wife to take up with a blonde actress and live flagrantly in opulent sin while said wife ran off to Europe and Asia on a punitive mission. Nobody even commented on the fact that Amelia Barr had left New York a brunette and now had turned up indisputably blonde.

Conversation in both men's and ladies' rooms, however, tended to active speculation—most of it disappointment—that there evidently was not going to be any divorce. Since most of the conversationalists were not without some smirch of civilized stain, it was finally decided over repaired makeup and straightened stockings that Amelia Barr was making the best of a flight of masculine summer madness, and that the Barrs once again would be available for cocktails and dinner and dull week ends in the country.

Alec's mind roved restlessly throughout the meal, repeating over and over Dinah Lawrence's advice to shut up and take Amelia to bed. So far he had performed in competent fashion on the first injunction, but he was filled with dread about the second section. It was of course natural that a man who had been deprived of a wife's physical affection for nearly three months should yearn for the returned body. It would be abnormal, otherwise, since Amelia was indeed a very attractive woman, very sexy, with her Nuyu-slimmed shape and her new blonde hair. Desperately, Alec wondered if he would even be physically able to perform the act of love. This caused him to order another brandy and a fresh cup of coffee.

He was tormented all the way home, frightened to feeble-wittedness, and it was Amelia who saved him. At this moment, Alec Barr came close to falling in love all over again with his wife.

"Sweetie," Amelia said as they entered the apartment, "I am absolutely beat from the trip, and most of me is several hours behind, like lost baggage. Also I think I'm starting the curse. Would you mind terribly sleeping in the guest room for a night or so, until I can get used to being back in this hemisphere? Lately I'm sort of unused to having a man in my bed, and you know how you thrash around. I really *do* need about fourteen hours steady sleep."

"Of course, baby," Alec said gallantly. "You get ready for bed. Would you like me to bring you a nightcap?"

"No thanks," Amelia said. "I think I'll just take a pill and die. The muscles in my legs are jumping, and I feel like over-all hell. You have your nightcap and read the papers, and I'll just quietly fold my tent." She kissed him on the cheek, carefully, and gave him a little pat on the shoulder. "Good night, Sweetie. Oh, are you in for lunch tomorrow?"

Alec thought rapidly.

"I could be. I had a sort of business date but I could change it if—"

"Don't. Dolly said the girls want to have a lunch tomorrow and hear all about the trip—you know, when you went to the boys' tonight she stopped off at the table and asked me. So go and have your lunch, and I'll tell all to the girls. Then we can start getting back on some sort of regular schedule with dinner at home tomorrow night. Okay?"

"Fine," Alec said. "Just fine. Well, good night. It's awfully nice having you back, Mele. Sleep tight, baby."

He stood in the center of the living room until he heard the bedroom door close and the sound of rushing water in the bathroom. Then he went back to the bar, mixed himself another drink, returned to the living room, kicked off his shoes, heaved an enormous sigh, and picked up the newspapers. It had figured to be, he reckoned, about the worst day of his life, in prospect, and it had really gone off rather well.

Evidently Amelia was more than ready to play ball. Whether she really had the curse or not he couldn't say—perhaps, in her basic female intelligence, she was as shy as he about resuming their physical intimacy with the barrier of Barbara Bayne still between them.

But she was not, evidently, going to make any great point of it—at least, not right now. Maybe she was going to settle for bygones being bygones and maybe—here Alec scratched his head—maybe she had a couple of peccadillos of her own to contribute to her reticence. He sincerely hoped so. He hoped she had found the biggest wencher in Singapore and that she had been screwed flat, if only as a gesture of revenge toward her husband. If that were so there'd be no trouble; if it weren't so, one of these days the name of Barbara Bayne would creep into the conversation and pow! Hold your hats, boys.

Well, Alec thought wryly, *if the worst comes to the worst, I can always run away again,* and then cursed himself for a cad at having such a thought on the first evening of the first day of the return of the wife of his bosom. He was relaxed now. Presently he nodded, went to sleep in the chair, and awoke shivering at 5 A.M. to seek the bed in the guest room for the first time in his married life.

And that, too, would prove to be a mistake, because after three straight nights of being able to fling his arms about, grind his teeth, snore, and more important, read himself into slumber without hearing Amelia's "Oh, for Christ's sake turn off the light and go to sleep," Alec Barr decided on permanent separate bedrooms.

73

They resumed a sexual relationship, as the strain wore off and body hungers reasserted themselves. But it was at best a sterile cohabitation, more in the manner of a midnight snack than of a gracious meal. It seemed that one nearly always importuned the other; spontaneity was lacking, and Amelia quite naturally blamed this on Alec's insistence on separate sleeping quarters. They partook of each other's bodies only when the act was not too distasteful to the consenting party. Otherwise, headaches and writing fatigue or early appointments made handy excuses.

Not once was the name of Barbara Bayne introduced into conversation, even when they wrangled over ordinary domestic problems. They fenced and parried carefully, stepping always round any topic which might possibly glide off into a confrontation of rankling fact. This delicacy was carried to ridiculous lengths; even the theater became taboo as a topic, as the Ritz was never mentioned again, as motion pictures involving Barbara Bayne were carefully avoided—avoided in each other's company, that is, although Alec was certain that Amelia went secretly to all of them.

Francis Hopkins was once more familiar to the scene, and Alec almost grew fond of him. Amelia had said that she knew Alec hated being cooped up in theaters for three hours, that he had enough work with words without inflicting more words on his already overburdened budget, so Francis became the automatic escort for all theatrical offerings that Amelia wished to attend.

Alec did not tease Amelia about her "house pansy" any longer. Kidding Francis was taboo, as the name of Barbara Bayne was taboo. One rough crack about Francis, Alec felt, would touch off the powder keg and blow their uneasy truce to hell.

Alec had tried to draw out Amelia on her trip abroad, and got little more information than he had extracted in the Carey limousine on the way back from the airport. Amelia was a damned funny girl when she wanted to be; she had a keen sense of the ridiculous and a stinging wit when she was discussing the foibles of anybody but Alec Barr. Alec was sure that a great many amusing things had happened to her on the trip, and he was equally sure that Amelia retailed them all to Francis, the eager listener, and to the girls, at their regular luncheons. But she entrusted her husband with no such slivers of raw meat, no chunks of nutty goodies that might have accrued to a woman traveling largely on her own in Europe and Asia. Alec was reminded strongly of his own secretiveness with his parents as a child, and of the Robert Paul Smith book *Where Did You Go? Out. What Did You Do? Nothing."*

And, he thought ruefully, in fairness to Amelia—why, goddammit, was he always thinking "in fairness to Amelia"? —in all fairness, he was no gift either. He would have liked to have told Amelia about the funny cop and the ashcan-kicking episode, or about Di Maggio sliding into third and tipping him the big wink. He would have liked to have told Amelia all sorts of things, but he clamped his mouth and carefully stepped around any confidence that might rouse the sleeping dogs of Barbara Bayne.

Perhaps there was very little of what all the amateur psychology buffs now were learning to call "communication" between them, but at least Amelia's presence gave

comfortable order to existence in the armed camp, as a kind
and considerate warder keeps an orderly cellblock. She had
Carl and Elsa whipped into excellent performing condition;
the house was always bright and cheery with flowers; she did
not accept too many invitations at which Alec's presence was
necessary. She did, however, accept a great many invitations
which she said she knew would bore Alec to desperation, so
she was asking Francis to take her. But at the same time she
was quite careful about Francis' presence in the house. She
saw to it that he was almost never there for any extended
period during Alec's nonworking hours. And she was always
at hand for an intelligent discussion of the day's news over
the dinner they invariably ate without guests when they dined
at home.

Life had settled into a calm, if strained, routine. Alec
rarely went out at night by himself. Once in a while he might
go to a boxing match or some authors' shindig, but mainly
he used his days for recapitulation and his night for work.
He harnessed the lunch and cocktail hours for business, and
the hours in between for phone calls which he invariably
made from one of three restaurants or his agent's office, since
it was too much trouble to go all the way uptown only to
come downtown again for a five o'clock drinking appointment.

But he worked well—not, as yet, on the new novel; that
was too big a chore. He had torn up everything he had
written and was starting to reassay its values afresh. But the
bread-and-butter money, the taxman's money, the apartment-
rent money, the restaurant money, the department-store
money, the Carl-and-Elsa money, the mother-and-father
money—*that* money was coming in again.

He had regained his old facile flow with the slick stuff. He
had vulcanized the two serials, finally, to the satisfaction of
Marc Mantell and the editors, if not precisely to himself, and
a big chunk of the useful green had lifted him momentarily
off the financial hook. He liked the idea of his new book,
but something basic in it eluded him, and it did not seem to
him that he was going to find it working until 3 A.M. in the
office, then.

"It *was* a great day," Alec Barr said with a happy sigh. He
loved this that burned in his brain at that hour.

And the same old boredom was beginning to set in again.
Each day was as predictable as the next: Up, shave, bathe,

dress, downtown, lunch, phone calls, appointments, home, cocktails, dinner, nap, work, nightcap, sleep. There didn't seem to be any gap in the day wide enough to drive a real idea through. And there was no doubt about it: he was drinking too much. Not drunk-drinking, not spree-drinking, not fun-drinking. Just sort of steady, slightly sodden dependence on the alcoholic rubber to keep him from running on the iron rims of his nerves. He didn't feel good, or bright, or funny when he drank now. He just felt slightly soaked.

December had come, and the bright leaves had molted. Feeling terribly apologetic, he had begged a week end off Amelia to go pheasant-shooting in Connecticut with Ben Lea. Amelia had been gracious enough; she had a week end she might just as easily fit in—with Francis—at the house of one of Francis' friends in Bucks County, and she said that Alec was looking pretty peaked and it would do him good to get away from the typewriter—and Toots Shor's—and breathe a little fresh air. In more than a month since Amelia's return, Alec had not been once to the house in Jersey, but had sneakily telephoned Luke each week to see that all was well. Alec was trying awfully hard to please Amelia. He felt in the depth of his guilt that he owed it to her to stay home and be a good boy. And Amelia, now she had Alec back, seemed quite content to let him go—if he showed no intention of straying too far. She almost never rang him after he went downtown for the day, but when she did have an occasion to telephone she seemed quite pleased to find him where he said he would be.

The week end in Connecticut came almost as a shock to Alec Barr. He had all but forgotten easy male companionship. Once free, in the light-snow-crowned green wood, it seemed to him that he had been locked up in the apartment forever. Ben Lea was, as usual, a joy to be with—consciously vulgar, brilliantly intelligent, carelessly easy. He was the only man Alec knew whose freckles matched his conversation. Ben didn't care much about shooting, but he liked to sit sprawled around a cheery-hearted fire in a log cabin of an evening, drinking whiskey and letting his spoken fancies crawl over any given topic. Ben knew a great deal about everything, from bulls to Beethoven, and especially he knew a great deal about a great many women—at least, from the only aspect of womanhood he considered important.

Alec had recently retired his Daniel Boone tendencies in

his effort to placate Amelia. Now, in the frost-nippy woods, following a brace of beautifully trained dogs over the Connecticut hills with their black backdrop of evergreen, snow-rimed forest, trudging through the snow-dusted stubble fields, he felt pleasantly alive again. The big-town boredom deserted him as a green-headed pheasant flapped squawking into flight, to be dropped in a cloud of feathers and dutifully retrieved by one of the setters. His appetite revived, and he let his whiskers grow. There was no daytime drinking; they only had a couple of nips before the early supper, and possibly a nightcap or so before tumbling exhausted into bed.

Now they were seated, comfortably weary, in the cabin by the little lake.

"Good day, today," Ben Lea said, the firelight making his brush of pink hair even pinker. He was sprawled in an old cowhide chair, red-stockinged feet propped on a battered leather ottoman. Wearing a plaid wool shirt and disreputable corduroy trousers, Ben Lea looked most unlike the popular image of a high-pressure public relations man. A bottle of bourbon and a half-filled glass sat next a half-empty box of shotgun shells on a low table beside him.

"It *was* a great day," Alec Barr said with a happy sigh. He loved this little shooting cabin, with its big rough-stone fireplace and its rackful of gleaming shotguns, its one rather mothbit moosehead. He dropped his hand carelessly on the head of the liver-and-white setter snoring at his side. "Old Ruff here had quite an afternoon with the birds, didn't he?"

"That he did. You had quite an afternoon with that little twenty-gauge yourself. That one shot you made over your shoulder, lying on your back in the snow, when you were trying to flush that pheasant for me, was the goddamnest thing I ever saw. You do that sort of thing often?"

"All the time. Nothing to it. Never shoot standing if I can shoot backwards, lying flat on my back under the bush in the snow. Sporting-type fellow, me. Toast of the munitions-makers and all that sort of rot, old boy."

"Bloody Boy Scout, that's what you are. Not a writer at all. Been rubbing any more girls together lately?"

"Not lately. Been staying home and behaving myself. Treading on eggs. Trying to work and pretend I wasn't naughty last summer. Not getting very far with it. Still get a very cold policeman's eye out of Amelia, although she never comes right out and says anything. But you can see her thinking. Makes things very tricky around the lodge. I suspect she believes that every time I leave the house now, I leap on a lass and bear her screaming to the earth."

"Hmmmm." Ben Lea reached for his glass. "You made quite an impression on at least one other lady this year. I don't know as I care much for you stealing my girl friends when my back's turned."

"Huh?" Alec blinked. The fire had made him drowsy. "Whayuh talking about?"

"Jill. Jill Richard. The lovely redhead from Blighty. I don't know what you fed her at lunch, maybe Spanish fly, but the last letter I had from London was quite childishly concerned with news about A. Barr, author."

Alec dragged himself up off the small of his back and refilled his glass.

"Oh, *that* one. She was a real winner. Pity she had to go home the same day—not that I was up to very much in the Lothario business the day I stood in for you at lunch. Barbara had just left by one door, and there was an indicated entrance of Amelia through another. Sometimes I think I was wrong in not staying permanently loose. I'm already chafing at the chains again. I keep wishing I was you—foot *and* fancy free. I guess I just had too much conscience to maintain the break."

Now Ben Lea sat up and blinked his blue eyes rapidly.

"Sometimes you really do amuse me, chum," he said. "You really do. You make a villain out of Amelia. You run away like a bad little boy. Then you jump around for a few weeks until your Puritan conscience gets you down, and then you want Amelia back. Then you get her back, and you want to bust loose again. One day you'll have to make up your mind one way or the other. I finally did—after five mistakes."

"You ever plan to get married again?"

"*Me?* Married again? Not bloody likely. I'm too old and full of whiskey. The idea of running another bridal kindergarten appalls me. What I *am* going to do, though, is go down to Mexico the first of the week, to check on a couple of accounts and see some bullfights. The Spaniards just came in for the winter season. Why don't you fly down with me, or is the book running too hot?"

Alec sighed again, this time not from satisfaction.

"Damned thing isn't running at all. I can't get it started. I thought maybe I could, when Amelia got back, but I feel like I'm picking oakum under the stern eye of the warden. As for Mexico . . . forget it. As for bullfights—I had some. All I'd have to do is run off to Mexico with a man of *your* known rotten reputation, and I'd be in more trouble than I was when I flew the coop last summer."

Ben Lea grimaced, not unhappily, and rubbed the gray-pink bristles on his chin.

"Well, I got to admit that there are three or four or five numbers, knockouts all, in Mexico City, a couple more in Cuernavaca, and smörgasbord in Acapulco. The idea had occurred to me—"

"Oh, no you don't. Christmas is a-coming on, and Amelia has old-fashioned ideas about trees and visits to the family and parties and all the rest of that Yuletide crap. Christmas, birthdays, anniversaries—that's when Daddy stays home and wraps presents and mixes eggnog and practices carols in the bathroom. There is something, I do not exactly understand what, about all feast days that brings out the very worst in women."

Ben Lea walked over to the fireplace and kicked a log into a shower of sparks. He squinted at his friend.

"You know something about you, Barr? I think you've got a latent streak of faggot in you. I don't think you really *like* women at all. Love 'em, yes. Screw 'em, sure. But *like* 'em? I'm not so sure."

Alec laughed. Ben was off again on one of his embroideries.

"Okay, so I'm a repressed fairy. Justify it, but you better not turn your back on me. I may be dangerous."

Ben scowled.

"It ain't all that funny. There's a twisted streak in you somewhere. You got this Mama complex about Amelia; almost a persecution complex. This girl never did you any harm. All she's done is love you, protect you, and maybe knock a few rough edges off you. Look, friend, I remember you practically from your first day in New York. You were bright but pretty hairy, if not exactly rough-hewn in the true Lincolnian image.

"You're very smooth, now—mighty slick. You've made a lot of money and you live in a big penthouse and you sit on the same park bench with Barney Baruch. You call Polly Adler 'Pearl' and Billingsley seats you automatically at Table 50 in the Cub Room. You pay a fat income tax and you hang out with classy broads like Barbara Bayne when you're on the cheat. Right?"

"Right. Now how does this make me a latent fag?" Alec's tone was still lightly bantering. "So I've been lucky. I'm an insider now, like you."

Ben Lea's voice became serious.

"Forget the fag bit. That was just a kid. But I'm not entirely joking about this persecution complex. Does it occur to you that perhaps without Amelia you wouldn't amount to a hill of rat sauce? No—" Alec had started to interrupt, and Ben silenced him with an up-pressed palm. "Hear me. *I* know Amelia doesn't write your stuff. I know she doesn't supply you with plots. I'm not accusing you of teething on her apron strings. But I am saying that a lot of the man you are has depended on and does depend on your lady wife. You've been married a long time, son, and when two people have been married that long a time it's hard to say where one person stops and the other starts.

"You run a fine house. You set a fat table. You know the very best people. You give some of the best parties in town —I've literally never known anybody to duck one from preference. You are asked to all the better homes and gardens, and you rank high, high, with all your assorted employers and, more important, their wives. Whose fault do you think this is—yours? Not on your bloody tintype."

Alec shook his head, his eyes hooded, lips pursed, fingertips together.

"Oh, I know, I know. I've heard the song before. Everybody sings it—you, Mantell, even Dinah Lawrence. I am Amelia; Amelia is me. The perfect team. Well, let me tell *you,* brother—"

"Let me tell you brother, nothing. We're *all* of us dead right, chum-boy. You married the girl—you've admitted it —as much out of a sense of security and solidity, after a pretty shaky youth, as much as from any other emotion. And she's made a solid, dependable friend for you ever since—a framework for the masterpiece, if I may go just a little bit gaudy.

"You've seen some of your famous friends' wives with their corsets eased. You know the ones I mean—the throwing-up drunks, the loud-mouthed embarrassers, the dinner-table dominators, the perpetual founts of knowledge of any and all subjects, the fist-clenchers and arm-wavers and cause-promoters. You've seen the kind that make Father say 'Mother's not feeling well, do you mind if I come by myself?' Or worse, 'Will you forgive us for leaving early?'—just after Mama has accused the hostess of whoring with her husband or of being a card-carrying Communist or something otherwise delightful.

"Amelia is none of these liabilities, boy. All she has done is make you a charming home, entertain your friends with taste and discretion, pry the built-in bores off your back, fend off the society sluts, dress quietly and well, stay sober in public and—for all I know—in private, and offer to kick the world in the nuts for daring to suggest that you may not be the greatest writer since W. Shakespeare." Ben Lea stopped and took a long pull at his whiskey.

Alec opened his mouth and again Ben Lea held up his hand.

"Wait a minute. You can talk when I've finished. Look. You're a hell of a ram with the ladies, I reckon. Certainly Barbara Bayne fell for you like a ton of bricks, and she's no easy bang. And if those letters I get from England are any indication, you've got a potential loyal client across the water. Did it ever occur to you that without Amelia in your background for all these many years, the chances are you wouldn't have gotten to first base with any of these dames? If you even managed to meet them in the first place?

"They used to say in the military that an officer's promotional potential depended entirely on his wife. I say the same, in effect, about you and a lot of other people in the public domain. A backdrop of easy elegance isn't lightly come by, friend. A great many important men run off and leave—outgrow, I mean—their wives, which is pathetic, with Charlie J. Tycoon apologizing for the little Nellie he married out of Poontang High. But Amelia has stayed right along with you, boy, whether you realize it or not. Most of the people you know don't think of you separately. They think 'The Barrs' or 'Amelia and Alec.' They *don't* think: 'That poor Alec, saddled with that pathetic Amelia,' or 'Poor dear Alec, *what* a pity he's outgrown his wife.'

"All I'm trying to say, and I guess I've said more'n enough, is that don't you ever forget that when you picked up Barbara Bayne on that plane and took her to bed, or when you made such an evident strike with my Limey friend, that

Amelia wasn't right in there running interference for you, directly or indirectly. The care and feeding of authors ain't easy for a woman, and I think Amelia's done a hell of a fine job on a difficult property. *Selah.* I've finished. Hit me in the chin, or pour me another drink."

Ben Lea sat down, puffing.

Alec smiled and picked up the bourbon bottle, tipping it into Ben Lea's glass.

"I'm perfectly willing to admit a great many truths in what you say," he said. "But may I, please, *may* I, say just one tiny word in behalf of A. Barr, the author who has received more good unsought advice than any writing man since the good Lord Jesus got the Word on the Mount?"

Ben Lea grinned and accepted the fresh drink.

"Pray do," he said. "The chair recognizes the gentleman from South Carolina."

"Did it ever, *ever*, occur to any of you lavish dispensers of wisdom and advice that maybe A. Barr's ass gets a little sore of forever being belabored with the allegation that without his ever-loving he will forget the alphabet? Does it ever occur that the lady is not without flaw, and that in final analysis it is *my* backside that applies itself to seat of chair in front of typewriter, and not Amelia's neatly girdled rear? That I get sick and tired of being told how lucky I am to have such a paragon to keep me straight? The only person who doesn't belabor the point is Amelia herself, and that's possibly because she's too busy peeking under the rugs and peering under the beds for nonexistent threats to her security in the nest. In the meantime what irks me most is that even *I'm* getting superstitious about Amelia. If I should leave her my luck goes with her—and what's happened since August is just a sample. For warners."

Ben Lea grinned at him.

"We only needle you because we love you. *Whom the Lord Loveth He Chasteneth* department. That and the fact that you're about to have a menopause. It affects different men in different ways. I think yours is tending to the self-pity, life-is-passing-me-by direction. Life isn't passing you by a damned bit, Buster. You've lived it a mite too fast, and it's just catching up to you, rather than the other way around. Who do you want to be, anyhow, for God's sake? Errol Flynn? Dylan Thomas? Lord Byron? Thomas Wolfe?"

Alec laughed hollowly.

"I suppose you're right. Very possibly there's enough Irish in my Scotch to make me a romantic, and I'm the wrong age for it. But man, I *do* get tired. I'm tired now. Come on, let's hit the sack. We must have walked fifteen miles today, and I'm out of shape for it."

Ben Lea got up and headed for the bedroom. As he undressed, he said:

"One thing more. You ever have this much trouble with a book before?"

Alec shook his head.

"No. I thought I was past it. This one needs something— almost anything—to make it sing. I just don't know what. I thought perhaps the fling with Barbara would have jarred me loose, but I guess I was wrong. I thought Amelia coming back would settle me down, and I guess I was wrong. I guess maybe I'll go on home and keep pounding away and maybe something will shake down. Maybe Santa Claus will bring me back my wayward talent. Good night."

"Good night," said Ben Lea. "Go back to them silken chains, chum, and batter that old machine. I'll send you a dirty post card from Mexico City."

74

Alec Barr actively hated Christmas, its preparations and its aftermath. He loathed the falseness of forced gift-giving, the down-to-Grandma's-farm spuriousness of the family visits, the snowdrifts of unwanted cards, and the rounds of overmerry parties which turned December twentieth to January second into a steady debauch you shared with people you would rather not see at all. Santa Claus entranced him not, nor did the people you met under Saint Nick's ho-ho-hearty aegis.

He was in a corrosively acid frame of mind when he got back to New York. Mexico with Ben Lea would have been fun—real fun, girls apart—and the Mexicans wouldn't be gathered under any family fir tree, oohing and ahing over unwanted handkerchiefs and nauseating neckties. Alec Barr was cantankerous in more ways than one; he hated turkey in all its forms, from hot roast to cold sandwich.

Amelia was not back yet. It was probable she wouldn't come in from Bucks until after the traffic thinned. The fag set always seemed to make a big thing of Sunday afternoon cocktail parties. He climbed out of his hunting clothes and reflected that it was a fine thing to be free, like Ben Lea, and as swiftly amended the thought to the fact that goddammit, he *had* been free, and after the first few weeks had been acutely miserable in his freedom. *He* had left Amelia; Amelia had not left *him*. She certainly could have stayed apart indefinitely if he hadn't sent that hurry-up-come-home-baby-needs-Mama cable. Which led him to a second annoying thought; do you suppose she really *was* fed up and planning to come back, or was that a lot of hogjuice? Was she maybe just playing cosy, sitting back and waiting for that reverse *dear-John* cable?

The whole thing was becoming ridiculous in his mind. He had wanted freedom, so he went and bought himself some freedom. He had wanted love, so he went out and found himself some love. He didn't like the freedom—he had itched for the harness. He didn't like the love, so he had gotten rid of the love. He had pined for Amelia's physical presence, and now she was back, he was already chafing again. If only—

"If, balls, Barr," he said aloud. "You and your bloody *if*s. You're not fourteen years old. Nine would be a better chronological age. But *if* only Amelia weren't so cool and collected, so obviously steering away from my backslide from respectability. If she'd just say something like: 'Was that blonde a better lay than me, and if so, why the hell didn't you keep her?' we could bring it all out in the open and quit this cat-and-mousing. The way it stands now, every time I hop into Amelia's bed I feel like some kind of paid fancy man, and I'm damned sure she feels like a whore. There's nothing left there—nothing."

Alec clapped himself dramatically on the forehead.

"And another thing, Barr," he said. "You simply must stop talking to yourself out loud."

75

In New York Amelia Barr was almost totally a miserably unhappy woman. She had been equally miserable during her trip to Europe and Asia. All the foreign sights and sounds and scenes had blurred in her vision, like a speeded-up motion picture. She was unable to concentrate on cathedrals, and cocktail chatter bored her. There had been several opportunities for casual amorous adventure, and she had spurned them all—although there were at least two men she might have considered likely candidates for serious flirtation if she had not been so intensely preoccupied with her husband's odd behavior.

The physical aspect of Alec's infidelity did not of itself overwhelm her. She and Alec had laughed too many times over the goatish caperings of too many husbands of their close acquaintance. Men were built like that, and an occasional unplanned lapse from marital decorum was to be expected. Amelia would accept occasional infidelity by Alec if she didn't know about it. But what ripped at her guts was the fact that she could not master a consuming suspicion, a compulsive possessiveness, that had bedeviled her all her life. The nagging doubts, the corrosive jealousies, did not apply only to the possibility that Alec, on a side trip, was tumbling some strange wench in alien hay. Amelia's self-torture applied to everything—old or young, male or female, country or climate—involving Alec Barr outside her personal sphere.

Amelia Barr was jealous of everything that closed her off from her husband's life, whether it was hard homework, conscious play, or even occasional male companionship. This jealousy was a thing she had tried desperately to control, and could not. She was dedicatedly magpielike in her accrual of half-truths and purest idle gossip, little insinuative bricks dropped here, sly innuendoes launched there. The women with whom she lunched and shopped and went to the hairdresser were curators of unverified titbits; their basic con-

versation over the martinis and Bloody Marys was always
devoted to the very *latest*. They were largely idle women,
well-to-do or high-social or a combination of both. Their
children, if they had any, were grown or nearly so. They
were long past housework or actual financial worry, and to
the last woman they had lost close contact with their husbands. Boredom was their bread and bitterness their meat.

There was the unassailable fact as well that most of the
group turned to the homosexual camp followers for companionship. Not the swishers, not the transvestites or the
screamers, but charming, willing, thoughtful homosexuals like
Francis Hopkins—ostensible men who were *really* interested in female doings. These boys were not bored by fashion
shows or concerts or opera. They adored the theater. They
were avid retrievers of gossip, and always, they were *available*. Nearly every girl in Amelia's group had her own reti-
nue of queer friends; wittily malicious friends who gave
amusing parties, who never sulked, who never yawned, and
who always made a woman feel important. This, Amelia
sometimes thought in a moment of painful clarity, was
basically unhealthy, if not downright wrong. But when your
husband of twenty years sealed you away from his life, and
bed became a bore, and there were no longer any small
private jokes, or eager aims, or confidences—even trag-
edies—to share, the faithful faggot became a fixture. At
least they *listened* when you had something to say.

Amelia was really worried about Alec. He had been acting most peculiarly since her return—peculiar in a different sense than from his initial panicked rush from the house
on that hot August evening. As a woman Amelia realized
that an accumulation of minor irritations could magnify
themselves into a full-scale temper fit. She herself was subject to haboring tiny bits of suspicion and scraps of dubious
evidence until the sum reached hysteric proportion. Alec's
dramatic departure didn't bother her very much as an action.
What drove her out of her mind was the recurring thought
that the wild-eyed exodus had been *planned*, and was all
of a piece with an affair that had been going on for God
knows how long; and, for all she knew, was continuing.
Or, if not an affair with Barbara Bayne, a liaison with any
one of a dozen possible women. Amelia found herself
looking at her luncheon companions with suspicion, remembering how Gwen Griffiths had swarmed all over Alec one

week end in Cuba, or how Alec and Polly MacAvoy had found an awful lot to giggle over in corners at parties. It was funny—perhaps "funny" wasn't the precise word—how the seeds of suspicion flourished once they were planted and even slightly fertilized.

Amelia Barr had been tearfully delighted to receive Alec's cable asking her to return to him. She had gone to Europe prepared to wait out the logical conclusion of whatever was chewing on her husband. She had rushed excitedly back to encounter indrawn remoteness on Alec's part. She had pretended a fatigue she had not felt, invented a menstrual period she did not have, in order to spare them both the embarrassment of bed on the night of her return. She had made a mistake there, it now appeared. Alec had moved into the guest room and in the guest room he had stayed, on the excuse that as "people grow older, they develop offensive sleeping habits which are just as well confined to separate rooms." Perhaps he was right; certainly he was a restless, noisy sleeper, especially when he was working hard. Perhaps she snored. She didn't know. Most adults did, especially if they drank.

They had drifted back into some pallid semblance of sex as their mutual caution subsided, but it was almost entirely unsatisfactory. Their sexual experience had never been wildly ecstatic, or even wild. Amelia Barr knew that there were all sorts of tricks to the trade, all sorts of things women—like Barbara Bayne?—did to titillate the waning appetites of their men, but she was afraid to deviate much from their old habit patterns. Alec frowned on too much distaff enthusiasm in bed. He objected, he said, to "gymnastics." Amelia wanted to give with all her body and heart, but she was school-girlishly afraid to attempt an overproficiency in the act.

Their physical life had become an occasional calisthenic, devoid of spontaneity. She had crawled playfully (and face it, girl, consciously erotically) into Alec's bed one Sunday morning, and had been more than rudely glared at. She felt that when Alec occasionally came to her room, he had been counting on his fingers and had felt that it was time again to do his dreary duty by the little woman. Most of the fun and nearly all of the games had gone out of their love-making, as she accepted his occasional rutting and he conveyed the impression that he was merely relieving himself. Amelia, in private tears, sometimes felt like a public comfort station.

She was prepared for a lessening of ardor—that happened to everybody after a while—but she was *not* prepared for the sudden cessation of jokes and confidences and intimate sharings of trivial daily problems. Alec Barr, when he was trying, could be one of the funniest men alive, in his own dry way. For all of their married life he had been wryly humorous about himself and others for her especial benefit. He now seemed to have lost all that humor, and went around with a face that was twice too long for a face, as he once had said, "that was twice too long already."

She had a fund of amusing incidents she might have expanded for his enjoyment, but she felt that he didn't want to hear about the European-Asian trip. She would have listened eagerly to anything he might have wished to tell her about his one sidestreet excursion off the marital highway with Barbara Bayne (and would have forgiven him without rubbing his nose in it, she firmly believed). But he kept that nearly three-month period sealed away. Insofar as anything Alec elected to confide, those three months had passed in a complete vacuum.

Amelia knew that her husband was having a horrid time with his work, and she wanted to be sympathetic, to invite confidence, perhaps even to offer a slight suggestion that might be useful. But merest mention of writing problems was enough to get her head snapped off; Alec didn't need any sympathy and wasn't accepting any offers of aid. Amelia wanted to take his unhappy head and cuddle it to her breast. But these days, except occasionally, almost impersonally in bed, he shied away from even a casual touch.

They sat, sometimes reading but often with Alec staring vacantly past her, for as much as an hour without speaking. Alec had never been very gregarious, but now he seemed to welcome outside interruptions. He was even amenable to cocktail parties, which he had always profanely avoided. She knew he did not like Francis Hopkins, but now he was excessively polite, almost hail-fellow-chum-buddy with Francis, on the off chance, Amelia sadly supposed, that Francis would take her out of the house and off her husband's hands.

Certainly they were both drinking too much, but there didn't seem to be much else to do. Alec had never been a quarrelsome drinker; now he was becoming a snarler. He had always been easy with the help, and now he was snapping at Carl and Elsa—critical to such point that Amelia wondered how long it would be before the couple gave notice.

She had talked most of this over with Francis—you *could* talk to Francis, where you didn't dare admit anything or confide anything in the company of the girls. Francis had been rather less than helpful.

"Of course, you could get a divorce, dear girl," he said. "There are certain to be grounds enough."

"I told you before I didn't *want* a divorce," Amelia cried. "I just want a husband back! I happen to love the man, and he's driving me crazy!"

"You could change the color of your hair again," Francis drawled. "Perhaps that blonde effect brings back too-fragrant memories of lost loves. Or you could adopt a child . . ."

"You're—you're impossible!" Amelia was near tears. "You're like all—" she caught herself just in time.

"Like all *what,* dear? What were you going to say?" Francis' voice was deadly.

"Like everybody else!" Amelia said wildly. "You never dig *beneath* a problem. "You're just like all the women I know! Tragedy in the house? *Change your hair style.* Baby drowned in the swimming pool? Buy a new fur coat. Husband gives you the gonorrhea he caught from his secretary? *A new string of pearls will cure it!"*

"Oh, pish-tush, there's no use talking to you in this mood," Francis said, offended. "Ring me when you're feeling better, and I'll take you to lunch. But," he said, rising to leave, "I was more than half-serious about that hair. You've out-Barbaraed Barbara. Why don't you let it go *all* gray, now, like that charming *newest* friend of Alec's with the pretty daughter."

"What—"

"Oh, nothing, really nothing, just kidding," Francis said. "But I think her name's Dinah Lawrence. A newspaper lady. I've seen her pictures in the paper. She has a byline. She's very attractive." And Francis Hopkins was swiftly gone.

The phrase *in vino veritas* came into Amelia's mind after Francis Hopkins had left. God *damn* the pansies. They had a way of bringing truth to light, just as gin fetched the hidden hatreds to the surface. Occasionally, *in faggot veritas* was apt. Adopt a child. . . . Better than a new hairdo or a vengeful trip abroad, better than a new mink coat?

Amelia didn't really like the way the thought struck. But a lot of people *were* doing it. And there was some great frustration in Alec about his sterility, some resentment of her as a result of what was really not her fault. All that business about temperature charts and wheat germ. . . .

It *was* very possible that Alec was frustrated because he couldn't be a father. Maybe the one thing that Alec lacked was a child—a little girl to spoil, a little boy to teach all that silly outdoor business. And maybe (Amelia credited herself with what she thought was honesty) it—or they—would give both of us something to do that didn't focus constant attention on each other.

Hank and Janie Holloway had been just verging when they went to that place—The Cradle, was it?—and found some charming children, and now they seemed happy as clams. They didn't even throw martinis at each other any more. And there was all that propaganda about foreign waifs. She'd seen some beautiful orphans in the countries she'd just visited —quite probably a lot of beautiful bastards as well. Especially in Italy, where the parochial schools were full of relicts of the second war.

She supposed there were masses of Japs and refugee Chinese as well—Germans, perhaps?—but it would be better to stick to something less fraught with eventual problems. No Jews, no Arabs, nothing with slant eyes or peculiar colors. There would be school to consider.

"I would grow to love it," Amelia said aloud. "I *would*. But you have to be practical on these things, particularly when you take into consideration a man as sensitive as Alec. I mean, I couldn't quite see landing him with a couple of Chinese orphans when English or Italian or French kids would serve as well."

That's a hell of a way for a potential mother to think, she thought, but you have to be practical in these things. I mean, adopting an American child would be fine, but what kind of American mother gives away her own baby?

It's not that I'm unmotherly or hard-boiled or anything like that. But there's not any point in adding complications to a marriage unless Alec is going to want it. I mean, being den mother and PTA and religious education and things like that—

"I'll sound him out on it, anyway," she said aloud again. "It won't hurt to try. Because we have to do *something*. All that trying to have a baby. . . . He hasn't been the same since."

"Alec," Amelia Barr said just before Christmas. "We have to do something about us." They were sitting quietly, reading, in the New York apartment.

"What?" Alec dropped his newspaper. "What say?"

"I said we have to *do* something about us. We've lost communication. We don't relate to each other any more."

"Now don't tell me you've been going to a psychiatrist," Alec said. "We've got trouble enough. What is this communication-relationship business all about?"

"I thought about it a lot in Europe and Asia. We're living selfish lives together. We've lost a common interest." Amelia's voice took a professional tone.

Alec struck his knee lightly.

"You haven't been to a psychiatrist. You've been doing those are-you-happy-with-your-husband quizzes in female magazines. Now what are you up to, exactly?"

"Just this. I want a child. I want something we can build ourselves around. I want—"

"You want something to hold us together, to cement the marriage, to give us something to talk about in our old age. Of all the—you know damned well I can't give you a child. We've been through all that. If we could have one I'd give you one. I'd give you six, or a dozen. But I can't. I'm sorry. So forget it."

He picked up his paper and shook it impatiently.

"No, now don't start reading again," Amelia said. "Please listen to me. I know it's not your fault—or *mine*," she said hurriedly. "Neither of us's fault that we can't have our own children. But we could adopt—oh, Alec, I saw the most *beautiful* children in orphanages in Italy. . . ."

"GI mistakes." Alec's voice was irritable.

"I don't care whose mistakes they were, they're lovely children. We could take one or two and—"

"And then I suppose we could take on a few Chinese and Algerians and Japs and you could call me Josephine Baker, and we could all live happily ever after with our own Little League of Nations. Just so it would give *you* something to do. Something to keep you out of the girl-lunch business. Something to improve my writing. When I'm stuck with a piece I can always teach somebody else's byblow the fundamentals of baseball. Well, forget it, friend."

"Oh, you—" Amelia was trying desperately to keep her temper. "A lot of people have made successful adoptions, and loved the kids better than—"

"Nobody finishes any sentences in this house any more. So I'll finish one," Alec said. "*No.* I will not take up the adoption of children as a fad; I will not assume the responsibility for strange lives just to keep you from being bored. I will not pervert a child into a substitute for this phony charity work you women take up as an excuse for martini lunches. And I will not, by God, be roped into a phony togetherness at the expense of a little stranger who will wind up being raised by nannies while Mummy's off in committee—or Europe, or Southampton, or Palm Beach, or wherever!"

Alec's voice rose.

"Damn you all for selfish bitches! You can't make it on your own with the husband and you think you can cure it all with this adoption business—especially if the poor thing has got slant eyes or a black skin, to give it chic! You think you can repair all the old ills and cure the bad consciences with the body of some innocent baby that you buy because everybody else is doing it! No, and no, and twenty times no! Kids of your own are tough enough to raise. We are not practicing any marital therapy in this house with a baby's body!" He pounded a fist into his palm.

"I only thought it might be worth trying," Amelia said coldly, dry-eyed. "So I was dead wrong. I'm ashamed of myself for suggesting it. I wouldn't want you for the father of even our own children. Certainly I wouldn't want to bring in a little child against an attitude like yours. Not even if I bore it myself."

"In this instance, you're dead right." Alec rattled his paper. "For household therapy I now intend to read Art Buchwald, if permitted. Go find a new committee to repair what's wrong with the world, and beg subscriptions in a saloon lobby. Give a charity ball. But don't buy me any strange children to ruin in a house that's already—" he hesitated.

"That's already *what?*"

"*Wrecked* was the word I had in mind," Alec said, and flapped his newspaper again.

Amelia got up and left the room. Alec dropped the newspaper. He walked over to the bar and poured himself a drink.

Poor, poor girl, he thought, twirling the ice. Everything else fails—for lack of a loving man—and now she thinks we can paste it all back together with somebody else's baby. Little Sunshine comes to our house to stay and makes everything peachy-dandy again between Mommy and Daddy. Shirley Temple on toast. Adopt the little bastard from some one-night wartime stand and make the old house a new home.

"What I need right now, real bad," Alec Barr said, and pounded the bar with his fist, "is somebody else's bastard to make my life complete! What I need is formulas and nannies and predigested spinach and the Little League if it's a boy and worrying if it's making out at age fourteen if it's a girl! What I need is sleep-in parties and cookouts and Boy Scouts and the Parent-Teacher Association! God almighty!"

Then he thought: *Poor Amelia. The last chance. Poor Amelia. But what we've got is sufficient to wreck us both. We don't need any added starters in the form of innocent victims.*

He took his drink back to his chair and picked up the paper again. Somehow Art Buchwald wasn't as funny as usual. Perhaps it was because Alec Barr could imagine the sound of sobbing from the back room, even though the actual hearing of it was acoustically impossible.

76

Dinah Lawrence. The name rang. Probably from the old days. *Dinah Lawrence?* Alec usually mentioned his vintage friends from the hungrier epoch. Why would he be secretive about an old buddy from the newspaper days? Amelia didn't mind his having *very* old friends whose acquaintance didn't include her. The hell Amelia doesn't mind, Amelia thought, furiously. So the Bayne bitch wasn't enough to keep him busy. He's got another steady lay on the side, which would account for—*of course*. It would account for a lot of late arrivals for dinner. How my boy has come on. *Cinq à sept* stuff. Afternoon quickies. I would not, really would not, have thought Alec capable of that.

All of Amelia's compassion for her harassed husband vanished. *The sneaky son-of-a-bitch,* she thought. He's probably had a quiet mistress for all these years, when he was being so damned noble about not going out nights with the fellows. Why the hell *would* he go out nights with the fellows, when he's banging himself blind every afternoon? No wonder he fought shy of my bed—the poor dear was *tired*.

I won't say anything to him about it. I won't I won't I *won't*. If he wants some grimy female reporter with ink under her nails he can have her, and welcome. But the sneaky bastard. All these years, and me, stupid me, never tumbling. I must have been born with rocks in my head.

So Dinah Lawrence joined the host of ghosts which trammeled Amelia's sleep. Dinah became one with Barbara Bayne, and led all the rest of the unnamed girls in Sydney, Australia, and Columbus, Ohio, and London, England, and Pittsburgh, Pennsylvania, that Amelia Barr would never know and always hate. Amelia nourished her fears with purest hatred, now; her hatred was fed by extra suspicion. And when Ruth Hazeltine kissed Alec Barr soundly beneath the mistletoe at a Christmas Eve party, under the combined influence of Yule spirit and gin, Amelia Barr stabbed her best friend with one poisoned look and announced loudly that she was bored to death and was going home. Alec could stay, or come, or drop dead, she couldn't care less. Alec chose to come.

They sat in frigid silence in the taxi all the way home. Alec was coldly angry and considerably puzzled. Amelia was tight-lipped, white-faced-furious. They waited tautly until they achieved the living room before the dam burst.

Alec shucked off his dinner jacket and slung it over the back of a chair.

"You want a drink?" he asked without any discernible interest.

"Yes," Amelia snapped. "I want *several* drinks. I would just as lief get stinking drunk."

"Save it until I get back with the booze," Alec said, walking toward the bar. In a moment he returned, and handed her a squat glass of straight Scotch on very few rocks.

"That should do you for a start," he said. "Now for Christ's sake, what bit you all of a sudden?"

"Nothing bit me—*all of a sudden*. It's been biting me gradually. It's been gnawing at me every day. And tonight I just got damned sick and tired of seeing you nuzzling that bitch Ruth Hazeltine! You've still got her lipstick on!"

Alec sat down and crossed his legs. He was wearing his best expression of injured innocence.

"I still don't know what's eating you. She's *your* friend, not mine. She was just a little drunk and got carried away and planted a smooch on me under the mistletoe. I doubt there was any great harm intended, except I wish she'd change her brand of lipstick. I never did like raspberry."

"Oh, cute it up, cute it up! Be a funny man! Another five minutes and she'd have had you in the cloakroom with your pants down!"

"Hey there, now, take it easy," Alec said mildly. "This is the season to be jolly. Peace on earth, and all that sort of thing. Noël. Noël."

"Jolly, my ass. I'm sick of all of it—sick of everything, sick of—"

"Me?"

"Sick of you, too. Sick of the whole messy, lousy—"

Alec put his drink down and leaned forward, resting his forearms on his knees.

"What is this all about? Something more than a wet kiss under the mistletoe from a broad I loathe and you know I loathe? What's under your blanket?"

"Not you, you bet. At least not more than once a month. *Who is Dinah Lawrence?*" the question came like a rifle shot.

"Huh? I don't get it. What has Dinah Lawrence got to do with all the fireworks?"

"Is she a better lay than Barbara Bayne?" Amelia spat. "Or have you lost count of all your women?"

"Now just you wait a minute, lady," Alec Barr said. "Sort of take a little reef in your sails, and let's have this from the start. It looks like the beginning of a long night."

Amelia drained her glass in long successive swallows.

"Get me another one," she said. "I need it."

"So fall on your face," Alec said. "It's your hangover, not mine." He got up and went to the bar again, leaving his full glass untouched on the table.

"Here," he said, returning with the second drink. "Now

let's see if we can't begin at the beginning. What brings Dinah Lawrence out of left field all of a sudden?"

"I'm asking you," Amelia said, her eyes glittering. *"You* tell *me.* How long have you been laying her?"

"I haven't got the first faint idea of what you're talking about," Alec said. "Believe me. How would you know anything about Dinah Lawrence anyhow?" He snapped his fingers. "Oho, of course. Our dear sweet friend has come to call again. Dear Auntie Francis and his portable cesspool. Am I very wrong?"

"For once you're not wrong at all. Francis *did* tell me. Evidently everybody in town knew about Dinah Lawrence but me. How long has *this* one been going on?"

Alec yawned.

"About twenty years. Befo' de wah. We were in the Girl Scouts together. You must be out of your mind, Amelia. Dinah Lawrence is a newspaper gal I've known most of my adult life. She's an old friend. I've covered a lot of stories with her."

"The way I get it, stories aren't all you covered with Dinah Lawrence," Amelia said viciously. "I'm just surprised I haven't heard about it before. If she's such an old friend, why haven't we had her here at the house?"

"I don't know what that little faggot told you." Alec's voice was growing angry now. "And I don't *care* what the little faggot told you. We haven't had her at the house because I haven't seen her in years. Dinah Lawrence is a friend of mine, like Ben Lea is a friend of mine, like John Barry is a friend of mine, like Marc Mantell is a friend of mine."

"Oh, so you screw them, too? That's a side of you I hadn't suspected."

"Now, that's quite enough. I don't know what's poisoning your well, but you can skip Dinah Lawrence as a threat to our dubious happiness. I like her. I was lonely while you were gone. I ran into her in a bar. She asked me to dinner at her house, with her daughter. I merely repaid the hospitality. I took them to lunch. At Twenty-One. You don't hide out in Twenty-One. I suppose somebody saw me—one of the Girl Gestapo doubtless—and it got back to your sailor-grabbing boy friend."

"My *girl*-grabbing husband is exactly right. He couldn't be righter. How old is the daughter?" Amelia's eyes narrowed as she zeroed the question.

"Nineteen-twenty, thereabouts. I don't really know."

"Old enough *and* big enough. Are you merely using her for a chaperone, or are you training her up as a summer replacement for when her old lady starts to sag? Waste not, want not?"

Alec's face whitened. He clenched his fists until the knuckles whitened.

"You deserve a real rap in the teeth for that one," he said. "That's bitchery of a high order."

"I'll take your word for it. You're the expert on bitches. What happened to your Barbara girl? Did she find out about your other lady friend and leave you, or what?"

Alec shook his head and sighed elaborately.

"There's really not much use trying to talk straight to you tonight, is there?"

"If you did it would be for the first time in years. I never fully realized that I had a practicing Casanova under the roof. I thought I was married to a dedicated writer. Write any good books lately?" Amelia's voice was growing harsher, more metallic, nastier, and she was beginning to slur her syllables. Alec closed his eyes. Thank God *I'm* sober, he thought. If I were drunk I'd think I was listening to Barbara Bayne. They all sound alike when they fight dirty.

"We'll ignore the last crack, I think," he said evenly. "It wasn't worthy of you even in your current state of agitation."

"Current state of agitation, my aching ass," Amelia said. "Sure I'm agitated. I'm agitated because the man I've been married to all these years walks out on me with practically no word and sets up housekeeping with a peroxide whore."

"What pretty blonde hair *you* have, Grandma. Natural, I presume?" Alec couldn't resist.

"Never you mind about *my* hair. Then I find out about this Dinah woman and your ready-made family. And as long as we're on the subject of the rich full life of Alexander Barr, what about your redhead?"

"What redhead, for God's sake?" Alec's voice was honestly puzzled.

"You know what redhead, for God's sake. The one you were climbing all over at lunch at the Laurent."

"Oh. *That* redhead. The one I raped on the carpet?"

"Yes, *that* redhead. I don't know her name, but I hear

she's very pretty. Is she another member of the harem?"

"I wish she were," Alec said bitterly. "At least she's pleasant-spoken and has nice manners. If it'll help you into the Christmas spirit—although you don't need much help, if it's true that it's more blessed to give than to receive—I only know the lady slightly. She's a friend of Ben Lea's. I don't know why I bother to tell you all this, but I was supposed to have lunch with Ben and he couldn't make it at the last moment and I got stuck with his other lunch date. She left for England that night."

"How very unfortunate for you. But I wouldn't have thought you need your precious Ben Lea to pimp for you. I thought you picked up your own talent," Amelia said.

"I think that'll be quite enough, thank you," Alec said, rising.

"While you're up, get me another drink," Amelia said, her eyes moistly glittering. "You must be good for something around the house. You're certainly no good to me."

"I'll get you your drink," Alec said. "And I'll even carry you to bed when it skulls you."

"That'll be the only thing you'll do about bed," Amelia called after him. "Carry me to it, I mean. Nothing else goes on *in* it."

Alec was back in a moment. He handed her the drink roughly, sloshing the whisky.

"I caught that last crack," he said. "You're really full of Christmas cheer tonight, my darling."

Amelia took a greedy gulp and fumbled in the box for a cigarette. She missed the cigarette end twice with the lighter flame, and jerked her hand angrily away when Alec attempted to guide the flame.

"Don't touch me!"

"All right, set yourself alight, if you wish," Alec said, picking up his drink and then setting it down again, still untasted.

Amelia finally got the cigarette going, and puffed furiously.

"My spies tell me you only stayed shacked up with the Bayne broad for a month, that right?" The voice now was deadly hard and cold.

"If it's anybody's business, that's right. Your information is more accurate than usual. So?"

Amelia spaced her words deliberately.

"Well, all I can say is that if you didn't screw Barbara

Bayne any better than you do me, I'm surprised she kept you on for a month!" Amelia took one look at Alec's face and said: "Go on, hit me! That's all we lack for the perfect Christmas Eve!"

"I'd like to slug you," Alec said. "God knows how much I would like to slug you. But I don't think I'll give you that satisfaction. Don't you think you'd better haul yourself together and see if you can make it to bed? Remember, in about ten minutes it's Christmas Day, and we have to make the annual pilgrimage to Washington to visit your folks. They wouldn't understand a black eye. It doesn't fit in with the eggnog-inspired orgy of good fellowship under the molting Christmas tree."

"You sarcastic bastard," Amelia said, getting unsteadily to her feet. "You nasty-tongued bastard. I wouldn't take you down to see my people if you were as hungry as you were when you first started eating off my people."

"The girl is really going for the groin tonight," Alec said. "That last one was real nice. *Sweet,* as Francis would say."

"Forget Francis. I think I'll take *Francis* down to see my folks with me tomorrow. At least he won't sit around all day and sneer at them."

"Take Francis to hell for all I care," Alec said. "Now you really should go to bed, Amelia."

His wife swayed in her chair.

"Go to bed when I goddam well please," she said, getting up. She spilled some of her drink as she took another gulp. "Why don't *you* go away somewhere? Maybe you need a rest from all your women. Maybe you ought to go someplace where you don't know any women and haven't got any pimps."

"Where would you suggest, Timbuktu?" Alec asked nastily.

"Not far 'nough," Amelia's voice was beginning to blur now. "Not nearly far 'nough. Gonna go to bed. But *you* not sending me, see? Going own goddam free will."

She turned and bumped into the corner of the piano. She seized the piano with one hand, and steadied herself. With the other hand she waved the glass, splashing whisky on the rug.

"Whyn't you go out to that goddam Boy Scout camp of yours and commune nature 'th that goddam sailor-stooge of yours? Maybe you can get whatsername, Dinah Lee, or somebody, to come out 'n spend holidays with you'n Luke.

'nless Luke's all company you need. I *heard* about sailors," Amelia said, and tacked off in the general direction of bed.

Alec Barr sighed, and walked over to the table on which sat his inviolate drink. He picked it up, and tossed off half of it in one gulp. He raised the glass to himself in the big Federal mirror.

"So now I'm a fag, impotent, and a whoremaster, all in one," he said. "What a talented fellow I really must be. Merry Christmas, Mister Barr. And a very happy New Year, Mister Barr."

He heard Amelia's door slam viciously. "Merry Christmas to all. And to all, good night."

He sat back in his chair and contemplated his glass.

"It's a damned good thing the Japs didn't have Amelia's intelligence apparatus," he murmured. "If they had, we'd have lost the war."

Presently he went back to the bar and poured himself a fresh drink. Amelia, in her current state, was going to exact a lot of heavy thinking from Alec Barr and he always thought better at night, with the room quiet and a glass in his hand.

77

Amelia was terribly hung over and reasonably penitent on Christmas morning. Alec brought her a tray containing aspirin, Bromo-Seltzer, and a large vodka Bloody Mary.

"Merry Christmas," he said. "Enter the junior member of the Three Wise Men, bearing gifts of frankincense and, you should pardon the expression, Bloody Myrrh. How are you feeling?"

"Godawful," Amelia said. Her face was puffed and seamed from sleep. *"Death.* Thank you for the Saint Bernard bit. I think I just may die. It was the martinis first and the eggnog second and the Scotch-and-temper last. Did I do anything real bad when I came home? I don't remember too many of the details toward the end."

"You were in fair form," he said. "Very fair form. Toward the end I managed to be impotent, a sex maniac, and a faggot all in the same package, which is pretty good, even for a man of my undisputed talents."

"Oh, God, now I *do* remember," Amelia said. "I was doing *all* of the drinking and most of the talking. But you were needling me pretty good, Buster. Pretty good." She nodded her head in grave affirmation.

She chased her aspirin with a slug of the Bloody Mary and hoisted herself to the side of the bed.

"I'm too feeble to take it up where we left off. But basically I was on sound grounds. Tell that Nazi in the kitchen to make a lot of hot, fresh coffee, will you? I'm going to see if a shower and this Bromo will bring me back to the land of the living. Oh." She looked at him through veined eyes. "Merry Christmas."

"Merry Christmas. I can't remember one when we didn't have a fight of some kind. If you live, there's a present for you. I'm going to get out of this dressing gown and into some clothes. See you later. I suppose we're still going to Washington?"

"*I'm* going to Washington," Amelia said, feeling with her toes for her slippers. "You don't have to go. As a matter of fact I'd rather you didn't. We'll talk about it after I've pulled myself together."

Alec thought hard as he dressed. She hasn't forgotten a bloody thing about last night, and I doubt if she was as drunk as she sounded. She just had her girl-glands going pretty good—and, as she said, she was on pretty sound ground. I'm just as pleased I didn't mention the week end Dinah and Penny spent with me in Jersey. What do we do now, Daddy? he asked himself, rejecting five neckties before he went back to his original choice. Something's got to give. That girl is really full of stored-up canker.

He thought then about the new mink coat—subject, of course, to exchange if she didn't like the color or the style, and *not* bought from Francis Hopkins' store—that he had carefully flung over the divan.

"They say you can cure anything with mink," he murmured. "Somehow I think this is the one thing you *can't* cure with mink."

He had a Salty Dog, the hallowed mixture of grapefruit juice, salt, and gin, to put him in a festive mood for the breakfast which he did not want. He was relentlessly pursuing a poached egg around the plate when Amelia joined him, wearing a flowered housecoat, her face made up.

"Gah," she said, frowning at the egg. "It looks horrible. I'll settle for fruit and coffee. And maybe another Bloody Mary."

"I'd cool it a little on the Christmas cheer if I were you," he said. "That's if you're really going to visit your family. I take it I'm not invited? You were serious?"

"I was serious," she said, attacking her grapefruit without enthusiasm. "After last night I don't feel very Christmasy, and I know how you loathe going down for the gift unwrapping. There's no point in both of us being miserable. I think I'll stay through New Year's. Incidentally, I'm sorry about some of the things I said—at least sorry about the way I said them—last night."

Alec dipped his head and said nothing.

Amelia took a sip of her coffee and made another face.

"Overpercolated as usual," she said. "Some day I'll kill that Kraut. Yes," she continued. "I'm sorry. But not very. There were a lot of things lurking around that needed to be said. I'm just sorry I was loaded when I said them."

Alec poured himself another cup of coffee, and still said nothing.

"There anything *you* want to say about last night?" Amelia pushed the half-eaten grapefruit aside.

"I think most of it got said," Alec replied. "There were a lot of words flying around. I don't think we left any private moan unturned."

"Don't for Christ's sake be funny this morning. I don't know what we're going to do. I'd rather let the whole miserable mess ride until after the holidays. Why don't you be a smart boy and go spend a week in Jersey—shoot a duck, catch a fish through a hole in the ice, chop down another tree? Maybe we'll both feel better after New Year's."

"It's an idea. Anything to get out of this cocktail panic for the next week. I think perhaps I will, Amelia. Please, could we possibly be a little pleasant to each other today, at least until I take you to the plane? It *is* Christmas, whether we feel much like it or not. And I haven't heard you mention your present."

"What present? I haven't seen any."

"It's on the divan in the living room. I thought you might have seen it passing through."

"I didn't see anything passing through. I don't think my eyes were open. What is it?"

"Suppose you go and have a look," Alec said. "I hope you like it."

Amelia got up, and he followed her.

"There," he said, pointing to the flung mink. "Merry Christmas."

Amelia looked at him swiftly, and he saw the tears forming. Then her mouth hardened.

"We can't afford it," she said. "You know we can't afford it. And I'll be goddamned if I'll accept bribery, Alec Barr!" She swept the mink to the floor with a furious gesture, burst into stormy tears, and ran for the bedroom. Again the door slammed.

". . . and a Happy New Year," Alec Barr said, as he carefully retrieved the mink from the floor, folding it gently along the length of the sofa. "Peace offering rejected. State of war existent. Situation normal."

He scratched his chin.

"I gather she didn't buy *me* anything for Christmas," he said. "At least nothing important enough for me to spurn."

He headed back to the dining room for another cup of coffee.

"Whoever came up with that mink advice is in the wrong racket," he murmured. "I'm glad I didn't buy her a car. She'd probably have run over me with it."

Amelia emerged shortly, dressed for travel. Her eyes were red and further puffed from weeping.

"I don't think we'd better talk to each other any more today," she said. "And don't bother about taking me to the airport. I've called a Carey. Go on out to the lake and try to have some fun. I'm sorry about the coat. But we really *can't* afford it, and I don't want to accept it under present conditions. Good-by, Alec. I'll see you in a week or so." Out of habit she held up her cheek to be kissed, then rang the elevator bell.

Alec went into her bedroom and got her bag, parking it on the floor beside her.

"Have a good time in Washington," he said, as the lift-door opened. "Give my best to your people."

He considered various things to do with his week. I suppose, he thought, I might nip over and say hello to Dinah and the kid, but Christmas Day is awkward to bust in on a family, and I didn't buy them any presents. I suppose I might even ask them if they want to run out to Jersey for a couple of days to help me catch fish through the ice.

"Don't be a nut," he admonished himself aloud. "Amelia'll have six detectives planted under every birch tree."

After a while he called the garage to send round his car. Then he got on the phone to tell Luke he was coming out to Jersey for a spell, and to be sure there was plenty of booze in the house. The buzzer then informed him that his car was at the door.

"*Christmas*," said Alec Barr, as he slipped into his heaviest overcoat. "Christmas. What a rotten day to get yourself born."

78

The lake was still not frozen in the middle, and ducks had rafted in the pools. It was pleasant in the country with the trees weighted with the snow, the hills like angel food, the thin ice of the lake snow-hillocked, and the deer coming daintily down to hoof holes in the crumbling ice to drink. Luke had laid in an enormous supply of firewood, and the house was lovelysnug against the cold. Alec let his whiskers burgeon and lounged around in red-checked mackinaw pants and zippered jumper. He briefly considered the idea of enticing Ben Lea to visit him for a couple of days, but rejected it when he remembered that Ben's job was nearly 100 per cent social and that this *was* party time in New York.

Two days after Christmas Alec was sitting in the kitchen, helping Luke clean the fish, when the phone rang. It was Marc Mantell.

"This is important." Marc Mantell made it sound important. "Listen. First, how are you getting along with Amelia?"

"Lousy. That's why I'm here. We had a hell of a row on Christmas Eve. I'm accused of screwing everybody in America but the Gish Sisters. It was a real dinger. She went to Washington on the annual family safari alone, and suggested that Timbuktu was much too close if it included me in it."

"That's good, then." Alec heard Marc Mantell chuckle. "Very good."

"What the hell's good about it?" Alec reached for a cigarette, and signaled Luke to bring him a match. "Get on with what's important."

"Well, it makes it all the easier. To leave, I mean."

"Leave what? For where? To do what?"

"Africa. East Africa. A little farther away than Timbuktu. Nairobi to be exact."

"I've *been* to Kenya. I was there year before last, remember? It costs money. I haven't got much money to spare for foolishness right now. Anyhow I got enough tusks and horns."

"This isn't foolishness. This isn't tusks and horns. This is business. Present money. More important—future money. Look: You've been reading in the papers about this Mau Mau business that's broken out in Kenya? The gang murders and rituals and such?"

"Of course. Scraps, anyhow. Nobody seems to know much about it."

"Exactly," Marc Mantell said. "Precisely. So I've got you a commission to go out there, ostensibly on safari, dig *into* and dig *up* the story, and write a couple of nice little lead pieces for *Life* with a *Digest* pickup guaranteed. All expenses paid; three months allotted. How's it sound?"

"It sounds fine if I know how much we get for this junket. I mean, they *do* cut off heads out there. How much is my head worth?"

"In this instance only thirty thousand dollars for the package, including the neck, plus the expenses of course. But if you're the Alec Barr I think you are, there must be enough novels and short stories kicking around to keep you busy for the next five years. Who knows? You might even get that current *War and Peace* of yours off the ground with a change of scene."

"Thanks for the heavy sarcasm. As a matter of fact, I think you may be right. I'm getting nowhere with it as it stands. It isn't a lot of money they're offering, but I can use *any* amount of money. When does this high adventure start?"

"Sooner the better. Right now. They've had a flock of Christmas killings, with more promised for the New Year. Troops have moved out from England. It's a big story, and they'll want a pretty fast wrapup on the first piece. You can take your time on the second."

"I'm a fiction man, remember? It's been a long time since I worked under the guns. Serious reporting is young man's work. I got weak arches."

"You haven't been writing a hell of a lot of fiction lately, may I remind you," Marc Mantell said drily. "Maybe it's time you took up reporting again."

"Everybody's been so very kind to me lately," Alec said, touching his heart for Luke's benefit. "It gets me right *here*. I'm all choked up. What do you imagine Amelia will say to my running off to chase savages, a mere month after she's back from her own exile?"

"From all I can gather she won't miss you," Marc said. "By your own admission you are remarkably short on peaches and cream in the household at the moment. Well, I got to tell the boys something. Yes or no?"

"Yes," Alec said. "Definitely yes. Ring up the British and alert them on the Kenya visa, will you? I'll bring the passport in tomorrow morning."

"Good man. What'll you do about Amelia? Fetch her back or go to Washington or what?"

"Neither. I'll bid her farewell on the phone. No point to any more doleful good-bys. It's not forever, after all, and maybe she'll welcome the cool-off period."

"Fine, then. See you tomorrow for lunch, and I'll put you on the plane. Anything else I can do?"

"One thing. Cable my safari outfit I'm coming—you have the address—and ask if Bronson or Duffy or Denton is free to white-hunt me. Any'll serve."

"Will do. Good-by."

"Okay," Alec said, and rang off. He turned to Luke.

"Let's finish the fish. It looks like you'll eat 'em, though. You heard most of the conversation?"

"I couldn't help it, Boss. You're really going to Africa on this deal?"

"I think so, Luke, I think so. I think it's exactly what the doctor directed. You know, when in danger or in doubt, cut a new set of orders. You'll hold the fort here."

"Sure, Boss. One thing: How's it be if I had the old lady and a few of the sisters down once in a while? We'll pay for our own grub and liquor. But it gets a little lonesome here by myself. And I skipped Christmas this year. I felt like I couldn't stand the confusion."

"You and me both," Alec replied. "Sure. Have all the folks down, as often as you want. And don't worry about the food and the booze, within reason. It looks like we ain't going to be broke for quite some time to come."

"I wish I was going with you," Luke said wistfully. "I sure would like to see that country."

"Maybe some day. But in the meanwhile you know the old axiom. He travels the fastest— Now let's you and me go nibble a drink—the fish seem to be cleaned."

79

Alec Barr's brain sang at the delicious thought that within hours he'd be off to Africa once more. The magazine assignment was of itself exciting; Alec had been scouring the papers for news about the native uprisings in a land he had come, through two safaris, to know a little and love a lot. He had heard stories, or rumblings of stories, about the various sects and cults such as the *Dini ya Msambwa,* started by a lunatic, and the *Watu ya Mungu,* whose "Men of God" merely murdered without using lunacy as an excuse. Years ago Alec's old friend Negley Farson had written a very perceptive book, discounting the cults as "merely the result of religious frenzy," and had pointed directly to what he regarded as a "common cause which is poisoning the bloodstream of the black continent." In retrospect Farson seemed to be right, if this new Mau Mau movement were anything close to what it sounded. And that, Alec thought, was not just a bunch of casual thugs and fugitive crooks knocking over an occasional farm and butchering its owners, but rather an organized political rebellion which had somehow gotten out of hand. The name of Jomo Kenyatta kept cropping up as the leader of the Mau Mau terrorist organization, and Alec Barr, the greedy reader, knew the Kikuyu leader to be a man of keen intelligence and extensive education, both in London and in Moscow.

"If old Jomo's the boar coon in this thing," Alec spoke his thoughts aloud as he and Luke gathered up his gear and guns, "this ain't just a bunch of misunderstood Robin Hoods up a hill."

"I don't get you, Boss," Luke said. "Come again?"

"Never mind," Alec said. "Where are the boots—the Bird-shooters?"

"Got 'em here," Luke said, holding up a pair of short hunting boots. "You're gonna travel pretty heavy—all these guns and stuff."

"Doesn't matter," Alec said, squinting down the barrel of a rifle. "I'm on expense account. You clean the shotguns yesterday?"

"That I did. Which—or maybe I should say how many"—Luke grinned—"are you taking?"

"Just the twelve-bore. The little twenty's fine for fancy work, but I got a strange hunch I'll be using more buckshot than birdshot."

"You don't want to do nothing foolish like getting yourself killed," Luke replied. "I'm too old for steady work. You got me to think of. I ain't got anybody else to be a dependent of."

"I'll be careful," Alec laughed from sheerest boyish exuberance. "By God, Luke, you can't know what it's like to be going back. Not just the job—but the country, the animals, the people—*the country*. I don't care if I shoot anything. It's just the idea of seeing it all again. You never really get enough."

"You look about twenty years younger since you got that phone call. Now business, Boss. Boots we got. Double rifle, three-eighteen, thirty-oh-six, three-seventy-five. One pistol, caliber thirty-eight, one shotgun, twelve-gauge. Three scopes. Binoculars. Two cameras, Hasselblatt and Rolleiflex. No hunting clothes at all?"

"Nope. Buy 'em from Ahamed Brothers in Nairobi, and give 'em to the safari boys afterward. All I want in the way of clothes is a dinner jacket—they still dress for dinner out there, you know. I'll pick that up in town. And that"—pointing to an old Harris tweedcoat—"some flannels and a spare suit, which I'll also pick up in town. Where's the medicine kit?"

"Here." Luke pointed to a square brown leather case. "I

been looking through it. You got one bottle of pills here that says 'Lion Bites.' Are you kiddin'?"

"No. People do get chewed up by lions once in a while. Toss us the box." He looked briefly at the contents and took out one bottle, which he threw to Luke. "Won't need those."

"But you always travel with sleeping pills," Luke said.

Alec shook his head. "Not on this journey, Chief. Out there I find it difficult to stay awake after nine o'clock at night. We generally rise and shine at five, in that cold black dark."

"I thought Africa was supposed to be hot."

"Depends," Alec said. "Oh, dig me up two pairs of those long-handled drawers, will you? In the South—either the Masai or Tanganyika—it's as cold as Vermont in January when those predawn winds sweep in off the plains. Only when you go North—everything is turned around out there —does it get hot."

"Well," Luke said, slapping the red flannels into the suit-case, "maybe some day I'll get to see it for myself."

"I wouldn't advise it," Alec said, starting downstairs with an armful of weapons. "It's a tough habit to kick once it grabs you."

80

The telephone call to Amelia had not been overpainful. She understood perfectly, she said—about both the money and the opportunity. She'd be fine. Drop her a note now and then, and be *careful*. Don't take any foolish chances. If it was all right with Alec, she might drift down to Miami from Washington and over to Haiti for a few days with the Dun-laps. They'd written and asked her to come. *And please take care of yourself, darling.*

Alec hung up and scratched his head. Perhaps he was see-ing things under the bed, but he was prepared to swear that a note of relief underlined Amelia's cool acceptance of Father rushing off to the wars once more. As if—as if maybe this was what they both needed to square them away again; to sweep the decks clean of Barbara Bayne and summer aberrations; of nasty, groin-kicking intramural rows.

"If it's okay with her it sure as hell is okay with me," Alec said, already thinking how wonderful a week end at Mawingo up close to Manyuki would soon be, with Mount Kenya peeking in your window every morning and the boys stoking the fireplaces with perfume-oily cedarwood. And Nairobi was forever fun. Somebody you already knew or were certain to like was always passing through. Which reminded Alec Barr of something else.

"What a sloppy son-of-a-bitch I really am," he muttered. "I made that fat promise about a Thanksgiving bash to Dinah and Co., and I haven't even bothered to give her a ring since she dispensed all the good advice. I'll rectify that right now."

As he dialed, Alec thought that what he actually wanted—needed—was somebody more perceptive than Luke to babble at before he embarked on a big adventure. Dinah was great babble-material. She never seemed envious of another person's fortune, and while she kidded you a lot, you never felt foolish when you bubbled over.

Penny Lawrence answered the phone.

"I thought you'd forgotten us," she said, after the hellos and how-are-yous. "Thought maybe you'd left town."

"Not left, *leaving*," Alec said. "Midnight. East Africa. Job of work. Thought maybe I might get a chance to crow a little while I buy you and your Ma that long-overdue dinner we planned for Thanksgiving."

"I'd love nothing better," Penny said. "But unfortunately my mother, the writer, had to dash down to Washington this morning and she won't be back until tomorrow. Some sort of vital research that only the Library of Congress could offer."

Hooked, Alec thought, but there's nothing I can do about it.

"Well," he said, "unless you're all freighted down with muscular boy friends, the dinner offer still goes. That's if you think your Ma won't mind her daughter going out with a dirty old man."

Penny's voice lilted.

"I'd love it, Alec. Please come around and tell me all about the Africa business, and tell me what to wear where we're going. And please—"

"Yes?" Alec was warmed by the girl's enthusiasm.

"Could I please ride out to the airport and see you off to Africa? I never saw anybody off to Africa before."

"Of course. Tell you what. I've got to go downtown now and see my agent for an hour or so. Put on your best black dress, and I'll stop off and pick you up. Then we can come on up here and you can help me with my final packing. All right?"

"Fine. I'd love to help you pack—and I'd love to see your *other* house. Not that I'll like it as well as the one in the country. An hour, you said?"

"About an hour and a half."

"Fine. That'll give me a chance to do something to my hair."

Well, well, Barr the cradle-robber, Alec thought wryly. What was the snotty crack Amelia made about Daughter being a summer replacement for Mommy dear? All wrong, all unfounded. She's a nice kid, a sweet kid, a smart kid, and there's at least one thing she won't have to worry about, no matter what Amelia might surmise. And that is, namely, me.

The brief conference with Marc Mantell was gratifying. Marc cultivated a delightful departure manner. He was like a good football coach, giving the substitute halfback a slap on the rump and sending him onto the field with his spirits two-blocked at the masthead. When Mantell bade you Godspeed, you just knew that you were coming back with a fresh Pulitzer and a million dollars in your hip pocket. What Marc Mantell had said precisely was:

"Christ, I never saw such a change in a man. You look like the kid who came to see me to learn about writing a thousand years ago. If just going off to get your throat slit makes you look like this, I'll see to it that all your future work is conducted exclusively in an atmosphere of chopped heads and poisonous snakes."

Alec bowed ceremonially.

"So said my faithful slave, Luke. I thought he was just snowing me. But you never snow me, do you, Maestro? Quite seriously, I do feel like a colt. I guess that once you've got the reporting monkey on your back, you never quite cure yourself of it."

Mantell rang for his secretary to bring the office bottle.

"All I can offer you is a farewell drink," he said. "Unless

you want me to drive you out to the airport? I haven't got any sound advice for you."

"No, thanks. I'm being escorted to the plane after dinner with a charming young lady."

"Oh, God," Marc Mantell said, "don't tell me you're—"

Alec laughed, and dispersed an imaginary cloud with a wave of his hand.

"No, no, none of that," he said. "Relax. This is the daughter of a client of yours. Dinah Lawrence's kid. I rang up the mother and got more or less saddled with the daughter for dinner. No rape intended."

Marc Mantell leaned back in his big leather chair and clasped his hands behind his head. He made an impressive sight, backlit by hundreds of bright-jacketed books, all written by members of the Mantell stable.

"You know I don't usually talk about my clients to my other clients," he said slowly. "But I can make an exception here. You've seen any of Dinah's book?"

"Only the first hundred pages," Alec said. "What she told me you sold to the magazine and the publishers. She mentioned that maybe there was a movie—"

"This is a winner. *Rich.* Why she wasted all these years scribbling for newspapers I cannot say. This is no one-book girl, not that this first one isn't a killer. This girl has enough books in her to keep her busy for the rest of her life. She's great, just great."

"I'm glad," Alec said. "Real glad. It's nice to know that nice people are occasionally capable of nice things. Usually it's the sonsabitches that grab the gravy."

"You're one of the nicer exceptions," Marc Mantell said. "That's not a joke, son. In my own peculiar way I'm rather fond of you, Alec."

Alec got up. Marc walked around to the front of the desk.

"I better leave now. You'll have me weeping in a second." He let his right hand drop briefly on Marc Mantell's shoulder. "I'll write you your first installment as soon as I size up the situation. If it runs to three I'll do the three, for no extra dough."

"You're out of your feeble mind," Marc Mantell said swiftly. "If it runs to three we'll get *paid* for three. Don't be silly. And don't get so carried away with this reporting job that you get yourself killed. Don't forget, you owe me a big book."

"That really *is* my boy," Alec said. "So long, Boss. See you in about three months."

"Watch out for those native women," Marc Mantell called after Alec. "You might just run onto a cannibal."

81

Alec held the taxi at the curb. The door to Dinah's apartment opened almost immediately to his ring. Penny Lawrence met him with a smile, and spun around on very high heels.

"My God," Alec said. "You're gorgeous. All this for old Unca Alec?"

"Of course, Alec. Really truly like?"

"Really truly." The dress was slim and classic and black. The pearls looked real. Penny touched her throat.

"Ma. My Christmas present. I guess she was celebrating the book. So to express my gratitude for the pearls—*real* pearls, I'll have you know—I swiped Ma's best black dress. I reckoned she wouldn't mind if she knew who I was wearing it for."

"Well, thanks, my pretty maid. Now let's steal her mink coat, too."

"Can't. She betrayed me and wore it to Washington. I'll have to make out with my own sheared beaver."

"You sound pretty bubbly," Alec said in the cab. "The pearls?"

"Some. But I do feel bubbly. I feel real Christmasy. I'm so darned happy about Ma and the book, for one thing. And I'm happy about you, too. You look—I can't tell you *how* you look. Like a brand-new man."

"There must be something in it," Alec said. "This is the third time I've heard it. Keep on telling me. I like it."

"I'm not kidding." Penny turned to face him. "A lot of lines have gone out of your face, the frowny ones, I mean. You look—well, you look *young*. And excited. Not," she added hurriedly, "that you ever looked so very old—"

"I know how I looked." Alec patted her lightly on the knee. "And I felt the way I looked. Funny we used the word *bubbly*. I want to bubble. *And* babble. That's why I rang up my favorite people. I'm terribly sorry to miss Di. I seriously wanted to congratulate her about the new book. I just left Mantell. If I hadn't known the old crocodile for all these years I'd swear he had a crush on your mother."

"It's wonderful to hear. But what does he say about *you?*" Alec smiled.

"He thinks I'm cured. He thinks that maybe this little trip is exactly what the doc designated to get Old Man Barr out of his personal literary Sargasso Sea. In short, he thinks all is not lost, and that some day I might be able to write a coherent paragraph again." The smile broadened. "As a matter of fact he was almost polite to me. Told me not to get killed, because I owed him a big book."

The taxi came to a halt and Alec paid the driver.

"I can't wait to hear," Penny said as they entered the building. "I don't know anything about what you're going to do, or how you'll do it, but I want to know everything. Ma'll murder me out of sheer jealousy."

"That I doubt." They entered the living room, and Alec helped Penny out of her coat.

"What a lovely room," Penny said. "But I still like your playhouse best. This looks more like a—a woman's room."

"You're dead right. But the office is pretty much me, and I suggest we have a drink back there in front of the fire. Quite frankly, I'm scared to death. It's been a long time since I went up against a straight reporting assignment."

"Oh, fiddle. Ma's told me something about you as a reporter."

"That's a nice comfortable perch," Alec said, pointing to his own leather easy chair. "What'll you drink, and what did she say? About me as a reporter, I mean?"

"Scotch on the rocks, please." Penny sat down and crossed her knees. "She said, quote: 'Barr at his best was incomparable. At his worst, he was better than the rest of us. What he couldn't borrow, he stole. What he couldn't jump over or walk around, he kicked down. He could cry, pray or curse, according to what the situation demanded, and if the situation was really demanding, he could also make love to a ninety-year-old frightwig—if there was a story in it.' "

"I don't believe she said it, and if she did, it's libelous. I was pretty brisk, I will admit, in my younger, juicier days, but as a matter of pure fact I couldn't carry Dinah's hand-bag as a reporter."

"That ain't the way I heard it," Penny said. "Now." She leaned forward. "Tell. Tell all about Africa and what you'll do."

"About the first thing," Alec replied, "is to find out who my white hunter is. A great deal depends on that. I've hunted off and on with three—Eric Bronson, Joe Duffy, and Mike Denton. They're all marvelous professionals, but Mike Denton is the more erudite member. That's to say he can read."

"But what *is* the situation? Why is a magazine like *Life* rushing you out to do a series of articles on this—what is it —Mau Mau business?"

"I imagine they think it's big—possibly a foreshadowing of a lot of trouble to come. More than just a brushfire. And as for why they're sending me—well, I partially explained it when I mentioned the hunters. I know my way around out there a little bit, and at least I know who to go to for in-formation. Trouble with most special correspondents is they wade in stone-cold and then rush off half-cocked."

"It must please you terribly to get asked to do a job like this," Penny said. "As a man, I mean, more than just as a writer."

"I have to confess it does. As you get older, unlikely as that may seem at the moment, you'll probably discover that it pleases you more for people to remember what you were good at when you were a kid than for them to dwell on what you may have accomplished as an adult."

"You mean you'd rather be known as Alec Barr, reporter, than Alexander Barr, novelist?"

"It takes some of the gray out of my hair."

"What'll you do when you get to—Nairobi, is it?"

"Very little for a bit. Hang around the Stanley and the Norfolk—those are the two major hotels—and buy drinks for old settlers. Listen a lot, and ask very few questions. Then I'll maybe run down into the Masai for a word with the game warden there, he's an old friend of mine, and then run up North to the desert country for another talk with another old friend of mine, who's game warden *there*. Mostly it's just a matter of developing *feel*—maybe smell would be the better word."

Penny sighed and shook her head.

"It sounds terribly simple, the way you tell it, and I'm sure it's considerably more involved."

"It really isn't. Reporting—or novel-writing, for that matter—is largely a matter of exposure to the scene. People read a lot of mysticism into the writing business, but mostly it's the simplest trade I know."

"I'll never understand it," Penny said. "But tell me about the country, and the people, and why you evidently love it and them so much. I read your last book—the one you gave me to read on the plane. You can taste the love in it."

Alec was unduly pleased.

"It's rather difficult to explain," he said, "but somehow you feel that there's no tougher place in the world to live. I'm certain the human race started out in Africa . . ."

Two hours later he looked with horror at his watch.

"Great God, girl," he said. "Do you know that I have been rattling on for exactly two hours, and that nobody's bothered to mix us a second drink? That apart from the fact that I haven't shaved, haven't dressed, and you haven't packed me. We have to get cracking, or history will march on without me."

"I'll fix us a drink," Penny said. "And Alec, please, could I ask another favor?"

"Ask away, if you'll accept my apology for all this garrulousness. You get me started on Africa and I get lost in the stars. What favor?"

"Let's please *not* go out to dinner. This has been so much fun. I'm fascinated with your Africa. If we go out you'll have to say hello to a lot of people and kiss a lot of women and I'll have lost you for the rest of the evening. There must be an apron in the kitchen, and there must be something in your deep freeze that I can broil or fry. Let's just stay here, *please,* until time to go to the airport."

"Of course, if you really want to—" He looked at her with genuine surprise.

"I'm glad there aren't any servants. You take me out to the kitchen, show me where's what, and then get on with your shaving and clothes-changing."

"Come ahead. I don't know any more about the kitchen than you do, but I think I can find it."

82

Once settled into his seat on the plane, detective story in hand, Alec Barr thought back on the evening. You gabby old goat, he said to himself. You ought to be ashamed of yourself. But admit it, it was fun to feel young and interesting and attractive again. No fool like an old fool, Barr, he said, and picked up the latest adventures of Mr. Philip Marlowe, Private Eye.

Alec Barr suffered from the writer's chronic fault. He knew an awful lot about a lot of things, places, and people. In large doses this dispensation of accrued knowledge could be a bore, and to a great many contemporaries, Alec was merely "on" when he grew anecdotally expansive.

Talking—monologuing, actually—with Penny Lawrence, Alec had feared no rebuff for the twice-told tale. The stories that Amelia had heard a hundred times gained crispness with new ears as target. The lore, folk and otherwise, was new to a charming young woman who was born on such a recent yesterday that she had been too small to see Paul Douglas in *Born Yesterday*.

Excited, happy, pleased as a child to be running off to Africa—stimulated, naturally, by the presence of a lovely young woman who devoured his every word—Alec had talked far too much for safety's sake. It was all too easy, he reflected, to bemuse a child with intimate tales of war and adventure, of colorful people in high places, of more exotic levels of theater and writing and politics and sport. The only trouble, he thought, trying to concentrate on Philip Marlowe's knee in somebody else's groin, was that the bemuser was apt to become bemused in the process of bemusing.

He thanked God because under the impetus of the really good dinner that Penny had pulled out of the kitchen reserve, under the tongue-loosening influence of several more drinks than he needed—but the Scotch tasted lovely instead of brownly boring—and under the stimulus of a captive audience, Alec had hit the red-signal danger point. He had begun to haul out scrapbooks, and had changed the LP records for some old 78s involving Hal Kemp and Ray Noble. That was when the doorman fortunately rang and said that the Carey people had sent the car to take them to Idlewild. They had driven, strangely and companionably silent all the way to the airport. When they said good-by, he kissed her lightly on both cheeks.

"One's for your Ma," he said. "And the other's for you."

It could have been the liquor, but Alec Barr's walk had a boyish bounce. *Time* magazine would have called his back ramrod-straight, and the man inside the body might very well have been described in his passport as lieutenant (jg).

Book IV/Jill

83

Six years later, six long years after Alec had left her at the airport, she walked through the door looking, for a moment, only vaguely familiar. A lot of pretty women came to "21," and they all looked more or less vaguely familiar, according to where they bought their clothes and which faggot teased their hair.

Alec was leaning on the bar, talking baseball with Henry, the corner bartender, who was considerably grayer. He had looked idly round the room, searching for a drinking companion while he waited for Marc Mantell. There didn't seem to be anybody he knew from the old days—how those days had passed—passed like a plume of smoke from the same fire.

And so here she was, his pretty Penny, wearing a mink coat and under it the body of a woman.

"You might not remember me," he said, as she came in from the lobby. "Old Unca Alec—from the dreary past. I was a pretty good babysitter, though."

Penny came swiftly and hugged him.

"You know it's been six years, almost to the day?" She stood away and held his arms. "Oh, Alec, why didn't you ever call?"

"I didn't think your husband would appreciate it. And"—

417

he paused—"I didn't know how recently divorced ladies react to old babysitters ringing up. How's your Ma?"

"Getting richer all the time. Books, films, magazines—but you'd know that, anyhow. Can we sit down and have a drink? Or are you waiting for someone?"

"Nobody that'll mind if we sit down and have a drink with the prettiest girl in the room. But I don't want to be attacked by any jealous suitors."

"Girl lunch," Penny said. "Have no fear."

"Boy lunch," Alec said, and took her by the arm. "Here, Vincent. I'm waiting for Mr. Mantell."

"You're always waiting for Mr. Mantell," Penny said after they were seated. "What now?"

"I'll have a pink gin," Alec said to the waiter. "And you'll have a Bloody Mary. Right?"

"Right. Now where have you been for the last six years?"

"Mostly in Africa. It seems I'm the expert on it." He shrugged. "It gets to be a bloody bore, consorting with cannibals, but it's a living." He smiled, and held up his drink. "Cheers. Also I love the animals."

"Cheers," she said. "You remember the last time you kissed me?"

"I do indeed. I was on my way to Africa. And you'd better kiss me again, because I'm on my way back."

"I'd be delighted to kiss you again." She touched his hand. "But why always on the way to Africa? What now?"

"Mantell. Some sort of big deal with magazines and a book and maybe a movie. I'm not exactly sure. Marc keeps his own counsel until the last minute."

"How long this time?"

"Maybe six months. Maybe a year." Alec shrugged. "It's a big country."

Penny leaned across the table and kissed him lightly, this time on the lips.

"That one's not for Ma," she said. "And six years is a long time between kisses. I'm a big girl now."

"You look like a big girl now." Alec lit a cigarette. "What happened to the marriage? I read the death notices."

Now Penny shrugged.

"Who knows? Too little, too much, not enough. Mutual boredom at the end. Nothing dramatic. I don't recommend marriage for marriage's sake. You can make a clumsy compromise, but after a bit it gets a little too clumsy to be borne. And that is the story of my life."

"I suppose," Alec said, "it's also the story of mine. Except I haven't had the guts to change it. Been too busy, I guess."

"Here come the girls," Penny said. "I'll have the other kiss for luck. Don't lose me for another six years, please."

"First order of return agenda," Alec said. "Love to Mama." He went back to the bar to brood.

It didn't seem so very long, these last six years, except when you started to count on your fingers all the places you'd been and who was dead and who was alive and who was married and who was divorced and who had graduated from college that was just a little snotnose the last time you saw him. Then a man looked at the encroaching gray which had quit being distinguished over the ears and now was merely dirty-looking and thin.

The people around you were changing all the time, but you didn't notice it until you read the papers, which carried more and more familiar names on the obituary pages. But you were losing your landmarks as you remembered this actor and that bandleader were dead and dusty; this athlete gone under, that politician put down. Even the gangsters had produced a new breed of name and a new kind of public image. The hoods were all businessmen now, with clothing and lawyers to match. Alec Barr was suffering a violent attack of the middle-aged blues.

All just yesterday, when he had taken off to play Injun with the Mau Mau in Kenya. But just yesterday was six long years ago and Alec Barr was forty-eight years old and an acknowledged expert on Africa. And it seemed very cold comfort to be an acknowledged expert on Africa when you still were busy trying to discover yourself.

Where had the time *gone?* Eisenhower was finishing his second term, and Alec had written a story on Eisenhower when he was bumped up from lieutenant colonel to general, at the start of the Big War. Alec's contemporaries owned grandchildren now, and Alec reflected wryly that he could very easily be a grandfather himself, several times over, if things had shaped that way.

So many faces were lost. Ben Lea, for instance. Alec still couldn't believe that Ben Lea was dead, cropped suddenly by cancer. Every time Alec walked into one of the old haunts, he half-expected to see Ben leaning on the bar, talking base-ball or bullfights or women with whoever was handy. Buying more than his share of drinks, and never, ever being dull or reverent. Of all the people who had gone, Alec missed Ben the worst. But he wouldn't go to New Orleans any more, on account of Owen Brennan's heart. He was leary of Houston, on account of Gran Adams' heart—hearts that had suddenly refused to work for no real reason known to any-one else but God.

Yet Alec felt himself unchanged, as Marc Mantell seemed unchanged, as certainly Amelia was unchanged. Alec still didn't know what color Amelia's hair actually was, as she seemed to adjust it to the seasons, but she had kept both her figure and her temper. Alec sighed, suddenly feeling ter-ribly tired.

The last half-dozen years had been a series of flights. On his return from Kenya, it was as if he and Amelia had signed a pact to avoid each other in the aim of staying together. Alec conducted himself faultlessly at home. He worked reg-ular hours and made regular trips to regular places.

He was, he repeatedly told himself, terribly happy about Dinah Lawrence's swift success. Her first book had been a runaway, and had branched into both movie and play. She had a fine feel for speech in her characters, and now was in steady demand for screen scripts. She had pulled one old piece out of the trunk, and it got turned into a musical that was still standing-room-only after two years. Dinah had waited until she was forty for the big leap, but then, Alec thought, Somerset Maugham was forty-four before he went winging on the short stories, the stuff that really made him famous.

And he, himself, Alec Barr, who had roared off to such early, flashy success, had settled down—face it, kid, he told himself bitterly—into a solid plodder. Consistent, surely; he had written the book which had been on his back at the time he left for the magazine assignment in Kenya, but it seemed to him that more people remembered the magazine assignment than recalled the book. It had, after all, been just another thick slice of slickness—serial, hardcover, Book-of-the-Month, paperback, and mediocre moving picture. The money came in, and the money got paid out. The government took most of it, and living claimed the rest. The flat cost a fortune, and it seemed that the place in Jersey demanded

more each year, but Alec stubbornly refused to give it up.
It was the only thing he owned (and that would include
Luke), which really seemed to belong to him.

Travel had become more and more a portion to his and
Amelia's lives, Alec thought—as necessary as the evening
cocktail or the trip to the hairdresser. Two months, three,
sometimes six months might pass in careful good temper
on both sides—some gossip, some jokes, some parties, some
real affection, very occasionally some medicinal sex. Then
the careful apportionment of guarded tolerance would show
signs of fraying, and Amelia would suggest that it would be
a fine idea if Alec took a sea voyage—Amelia *hated* ships—
or possibly that she, Amelia, felt like another trip to Europe
or to Jamaica or Mexico. She'd be fine; Ruth would go with
her, and if Ruth couldn't find the time, there was always
Francis. Francis had now become as standard equipment as
the trip to the hairdresser. He had gone gray too, but had
weathered well, watching his diet and keeping his figure
elegantly slim. God Bless Francis, Alec thought. I'd go mad
without him taking Amelia off my back.

He leaned hard on his corner of the bar and waited for
Marc Mantell and considered the six years that had passed
since last he had seen Penny. Alec had never had a daughter,
so perhaps it was that as much as anything which bothered
him about Penny—first her wedding, then her divorce.

In the parental sterility of his mind, Penny had been close
to daughterhood. Certainly she was the only young thing with
whom he had been associated, even if sporadically, almost
from birth.

He wondered with the self-imposed cruelty of adult retrospect what Penny had seen in this Donald type that led
her into his arms and bed. And then he turned and fought
himself for the constant feeling that all young American men
seemed to be stamped from the same soft dough with the
same cookie cutter. They all were crew-cut, and even the
thin ones looked fat. They seemed terribly old in a time of
youth, and when they passed thirty they all looked impossibly
immature, even with the white in their hair and their vested
bellies bulging. It was impossible to imagine them actually
taking a woman—actually *making* a woman of a girl.

Alec closed his mind to the idea of this soft-cheeked
hobbledehoy, Donald, bedding painfully and sweatily with
his pretty Penny. His pretty Penny had deserved a man, and

she had married a boy, and now the divorce was testimony
to her lack of a man to fill her mind and body. Or so Alec
thought defensively, as if he himself were a guilty party to
the plot.

And now, by God, he should be sad but was instead terribly glad about the divorce. This Donald Something hadn't
really touched her, and Alec had his pretty Penny back again
to ask him respectful questions and warm him with slavish
attention to his adult sagacity, of which no *young* man ever
would be capable.

Great God above, Alec Barr thought, senility has really
set in. If this kind of thinking signposts the inroads of age,
marks the deep runnels of frustration, you are well on your
way to the boneyard. Pretty soon everybody but you will be
wrong about everything, and you will start recalling the nonexistent plodding through the snow to the little red schoolhouse.

But damn it all to hell, you didn't like the idea, Barr, of
the most perishable of all commodities passing to a male with
no more man built into his face than he had brim to his hat.
Brooks Brothers was an obscene party to the defloration.
At least the coat should have been custom-cut.

How had he touched her? When, the very first time? Before
or after the vows? Or perhaps in a car, in a nest of crushed
flowers in a park? On a beach, the salty-sun-warmed-girl-
smell rank on a towel that accumulated sand? Under a
blanket of blue, and whatever *did* happen to the Casa Lomas?

You're a father, Barr, Alec thought. A father physically
jealous of the young man who takes from your daughter
what you took so lightly when it was somebody else's daughter, in a front seat or on a beach or under a blanket of blue.
And you ain't anybody's father at all. You're an ancient
adolescent who still wants to fall in love. You lament for
youth, which somehow passed you by, and you are pleased
about the failure of a marriage which all youth's easy buttresses couldn't support.

And you think like a bloody writer in search of a plot for
one of the magazines which respects its advertisers' sensitivity
more than its writer's concept of structure. There are no
wicked women in the world, and divorce is disallowed, because there are no wicked men in the magazines, either, and
everybody lives happily ever after.

My life with Amelia would make a marvelous piece of

nonsalable fiction, Alec thought. The friendly enemy. The nonconfiding confidante. The absent presence, the present absence. Which way to where, and if any, when? Who's on first base and what's the score?

Time to travel again, Barr, Alec thought. Time for the fresh horizons to renew the tired blood. Christ, if they would rig up a really decent sort of war, where you cared about the people you kill. Korea was a half-assed nothing war. You weren't allowed to cross the Yalu, and killing Koreans was about as pointless as going to school with them. Against the law to kill the Chinks, and all the Korean girls had cross eyes and a species of untameable clap. Even the war correspondents were retreads, and there wasn't anything quite so useless as an old war correspondent.

And there was Mantell walking into his field of vision. And when the wide mouth opened it sounded just like Mantell and it warmed Alec's cold heart. "Alec, you look like hell."

"And that is who?" Marc Mantell asked. They were seated in the unchic room, where it was quieter. Penny had waved from the door.

"A ghost," Alec said. "A very young ghost from my old past. She's Dinah's kid. Just bought herself a divorce. Pity, a very nice girl. Except she's wrecked my day. It's been, great God, six years since she saw me off to Africa."

"Well, we might as well get stuck into it," Marc Mantell said. "This time it's a real big one. I'll have a hamburger," he turned to the waiter.

"Give me steak *tartare*," Alec said. "I might as well get used to raw meat again. I am suffering from a chronic complaint. I have been thinking, and it all comes out backward. Thinking does not suit me. I am a reactor. Basic Barr. Add a little whisky and it all spells MOTHER. Met any interesting Whistlers lately?"

"All right now, stop," Marc Mantell said. "I never handle comedians any more, except me. You have to be a kind of comedian to be an agent, on account of the people you associate with. Your old joke. It only hurts when I laugh. You want to travel, enrich your life, earn while you learn?"

"You interest me more than strangely. It's miraculous," Alec said. "Pray proceed."

"We are serious now. I'll spell it out. You may remember Ray Schell, of *Cosmic?*"

"I should think so. We used to sell him pieces to be run in glorious Technicolor, like in *The National Geographic*. We haven't done much business with him lately. So what about Ray Schell, he should enter my life again?"

"You aren't drunk?"

"No. Sober as a boxful of Mormons."

"Well, you sound a little unearthly. There is this about Ray Schell. He just phoned me from London. He's been talking to some members of Parliament, I imagine, or some book publishers, or colonial-office types—I don't know. But he's suddenly got this wild hair about Africa. He wants to do a whole year's front-of-the-book on emerging Africa."

"A whole year's FOB? Twelve big pieces? That's an awful lot of Africa to set before the public. The public still thinks the Congo is located in a country called Nairobi."

"Exactly. Ray reckons that the whole country's going to be the most important real estate development in the world, with all this freedom business going on—the conference in Belgium, all of that Mau Mau stuff left over in Kenya, old Kenyatta still in jail, that African news that's creeping into the papers more and more. And he wants, as he says, to do a real massive job on it."

"Highly commendable, and about time, too. But how does this affect me?"

"It affects you thisaway, chum. Schell wants *you* to write the whole job. Cover *all* of Africa. Dine with the potentates and eat with the poor folks. Write the country the way it *is* —and in such a manner that even the rednecks in Georgia will know the difference between the hippo and a hydro-electric dam. Interpret the winds of change; sound the knell of colonialism, foresee the future when two hundred million Africans suddenly come unprepared into pants. More or less."

"Are you quite sure *you're* not drunk? That's not an assignment for one man; it's a job for an army. And why me? I'm no real authority on the place. This is a straight reporting deal, anyhow, not a job for a fiction writer."

Alec could feel impatience in his agent's voice.

"They don't want a reporter to go out and just skim the surface. They want a bookman to do it. They want it covered in depth and written in dimensional prose, not journalese. They want you to take a year, if necessary. They want you to write a real *book*, not just a series of articles."

"Let me get this straight. They'll give me a lot of time,

and they want a running series of articles, once I'm clued in, but they want it written as components to a future book? Which they, of course, as owners of Cosmic House, will publish? And will republish, I should imagine, in their own paperback, eventually?"

"That's the size of it. And they seem to want only you, because at least you've kicked around the place a few times, and know something about the people and the country."

"Very flattering, I'm sure." Alec paused. "Here is where I'm supposed to ask: How much? Well, okay, *how much?*"

The chuckle was louder this time.

"You'll like it. They'll pay a hundred thousand for twelve articles, with full expenses. We have the usual book deal, but the hundred thou is your advance against it. And we got a whackeroo for the paperback—another hundred thousand against fifteen per cent. That's a guaranteed quarter-million, my boy, figuring the book will sell at least fifty grand's worth for your share, and a year's lush living on the expense account."

"When does this big deal start? And what are the catches?"

"There's one catch. It starts *now*. Right now. Immediately. Somebody's told Schell something about this upcoming meeting in Belgium to discuss the Congolese freedom. He thinks it's not going to be a matter of years, but only a matter of months, and that everybody else will dash headlong on the heels—Somalia, Guinea, Nigeria, the whole kit and kaboodle. One great big minstrel show. Schell wants to buy in early. What do you say?"

"I'll have to think," Alec said slowly. "It's a hell of a big job. Fascinating, sure, and a challenge, sure, but one hell of an enormous task. You know how big that continent is? *I* do. And it's a long time since I worked at any serious reporting. That's young man's business."

"Maybe you need some young man's business. Maybe it's time you took up reporting again. It'll make you feel younger when you get back to fiction."

"You got a point," Alec said. "A very potent point. Well, I'll think it over."

"Do better than that. *Pack*. Schell will be in London until New Year's only, and after that he's off on a swing to Cambodia or some other pest-hole. He stressed very keenly that he wants to see you immediately, to block out the whole campaign."

"Immediately like when?"

"Like day after tomorrow. You can get your necessary shots in London. And I might as well tell you, I was so sure you'd leap at this one that I told Schell to have his staff go ahead with the various visas you'll need, from the London embassies and consulates."

"That was bloody presumptuous of you." Now there was great good humor as well as excitement in Alec's voice. "Well, I'll buy."

"Fine. I really think you ought to do this, Alec, for a lot of reasons. Among others, we need a fresh image. We're getting a small touch typed, and I don't want it to happen to us. Okay?"

"Okay," Alec said. "What else?"

"You're booked on tomorrow night's jet for London. You're also signed in at the Savoy. You won't have a hell of a lot of time in London. I think Schell's leaving on the second, and those conferences start in Brussels next week. You'll want to catch them; all of the hotshot politicians from Léopold-ville are in town to tell poor little Baudouin where to head in, and they're loaded for bear. Then I'd suggest a fast run to the Congo, and after that you're on your own. All this, of course, you'll clear roughly with Schell."

"Tell me one more thing, Boss. Why do they actually want *me* on this job? A lot of people—Steinbeck, Hemingway, Gunther, Stuart Cloete—a lot of people's mouths would water for a shot at an assignment like this."

"You mention some good men there," Marc Mantell said. "But you forget something, Author Barr. You're still remembered as a hell of a reporter from the Mau Mau job for *Life*. And this job calls for reporting first, before you fall into the deep-dish end of it."

"Well, it sounds pretty wonderful," Alec said. "I'm to have a year, if necessary?"

"That's right. More if you need it. And if you choose to stay overseas for the full eighteen months, the tax structure favors it. It's keeping money."

"I may just do that. You know it was six years ago you sent me off to die with the Mau Mau? This week, I mean? How come you never send me any place *before* I do my Christmas shopping early?"

"I don't want to wreck Amelia's schedule with the old folks at home. I'd hate to have you miss that Christmas orgy under the elms, so to speak. Who'd peel the ribbons off the Santa Claus donations? Who'd exclaim happily over the handkerchiefs?"

"Oh, go to hell," Alec said. "I'll see you tomorrow, and now I'll go and break the news to the little woman. I suppose if this tax thing works I can always send for Amelia."

"Yes, there's always that," Marc Mantell's voice was dry. "You can always send for Amelia."

84

Well, the talk with Ray Schell had been as painless as the trip over. Alec still marveled at the kind of service the jets were finally giving after so much frustrated promise. You got there almost before you left, if you timed your hemispheres right.

Schell was easy. All he wanted Alec to do was employ ship, plane, jeep, camel, and foot to be everywhere at once on the sub-Saharan continent. Alec tried to explain that Addis Ababa was not really closely allied to Léopoldville, what with a few Rhodesias in between, but was dismissed by a large wave and a larger letter of credit.

"Play it your way," Schell said. "I don't know the first goddam thing about the country except that it smells like solid news for the next century. I remember your stuff from six years back, which is why I want you for this job. Start the pieces as soon as you got a good grip on the situation. I'll stay in touch with your man in New York. Happy New Year. I got to be in Bangkok Monday, and right now I got a date to lay a lady."

He left, a florid, round-faced, white-haired, tough-voiced, exuberant man in yellow shirt and black knit tie. His father had founded a fortune in oil. Ray Schell was spending it in another speculative field, magazines. And looking at the amount of the letter of credit, Alec was pleased to reflect that a good bit of the oilfield fortune was being expended on Alec Barr.

London was deader than the late Mr. Kelsey's knuckles.

It was the second day after Boxing Day, but the town was still out of town. Now that Schell had left him to "lay a lady"—Alec chuckled at the line—he was all by himself and nothing to be done until the talks in Brussels started after New Year's. And New Year's seemed a month instead of three days away.

Alec loved London, but for a very real reason he'd spent little time there since the war. And it wistfully occurred to him, as he sat in his suite at the Savoy, that children born in the Blitz now had children of their own, and that most of his contemporaries were dead or emigrated or rejuggled in the marital numbers. Alec Barr's head was all gray now, as gray as London, and the thought that he had once had that particular date broken, because of the bomb death of one very pretty girl, made him feel older and grayer and sadder and even more unwanted in a town which had shut down tight for the holidays. What was the name? The name was Sheila. That was the name. *Sheila*.

There was no point in going to Brussels until the conferences actually began, because the first sparring would be all cocktail fight. At least there in London the movies were in English, and there was television and room service. But it would be nice to say blithely "I've got a date to lay a lady"—and mean it.

Alec Barr snapped his fingers. Six bloody years it'd been, six years of muddled time-passage, but he could see her as clearly as he remembered the freckles on her nose. Jill Something. Ben Lea's Limey lady. Jill—not Esmond. Jill—funny last name. Sounded singular when the Joneses all had *eses*. Pritchard? No. *Richard*. Of course. *Jill Richard*. Lunch at the Laurent when Ben couldn't show and her late husband had been in import-export in the East and it was two days after the monumental battle with Barbara. Jill lovely Richard.

He wouldn't have been smart enough to have kept changing the name and address in his little book, even if he'd written it down in the first place. And poor old Ben wasn't here any more to help him. In any case a girl that attractive would be bound to be married again. But what the hell, Barr, give it a whirl. He picked up the directory with the *R*s in it, and would you believe it, right there in the book. Chester Square. Couldn't be but one Mrs. J. Richard, and still unmarried if she was wearing her maiden name behind the Mrs.

The voice was as cool as he now remembered in a burst

of recaptured recall. He could see the emerald eyes and the
sunburst of hair and the tiny splotch of freckle.

"It'll be too much to expect that you remember me," Alec
Barr said. "After all these years. Barr. Writer friend of Ben
Lea. Six years ago to be precise. Six years too long."

"Of course I remember you." The cool voice hadn't
changed. "How are you, Alec, and what ever happened to
that urgent business trip you were going to make to London?"

"I think that possibly I could explain better in person,"
Alec replied. "I'll be sufficiently embarrassed face-to-face.
That's of course if nothing—your personal life I mean—might
prevent us from having a drink or dinner?"

"I'm still a lorn widow, if that's what you mean. And I'd
adore to see you again. Will you be here very long?"

"Until after New Year's. I'm off on a devilish long jaunt to
Africa, matter of business. I suppose you're terribly caught
up with the holidays?"

"Point of fact, no. I suffered a very long Christmas-cum-
Boxing Day week end in a very drafty stately home in Sussex,
and I'm only just back in town to get myself warm. I wonder
if you'd care to come to dinner tonight if you're free? The
town is so desperately sad in the public places, and at least
here at home I can offer you a functional fireplace and an
absence of cheerless faces in a supposedly jolly season."

"I can think of nothing I'd rather do. Will we be just
us, or is it black tie or what?"

"Just us. And it won't be a very grand meal. Come in what
you stand in. I must warn you that I'll be doing the cooking
myself. Staff all off hanging various personal halls with
holly."

"I'll wash the dishes myself, and offer all manner of useless
advice in the kitchen," Alec said. "How early may I come
to call?"

"As early as you like. Say fiveish for a drink or so?"

"Only the complete breakdown of the transit system will
prevent."

"Good then. It'll be nice to see you again."

Alec said good-by and went immediately to bathe and
dress. His hair had been cut last week; he wondered if another trim might be in order, and decided against it. He rang
the valet and ordered a swift press in his best black mohair
and debated the advisability of flowers. *No.* Not to be overeager, laddy. The flowers could be sent round tomorrow.

He whistled loudly, then sang in the shower. He shaved ever
so carefully, and gave acute attention to his nails. The suit
was back, as sharp as Signor Brioni in Rome could cut it
and the valet could refurbish it. He fretted through a rack of
ties and decided on a dove-gray satin. It occurred to him that
it had been a very long time since he had devoted this much
attention to garb—not, actually, since that long-past day
when he was sweating out Amelia's return.

He gave himself a final dress inspection in the mirror.
There was a semblance of tan remaining from some autumn
shooting. The all-gray against the tan made him look younger
than the old white splotch over the ears. Like Dinah's all-
white, he thought. Strange how one gets so used to a face
that you never see it even though you wash it and shave it
and brush its teeth daily, he thought. It's not such a bad
face when you come down to it. Too long, a bit horsy, but
Leslie Howard was foxy and fawn-eared, and Gable is round-
faced and bat-eared, and Coop is as lean and melancholy as
I. Poor old Bogey spoke with a hissing lisp and had very
little hair on his head. Cary Grant goes on forever, and so
does Jim Stewart, who's whiter than me. And they've lassoed
the ladies in droves for years. Thank God I've kept my
shape, Alec thought, patting the sheeny mohair over his
hips. I swear I haven't gained or lost a permanent pound in
thirty years.

But God Almighty, he thought. Jill's almost as old as me.
D'you suppose she's come apart at the seams as she heads
for the fifties? And why wouldn't she be married, no matter what she said about being a relaxed widow lady? It'll be
dreadful if she's run to fat and vertical wrinkles—but not
with that face, not with that fine lean frame. Never, nay,
and no indeed.

85

The house was tall and slim and Georgian, standing coolly
in the quiet square. Alec heard a gong as he touched the bell.
The door opened swiftly.

"I needn't have worried at all," he said. "Hello there, Jill Richard." They shook hands formally.

"Hello there, Alec Barr. Needn't have worried about what?"

"*You*," he said. "You're permanent. Ageless."

"I'll just take your topcoat and lead you to the drink tray," she said. "And then perhaps you can expand your appraisal."

A fire hissed with blue flame in an Adam fireplace, its mantel regimented with gilt-edged invitation cards. The room was white-wainscoted, painted in off-apple-green. One wall was bright with books. The brown pool of fine furniture reflected candlelight from the adjoining room. "There," she said, and patted one half of a shaggy white split-divan.

She sat facing him before the fire, on the other half of the white divan. She was wearing slim black velvet pants and a Pucci blouse of shaded ivory. The eyes were just as green, the hair just as red, and the mouth still turned up sharply at the corners. The sandals were twisted cords of gold.

She lifted her drink. The teeth were still dazzling.

"Welcome to my wigwam, as the Americans say."

"It was a very long interval, as the British say. You look lovely, you know."

She laughed, the clown's mouth curving.

"A wrinkle here, a wrinkle there. Perhaps a slightly larger bill at the hairdresser's. One ages. You look marvelous yourself, Alec."

"I'm alive. We've lost a few friends lately. Merely being around has its compensations."

Jill Richard's face clouded.

"I heard about Ben. What a pity, a very real pity, so full of life and fun and to—well . . ."

"Not now. This is a celebration," Alec sighed. "I can't say what's happened to the last six years. *You* talk first. How do I find you still in a state of single harness?"

She shrugged.

"You know. A gentleman here, a gentleman there, perhaps even a beau. But not enough of a real beau to uproot me from this." She swept a hand. "It's quiet here. It's simple here. There are books and a fire here. And there's just enough money not to make me fight the battle of matrimony for commercial reasons. I finally got my husband's estate settled in a mild sort of manner. There's been nothing I needed to do—nobody I wanted enough—to spur me on to future risk of soul and sanity. One travels; one goes to the pictures and plays about with a chafing dish on Sunday when it's invariably raining. There is always TV. Now please, *you.*"

"I'm a sort of literary eel in aspic. I've traveled. I *am* traveling. I work. I take in writing. I'm on a challenging assignment now, a mild little chore called 'All of Africa.'"

"I read your Mau Mau articles, and the last two books." Jill's voice was careful. "The Mau Mau was absolutely first class. The books were very good."

Alec grinned.

"I know the tone. Another lady I know—an actress—once described herself as 'adequate.' I've been an adequate bookwriter since I saw you last. I wouldn't give it much more."

"Oh, now, please, you've held together beautifully," she said. "But I have a feeling that you haven't been satisfied. You were quite sparkly the day we met. I have a hope that you've kept something back for when it's ripe and good and ready. That's not meant to sound patronizing."

"You couldn't be righter." Alec's voice was dry as old leaves. "It's just that I seem to now know *what* is ripe and good and ready. In the meantime I work. There's a large literary octopus called *Cosmic* which wants me to spend the next twelve months racing around Darkest A. Series of magaziners and then a book. I dunno. This is the first leg of the voyage. Next stop Brussels for a conference, and then down to the Congo for a looksee. Then a general reccyrun from Cape to Cairo."

"You do make it sound rather like a chore instead of adventure," Jill Richard said. "I'd be wild with excitement."

Alec grinned, his face lighting.

"I *am* wild with excitement. There's something about Africa that pulls my personal phoenix out of the ashes. I get reborn every six years, I guess. Just when I am feeling very wan and completely tiny and used up, my agent telephones and says that some good fairy's offered me another chance to exercise my fiddlefoot in my favorite continent."

"What is there about the place? I read a lot. Alan Moorehead, for instance, all his background of Baker and Speke and the rest. Africa sounds almost like a communicable disease."

"I wouldn't know how to explain it. I talked about it a solid two hours one night six years ago to a charming child named Penny who was quite thrilled that she was going to drive me out to the airport because she'd never seen anybody off to Africa before. I don't think I made it through her comprehension barrier, though. Maybe you could sum it in a phrase, but a hundred books will never tell you."

Jill Richard got up and stirred another drink.

"See if you can sum it in a phrase. You can write the hundred books later."

Alec ran his hands through his hair and stretched out his legs. He took a careful sip of his drink.

"I don't know how to say it. Perhaps because it's so much contrast. The heat is so hot, and you'll freeze the same night. There is always death in your life—each moment a reminder of the inevitability of your impermanence—but somehow you've never felt so much alive. The hyena is the angel of death, and I find his howl more soothing than a robin's chirp. The stars hang lower, the moon swings closer, the firelight is brighter, the air crisper. A lion is gentle as a dog, and an elephant always seems to be regretfully departing—except when it screams and comes straight for you. Gin tastes better. There are bugs and snakes and hunger and thirst and all manner of revolting diseases and, my God, there is filth. But I never feel dirty when I'm filthy, and I can feel dirty in New York or London when I'm only dingy. There is a thing of bright morning and swift-falling night and the promise of a fire which to me is more exciting than the expected embrace of a woman you love. I can think of nothing more violently rewarding than showing it to someone you love, but all the time you would be miserable in case she didn't see it your way, didn't love it your way. This is a pretty long paragraph, but the country in all its varied aspect is too huge to generalize. And this impression," Alec shrugged, "is what my masters want me to transmit to paper in the next year."

"I'd say you're off to an excellent start. I'd love to see it through your eyes some day."

"It's really a huge risk to take, showing off the country to strangers. Some people only see snakes and bemoan the lack of ice, complain about the dust and swell up from insect bites. A night noise is a menace, and the locals a source of contagion. Other people see the same thing as sheer beauty, and can only walk through paces in their own lands until God is good enough and the money sufficient to send them back to the desert wastes and the stinking swamps and swarming mosquitoes and savage people."

"Hemingway caught your view of it, I thought, in 'Snows

of Kilimanjaro.' He also captured the risky view, the other side, in 'The Short Happy Life of Francis Macomber,' when it all seemed a waste of time to bring the girl there in the first place, whether or not she shot you in the neck."

"Ernest got it, but I think superficially. He was never there long enough in a single stretch, and he was always on some sort of houseparty, with a new woman and a reputation for he-mannishness to maintain. He was writing it *before* he did it, before he really saw it—preparing himself for what he hadn't seen yet. He suffered from a complaint common to most writers. They remodel the landscape to be sure it'll fit the print. They shape their characters mentally before they give the characters an opportunity to define themselves. Also Hemingway never hunted elephant, any more than he was ever really in a war."

"That aspect of the man is not generally held by the public," Jill said. "And do I detect a touch of bitchiness?"

"Not meant," Alec said, and lit her cigarette. "It's just that there are two kinds of war, one for volunteer ambulance drivers on a joke front and famous war correspondents who roar in for the kill after the real fighting's over and don't sleep in the mud. The other kind of war is where you smell bad and don't have any whiskey and may or may not trip over your own guts, physical and mental. That kind of war lasts a dreadfully long time, and is almost one hundred per cent unpleasant."

"And what sort was yours?"

"Mine? I was well-fed, well-boozed, a uniformed civilian in my own service. I heard shots fired in anger, but fled in fear and won no medals. I went in early and got out fast, and killed nobody personally that I can recall. I didn't even get wounded."

"That makes your appraisal of Hemingway a little less subject to criticism. But what was the thing about elephants?"

Now Alec grinned.

"On that one I'm home. Until you have hunted elephant you have not hunted man, nor have you known humility and fear and reverence and the short length of life, the measureless depths of death. I do not think this can be explained to anyone but another elephant hunter."

"And you are an elephant hunter?"

Alec dipped his head.

"Begging your pardon, I am an elephant hunter. Not an ivory shooter, but a seeker after big teeth. There is as much difference as in bullfights or wars."

"I don't understand the elephant mystique, although I think Ben pretty well clued me on bulls. How did Ben . . . ?"

"After dinner, if you don't mind," Alec said. "I discuss Ben better over a brandy. I'm still not used to the idea that he's gone."

Jill pointed to his empty glass.

"Another before my feeble effort at food?"

"Thanks, I won't. I don't really seem to need much extra stimulation with you. I go on my own steam. You'd really like to hear more about Africa? It's a lengthy topic."

"I really would like to hear something more about Africa. And then I would like to hear something about that book you may just be ripe enough to write."

Alec waved his book away.

"I'd rather talk about a man named Melville, and *his* book, and give you a back quote from Hemingway's 'Green Hills.' Occasionally, a man learns something about how things really *are,* such as whales. To the best of my memory, Ernest was talking literature to some character and the topic of Melville arose over the campfire. It seems to me, and I have a frightening mind for this sort of thing, that Hemingway said: 'There have been writers who've had the good fortune to find a little of how things can be, from voyaging or other people's chronicles—whales, for instance. This knowledge is wrapped in rhetoric like plums in a pudding. Once in a while it stands there alone, unwrapped by pudding, and it is good. That was Melville. The people who praised it praised it for rhetoric, which is not important. They put mystery in it which is not there.' That's not exact, but close."

Jill Richard looked lovely in her black pants and white blouse by the firelight in the green room with the candles glowing like a distant campfire from the next room. She was leaning forward, elbows on knees, much as Alec rode in a Land Rover when somebody else was driving. She was keenly intent, and Alec felt that she actually cared about what he was saying—not impressed because *he* was saying it, but cared for what he was saying.

"They say man is God's masterpiece, and I never believed it since I saw my first elephant. Perhaps whales. . . . I never met a whale at first hand, but I know what Hemingway was trying to say when he talked about Melville and Moby-Dick. The elephant is Moby-Dick for me, but not because the elephant has chewed off a leg or anything like that.

"But when you see the futility of politicians, the needlessness of wars, the utter damned stupid cruelty of man to himself, the elephant stands as a monument to God in His Wisdom."

"And so you shoot him for his teeth?"

"I shoot him for his soul, and his teeth are the monument, as the Cross is revered in Christ's name. And I shoot him when he is ready for heaven, and I don't want him pulled down by *people*"—Alec almost spat the word—"people who don't deserve him. People who would reduce his flesh to tortured tatters and his tusks to stupid religious carvings, billiard balls, or bangles for some Indian wench's wrists. I shoot him to keep him, him and the memory of how he actually was."

"That's playing quite a lot of God."

Jill Richard's brow wrinkled.

"Everybody plays a lot of God, one way or another. Some do it more stupidly than others. And I do not shoot all the elephants I see. When I shoot an old elephant I shoot the memory of man and my particular hope of Heaven, which would be to be put down at ultimate prime by any man— or beast—like me. I could cite you a crippled lion beset by hyenas; I could cite you one particular bull elephant. Romain Gary was touching on it in *Roots of Heaven*, which made a very lousy movie. Ben Lea was touching on it in more ways than one."

Jill stood up.

"I would like very much to have you cite me one particular bull elephant. But at this moment I must bestir myself and see to the chafing dish, if we're to feed at all. The gentleman's retiring room is over there, and I shall switch on a little moody music."

"May I help at all?"

"Rather not. There's *The Times* and *The Express* and your own *Time*. Make yourself at home, whilst I get myself to the scullery."

Alec sat back with a fresh drink, listened to some high-fidelity Debussy, and briefly closed his eyes. It was almost like being back by the campfire again—the campfire he would be seeing soon, he hoped, despite the business of politics

and emerging nations and datelines and travel. This Jill—
there was a woman to talk to, and you didn't feel she was
listening politely. After dinner, which was certain to be delicious, he would see if he could tell her something about
what the country meant. In a way, it was a practice swing
for the job he was about to do for the book he might write
some day.

He could hear vague clatters from a kitchen, but with the
restlessness of all attendant males arose from his chair and
prowled the room. Unerringly he headed for the bookshelf,
and liked the company he found himself in. There were a
few standard sets, but they were hand-rubbed, not standing
stagnantly in stiff bargain-basement covers. Not unused the
Dickens, not the Poe, not the Hemingway, not the Proust,
not the Steinbeck, not the Twain, not the Kipling—and, certainly, not the Alexander Barr. All the Barr was there except
the last one. She'd said she read it, but? Well, somebody
stole it, because Jill Richard seemed an unlikely borrower or
a library-card literata. Make a mental note, Barr.

He strolled over to the lovely slim fireplace, standing ivory-
gracile against the palish apple walls, the deeper summer
green carpeting. What a lot of cards there were. Guiltily,
listening for the kitchen sounds, he picked up one, being extremely careful not to disturb the rigid military array in
which the invitations guarded Jill Richard's social life from
harm, like the busbied soldiers who marched sentry-go in
front of Buckingham Palace. Just a peek.

*Colonel and Mrs. request. General Sir and Lady request.
John and Wendy would be happy if. Lord and Lady request.
Mary and Peter would be delirious if. Sir Bertram* [no lady]
asks the pleasure. Cardcardcardcardcard. And *Darling Jill if.*
And *Jill sweetie if.* And more *cardscardscardscards.* Until
this *It'll be a tragic way to start the New Year without you
so please be kind. Love ever Miles.*

"Miles, eh?" Alec's brain snarled. "So who the hell is this
Miles, with his tragedy and his New Year and his love-bloody-
ever?"

He heard footsteps and managed to be back in the chair
with *Time,* whose cover was a picture of some African politician (Mboya, he glanced hurriedly at the caption) when Jill
entered the room.

"Dinner, such as it is, is served," she said. "I hope you
weren't too bored waiting."

"I wasn't bored, actually." (I'll say I wasn't bored. You and that bloody Miles and that bloody tragedy if he can't start the New Year without you.) "I'm afraid I sort of succumbed to the music and drowsed off a bit. Hard flight; you know. Big day at the office."

86

They sat now in fire-and-candlelight, Jill with her legs tucked under her on the white divan. The dinner, for all her disclaimers, had been simple and superb. They had stacked the dishes in the kitchen for the daily who, Jill said, had promised to come in for a lick and a promise tomorrow. Peace hung like woodsmoke around Alec's head, and the brandy was smooth on his tongue, the coffee hot and delicious. The hearthfire had burned down to a bed of ruby coals.

"Now," Jill Richard said. "Tell me more about Africa. Tell me exactly as if you were seeing it for the first time—exactly as you'd write it—if you wrote it. I won't interrupt, I promise. I listen well."

"All right," Alec said. "But it'll be quite lengthy. I've been in the prose business so long I find it difficult to cut my speech and am apt to go a little flowery on description. If you can stand it, here goes."

"I can stand it," she replied. "Fire away."

This was a very important trip for me, Alec said, *I was having my first real look at the land I was coming selfishly to love, after a couple of ordinary safaris and some once-over-lightly journalism.* (Alec closed his eyes. Just talking it over was almost like being back in the bush again. Alec was sitting in memory on the veranda of Cottage Four in the back courtyard of the Norfolk Hotel on Government Road in the city of Nairobi in the Crown Colony of Kenya, in British East Africa, in mid-February of the year 1953. The ashtrays, as always, were too small for a man who smoked while he worked, and the usual uninvited dogs were prowling the cobbled compound.)

Alec Barr was burned to boot-color and his hair was sun-bleached sufficiently to meld into the white patches over his ears. He was a few pounds thinner; food had been rather more than slightly irregular up the tall hill. He was wearing a khaki hunting suit, *dhobie*d almost white by the pounding of the safari personal boys, and a smile of professional satisfaction. He had just written *endit* to Section Three of a series on the Mau Mau uprising. At hand, weighted to the railing by a Scotch bottle, was a cable from Marc Mantell which said: BOYS DELIGHTED FIRST TWO ARTICLES ALSO ART STOP EAGERLY AWAITING THIRD PIECE STOP HOW ABOUT THAT BIG BOOK QUERY BANK ACCOUNT AMELIA PARENTS ALL HEALTHY STOP WE MISS YOU SO COME HOME STOP BUT SHOOT ME SOME TUSKS FOR OFFICE FIRST BESTEST MARC.

He shuffled the fresh pages into a neat bloc and dipped into a brief case for the carbons of the forerunners. It all seemed to fit, he thought, but maybe he'd just read it again to see if he'd left out anything really important. He liked the way the magazine had handled the first piece. It had been a quick-and-dirty, but it had been given the cover plug and a lot of picture play, considering that he had been forced to use amateur photographers, his hunter and himself. It certainly packed enough authenticity. There he was, Old Hero Barr, wearing a bloody great pistol in the midst of a bunch of Mau Mau prisoners. He looked hairy enough even to convince *The Reader's Digest* that he hadn't made the whole thing up.

My God, the story'd been easy to cover, he thought, as he automatically recopyread the carbon. Walk right straight into those murders on Kinangop; bang into blood-soaked homes of people he knew. Then the sweep by the *sub rosa* vigilante force, when they flushed a huge covey of Kikuyu terrorists out of a mountainside. And the characters, my God. . . . As the Australians used to say, you wouldn't read about them.

Such as this particular character now, who was leaning over the wall of his cottage. He seemed to be nine feet tall at least, and he owned mustaches lush enough to hide a flock of sand grouse.

"They told me you worked for a living," the monster said. "I refused to believe it. I say, you wouldn't ask a thirsty chap in and stand him a drink, would you?"

"I'll make an exception in your case," Alec said, getting up and shoving a hand at the big man. "And how'd you be, Mate? Kill any interesting people lately?"

The big man shrugged.

"Business was a little slow after you left. I suppose they staged this whole nonsense for The Press, anyhow. Or maybe we ran out of targets. Well, gully-gully." He raised his glass.

"Gully-Gully, and here's blood in your eye," Alec said. "Come in. Take a pew."

"What's all this bumf, the last batch of inaccuracies?" The huge man gestured at the carbons.

"Last batch. I have whored my way out of a tight corner," Alec said. "The entire world will now know what is going on in this miserable little stronghold of free love and heavy boozing. I've given the Micks all the best of it. I wouldn't be surprised if Kenyatta doesn't make prime minister one of these days."

"Jolly good," the big man said. "We can use a man of Jomo's inventive talent, in light of what we've got in the Colonial Office. I say, where're all your tame white hunters? I thought when I saw the whisky at least one of the heroes would be lurking about to see nobody stole it off you."

Alec made a scattering motion with his hands.

"Gone. *Kwaheri* the lot. Metro-Goldwyn-Mayer has supplanted Mau Mau in the national interest. They're making *Mogambo,* whatever the hell that is, and my brave buckos have all rushed off to see that no hyenas eat Grace Kelly. For pay, of course. They look after Ava for free."

The big man shrugged.

"I prefer the Mau Mau to the movies," he said. "The ceremonies are less gruesome. I stopped off to make you an offer, *rafiki.*"

"So I'm a friend, am I, a blood brother?" Alec grinned.

"*Bloody* brother, more. And don't be so bloody rude. Look, Alec, I'm sick, and I suppose you are, of all this murderous nonsense of the last couple of months. Government have taken proper retribution out of our hands. Not nice to cut off *their* heads any more in purely private enterprise. They've brought in the *Black Watch* and the Buffs to do it for us. All legal now. We're in a war even the ratepayers can understand."

"You sound like an editorial writer," Alec said. "What's the offer, Sandy?"

"I'm packing in the hero business, and heading back to

my animals in Southern Tanganyika. The offer—which I may
withdraw unless you furnish more whisky—is for you to
come down with me and play assistant game warden for a
spell. I need the blood off my hands and out of my heart, and
so, I suppose, do you. After this last month. You still a Yankee citizen?"

"Not if they find out what I've been up to," Alec said.
"But your offer is accepted with considerably more than
alacrity. Be nice to see a hyena again who isn't human, black
or white."

87

They called Sandy Lang "Lang Sandy" often as not. because
of the six feet four he measured from cotton crest of the big-
footed stride on the East African ground over which he had
walked a million miles—when he had not measured it by
oxcart, or latterly, by Land Rover. Bar the war, Sandy had
lived in Africa all his fifty years. Some thirty of those years
had been devoted to various aspects of the Game Department. In Southern Tanganyika, where he ruled a tremendous
stretch of territory, he was called simply Bwana Game by native and white alike.

He was married to a tiny blue-eyed woman half his
height, who was only slightly tougher than her husband. The
kids had grown and gone; Sandy ran his office officially from
Musoma, but he was rarely in the office. He actually administered his vast acres from a *boma* outside a tiny settlement called Ikoma, near the site of the old pre-World-
War-I German fort, just on the lip of the Grummetti River.
Sandy Lang's best friend was an almost-carbon copy, who
was also called Bwana Game as a result of his nearly thirty
years as chief of the Southern Masai of Kenya which joined
Sandy Lang's Tanganyika area. Between them the men ruled
terrain the size of Texas. They lived by simple code: Cherish
the animals mercifully and prosecute the poachers merciless-
ly. It was said of both men that they would jail their dear
gray mothers if they caught the old ducks shooting a foot

less than the dogmatic minimum of two hundred yards from a hunting car.

"The way this Mau Mau thing is going," Sandy Lang was saying now to Alec Barr on the porch of Alec's Norfolk cottage, "we are bound to close the Masai and a good bit of my area, I shouldn't wonder. Too many of the laddybucks are denning up in the Masai and spilling over into my country. It'll not be poachers we're hunting down there pretty soon; it will be the Mickey Mice again."

"I suppose so," Alec said. "What've you got in mind?"

"Nothing of a great deal of importance except to me—and, judging from the cut of your jib, maybe you. I thought perhaps you might like one last look at paradise before the political necessities of this filthy world wreck it entirely. I have a lot of work to do—must count my lions, must break up a few poacher gangs, must fix some bridges we lost in the rains. I thought maybe you might just like to come along for a few weeks on a bedroll, no-tent sort of safari."

"I couldn't think of anything I'd rather do," Alec said, gathering up his papers. "It's a great compliment. Rather unusual, too, isn't it?"

"First time in thirty years," Sandy Lang said. "Bar the odd Very Important Persons or some royal relative the Governor occasionally saddles onto me for a week end."

"Let me mail the last piece and send a couple of cables," Alec said. "Then I'm your man. What does an assistant game warden do?"

"He drinks gin and shoots birds with the chief game warden." Sandy Lang grinned again. "And listens to a lot of lies about the war in Burma without challenging their probability. From time to time he may be called on to change a tire or shoot an old cow elephant with a nasty disposition and a talent for wrecking mealie fields. But mostly he just comes along for the ride."

So Alec had come along for the ride, and it seemed to him he had never enjoyed anything quite so much as the sunbright days in the high cool meadows—you couldn't rightly call them plains—of yellow grasses and the orchardy-looking scrub forests that held so many millions of animals. The Ikoma area joined Kenya's Masai on the one hand and Tanganyika's Serengeti Plains on the other. It was the natural channel for the migration of zebra and wildebeeste, the huge herds which searched for the tender grass that was always edibly short in the Ikoma area. The cats followed the herds, and Alec came to know several score lions on a friendly, personal basis.

There was no desire to kill, although a certain amount of daily shooting was necessary to feed the camp. Sandy Lang traveled with an entourage of half a dozen game scouts, ex-poachers all, dedicated wardens now they had been bailed by their original captor from the Kingi Georgi Hoteli, or jailhouse. Alec and Sandy shot francolin and guinea fowl for their personal table and an occasional big piece of meat for the boys. But mostly they wandered happily, rebuilding a washed-out bridge, performing public-works repair on damaged drifts that crossed dry streams, always keenly checking the area for poacher camps.

The only notable creature Alec had shot on this trip was a lion. They had followed some hyena hysteria, and a slow circling of vulture, and they came upon the lion in a little shady glade. He was starving, that was clear, as he lay fly-clustered under the dappled-yellow fever trees. His hide hung in folds, and his ribs showed like staves under the fang-scarred, thorn-tattered skin. He was ringed round by the hyenas—hyenas squatting, doglike, tongues lolling, as they waited. Occasionally one of the hyenas ventured closer, and the old male would attempt to drag himself by his forepaws toward the hyena. Sandy Lang dropped his thonged binoculars thumping on his chest.

"Poor old bugger," he said. "That'll be Brutus. I wondered why we hadn't seen him. You know the full story on this little tableau?"

"Appears to me his back's broken, and the *fisi* are just sweating him out, waiting for him to become weak enough to warrant a fast finisher."

"You're dead right. I really should have put two and two together when we saw that handsome young chap licking his wounds the other day. It was evidently a hell of a fight. Younger male kicked the old man out of the pride, and broke Papa's back in the process. But he's still king here, though. Look."

Another hyena had edged closer, and the old lion growled feebly, hunching his shoulders in an ineffectual effort to get at the emboldened scavenger. The hyena retreated.

"*Bunduki,*" Sandy Lang snapped over his shoulder to one

of the game scouts. *"Bunduki ya Bwana."* He turned to Alec. "I imagine from the look of him the old boy's been without food of any sort for a week, and has kept himself barely alive from the dew off the grass. He couldn't have crawled to any water. Would you mind finishing him for me, Alec? He's rather an old friend of mine—sentimental of me, I confess, but I've known him a good fifteen years."

"Of course." Alec took the rifle from the gunbearer. They walked up to the little glade, and as they approached the hyenas gallumped away, their inherently crippled hindquarters making an obscene parody of the old lion with the broken back. Vultures, perched in the thorn trees and sitting on the ground well back from the hyenas, rose with a creaking of wings.

The old lion swung his great maned head as they approached, and turned his sad yellow eyes toward the men.

Sandy Lang made the lion-coughing sound in his throat. "Poor old Brutus, poor old chap," he said, merging the words with the lion-talk. "Poor old fellow. Good-by, old boy. Take him in the ear, Alec," he said and walked away until he heard the flat crack of the rifle. Then he stopped and turned.

"Well done," he said. "We'll leave him to the hyenas and the birds now. No!" he said to one of the game scouts, who was approaching the dead lion with a knife in his hands. *"Hapana kata ndefu!* Leave his whiskers alone!"

"They'd strip him clean if I'd let them," Sandy Lang said. "They'd have his balls off him—broiled lion testicles make you brave. They'd have his whiskers—lion-beard ground up and taken in tea cures impotence, like powdered rhino horn. If he had any fat on him they'd have that, as well—to sell to the Wahindi—because lion fat cures gonorrhea. Off would come the mane to be sold, and the claws and teeth for jewelry. Leave him!" he said again to the game scout. "I'd rather the hyenas and the birds had him entire than let some bloody Indian *dukah-wallah* buy his spare parts."

They were waiking back to the Land Rover now. Over his shoulder Alec saw the hyenas moving in, the vultures beginning to land with a bump behind the hyenas. Sandy Lang stared straight ahead and spoke, almost to himself.

"I don't know," he said. "I really don't know how to explain it. You were up the hill the other week when we rather arbitrarily rid the world of a few dozen local gentlemen. Didn't bother me at all, although you will also remember that

I gave the order. But I'm always tremendously saddened when I have to polish off one of my friends, like the old gentleman back there. That's the chief trouble with this wonderful goddam country. There's no such thing as a decent finish, for animal or man. The only wild creatures that profit from death are the hyenas and the vultures, and they cop it as well, eventually. The hyena even eats himself, poor chap. God on the Mountain must really have been in an evil humor when he made *fisi*—the hermaphroditic freak with the lion's jaws and the crippled spine. Makes you wonder about it all."

"I think we'd better open the chopbox and sprinkle a little gin on your friend's memory," Alec said. "Wakes are customary in most portions of the world."

Sandy Lang grinned again.

"I guess I *was* being a touch heavy," he said. "After all, everybody winds up inside the hyenas. One way or the other we lose the balls and the fangs and the claws. Even the whiskers. I say, this *has* been a doleful day. I suggest we take out the shotguns and relieve our feelings with a few murdered sand grouse at the nearest waterhole. Somehow, the sound of a shotgun tends to cheer one up."

88

"This is where I do my heavy thinking," Sandy Lang said. "This officially belongs to Her Majesty. Unofficially it belongs to me. Even more unofficially it belongs to Meg, and one cross-bred Gyppie goose, plus a few imported peacocks and some relocated pheasants and tame local guinea fowl. Pretty?"

"Gorgeous," Alec Barr said. "I'd never want to leave it."

"I don't—for very long. Once in a while Musoma or Arusha calls and I must heed or lose my job, but basically this is home."

They had made a huge circle, involving two weeks, and now were back at the *boma*—the barriered game post. Smart, khaki-*kepi*ed *askari* saluted sharply before they raised the barrier pole.

"Memsaab *iko?*" Sandy Lang asked the *askari* sergeant.

He shook his head, his hugely pierced earlobes swinging. "Arusha. Back tomorrow, she said."

"Good enough." Sandy Lang slipped his clutch and turned to Alec. "We'll head for the house and have a real bath."

"If there's a heaven above I should think God took a couple of practice swings here," Alec said as they crossed the river, turning into a hard-packed clay track. Great trees —the tallowy, leopard-mottled fever trees with great frothy tops, huge sky-searching fig, pulpy purplish baobab—leaned toward the river. A flock of metallic-blue guineafowl scuttled across the road, and doves rose, settled, and flew again before them. There was a quack of Egyptian geese from around the river's bend, and a herd of bright golden impala stood unafraid, solemnly staring until the entire company leaped like a ballet chorus. One female warthog, ludicrously dignified with her antenna-tail erect, trotted into the side-bush, followed by a squad of four piglets. A waterbuck stood squarely in the track, long-horned, thicknecked, and shaggy in his rough tweed coat.

"Stuff's awfully tame," Alec said.

"Practically members of the family. You noticed the sign said no shooting within five miles of the *boma*. You're apt to find a lion or two on the lawn. Meg feeds them, and they follow her home."

They pulled off the track onto a patch of emerald lawn that rolled gently to the river. The square house, native gray stone with the classic red tin roof, nestled under a huge grove of the yellow-thorn acacias. The house was almost choked in a jungle of flowers—smothered by golden-shower creeper, rimmed by a riot of red and yellow cannas, outbuildings buried in purple bougainvillaea. Beds of zinnias snugged the boundaries of the lawn. Trees of pink frangipani and lavender-weeping jacaranda and brilliant Nandi flame studded the broad vista of lawn. Hibiscus and poinsettia made crackling scarlet accents in the glossy croton hedges. An acre seemed to be devoted exclusively to petunias.

Two Rhodesian ridgebacks, a dachshund, and a cocker spaniel rushed up barking, and a lion cub got up lazily from a nest in the flower bed to swagger sleepily toward the car. Troops of guinea came trotting, and a peacock strutted close, making a huge fan of its tail. Mongolian pheasant mingled carelessly with native yellownecked spurfowl. In the center of the lawn, as if daring the visitors to enter, a species of half-wild goose stood on its tiptoes to shout a war cry. He was answered by a gaggle losing altitude to land at the river.

"Where's your ark?" Alec asked. "You seem to have all of its components here, Bwana Noah."

"We *do* run a little heavily to wildlife," Sandy Lang said. "Especially since the kids grew up and wandered off. The Memsaab seems to have turned all her energies to pets and flowers."

"I'd not be far wrong in guessing the color of her thumb," Alec said. "I never saw such flowers in my life. My God, are those actually roses? They're big as cabbages."

"Meggie takes pride in her garden," Sandy Lang said. "I swear she could drill a hole in a block of granite and something would sprout. Just as well, too, because the local antelope-gazelle population has developed a taste for exotic fodder."

They walked toward the house, where a barefooted, red-*tarboush*ed houseboy in a long, white, nightgownish *kanzu* held the door open. The lion cub—not a bloody cub, Alec thought, as the thing leaped playfully onto the small of his back—seemed secure in its intent to accompany them into the house, together with the four dogs and half-breed goose who was waddling up in the rear.

"Shoo, the lot of you!" Sandy Lang booted the lion lightly in the behind, and made sweep-out gestures with the back of his hands at the dogs and the goose. *"Sa!"*

He shook his head at Alec.

"Buggers'd follow me into bed if I allowed it," he said. "They're here alone a lot with the Mem, and she gives them the run of the place. Come into my castle. I see Molo's got the ice out; he must have heard the car. Gin, I presume?"

"Indeed." Alec looked around the room, which was more or less standard East African farmhouse. Leopard skins draped the backs of cowhide divans, and climbed the cedar-paneled walls. Fireplace, heads, tusks, horns, hides, books, pewter mugs—Alec laughed happily.

"I might as well be home," he said. "I've got a place like this in New Jersey. We're a little short on livestock, though. Tell me, how do you keep the local carnivora from chewing up your pets? I should think the mortality would be considerable."

Sandy Lang finished pouring the drinks and handed one to Alec.

"Not too difficult. There's a boy looks after them. It's an easy job. He's got just one duty—to herd all of the feathered friends into a rather solid fowlhouse before nightfall. Otherwise the civet cats and leopard and jackal. . . . The dogs sleep in the house, and the little lion—by the way, her name's Sheba—wanders around on her own. When Meg's here the lioness sleeps with *her*. She doesn't fancy me overmuch."

Alec slumped in a mottled cowhide chair and stretched his long legs toward the fire, which Sandy Lang had kicked into life.

"I met a lot of rich people in my time," Alec said. "But after this last couple of weeks . . . ," he shook his head, almost in disbelief. "You're the richest man I know."

"I quite agree," Sandy Lang said cheerfully. "At least in my own domain I am emperor of all I survey, and there's a hell of a lot to survey, when you consider I have to pay for my own petrol. Hey, Molo, *kuja hapa!*"

The houseboy entered and stood, arms folded across the white *kanzu*.

"*Bafu wawile. Bwana Alec kwanza. Maji* plenty bloody *moto, sikia?*"

He looked at his wrist watch.

"We'll have a bath, I think, before we eat. I was standing downwind of meself and didn't like the smell." He turned again to the servant. "*Na leti chakula saa nane.*" The boy bowed and left the room.

"I get the *plenty bloody* and the *moto* and the *maji*," Alec said. "But the time business always defeats me. When did you tell him we'd eat?"

"About an hour and a half from now. *Saa nane* is two o'clock, one way, since it's eight hours from six A.M. Leave it. One fine day, after the Exchequer has done away with the pounds, shilling, pence business, we'll teach people out here to count in a less complicated fashion. We still have time for another gin while the boy heats your *bafu*-water."

Alec settled himself deeper into his chair, wriggling in conscious comfort. He watched his friend rolling the angostura bitters so that it spread evenly in the glass.

"You know," he said. "This kind of life is really too good for the people involved." He waved at the wall of books, mostly leatherbound, yellowed pages crisp from age, except for the one loud line of modern paperbacks. He pointed his chin at the fire.

"Those poor, downtrodden blacks that you colonials beat to death daily. All those horrible flowers cluttering up what might just as easily be cement instead of grass. The lion lying down with the dogs. Booze on the sideboard, bath coming up, food in the offing. Nothing to do but admire the scenery and count your peafowl when you've finished counting your lions. And for this you also get paid."

"Don't tell anybody," Sandy Lang smiled. "I've been frightened for years that they'll find out what I do for a living and take it away from me."

They bathed in iron-rusty water and ate cold partridge with salad, and Alec sought bed while his friend went off to the little office to deal with government correspondence. Alec rose about four and found Sandy Lang on the lawn, talking to a delegation of Wa-Ikoma warriors—ocher-painted like the Masai, spear-leaning as the headman gestured. Cow skulls, foul-smelling and still partially clothed in rotted meat, lay in a heap.

"Problem with the locals," Sandy Lang said. "Cattle-killer in the area. I don't believe a bloody word of it, mind you. They get government compensation now for slain stock. What they actually do, I think, is kill it themselves and eat it and bring me the head and horns, and blame the whole business on the poor old *simba*. All right, all right!" He spoke in Swahili to the grizzled elder. "Show me where he killed the last cow, and we'll sit up for him tonight."

Turning to Alec, he shrugged.

"It's nearly always like this when I'm home. This old bugger's got a bee up his nonexistent britches about a cattle-lifter. So I—we, if you can stand the idea—have to go sit up over a smelly carcass and do in some hapless lion. Else the headman'll create a flap with the District Officer and the DO will land it on the DC and when it gets to Dar-es-Salaam and Arusha it will rocket back to me with six new political bows tied on it."

He swung to face the chief, smiling.

"*Kwaheri*, damn your bloodshot little eyes," he said in a

voice replete with charm. "Bugger off, and I hope your youngest wife catches the clap from her latest lover and gives it to you."

The chief smiled happily, bowed, and stalked off, striding storklike on white-scabbed, lean brown legs, his red cape swinging to expose half his body.

"You understand," Sandy Lang said to Alec, "I really didn't mean what I said in English. They're quite a pleasant people, these Ikoma chaps, but they're beginning to spoil— going very political like everybody else. The old boy'll be wearing pants and a hat in another couple of years, once the tall tales of political progress filter in from our friends in the Kenya mountains. Meanwhile, dammit, I suppose I have to go and shoot something to appease him, or he'll have his lads out killing *all* my lions with spears or poisoned arrows."

"Pity we didn't bring in the poor old boy with the broken back," Alec said. "We could have pretended he was the culprit."

"Once in a while, very rarely, I make a mistake," Sandy Lang said. "Come on, let's see to the big *torchi* and be off to the scene of the crime."

"Spotlight? That's against the law."

"It's against the law if *you* use it," Sandy Lang said. "It is not against the law if I use it. If you think I make any sport out of clobbering my friends, you're wrong. We sit up over the kill fairly comfortably in the Rover. The lion, if any, comes to the kill. We flash the light in the poor beast's face, blind him, and shoot him between the eyes. Then we carry the carcass to the chief and go home for— if we're lucky—a nightcap. If I have to do it at all I might as well do it sensibly."

They—or rather Sandy Lang—shot the lion, which turned out to be a lioness with two canine teeth missing and a crippled pus-swollen paw from the presence of ancient porcupine quills. She was old and, as Lang said, only about one month away from becoming a maneater.

"Wouldn't be very much left for the old girl to feed on," Sandy said, flashing the big torch on the corpse. "I'm surprised she was able to kill even a very small cow. Next step would be the herdboy, and then we have more politics from the cityfolk. Pity she wasn't a male. They could have made a new bonnet for the old man out of the mane."

They bumped over the plain, homeward-headed, after dropping the dead lioness in front of the headman's compound. The moon was high, and Alec was surprised to hear his host singing, very much off key.

"Moonlight causes me to bay," Sandy said. "Also I'm pleased we're getting home early. We'll make it to bed before midnight, and be lovely and fresh for the Mem when she tootles up tomorrow."

"I told you," Alec said as they rattled over the rough hoof-pitted plain, "that your house reminded me of mine— the country place in Jersey. I spend half my life trying to explain to visitors that the things I've hung on my wall were like the things we've shot—old, unhappy, past breeding, and generally miserable. Or else they wouldn't make a trophy. Most old people need a wall to preserve themselves for posterity, or they wind up like the back-busted lion, or that poor old girl tonight."

"It's true, you know," Sandy said. "I suppose I shoot half a thousand animals a year in the interests of preservation. You get the elephant migration, all the way from Addis to the Rhodesias, and some of the old outcast bulls are always rogue, some of the old dry cows maniacal. You get the sick and the lame and the halt and the half-blind, and they all want extermination."

"Pity we don't have game wardens for people," Alec said. "Except who'd like being put down for his own good?"

"Not me," replied Sandy Lang. "It wouldn't occur to me that anybody was doing me this great favor."

"Me neither," Alec said. "Oho, Bwana Game. There seems to be activity at the *boma*."

"Problems, always problems," Sandy Lang said.

They drove swiftly to the barrier, and the *askari* spoke excitedly in a strange language that Alec learned later was Wa-Chagga. Sandy cursed and tramped the accelerator, spinning his wheels as the Rover leaped away.

"What did he say? You were in a great good humor five minutes ago." Alec's question was met with a string of curses.

"So help me I'll kill him, I'll tear him to pieces with my own hands!"

"Who? What about?"

Sandy Lang ground his teeth.

"Wait. I want to see the extent of the damage first." He

whirled the Rover into his back yard and leaped out, leaving the motor still running. Alec leaned over and switched off the ignition key.

The headboy, Molo, was standing at the door, but this time his arms were not folded. He was wringing his hands, and according to the light that came from the acetylene lamp he was holding, Alec was prepared to swear that his brown face had gone greenish.

"Where? God damn it, where? *Wapi?*"

"*Nyumba ya kuku.*" The boy pointed to the chickenhouse.

"*Ngapi?*"

"*Yote,*" the boy replied, cringing as if he expected a blow.

Sandy Lang snatched the lantern out of the boy's hand.

"Let's look at the carnage," he snarled from a tight mouth. "Christ, I don't see how I can face Meg when she comes back. *All* of them——"

Alec hurried along, trying to match the tall man's giant strides. He tugged at Sandy's sleeve.

"You wouldn't mind cluing me up on what's got you in such an uproar, would you?"

"No," Sandy snapped, "I don't mind, but I'd much rather I didn't have to. What's happened, as I gather it, the chicken-herdsman got drunk or smoked too much *bhang* and forgot to lock the fowlyard gate. A honey badger forced the door and killed the lot, the boys say."

Sandy Lang plumped the lantern down by the henhouse door and looked at the clawmarks.

"Ratel, all right: The little bastards can scratch their way through a two-by-four. Claws like bears."

He picked up the lantern again and beamed it inside the fowlhouse. It reeked of blood and feathers and dung. Everything in it was dead. None of the dead fowl had been eaten. They lay in heaps, the peacocks, the pheasants, the guinea fowl, the geese, the tame francolin, the ducks. Each throat had been torn out.

Sandy Lang pressed his hand to his eyes.

"Come on," he said. "Let's go back to the house and have a drink to about ten years of lost effort." He held the lantern high, and Alec could see tears in his eyes.

"Look. Just *look*. God-damned brute doesn't even bother to eat what he kills. Just kills it for fun and takes off to other fields. Like human beings. Come on! I don't trust me to talk to the fowlherd-boy tonight—I think I might just beat him to death."

Sandy Lang's hands shook as he poured a stiff hooker of Scotch into two glasses.

"Excuse the operatic exhibition, Alec," he said, and his voice had calmed. "It's not the dead fowl, although God knows Meg's heart'll break when I tell her that all her work —all the *time*—has been wiped out in one night. It's the bloody people that drive me up the wall. That stupid *nugu* has just one job, to lock up the birds, and he smokes another pipe of hemp or gets himself drunk off *pombe* and the whole purpose of his life is forgotten."

Sandy Lang threw himself into a chair.

"You can't understand it, really—the frustration one acquires from dealing with Africans. I suppose nobody outside of us old-timers does. But you can't trust them with anything that makes common sense. Send a boy to fetch your hat and he chases a butterfly. The only thing the African does competently is wait. Ah, to hell . . ."

He clapped his hands. The head boy appeared, still frightened.

"Mambia askari leti gin-trap," he said. *"Upese!"*

"The thing'll be back," he said. "It hasn't had its fill of blood."

"Look," Alec said, after the *askari* had come with the trap and received instructions. "This has all been a little violent. Some dead fowl—"

"Fifty-eight dead fowl, and me having to account for the accident to the Memsaab." Sandy gritted his teeth again.

"Well, I need a little brushing up on natural history. What the hell is a honey badger, exactly?"

"It's called a *ratel,* properly. It's a species of big weasel. Lives in Africa and India. It loves honey—and any kind of fowl. It's not very big—about the same size, I'd say, as one of your wolverines. Same characteristics—long claws, sharp teeth, tough hide. And brave, my oath, how bloody brave. As well as a cold-blooded killer for sport." Sandy Lang said again, and bared his teeth, "Like you and me. Except he's braver."

"What makes him so brave?"

"I don't know. The natives have a story that his hide is so tough that when he tackles a beehive nothing can sting him except in the asshole. They say that he has a special fermentation in his bowels that allows him such a lethal fart that he can back up against the beehive and anesthetize the bees with his wind. This I don't know about; all I know is that he can and will tear apart a bee colony that would sting a lion to death."

"Sounds like quite a beast for such a small fellow. What else?"

"Pound for pound he's probably the strongest, most evil-tempered animal in the world. And he differs in his method of attack from most animals. The average carnivore, cornered and fighting for his life, will go for the jugular. Not the little honey badger. He heads straight for your balls. The Wogs are scared stiff of him on that account. They've got an overdeveloped testicle-consciousness anyhow."

"Sounds like a nasty bit of work, your honey badger. Reminds me of a few people I've known," Alec said. "More?"

"Very little. I wouldn't mind anything the little bugger did, even at the risk of possible castration, if he killed to eat. But he kills for fun and de-nuts out of sheer malice."

"I've seen it happen with squirrels, in America," Alec said. "A boar squirrel definitely follows the castrating technique. I suppose the weasels and the squirrels—and perhaps today's American womanhood—have something in common. My mother did a magnificent job on my old man, and her mother on my grandfather before her."

"I wouldn't know about that," Sandy Lang said. "What I do know about is this." He walked over to the fireplace and took a gnarled clublike walking stick out of an old brass six-inch German shell case.

"I'm not going for his *balls* when we catch him in that trap," Sandy Lang said. "I'm going to beat his brains out with this *rungu*. It'll be a small satisfaction for the look of Meggie's face when she hears the news tomorrow, but better a tiny revenge than nothing. At least it'll make *me* feel better."

He rested the knobkerrie alongside his chair.

"You can go to bed if you want to, Alec," he said. "But I'm waiting up until I hear that trap snap and a certain type of growl coming from what it's caught. If you're interested in cornered animal savagery, I suggest you wait up with me."

"I'll wait up," replied Alec Barr. "On that you can rest assured. It's so seldom these days that you can trap a villain and personally beat his brains out."

89

They needed no rapping on the door to tell them the trap was sprung. The dogs had alerted to the snarls which came from the chicken pen. Once the door was flung open to admit the night, the hissing hatred came clearly from the fowlyard.

Sandy Lang picked up his *rungu,* a thick shillelagh which might have been borne by an early ancestor.

"Our little friend has returned," he said. "And from the sound of it, he isn't caring too much for his current condition. Mind grabbing a shotgun from the cabinet, Alec? He might just manage to chew a paw free from the trap, and I'd hate to have him dig into my crotch."

Alec took down a shotgun, checked the barrels, and looked inquiringly at the gun's owner.

"You always keep these things loaded with buckshot?"

"Indeed. I can think of nothing less useful on a sudden night alert than an unloaded gun. And anything you have to shoot at night wants buckshot."

They walked through the yard and back to the fowlpen, from which the mewing, growling, hissing combination of hate and hurt grew louder.

It was amazing that such a small beast—it could not have possibly been heavier than forty pounds—could contain such fury. The eyes burned with hatred. When the men approached, the burly body launched snarling at them, carrying the heavy gin-trap the full length of its chain.

"Gutty little brute, like I told you," Sandy Lang said. He hefted his club, and started toward the animal.

"I'm sorry," he said, stopping suddenly. "I suppose I'm not that much of an African yet." He extended the club to Alec. "Give me the shotgun."

The small tawny-gray beast with the black-patched back leaped again, his bear-claws hooked, his mouth drawn back from the needle teeth. He leaped again to the length of the chained trap, turned to chew savagely at his feet, clamped securely in a trap large enough to hold a leopard. Once more furious at the sight and smell of man, he launched himself in a dead aim for the groin of Sandy Lang. The chain snapped him back.

Sandy Lang blew the animal's head off with the shotgun.

"I suppose he was only acting according to his lights," he said, and his mouth shaped a faint flicker of smile in the lamplight. "The criminal back to the scene of the crime, and everybody in the world wrong but him. Here," he said to the houseboy, extending the gun. *"Chukuwa."* He touched the animal with his foot.

"Kufa. Dead. Finished. And tomorrow night, or any other night, when we leave the door unlocked, there'll be his brother or his cousin to remind us that you can't really protect anything permanently in this bloody country."

They walked back toward the house.

"You know," Alec Barr said. "I'm really pleased you didn't beat it to death with the club for the sin of acting according to its lights."

"I grow soft with age," Sandy Lang said. "I only get really angry when I deal with humans. Actually I'd rather have shot the man who left the door open."

"One thing," Alec Barr said as they entered the house. "Would it be terrible trouble to have one of your boys drive me to Arusha early tomorrow before Mrs. Lang gets back? I have to leave in a day or so, anyhow, and somehow I don't fit nicely into private griefs."

"You're a man of rare understanding," Sandy Lang said. "If there's no guest in the house there'll be no stiff upper lip. She'll merely cry, and find a fresh fault in *my* personality. Come back any time, Alec. You've a home in the country until the politicians make it impractical."

"I'll need it," Alec Barr said. "I'm heading back to some honey badgers of my own."

90

Alec stood up and stretched. He swallowed a yawn.

"Christ, I talk too much, or maybe you listen too well. But the thing is all hooked up somehow with Ben. With Ben, with the old lion I shot in the ear, with why I have a tendency to despondency from time to time. You asked about Africa. I think you have already lived to regret the first question."

"Don't be entirely silly," Jill said. "I've been fascinated and you know it well. You haven't written the old lion or the honey badger? You haven't told it to anybody the way you told it to me?"

Alec shook his head.

"I suppose I was a little—perhaps—shy. Maybe I wanted to keep it for myself. I wouldn't have told it to Ben, really, because he was the funny man, the bright fellow, the semiserious kidder who wouldn't even see himself as an old male ready for the reaper." He looked at his watch. "It was a gorgeous evening, but honestly, I must run and let you get some rest. When I get started I—" he waved helpless hands. "It's so damned seldom I find a listener."

"Now, one nightcap in aid of our dear Ben. How, actually, and why? You haven't fooled me with all the fascinating African evasions, you know." She spilled a tot of brandy into his glass.

"I know. It was pretty simple. Ben was a fast guy—fast with his head, fast with his hands, and faster with the check. He was like the better bullfighters he loved. Straight in over the horn and hope for the best. It was that kind of cancer. I suppose he could have stretched it out for a few more years."

Alec swished his brandy.

"I went to see him in the hospital. It was ghastly. We'd been to Madrid and had a brave *fiesta* a few weeks before. The man Ben Lea that I knew had gone and left merely a stranger's face. He turned to me and said—does this bother you much, Jill?"

"Not at my age and time of acceptance. I've had a few of my own. What did he say?"

"Ben said: 'They tell me I can't drink, I can't smoke, I can't screw, and I go to the bathroom in a bottle. I'm better dead than how I am, temporarily propped up by science. So I'm going to die. I've told the doctors to cut. So long, chum. For this they got to award me both ears and the tail. *Mine.*' "

Alec shrugged.

"They did cut, and he died with his face to the wall. Ben didn't try to stretch it. He knew about the bulls that killed matadors. They only make it from the ring to the abattoir."

"I can't weep for him," Jill said. "He used to say, when I first met him, 'I'm no man to hang around where he ain't wanted.' Cheers to our chum." She raised her glass.

"I'm a man who knows when he ain't wanted, too," Alec said, rising. "Perhaps the choice of verb is wrong. I'm off to the dear old pub. Question: My time is short. How much of yours is mine?"

"I rise pretty early," she said. "I'm dead tired tonight. We older ladies need our beauty rest, or we go all wrinkly and horrid."

Alec nodded, and his face grew an inch longer. "I've observed your mantel. I know that you must be absolutely crowded at this season."

"I'm crowded at this season. I'm always crowded at this season. Everyone gives parties for the same people who attend their own parties. There are some nice ones. . . . How long will you be here, do you imagine?"

"I hadn't really thought. I hadn't counted on finding you. Just that I thought you'd be occupied, matrimonially or otherwise, and . . ."

"And now that I'm not?"

"I'd selfishly like to claim every moment of your time."

Jill Richard looked at Alec coolly. Deliberately, she raised her hand and slapped the serried array of invitation cards. Each diagonally placed sentry nudged another, and the entire battalion of expensively uniformed social soldiery ran out of mantel terrain and fluttered futilely to the floor, without firing a shot.

And that includes dear bloody Miles and his tragedy, Alec thought.

91

Alec Barr whistled a merry stave as he dressed. Sweeping the entire cavalcade of cards fluttering to the floor had been a wonderful gesture. Of course there must have been men—lovers, possibly some serious—in her life over the last six years. These anonymous rivals bothered him not at all. You didn't hit the middle forties without a series of happy and unhappy—how did the Spanish say it? *"accidentes del tráfico de la corazón"*—in between. He had written the book on that one.

He clothed himself for Britain-by-day (or Alec Barr for the old Ritz-Carlton) in gray flannel, brown suede shoes, and rakish blue trilby. He found a copy of his latest book at the enquiries newsstand while he was waiting for the florist to rape her supply of hothouse roses. Jill had said she had read it, but he hadn't seen a copy on her bookshelf. He decided to go completely American, and as the licensed victualers had just opened, bought a magnum of Mumms. Another thought struck him:

"Stop at Fortnum's," he said to the driver. "I won't be a minute."

"Tyke yer time," the driver said. "Business is slow, Guv."

At Fortnum's Alec bought a vastly red-ribboned five-pound box of chocolates and a covey of tins of caviar.

"Christmas was last week," the driver said, noting the armload.

Alec laughed.

"I overflew it," he said. "Saint Nicholas passed me by. Drive on, chum, to Chester Square."

Alec hummed. Now it was "Jingle Bells."

The driver glanced backward through his slotted window.

"I fought we settled that Christmas was over, Guv," he said. "There ayn't no bleedin' snow. Only this bloody slush."

"It may be slush to you," chum, Alec said. "But you're driving a one-horse open shay through country snow. Press on to Grandma's farm."

The driver shook his head. The passenger looked English, dressed English, and his voice was almost English, but he 'ad to be a bloomin' Yank. Bloke was singing something now abaht it wasn't ryning no ruddy ryne to 'im, it was ryning bloody violets. All Yanks were barmy. No wonder they was all so bleedin' rich.

Alec looked out the window. The gutters fresheted with slush, the sidewalks were murderous with scummed patches of ice, the streets barnyardish with the drab droppings of festive Yuletide snow. The sky was broodingly overcast and as glowering gray as his suit. The roofs of the buildings were still gaily snowbonneted, but dripping icicles, like long dirty fingers, pointed from the eaves where the pigeons walked, feather-ruffled, to keep warm.

"Pull up the horse," Alec said. "There's Grandma's farm, that house there. What is on the clock? I can't see over the flowers."

"Fourteen bob, wif the wytes," the driver said.

Alec pushed a five-pound note through the window.

"Stack me up with these parcels and keep the change," he said.

"But you've 'anded me a bleedin' fiver," the driver said.

"I only wish it was the inside straight gen on the football pools," Alec said, his arms mountainous with bundles. "I wish you good morrow, Cupid. Unless perhaps you'd like to wait a few minutes more?"

"For a fiver I'll wyte a few *hours* more, Guv. Tyke yer own good time."

The driver stood in the slush, waiting for the door to open to Alec's ring. He saw a redheaded woman in a green-velvet housecoat greet Alec with a flashing smile.

"Oho," the driver said, climbing back into his hack. ' 'E ayn't barmy arfter all. The poor bloke's in bloody love. 'E's bloody well insayne, at 'is ayge."

"What on earth is all this?" Jill said. "And you're very early. I haven't finished dressing yet. Here, let me help you."

"Take the flowers, I'll handle the rest. *What is all this*? I'll tell you what all this is. Young Barr come acourtin' in the best juvenile fashion. If you had a fence I'd walk on it, bundles and all."

"You're insane. Chocolates. Caviar. Flowers. A book. *Champagne*. Oh, Alec, you *are* an idiot."

"As Charlie MacArthur once said to Helen Hayes, when he offered her a bag of peanuts, I only wish they were emeralds." He brushed a pouted kiss barely against her cheek. "Let me help you stow this clagger away, and then hurry and dress. I intend to ply you with fine viands in a cavern snug against the bitter cold, and there is a one-horse open shay awaiting without."

"You sound as if you've been drinking rather early in the morning," Jill said.

"I have, but not alcohol. Now. Get me a great big vase and I'll stick all the flowers in it. Then you go and dress. You can arrange them properly when you get back."

"Yes, milord." She handed him a large vase, and then kissed him lightly on the lips.

"Hmm," she said. "It isn't alcohol after all. Cocaine?"

"Headier stuff than that. I've come to collect you, just as I thought six years ago."

"I really believe you have," she said, and walked to the hall. Alec stood and watched her ascend the stairs, noting the steady set of shoulders, the sweet narrowness of waist, the trim hips firmly molded under the flow of green velvet.

He walked back to the living room, and looked again at the almost-bare mantel over the Adam fireplace.

Only one card, a square white one with overlarge writing, adorned the mantel which yesterday had been garrisoned with gilt-edged invitations.

The card said simply A. BARR—DURATION OF STAY.

Alec smiled and went over to the table where he had dropped the book. He got out his pen and wrote: "Collection Day six years overdue, but well worth the wait, if not extended too much longer." He signed it: "S.S. Barr."

She came down swiftly, beautiful in green wool with creamy jabot at the throat. The red hair was almost alive.

"You look lovely," he said, and held out both hands as she reached the bottom of the stairs. "I saw the card on the mantel. Thank you. And I wrote something in the book."

"Oh, do let me see." She ran over to the table.

"The first part I understand. But what do the initials stand for? Certainly not Alexander."

"They stand for 'September Song,'" Alec said. "Perhaps you've heard it. It used to be very popular."

"I've heard it," she said, and came swiftly into his arms. "I love it. If you think the cabbie can wait another minute, this lipstick doesn't rub off. Not very much, anyhow."

"The cabbie can wait another year," said Alec Barr.

92

The temptation had been great to allow the cabbie to wait that other year, but Alec was still feeling strangely shy. He felt like a child, when the kids competed to see how long they could make the all-day sucker or the soft drink last. It wasn't fair to have only five cents to spend and then to gobble up the lollipop or swill down the drink. After a moment he pushed Jill gently away.

"The Jews have a saying I like," he said. "Eat first, then talk. I came to take you to lunch and to lunch we go. The only trouble is that, apart from a few standbys, my time in London Town has been so brief since the war that I know very few of the cosier places. My master fed me very well at the Mirabelle yesterday, but I wouldn't call it very snug. And in Les A., I'll know everybody, and they'll all be from New York or Hollywood. Suggestions?"

"There's a private club on Curzon Street I think you'd like. Velvet-curtained and dark-paneled and sort of nooky. Like your Laurent. It'll scarcely be overrun in the middle of the holidays, and in any case Victor loves me. He'll surely not plant us in the middle. The quietest corner will be ours."

Alec felt the barest twinge of jealousy at the intimation that Victor, who he assumed was the headwaiter, had vast experience conducting Jill to the quietest corners if he knew her well enough to love her. But there again, that battalion of invitations he had so shamelessly spied on told him that this lady got around, and what headwaiter—or anybody else— could possibly help loving this snubnosed freckled maid with the harlequin smile?

Everyone from the doorman to the headwaiter to this Victor and this Leslie greeted Jill with friendly respect and very polite intimacy. He felt precisely as he imagined Penny might have felt when he was preening himself before her in "21," because Jill was getting exactly the same treatment. Mr. Victor insisted on buying them a drink at the bar, and then said a moment later:

"Your table is ready now, Mr. Barr," and Alec would have sworn Mr. Victor stopped himself from saying "Your table is ready now, Mrs. Richard" and that he had probably chased a couple of less steady customers from it.

93

It was just coming on for dark, winter-gloomy dusk, when they arrived at the house in Chester Square. Jill flicked on the lights, then drew the draperies. She nodded toward the fireplace, where the makings of a fire had been laid.

"Missus Thing has been and done and gone, I see," she said. "Be a sweetie and light me a fire and find some music while I go rescue those poor lovely roses from their ugly jug. The recordings are in that chest there. The player is one of the simpler ones. You know how to operate it?"

"I think so."

Jill headed toward the hall, and turned at the foot of the stairs.

"It's really such a filthy day out, would you mind terribly taking pot luck here again? Perhaps just some scrambled eggs and a dab of your Christmas caviar? I'll put the champagne on ice now."

"I'd love to. I can't think of anything nicer than not seeing any more people today. People make me nervous. You may have noticed at lunch. Of all the uninspired conversations until we both broke up and disgraced ourselves . . ."

"Don't give it a thought. I wish I had some carpet slippers to offer, but I haven't. However, I don't object to stocking feet. As for me, I intend to get straight out of this girl armor and into some slacks before I fix the flowers. Pretend you're home. Fire, please. Music, please." She disappeared.

Alec took off his coat and blessed the fact that people in America mostly wore belts instead of braces these days. He bent over to light the fire and thought: *Christ, I'm scared stiff. I feel like a bloody bridegroom.* It's all so easy when it's late-night and drunk-spontaneous, and you just leap into each other's arms and fall automatically into bed. Then you don't really care if you're any good or not, and generally you are. I wonder if women actually realize that the burden of proof is really on the man, and how horribly frightened the poor bastard is that he'll be rabbity on the first one and won't be able to raise the necessary armament to disprove it on a second shot?

The fire leaped into a strong blaze. Alec switched off the louder lights and turned on some lamps. The low-pitched mellow lighting made him feel a tiny touch braver.

It's here, and I know it's here, he thought. But damn me if I know how to set about it. I can't just grab her or suggest coldly that it would be a fine way to kill a winter's afternoon if she whipped off her clothes and led me to the hay. It must be a fact, he thought, that most seductions occur at night, when you're full of booze and food and music and euphoria and it's late and dark and you get the word right away if she asks you up for a nightcap. But here it is barely four of a dying day and everybody's sober as ten judges and we didn't even eat much lunch, just shoved the food around while we felt each other out with a flock of clichés.

Music. The timorous seducer's friend. The handy aid to intercourse. Touch 'em on the gentle ganglia. Hal Kemp and Ray Noble and Glen Gray and honeysuckle on the petting porches of Fraternity Row. "The Very Thought of You." "Talk of the Town." "Heart of Stone." I wonder what they were playing in England when Jill came along? Certainly Noble. Al Bowlly, be my friend. Evoke me a lost piece of poignancy. Sinatra, aid me. Where are you, Kenny Sargent? And oh, God, Kern and Gershwin and Mercer and Arlen, Burke and Van Heusen, Matt Dennis and Sammy Cahn, Weill and Loesser, be my buddies tonight. Like in that song of Loesser's from *Guys and Dolls.*

He was thumbing through the record file. Thank God her tastes were catholic. There was a lot of classic and semi-classic, but there was also some Lena and Ella and Frank and Louis and Sarah and Pearl. She liked piano, evidently, apart from Debussy, for here was Bushkin and Sutton and Short and Tatum and Garner. Play, Sam, like Bogey said in *Casablanca.*

Try Sinatra, the old nostalgia king. Eeny, meeny, miney mo. *This one*. Luck be a lady tonight. Alec smiled. He felt about eighteen years old, hoping for the best on a first date and fearing the fracture of a mood. Because they *did* get along. She listened about his elephants, and they laughed together at the shyness which made the luncheon conversation a travesty on a travelogue. But you couldn't go on forever with a steady diet of zoology.

This one. Sinatra. And *what* a collection for a blind choice! The all-time creamers. "When the World Was Young." "I'll Remember April." "September Song." Jackpot, for very damned sure. And "A Million Dreams Ago" and "I'll See You Again" and "There Will Never Be Another You" and "Somewhere Along the Way" and "These Foolish Things" and "As Time Goes By" (play, Sam, it got Bergman) and "I'll Be Seeing You" and "Memories of You."

Barr, you incredible man. You and that "September Song" knock with the book signature. Thank you, Frank Sinatra. Thank you, Capitol Records. And thank you, thank you, thank you, all you wonderful composers with your little old tune-pickin' fingers. God bless ASCAP.

Alec twisted the various knobs. "I'll start with good old 'When the World Was Young,' and hope she can hear me in the kitchen, wherever she's at, and maybe that'll fetch her with the flowers," he murmured, and turned up the volume on Axel Stordahl. The fragile music touched the haunting button in him, as the better old ones always did, and he sat down and brooded happily into the fire. The brooding called for a drink, and he went over to the whisky tray. Ice, he noted, had been freshly placed in the copper bucket, an unusual happenstance in an English home. Mrs. Thing was obviously well trained.

She was by God a wonderful girl; veteran of the wars, bedwise if not bedworn, and *simpática* in all the ways he had sought. There seemed to be that sincerely honest interest in him, no signs of possible jealousy, and an intuitive knowledge and understanding of his marital posture. They hadn't gotten onto the topic of Amelia yet, but her cool acceptance of his presence argued that she knew damned well that he and Amelia were merely formal partners in a dreary marital dance.

"World" had quit, with Frankie's fine glissandos in full form, and now "I'll Remember April" was beginning. Alec rose and turned up the volume a little louder. This was a real goose-pimpler, too, if you were old enough. And she was old enough. You didn't have to *explain* things like depressions and wars.

Alec sighed. This modern generation, he thought, and was shocked to realize that he was no longer referring to his own age group. He did not, positively did *not* know what they thought or felt or did. They had not known poverty, not known war, not known real fear. They worshiped speed, hot rods, and motorbikes, dressed sloppily in each other's clothes, ruined their eyes on TV, got engaged at twelve and married at fourteen, listened to nasal music that would stampede cattle, and appeared to be unable to read or even talk coherently. Young Penny—*young* Penny, my foot—had been a pleasant exception, but then young Penny was old enough to have been to college, to be married and divorced, and young Penny had been reared by a wise mother. *This is a hell of a time to be thinking about a couple of other women,* Alec thought. Well, here it comes, good old "September Song." *Where the hell is Jill?*

Sinatra's voice eased into the room, tenderly cultivating each word of the lyric. It didn't have the rough sincerity that John's old man, Walter, had given it in *Knickerbocker Holiday,* but then Walter Huston *was* an old man and had spoken the lyrics in tones cracked with true emotion. Sinatra was only Alec's age, and his phrasing was smoother than anybody's. And on this one Sinatra was trying. The words came slowly, beautifully; and then the ones so well remembered:

> For it's a long long time
> From May to December
> But the days grow short
> When you reach September . . .

She entered the room before the reprise. Sinatra was backtracking slowly into:

> September, November,
> And these few *precious* days,
> I'll spend with *you* . . .

She was wearing a simple, clinging, ivory-velvet housecoat flaring from her hips and flowing graciously to the floor. Her face came sweetly as a flower from the high neck of the gown with big buttons down the front.

Her hands hung straight by her sides, palms out, fingers slightly curled.

"I've come to be collected," she said.

94

"Your timing was absolutely perfect," Alec said, much later. "No, not *that*. I don't mean what you think I mean."

"I know exactly what you mean, darling," she said. "I knew it was Number Three on the recording. I played it several times last night after you left, and had difficulty in not rushing straight over to the Savoy. From 'When the World Was Young' takes exactly sixteen minutes to the reprise of 'September, November.' It barely gives a girl time to make herself presentable. But I must say you were terribly decent about making the fire and shuffling through the other records."

Alec sighed.

"You really can't beat 'em. You just have to join 'em."

"I'd say we've joined very nicely," she said, and giggled.

Alec raised his head from the pillow and slung his legs over the side of the bed.

"What about the roses?"

"I suppose the poor things are still lonely in the kitchen. I haven't given them a thought since we got home."

Alec lit a cigarette.

"Don't you think something should be done about the poor roses?"

Jill took the cigarette out of his mouth and crushed it out. She drew him gently back to bed.

"Let the bloody roses dwindle down to a precious few," she said. "We haven't got time for a waiting game."

"This could never happen in Paris," Alec said against her mouth. "Not even in the springtime."

They had dined magnificently on caviar and champagne

and Danish-ham sandwiches and the other side of the Sinatra record. The talk was free and easy, and the jokes were fewer, and there had been no probing into pasts, no mentions of dead or divorced husbands or lovers, no inquiries about Amelia. There was no more pointed reference to "September Song" or dissections of why they had come so easily to couch. At a very early hour they yawned simultaneously and Alec followed Jill obediently to bed again. The last was as easy as the first, and Alec slept without thrashing, his hand cool on Jill's warm flank, buttock occasionally turned companionably to buttock. He had awakened feeling fresh, and very, very loving, and now here it was the last day of the year.

95

Alec walked over and gazed out of his broad window toward Festival Hall. He occupied one of the better river suites in the Savoy, and the Thames, framed by frosted trees, rolled smoothly black and wintry to his view. The Savoy, God knows, was old and faded-shabby in some of its quarters, but it never failed to excite him—just the idea of actually being in the Savoy excited him. Today the Savoy didn't excite him.

Jill had gone off to the hairdresser's after a long lunch at Les Ambassadeurs—they had finally gotten around to outside movement—and Alec had returned to his hotel to read the papers and, later, change for New Year's Eve. He was keeping his suite, although his nights would be spent in Jill's house. He thought, rather primly, that moving in bag and baggage was more than a bit presumptuous.

It worked well, actually. Leaving after breakfast, the trip back to the Savoy gave Jill a chance to go about the things women did, and it gave Alec a chance to shave and shower and dress for lunch. Women were fine; women were wonderful, but the luxury of bathing and dressing leisurely apart from female presence was an important thing to a man. Alec felt at ease in Jill's bed, at home in the drawing room, and comfortable in the kitchen. But there were too many girl-things in the bath for close communion between the sexes, and they ran collision courses in the bedroom when Alec was struggling back into his pants. It seemed simpler to return to the Savoy with a shadow of whisker, to stare down the doorman as he entered in last night's clothing.

There was the selfish time, too, of unshared newspapers, and perhaps one pink gin in the American bar before he took the cab to meet Jill for lunch. Seeing her freshly was an evocation of the first meeting—watching her face come brightly through the door promised pleasures already enjoyed but not yet fully explored. The thought *This is my girl* delighted him as he rose to meet her.

The prelunch selfish aloneness was marvelous, but this latish-afternoon aloneness was another thing entirely. He stalked his suite on leopard legs, scowled at the afternoon newspapers, and hurled a copy of *Time* across the room. He had, he thought, more than enough time on his hands, and not even a dentist's appointment to fill it.

"Face it, friend," he said. "You're stuck. You're lonesome for a woman who has only been out of your sight an hour. You won't be seeing her until six, and it is now only four."

Suddenly the marvelous, wonderful, twenty-two-guinea-a-day Savoy suite with its view of the coconut-icinged trees and the black rushing Thames and the Festival Hall oppressed him. He was lonely, just plain damned lonely, for a woman with whom he had only just slept last night, with whom he had breakfasted in the ridiculous skimpy robe she had lent him, with whom he lunched at Les A., and without whom he had spent all of his life until now.

He put on his overcoat and walked down the passageway and out into the Strand, past the Coal-Hole entrance, past the chemist, past the haberdasher, past the pipeshop and gun-shop and bookstall. He could think of nothing to buy, for himself or Jill. Presents for Jill would come later. Presents for himself he didn't need.

London's inviting winter dusk did not as usual rouse him. In past years he could have spent hours caressing weapons in Westley-Richards or Purdey's, or he might have gone to Rowland Ward's to browse the books and chat with the manager about trophies and records. He had a guest membership in Buck's, and there was always the British Museum. Now he strode the Strand, on one side, crossed the street at the bottom and walked back on the other side, counting milk bars and clothing stores. He might have gone to Hatchards to wander among the books; he might have rung up his London agent or his publisher. He was acutely miserable, and the minutes stumbled by on club feet.

Finally he went back to the Savoy and ordered a corsage of ivory-and-green orchids. He rechecked to see that his table for the evening's festivities was correctly booked. Then he walked down to the press relations office, hoping that someone he knew was in, but Jeannie had gone off to America and there were only new faces. When Jeannie was around she was always ready for a drink and a chat, to fill an idle afternoon.

He went to his room and picked up the *Time* from where he'd flung it, and read the same story three times before he rang for the room waiter and some ice. He mixed a drink and checked his evening wardrobe—no tails, or perhaps he might have wasted some profitable time buying a topper from Chipp. The dinner jacket was freshly pressed. He counted his studs and looked to his pumps. Then he grappled with his big decision.

And Alec had a big decision to make. He had decided to spare himself the first week of the conference opening in Brussels, and had so informed Jill. But the time seemed so dreadfully short. It seemed so foolish to desert such a fresh fund of loving companionship to push off to a chill dull city of which he knew nothing except that it owned a famous post-card statue of The Pissing Boy and a rather myopic, involuntary young King. Leaving London to hover over endless conferences which would all be covered in the overnights he could easily read in the papers or pluck from the file at the United Press seemed bloody stupid, especially when he held Jill warmly close. Nobody ever learned anything covering conferences. You went to the places which the conferences might affect and dug for the reaction there. There was a valid excuse for delay too. He needed several visas for exotic hogwallows like Sierra Leone, the Cameroons, and Gabon, and some had not as yet been granted. He couldn't afford *not* to visit Doctor Schweitzer.

Until now he and Jill had contented themselves with surface discovery of each other. They chatted and related anecdotally from the past, but the chats were beginning to bend toward pointed talk, and the relating to relationship, and the anecdotes moving to the threshold of serious plan.

Alec could sense it; he could smell it and touch it. This was no one-night, one-week, one-month toss. There was too much woman to consider, and all the woman that was there he was prepared to love—no, not just love. To really be in love *with*.

Bed was great. Bed was fine. Bed was dandy. Their bodies came as easily, sensitively, together as their adjustment to seriousness, sharp wit, or silly damfoolishness. Nothing she did in or out of bed grated on him.

She was no sexual gymnast, and bed with Jill was no formal exercise in amatory calisthenics. There was no frightening atomic explosion, where all the stars fell down and the earth sundered, but rather one long, mounting, conscious climb to the summit of a blissful hill with a final plunge over the edge of joyous life into ecstatic death, but always with the sure knowledge of immediate fleshly reincarnation after an eternity of consummate spiritual peace. Sex with Jill, Alec thought, was no brutal encounter. It was a long loving stroll, hand in hand, toward an absolutely certain destination.

Out of bed she was considerate, pleasantly ribald, occasionally caustic, serious when it matched his mood, and deliciously able to pierce solemnity with a bright sunlit shaft of ridicule. She liked to do small things for his pleasure without making them appear to be a chore. And Alec had the feeling that in any crisis she would cope without hysteria; that, once decided, she would proceed directly on her own charted course with complete disregard for consequence. There was a toughness seeded in her gentleness that one felt instinctively, like heat radiating from the internal wires of a warming pad.

Alec Barr had no easy explanation for the electrodynamism which had drawn them straight into each other's arms—a thing that Jill now confessed she had felt that night in Clarke's, even before introduction.

Of course there was the purely sensual pleasure of watching her. She had unusual brows and lashes for a bright redhead; they were not of the pinkish persuasion, but a very dark roan, and needed very little in the way of assistance. She looked as well with a scrubbed morning face as she did when she was made up for the street. Naked she was a revelation, but to Alec she was more exciting when primly clothed. There were no bolsters or buttresses necessary to her body; the breasts were high and firm as a girl's, and when she wore Capri pants without a girdle her backside marched trim and unjiggly. The long legs delighted him even more in stockings or trousers than when he stroked the complete extension.

He loved to watch her walk; he loved to watch her sit and cross her knees; he loved the fluidity with which she left a room or climbed a stair or entered a taxi. Whether she lit a cigarette or touched her hair or fixed a flower, the motion was one great gracious ripple. Everything she did gave him enormous pleasure, and he found himself thinking in terms of Cole Porter.

Reflecting on her essence, watching her with people, even in these few days, Alec decided that her chief attraction was the generation of purest delight. She lit a room when she entered it. She was not beautiful; the nose was snubby and the mouth too wide and funny-tipped at the corners, and the hair was really carrot when you came down to it. But she glowed from within, and the world warmed itself in the incandescence.

On the strength of precious-few days, Alec Barr was prepared to spend the rest of his life being in love with Jill Richard, and now the decision-business arrested him again. Spending the rest of his life being in love with Jill Richard involved divorcing Amelia, and Alec Barr shuddered at the idea. He was about to become a busy boy again. And he was, Alec forced himself to admit, a selfish man. Divorces were rare in his background of raising, and never pleasant. Divorces represented the subdivision of dogs and children, if you had any; the fission of library and furniture and money and everything which had been mutually built, including the flowers in the garden and the plants in the pot. Divorces involved scenes, and nasty ones at that. And divorces involved lawyers and courts and custodies and money and tension. Divorce was not a healthy climate for a writing man to work in, but Alec knew few writers who had cloven to the same woman. Hemingway was on his fourth; Steinbeck on his second or third; and the only thing that had saved Fitzgerald from multiple matrimony was his wife's lunacy and the alcohol that killed him. Scott had lived ostensibly happy, if painfully sober, with Sheilah before he pegged out, according to her own account. Perhaps Sheilah was content to be a mistress. One thing you can bet your life on, Alec thought grimly, is that my girl Jill, no matter how easily we came to bed, will *not* be content to be a mistress.

"And there, Barr," said Alec, "is your big decision. It's a little larger than a flock of Congolese coons in a blackmail conference in Brussels. Will we wed the wench, or will we keep right on being part-time lover boy and full-time jerk?"

One thing for certain, there'd have to be some strong summit talk. They had avoided the close personal inspections of the past because they had been too busy jabbering happy-talk and making happy-love. There were a great many items on the agenda. Who wanted to love where, and how much? Alec had no idea what a divorce would cost, but he did accept with basic fairness that his marriage with Amelia had not been one of those Hollywood-type one-night stands, and that she deserved full fair portion of his goods and chattels. The Jersey house would have to go, he thought, it cost too much, and Amelia would surely want to keep the big penthouse. Authoring was a dicey business at best, and now Alec wondered if he could even afford a divorce. If Amelia hit him for a really big settlement. . . .

Finally six o'clock came, and there was Jill at the door, wearing a three-piece, very heavy green tweed outfit, cheeks blazing from the cold, hair sparking from the hairdresser.

"You're two minutes late," Alec growled. "If you think I've got nothing better to do with my time than hang about waiting for women to go to the hairdressers you're—"

"What?"

"You're dead right." He smiled. "My God, it's been a long afternoon. I've missed you horribly. Is that wrong?"

"That's right," she said. "Are you going to buy me a drink or just make me stand here or what?"

"*What,* I think," he said, and kissed her cheek. "After the drink. But then you'd have to dress again, and then go home, and undress again, and then I'd go home with you, and have to undress and dress again and then come back here and put on my fancy pants and so I suppose we'll just settle for a drink. God, modern living is complicated."

"I think you're an idiot," she said. "But I have a sound suggestion. You put on your fancy pants and then come home with me and we'll smear a little more of that caviar on a piece of toast and then you can talk to me while I dress, but only through the door. No peeking permitted. I bought something special I've been keeping for a treat and no treat has come along until now."

"I'm the treat?"

"You're the treat."

"It would be a pity to muss that new hairdo."

"Don't worry, young man," Jill said. "I'll keep until after midnight."

96

Alec had turned on the hi-fi and was down in the kitchen prowling through the pantry and the frij. Jill kept a nice bachelor house, he thought. Her pantry was a fortress, full of savory things from Mr. Fortnum's masonry. There was a deepfreeze laden with basics against a long cold winter. The booze stood in honest ranks along the shelves, and there seemed to be enough pickles, relishes, cheeses, biscuits, olives, tinned seafood and *pâtés* and tongues and chili and similar staples to make eating less than an arctic adventure. He lit onto a can of chives, found some lovely-looking brown bread in a pressure tin, uncovered some fresh onions and celery and hard-cooked eggs in the refrigerator, and decided to play chef. His caviar tray, when he finished, would not have shamed M. Henri Soulé in New York's Pavillon. He buried a bottle of champagne in a bucket and popped a couple more into the deepfreeze against future need. This seemed like vodka night, so he stuck a bottle of vodka as close to the freeze unit as it would fit.

He whistled as he created confusion in the kitchen. This was fun, picnicking out of somebody else's storehouse, coat off, a ridiculous apron of dishtowel around his waist. He would prepare this fine tray of caviar and half-frozen vodka and plump his green-ivory orchid spray in the middle, and serve it with a heraldic flourish to some appropriate New Year's Eve rondelay on the hi-fi.

He was not bored now, in his boiled shirt and apron. He had fixed the fire—that was fun—and had fixed the music— that was fun—and now was fixing the caviar with trimmings, which was also fun. More fun than those thousand parties they'd been invited to—*she'd* been invited to—and had turned down for a table at the Savoy.

Damn, but the lady was taking a lot of time over her toilette. He had yelled a few rude things at her, up the stairs, and once had fetched her a drink, which she took with a bare anonymous arm through a cracked door. Peculiar little brutes, women. Shameless mother-naked, but very wary of letting the male animal observe the processes of raw-material transformation into a work of public art. Be a very strange thing to be a woman. A lot of unhandy aspects to be complete package of sugar and spice.

Alec wished it was New Year's Day proper, and over, and they were out of the crowds, and back here in front of the fire. Contrived festivity horrified him, but on New Year's it was necessary to get yourself all starched and shiny to go out and kiss a lot of people you didn't know and yelp "Whoopee!" at the top of your lungs.

He arranged his caviar tray to his satisfaction, set the glacine-boxed corsage in the center, gave the champagne another twirl in its bucket, and poured the vodka in tiny glasses nesting in ice-filled coffee cups. He took off his tea-towel apron and put his dinner jacket on again. Then he went to the foot of the stairs and yelled:

"Which New Year's Eve did we have in mind?"

"This one," she said. "Retreat to a respectful distance. I may be overpowering."

She paused at the head of the stairs, and twirled.

She was wearing a dress of simple black—velvet, it appeared—with a deep V which displayed the top halves of her breasts. There was a necklace of emeralds depending to the hollow of those breasts, and emeralds in her ears, emeralds around her wrist. The fresh-wrought hair was swept high, and the effect was symphonic; cream and green, eye and gem matching, skin ivory against the velvet, the red and green and the cream and the black steeping straight out of a portrait of a highborn lady.

Alec bowed, deeply, ceremoniously.

"Your humble servant, Ma'am," he said. "I am stunned."

"You were meant to be stunned," she said, coming slowly down the stairs. "That's what took me so long. Like the special frock?"

"Don't call that extra layer of furry black skin a *frock*," Alec said. "Anything under it?"

"Don't be rude," she said, and held out one hand, high, to be assisted from the last step to the hall floor. "Of course there's something under it. *Me*."

"I never danced with a duchess," Alec said. "Now I don't need to."

"That was sweet—and so is this!" She had seen Alec's elaborate effort at cocktail presentation on the coffee table. She kissed one finger and touched his nose. "I never knew you'd be so handy around the house, and oh, bless you darling, I hadn't noticed the orchids."

Alec shrugged.

"Flowers for you aren't too hard to select. Orchids with freckles to match the ones you've tried to conceal this evening."

"Why bother to go to Africa? Why don't you just stay on and run the house, choose my clothes, supervise the kitchen —you know, make a career for yourself?"

"I am a writer," Alec Barr said proudly. "And also, I'm too pretty to work."

97

The little ormolu clock on the mantel chimed.

"My God," Alec said. "We've been sitting here for three hours and three bottles of champagne. Where could the evening have fled?"

Jill yawned.

"Happy evening. Fire and music and caviar and champagne and handsome fellow. Very much talk." She shook her head. "I never knew two people had so much to talk about. I expect I'd better run a comb through my wig if we're going to get to the Savoy. It's *eleven* o'clock."

"We missed several hundred parties," Alec said. "If we hurry we can get to the Savoy just in time for the duchesses to start putting on paper hats, and well before people start pinching other people's bottoms. You hungry?"

"After all that buffet you fixed? Scarcely. Well, up and away, I suppose." She got to her feet. There was a fireflush in her face, and the hair was touched with gold.

Alec took her by the elbows.

"I wish . . ."

"What do you wish? It's a little early in the evening for wishing."

"I wish—I wish we didn't *have* to go to the Savoy. You're much too lovely to share with a flock of noisy drunks all singing, 'Auld Lang Syne,' popping crackers, hurling confetti, and wearing silly hats and kissing strangers. I wish I could keep you here, all to myself, so that we could own a private piece of the New Year."

Jill looked at him steadily. She drew her fingers lightly over her hips and thighs, touching the velvet softly, caressingly.

"After all this effort, all this production, you really don't want to go out and show me off to the howling mob? I'm to consider all the fancy costumery wasted?"

"Not *wasted*. Richly spent on a man who loves you, to the exclusion of all others, and who doesn't want to share you with anyone tonight, not even by so much as a glance."

"In that case," Jill said, "in that case, I don't see why we should worry any more about my makeup. Would you say we had to wait for the stroke of twelve for the New Year's kiss?"

A moment later Alex said:

"I promise you I'll even sing 'Auld Lang Syne' if it'll please you."

Jill sat down and kicked off her shoes.

"I'd rather hear 'September Song' again," she said.

Well after midnight Jill said:

"Was that thing you said about 'the man who loves you' a figure of speech?" Her previously carefully coiffed hair was tumbled, her eyes very bright. Earrings, necklace, and bracelet were heaped on the coffee table.

"It was not a figure of speech, God help me," Alec said. "I *do* love you—am so in love with you—and want to marry you. But there are a thousand things we have to talk about."

Jill shook her head.

"No. No plans. I am too full of bubbles and firelight.

Serious talk is for the cold gray light of the new day. Dance with me. Kiss me. And tell me again that you love me."

Alec held her lightly, swaying, murmuring against her hair. Suddenly she giggled, the little girl's giggle.

"I'm a touch tight," she said. "I see all sorts of sparkly things before my eyes. And we haven't even made any resolutions yet."

"I have," Alec said firmly, steering her toward the stairs. "One."

"I'll just have to share it with you," she said, leaning against him as they walked in stocking feet into the hall. "I haven't any resolutions of my own."

98

They almost never went out at night, but settled into a domesticity that was as homely as if they had been practicing it for years. Alec had decided to add another week to his London stay, bur refused to move his basic equipment from the Savoy. He wanted a formal address, and in any case he had to check in at the United Press offices once a day, just around the corner in Bouverie Street. There was certain other work as well: the finishing off of his visas, some reference chores at the library; lunch with the publisher at the Garrick, a drink with his London agent, and a couple of transatlantic conferences with Marc Mantell.

Jill had asked him to move in, she didn't care a damn for what the neighbors thought, but Alec stubbornly refused. He was happy to spend his nights there, and a good portion of the mornings.

Their routine was almost invariable. Up, breakfast, out, hotel, bath, shave, dress again, appointment or United Press, meet Jill for lunch, another appointment, meet Jill for cocktails or early movie, and then home to Chester Square for a lazy evening by the fire and something simple from the kitchen. Occasionally they watched television.

Mostly they talked. There seemed to be a thousand things to discover, a thousand plans to be made in the short time

Alec could devote to London. Alec had asked her if she
would like to come with him to Africa. She shook her head.

"I'd love it—some other time. But you've work to do and
you need freedom of foot. No, my love." She shook her head
again. "You'll travel faster alone. Get the work done faster,
and come back to me faster."

"It'll be a long six months—maybe even a year," Alec
stubbornly. "I don't know if I can make it without you for
a year."

"There's no real reason why you couldn't come back here
to finish your articles, put the book in shape. And then you
could start the machinery on the divorce."

Now Alec shook his head.

"This divorce is going to be tricky enough without giving
Amelia any easy ammunition. We will have to play it very
cool until the settlement's made. My marital track record
hasn't been exactly without blemish," Alec said. "If she gets
the idea that I want this divorce very badly . . ." He
shrugged.

"Beating the income taxes on this," he said, "is about
the only way I'll be able to afford both Amelia and you. If
only . . ." he let his voice drift.

"If only what, darling?"

"I know Amelia doesn't really like my Jersey house. If
somehow I could salvage that from the wreck. . . . Would
you mind terribly living in the country for most of the time,
if we could keep a small flat in town for late nights and
theaters and things?"

Jill rose and kissed him.

"I've always lived in cities," she said. "But I'll still live in
a tent, if necessary. All I want is my clothes, about six
books, and to be with you. But maybe we might even decide to live here in London permanently? I mean, if she
takes the Jersey house?"

"No," Alec said. "America's my home. I don't think I
could play the expatriate bit very satisfactorily for very long."

"All I want is the rest of my life with you," Jill said. "I
don't care where. Just hurry, please."

Alec turned to face Jill.

"Amelia and I have been married a very long time. You
just don't knock an association of long duration in the
head, like you'd slaughter an ox. It's a distracting business,
from all I've observed. Did yours distract you much?"

It was the first time they had really discussed personalities. They had continued to skirt each other's past incumbents with a delicacy touching on fright.

Had her voice stiffened just a little?

"It was very painful *before* the act," she said. "My first husband was an impossible man. I felt dreadfully sorry for him but I was quite young and could see no point to both of us going insane. Nicholas? I don't really know. I had lost a lover in the war, and when Nicholas came along and wanted to marry me I suppose I married him because he wanted it. I was still in a sort of state of shock over Martin, the—the man I loved very much who was killed.

"But no divorce is very nice. Somehow when the lawyers finish pawing at it anything that had been nice has gone. Divorce is quite a price to pay for a new love." She narrowed her eyes. "It has a way of winging home to roost, sometimes, when the new love for whom the divorce was bought might not seem really worth the effort."

Alec watched her face. She paused, and then went on.

"The last venture with Nicholas certainly put me off the marriage idea until now. I've been happy. I have friends— good friends. I never lacked for—for beaux to take me out if I wanted to go out. And I didn't go out very much. I did not want to muck up my life again. I wanted serenity, and I still want serenity. But now I want somebody to be serene *with*. I felt fated toward you. I feel we're right, with most of the mistakes behind us."

"Amen," Alec said. Then, lightly, "What's going to happen to all your host of admirers—the card-senders that you so blithely swept off the mantel the other day—when you take up steady with a bloody Yankee author?"

Jill smiled.

"There's only one really persistent chap. He's terribly nice. Quite a bit older, widowed, well-off, social, kind, and very-very punctual. The only thing is that he's a stockbroker and goes to The City every day, and I never could abide bowler hats. Also I don't love him."

"Poor Miles," Alec said. "How do you feel about ancient authors with a square mile of unfilled white paper to fight?"

"I'd like a chance to marry one," Jill said.

99

They were sitting before the fireside a few days later when the phone rang.

"Oh, hello, darling," Alec heard Jill say. "Of course. And Happy New Year to you, too. I only just got back from Paris." She rolled her eyes at Alec, and covered the receiver. "Miles."

"But of course *not*. Now? I'm having tea with a friend—an American friend who is just passing through. On his way to Africa. You may have read his books. *Barr*. Alexander Barr."

She nodded at Alec, lifting her lids again.

"But I'd be delighted to give you a drink, and I'm sure he'd be delighted to meet you, too. But please make it soon, darling, as I really must rush out, and I haven't dressed for dinner yet. I was just going up when you rang. Of *course*. Good-by, darling."

She cradled the phone and turned to Alec.

"Not very much I can do about that," she said. "He's just across the way, and he rang to see if I were back from *Paris*. He wants to call by for a drink and to meet you. D'you mind terribly?"

Alec smiled.

"Of course I don't mind. I've got the girl. And I confess I'm curious to see what my rival looks like."

"Ex-rival. And as I told you, he's really quite sweet. But he's Old Etonian and has several medals and was a colonel in the war and is apt to chuff-chuff a bit. I rather imagine you'll like him. *I* do."

"I shall stone him with a martini," Alec said. "And then I'll steal his old school tie. But I will not buy any of his bloody bonds and shares."

"Chances are he wouldn't try to sell you any. He'd think it frightfully infra dig. He has *persons* who handle the more sordid aspects of his profession."

Alec thought privately that Jill had rather played down her

481

boy friend's qualifications. Miles was quite florid, certainly, but his mustache was close-clipped and gleaming white against the slightly sirloin skin, as was the abundant silver hair. His eyebrows were black—dye?—and his blue eyes were very keen and completely steady. He was a bit overweight and not too terribly tall, perhaps five eight or nine, but his blue pinstripe testified eloquently to the best of British tailoring, his hard collar sustained the old school tie, and a carnation couched crisply in his buttonhole.

Jill held up her cheek to be kissed, then turned to Alec.

"I should like you to meet an old friend, Alexander Barr, Miles," she said. "Alec, this is Colonel Miles Chalmers, a very dear friend."

Colonel Chalmers' grip was firm and dry.

"Not meaning to intrude," he said. "But I was only just passing by. Worth risking a ring. Terribly pleased to meet you, sir, and honored. I've read everything you've written, I believe. Jill tells me you're on your way to Africa?"

"Correct." Alec liked the look of Jill's colonel. "Rather an impossible task. I'm supposed to cover the entire continent and reduce it to simple arithmetic."

"Sounds slightly staggering." The colonel turned to Jill. "Yes, I'd love a martini, if that's what you have in the mixing glass there."

The colonel stood in front of the fireplace, legs spraddled, as if he had stood there more than once before. He twirled his glass in his fingers.

"Never spent any time in that sub-Sahara theater," he said. "Spent hell's own time in the Western desert, though. Always had a craving to see black Africa. I envy you," the Colonel said. "I truly envy you. Not to shoot, but to see."

Alec nodded. "I feel the same way. Although I've shot."

"Shouldn't think you'd care for it much once it was dead," the Colonel replied. "Like foxes. Fun to see 'em run. Dreadful when the hounds have draggled 'em."

"Lions rumple very easily," Alec said.

"So do Japs," the Colonel said. "I switched to Burma after the desert. Germans don't seem to rumple as easily as Japs."

"Leopards don't rumple as easily as lions," Alec replied.

"Or girls," Jill interrupted. "Whatever are you gentlemen talking about, anyhow?"

"War," the Colonel said.

"And Peace," Alec added.

Jill advanced with the martini pitcher. The Colonel held out his glass.

"Just one more, and then I must dash." He looked at his watch. "Must meet some people. Hope you'll dine with me soon, Jill. You as well, Barr, if you're here any length of time at all."

Alec smiled. He liked Jill's brisk little stockbroking colonel.

"Perhaps on the return trip, sir," he said. "I'm afraid I'm about to snatch up my mack and my portable and do a dash in the next couple of days, which'll be fairly busy. Meanwhile I'm trying to monopolize as much of our hostess' time as possible."

"Can't say I blame you in the slightest. Well, I really must fly. Ring me when you've a free moment, Jill darling, and I shall buy you a bean." He pushed out a firm hand once more to Alec Barr. "All the best in Africa," he said. "And I should really like to hear about it when you return. I'm findable either at the office or at White's. Good night. *Bon voyage.*"

"Good night," Alec said, and walked to the fire while Jill escorted the Colonel to the door.

"Well," Jill was saying. "And what did you think of my best beau?"

"I liked him," Alec said. "I liked him a lot. I shouldn't want to go up against him in a proxy fight in a takeover deal. Or in a dark alley. Or in a war. I'm frightened of middle-sized round men. They don't have any edges you can knock off."

"Miles is rather a sweetie. But he does the pass the port to the left, and he will wear the round hat, and he will *never* tell anyone how he happened to win an MC and bar. And he is so punctual."

100

It seemed to Alec Barr that he had never lived permanently in any other place but the Norfolk or New Stanley hotels in Nairobi. He dwelt in one or the other according to the shortage of space. Sometimes he was lucky and got a cottage in the Norfolk. Sometimes he settled for a suite or a room in the Stanley. Sometimes he slept on the manager's divan. Nairobi was working headquarters, and the hotels were where he left his excess baggage and where his mail was held. He had grown very fond of the manager, a plumpish Liverpool Irishman with a big nose.

The manager, whose name was Burrows, was rapping on his cottage door. He held a brown envelope in his hand.

"Cables, Bwana," he said. "Your accrued mail is in my office at the Stanley. There's about a bushel of it."

"Come in," Alec said wearily. "I'm in the tub. How are you, chum? Would you be a nice guy and call a boy for some ice? There's a bottle of whisky there on the table. Jesus, I'm beat. Straight through from Angola. Read me the cable, will you, while I scrape some of this Africa topsoil off me. Who's it from?"

"The first is from your own true love." Burrows cleared his throat. "The second is from the office. You aren't going to like either. "Says, quote READING ABOUT CONGO FIGHTING AND TERRIBLY WORRIED STOP HAVEN'T HEARD YOU THREE WEEKS ARE YOU ALL RIGHT QUERY LOVE JILL. Unquote. Other one: JOB TOO BIG ONE MAN STOP EXPRESSING LARRY ORDE FOR ASSISTANCE. SCHELL. Unquote. And I already ordered the ice."

"Oh, God," Alec said from the bathroom. "Women and war. I suppose I'd better phone her. Any chance of getting a call through to London now? And this new boy? Guess they think the old man's getting weak in the legs. It's a kind of a slap in the face."

"Not now," Burrows said. "The exchange closes, you know. But I'll book one for you tomorrow."

"Tomorrow? Christ, I'm supposed to catch a slow camel for Somalia tomorrow. How long have I been gone this time?"

"Since they shot Verwoerd," the manager said. "Postpone the slow camel to Somalia and reassure the lady. Anyhow you got to wait for the new boy. Here comes the ice. Mix you something?"

"Anything, just so long as it's double," Alec said. "You know I've been out here eight months since I kissed that gal good-by in London? Seems like eight minutes."

The manager brought a glass of whisky to the bathroom, where Alec was toweling himself.

"Must say it agrees with you," he said. "You're a little skinnier, but you're as brown as a boot and seem healthy enough."

"Thanks, both for the drink and the physical check-up. Actually, I've never been happier in my life. Up to now I supposed I'd been working well and seeing the country. But, oh my God, this is a large hunk of land. Dinner tonight?"

"On the house. See you in the Grill. I must be off: I've complaints to deal with. I'll book your call for five tomorrow afternoon. You need a few days off, chum. The crumpet crop's not bad. There's a little—"

"Skip it. My conscience still tingles from a lady in the *Relais*. That's in Brazzaville, peasant."

"White lady?"

"I don't really remember. Winds of change, you know. It was all sort of vague. But I seem to recall she was a charming air hostess I met at the Club Caiman. She left early."

"I know, I know," the manager said, retreating. "She had a plane to catch."

101

Alec dressed slowly, savoring his drink. It was nice to be home again, to see Burrows again—what a nice guy he really was—and to get into some unsweated clothes once more. He'd been living out of one bulging suitcase for too long a time. Bush khaki was all right as a steady working uniform, but once in a while a fellow yearned for a white shirt and a press in his trousers.

Eight months. Eight months of what they called MMBA —"miles and miles of bloody Africa." But he wasn't kidding. It was all worth it. He had never felt better, although he supposed he'd been down with most of the aches and agues they produced in this bug-ridden paradise. He had lived off gin and paludrine, and in the absence of paludrine, merely gin. But he was writing reasonably well, and happy in his work.

He supposed he was overdue in his personal correspondence, and he felt like a heel about Jill. But somehow when you were desperately busy, catching a native bus one day, waving down a charter plane the next, lassoing a camel the next, tooth-jolting along in a jeep the next, you were more concerned with crotch rot and athlete's foot than with women. The women, even your far-off beloved woman, became misty in the memory, and it was strange how you didn't really miss them. Not so strange, come to think of it; he never missed them much during the war when he was at sea or stuck on islands for interminable stretches. And you got a proper set against hand-writing post cards when you were typewriting prose.

He had read and heard about white men and their dependence on native women in the tropics. He had been up and down and across Africa, north and south, east and west. Names jumped in his brain like electrical impulses: *Mogadishu. Addis Ababa. Luanda. Ruanda-Urundi. Luluabourg. Lizville. Stanville. Accra. Léo. Brazza. Kampala Nairobi, Mombasa, Dar-es-Salaam. Lumumba Gizenga Kalonji, Mboya, Kenyatta, Kasavubu, Balikongo, Tshombe. Verwoerd?* He'd been in Joburg the day Pratt shot him. And that poor old fat King, Mushenge. *Togoland.* Who the hell ever heard of Sylvanus Olympio before? Or Sekou Touré? Or Abbé Youlou? Or all of the new black faces and places that kept cropping into the news? Who had seen the ash-smeared women marching naked through the streets of Luluabourg? Who had seen the fighting outside Bakwanga? Who, for Christ's sake, had ever heard of Bakwanga before?

"Me," he said, knotting his tie. "Old Doctor Livingstone Barr. And it certainly seems to agree with me, like the man said. Even if I haven't grown a beard and taken up a life of shame with black *bibi*."

He hadn't been tempted, hadn't felt frustrated, even though the Congo was full of Belgian and French women, and Nairobi, on his frequent trips back to regroup, was populous with pretty English girls in short shorts. God knows Capetown and Johannesburg and Durban were overstaffed with females. But the only time he had fallen from fidelity was in the Hotel *Relais*, on the French side of the Congo, and that with a pretty Sabena lass who, like the man said, had an early plane to catch.

It had been all too wildly busy since he got off the plane in Nairobi, after deciding that nothing would break in the Congo until after Independence on July 1. He was dead right about that hunch. Sometimes using a white hunter as chauffeur-guide, sometimes on his own, he had scoured the closest country—by jeep from Nairobi to Somalia, plane to Ethiopia, down and across again to Portuguese West, Angola, cutting back to Gabon to spend a week with Dr. Schweitzer in Lambarene, meeting some rare and wonderful lepers, tame bongos, and Jewish refugee doctors.

The copy had written itself smoothly and piled up quickly when he occasionally took a week off and hived up in a hotel with his portable. The few cables from Marc Mantell were complimentary. Evidently the editors were happy with his file. Being around when Pratt shot Verwoerd had been a stroke of lucky timing. They were about to hang an Englishman named Peter Poole in Nairobi for killing a black man; he'd be around for that execution as well. It was the first time they'd ever strung up a white man for the sin of shooting a native in Kenya. If everything was going along so well, why were they shipping out an assistant?

Alec could see the collected pieces forming into a good, solid, comprehensive nonfiction book on Africa, the new Africa. It would have a great many nuggety things in it that the once-over-lightlies didn't know about—like the old chief with his five hundred and fifty wives; like Albert Kalonji, who declared himself King inside a budding democracy; like what he knew of the Jap leprologist with Schweitzer, like the wholesale castration in Ethiopia and Somaliland, like the border fights among the Turkanas and the Suks and Karamajong. . . . It would be a good book, even if it were basically compounded of magazine pieces.

But *somewhere,* planted more deeply, there was the book to be written—a novel—that was still evading him. Sometimes he thought he almost had it, and then it slipped away again. One day, he thought, the penny would drop and then he would have The Book, The Big Book, the one which had been sliding through his fingers for years. All of the rich stuff of old and new, of life and death, of black and white, of yesterday and tomorrow was here in changing Africa, and he, Alexander Barr, was going to stick around until he bloody well found what he sought.

102

Alec decided he would stroll slowly in the dusk down Government Road and savor the refreshing chill that came swiftly to Kenya at 7 P.M. He wouldn't pause for a drink here; the Norfolk veranda would be full of yahoos in pipestem cord pants and rolled-up shorts, all talking about returning to South Africa and all yapping at the top of their lungs. The people he had known in the country before didn't come to the Norfolk so frequently any more. They seemed to fancy the New Stanley since Burrows had moved his headquarters there, and the Grill was really a fine restaurant now, better than anything in Africa, almost as good as anything in London.

God it was good to be clean again, going to dinner in the dark quiet Grill, counting on seeing some nice chaps he kept meeting all over the continent. Nairobi was the nerve center of African coverage; you could only stand so much Congo or West Africa before you came back for a proper haircut and to get your face dry-cleaned. The town had grown enormously in ten years. It didn't even seem strange to see black faces in the Grill or the upstairs dining room now—black faces seated at the tables instead of waiting on them.

Let's see. Tomorrow he'd put through the phone call to Jill, although he dreaded it. He had phoned her several times before, from various cities on the continent, and the result always seemed the same. After interminable waiting, communications invariably broke down. The line faded and squawked and you wound up in frustration, as some African or Asian operator cut the connection just as you reached a pregnant point in your conversation. They'd chopped him off once—and it had stayed cut for two days—just as Marc Mantell was saying: "And the movie price is——" Try going to bed with that gap in your life sometime, he thought, particularly if you need the money.

Yes, tomorrow he'd surely ring Jill, who must be having a dreary time of it as his absence stretched into extra months. Unless the good Colonel, what was his name, Smathers or something like that, was still squiring her about. The Colonel—the name was Chalmers, he remembered now—made a beautiful stodgy stand-in for the kind of vibrant excitement that Alec Barr was supposed to generate. The Colonel wore a bowler hat, and Alec Barr wore a double-trimmed *terai* or a rakish police beret. The Colonel sold stocks and bonds and went to The City every day, while Alec Barr drank warm Bénédictine in the jungle with a fat native king and wrote magazine pieces and plotted bigger and better books and— you devilish dog, Barr—occasionally tumbled into bed with a passing acquaintance in a Congolese hotel whose portals were guarded by two enormous ebony gods. The Colonel wore an old school tie, and Alec Barr wore an air of debonair swashbucklery. But the Colonel was useful, and Alec was sincerely glad that at least his lady love had something to do with her evenings while Alec Barr was rattling around like Sir Richard Burton aprowl for high adventure.

Tomorrow he'd get himself thoroughly reorganized, and while he was putting through a call to Jill, he'd see if he couldn't get onto Amelia as well. If Jill were worried over his welfare—and that Congo fighting must be making an awful lot of headlines, with the United Nations all mixed up in it—Amelia must be more than slightly concerned. And it had been at least six weeks since he had written Amelia. If he didn't phone her—and it *did* seem difficult to talk to your wife and your lady-love on the same day—at least he'd flog off a wire saying nobody'd dined off him yet. Better cable Marc, too, for the inside on this new assistant.

That would be after he sorted out the mail which was doubtless arriving at his Norfolk cottage now. He didn't want to open mail tonight and consider nagging problems on the other side of the world. He didn't want to know the latest news about the misconduct of his mother and father and brother. He didn't want to hear any complaints from the Amelia front—and, oddly, he didn't want to read any recounts of the London social season or any edged importuning about his imminent return. He especially did not want to read any reminders about the contract to set the divorce machinery in motion once this assignment was up.

For a moment, Alec Barr hoped devoutly that the assignment would never end.

Well, here he was, at Hardinge Street, and there was the Thorn Tree, cluttered with outdoor drinkers still, in front of the brightly lit New Stanley. He'd go to the upstairs bar, not the Long Bar, which would be full of hard-core, seamy old-settlers bemoaning the winds of change, and have a couple of drinks with the transient gentry. There was bound to be somebody he knew—Peter Younghusband from the *Mail*, Ross Mark from the *Express*, one or the other of the newsmag boys. It would be pleasant to exchange a little gen—you couldn't cover everything in Africa at once. Maybe they were right about that little help: that extra pair of legs.

Then the expectancy of a good dinner with Albert smilingly polite, the native waiters happy to see the Bwana home again, and he knew exactly what he was going to have. He was going to have about thirty-six tiny Mombasa oysters, a Dover sole as big as a bathmat, a green, green salad, with Roquefort, and a *coupe* Denmark with three thousand calories in its chocolate sauce. He was going to drink a whole bottle of Chateauneuf du Pape, despite the fish, because he craved red wine tonight. And he was going to have a couple of brandies, and he was going to be very happy about the whole thing because his friend Burrows was paying. Then he and Burrows would go to the Equator Club for a while, and finally wind up in the manager's suite, drinking the manager's whisky, and playing the manager's music. He would get drunk and not go back to the Norfolk, but tomorrow he would awake with a hangover and face the chore he hated most—to get through to London to tell Jill Richard that he wasn't exactly coming home right now.

103 / Larry

The least he could do would be to meet the punk, Alec thought, and disliked himself for even thinking the word *punk*. Larry Orde was no punk. Young, yes, but punk, no. Nobody who graduated from the United Press' select finishing school called The Downhold Club was any part of a punk. Not if you worked for Baillie in New York and Lyle Wilson in Washington and Fergy in London—and didn't get canned —would you ever qualify for the word *punk*. No, Sir.

I'm getting old, Alec Barr thought, as he waited at Embakasi Airport for the big South African jet to flop in—he hoped, with better luck than just recently, when it skidded in with the wheels still tucked into its big fat belly. I'm getting old if I even *think* punk; I'm getting old if I resent assistance. Of course this goddam continent *is* too big for one man to blanket. I *do* need another pair of young legs and some bright keen eyes and some muscular enthusiasm that hasn't been entirely blunted by too many wars, too much booze, and too many women, not to mention over-scheduled airplanes.

Well, he shouldn't be hard to spot, and there he is. The red-hot assistant. God, but he looked so very young as he shambled across the blindingly white airfield, with the blazing Nairobi sun striking sparks off his roan hair, mildly haloed in the morning wind.

Alec whistled. He gestured from his perch on the wave-off platform, and pointed downstairs with his thumb. Orde grinned, dropped his portable typewriter, and shook his clasped hands over his head in the prizefighter's salute. Alec turned and went downstairs to wait outside customs. Orde wouldn't have any trouble. The typewriter would be battered enough to be classified as nondutiable, and if he knew young writers, Orde had made the weight allowance on baggage. He'd have to fix the clothes thing; Ahamed Brothers and the African Boot Shop would fit out the youngster in a hurry.

"Orde," the young man said, and stuck out a freckled

491

hand on which sun-whitened hairs were still restless from the wind. "You've got to be Mr. Barr. Nobody else would be meeting me."

"Barr's right," Alec said. "Welcome to our village. Been out here before?"

"Nope," the kid said, and grinned, showing square white teeth in a freckled snubnosed face. Wind or no wind, that red hair would never need a comb. The blue eyes were direct. "Harlem's about as close as I've come to it, unless you count Mississippi. I come to you pure."

"That sounds like a bloody lie, for starters," Alec said. "I read your big piece on the spy trial in Moscow. I used to read your daily stuff when you were UPing all over the place. Beirut was very specially good."

The kid's face lit.

"You read the Beirut? I had a lot of fun out there. I was a Marine myself once—in an old war. Korea."

Jesus God, Alec thought, feeling his whiskers turn snowy. An *old* war is *Korea?*

"I was almost a Marine once," Alec said. "I got lent to Larson on Guam. I guess I didn't quite cut it. First thing I knew they gave me to the Air Force—the Baker Two Nines —and then I guess I didn't make it with them, either. They gave me to the British Pacific Fleet, figuring I couldn't do much harm in Australia. That was in an *older* war." He grinned, trying to take the bite out of the adolescent attempt at establishing adult status.

"Come on," he said, and could not resist speaking Swahili. He clapped his hands at the porters and said: *"Sikia! Lete sunduku motocar yango, upese sana!* How many bags have you?" he asked, turning back to Larry Orde.

"Two. Valpak and an ordinary."

"Sunduku mbile," Alec said to the porters. *"Ile mkubwa na ile kidogo."* He pointed. *"Hapana hapa! Hapa pandi hi! Pandi hio!"*

"I think they search the local schools for dropouts for these porters," he said to Larry Orde. "Bloody *nugus.*"

"Your Swahili doesn't sound like mine," Orde said. "I guess I got the wrong book."

"Mine's what they call *ki-settler* Swahili, like Kitchen Kaffir. Baby talk. Trade language. What's yours?" He looked at the young man with fresh interest.

"I gathered," Orde said modestly, "that you were telling

the boys to put the little one and a big one in your car, and
that they weren't on this side of the customs bay, but on the
other side, and to hurry up?"

"That's right," Alec said, and felt rather small.

"Well, it wasn't all wasted then," Orde said. "I took a
month's crash course when I signed on for this job. But the
stuff they taught me sounded more like pure Arabic. Lots of
changeable prefixes and suffixes. Like one knife is *kisu* and
two knives are *wisu* and *mbile* gets to be *wawile*. Right?"

"God bless us all," Alec said. "We will stop for a drink
while they lose the luggage. You speak some more languages?"

The kid laughed and touched his outflanged ears.

"I'm a rabbit," he said. "I speak more languages badly
than any living man. The only thing that ever really beat me
was Basque and maybe Albanian. You can't tell my Russian
from my Italian, really, but I'm pure hell with sign language.
The French isn't really too bad, and the Spanish is passable,
and I can make it in butch Arabic, like *Hamdullilah!* Or
possibly *emshi!* The rest of it is 'nice clean seester.'"

"Well, they'll all come in handy," Alec said. "Africa has
been moved in on but very good in the last few months.
How's your Red Chinese?"

"That I ain't got—yet," the kid said. "But it'll come. You
have any ideas about where I stay while we sort out what
exactly I'm supposed to do to keep out of your hair while
I'm earning my pay?"

They were walking now toward the hire-car. Alec tossed
the porters two shillings each. The porters bowed and said
"*Asante sana, Bwana*" and departed.

"You won't hear that 'Bwana' very much pretty soon," Alec
said, sliding under the wheel. "It's going out of style, like the
kanzu and bare feet. As to your housing, I've got a suite.
It has two beds in it. I'd thought you could bunk in with me
—it's a cottage really—until we decide who's gonna do what."

"Fine," Larry Orde said. "My God, zebras! And those
things like buffalo, with the manes—wildebeest?"

"Right. Until very recently—at the old airport, especially,
they used literally to have to shoot them off the strip. White
hunters were called out an hour before plane arrival. I go
back *that* far," he said, again with a guilty sense of com-
placency.

"What's a *kanzu?*" the kid asked. Alec slid a curious glance out of the corner of his eyes. Boy's retentive, anyhow, he thought.

"A *kanzu* is a kind of nightgown that is classic on the Arab-leaning Coastal Strip, Mombasa–Malindi way, and it became the official uniform of the servants. White *kanzu*, red sash, and bare feet. Now the trade unions clamor for pants and tennis shoes, and you can't really make many African friends yelling 'Boy!' any more. Winds of change, and all that. Things've changed since Tom Mboya got his picture on *Time*'s cover. Big deal."

The rubber squished sweetly on the straight concrete road.

"Pretty flowers," Larry Orde said. "All this looks very new."

"It is, reasonably. They did it specially for the Queen. Those bougainvillaea are pretty special. Pretty soon it won't be the Queen's High Way any more. More likely Mboya Boulevard."

"What's he like, this Mboya?"

"Smart. Too smart by half, as the British would say. Power-seeker. Got very mean eyes. Slanty. Like a leopard. I think he really *hates* being black. That's possibly why he surrounds himself with so many white people. I think he *sees* himself as white, and one day he'll kiss his elbow and turn into a Swede. He doesn't really care very much for me."

"Any particular reason?"

Alec grinned.

"One. A few months ago His Imperial Highness, Kwame Nkrumah the First of Ghana publicly dumped him, and I asked Mr. Mboya how it felt not to be Nkrumah's bum-boy any more. I'd forgotten the British connotation. Mboya hadn't. Trouble with Mboya is he looked down on savage Africans. In his own words, he 'doesn't like naked niggeers with spears.' They've got to go. You won't believe it, but he even used the old cliché about breaking the eggs to make the omelette. This is going to be a mighty fine omelette, one of these days, when the real nut-cutting starts."

"I've been reading your stuff with a double-strength pair of glasses." Larry Orde was serious. "You really do know a hell of a lot about this piece of real estate, don't you?"

"Flattery will get you everywhere." Alec threw back his head, laughing. "It might even lead us into a serious discussion. I'd like to know if I'm being gently fired, replaced, or assisted. But it'll wait. I want you to meet a couple of chums of mine. One of them's the manager of the hotels. The other's the game warden. And there's a couple of local stringers around who can be helpful."

"Anything, anybody at all," Larry Orde said. "I'm out of my depth in a strange land and I feel like a jerk coming out to help—to assist—what the hell would the right word be?—to muscle in on your turf. Bear with me, please, Mr. Barr. I'm a young thing who cannot leave her mother. Or something."

"I ain't brooding about you," Alec said, turning right off Government Road to pull into the Norfolk Courtyard. "Here we are. Dear old Cottage Seven. If walls could talk—boy!"

"That bath you mentioned sounds just fine," Larry Orde said. "Maybe some people fly without feeling crummy. Not me. Even my fingernails smell bad. Forgive me if I ablute?"

"It's a nice use of the word," Alec said. "You'll find me on the veranda, counting Belgian refugees. We get a lot of customers out of the Congo these days. Happy sailing."

They sat on the veranda after lunch, comfortable in wicker chairs, feet propped against the half-wall that rimmed the porch.

"The letter explain anything?" Larry Orde asked. "My Lord, that was quite a curry. I'm still blistered on the innards."

Alec flicked the letter with a casual forefinger. He shrugged.

"Yep. It sure did. It told me what I already knew." His smile tugged downward at the corners of his mouth. "I'm too old for the racket. It didn't spell it, but it said it, loud and clear. And you know something, Larry? He's dead right. It's a young man's business, and the place is too big for one old gaffer."

Orde took his feet down, carefully, from the wall, and leaned forward, forearms braced on knees. The blue eyes were very candid.

"Tell me," he said.

"Some more coffee?"

"No thanks. Had enough. *Tell* me."

"You're running into a sad preview of *you*, twenty years from now," Alec said. "Strange as it may seem, full of piss and vinegar as undoubtedly you are, the *me* you're sitting with is a dreary foreshadow of *you*."

"Maybe I understand, maybe I don't," Larry Orde said.

"Make it easy for me, Alec. You know Schell. He didn't tell me much except to get off my ass and on my horse and rustle out here to work with you. He said you'd sort out the arrangement." Orde grimaced. "You know yourself, the money talks. I'm staff, not special. I go where the man says unless it gets entirely unbearable."

"In a very small nutshell," Alec said slowly. "You do the work. You get on the wild horse. I sit here—or very possibly in Léopoldville—on my ass. You are the legs; I am the backside. You report. I write what you report. We are back in the bureau business. I get the byline. You do the work. I feel like a pimp and you're supposed to feel resentful. You are my legs and I am your fingers. And the byline will read 'by Alexander Barr,' and it'll be your work, molded into passionate prose by old Dad here, as he sits in the breezes on this cool veranda while you die of crotch rot in the jungle. Like it?"

"No, I don't like it, but for a reason you may not have suspected." Larry Orde grinned crookedly. "I don't like it on *your* account."

"That's charitable of you," Alec said, and saw swift anger in Larry Orde's eyes. He held up a pressing palm. "No. Stop it. I didn't mean that to sound either condescending or snotty. I meant it in a true sense, like you used the word *ablute*. It's damned decent of you, Orde, to see my side of it. It isn't really very nice to be pastured because the arches are sagging and the old pezazz isn't there any more, particularly when you've spent the last six months trying to persuade yourself that you *are* thirty years old with a lot of ginger under your tail."

"Well, I didn't mean to be condescending, either," Larry Orde said. "I just meant to say that I don't mind doing the leg bit if you're happy to trust what I shoot you in the way of rough report. I don't care about bylines on this one; what I want to do is learn. And if the stuff I file is good enough for you to hang a byline on, I'm happy to be the unheralded half of the team. Okay?"

"Shake," Alec said, and shoved out a hand. "I think we will go far as an entry. Maybe as far as the bar."

Orde grinned again.

"For the moment that's far enough. Now that you're not going to have me poisoned by a pet witchdoctor, there are several million things I don't know that you can tell me."

"I pump easy," Alec said. "Brainwash me. It's your expense account now."

Young Larry Orde grinned again.

"Maybe they made a mistake in sending you a helper. That last crack sounded like you're just pushing into your prime."

"I been in the racket a long time," Alec said. "Just about as long as you are old. Frightening, ain't it?"

"It will be when I run into the same situation twenty years from now," Larry Orde's voice was quiet. "I hope I handle it as well. This could have been a bitch, you know that?"

"I know that," Alec said flatly. "Now let's stroll down life's pathway, hand in hand, to the bar, and bring your notebook. If you got questions, I wouldn't be surprised if I didn't have answers. Some, anyhow. We start out with Grandpa's first injunction: Never get mixed up with red-haired women who wear black underwear."

"I really don't want to sound like a Foxy Grandpa," Alec said. "But I have put in some time, as you freely suggest. One of the things you don't want to do is get yourself killed foolishly. And this is a foolish country, with a foolish war, run by foolish people. Nobody knows who's on first base from one day to the other."

"Wouldn't it be kind of hard to get hurt in a fracas like this? I mean I saw some iron and heard some noise elsewhere." Young Larry Orde dismissed the Congolese fighting with a curve of his hand. "It must be just a bunch of looters running around loose, and very probably drunk."

"You hit it right on the head," Alec said. "That's the trouble with it. They've got no defined front, no proper armies—hell, the commanding general was a medical attendant only a few months ago—and everybody's the same shade of black. But the risk is there, always because some self-styled patriot with a sewer-pipe musket thinks you're a Belgian spy."

Larry Orde grinned and his freckles spread, making Alec think suddenly of Ben Lea.

"I'm taking care of that," Larry Orde said. "I've got a United Nations armband and a tin of shoe-blacking. I aim to steal a blue helmet, give my face a high polish, and sort of melt into the scenery." He hummed a last line. " 'Dat's why de white folks call me Shine.' "

"What you haven't considered," Alec said, "is that the native runners haven't panted in with the latest bulletins. Either they are fighting in Kasai or not. Either that bearded jerk Lumumba had accepted a Red offer or he hasn't. Tshombe has just been captured, or is marching on Léopoldville, or is defending Katanga to the last copper mine. Believe it or not, they shot at Dr. Bunche the other day."

"Ralph's a little light for this area," Larry Orde grinned again. "I aim to be darker. What'll I do first, Boss-man?"

"I could suggest you go to Léopoldville and get yourself put in the picture," Alec said. "But the picture will change before you get yourself put in it."

"It sounds livelier in the Kasai, and one way of getting there is via Luluaburg. There's a plane out for that joint tonight."

"That was lively when I left," Alec said, signaling the waiter. "A lot of Lulua women marching naked through the streets."

"Sounds like the place for me," Larry Orde said. "Start with naked broads and hope for the best."

Alec tapped his shoulder with a finger.

"There was one thing a little different about these naked broads," he said. "When they marched through the streets they were smeared with ashes, and had just declared war. The next day they ate my chauffeur."

"Sounds like a fine town to start in, knowing nothing at all," Larry Orde said, and got up. "Léopoldville would only confuse me. I think I'll sling my junk together and head back to the airfield."

"No dinner? There are a couple of nice guys just back from the area who might be helpful . . ."

"No dinner. I wouldn't want to miss all those naked ladies marching through the streets. I'll keep in touch, Alec. File to you here?"

"Care of Burrows, the manager. He screens all my stuff and keeps me in touch if I'm off on my own. Take care, Larry. It's a big piece of real estate, and it buried a large number of white men."

"I'll take care. I'll take care, and you take it easy. I got long legs and small brains. I'll feed you whatever I've got as soon as I've got it. And say . . ."

"What?"

"I hope I don't let you down. If I do it won't be for lack of legs."

The waiter appeared with the check.

"Mine," Larry Orde said, threw a bill on the table, and walked away.

Alec Barr looked at the tall young body.

"I suppose I used to look like that—once," he murmured, and went off to the Grill to find his dinner companions.

104

Alec Barr got up from his typewriter, stretched, and dug his fingers into the dull ache over his right shoulderblade. He flexed his right arm, pumping it up and down. He could always tell when he had written a hot piece even though he'd been out of fast journalism for a long time. Today, nearly twenty years later, whenever he slung savage punches at the typewriter when he was angry at the story he was writing, the shoulder ached and his back felt terribly tired. And he was sore as a boil today.

"A pretty good topical piece for an old book-writer," he murmured, and walked over to the table to touch a silver coffeepot. The pot was cold. He shrugged, kneaded the aching shoulder once more, and then poured two fingers of Scotch into a slightly clouded glass. The ice had melted in the bowl, so he tipped the cold water into his glass. He took a sip and lit a cigarette. "Pretty good piece," he said again. "I wonder if anybody'll read it this year?"

His lips moved now as he slashed with the pencil, and occasionally his shoulders jerked slightly as he came to a tough verb or an apt adjective. This was what the office used to call a "Barr's-fed-up-again" kind of piece in the older, more satisfactory days.

"That'll do for a start," Alec Barr said as he folded the corrected pages and tucked them into a rubber-stamped brown manila envelope marked "first copy" in a corner, and then placed the corrected carbons in another envelope marked "second copy." The first plane might crash; the odds against a later mail not arriving were a million to one. He reached for the telephone to ring for a boy to collect his piece, but the operator's voice cut off his request before he began.

"I was just ringing *you*, Mr. Barr," the telephonist said. "It's Mr. Burrows."

"Put him on," Alec Barr said. "Come on over, Brian. I just finished some honest toil. I am a writer of leisure these days, now I've got myself a field assistant."

"That's what I rang about," the manager said. "I have a cable for you. You don't have an assistant any more. He just got himself killed. I'll bring the cable."

There was Burrows, looking pale and grim. Alec handed him a drink and took the cable to the light. He read it aloud, from habit, as if to convince himself that there wasn't any hidden stuff. It was marked G371 WASHDC 4545665 121P TRDIO. It said:

ORDE KILLED CONGOLESE ARMY MACHINEGUN COVERING FIGHTING BAKWANGA STOP ETRUSHING NEW ASSISTANT GOOD MAN ETUNDER YOUR DIRECTION HOW QUERY PREFERENCE SPECIAL QUERY BEST SCHELL.

Alec Barr reread the cable, then crumpled it and tossed it into a wastepaper basket.

He walked over to his typewriter and slid a cable blank under the roller. He punched rapidly at the keys, and ripped out the cable blank. He handed the cable blank to his friend, Burrows the manager.

"Send it for me, urgent," he said.

Burrows flipped a sloppy salute and went out the door. "You people do believe in saving words," he said.

The room boy came, deposited ice, accepted his tip, and left. Alec Barr built himself a new drink in a fresh glass, and sat down on the divan. He put his feet up on the coffee table and turned on the switch of his mind. Then he reached for the piece he had just written but had not mailed and reread it slowly.

There was the necessity of an Orde obituary in that story. It would fit nicely in the article. A dust-to-dust piece. Africa takes back its own. All men equal under six feet of dirt. Or at the end of the rope. There came that poor Peter Poole again. Would one fit the other? Could they be made to merge? What did they share, apart from the African earth? Poole had killed and had been killed as punishment. Africa had killed Poole as surely as Africa had just killed young Orde—as surely as Africa had killed missionaries and settlers and its own savage people in bloody tribal wars, in storms, in famines; bringing death by wild beasts, by fevers, by snakes, by arrows and spears and boredom and black-water fever and dysentery and malaria and sleeping sickness and booze. Africa wrapped everything in its great wet embrace, its hot, stinking, sweaty arms; like one huge jealous mother, willing to let her children stray just so far before she reached out and hauled them back to smother them.

I suppose they'll bury him on the spot, Alex thought. *Meat doesn't keep well in that climate.*

What did he know of young Larry Orde? Larry Orde was in his late twenties, maybe he was even thirty. The kid was just starting and had been frankly picking his seniors' brains. And Alec Barr remembered a long while back, when he had breathlessly combed over another man's whiskered knowledge because it all seemed so difficult then and too exciting to be borne. The short happy life of Larry Orde, who couldn't wait to die.

Well, he was a nice kid, big enough to have been a good Marine, maybe—too young for the last big war, and almost too young for more than a little piece of Korea. He was smart. There wouldn't have been much you needed to tell him. He undoubtedly came from a good family, but would have been tortured by the newspaper itch, and especially, very specially, he would have wanted to be a foreign correspondent. He had undoubtedly read all of the books and seen some of the movies. The laughing man in the dirty trenchcoat with the crushed fedora and the portable mill—that was the cynical hero who strode the earth, nourished by blood and soothed by the thunder of distant guns.

Alec didn't even know where Orde had gone to college, or even *if* he'd gone to college. He supposed he had, because everybody had money enough these days. He came from somewhere out West. The kid had obviously worked on one of the hick papers, and then had come to the Big Apple as a very young Washington correspondent for one of the chain's Western outlets. After a while he would have been kicked upstairs to work for the Bureau. In a very short time he would leapfrog over the other, wearier men, and would have been—had been—until just now, the top spot-news exclusive-type errand boy, for his enthusiasm was limitless and his digestion perfect.

It was a lovely life for a young man with no woman to

hold him at home. Foreign correspondence captured all the excitement of war, except that you were not so personally involved when you watched other people's battles. But the danger was there, if you were a good one and constantly went to where the shooting was.

Now Larry Orde was dead. Dead by the hand of a man he never knew, probably a man who doesn't even know who or what he shot at or if he hit it. Killed dead by some jungle brute who'd probably carve a steak off him if he had the time. Orde might have been killed by a bow, a spear, a poisoned stake in a gamepit, or a trip-noose. But killed dead, by God, as dead as if Adolf Hitler or Hirohito or Joseph Stalin or Mao Tse-tung had seen to it personally.

There is nothing deader than dead, Alec thought, whether they stretch your neck or strap you into an electric chair or hit you on the head with an H-bomb or introduce you to an unfriendly virus. Lawrence of Arabia lived a long time and copped it in a motorcycle accident; the banana peel and the bathtub beckon daily to the grave. Thinking of all the people he had known well who were dead, Alec Barr suddenly felt very old and tired and lonely.

Then Alec brought himself up short. Maybe Larry Orde was destined never to live long enough to grow cynical about anything, including the possibility of dying.

Being dead, in terms of permanency, meant no more women, no more rare steaks, no more moonrises and sun-sets; no more consciousness of autumn's clean woodsmoky tang; no more spring's tender-maiden vibrancy; no more winter's cold, smooth womanly serenity outside the fire's rosy core; no more pleasant, sweaty, sex-spent August lethargy.

He wondered idly about the girls Larry Orde had known. Young and handsome as he'd been, he must have known many. Of the hundreds how many would weep? More than one must have set a desperate cap for him. Some had known the warm presence of that young body, the first fumbling hands and hurried kisses, later the knowing assurance of habit, the it's-your-turn-to-bring-the-towel intimacy. No more of that for Larry Orde, no more sun-blessed picnics on the beach, with the warm, clean, salty-wet girl smell; no more the stroking snug of a well-cut dinner coat over the starched cool caress of a dress shirt and the cold-burning bounce of a martini before dinner. No more golf, no more water-skiing, no more bird-hunting; no more pleasant whiskey conversation over the lazy flutter of fire. No more thrills as the plane took off for strange, far places; no more stomach-twisting excitement as you came to ground in this new, strange, far place, to grapple with fresh problems; no more farewell waves, no more hello smiles. *Nothing*. No more sight, sound, smell, taste, feel. Just the great black void forever oblivious of the plodding passage of daily time into infinity.

Well, all the same things were common to a man like Peter Poole, weren't they? He had killed more than one African; some, perhaps, with justice. But the last one he had killed unjustly, as Larry Orde had been unjustly killed, so they had hanged Peter Poole last night for it. But they were both dead, and all the voids that applied to Larry Orde would apply to Peter Poole as well.

This was getting him nowhere. He placed paper in the machine and rubbed his palms together, polishing his thoughts, waiting for the lead to phrase itself. It was just like being in the newspaper business again. The lead always came. Somehow, it came. Now it came:

"Larry Orde was a young man of ambition and ability and luck," Alec wrote. "He was lucky because he did not live long enough to become cynical about the thing he loved, his work, which killed him in the jungled bush near the little town of Bakwanga in the Kasai Province of the Belgian Congo. He was joined in death by a young Englishman named Peter Poole, who was hanged last night in Nairobi Jail for the crime of killing an African. The young men had one thing in common: Africa killed them both as Africa has killed men since time began, regardless of their guilt, their innocence, or their color.

"Larry Orde . . ." Alec tapped his keys steadily. It would not be a very long insert, because he knew so little of the dead man he was writing about. But it would fit beautifully into the earlier piece. And what he knew about the country was too long, too complicated, to put into one story about an eager young man suddenly being forever stopped in time by a howling savage's innocently errant bullet. It seemed only a few short minutes before he was finished, as short as a life in present time.

He closed his typewriter case, poured another drink, and rang down to the desk to check airplane schedules to the Congo. Cradling the receiver, humming a monotonous tune, he began to pack, as he had packed a thousand times before. There were no farewells to be said: he would go to the Grill now for dinner, then he would go to the Equator Club for a few drinks, and then he would rise early enough tomorrow to snap shut his suitcase, sign his hotel bill, and fly off to the Congo again. He would know some of the men there. It suddenly seemed very important for Alec Barr to go to the Congo. One of the reporters would fill him in, and he would write another piece giving the exact details, so far as it was possible, of how Larry Orde met his death. And then he would begin to scout around for some more stories which would not be covered by the wire services and the straight-news reporters who were filing daily frontpagers on Patrice Lumumba's changes of mind.

When his leather shoulder-bag was packed with the necessities of writing, plus a carton of cigarettes, a bottle of whisky, and a couple of paperbacked novels; when his Valpak was stuffed with his spare suits and shirts; and when his scuffed typewriter case was latched firmly shut, Alec Barr, novelist, itinerant magaziner, would leave Nairobi to take up Larry Orde's adventure where it had ended so abruptly with a bullet from the gun of a Congolese soldier who was gulping greedily for the first time from the poisoned springs of licensed independence.

Automatically he checked the room. There on the writing table was the carbon which somehow had not been tucked into the office bag. Alec picked it up, and reread it out of old-packing habit. It said:

COSMICPRES WASHDC PARA SCHELL UNSEND REPEAT UNSEND NEW ASSISTANT EYE KILLING OWN SNAKES ETEYE KASAIWARDS SOONEST STOP YOU UNWANT ME SOLO SEND NEW BOY THEN UPSTICK JOB ASSWARDS STOP OTHERWISE UNHOW BARR.

Alec threw the cablesed carbon into the wastebasket. It was only on the plane that he remembered he had not yet been able to complete the phone call to Jill Richard in London.

105 / Alec

Mike Denton was a professional hunter. He was currently without client. Alec Barr had hunted with him before. Now he hired him as assistant reporter. Mike Denton was tall and broad and thick. He had wrists the size of other people's ankles, and if you needed a jack for a sick jeep and didn't happen to have one, Mike could lift the jeep while you changed the wheel. Mike's square-tipped fingers were sensitive to the aching innards of any vehicle. His bump of direction was nearly infallible, and what he couldn't find by sun and stars and terrain he could backtrack. He was a man of the bush, acutely aware of the presence of people. Alec reckoned that if Larry Orde had had a Mike Denton by his side, the chances are he wouldn't have run into the ambush that killed him. Mike Denton, tall, dark, sun-scorched. He smelled first, then thought, then acted. He was a very useful man to have around in a piece of real estate which didn't even know its own name, let alone its motivation.

Mike's animal sensitivity came in very handy on more than one occasion. For one thing, he would work the other side of the street. He had large, trusting brown eyes; soft brown eyes that belied the keen brain behind. People talked to Mike where they were likely to be wary of Alec, whose press credentials were known. Their evening cross-checks of information over a whisky were most revealing. Somehow the evaluation of what the same people had told them both, poles apart, watered down to an approximate truth. In more than one sense, Mike Denton was supplying what Larry Orde had been commissioned to provide—legs and ears. And a not inconsiderable extra asset, apart from his Swahili and Shangaan and Kitchen Kaffir—was a foretaste of trouble before it bit you.

They were cruising around outside Bakwanga in the Kasai retracing the area in which Larry Orde managed to get himself killed. Some sentimentality was involved, more curiosity. The day was sunny. The lianas hung ropy from the trees.

505

Monkeys chattered; birds called. It was the kind of day which, in other parts of Africa, called for an early halt for a slap of gin and picnic lunch.

"Gorgeous day," Alec said. "Almost like in the Masai."

"I don't like it," Mike said. "Something too altogether bloody nice about it."

"What?"

"I don't really know. But all the monkeys seem congregated here. All the birds seem to be here. They all sound *nervous*, like as if they were keeping each other company. You know, Alec, you've hunted leopard, how all the normal noise gets driven down the *donga* as the leopard moves along? The noise moves ahead, and then stops. Seems to me it's moved ahead, and then stopped . . ."

"You guys are all alike," Alec said. "Outdoor mystics. Sermons in stones and all that . . ."

"Maybe not in stones." Mike Denton's voice was serious. "But maybe in grass. Look: you've a gun. Stay here and shoot anything that isn't me. I want a little reccy, and I do it better when I'm not accompanied." Now he grinned. "Those big noisy city feet of yours."

"Okay," Alec said. "I've got a detective story and will keep custody of the liquor. Try not to get eaten by anything large and ugly. I'll never be able to find my way back home if you do."

"Right. But I'm serious again about shooting anything that isn't me, and if there's any doubt, shoot anyhow. These people don't know who's killing who, right now—and apart from that a white face is a white face and a Land Rover is big loot. I'll be back, and you'll hear me whistle before I break cover."

"Go play cowboys," Alec said. "Want a drink first?"

"Never use it in the daytime," Mike said, and melted into the embracing bush. Alec considered the use of the word *melt*, which he had never fancied. But that was what you did out here. *Melted.* Here you were, in full sight, and in a second, bam! No person. Literally melted into the bush.

Alec tried the detective story, which amused him briefly because it contained a character named Biggie Burrows who more or less resembled his friend the hotel manager. But Biggie met a sticky finish, being thrust from a speeding car, and Alec lost interest in the rest of the yarn. He yawned, and yawned again, and presently slept.

What woke him was a salvo of rifle shots.

He reached for his rifle and checked the load. There wasn't anything else to do until Mike showed or didn't show. The magazine was full; he jacked a bullet into the chamber and tried the safety for size.

Now time stopped; the wait seemed interminable. No bird sounds, no monkey sounds, just slow time going nowhere.

After a thousand years, compressed into fifteen minutes, he heard a whistle. It was a whistle no African was likely to make—the first few bars of "Colonel Bogey." In a few seconds Mike Denton burst out of the bush. His face was red, sweating. He jumped into the jeep, reversed, spun, and roared off in the direction from which they'd come.

"I don't suppose you'd like to tell me what this is all about," Alec said. "I mean, I only work here—"

"You almost *didn't*, chum. I almost went out of business as well. These bastards are getting smarter all the time. This time they had an outflanking patrol—behind, not ahead. There's a whole company of ragged-asses up front, waiting happily with those nice little Czech machine guns for any of the local unwary with the other Czech machine guns. What the flankers found was merely me."

He slowed speed.

"I'll appreciate that drink now. *And* a cigarette," he said. "It was pretty busy for a bit, and anyhow I lost my lighter."

Alec lit a cigarette, and then handed Mike a bottle of Scotch.

"Don't tell me anything that I can use," he said. "I only came here to write about this bloody war. Keep your own counsel."

Mike coughed from the whisky, took a deep drag on the cigarette, and grinned.

"Man, it was rough there for a minute. I wished you'd come with me."

"So do I," Alec said shortly. "And then?"

"It's hard for a company of Wog soldiers to move without disturbing a little of the foliage. They disturbed plenty. By all signs they'd been and gone a couple of hours ago. But I hadn't reckoned—stupid bastard me, it'll get me killed, or what's worse, kill a client someday—I hadn't reckoned on the rear guard.

"I was tracking a good hundred yards ahead of myself, looking for a couple of hundred men, and then suddenly I stepped smack onto somebody's stomach. The outriders were taking a little ziz, and I jumped right onto—I suppose he might have been the sergeant. Didn't seem to take kindly to it. Woke him up from a dream full of booze and women. Had a nice Belgian rifle with him—Mauser action, I'd surmise."

Mike Denton stopped the jeep.

"Let me have another go at that bottle," he said. "It's been a thirsty hour or two."

Alec sighed in exasperation.

"I'll have one too," he said. "Then, for Christ's sake, what *happened?*"

Mike Denton smiled happily, brightly, as a good child smiles when teacher gives him a gold star.

"Well, I made a certain amount of noise curing this chap of his troubles, and the whole bush leapt up at me. Wogs to the right. Wogs to the left. I hate to confess it, but after I shot the old *bunduki* dry, I took to me heels, trying to reload as I went. Difficult, reloading while you run.

"Then I took up a strong position behind a stout log, and let the rest of the pack find me." He smiled again, and now the smile was no longer childish.

"I think we got some of our own back for young Larry Orde," he said.

"How many?"

Mike shook his head irritably.

"With half the Congolese Army on my heels, did you expect me to stay on and collect the bloody headskins?"

"I'd like to have had a crack at the buggers," Alec Barr said rather wistfully.

"Forget it. You're the writer. I'm the professional hunter on the scene. You stick to your job, I'll stick to mine."

"I know. I'm the head and you're the legs. Everybody keeps reminding me of it. I feel like a kind of ancient child."

"No offense meant, Alec. But legs is legs in this cat-and-mouse business. I'm slowing down a bit myself. Been chased by too many elephants. And, occasionally, people."

"All right. But the next time we have to go play war, I want to come too. I get lonely sitting in jeeps while you have all the fun."

"Don't be sore. Next time out, you're invited. Promise."

106

Legs. Alec Barr cursed. "Bloody legs," he said. "Goddamned legs. The legs I haven't got any more."

Funny how a reporter's feet were more important than his brain. The kid had said it—young Orde, now dead and legless himself—had promised that he wouldn't guarantee brain but that he was long on legs. Schell had sent Orde out to supply legs for Alec, and now Alec, out of middle-aged arrogance, was trying to supply his own legs as well as brain.

"Jerk," Alec Barr said to himself, and tottered into a scabby tin bath.

Alec Barr was not quite conscious of what bath was in what hotel and what town of what country he was momentarily occupying, in some sort of fruitless search for youth—some sort of idea that if you combined revenge with superhuman activity, you too could be a Larry Orde again. Not that you'd bring Larry Orde back, of course. But you might bring Alec Barr back in Orde's clothing. With legs. Goddamned *legs.*

Alec considered legs, as he lay in his bath. In the newspaper business, they had a word—legman. Legman was what Alec Barr had been, at the very first, a fellow with strong arches and a limitless ability to scurry around, waiting for something to happen.

Now legs meant more. Legs meant how often you could be sick with the creeping crud in how many hotels—or lack of hotels. Legs meant your lack of tolerance for the local garlic, the local water, the local booze. Legs meant how many aircraft you could miss in a given day—how many telephone connections you couldn't make, how many pieces you couldn't get filed through the local post office, how many cars you couldn't hire. Legs meant how many things you had to buy, and bribe for, and occasionally, steal.

Alec Barr surveyed his legs. He was in the only tin bath of the crummiest—and only—hotel in a plague spot called Kismayu in Somalia. A black whore, earlier on, had de-

manded money as he sat in the lousiest bar of the lousiest
hotel in the lousiest town of one of the lousiest stretches of
camel country in the world. She had demanded the money,
because, she said simply, "I am black."

He had just emerged, alive, from a knife fight with a noble
harka of Somali *shiftas*. The *shiftas*—border raiding bandits
—had desired Alec's water, which was preciously contained
in jerry cans on his jeep. They had *barrak*ed their camels and
made a proposition, with knives. Alec had no weapons except a *panga*. A panga, he reflected, is all right if it isn't
made out of tin, and mine was purest tin. But it looked
fierce, anyhow, when I waved the old cane-cutter at the
camel jockey. At least it distracted his attention sufficiently
for my white-hunting companion to hit him over the skull
with a flashlight. I don't know exactly what Mike uses for
batteries in that flashlight, he thought, but they must assay
very heavy on the lead quotient.

We have only been in jail three times today in this lovely
Somalia, now it's come free, and all the visiting educational
assistants are Army officers from Cairo in a kind of cultural
drag. At least they snap to and salute in a way no educational assistants ever learned.

So I got to go to jail again tomorrow, Alec thought. I am
weary of going to jail while they read *documenti* upside
down. What the Wops wanted with this goat paradise I can't
imagine. Small damned wonder they want to stake out the
Northern Frontier of Kenya. There's more room for the
camels, even if they have to kill the elephants.

It seems a little silly, this going to jail, but as long as Mike
and I take it turn and turn about, they seem satisfied. Old
Mike was a hell of a fine idea, even if he does pad the expense account. Never knew a guy so free with his flashlight.
So now I'll go back to jail and maybe they'll let Mike come
and have a bath. Jail very short on bathroom facilities, I
believe. I wonder what the jails are like in Mogadishu? Don't
tell me; I'll find out.

"They just put our lawyer inside," Mike said in the Agha
Khan suite of the Hotel Langham in Johannesburg. "Do you
think it might be time we left?"

"I think so," Alec Barr said. "You know the old line about
'when winter comes, et cetera.' How about reservations out?"

"Unbeknownst to you I've been sleeping with a steward-
ess," Mike said. "We're on the express run to Nairobi."

"Look," Alec said to Mike. "This is Ethiopia, and the old chap is the King Emperor. You are supposed to bow your way in. Try not to trip over the house lions as you bow your way out."

Mike rolled his eyes.

"And to think I used to shoot them for a living," he said.

"Shoot what?"

"Lions and Wogs," Mike said. "I suppose we need a necktie for this?"

"Definitely. You can't go up against a King Emperor without a necktie. Not to mention the palace lions."

"I hear the VD rate is ninety-seven per cent here," Mike said.

"I wouldn't know. But the real estate is ninety-seven per cent homeowned. He has it in his wife's name. Including this hotel."

"How about the gold mines, with the slaves?"

"*Not* in his wife's name. The loot goes out weekly to Switzerland on his own airline."

"Will they fly us to the Ogaden?"

"Oh, God, no." Alec's voice was horrified. "That's off limits. That's no-man's land. Not even the King Emperor goes there, or they'll cut off his—"

"That's good enough for me," Mike said. "Only two to a customer, and I'm my own customer. What about the Russians here?"

"You can see their new house," Alec said. "Lend-lease."

"But the currency isn't worth anything, even in its own country," Mike said.

"Of course not," Alec answered. "They make it in Czechoslovakia."

"But this is Guinea."

"They still make it in Czechoslovakia."

"What do they use for cash?"

"Dollars," Alec said. "Or maybe Swiss francs. But you know something?"

"What?"

"Don't throw away the old Somali money. It fits the Nairobi parking meters just fine."

"What country are we in now?"

"I don't know. Haven't checked my passport. We are either in Ruanda-Urundi or East Prussia. Actually I think Angola. With luck, the main drag."

"What's its name?"

"Either Usumbura or Luanda."

"I thought Luanda was in Buganda."

"Don't be stupid. Buganda is in Uganda. Impala, or Kampala, or some such. Right next door to Dar-es-Salaam."

"But Dar-es-Salaam is in Yemen, across the river. Where all the old Somalis go to die. That's where the British make believe they own Aden."

"Oh, no, the British make believe they own Singapore. And perhaps the Kahawa base in Kenya."

"Where's Kenya? I remember the name vaguely. I think I used to work there."

"Kenya's in the Congo. The capital is Schweitzerville."

"That across the river from Léopoldville?"

"Oh, no, Léopoldville's in Zanzibar. It's a colony of the Coastal Strip in the Gabon."

"And the Gabon?"

"I dunno. They put in another *o* and named a viper after it."

"Whatever happened to the rest of the world?"

"The Russians bought it so that the Red Chinese could have some place to expand, now that Hungary's taken."

107

It was tough losing Mike. But a hunter was a hunter and a client was a client, and after all Mike had those three kids to feed. Mike was booked firmly and he had to go back to the client. His business was not journalism—it was killing things for people to stick up on country-house walls—and anyhow, he'd overshot his license in that dicey business in the Kasai. Alec missed Mike's company around the fire or in the hotel lounge, but in one fashion he was relieved to be entirely on his own.

Mike was too close to young Larry Orde for permanent adult comfort. "Let me do it," Mike would say. "I'll just nip off and—"

Alec Barr was all alone, really by himself, now. There was no Mike to do it, no Larry to do it, only Alec Barr to do it.

And legs or no legs, he liked doing it. He felt just fine, just doing it—fighting with the dialects, haphazarding around, coping with what he had to cope with.

The copy flowed easily. No strain, the old Admiral would have said. It was nice to be a Boy Scout again, all on your own in Darkest A.

108

Serves me right for getting interested in bat manure, Alec thought. That's all I need to make my life complete, a full knowledge of caves full of bat dung. No Bukavu, no Lake Kivu, for this boy tonight. No little Switzerland-in-Africa, no hot bath, no friendly bar. Not with this clapped-out travesty of a jeep and this pathetic imitation of a driver-mechanic and that bloody Lualaba River up over its banks. Stanleyville, wherefore art thou, and when? Not that the Mount Hoyo bat caves aren't interesting, if you had a passionate interest in bat guano.

"Cas de passage not too far," the Congolese driver said in baby-French. "We stay night there, work on *jip,* maybe river go down in day or two."

Alec made a face.

"I suppose so," he said. "It's a cinch we can't go much farther on three wheels and a stick. You savvy bearing assembly shot to hell?"

"I fix, first light tomorrow. We stop *cas de passage, hein?"*

"Beggars, choosers," Alec replied. "We stop *cas de passage.* Me Tarzan. You one hell of a poor substitute for Jane."

"Oui," the driver said, smiling broadly, and Alec thought that he never expected to hear the French language spoken in American Indian grunts.

At least the *cas de passage* would have a roof on it, and some sort of bed, and with luck, even a dining hut. No soap, no drinking water, no food, no bedclothes, but at least a circle of plaster-and-wattle huts and possibly some muddy washing water. They could tinker with the car tomorrow, let the river drop, and he could get some sort of a plane out of Bukavu for Stanleyville. He was tired of swinging from limb to limb in this tin tragedy of a jeep.

They limped into the *cas de passage*—a dismal cluster of huts—just at dusk. There was nobody there but the caretaker and a couple of his wives. The caretaker was well along on his daily ration of palm-toddy, but there was a fire of sorts to heat some water, and Alec managed to acquire a couple of feeble-wicked smoky hurricane lamps. The rest hut was like most he had seen—a big cracked mud-plaster beehive with a peaked thatched top from which lizards would peep—and, occasionally, a snake would fall. The beds were of rough planking, with straw mattresses slopping over interlacings of tire-tube stripping. The two chairs had been constructed from packing boxes by an idiot, and the one table *was* a packing box to which legs had been added as an afterthought. There were hooks on a crossbeam for the lamps, however, and a chipped graniteware basin sat on the table.

"Home," Alec said briefly to the chauffeur. "Bring the *equipage* from the car."

The first bit of *equipage* was the case of booze, half gin, half whisky, which had top priority of movement. Then came the *chaguls,* the water-bags that tied to the jeep fender fore and aft, canvas sacks of sustenance. Then came the jerry cans of petrol and more water, then the chopbox full of tinned food, the cartons of cigarettes, the pistol and small rifle and ammunition and finally the bedroll. Alec knew by now what people stole first. The typewriter came last.

"Go steal some fire," he said to the driver, "and we'll have our own little Campfire Girl pow-wow over the roaring blaze."

"*Comment?*" The driver, a Bakongo with a very flat pockmarked face, look mystified as usual when Alec spoke to him in English.

"*Apporte-moi du feu,*" Alec said. "*Prends-le de l'autre grand feu.*"

"*Oui,*" the driver said, and came back shortly with their combination shovel-entrenching tool full of coals.

"There," Alec said, pointing in front of the hut. "Now go steal some wood to put on it. We'll have a jolly picnic."

He poured himself a very large hooker of Scotch into a red plastic glass, cut it slightly with water which was only slightly warm, pulled a chair out in front of the fledgling fire, and hung one lantern from the branch of a nearby tree. Presently, after another drink, he would eat something from the tins in the chopbox—sardines, crackers, Vienna sausage, tinned cheese, pickles, cold beans, or that awful canned mixed potato salad with the clammy mayonnaise in it.

He was not unhappy. A slice of moon was playing hide-and-seek with some frisky clouds, and the stars peeped coyly in and out of the scud. The fire now had caught firmly hold; so, too, the whisky was beginning to establish itself in his stomach. You learned a lot about simple pleasures from rattling around the country on the ground that you could never appreciate if you just flew over it.

Some sort of nightbird called, and was answered by an animal, possibly a night-ape of unknown species. Crickets performed in all tones and keys. A hyena giggled, far away, and there was a grunt of hippo well down the river. There were mosquitoes, still, but Alec had learned about canvas gaiters for the tender ankles, and his wrists and neck had grown fairly salted to insect bite. The mosquitoes would knock off after a bit. He never bothered with a net any more. No matter how carefully you fixed it, one mosquito always managed to stay inside it with you.

It was amazing what you learned to do without, if you kicked around long enough. He had sufficient medicines in his Red Cross kit to cure anything short of a bullet through the heart. There was whisky, and cigarettes, and water, and fire, and bedroll, and a stout canopener—*tinnikata*, it was called in Swahili. There was a big *panga*—machete—which served to pare nails and also to cut firewood. Alec had plenty of blankets for his bedroll. So he stank, and his whiskers itched, and his bush jacket was wrinkled and greasy and roughed with dust, but it had been a rewarding trip, all round. At least he was alive. And he had seen a great many dead people in the Congo since *l'indépendance*.

Alec stretched his feet toward the fire, took another sip of his drink, and reached into his jacket pocket for a fresh packet of cigarettes. The fingers touched paper. Oh God, that last letter, Alec thought. *And I haven't answered it yet.*

He pulled out the letter and looked at it with absent eyes. The envelope was creased and crumpled and greasy with bug-dope. He had read it several times, but as yet had formulated no answer.

He got up and poured another tot of whisky, and then hitched his chair more closely to the hurricane lamp. He read slowly, as if seeking hidden meaning in the tiny-charactered schoolgirl's script.

My darling:

It's been four weeks since I last heard from you from Stanleyville and frankly I'm frightened rigid. I can't imagine that you would not have written in all that time, and I can only assume that the letter has gone astray or that you have been ill. The papers are full of atrocity stories from the Congo and I am refusing to let my imagination run riot about the risks you must be taking. I've read everything that I can rake and scrape on Africa, and my dreams have all become nightmares.

It's been nearly nine months since you left, and I had hoped that you would have been back by now and that we could press forward with our plans. I know you hate reading this, but please don't hate me for writing it. Having found you only to lose you so swiftly and for such a long time makes me acutely miserable, apart from sheer panic at the risks you must be taking. It seems to me that you have more than fulfilled your part of the contract with your publishers, and is there much more to be gained by repeatedly stretching your luck?

Do come home darling, and soon, while I can still remember what the man I love looks like. The snapshot on my dressing table is a poor substitute for my real Alec.

I had thought, British climate being so vile, and you being so accustomed to the tropics by now, that it would be nice if we took sort of matching little villas in Spain or Italy (no compromise whilst the dreaded machinery is in process) whilst you finished the hard work on your African book. I promise not to molest you during working hours! But wouldn't it be lovely darling if all went well with the divorce and it came through about the same time that you sent the last proofs off to the publishers! It's all the wedding present I'd ever want!

Please please do take care of yourself and hurry home to Ever your

    Jill

P.S. I positively loathe myself for saying this, but I don't think I could bear the idea of going on and on hoping if we are not to be. I am accustomed to living without you now, and find it bearable if I can think and plan and reassure myself that all will go well, that you have not stopped loving me, and will come back and get on with the details of your divorce, much as I know you will hate the idea of breaking up with Amelia after all these years. I re-

*spect you all the more for your consideration of Amelia,
but I can't drag on with only vague hope to warm my heart
and my bed. If we are not to be, please tell me now while I
am still used to living without you.*
All my love,
  J

Alec folded the letter, stuffed it back into his pocket,
and heaved a sigh. The cricket symphony rose now in giant
crescendo—fiddles, oboes, bassoons, kettle drums. Somewhere darkly distant from the compound a real drum
throbbed softly, meditatively. Giant moths flew into the hurricane lamps. Again the hyena keened, closer now, possibly drawn by the smell of meat, for the drunken caretaker
—and Alec's driver—were hunkered over a fire toasting bits
of meat on sticks. The hippo spluttered, snorted, and then
roared. The moon had come out of the clouds and was
hanging, steady in the sky, and the skies were constant.

Alec got up, kicked a log deeper into the heart of the
fire, and poured himself another drink.

"I *can't* leave it right now," he said. "I cannot and will not
leave it right now. And I might as well take the bull by the
horns and tell her so, while I'm full of whisky and night
sounds. At least I can mail it when I get to Stanleyville.
There's so much—so very much—I haven't seen."

His voice sounded strange on the night air, as if he were
eavesdropping on a stranger.

He walked into the hut and unzipped the cover of his
portable, squaring the machine on the packing-box table.
He dipped into his office-bag and produced paper and carbon. Placing his drink carefully on the hard-packed clay beside him, he lit a cigarette and massaged his hands. He
scratched his head, and filth came away under his fingernails.
This was not going to be easy; not going to be glib, not going . . .

He approached the machine cautiously, circling the keys,
and began to write:

Somewhere in the Congo

Jill darling:
*I cannot apologize enough for being such a lousy corre-
spondent, but in most of the places I have been lately we*

are remarkably short on mailboxes, and on the rare instances that I can reach reasonable post-office facilities, I have a hunch that every third letter is robbed of its stamps and thrown in the wastepaper basket. I have been making half a dozen carbons (and goddamn how I hate carbon paper in this sticky climate) and firing off duplicates of my stories from various towns on the off chance that one will get there. But it is true that I find steady correspondence difficult out here, as there doesn't seem to be much to chat about except the latest batch of ravished nuns or the latest bunch of priests who had their ears sliced off. It doesn't make very good small talk and I hate to burden you with accounts of my latest attack of hookworm or WAWA, which in our strange sense of humor means "West Africa Wins Again." So far I have not contracted leprosy or taken up with any local squaws.

Seriously, it is difficult to explain how this dreadful country seizes hold of you. I am gradually acquiring that most awful common complaint, Africa-jealousy, which is to say that if you stay out here long enough you are furiously jealous of anyone who has been places you haven't been or who knows things you don't know about this horrible sprawling piece of real estate. I always have the feeling that there is something new just over the next hill or in the next village, and the habit patterns of this enormous cruel child which is Africa are positively sinister in their fascination.

I have seen a great many things, mostly horrible, some staggeringly beautiful, and an awful lot of naked life and death. I think the death of young Larry Orde, of whom I wrote, hit me harder, in terms of man's impermanence, than anything since the war, and the casual way that life is dismissed and death computed in today's Africa is a shocking experience in terms of the old nightingale in Berkeley Square and tea and scones in front of the fire. I suppose you'd say I'm hooked. I risk boring you with this long preamble as an answer to your last letter, but I think that I'm on the verge of finding the big book I've looked for all my writing life and I don't see how I can come home at this very moment, when there is so much ferment going on around me. Putting the magazine pieces together in the contracted book is almost academically simple and can be done with Scotch tape and a quiver of pencils, but the book I want to write is bigger and deeper and much more dimensional than the tricked-up journalism I've been practicing for the last nine months.

I hope I can make you understand that this is going to

take time and concentration, freedom from tensions and distractions. I want to start this big book soon, and as you must know, darling, from your own experience, the climate of divorce procedure is not precisely conducive to serious literary output. Nor is the idea of being a part-time writer on an informal honeymoon in Spain or Italy exactly ideal for an effort that will take everything that I've got for the next six months of concentrated labor that I'll have to devote to what I feel is my one chance to do something really big in my chosen profession.

You don't know a great deal about writers, my love, but they are curious beasts at best, creatures of odd whim, fixed habit, and unpredictable temperament. I can write a short story or an article in a hotel room or strange house, but a big book demands the maximum in household gods, well-used facilities, and accustomed surroundings. So I suggest, and hope that you will agree with this proposition that I'm about to offer, that I go back to America and to hell with the tax loophole, settle into my accustomed haunt in Jersey with my reference books and other props to literary production, get this big book off my back, and then go up against Amelia for the divorce with my hands free and my brain clear. It will only make a difference of a few more months, which in a way seems unimportant in terms of all the years we have not been together, and all the years we hope to be together in the future.

Please understand this, darling, I'm not really being a coward or trying to avoid facing up to Amelia and the divorce with all its unpleasantnesses, but as I think I mentioned, you cannot write a book while you're subdividing the dogs and tearing the library in half, counting the furniture and closing bank accounts and spending most of your waking hours with lawyers and your sleeping hours dreaming about lawyers. There is also the fact to consider that I really cannot arrange for this divorce by long distance and will have to face the awful necessity of thrashing the whole thing out with Amelia.

The book is important in more ways than one. Financially Amelia will pretty nearly clear me out, as is her right after all these years, and a really big book uninvolved in the Amelia settlement will give us a sort of dowry to start our life together. But that's not the most important aspect. Before I am anything else I am a writer, a professional writer, and unless I do justice to this book which is boiling inside me at *the moment, I would not be much of a husband for you or any other woman. I hope you can understand this, lame as it may sound, and will agree that a few more months apart won't make a vast difference in our lives, and will allow us to start clean and fresh in all aspects.*

I should finish here in a couple of months, and will come immediately to London where we can discuss this whole thing further. I would then plan to go straight back to New York to get on first with the book, then with the divorce, and then we can take that castle in Spain or the villa in Rome, because I do love you and I do want to marry you and do want to live happily ever after.

Keep writing me care of Burrows at the New Stanley and please be patient a little longer with your wandering boy who sends you, even if by cleft stick,
All my love
Alec

Alec Barr reread his answer, penciled it automatically, and decided not to try to improve on its loose construction. He hated writing personal letters, particularly answers to letters which were somewhat less than slyly importuning. Of course he understood Jill's point. He had been out long enough, far too long; he really should go home and face up to Amelia. He had more than done his job; he had amassed material enough for two dozen articles instead of for the contracted twelve, because he had really roved the continent, nearly always lone-wolfing, purposefully avoiding the herds of imported reporters who fed incestuously off each other in Léopoldville and Nairobi and Stanleyville and Johannesburg. He had refused most formal interviews and all press conferences. He was stuffed, crammed, chock full of Africana, and still he wasn't satisfied. He had not, for instance, found sufficient time to tackle Mozambique as yet, nor had he been to the Seychelles. He had barely scratched the West Coast. And there were several parts of Kenya he hadn't seen—Lamu Island, for instance, the old Arab slaving settlement off the coastal tip.

And of course the Congo—the Congo was changing daily, sometimes with double government, and a great battle for power between the wild-eyed Lumumba, the colder eyed Gizenga, the stodgy Kasavubu, that canny Belgophile, Tshombe, in Katanga, where the big money grew in the caves of the *Union Minière*. Hell would surely pop in Katanga, which had seceded from the new government, because Katanga owned most of the riches of the Congo, and Moise Tshombe wasn't about to give up without a battle. The next big story would be Katanga, and he didn't plan to miss it.

Alec addressed his letter, sealing the original and two carbons (which he would mail in various towns) and went back to his fire. He was hungry now that the letter and the decision were off his neck. He rummaged through the chopbox and settled for Vienna sausage, canned Australian soapy-tasting cheese, and a tin of sardines. He poured another drink of Scotch, to serve as a table wine, and munched happily under the stars, thinking idly that he hadn't suffered from indigestion in ages, and he had eaten everything from fried grubworms (not bad, actually, rather like batter-fried shrimp) to what he strongly suspected was a soup that used a human shinbone for stock.

Alec felt marvelously self-sufficient, exuberant even, although the exaltation could possibly be credited to the three stiff drinks he had taken. He got that special thing from Africa, that exaltation, and he could understand how the old American mountain men had felt about space and an absence of people. Guthrie had written it so very well in his *The Big Sky*. A man must be happy forever with a monument like *Big Sky* to his name. He wondered where Guthrie got the feel. Guthrie was a modern, and of course there was a ton of research available, but feel was something you had to find for yourself, and it wasn't in books. Alec thought that he had acquired some feel, now, and he gave full credit to his African vagabondage for its acquisition.

He was ready for his big book, he thought—not just one, but a series, an interlocking saga, a tracing of a single family. The basic idea of course was not new; Galsworthy had done it, and so had Faulkner, but nobody had done it on Africa, not through the clear eyes of people who looked at mountains named after themselves. It was a tremendous crucible, this Africa, and it forged writers if it killed people in the process.

Alec finished his drink, went inside and spread his bedroll on the rubber thongs of the bedstead. He had tossed the straw mattress into a corner. God only knew what sort of wildlife it housed. He lay down, thinking that tomorrow they would try to glue the jeep together sufficiently to limp into Bukavu, and then closed his eyes. But his brain remained incandescent, and he twisted and turned in his blankets as sleep forsook him. Bits of plot structure raced through his mind and excitement mounted, wakening him further. Then he reviewed his letter to Jill and told himself once more that he was right. Even admittedly selfishly, he was *right*.

He could not undertake a big project, especially the first volume of his planned saga, his big body of work, in a madhouse of legal complication, wifely tears, and shouted recrimination. He could not embark on his big work with a bitter taste of an old marriage combining with the nagging necessities of a brand-new marriage, in brand-new surroundings, under completely brand-new circumstances. When Alec worked he was a dedicated laborer. He was neither a lover nor a drawing-room wit. He was preoccupied, withdrawn, and completely obsessed with his characters and their doings. That is where Amelia had really been so good. She had never attempted either to intrude or to share, in little-womanly fashion, his literary labor pains.

He had tried to explain in the letter to Jill, and not very well, that writers were not as other men, bankers or—say stockbrokers. Atmosphere *was* important. It wasn't a matter of mere temperament, so much as it was of calloused custom. Alec needed Luke when he was working hard. Luke did everything that Alec didn't want to do or have time to do. Alec needed his books—and on this big new project, he would doubly want his books.

His mind's eye could see them all right now—not filed alphabetically or by category, but arranged according to use and need. He could walk unerringly to any volume he wanted and strike within a page of putting a finger on the exact matter he craved. He had accumulated a vast and expensive library on Africa since he had become a buff, after his first safari, and he would need it all, from Baker to Speke to Selous to Teleki to Burton to Gordon, the oldsters, to Huxley and Cloete among the moderns.

He would need his fire, and his lake to refresh his mind, and Luke to retype the daily copy which Alec filthed with his pencil. He would need Luke to talk *at*, when he was vocally forming half-born ideas. He would need Luke for the comforting chat at the end of a long tough day, and he would need the presence of a nonobtrusive person whose cigarettes did not have to be lit, whose drinks did not have to be mixed, and who did not have to be made love to when the writer's head was full of plot and history and dialog.

That, he thought, is why he had written the literary Dear-John letter tonight, in the middle of a howling jungle, pecking away on a packing-box desk in a verminous *cas de passage*. She was such a wonderful woman, Jill. He tried to visualize her in his mind, but the image failed to come clearly. He had been away too long, he thought; he couldn't see Amelia at all. His mind was a crazy quilt. He could see Larry Orde quite clearly, and he remembered Jim James as if it were yesterday. He could see Fran Mayfield, even to the flush that dyed her cool brown skin, high on the cheekbones. This was not going to be any sort of night for houses.

Alec got up and dragged the bedstead outside by the dying fire. He poured himself another light nightcap, sipped it through the life of one cigarette, and lay down under the snapping stars. It was cool; mist was rising from the river. The mosquitoes had all gone to bed. A hyena cried and was joined by another, who giggled. The crickets stepped up the volume of their concert. This time Alec drifted easily off to sleep.

109

The old New Stanley looked like home and mother, if you had a home and liked your mother. He would surely have a reservation; he had wired Burrows from Musoma a few days back, and had received a return cable: HOTELS FULL BUNK WITH ME. The manager had a penthouse suite with a record player and functional bar and a fine view of the city. At these prices I could do much worse, Alec thought, feeling a warm glow as old John, the late porter, greeted him with a *Jambo Bwana* and the pretty receptionist said: "Welcome back, Mr. Barr. Mr. Burrows has left the key and a note for you."

"I'm glad I cabled," Alec said. "No self-respecting hotel would let me in without a *laissez-passer* from the manager." He grimaced and indicated his travel-stained khaki, the battered and dented tin safari box, the dust-impregnated shoulder bag, the tattered typewriter casing.

"A hot bath'll fix all that," the pretty young lady said. "Oh, and the housekeeper has unlocked the spare room with your clothes in it. Here's Mr. Burrows' note."

The note was a hurried scrawl: "Duty (female) calls. I'll be back about six. Your mail's locked in the safe. There's booze in the bar, ice in the bucket. Welcome home. B."

The manager's suite was big and square and slightly barren of furniture, but it had shelves with books and he could see the tall ice bucket at the corner of the bar, and the coffee table was stacked with fresh newspapers and magazines.

"Put the box there," he said, pointing to the spare room whose door now gaped open. He tipped the boys and then walked out on the little balcony to see if Lord Delamere had been moved from his pedestal or if anything had happened to the Khoja mosque in his absence. And, by God, it had been an absence. Compared to me, Alec thought, the Wandering Jew was a basket case.

There ought to be masses of mail, he thought as he undressed, tossing his filthy clothes in a corner for Murungwa to collect and *dhobi* tomorrow. I haven't heard from anybody in two months, but then I haven't exactly been anyplace where I'd be likely to hear from anybody in the last two months. There isn't any sort of postal service left in the Congo, and I didn't even know I was going to Lake Victoria until just before I cabled Burrows from Musoma. Well, no news is good news, somebody once said, he thought, and sank blissfully into the bath. From time to time he sipped at a gin-and-T, and reflected that godliness ran second to cleanliness in importance. Half an hour later, when he climbed out of the tub, there was a clinging rim of earth that reminded him vaguely of the Indian Ocean outside the Tana River when the heavy floods washed the Kenya topsoil out to sea.

He brushed his teeth until his gums bled, and shaved twice. The nails still demanded some excavation, but eventually, clad in a fresh *kikoi*—the all-purpose Somali sarong —he padded happily barefoot around the flat and turned on the record machine. By God, it was good to be back in Nairobi, legwork finished, job washed up, big books framed firmly in his head, bound back to London and Jill and then home to Jersey and Luke and the deer drinking in the evening and a great, big, fat Book One just squalling to be born. He had been out almost exactly a year, and there were only two more articles owing on his series. He'd slap *that* book together, then really get stuck into his own pet project. Alec

Barr was feeling very young and not a little lightheaded when his friend Burrows, the manager, came bull-like through the door carrying what seemed to be a bale of correspondence. He tossed the bulky cord-bound bundle on the coffee table.

"Well, well," Burrows said. "The prodigal son. *Habari?* I thought maybe you'd wound up in a cookpot in the Kasai until I got that cable from Musoma. Whatever took you to Tanganyika?"

"I was trying to find out if Lake Victoria was actually the source of the Nile." Alec grinned as they shook hands. "I don't trust them old-fashioned reporters. What's new? Has Columbus discovered America yet?"

"No, but I hear Gladstone's dead," Burrows said, mixing himself a drink. "Welcome to the busy village. Job all wrapped up?"

"Job all wrapped up. Write a couple of pieces here on the local *uhuru* expectancies—that's what really took me to Tanganyika—and then off to London and then New York. I got me some big projects, man, some big projects."

"Why London?" Burrows made his voice very careful. "Why not straight through to New York?"

"You must be crazy," Alec said. "I got a *girl* in that London town. The girl I'm going to marry *lives* in London. I have been celibate so long I wonder whether I'm a boy or a girl. Where else but London?"

"Sit down," Burrows said. "Rest your feet. You didn't get any cables I was flogging around—Léopoldville, Stanleyville, Usumbura—places I thought you'd be likely to touch?"

"Nary a cable," Alec said cheerfully. "What the hell's the matter with you? You look like somebody stole your rubber duck."

Burrows got up and undid the cord which controlled the correspondence. A newspaper—the London *Daily Express* —had been used as a wrapper to contain the mass of mail. Burrows picked a brown cable envelope off the top of the heap and handed it to Alec.

"Then you didn't get *this*," he said. "I'm sorry, chum. You're not going to like it."

Alec frowned and opened the envelope. His eyes narrowed as he read.

YOUR LETTER TERRIBLY CLEAR GOODBYE AND GOOD LUCK WITH THE BOOK JILL. He read it again, unbelievingly, aloud.

"I'm awfully sorry, Alec," Burrows said. "But I thought

you would have known. I thought that if I sent copies to the various consulates and hotels . . . evidently you didn't."

"I didn't," Alec spoke through tight teeth. "I haven't had a word since I wrote that one letter. It didn't bother me. I expected to find a pile of mail here—I *have* written two or three times since and mailed it when I could from where I could. I wasn't expecting any answers. I certainly wasn't expecting *this*. Sounds final, doesn't it?"

"That it does. Very final."

"Well," Alec snapped. "Let's get cracking with a priority phone call to London. It can't be all that final. It can be fixed. It has to be a misunderstanding—too long away, you know what letters are when you've been away, you lose touch, you write less, she would—"

"I wouldn't worry about the phone call, Alec. It's *that* final. Here. Have a dekko at page three. William Hickey's column. Feature picture. I'm sorry."

Alec took the *Express*. FINANCIER WEDS. In caps. The top three columns of the gossip page were devoted to a picture of Jill, *his* Jill, leaving a church with the gallant colonel, Miles Chalmers. A Rolls-Royce stood gleamingly handy. The bride looked radiant. The groom looked very young despite his trim white mustache and snowy hair. The bride wore what was probably green, and her corsage was probably ivory-and-green, doubtless freckled, orchids. The sturdy groom, who was described as D.S.O., M.C. *and* Bar, was wearing a carnation in his carefully cut lapel.

"I guess she just got tired of hanging around," Alec said dully, after a moment. "I guess women don't like to depend too much on compulsive truants. I guess—"

"I guess you better have a large pink gin and get rid of that tonic," Burrows said. "Tonic is very bloating."

110

Alec shook his head like a boxer trying to clear his brain after a punch.

"But we might have talked it over. She could have waited a little longer. I could have changed my mind, changed my plans—the hell I could! The hell I *would!*" He glared at Burrows.

"Don't bite me, *rafiki,*" Burrows said. "*I* didn't jilt you."

"I'm sorry," Alec grinned feebly. "It just sort of hit me in the stomach. This I wasn't really expecting."

Burrows gestured at the mass of mail.

"You'll probably find a long explanation in *that,*" he said. "Look, I imagine you'd like to be alone—sort out your mail, get yourself clued up. I'll just run along and—"

"You make a move for that door and I'll snap your spine, so help me," Alec said. "This is one night I don't want explanations, amplifications, United Nations, or any other kind of God-damned-nations. I don't want to open any mail. I want to get good and drunk and maybe pick up a girl and maybe—Hey!"

Burrows walked over to the record player and turned the stack over.

"Odd," he said. "This one is a Nat Cole number. It's called 'Welcome to the Club.' *Hey* what?"

"You know what I feel like?" Alec said. "I feel maybe just a little bit relieved. Things are suddenly simplified. I feel like going fishing. I feel like chartering a plane tomorrow and flying up to Lake Rudolf to that Samoan village Bob Maytag built for Miami University. I feel like catching a fish and shooting a whistling teal and chasing a croc and bathing in that nice hot pool and drinking a little booze and absorbing some of that NFD sun for about a week. And I feel like you going with me."

"It's a lovely idea," Burrows said. "Except I do happen to run a couple or three hotels in my spare time. I can't take a week."

"The hell you can't. Call it compassionate leave. Compassion for me. How would you feel if I blew my brains out because you wouldn't come fishing with me?"

"Terrible," the manager said. "Bloody awful. Especially if you did it in the Grill or the upstairs lounge. Maybe I can squeeze a week, at that."

Alec extended his hand with an empty glass in it.

"More pink gin, boy, while I celebrate. What, as a Mr. Collings of the newsmagazine world once asked me, is the crumpet situation at the moment? I have been womanless much too long."

Burrows scratched his blue-shaven chin.

"Well, there's a couple of likely leftovers from the last

Metro-Goldwyn-Mayer picture, sort of loose-ending around at the moment. One is not overugly. The other is not excessively gorgeous. But they are definitely girls, judging from a distance, and they have a decidedly non-virginal aspect. They look clean, in any case. You had what in mind?"

"This in mind. How would it be—and you *are* the manager of this marvelous hotel, with a certain *cachet*—how would it be if you broached the idea that a Famous American Author, with the look of eagles in one eye and a secret sorrow in the other, was desirous of asking them to go for a riotous evening at the glamorous Mount Kenya Safari Club, on the off chance of seeing Bill Holden, a personal friend of the Author's, and then to progress by easy stages to the palm-thatched paradise by the magic lake of Rudolf? It took Teleki two years to walk there. We can fly it in an hour from Mawingo."

"You better take it easy on the gin, it's beginning to snap back at you," Burrows said. "I think we can play down the fishing angle, and concentrate on the swimming pool side. These wenches don't impress me basically as the outdoor type."

"My destiny is in your hands," Alec said. "I shall anoint myself with oil and meet you *and* the Hollywood vestals in the Grill for champagne and caviar, later to the Equator, gator, thence to the wild blue in one of the Wilkens Airways' better charter jobs."

"Watch the gin," Burrows said. "Or there won't be much point to my marshaling the troops." He clapped Alec on the shoulder. "I *said* I was sorry, friend. Don't let it bother you too much. Now," he said briskly, "what about the mail?"

"—the mail," Alec said. "Leave it here. There's nothing in it I want to consider. I'll read it all when I get back. This is a holiday."

"I couldn't help noticing three or four letters from your wife," Burrows said. "Maybe—"

"She wouldn't have anything new to tell me, and right now I want to be cosseted with crocodiles, or something, because I am sick of love. It'll be nice to smell a cedar fire and see the Mountain again, nicer to set out in the gallant old *Lady of the Lake* and catch a perch."

His glandular activity subsided somewhat, and now hurt showed soberly in his eyes.

"You know, Mr. B.," he said. "I really didn't think she

was a bolter. I really thought I'd found the final one who'd maybe understand."

"What you need," Burrows said harshly, with affection, "is to find yourself a gypsy. Now get yourself dressed and we'll go and collect the crumpet. Past the point of collection, you're on your own with this business of a dirty week in the wildwood."

111

Alec and Burrows simply went fishing. The girls had proved better than Burrows described them; pretty, nonalcoholic, and one of them, Sheila or Sonia or something, had demonstrated signs of intelligence. It could have worked into quite a nice week-long revel, possibly, except Alec's false endocrinal excitement had subsided into a polite glumness as the evening wore on. The girls were quite willing to play; Burrows was full of fun and quips, but Alec was simply lumpish through the dinner and after, at the Equator, where the floor was crowded and the music much too loud.

In the men's room, Alec said:

"Apologies, friend. My loud brave talk was for nothing. They're nice kids, but I don't think I could really spend a week explaining why North is hot and South is cold in Africa. I love capped teeth, but these girls have entirely too many. Maybe some other year."

"I thought the adrenalin would wear off," Burrows said.

Alec bent over the handbasin. He wet his breast-pocket handkerchief and swabbed his brow. The towels on the roller seemed a trifle suspect.

"To my shame, *compadre*, no plans. I suddenly ain't with it. I've always had a kind of shy about strangers. They're very nice kids, but if it's all the same to you, I'd just as lief we went fishing stag, and for tonight, saw the ladies to their door with a flourish and a kiss of the hand. I guess I'm still carrying a kind of middle-aged torch."

Burrows straightened his bow tie.

"Tell you what. We'll go back to my flat and have a nightcap. You can suddenly be the very tired explorer. I'll see that the girls get back to their quarters—and I might even supervise one of the troop movements personally." He grinned wolfishly. "I'm a bachelor—with no lost loves in London."

112

The girls had been very nice about *not* being white-slaved into the Samburu Country. The prettiest one, Shirley or Sonia or whatever, seemed a mite disappointed that the distinguished American author was so *square,* and seemed always to be looking past her when she was performing at her very cutest, like Shirley MacLaine. Mr. Burrows was as cute as he could be, but he was only a hotel manager and somehow she had always thought authors would be different. This author looked like he was seeing ghosts over her shoulder, and he wasn't making sharp with the dialog at all. None of those swift cracks like Noël Coward. All this author said was: "Huh? Pardon me," when he came back to the land of the living. Nairobi was a poky town. Norma or Gloria bet it was different when Ava Gardner was making *The Snows of Kilimanjaro* or Stewart Granger was making *King Solomon's Mines.* Not to knock him, really, but this author, this Mr. Barr, seemed a little *dim.*

The dim author, Mr. Barr, had a marvelous time at Rudolf. The fish bit voraciously, the shores were lined with the most delectable waterfowl in the world, the black-and-white whistling teal, and the swimming pool, blasted out of solid rock, was so warm that you froze when you came out into a temperature of 120 degrees Fahrenheit, with the strong lake wind blowing. South Island, the haunted island, was there across the way, and the crocodiles lay like jetsamed lumber on the pebbly beaches of Molo Island. The air was so dry, the temperature so hot, that you scraped the dried salt sweat off you with the cutting edge of your hand. Alec caught one good perch, a million-to-one mutation, a hundred-pound goldfish. As the metallic-scaled fish rose out of the green water, shook its great head, and then came meekly to boat, it had all the appearance of Mae West in a gold lamé gown.

"I think I'm cured," Alec said to Burrows, on the last day, as they sat inside the cool, Polynesian prototype of thatched hut, drinking iced tea and waiting for Freddie to come into the windsock with the ordered charter job. "I think I got my vitamins all back in a neat little row. Regard me, Barr, the reformed lover, Barr, the dedicated writer, Barr, the testimony to clean living and pure thought and at least one hundred-pound goldfish."

"The palm trees creak in the winds of overconfidence, says the Koran," Burrows said, still wearing his floppy panama hat inside the house. "*Hamdullilah!* So do the knees." He looked like a very dissolute pasha from the ancient court of the Grand Turk, with his large Irish-Iberian nose burnt cordovan by the smiting Rudolf sun and his dark spaniel eyes non-Hibernian in their heavy pouches. He waggled his head wisely in the Indian fashion. "Man who is speaking through backside sometime fall in dung." Then, seriously: "What now, Alec?"

Alec moved to the bamboo bar.

"First, I think we switch from iced tea to gin. Second, I'm off, Brother B. Back to the plow. Remember, I've had two shots at the short happy life of the middle-aged lover, and it didn't fit my face. Well, I settle now. I settle for a lot of things. But mostly I settle down. I got books to write, and I require a passel of peace. I'm going home to the old accustomed andirons, and shall toast my literary talents before my own fire, in my own wigwam."

Burrows, looking more somber than ever, said:

"Amelia? What about Amelia?"

"She's a way of life," Alec said, and spread his hands. "She's Amelia. She's there. She'll always be there. I've tried to run away once too often. I'll go back to Amelia and write books and forget I'm what a guy you'd have loved once called a 'grizzled adolescent.' His name was Ben—Ben Lea. He also told me I was too square to be a lover."

"I am not the man to say he had a point. But I like the idea of work. You're very high on this sort of *Forsythe Saga* of yours?"

"I got it all made but the writing," Alec said. "All I need is pad and pencil."

"Hark! I hear the plane," Burrows said. "That'll be Freddie, wanting to catch at least one fish before we depart." He checked the watch on his black-haired wrist. "One fish for

Freddie'll be another couple of drinks for us, and we can just scrape into Nairobi in the cool of the evening."

"I really do have to sort that mail," Alec said. "This has been the first properly stolen week I've enjoyed in a year. I'll hive up in your quarters again for a couple of days before I'm on my way, right?"

"Right. Now we'd best send the car for the noble aviator, who will have his fishpole in his hand."

113

They sat, sunburnt-crisp and shivering in the Nairobi cold. Alec was sitting on the floor. He was once again wearing a *kikoi,* but with an old sweater slung over his shoulders. He was surrounded by a slagheap of discarded correspondence. The hotel manager was seated on the divan, reading a copy of *The East African Standard.* Suddenly Alec Barr began to laugh—to laugh madly. He waved a letter in his hand.

"Have you blown your bloody top?" Burrows asked. "The Rudolf sun isn't all that potent."

"Here," Alec said. *"Here.* It's been all here all along, for God knows how long. *Here!"* He collapsed with laughter, as he scaled a letter toward his friend.

"What's so bloody funny?" Burrows said, picking the letter off the floor.

"Read it! It'll kill you. It's from Amelia. She doesn't want to be married to a will o' the wisp any more. She's suing for divorce because she's fed up, and the whole thing is dated before I got the cable from Jill, before Jill married the colonel! And *I* was ducking a divorce!"

Burrows read the letter carefully.

"You poor son-of-a-bitch," he said. "What will you do now?"

Alec Barr looked at him, the false laughter gone. His nostrils were pinched white, and the eyes cold.

"Like I bloody well said. *Go home and write my book."*

Book V/Penny

114

It wasn't surprising that the phone should ring at the exact moment Alexander Barr ripped a page out of his typewriter and hurled it hatefully in the general direction of the wastepaper basket. This time the ring came as a relief, no matter what the implied catastrophe. Alec reckoned that over the years most of the vital information which influenced his activity—professional, social, and emotional—had been prefaced by a tinny jangle like a nervous laugh when he was doing something he didn't want to do.

It was midmorning in New Jersey—a sparkling, breezy, sun-warmed July. It was the kind of day that people often said made you glad to be alive. The fish were jumping, and the locals were high. But for Alec Barr the living was not particularly easy. For one thing, Daddy still wasn't rich, and there weren't any Ma around to be goodlooking, and there didn't seem to be anybody but Luke standing by. And Luke was nobody's Sportin' Life.

The Big Book had seemed so easy of commission when he had plotted it roughly in Africa. He had, he thought, all the ingredients for the fruitcake. He had earned the eggs and flour and milk with his basic background toil. The more pungent bits of his life, God knows, could provide the citron and cherries and nuts and raisins and the final splash of brandy. But he had no fruitcake. All he had in front of him was a lot of soggy unmanageable dough, and the kind of dough he owned wasn't spendable.

He looked across the lake—it shimmered in the morning sun and dimpled in the wind. The door was opened, and he could hear the whisper of the breeze as it stirred the trees. The wind was in his direction; he could hear the plop of a bass as it rose to strike a bug. Any number of birds sang close by. He could hear the calling of quail in the backbush across the lake. A cardinal sat by the poolside and sneered at him, its topknot raised arrogantly.

When the phone rang, Alec rose to answer it with all the built-in dread of modern warriors who live by the Bell System.

"Bad news. Hemingway's dead," Marc Mantell said harshly, without a prefatory hello. "Killed himself. Blew his head off."

"Jesus," Alec said. "When?"

"Just now. Hasn't made the papers yet. Got it off the radio. One of my office girls, the kind that take transistors to work —I thought you'd want to know. How's your book coming?"

"Not well. About as well as your phone call suggests. Maybe I'd better look for a gun too. What did he use?"

"Shotgun. Rather a thorough job, I understand, if you can believe the early reports."

"Where?"

"That second home of his, after Cuba. Ketcham. Idaho. And in the living room or library. On the rug. Quite messy, I believe."

"Poor bastard. Any easy explanation?"

"I dunno. He'd been in that clinic. Insulin shots, somebody said. Must have been a nervous thing. Booze. High blood pressure—you know."

Luke walked through the room, and looked inquiringly at Alec. There hadn't been many phone calls lately. Alec covered the receiver.

"Bring me a Scotch and a cigarette," he said to Luke. "Friend of mine's killed himself."

Luke nodded, disappeared into the bar.

"Fortification," he said into the phone again. "I just sent Luke for a drink. I know it's early, but what do you really think?"

"I think he was tired of trying to cope with it all," Marc

Mantell said. "I think it all got to be just too much trouble."

"He isn't exactly unique," Alec replied, holding out his hand for the drink Luke had produced with miraculous speed. "Excuse me. I'm drinking a toast to a good guy. Ah. *Better*. You hit me with a shock."

"I know. I always thought of Papa as indestructible."

"You know I never called him Papa," Alec said. "I never even called him Ernie. Ben called him Papa. The latest Mrs. Hemingway calls him Papa. Leonard Lyons calls him Papa. Everybody called him Papa. I always sort of thought of him as 'Mr. Hemingway.' He called me Alexander."

"So did I," said Marc Mantell. "So did I think of him as 'Mister.' But then I never really thought of Sinclair Lewis as 'Red.' Instinctive dignity of accomplishment, I suppose. Even when Lewis lost it, *I* kept it. I don't suppose I really would have called Maxwell Perkins 'Max' or Thomas Wolfe 'Tom.' "

"How do you think of me?"

Alec could hear his agent chuckle slightly.

"Mister Alexander Barr, Pulitzer-Prizer and potential Nobel winner. How many pages we got?"

"Not enough for a Nobel. Not enough for you. Not enough for me. Just not *enough*."

"Any difficulties I'd be useful at?"

Alec shook his head characteristically, even though he realized as he nodded that the agent couldn't see the gesture.

"You just shook your head in doubt and torment," Marc Mantell said. *"Didn't* you?"

"You're too smart by half," Alec said, and blew a razzberry into the phone. "That's English for 'we've been working together too long.' Yes, I did shake my head in doubt and in torment. And will again. I'm trampled by a giant, this time, Father. It used to be the midgets that nailed me. The guppies nibbled me to death. I am now attached to a tiger shark."

"They're both members of the fish family," Marc Mantell said. "All you need to catch them is the right hook."

"You've used the correct word," Alec said, "but I don't know if I'm the right worm."

"Skip the gags. Anything new from Amelia?"

"Nothing really since the divorce. I think she's in Acapulco. Ask the lawyers you send the alimony to. They always know."

"Anything from . . . England?"

"I believe she's too old for childbearing," Alec said. "What else?"

"When can I see some copy? You got me crazy with this secret approach to a book. You used to ask me out to play Scoutmaster—"

"I'll show you some copy when I got some copy I can stand to show you. And right now, Boss, what I got in hand ain't that kind of copy."

"I suppose it's a waste of time to ask you if you're happy, in or out of your work, now that you're singly blesséd?"

"You were never righter," Alec said. "Dead waste. But then, who ever knew a happy writer? Married *or* unmarried?"

"Not me," Marc Mantell said. "And I've been hanging around the racket forty years. Just don't blow your head off with a rifle, hey?"

"At this moment," Alec said, "I don't even think I could hit it with a shotgun."

115

This is, Alec thought, the Big Casino. The Real Riffle. The Last Flutter. All the things you are, you no longer are. It is a state of existence called Ain't. This is all what you is. *Ain't.*

I call it downright uncomradely of my old chum from Pamplona and Madrid, my hero from the old gay days in Paris, the man who taught me that you could bait a fishhook as lovingly as you describe a countryside, to go and blow his bloody head off to a point where *Time* says there is nothing left but the lips. It is not fair to do it the easy way; to quit your responsibility. And Ernest had a responsibility. He had invented a new world, for one thing. Luke had asked about that after Marc Mantell had hung up a few days ago.

"Shake you a lot, huh, Boss?" Luke said. "Here, gimme the glass. You want some music on the noisemaker?"

"No sad songs for me," Alec said. "And nothing from that other world. Drink, yes, thanks, Chief. Music, no. All the good music got itself invented about that time."

"You got a thing about music, Commander. I notice it a lot. The book goes good, we play one kind. The book ain't steaming well, we play another. When we were in the divorce foul-up—"

"Leave it," Alec said. "I don't need the music to remember. They wrote a new kind of music for divorces. Most of it is for percussion with no horns."

Luke walked back from the bar and handed Alec a fresh drink. He sat on a yellow leather Moroccan *pouf* by the fireplace and said:

"What kind of a guy was he really, Boss? You read all that crap in the papers. You don't really know what to believe."

It seemed to Alec Barr that the older he got the more he swung his head, like an old and puzzled lion. He swung it now, looking through the window toward the breeze-pouted little lake.

"I don't know, Luke," he said. "We all come from other places, other times. Some people belong to a particular epoch, an era, like a war. Some people can only find themselves in the time of their involuntary choosing. Some never find themselves at all. You do remember the war? Remember Genial John? The Admiral?"

"Oh, boy, do I not, Commander! That sub-tending flagship in Saipan. Do I *not*. Him and Henry Fonda."

"Genial John was perfect for his time. So was the Bull. So was Mush, with the submarines, and Slade, with the submarines. One died and one didn't. Mush took the *Wahoo* down, and he took her down all the way. I wonder what would have happened to Mush Morton if he *had* come up. I know what happened to Marshall, who came off that sandbar and got passed over for promotion. He's living in Mexico. I hope he's happy."

Luke raised his beer.

"It was a pretty good time, Commander. Seems like it was about the best time I ever knew. You still ain't answered what I asked. What kind of a guy was he?"

"I wish it was winter so we could have a fire," Alec said. "What kind of a guy was he? Well, let us consider Ernie Pyle. With all the trouble he ever had, he lived the only perfect life that a writer ever had. Hemingway was a joke warrior and a joke war correspondent. He called himself Ernie Hemorrhoid, the poor man's Pyle. Pyle was perfection. The world swung right spang around and stopped in front of a funny little frightened man who couldn't hold his liquor, was no good with his wife, who was a real drinker, and a wild one—"

Luke held out a protesting palm.

"You can't say that about Mister Pyle," he said. "Why—"

"*Why* my ass," Alec snapped. "Lee Miller said it better than me in his book about Pyle, and he was Ernie's best friend. I wasn't Ernie's best friend, but I damn well wrote his copy on a couple of islands in the Pacific when he was too tired to function. Ernie had plain run out of gas. He didn't want to come out to the Pacific to write about an already-won war and to get his brains blown out by the last bloody Jap on the last unlikely island. Which is exactly what happened to Ernie at Ie Shima. The War was over, and so Pyle achieved perfection. Valhalla, laid on."

"I remember Ernie Pyle, but I thought we were talking about Mister Hemingway." Luke's brow creased. "You are kind of left-handed around corners, Commander. This Valhalla is an island I never made."

Alec smiled briefly. His voice was very soft.

"Excuse me, Chief. But I am not really talking around corners. I am making a weary oblique point. Look: Pyle was a folksy writer doing travelogue pieces before the war. He was the quintessential Little Man. Nobody paid much attention to Ernie except his hometown sheet and a small bunch of hicktown client papers. Ernie was too little to be considered by the bigger papers, such as his New York outlet. He was pure local boy. He was corny. He was a *little* man, who wrote funny little pieces about getting his zipper jammed. Also he had quite a lot of backhouse humor."

Alec paused, and extended his empty glass toward Luke.

"That day in Australia when I picked up the paper and saw a headline that said a famous war correspondent had been killed in a ratbag island called Ie Shima I knew it was Ernie before I read the story. I had that old feeling about him on Guam."

Luke handed him back the replenished glass.

"He drunk a lot, Hemingway, huh?"

"We all drink a lot. So did Ernie Pyle, even though he was

so fragile he couldn't handle it very well. Hemingway wasn't fragile—not until the end. Then he got fragiler. But Ernie . . ."

Poor little brave scared bastard, Alec thought, his mind traveling back to the last days on Guam, just before the Iwo kickoff, poor little scared brave drunk bastard, with a tame light commander to run his errands, to cover his waterfront, Max Miller the name was, and people like me to help with the copy. Copy which was pretty bloody awful copy, even in view of the fact that Ernie didn't want to be there anyhow, but the Navy had made a Presidential point of it, and so had the Baker Two Nines, and everybody was quarreling over Ernie's still-living body. Like drunks fighting over the only whore in the saloon. Military brass, and theaters of war—*yah*.

"Ernie committed suicide with his presence in the Pacific," Alec said slowly. "You couldn't understand it, Luke. You lived clean and fat with the professional admirals. But Ernie had kicked off with the worst blitz in London. He went all the way through North Africa. He made all Sicily and he made all Italy and he made the invasion in France and stayed there until the Krauts quit. He didn't weigh any more than a bottle of Scotch. He had a rotten bad belly—he used to say that he had been sick in more hotel rooms than any living man, and this was *before* the war."

"He musta been a helluva fellow," Luke said. "I only just seen him a coupla times on Guam with that tame civilian commander."

"He by God was a helluva fellow. Ernie really liked to live like an officer, a general, and instead, he made himself live like a dogface rifleman, even though the generals were kissing his ass and all the theaters were screaming for him to cover them. He slept in the mud with the scared men. Ernie was bigger than Bradley, bigger than Eisenhower. There's never been anything or anybody in a war as big as Ernie Pyle. Including Alexander the Great and Napoleon."

"Why?" Luke asked. "Why? There was a lot of other writers around."

Alec twitched a lip-corner upward to match his quirked eyebrow, and blew a cloud of smoke.

"Ernie was Ernie because the whole world stopped turning one day and focused its entire attention on The Little Man. It was exactly like the world had been blind and somebody suddenly turned on the lights. The world was full of little men and Ernie was *the* Little Man. He was damned near close to being Jesus Christ in the eyes of the poor lousy guy in the foxhole and in the eyes of the people back home."

Alec shrugged his shoulders and spread his hands.

"All I can say to try to explain it is that Ernie was *America* —Ernie was the world at war. He had the knack, the wondrous skill, of writing about all the toilet paper you saw scattered around the dead body of a nineteen-year-old GI from Ohio, or a dead Polack captain coming down an Italian mountain roped to a mule. He knew about hot and cold and wet and dry and fear so horrible that he couldn't push a pin through his asshole. And so did Hemingway, but in another time, in another country, in another kind of war."

"A Jap killed Pyle," Luke said. "Mister Hemingway shot himself."

"Very little difference in the method. They both gave themselves wholly to a time. They both more or less died for their country—not their own country, precisely, but for their *age*—their *time*. Some people are foredoomed to die when they've outlived their usefulness. Pyle would have been useless after the war that made him so important. Hemingway decided he had become almost useless. A Jap did a speed-up job on Ernie. The other Ernest just got tired of the whole damned mess and did the job on himself. I shot an elephant once . . ."

"Yeah, you told, Boss. The old, old boy."

"That's right," Alec said. "I did the same job for the elephant that the Japs did for Ernie Pyle. I did the same job for the elephant that Ernest Hemingway did for himself with his own gun."

116

The whole thing was pretty creepy, Luke had said. Creepy wasn't the word for it, Alec thought. Inevitable, yes. But to think of Hemingway, all that special kind of talent which was suited to one age, the age of writing discovery. All the wasted words he never wrote, that Fitzgerald never wrote, that the whole gang never wrote because they were so bloody busy sitting around the *Dôme* and the *Deux Magots* that they couldn't take time off from talking to write.

Pyle at least got killed at his working peak. Ernest hung around too long, like the old bull at the waterhole at Illaut in Kenya. Everybody had heard all the jokes and he couldn't travel very far from his water any more.

And where the bloody hell does that put you, Alec Barr? What waterhole have you hung around so long that you can't make love, you can't write, you got no wife and you got no girl and all you've got is bloody fanny adams, a polite English euphemism for a coarser expression.

And sweet FA is not the correct word for it. Do-nobody is better. Being free, unchained from matrimony's chafe, is a fine thing, and so you take your old prestige and your middle-aged good looks (a touch of gray over the temples, perhaps, but Alec keeps his figger well) into the market places, and everybody, but everybody, wants to buy.

And what are you, Alec Barr? An old, mangy lion with his spine snapped. You got no wife. You got no girl. You got no book, really. You can't drink like you used to drink, and you can't function in bed as you used to function, and all of the cheap love you used to think would be fun to sample isn't fun any more because:

You can't get it up, any more, Alec Barr. Neither your talent nor your cock. *You just can't get it up.*

And when you can't get it up you might as well be dead, as Ben Lea said when he opted (what a bloody awful bunch of words were creeping into the language these days, *opted* for Christ's sake, you might as well say *escalated* or that awful thing, *contacted*, or that worse thing, *positioned*) when Ben Lea opted to be sawed in half because there wasn't anything he could do including go to the bathroom except in a bottle. Ben said the hell with it, and died. Ernie said the hell with it, and got shot by a Jap who probably couldn't have hit his foot for a self-inflicted wound. And Mister Hemingway couldn't take a lot of it any longer so he stuck a 12-gauge shotgun down his gullet and blew his own head off.

Alec got up and massaged his back. There seemed to be more aches than there used to be. He felt terribly depressed. Life was assuming, more and more, the guise of that well-remembered honey badger. Life went instinctively straight for your groin and then killed you for fun. It was like booze. You develop a taste for good wine and all of a sudden they tell you that you've got a lousy liver. Alec felt alone and terribly sad. He was remnanted like an oversold book from all the nice people he had met in a lifetime. He felt saddest of all about Amelia, sadder than about Barbara Bayne, sadder even than about Jill Richard. He had not expected that Amelia would ever divorce him. He had *counted* on Amelia. He had thought many times, and said many times when he was depressed, in the early days, that if the worst came to the worst he could always go back to sea. He could always go home to Amelia.

He had been shocked of course when Jill rejected his procrastinating, sent him that cable and then wed the steady stodgy fellow who would come home nights—some fellow who was not always selfishly concerned with himself and his own little professional picknose problems. The only thing that would concern Jill's new husband was the state of the stock market, and when the Exchange closed he would always come home to Jill and the petunias. Perhaps in reverse order, but he would surely come home. Like a pigeon.

But Jill's summary dismissal had not delivered the same wallop in the guts. Amelia's letter was a sneak punch, but very legal, very logical. Amelia had written that she was damned sick and tired of being married to a matrimonial fugitive; that what she wanted was a man around the house, not a literary memoir. And she was going to get out while she was still young enough, still had looks enough, to find herself that man. She would always love Alec very much, but they had gone too far past each other for repair. The names of her lawyers were. . . .

The divorce had not provided any field day for the press. There was no other woman involved—Alec grinned ruefully as he thought, I'll say there wasn't—and they had made a decent, dignified thing of the financial settlement. Amelia had gone off to Reno, and it had been reported only in a few paragraphs in the papers and newsmagazines. But the predivorce details had been emotionally unsettling; the repeated conferences with the lawyers, the tension between Alec and Amelia when they were forced to meet to skirmish and niggle over details had done nothing helpful to speed the commission of the Big Project.

Alec Barr was too much a professional not to finish up his Africa series from his more-than-copious notes. He revised the articles into smooth book form, consulted with the editors on cover and photographic content, wrote captions, and finally read proof. He appeared on television shows and gave interviews. He was able to perform these chores almost absently, academically, with his mind miserably free to rove over his own self-obvious inadequacies as a human being. In this instance he was sad but not sorry for himself, and he blamed neither Amelia nor Jill for abandoning the S.S. Barr. In this case, Sinking Ship Barr, no longer September Song Barr.

He took a brief vacation after he had wrapped up the articles and the book for Ray Schell's publishing house. He flew down to Mexico City and saw some bullfights, but somehow they lacked the *alegría* associated with Carlos Arruza and Silverio and Gaona and others from the past. The new boys didn't seem to care about the bulls. He also missed Ben Lea as a jolly drinking and occasional wenching companion in the city and in the outside-D.F. fun towns. Overbuilt Acapulco no longer bore the slightest resemblance to the old days.

The vacation hadn't injected any fresh blood into his emotional veins. He drank but did not enjoy drinking, as he did not really enjoy the bullfights, because there was nobody there to enjoy anything with him. He had thought to invite Dinah Lawrence for the holiday, but Marc Mantell informed him that Dinah was off movie-making in Spain or Palestine or someplace, and he couldn't think of anybody else he wanted to ask. He took off feeling full-squeezed, sucked dry, and he came back feeling the same way. There had been one woman—a very pretty American *turista* he had met with some dull people at an Embassy cocktail fight he'd got roped into—and that had developed into a great big nothing, as well. After the usual polite preliminaries they had gone to bed, and Alec found to his horror that he was completely impotent. The week end ended early by mutual consent.

One thing was fortunate: Amelia had been reasonable in the financial aspects of the divorce settlement. She had of course been granted the apartment and its furnishings, but had shown no interest in the Jersey house. When the final bills of divorcement were signed, Alec settled for fifty per cent of their net worth, and third of future possible earnings. Royalties from backlists would assure that Amelia would not have to forego the girl lunches at "21" and that she would be able to maintain the East Side penthouse without seeking a roommate.

Alec hadn't bothered as yet to look for a permanent Manhattan roost. A variety of apartment hotels had seen him through the divorce, when his physical presence in New York was absolutely necessary. Carl and Elsa had been disposed of by Amelia; she would in future make do with a daily maid.

It was damned ironic, Alec thought, that he had arrived at the sublime stage of seeking—complete freedom, clear title to the Jersey house, less involvement with Manhattan social life, plenty of working space uncomplicated by either romantic or domestic fuss, all the opportunity in the world to fill his Jersey retreat with luscious concupiscent ladies—and all he really had was himself and Luke in Jersey and Marc Mantell on the other end of the phone.

"What we need here," he said to Luke, a few days after the Hemingway suicide, "is a fat pussycat and a rubber plant. You know, we're nothing better than a couple of old maids?"

"It's all right with me," Luke said. "It's real nice and peaceful. We ain't figuring on getting married again any time soon, are we, Boss?"

"Great God, no. For starters we can't afford it. And anyhow, like the old joke says, who'd marry us?"

"You got a point," Luke said. He was watering some of the indoor split-leaf philodendrons. "And we got enough plants. Hey, what ever happened to that nice Mrs. Lawrence? With the pretty daughter?"

"That nice Mrs. Lawrence, according to Mister Mantell, is in Europe working on a picture. And that nice pretty daughter is—or *was*—married and divorced and for all I know, married again."

"She was a real humdinger, that daughter. How old'd she be now?" Luke kept his voice very casual as he started placing some cut flowers in the bar vase. "You like anything to drink, Boss?"

"No," Alec said. He looked keenly at Luke. "The daughter'd be pushing thirty now—twenty-seven, twenty-eight, I forgot exactly. What are you up to, Chief?"

"I ain't up to nothing, Commander. I just thought maybe we could do with a little life around here, and if that Miss Whatsername is old enough to be married and divorced—

well, they don't stay kids forever, do they, Commander?"

Alec got up from his desk and walked into the patio room.

"You've got all the makings of a prize pimp," he said. "I believe I will have a drink after all. How about a Pimms'? We got any cucumbers?"

"We got cucumbers. Mind if I join you? Fixing flowers is really a woman's work. It makes a man thirsty."

Alec laughed his first hearty laugh since Marc Mantell had phoned him with the news of Hemingway's death.

"By God, Luke, you're about as subtle as a depth bomb. What are you doing, trying to marriage-broker me into a new set of problems?"

"I ain't trying to hustle you *into* anything, Commander. I'm trying to hustle you *out* of something. You been moping around with your head hanging down like a sick chicken. You're too young to not have any fun. The world ain't all ended."

Alec looked out at the blue lake, at the clear, cloud-dusted sky, at the carnivorous greenery around the pool, at the flowers flaming in the yard.

"You're a good friend, Chief Yeoman Luca Germani," he said. "I'll take your advice under consideration, and possibly forward it to higher authority for action."

Luke disappeared into the kitchen and came back in a moment with a bowl of sliced cucumbers, apples, and a glassful of mint sprigs.

"That was a good idea, that Pimms'," he said. "Makes the summer kind of more festive than a gin-and-tonic. Like a girl in a pretty sunsuit sitting by the pool."

"All right, all *right,* you made your point." Alec got up and walked back to his desk, and took an address book out of the left drawer. "I've forgotten her married name. I don't even know if she's living with her mother any more."

"Yes she is—" Luke stopped suddenly, and pressed a hand over his mouth.

Alec dropped the address book and walked back into the patio room. His fingers vised Luke's shoulder.

"What the hell is all this all about, precisely? What kind of bloody nonsense are you up to?"

Luke wriggled away. He rubbed his shoulder.

"You got strong fingers, Boss. I ain't up to anything, really. But a lady—a Mrs. Montgomery—called up while you were taking your morning walk, and left a number. She said to tell you it was Penny calling and that she'd like you to call her back. I just sort of remembered that Mrs. Lawrence's daughter was named Penny. So I looked in your address book, and it's still the same old number. That's why I knew she was living—"

"Oh, skip it, and finish the drink," Alec said. "But for Christ's sake don't go coy on me any more."

"Here." Luke extended the frosted glass as a peace offering. "I didn't really mean any harm, Boss. I just sort of thought I'd sound you out. Kind of foc'sle politics. See how The Man's feeling before you put in the paper for that forty-eight-hour leave."

"All right. You might as well finish your Lovelorn chores. Get Mrs. Montgomery on the phone for me, will you? And it's a damned good Pimms'."

Alec sprawled into a chair and gazed at the lake again. Was it all that obvious, so obvious that even the faithful Luke was taking him to raise? Nobody's played the pimp for Alec Barr in his entire life, and here was Luke talking bad fiction and practically bridling over one lousy phone call. Alec sighed. He wished that it had been Barbara Bayne instead of Penny who'd left the call-back request.

117

"I thought you might be feeling a little low," Penny said. "Your friend Hemingway, I mean. Ma used to talk about you two. Anyhow, I took a chance."

The voice was completely different. The eager girl was gone. The voice now was smooth and contained and more than slightly sophisticated. It went with velvet Capri pants and silk blouses and a tolerance for martinis and another kind of tolerance for men.

"It was terribly kind of you," Alec fell into the British defensive cliché. "I'm fine. How are you? And what do you hear from your mother?"

"Nothing could be finer than our Dinah. Gets younger to a point where everybody thinks she's the daughter. I believe she's in Greece right now. The picture keeps moving around, and Ma has to fix a new script every time they fire a director. As for me, I am a brazen forward hussy. I was about to invite myself out for the week end. That's if I heard any encouraging sounds on the other end of the phone."

Alec sat on the corner of his desk, swinging a foot.

"The voice you hear is the voice of encouragement. You have just remade my morale."

The other voice lilted nicely, not too falsely.

"I've never forgotten one tiny week end," it said. "The week end when you asked Ma to come and stay with you while you both worked on a book. This is a terrible thing to say, Alec dear, but I wondered—I *have* been through the divorce thing, and it's not nice—I wondered if maybe this wasn't the right time for at least one member of the family to stand up and be counted. In case—"

"In case?" Alec's voice tightened.

Now the voice was completely level and sincere.

"In case you were lonely, and sick at heart about your friend's suicide, and maybe having work trouble—nothing special, really. Just that maybe you might want somebody around to fry you another kind of egg."

"I think you're terribly sweet. Shall I come and fetch you, and when?"

"Of course not. I have a little car. I can at least find— what is it, Wykcoff?"

"That's right."

"Then if I can't trace my way after Wykcoff I'll ring you from the filling station or something and you can send Luke down to lead me in. And Alec?"

"Yes?" There had been another, a rather crumbly change in her voice.

"This isn't any sort of juvenile altruism born of old baby-sitting or ancient family friendship. If you want the barest truth, I'm miserable. I want a knee to rest a head on and a hand to hold that isn't straight up my skirt because I'm young and divorced and fair game. This probably sounds awful over the phone. But I loved your house in autumn and I loved seeing you in it—and, well, I guess I just got the lonesome blues and picked up the phone on a hunch."

"Your hunch was entirely correct," Alec said.

He put down the phone.

"Pull in your ears, Chief," he said. "And change the spare

bedroom to something reasonably suitable for a lady."

"We're in business again, huh, Boss?"

"We are *not* in business again, you miserable scavenger. We are merely having a young lady out for a long week end. And you better go to town and find us something fairly fancy in the food department."

Luke saluted smartly.

"Aye, aye, sir," he said. "Will do, Commander. And Boss?" Luke grinned.

"We got just time enough for me to give you a haircut."

118

Life proceeds in sevens, somebody said, Alec thought as he stood in the drive and watched Penny Lawrence—the hell with that name Mongomery—climb long-legged from her little MG. This is a big, big seven, which started with the first and now is knocking on the fourth. This was a most staggering young woman of twenty-seven or -eight, mature as he remembered her mother from the early days, ripened by marriage, full of juice as sun-warmed fruit and with the first tiny lines of saddened wisdom showing at her eyes. The eyes were no less blue, but the once-riotous black curls were tamed into a more matronly coif. There had always been a figure and a face. The baby fat was finally gone from both.

"I believe in God," Alec said, and kissed her on the cheek. "Seek and ye shall find. This was a day when I was fresh out of green pastures. Come in, come in, and I will maketh you to lie down beside a mint julep. This is a Twenty-Third Psalm sort of day."

"By golly, Unca Alec," Penny Lawrence said. "You don't look so down. You sound right bubbly, like the last time I saw you. I can't stand it if you're running off to Africa again. Hello, Luke. There's only the one little bag. Mind if I run straight off and climb into some shorts and a shirt, Alec? Where am I, same room?"

Alec ticked at his fingers.

"I am *not* so down. I *feel* right bubbly. I'm *not* running off to Africa again—or to any place else. You *may* run straight off and climb into some shorts and a shirt. You *are* in the same room."

"Aye aye, sir," Luke said. "See what I mean, Boss?"

"I see what you mean, all right, and you've just been busted to seaman second for being too goddam fresh," Alec said.

Alec made the julep in a frosted pewter mug. He took his time with the simple syrup and then bourbon and the shaved ice and the mint sprigs. It was amazing, that passage of time. Yesterday he had held her on his knee and she had called him Unca Alec. Today she called him "Alec dear" on the phone in a woman's firmly rounded voice.

"Practically contemporaries," he mumbled, watching the frost thicken on the pewter. "How dat ol' time do fly."

"What?" a voice said behind him.

"Old man's bad habit," he said. "Talking to myself. Find it easier to think that way. I say, child, you do look a sight for any eyes."

"I'm too fat." She was wearing powder-blue short-shorts and a lighter shade of blue silk blouse. The thighs were firm, the full breasts no longer perky young, and she was tanned a biscuit-brown. She was a big girl—woman—his pretty Penny now. She would stand about five seven and weigh a compact one-thirty, thirty-five. "It's pure boredom. I've become a secret icebox raider."

"You're not too fat at all. You're a beautiful hunk of babe," he said. "Have a julep and tell me the story of your life."

"You just used the word I had in mind to explain the story of my life," she said. *"Contemporary.* Are we inside or outside by the pool?"

"Inside, I think. That's a comfortable chair—" remembering sharply the evening in his office in the town apartment when he'd said almost the same words. *"Contemporary? How?"*

"I made a simple mistake. I married one. It took me two years to find out that you can't marry contemporaries and make it work. Somebody has always got to be older than somebody else. In this case it was me. And you know something?"

"No. Tell me."

"I blame you and Ma. Ma always raised me like an equal

and you always treated me like a woman. Even when I was a little girl, I was used to being around adults, and I married a male bobby-soxer." She made a face. "I still don't know why except he was awful good-looking and I was getting on for being an old maid."

"I remember." Alec rubbed his chin. "I don't suppose you do, but we had quite a long chat about it. You said at the time you had an idea that you wanted to make a career of making some man a good wife."

"I remember very well. But I said *man*. I made a mistake. I married a boy. We seemed to be a little short on available men in my league. They were all married."

Alec got up and walked out to the far edge of the pool, where the hill fell away to the lake. The conversation had started awkwardly, brusquely, bluntly, almost as if—

"Thank God," he said to himself. "Here comes Luke with some *hors d'oeuvres*." Then aloud: "Thanks, Chief. Over there. What are we eating tonight?"

"Goodies," Luke said. "All laid out and ready for the chef. Strip steak and sweet corn and new tomatoes and all manner of stuff. But Boss, I got to beg off. I already had a word with Miss Penny. She's standing my galley watch for me. There is a chick in town that— Well, I promised I'd take her and her mother to a show and she's got the tickets and . . ."

You scheming son-of-a-bitch, Alec's eyes said to Luke. *You and your bloody ten-cent conniving.*

"You could always ring up and call it off," he said.

"Boss, you always say yourself you never need me at night," Luke began, and Penny cut in.

"Oh, for goodness' sake, Alec, I'd love to cook dinner for you. As a matter of fact I had a private chat with Luke and we decided that you're both sick to death of the sight of each other, not to mention the cooking," she said. "I *want* to cook your dinner, Alec. Remember the last time?"

"Have a good evening, Seaman Second," Alec said to Luke. "You may very well be cutting yourself a new set of orders pretty soon."

"Before you say it, this is a clear case of collusion," Penny said. "Don't be mad at Luke. I've only ever had one chance to be with you when nobody else was around. I told him we had a lot of things to talk about and it would be just as well if he took himself off. If that's brazen, call him back."

Alec sat down in the facing chair and rested his elbows on

his knees. He looked upward through bushy grayed brows.

"It's brazen, and you're a proper baggage, but I won't call him back. I'm complimented. You want a swim before the sun goes? It gets chilly out here in these hills, even in July."

She stretched and wriggled slightly in her chair. Her golden skin sweated tiny diamonds of moisture in the sun.

"Nope. I just want to sit here and hear about you. I don't really *know* anything about you any more. And now I've got you all to myself. Finally."

119

Alec was sleeping soundly when the light rap came on the door. It had been a fine dinner, gracefully served, with candlelight and slow music. He had talked himself hoarse, both before and after. For the first time he had felt—perhaps the brandy had helped—had felt like trying to put it all down, step by step, including the Jill business and the Amelia letter and the African itch which had vastly overextended his stay, his plans for the big body of work—*everything*. Twice he had called Penny Dinah by accident, and once his tongue had slipped and barely stopped a Jill. He had been thoroughly, gratefully weary, and not a little befuddled by brandy and his own rhetoric when he kissed Penny good night at her door and went off to bed.

There was the tap again. He snapped on the light and looked at his watch. Four A.M.

"Wha'? Luke?" His voice was still thick with sleep.

"Not Luke. *Me*. Penny."

"What's the matter, Sweetie? Sick?" Alec dragged himself to a sitting position.

"No. Not sick. But I had the terrible white awfuls. Couldn't sleep. May I come in for a moment please for a cigarette? I'm not really out of my mind."

"No, I don't think you're out of your mind. I've had the awful-awfuls myself. Wait a moment while I get into a robe. I'm completely raw. Go on downstairs and we'll light a little fire and have a port or something."

"All right," her voice was very tiny. "I'm sorry, but I—" the voice dwindled and died.

"Forget it. I'll be right down." Alec got out of bed, reached for a pair of trunks, and groped in his clothes-press for a robe. He shivered. It was damned chilly, July or no July. *Women, Jesus.* He put on a light flannel robe and found some slippers and stopped in the bath long enough to scrub the night-fur off his teeth, douse his face, and scrape a brush over his hair. *You don't suppose this kid's gone a little peculiar in the last few years?* he thought, heading downstairs.

She ran to him and pressed her face against his shoulder. She was wearing a thin robe, and a nightie under it, and he could feel her quiver.

"Please just hold me a second," she said. "I want to be held for a second. I needed badly to be held for a second." She had looked large in her shorts, large and healthy and almost robust. She felt very small in his arms.

He gave her a little pat, kissed her forehead lightly, and pushed her away.

"Curl up in that chair while I fix the fire. Then I'll get us a drink."

"I don't want a drink. I just want to be close to someone." She pulled one of the leather *poufs* close to the fireplace. "It's a long time since I've been close to anyone."

Alec brought some kindling from the kitchen, wadded a newspaper, and touched the permanently laid logs into boisterous flame. Then he went to the bar and fixed a large glass of cognac and port, half-and-half.

"This is the best sleeping pill known to man," he said. "We'll make it a loving cup."

He sat down in a chair. Penny dragged her *pouf* backward from the fire and sat at his feet, resting her head on his knee. She took a sip from the glass and made a face.

"Strong medicine," she said. "I don't really need a loving cup. I need a loving man."

"Strong talk," Alec said, and passed her a lighted cigarette. "Very strong talk from a little girl."

"I'm not a little girl! I haven't been a little girl for a long time! I'm a grown woman, Alec Barr. I've been married and in what I thought was love—more than once, you might as well know that. And it suddenly occurred to me that I had been wasting my time on the wrong people. I love you, Alec

Barr. I loved you as a child and as a gawky girl and now I love you as a grown woman, if that's what I am. I thought the time had finally come to tell you—because if you don't want me, I'm wasting my time."

Penny Lawrence bit her lip, then took a drink from the glass. She held up a hand and touched him lightly on the shoulder.

"I know all the things you're going to say. I have been reciting them over and over to myself ever since I went to bed. And I know that I could have gone about this differently—good dinner, brandy, moon over the water, music, seductive perfume, propinquity, no Luke, nightbirds calling—the hell with it. It's too easy to confuse moonlight and wine and roses with what I wanted to tell you. I'm a woman; we're both lonely. . . . The hell with it again. There's so little time, Alec. I don't want to waste it. And that's why I couldn't sleep. That's why I beat on your door.

"Here is where I could start to cry, and where you say 'Here, blow your nose, like a good girl, and I'll take you home to Mummy.' And I'll leave if I've embarrassed you, but not to go home to Mummy."

"I don't know, I really don't know." Alec twisted and untwisted his fingers. He smiled faintly. "You must admit you came at me rather violently. I feel a touch maidenly—'la, sir, this is so sudden.' There are other ones I could fall back on such as 'I didn't know you cared.' And I didn't. Or at least I didn't think about it. But I really don't know what to say. I hadn't planned anything."

He tipped up her chin with a gentle forefinger.

"There's the age difference. I've known you since I almost, but not quite, changed your nappies. I won't say I've always —not in recent years—thought of you as just a little girl. I was almost actively jealous when you got married, but I put that down to a fatherly—"

Penny flared. She sat straight up in her chair, knees tightly together.

"It wasn't fatherly a damned bit! That night, seven years ago, when we had dinner at your apartment, if you hadn't had to catch that plane for Africa, I could have had you—could have made you take me—then! And you know it, Alec Barr! That last kiss—and I quote, 'One for you and one for your Ma but the last one is for *me*'—*that* wasn't any fatherly anything. You just ran out of minutes and the kiss was an apology for the unfatherly pass you never made!"

"Here is where I say 'You'll have to give me a little time,'" Alec said. "And 'Are your intentions honorable?'"

"Not a goddamned bit," Penny said.

Alec got up, took the empty glass, and moved to the bar. Daylight reached rosy across the lake.

"You could at least wait until nightfall," he said. "I feel so shy in the daytime," and was vastly relieved when she threw back her head and laughed. The line of her throat was lovely, exquisite, Alec thought, and thought also that he had no right to think such a thought, and that once more he was panic-stricken at the necessity of proving himself in the minutes ahead.

"It really is time for beddy-byes," he said. "Luke'll be stirring soon. It's time we sought our various beds."

"I don't want to seek our *various* beds," she said, getting up and walking close to him. "I don't ever want to be alone any more."

120

An overpowering guilt assailed Alec Barr when he woke at near-noon to find Penny still sleeping, rosy-faced, black hair tumbled, in the crook of his nearly paralyzed arm. Great God Almighty, he thought, brain suddenly electrically awake, I have despoiled a child—and then thought as swiftly that he had not despoiled a child; the child had ravished him. But what a delightful ravishment, and what a wondrous woman and not a child at all.

He withdrew his arm as gently as possible, and she moved, smiled, and snuggled voluptuously closer. Fingers touched him, knowingly, and it seemed pointless to get out of bed at that moment. It was not until Alec Barr went to the bathroom to shave and shower that he was struck full force by a massive revelation.

Alec Barr is a man again, he thought, a right good man at that. The proof of his manhood was whistling as she moved about the guest bathroom, drowning out the clatter of Luke's noisy housekeeping below stairs. It was a happy song, too, and so was Alec Barr's off-key caroling from his shower. It was so good—it was bloody wonderful—to feel himself a man again in the one vital area that really mattered. The nagging ache had left his back, and the more persistent ache had departed his soul. His head was clear, and he felt good, strong—he felt like work and he felt like play—and he suddenly felt an awful sense of grateful responsibility.

Penny was glowing when she came down to lunch, dressed in black stretch pants and bright red sweater.

"You look like somebody died and left you a million dollars, Miss Penny," Luke said. "You look like a lady with a fine night's sleep."

"You never said a truer word," Penny said. "What's for breakfast—brunch—Luke? I could eat a team of horses."

"The Boss ain't down yet, but he usually starts off with whisky sours on a feast day," Luke said. "So I made some. And then we got some deep-froze quail from last fall's shooting—with that cream gravy with mushrooms the Boss knows about. He's a pretty good cook, the Boss, on some things. We got scrambled eggs and little pork sausages and hot garlic bread and very light wine, rosé, and a salad and some fruit and some cheese. That sound all right?"

"I was going to hold out for scrapple," Penny said, as Alec entered the room. "But Luke has dissuaded me. Sleep well, Commander?"

"Had some delightful dreams, thank you very much. And thank you, Luke, for defecting last night. Miss Penny is a real cook."

"She was never in the Navy," Luke said. "Have a little torpedo juice, Commander. Do you a power of good."

"I've been done a power of good," Alec said.

121

"There is a thing to consider, darling," said Alec Barr, three days later. "We have had a honeymoon. Would you consider it very rude of me if I inquired as to your plans for the future—such as marriage?"

"Marriage, and I swear it, was not my original intent," Penny said. "And I am lying in my teeth. I would love to marry you, and don't you dare give me any calloused old arguments about that corny age-difference bit. That strange man who has been invading my privacy is a positive shocker. Wow!"

"Wow yourself. There is the stark fact that I am forty-eight and you are barely twenty-eight. I was your mother's friend, and—"

"*And I am young enough to be your daughter,*" Penny's voice mincingly parroted. "And when I am thirty-eight you will be fifty-eight, and when I am forty-eight— Oh, come off it, chum, as you would say the British would say. You don't have to go grandpa-defensive on me. You are not obliged to marry me because we have been sleeping delightfully together on account of I snidely planned and plotted to lure you to my bed. It's just that if you don't mind terribly I'd love to marry you, if only so we wouldn't have to hide things from Luke."

"How'll we ever tell your mother?"

"Mummy's a big girl now. I think she's old enough to face the facts of life."

Alec winced inwardly.

"I wasn't thinking so much of Mummy being a big girl now and being able to face the facts of life. I was just thinking that it might occur to Mummy that she might have hired a different sort of babysitter quite a lot of years ago, and Mummy might just not approve of one of *her* contemporaries—"

"Despoiling her little daughter? Of being mother-in-law to an old boy friend? Of being laughed at in the literary saloons because daughter copped the prize? Don't ever be that kind of silly, darling. There is at least one thing women have in common, and that is a general respect for no-holds-barred procedure on the acquisition of men."

"Call me No-Holds-Barr," Alec said. "Will you for God's sake marry me, then, Miss Lawrence?"

"Right gladly, and as soon as practically possible, as long as you aren't playing out a guilt complex about your 'pretty Penny,' as you used to so nauseatingly put it. You'll only be marrying a wily wench who trapped you first into bed, and then into a narrow corner."

"You write all the fast lines," Alec said. "So I'm cornered. When and where?"

"There are certain ladylike aspects of a fresh marriage I have to consider," Penny said. "There are things like clothes and where do I send them and do we live in town and letting Ma know I've pinched her oldest beau. Would three weeks be asking too much for the formality, if I granted another pleasant informality now?"

"You got yourself a boy," Alec said, and then flinched again when he remembered whose phrase he had used.

"Something touched you there," Penny said. "What?"

"An old newspaper expression," Alec said. "I expect we'll have to consider engagement rings shortly?"

"I'd rather have a dedication in the front of a big book. Kiss me big and take me away to the Casbah and—oh, Alec, I do love you so! Don't make me ever keep it light and frothy and flip! I do love you so!"

"I am past the age of wanting it light and frothy and flip," Alec said. "I want it solid and sincere and as corny as you please. I've made up enough light lines in my time. I don't want to make up any more."

They were married in Greenwich, Connecticut, the following month. The bride's mother did not attend the wedding. Picture business claimed her on the Coast.

122

They were, Alec supposed, gloriously happy. Certainly his ego was inflated. It was exhilarating to introduce this glowing girl as Mrs. Barr, to feel the stir she roused when they entered a restaurant or walked down a theater aisle or sat at a night-club table. Penny was absolutely wonderful about *not* going to restaurants and *not* walking down theater aisles and *not* going to night clubs. She loved living in New Jersey, she said, and she got along with Luke, considering that Luke was no longer Chief of the Boat. Penny had swiftly taken over most of his duties and thus had destroyed a great many of his privileges. But it wasn't as easy as it used to be, and while Luke took his major meals with them, at first, the awkwardness was so marked that he very swiftly began making excuses not to appear at table. There was very little coarse Naval reminiscence any more, and not a great deal of relaxed joking betwen master and man. Luke had never been a servant, but more of a hunting companion, and now the imposition of a permanent female presence made him largely superfluous in any capacity except that of secretary-handyman. The atmosphere was, to say the least, strained until after Luke drove into town or eased off to bed.

Alec was working very hard, and Penny was marvelous about that, too. She remained as quiet as a shadow, read much, and otherwise occupied herself with making mild changes in the house. Under the slack stewardship of Luke, with Alec's frequent absence and lack of keen interest in the details of housekeeping, a remarkable number of things like towels and sheets and ashtrays and curtains and lamps and crockery had fallen into obsolescence. It seemed, with a woman taking fresh interest in the house, that practically the whole building, inside and out, was standing in sad need of drydock and complete overhaul. The constant activity of plumbers and painters and parcel deliveries made Alec nervous, even though they confined themselves to other parts of the house.

It evidently made Luke nervous, too. He approached Alec one day, when Penny had driven off to the village, and cracked his knuckles. His lean Italian face was deeply troubled.

"Mind if we have a little coffee-time conversation, Commander?"

Alec looked up from his desk, mildly irritated. He had been editing the latest batch of fresh copy, and it seemed that he had cut more than he left.

"What's on your mind? And quit cracking your knuckles."

Luke gazed at his feet, and put his hands behind him.

"It's kind of hard to say, Boss, but I been doing a lot of thinking. It's not quite fair to the new Missus for me to be here."

"What the hell are you talking about?" Alec was acutely irritated now. He pushed back his chair and walked into the patio room. "Come on in here and sit down. What about the Missus?"

Luke looked miserable. Now he shuffled his feet.

"The Missus and I get along fine, I didn't mean anything against Miss Penny. But—well, hell, Commander, I ain't exactly a regular servant. I ain't exactly anything in real particular in this house. It makes a strain on Miss Penny, and it puts me in a kind of funny spot, too. *She* doesn't want to give me orders to do most things a servant would do. So she does them herself. I'm a kind of third thumb. I ain't neither flesh nor fowl."

"I hadn't noticed it." Alec's voice was crisp.

"You been very busy on the book. But you got to face it, Boss, no new bride wants a permanent houseguest, around all the time for meals and things, always somebody strange in the house. Maybe you haven't noticed it, but I always feel like I'm being made polite-to on purpose and that makes *me* nervous. There ain't anybody in this house but just us three, and three's a crowd."

"So what are you driving at?" Alec drummed his fingers.

Luke sounded more miserable.

"I think I better hand in my papers, Boss. I think I better take off. This is fine out here for a couple of bachelors—" Luke gestured helplessly. "For two men it's fine, sort of roughing it, but I just don't fit into a steady domestic threesome. It's all right once in a while, week ends, like in the old days, but—" he gestured again. "I think I better look for a new job, Boss."

Alec leaned back in his chair and scratched his head.

"Buy us a beer, Chief," he said. "Let's talk about this a little more. Where'd the Missus go?"

"She said something about the beauty parlor and a couple of other errands. You were busy and she didn't want to bother you."

"Well, if it's the hairdresser we've got plenty of time to sort this out. First the beer."

"Aye aye, sir."

"Now," Alec said, with a mug of beer cold in his hand. "Anybody done anything to hurt your feelings?"

Luke shook his head violently.

"No, no, Boss! Please don't misunderstand me. I think Miss Penny's wonderful. It's me that's the extra spoke in the wheel. You can't make a steady household out of a hunting camp—excuse me, but it's true. When you were married to Miss Amelia she practically never came out. She certainly didn't live here. The place belonged to you and me. Alone."

Alec took another sip of beer and lit a cigarette before he spoke. He massaged his chin.

"You could have a point. I've been thinking of it some myself—but that doesn't include you quitting, Luke. You got to admit that it's damned lonely out here for a young woman, with me bashing the typewriter all day and nothing but loons on the lake to talk to. And you aren't exactly my idea of the perfect lady's maid."

Luke grinned faintly.

"I'd be the first to admit it, Commander. And so would Missus Barr."

"What we had better do, I think," Alec said, weighing his words, "is find a flat in town—small sort of place, and easy to run—and return to the old routine. It'll give Penny more things to do, and more people to do it with. She loves this place, Luke, so we can come out for a lot of week ends, maybe every week end. And when I've got a helluva lot of work, I can sneak out here in the weekdays and leave the Missus in her Ma's capable hands. They can both come visit us on the week ends, and we can all play Injuns together. How's that sound? I really don't want to lose you."

Luke's troubled face lit.

"It sounds just dandy. I'll keep the ship taut through the week and sort of disappear on the week ends, unless you really need me. And—don't get sore, please, Boss—I want to take a pay cut. I've come to kind of consider this place as my home, too. I don't want to leave it, but I know you got—got other considerations. They cost money."

Alec clapped his old chief yeoman on the shoulder.

"Forget it, Chief, I ain't that broke. Not at all. But take an even strain for a while, hold her steady, and the Missus and I'll see what we can work out in the way of townside facility. Okay?"

"Aye, *aye*, sir. Sorry if I talked out of turn."

"You didn't. I should have brought it up myself. Let's get back to work. I've about finished that last stack of copy."

123

They had found the flat through a stroke of blind luck—downtown this time, just off Gramercy Park. It was a sub-lease on a cooperative, and not nearly so grand or spacious as the old penthouse, but bright and airy and tastefully furnished. It would do, Alec and Penny told each other, for the next couple of years, until they found something really fine of their own, and then could start to build its furnishings from bottom to top. Alec silently thanked God; he had paid for the furnishing of two houses and was aware of the excruciatingly high cost of ashtrays and curtain valances. They had two years' grace on this flat from its owner, a recently widowed lady who was going abroad to forget the last husband and ferret out another.

It was rather odd, living back in town again after a year of African bush and months in New Jersey by the lake. It was so—so *noisy*. It was filthy as well, and the traffic seemed perpetually snarled. A drop of rain disrupted all transport; an inch of snow brought the city to a complete standstill. You couldn't get a taxi even on fine days until after 10 A.M. and any fool who tried at five or during the theater hour was mad. New York was full of dingy pigeons and dingier people and Asian flu, of strikers and snarlers and paraders. Alec thought of fireside nights in Africa, of tranquil days by his lake in Jersey, and sighed silently. But he was willing to put up with the abrasion to his nervous system, because his bride seemed rapturous at being close to the hairdresser again. Living in Jersey, Alec had felt no particular strangeness at being married to a girl half his age. In New York there was a difference—a very palpable difference. He didn't get around much any more, and when he did move outside the new flat, it was seldom in the homes of people he had known —such as the Hazeltines, he thought wryly—but only in the public places. Age disparity *did* make a difference. The people he waved at or blew a kiss to in the restaurants were of his age and older. They looked appraisingly at the new

Mrs. Barr and stopped at the table to say hello, but they rarely offered invitations to drink or dine. After all, they had their set circles in Greenwich and Bucks and the Hamptons. Alec supposed rather ruefully that they would no more consider close association with his wife than with his daughter, if he had one. In "21" or The Colony or in the older Third Avenue haunts like Clarke's and Costello's, he felt rather embarrassed, as if he'd brought a child to a grown-up party. The waiters looked at him with a sort of tut-tut-Mister-Barr expression, and Alec felt that Tim, at least, would shortly admonish him against what the senior Costello called "neck-archin' in my shebeen."

Alec felt himself to be repeating the old trips to the Zoo with Penny. He was taking a child for an outing, arranging for a Saturday picnic or a party for a rainy Sunday to keep the child amused. Which was, in a way, entirely unfair to his wife.

Penny was the perfect concept of an author's model wife. She tiptoed noisily around the new apartment. She ostentatiously never intruded into the little room he called an office. It was not much of a room (Alec sighed again when he remembered the vast expanse of the penthouse den, with its bar and hi-fi and long rows of books, the separate set of *Encyclopaedia Britannica*), but at least he had a desk and a typewriter and some short bookcases and a comfortable green leather chair and a sort of love seat that Penny identified as the "tangerine divan." But there wasn't room enough in it to pace out the plot; not enough room to accommodate a secretary or, for that matter, to swing a cat. It had no fireplace that worked, no place to really scatter papers in ordered confusion. And the whole building had been modernized when it was chopped up and went cooperative. You could hear the toilets flush all over the place, and other people's television programs intruded on your conversation.

It was an apartment to get out of. It looked like everybody's adventure into *House and Garden* good taste, and the ashtrays were too small. If you got up and stared out of a window all you saw was a pigeon on the sill. Papers and magazines stacked up unbelievably on the coffee tables. It had a small bar with funny Steinberg pictures on the wallpaper, and no place, really, to put the glasses and bottles where the bartender could reach them. It had framed reproductions of cartoons from *The New Yorker* also on the

walls. It had everything but a large brass spittoon to give it
an air of false conviviality.

The whole damned place made Alec nervous, and because
he was nervous, he entered into a strange new life with his
wedded wife. It was a reprise, he thought, on Barbara Bayne
—he was now escaping for the same purpose which had
taken him to so many dives and driven so many hobnails
into his liver.

It *was* true. He felt a responsibility to amuse Penny in
the evening hours, after a rough day at the machine or with
the pencil. It was not fair, he thought, for the girl to mouse
around all day, for fear of disturbing The Great American
Author at his chores, and then confess that his back was
deviling him, he had a constant ache in his shoulder, and
what he would really most like to do would be curl up with
a drink and the early morning papers and then fall into bed.
Nor was it fair to replay the recent performance on paper—
watch her eagle-eyed when she uneasily read the stuff she
couldn't possibly evaluate not so much from inexperience
as because *he* didn't know what he was going to write next
either. A writer wrote all day. He didn't have to talk about
writing all night if he had a young and pretty wife.

And there was something else. He used to say jokingly
that he could write or he could drink. Now he was forced
to admit flatly that he could be either a writer or a lover,
but the combination was nearly impossible. If he was writing he took too many strange characters to bed with him. If
he was loving, he forgot what the characters were like—what
they were apt to think or say or do. He'd had that trouble
with Barbara Bayne, that shattering distraction of a woman.
Now he was having more of the same with a brand-new
wife, who was even more distracting because of her status,
and also—here it came again, boys—that dreaded disparity
in age.

The truth of it was they didn't have much to talk about
except each other, her mother, and the bloody book. He was
rapidly running out of current ancedotes, and she didn't dig
—she would have said—most of the background to the old
ones. Their social life was confined almost entirely to her
friends; his friends were also Amelia's friends, and while
they were polite enough . . . well, in fairness, they didn't
want to risk an embarrassing *contretemps* with Amelia, and

they had very little interest in a new wife who was younger than their own daughters.

Alec Barr could have wept in frustration, if he'd been the weeping type. Since he was not, he invented games for a child who could not (he thought) possibly comprehend the wealth of his background in terms of the rich conversations he might have held with Ben Lea, who was dead, or with Marc Mantell, who was still alive. You had to explain it step by step, such as why Lou Gehrig was called the Iron Horse, and who Damon Runyon was before he became posthumously famous by way of Abe Burrows' adaptation of "Guys and Dolls."

This latter aspect had become painfully obvious one evening when Marc Mantell stopped off for drinks. Alec was feeling quite jubilant. His agent had read the first half of the new project and was plainly excited. Perhaps the first two martinis hit him a little more happily than usual, for he and Marc Mantell had drifted into one of those good-old-days-remember-when conversations. It had all started with some idle remark that Marc Mantell had made about writers dating themselves—always a favorite topic—and the difficulty of adjustment to the editorial tastes of the current crop of magazines.

"Sometimes I feel like I'm still back in the cod-liver oil period," Marc said. "Or the Fletcher's Castoria phase. What babies get fed cod-liver oil or cry for Fletcher's Castoria any more? Who today ever heard of a Locomobile or a Pierce Arrow?"

Alec chuckled.

"You, me and John O'Hara, I suppose. John's got total recall, and he makes the readers hold still for it."

"Yeah, but he's writing period stuff on purpose, and he's good enough to swank it up by calling galoshes 'arctics' and clothing his women in middy-blouses and spitcurls. Technocracy is still real to Jawn."

Penny sat silently in a corner, following each speaker like a spectator at a tennis match. She had folded her hands in her lap, placed her knees primly together, like a nice child in the presence of her elders. She adopted this pose in a valiant effort to repress a yawn.

"God, sometimes I feel old," Alec said. "Even when I see names in the paper from the old New Deal days. You read where all the bright Young Turks—Corcoran and Landis

and Bill Douglas and Fortas and Henderson and Frankfurter
are in their fifties and sixties, and when I was working
Washington they were regarded as dangerous young radicals
or something, throwing bombs at the economy. And all the
old generals and admirals from *my* war are dead or largely
disappeared. All the generals and admirals from the Korean
War are about to retire. The junior senators are all chairmen
of their committees now, or have just been elected President
of the United States."

"And I got about fifteen years on you," Marc Mantell said.
"My first car was a Stanley Steamer, and I was a man grown
when Gene Austin started singing 'My Blue Heaven.' I remember free lunches in saloons and station KDKA and
Grover Cleveland Alexander as a young pitcher. Not forgetting Ty Cobb."

"You remember the Doodlesockers, and the first Amos 'n
Andy and the Two Black Crows and gooper feathers? And
Jones and Hare? I was a kid, of course, but Cab Calloway
was just coming up and so was Little Jack Little."

Marc Mantell laughed.

"Hell, my set regarded them as brash intruders, products of
Prohibition. And that included Jack Benny and Rudy Vallee.
I am an old Jean Goldkette, Coon-Sanders man, and I could
still do the Bunny Hug if somebody bet me. Or at least the
original Charleston."

"It seems so close and yet it's all older than Penny."

"And it occurs to me that we're being very rude to Penny,
two old gaffers cutting up ancient touches. You understand
any of this maudlin nonsense we're talking, child?"

Penny smiled a trifle hesitantly.

"I'm afraid I don't, but don't let that bother you. I'm getting an education. I've been backreading Alec's books, and I
do know about Al Capone and Prohibition and some of the
more dismal aspects of the Depression."

"She knows about the Depression, all right." Alec patted
his wife on the knee. "I've bored the living drawers off her
with my oft-repeated stories of what happened to me on the
way to the Little Red Schoolhouse. Poor child. She's very
brave. In any case her mother's due back from Europe pretty
soon and I'll have a grizzled audience for what used to happen back Befo' de Wah."

"I'm really terribly interested," Penny said. "Alec's got
pretty close to total recall too. It seems to me that there was

an awful lot going on in the world before I got out of mary janes. I feel sort of stupid not knowing more about it."

"Don't. We're both a couple of bores. I don't suppose you'd make an old bore another martini, would you? The old bore's bones ache." Marc Mantell grinned at her.

"I'd be delighted. And you're staying for dinner. It's the maid's night out, but I've actually learned how to cook other things beside steak, haven't I, Alec?"

"*Cordon Bleu,*" Alec said, giving her an affectionate tap on the rump, "with the help of Fanny Farmer. You can fill this old bore's glass, too, darling, while you're still young and healthy."

Penny brought the fresh drinks and then excused herself to go to the kitchen. Alec watched his agent's eyebrow raise quizzically.

"Problem?" Marc asked.

"Sort of," Alec said. "Tonight was fairly typical. Penny's been overplaying the author's loving wife a bit. She's been trying to stay out of my hair so damned hard she's actually getting *in* it. She tippy-toes around and sort of doesn't do things a great deal louder than if she actually did them. And she's so constantly sweet about things like tonight, when I forget she wasn't born when most of the things we mention were happening. Sometimes I wish she'd scream and curse and throw things when I get going on the war or the WPA."

"It's a rough one. But the girl loves you and she's new at the job and she's trying hard to please. Maybe she's over-trying. She'll get over it. She'll gain on you, and you can recede a little."

Alec scratched his head.

"Don't take me altogether wrong. She's marvelous. The only thing is that when she has her friends around—not very often—I generally don't have the faintest idea of what they're talking about. I know there are such things as *nouvelle vague* and Brigitte Bardot and all that jazz—you see, it *is* catching—but my sex symbol was Jean Harlow and my director was Frank Capra, not some Frog named Roger Vadim. I don't know what the hell Françoise Sagan is writing about, and these new, up-and-down piano players defeat me. It's like the old days when I was doing the town with Barbara. I felt like Alice in Wonderland. Now I feel like Alice in Wonderland in reverse."

"How do you suppose *she* feels, when every time some old

sweat like me comes in and we start talking about Lefty Grove and Ray Noble and John Gilbert? Unless this girl's seen him at the Museum of Modern Art she's even a little young for W. C. Fields. To her Frank Sinatra is an elder statesman, and Bing Crosby is only a wealthy golfer."

"Well, I hope Bing's making out better conversationally with Kathy than I am with *my* teen-ager," Alec said. "But seriously, it does put a crimp in my conversation. I keep feeling that I need to explain what I'm saying, or else I'm being rude to my little gal. And I love my little gal. It just makes me nervous, that's all."

"Well, Daddy Longlegs, I have no advice," Marc Mantell said. "Bing keeps Kathy pregnant a good bit of the time. Maybe you could adopt that as a solution. Or else just tie her in the kitchen. Judging from a faint smell she's well at home there. At dinner, let's try not to talk too much about Libby Holman and Harry Richman and who won the 1924 World Series. We might also give the book a rest, as well."

Alec grinned.

"You've asked for a tough one there. What else does an author talk about when he's writing a book? Seriously, what do you actually think?"

"By God, you're as bad as all the rest. I *told* you. From what I've seen I think it's great. If you can sustain the pace you've got a marvelous book. The subject's fine, the family's fine, the country's fine, and the time is ripe. Now how the hell can I tell you any more until you finish it?"

"Corrected I stand. I shall go back to the plow with renewed enthusiasm tomorrow. Meanwhile, there's time for one more delicious martini before chow call."

"I'm game, but I'm not a writer. An agent can drink and go home. How much of that hard stuff are you using these days?"

Alec shrugged.

"Not much. This is a special occasion. Nothing during working hours—well, maybe one before lunch—and perhaps a little more at night than I really like. But we do go out quite a lot, and you can't just sit in a saloon with a glass of milk. At least I can't."

"Penny like going out all that much?"

"I don't really know. But she's *young*, Marc, and it's damned dull for her most of the day. And I feel like I ought

to show her a little fun, if only—if only in grateful payment
for . . ."

Marc Mantell lifted a hand.

"Stop it, son. She's got what she wanted. Don't for Christ's
sake go defensive because she did you this great favor. She'd
be the last to want it, I promise you. She didn't marry a
bum, you know. She's a big girl. And you ain't all that old."

"I know." Alec's voice was sheepish. "Well, let's skip it.
Here she comes, apron and all."

Penny's face was flushed from the kitchen, and she looked
very French-maidy-fetching in a little ruffled apron over her
cocktail dress.

"Dinner," she said, "is served. If you'll just let me fix my
face."

"I see nothing wrong with it the way it is," Marc Mantell
said.

124

While the men chatted in the living room, Penny Barr went
about the routine of preparing the maid's-night-off dinner,
pacing automatically through table setting, frigidaire inspection, stove adjustment, condiment assembly—tasks that required no thought and allowed her brain to wander.

They had, she thought, been married almost six months.
Christmas was just over, New Year's just past, Mr. Kennedy
had been installed for a whole year, and it was now, cold,
1962. Something was already askew with her marriage, she
thought, taking the salad fixings out of the refrigerator, and
it must be, it had to be, her fault, because Alec, her Alec,
was the same Alec she had practically assaulted that July in
New Jersey, that Alec she had collected on his rebound from
Amelia—that Alec she had dragooned into marriage out of
a mixture of father-fixation, personal loneliness, old-young
physical attraction and yes, better face it, Penny, the usual
daughter-mother rivalry the psychiatrists were always yam-
mering about. Daughter-wants-Mommy's-man had been built
in a long time.

She had played it wrong, she thought, peeping into the casserole and adjusting the oven temperature. She had played it wrong in her first marriage, when she discovered she'd wed an adolescent. She had taken the lead, she had assumed the trousers, she had waxed while her husband waned. At the end there was nothing at all except Mommy leading Baby around by the hand, pushing him in a psychic pram, and she had wearied of being Mommy and had cut the umbilicus by way of a divorce. Nothing, although she had dabbled at the sort of inescapable affairs one encountered if you were out on the night in Manhattan, had happened to impress her with a fresh possibility of mating until she had read that Alec Barr had been divorced by his dear wife Amelia. She knew quite a lot of *that* history from her mother, and determined not to reprise it. She didn't want Alec Barr running off to far places, or even dropping by for a cup of coffee (cup of coffee!) with her mother, and taking his pretty Penny to the Zoo. She wanted him home and happy and boss of the lodge. She also wanted him in bed.

She had watched her mother work enough to know quite a lot about writers. She already knew enough about men, generally, to know that she had forced Alec's hand on the marriage—she knew that, if given sufficient time to rebound, Alec might quite reasonably have married her mother. She had harvested her man at a time when he was sick at heart from the disruption of a potentially serious romance and the completely unexpected divorce by a woman on whom he had always depended for stability. She had pounced when she suspected that he was terribly depressed by the death of his friends Ben Lea and Ernest Hemingway. She suspected furthermore—he had never told her in so many words—that sexually he had been impotent as a result of combined shocks. That was possible in all men (dear divorced Mr. Montgomery had taught her that, to her considerable frustration) and that Alec had been renewed through her vibrant young body. That at least she had given him.

And she had given him something else—a refreshed potency in his work. This big book, this first of a projected four, was going slowly but well. Marc Mantell had said so. So far so fine. Except that the work was stealing the body from the bed.

She had made one mistake, a very big mistake. She had been too damned overmuch the little woman, the quiet homemaker, the author's understanding wife, the patient little hand-holder, while the grownups talked on and on. This was out of character for that vibrant girl—not stupid, not unsophisticated, not unschooled in either sexual arts or social sciences—who had practically raped the man she knew would marry her. And *why* had she known he'd marry her? Guilt complex, as much as anything, for the act of deflowering (huh! Penny snorted, and took a saucepan off the fire) a tender maiden. Guilt complex, an adult gratitude and male conceit, of course, and a genuine tenderness. But if I'd been thirty-eight instead of twenty-eight, I doubt very much if we'd have rushed to the parson with such speed. (Where the hell did that maid put the new olive oil?)

So I made the mistake. With my loving ex I made the mistake of overaging me. With the gentleman I love and am married to I've made the mistake of milkmaiding myself back to a tender simpering nineteen. I am altogether too goddamned understanding and submissive and yes-milord, with the result that he thinks he has to take me out at night, like some debutante, for fear of boring me if we stay home like old married folks. And why does he fear boring me?

(Ah. There's the olive oil.) He fears to bore me because he suspected I thought Lou Gehrig was a woman or Babe Ruth was a candybar, or that the Louisiana Purchase was something Huey Long bought, when he's talking to people his own age. I can't help it if I really wasn't grown up in the Depression, which you'd think he owns personally, or if I never heard somebody named Deane Janis sing "Remember That Forgotten Man." I saw it on television, but *My Man Godfrey* still lacks social significance because I never lived in a Hooverville. I hadn't even seen anything of William Powell until he played the doctor in *Mister Robers*. Greta *Garbo?*

That doesn't make me hopeless. I don't see why I'm supposed to do crossword puzzles when he talks to his friends, even though I'm so goddamned bored I could scream at doyou-remembers like tonight. They're so *bloody* patronizing, these graybearded elders, when they sort of look at you and sigh that Little Sister here can't possibly understand about Home Run cigarettes and Home Run Baker, whoever the hell he was.

Bending over this hot stove is making me hot inside *and* out, Penny thought. I really cook better with a good temper. But what my fellow doesn't understand is that I *do* understand that he can't write his brains out all day and then be a night-clubbing playboy for most of the night and a hotrod lover the rest of it. The loving's fine when it happens; I got enough sense not to want to compete with a bed full of fictional characters. I can always wait until Sunday.

But something's got to give. I've got to stop playing wifie-wifie, and he's got to quit this resigned I-must-amuse-the-child bit; this we-can't-talk-freely-because-we'll-bore-little-Pen-ny-who-is-too-young-to-know-what-we're-talking-about *JAZZ*.

Penny burned her finger just then and said, resoundingly, "Shit!"

I'll go in and fetch them to supper, she said to herself, and the first one that remarks that I couldn't be expected to know who was Calvin Coolidge will get hit right over the head with the *soufflé* potatoes.

"Dinner is served, gentlemen," she announced, emerging, and knew that she looked very sexy in her frilly apron.

125

The younger folk came more and more to the house—bouncy girls with Bardot hairdos, crew-cut baby-cheeked young men, people who did nothing, seemingly, but ski and talk about skiing. Alec was well past skiing, as he seemed to be well past the appreciation of most of television that didn't deal with news or old Westerns. There didn't seem to be anything to *say* to these young friends of his wife's, except hello-have-a-drink, although he tried valiantly to share the conversations. The thing that irked him most was being called "sir," more often than not, and being dismissed as if he couldn't possibly be expected to understand the inside quips and references. Suddenly he felt the reverse through-the-looking-glass thing—they were doing to him exactly what he had patronizingly been doing to Penny. They made his back hurt worse.

They all seemed so damned healthy. There wouldn't be an aching back or a malevolent sinus in the lot. They mostly had three or four children each, the marrieds, and dressed very well, and lived in Scarsdale or Westport or Bronxville—and none of them was thirty. They had largely given up cigarettes—the men invariably fumbled with pipes or elaborately cherished cigars—and they tended condescendingly to a glass of sherry if they drank at all. And if they didn't, they made a loud point of it.

They talked stocks and bonds and advertising budgets and television ratings with the same passion they devoted to skiing. They dwelt long on security—retirement plans, fringe benefits, Blue Cross, mutual funds—with desperate eagerness. The jargon was a bad blend of Madison Avenue and suburban *ersatz* elegance, always spoken nasally. If they talked of music it was folk singers, or Dave Brubeck, or Gerry Mulligan. If they discussed plays it was lengthy revivals of moldy Eugene O'Neill or of the one-act things that occurred in "the round" and off Broadway. They were seemingly not interested in baseball, or in any writer of vintage more mellow than Edward Albee. They argued over saturated and unsaturated fats as murderers and thought all blood sports barbarous. (A week end with two tweedy couples in the Jersey house had been disastrous. They had looked at the trophies, the tiger and the leopards and the antelopes and elephant tusks, and, it seemed to Alec, regarded him as a monster.)

Psychiatric tags—relate, in analysis, sibling—strode their conversation, and their acute appraisal of the psychological mechanics of the female orgasm made Alec writhe. He was an outsider now, exactly as he had been an outsider when he was so dingily poor in school. He felt himself to be what once he had jokingly called himself— "dirty old man," and stupid as well. And he was infuriated when Penny's friends spoke blandly over his head—exactly as if he were not there, weren't handing round the drinks and the tea; exactly as he had seen Southerners talk through servants or adults speak over the heads of children who must be too young to understand.

One thing that annoyed him especially was that the entire pack seemed to have arrogantly risen above the news of the day. To Alec, "Did you see in the papers?" was the wedge in nearly any conversation, and going to bed without listening to the late news or buying a bulldog edition was unthinkable. He read *all* the papers, morning and evening, as well as the newsmagazines, from weather forecast to the lovelorn columns. News was bread and meat and drug to Alec, but Penny's group ignored it as a bore that would only be repeated again, slightly revised, tomorrow. If they read any books it was a Mickey Spillane skimmed on a plane trip, or some un-reviewed and largely unsold work by a limp-haired lady psy-chiatrist or a hornrimmed economist.

They dwelt vastly on the atom and the astral world; they talked extensively of child care and education, and Doctor Spock was very big, but Alec was prepared to bet his literary future that nobody in the room had read *Huckleberry Finn*, *Madame Bovary*, *Anna Karenina*, or even *Vanity Fair*.

Penny, loving Penny, labored mightily to fetch Alec to the fold, especially by drawing Alec out on Africa. But the effort was largely unsuccessful. There seemed nobody to talk *at*, and if Alec did get going on the one topic of which he was the modern master, he felt himself a crashing bore and lamely changed the subject. You could not talk tribal rivalry, African insecurity, African jealousy and greed and cultural conflict to an audience which only had the one fixed idea: All colonials were monsters and all rebels (even including ter-rorists) were fighting for the right. Alec felt guilty about the books and articles he had written, as if he were part of the brutal colonial scheme to enslave the world, and he doubted very much if anyone present would credit the fact that some "freedom fighters" ate baby brains, drank menstrual fluid, and had intercourse with animals in their "freedom-fighting" rituals.

It was all sad, all very dreary, and Alec felt more and more constrained to excuse himself with a muttered "Some more proofs to finish—deadline you know—if you'll please pardon me," and flee to his little den to read *Field and Stream* and doze in his chair until he heard the good-by noises in the hallway.

"I'm sorry," Penny would say when they'd left, bending over to kiss the top of his head. "They must be dreadful bores for you, but they're about the only people I know, and in a way they're pretty good at their various trades. You must admit that Vera is the best modern stage designer we have at the moment, and Roger has literally soared in Belton, Bratton and Knowles. Kenny's the best decorator in the busi-ness, and if Ian ever gets the right break, his plays will be fabulous . . ."

"I know, I know, Sweetie, but it's just that they make me

feel so damned old, and I don't understand half of what they're talking about. Come on, be a good girl and mix the old man a nightcap, and let's hear a little slow something on the squawk box that isn't Mulligan or Brubeck."

"Ella or Sinatra or Nat King?" Alec could feel the smile behind him, as she leaned over the chair and stroked his cheek.

"Any or all three," Alec said. "I'm sorry I'm such a stick-in-the-mud. But I belong to another—"

"Shush," she said, coming round to sit in his lap and closing his mouth with a kiss. "Where it counts you're younger than springtime."

(And I wonder how she meant me to take that crack? Alec thought, as she went off to fetch him his drink.)

Peter was one of the few unmarried members of the Penny group that came for tea and talk. Peter was something in advertising, mostly to do with television, and he was, Alec forced himself to admit, a sight for sore eyes, masculine *or* feminine.

Peter had a carved Indian profile, with hawk nose perfectly complemented by long jutting jaw and a sensuous lower lip. His skin was coffee-colored, almost, and only some of it was from the tan he received from skiing in winter and water-skiing in summer. He had opaque eyes, as deeply black as Greek olives, and perfect, brilliantly white teeth. (Alec was prepared to swear that they were all capped.) Peter had the kind of close-growing black hair that rippled as smoothly as sealskin, fitted him like a helmet, and was always in perfect trim over the small, neat ears. Peter's neck was long and thick and corded, and his clothes never seemed capable of either bag or crease. In dinner jacket or in the decent gray flannel of his trade, Peter still seemed to be wearing a cable-stitched turtlenecked sweater with green reindeer worked into the woof. Peter was two kinds of skier, a tobogganer, a tenniser, and now that the Kennedys were in, very possibly a keen touch footballer. Certainly he golfed in the seventies, and played a very decent slow piano. He worked with the weights at the New York A. C. just to keep his muscles in tone.

Peter kept his sloe-eyes clear. He traveled with the pack, but he never seemed to have any steady companion in it. Peter was a confirmed bachelor, a compulsive collector of women, and evidently he only wore them once or twice before throwing them away. Alec was quietly impressed by the diversity of the pretty playmates Peter brought to the flat and who accompanied him on the skiing week ends. Alec had been denied an affluent bachelorhood, and the steady succession of nubile females Peter presented constituted almost a lecture with slides on the potential of a handsome young dog who made upwards of $20,000 a year and worked easy hours. Young actresses, models, society nymphets, chic secretaries, slightly weathered divorcées (and quite possibly some covert still-marrieds?) accompanied Peter on his rounds. One of the things Alec admired most in Peter was that he usually left the party early—very possibly, as Alec once remarked to Penny—to bed, if only to rise.

Yet Peter did not own all the aspects of classic wolf. None of his women was tawdry; he was exquisitely polite to them all; he never leered or implied intimacy. He was merely handsome Peter, Peter the Profile, with a new redhead, brownhead, blondehead, dyed-head, tall, thin, plump, short, stacked, blue-eyed, green-eyed, brown-eyed, black-eyed, invariably well-dressed and well-spoken woman on his arm. He kept himself and his women notably sober, and made no public passes at anybody, his own or anyone else's woman. But his women drowned him with their eyes.

Alec had resigned himself to the skiing set. With gratitude he encouraged Penny to go off on New Hampshire and Vermont week ends with the boys and girls to strap on laminated staves and slide down snowy hills. It relieved his conscience a little, for it was bloody dull for a young girl to sit around with *The Times*' book section while Father was holed up in the back room with The Book. Selfishly, he enjoyed the brief spate of relief from the necessity of worrying over whether Penny was bored to death—and also of the necessity of performing his one athletic feat which might prevent her from being bored to death. Bed could also become tedious, he thought, if it constantly took on the aspect of parlor trick or planned picnic.

Mostly the skiers left on Fridays, early afternoonish, and returned late Sunday, wind-flushed and winter-sun-tanned, glowing with rude health and prickling with anecdotes about who did what on which slope and spouting expert appraisals of the snow. (Snow, to Alec, was a dirty off-white something the New York City maintenance people really didn't know how to handle because they didn't have any place to put it.)

But now he was very fond of snow, and he read the papers to see what its condition might be in the neighboring hills, and he often wondered why the skiers didn't have three or four sets of skis, so they could leave them in a variety of areas, instead of always packing the bloody things back and forth. Snow freed him for calm week ends with Luke in the Jersey place or left him to blessed peace with his books in the flat. Alec found himself thinking dismally that when spring came, he would be forced to invent some new games for his lovely girl-wife to play—at least until it was warm enough for water-skiing.

Penny, at the same time, was not nearly so keen on the outdoor life as she appeared to be. But there was a growing guilty suspicion that her presence kept Alec from full concentration on his work, and she was also beginning to suspect that Alec's visits to her bed were assuming a proportion of duty-dance—a hushpuppy thrown to keep the hound dogs quiet. As the days between the visits increased, as the work on The Book became more intense, she was just as happy to work off her animal energy on a ski slope.

Alec knew something of the *après*-ski atmosphere, when the girls changed into buttock-squeezing stretch pants and bejeweled chunky sweaters, and the hot fire mingled with the hot music and the hot grog and the cold night and the snapping stars and the fur rugs in the sleighs whose bells jingled merrily as they chased the moon. He did not worry about Penny, or her odd-girl-out status on the week-end trips. There would always be some lean young man about, even if he were only a ski instructor, and Alec rather fancied that his Penny wouldn't be wasting her physical substance on lean young men *or* ski instructors. And ski people *were* different. They didn't pair so much, and they were usually good friends in town as well as out. Young marrieds these days seemed to fancy the extra girl as well as the extra man, even if it was only for a cookout or a Sunday brunch.

It was a proper pity, Alec thought, that he couldn't work up enthusiasm for these safaris into the snow, but he'd never learned to ski, was too old to start, and did not repeat *not* fancy breaking an arm to the detriment of his work. Alec found himself getting carefuller and carefuller, instead of curiouser and curiouser, as the years raced on. He was even wary of such things as fire tongs, shower mats, and other hazards to navigation. No man can write fact with a sore finger or fiction with a burnt hand.

It was Friday, and Alec had an early date with Marc Mantell—prelunch, to talk to the lawyers about some very fine print in a movie contract. He collected his papers, popped them into a brief case, and went out to say good-by to Penny, who was very shortly off to New Hampshire with The Group again. As he passed through the foyer, seeking Penny in the living room or kitchen on the other side of the flat from his office, the doorbell rang. Funny, the acoustics in these new chopped-up apartments. You couldn't hear the doorbell from the living room, but it sounded like a fire siren in the office, and every time a neighbor flushed a toilet next door you felt like yelling *"Olé!"*

It was Peter the Profile. Peter looking tanned and ruddy and neat-headed and very sporty in a greenish Harris-tweed confection that never saw a wholesale house. He had his overnight bag and his skis with him.

"Hey, come on in," Alec said. "Ain't you kind of early for the pneumonia circuit?"

"I am, I guess," Peter said, leaning his skis against the wall. "But I'm stagging it this week end, and got delegated by the mob to come and collect your bride. We've got a chartered airplane this time. People drink too much on those ski trains. So I thought I'd come around and raid your bar a little bit while Penny got her togs together."

"The bar is eminently open to pillage," Alec said. "Shed your coat and I'll buy you the first one, but then I really must run. I got lawyer business today and I'd much prefer the dentist. Penny!" he shouted. "Company!"

There was no reply.

"She's got to be here," he said to Peter. "The trouble with these flats is that you can hear everything from one end and nothing from the other. Come and sit. I'll dig up the old lady."

He found Penny in the kitchen, hair-turbaned, waist-aproned.

"Your boy friend's early," he said. "Seems like you've got a new means of transport. Chartered aircraft. Darling, I must rush off. Mantell's got a whole fleet of lawyers convened, and I'm part of the act. Have a good time, and please come home early. I'll miss you."

Penny touched her bandanaed head, and frowned.

"Who's the boy friend? And me with the curlers still in."

"Tried and Trusty. Old Faithful. Pete. The Profile. It seems he ran out of women—although this to me is incomprehensible—and has been delegated as your squire. Do me a favor and try not to get seduced in the snow. I'm told it's bad for girls—snow, I mean. And have a good time watching the necks break. 'Bye."

He pecked her cheek briefly and passed back through the living room.

"You know where the bar is," he said to Peter. "Mix your own. The Memsaab is in a swivet. She's still got her curlers on, so you're on your own for a bit. Excuse me for the rush, and don't fly into any New England hills. So long, Pete."

"So long, Alec. I'll manage."

Alec grabbed his topcoat and push-buttoned the lift. He snatched up his brief case, and descended to the street, where the doorman—as usual, as in all New York apartments —was off about some other business. Eventually Alec found a taxicab and sat impatiently, swearing at the traffic, on his way to 30 Rockefeller Plaza. From force of habit he riffled through the brief case.

Precisely at 46th and Park he discovered that the one vital sheet of statistic that Marc Mantell's lawyers wanted was missing—a signed quit-claim on a fictionalized real-life person who might just possibly sue for invasion of privacy.

"God damn it!" he roared. "Driver, we've got to go back downtown. I forgot something valuable. Sorry."

"All the same to me, Boss. The flag's down. The clock ticks. Uptown, downtown, who cares?"

When they reached Gramercy Park, Alec said to the driver:

"Do me a favor and wait, will you? I won't be but a minute. There's an extra buck in it for you."

"Dee-lighted," the cabbie said. "Take your time. I got nothing better to do. Kennedy don't need me today."

"Thank you." Alec got out, and for a moment his mind raced back to London and the Cockney hacker who said 'e'd wait a bloomin' year if necessary, outside Jill Richard's house. He shoved that thought hurriedly out of his mind and let himself quietly into the flat. There wasn't any point in going through the same good-bys again.

As he entered the foyer silently, he heard a voice. It was Peter's voice, low, urgent.

". . . . But we don't *have* to go with the others," Peter was saying. "There's this little lodge where we can be alone. It's marvelous, fire in the bedroom, wonderful food, and the people live in another house. The snow's better, and there won't be all that clutter of—of *everybody* in everybody else's pockets."

Penny's voice came loud and clear.

"No, Peter. Absolutely not. I don't know what gave you the idea that you and I might just fit in a sneaky lost week end."

Peter's laugh was a snort.

"You don't know what gave me the idea? That sleighride last week end gave me the idea. That good night kiss at the bedroom door gave me the idea. And you weren't exactly playing five minutes ago, or is my lipstick all smudgy just because I'm careless?"

Silence. Then:

"All *right*. I kissed you in the sleigh. I kissed you when you took me home. And you just kissed me here, and I—I suppose I kissed you back. You're a very attractive man, Peter. I'm only human."

Peter's laugh was gay, now.

"I'll say you're human. And too much woman for—"

"For *what?*" Penny's voice was sharp.

"I was only saying that you're too much of a woman to go unappreciated."

"That doesn't mean anything. And it wasn't what you started to say. Certainly I kissed you. But I didn't invite it. It's just that I'm too old to scream when the kisses don't mean anything."

Now the soft chuckle, velvety, stroking.

"You're a little liar, and you know it. You've been married twice. You don't kiss a man that way unless you're leaving the door open for something else. Something better, bigger. That's why I asked you to go away with me for the week end. You were *asking* me to ask you."

"I suppose you're right, according to your lights," Alec heard his wife say. "And I'm dead wrong. It was a good night after a good day and there was a lot to drink and—"

"Oh, nuts, let's try it again for size and see who's right and who's wrong."

Alec stood, fascinated, and certainly not horrified. There was, he thought, no point in playing the outraged husband rushing in, brandishing *what*—a gun, an umbrella?

"You see," Peter's voice was softly triumphant. "You liked it. You'll like it better still. And old Somerset Maugham back there in his cave couldn't care less. Old Pops won't mind if you have a little innocent outside fun—"

That was a flat crack, sharp as a pistol-shot.

"Get out of here! Get the hell out of here—now! And I never want to see that smirking face of yours again!" Penny's voice was angry, tearfully furious.

"Oh, yes you do, yes you will," Peter said. "I don't mind the smack in the face. I was out of line about old Daddy-O. But you'll see me again, because you'll want to see me again, and because old Pops isn't any good to you, and you—"

Crack!

"I guess you may be serious at that," Peter said. "That's two in a row. You must be mighty disturbed about your own feelings if you belt me twice."

"Get out! Get *out!*" Penny's voice reached a scream.

"Okay, okay, cool it, baby, I'm on my way. But when you change your mind, and you want to kiss it and make it well, give me a ring. Old Daddy-O really won't mind. Not from what I've heard. He'll be glad to have you off his hands. No, now, don't hit me again," the voice mocked. "I'm really going. Give my regards to Foxy Grandpa."

Alec faded into his office as he heard the angry footsteps coming toward the foyer. *Pops,* his brain said angrily. *Daddy-O. Dear old Dad. Foxy Grandpa.* I ought to beat the son-of-a-bitch to death with his own skis. So this is how they think of me. *Foxy Grandpa. Daddy Longlegs.*

Alec's stomach writhed as his fists clenched.

"And if I make a scene," he said to himself, "if I make a great big manly thing, this beefy bastard will beat me to death in my own house, and my wife will never forgive me for two things—overhearing her little drama and being beaten up in my own house. And the guy's not worth shooting, nor is the offense worthy of that much bad melodrama. Best thing to do is sneak out again and forget I ever mislaid a piece of paper."

He found the forgotten document, shoved it into his brief case, and waited a full five minutes after he heard the lift arrive and depart. Then he went carefully to the fire stairs and walked down to the street.

His cab was still waiting.

"I lost me a fare," the cabbie said cheerfully. "A guy come boiling out with a suitcase and a pair of skis, and damned near hijacked me. I told him I was waiting for a gentleman who lived in the apartment, and wasn't for hire. But boy, was he mad at something!"

"You know how these athletes are," Alec said. "Temperamental. Now let's go back to 30 Rock as fast as we can. I had some trouble finding out what I needed to know."

"Anything you say, Boss," the cabbie said.

Well, there it is on the plate, Alec thought, as they rode uptown. There is the inevitable picture. *Pops. Old Dad. Foxy Grandpa.* Beautiful young bride and dull old dog smelly in the back room. Frustrated young ewe amid the ravening wolf pack. If it's not Peter it'll be Paul—or Matthew, Mark, Luke (not my Luke), and John. I let myself in for the one problem I should have let myself very much out of, that May-and-December jazz. Oh well. Now the lawyers, and then back to the plow.

I won't put her on the spot with any eavesdropped knowledge, he thought. I'll just slink back to the office and start pounding "the quick brown fox jumped over the lazy dog" and "Peter Piper picked a peck of pickled peppers" on the Iron Maiden. When she's sufficiently reassured by the sound she'll come back and tell me she's bored with skiing, has a headache, and decided she didn't want to fly.

Later, Alec looked up from the machine.

"I didn't hear you come in, Sweetie," he said. "I thought you'd left for the pneumonia pastures?"

"I'm not going skiing any more this year, darling," she said. "I'm fed up with the whole business—the people and all. Let's go out to Jersey and play with Luke and catch a fish through the ice or something. Unless you're in a working scene where you can't stop?"

"I can stop right now," Alec said. He got up and took her in his arms. "I can stop right now. And later, let's go out and beat up the town a little bit. We haven't been to '21' in ages, and there's a new singer at The Blue."

"Oh, I love you!" Penny said. "I really do love you!"

"There's no point in crying about it," Alec said, and smoothed her hair. "It's completely legitimate among married folk."

126

Alec Barr was well acquainted with the old saw that the eavesdropper never heard any good of himself. He was also equally aware of the fact that he had a good and loyal—and young—wife, who had brushed off (indeed, knocked flat) the first of what was inevitably going to be a series of assaults on her fidelity. Alec was neither overproud of her rebuff of the All-American boy nor overperturbed by the fact that she'd allowed herself to be kissed by Mr. Peter Profile. Alec knew more than a little of those things; chiefly, he knew they were inescapable unless you fettered your creature and locked her to your wrist.

He, Alec Barr, was old, and growing older. And she, Penny Barr, was young, and growing riper. He would only become sere; she would merely secrete fresh juices. At the moment Alec was master in the bedchamber and his name was on a variety of dust jackets. Quite swiftly his only need of bed would be for simple slumber, and the dust jackets would turn into paperbacks. And Penny? A succession of Peters, all pounding on the ramparts? And himself, with nothing to offer in the drawing room but ancient, wheezy reminiscences, and nothing at all to offer in the bed?

Alec ground his teeth and decided that literature had used enough of his time this day. He'd go out for lunch. The flat was empty; Penny was off to the hairdresser's or Macy's or someplace. Alec decided that what he really needed was some hearty male talk, not to do with work or money. He would ride up to Toots' establishment. Maybe Di Mag or Conzelman or Holden or Horace MacMahon or some of the other old sweats were in town. Pity Herman Hickman and Julie Garfield and Johnny Hodiak were so untimely gone. It was getting tougher and tougher to find an old face in Toots' place unless you wanted to talk to Pat O'Brien.

A big unseen fist punched him in the belly.

The hair was still the same, the fluffy-yellow-duckling hair. The backside was a little broader, but the neck was still delicious. She was sitting on a barstool, talking animatedly with Ziggy, but there could be no other head, no other neck, and in front of the hair and the neck there would be the clean cameo features and the deep dimple and the sharp-cut up-turned lips.

"Buy an old friend a drink, Barbara Bayne?" He made his voice low and casual.

"Buy the gentleman a drink, Zig," she said without turning. "I have always greatly admired his work. This wouldn't constitute a pickup, would it?"

"No ma'am, Miss Bayne," the bartender said. "What'll it be, Alec?"

"Anything at all," Alec Barr said, and turned Barbara Bayne around on the stool. He kissed her lightly on the cheek and said simply: "My God, more beautiful than I remembered."

"Now that's a damned lie," Barbara said. "How are you, Alec? It's been a little over two million years. I hear you're happily married to a charming young lady. All my heartiest congratulations."

Alec slid onto an adjoining stool.

"Thank you, but tell me all about you," he said. "What you've done, what you're doing, what you plan to do?"

Barbara deepened the dimple with a smile.

"Barr, the same old smooth operator," she said. "You haven't changed any. 'Tell me all about you,' for God's sake. Get 'em to talking about themselves before you grab them by the leg. Well, in order: One more marriage down the drain since last we met. Working steady in a dubious medium called television. Future plans? To lose ten pounds. I had a lush vacation and ate myself out of shape."

"I like you lush," Alec said. "What's the lady drinking, Zig? I'll have the same."

"Gin," said the bartender. "What else? How'll you have it?"

"Pink," Alec said. "To match my eyes."

"Still with the gags, huh?" Barbara said. "Still hiding the breaking heart with the flip chatter?"

"I suppose so. Maybe I should have written for your medium, but Fred Allen's dead, and I'm a B. S. Pulley reject."

Barbara Bayne got off the barstool.

"I was about to have a spinster's lunch," she said. "I've got a taping date pretty early in the afternoon. Would you care to join the ladies—namely, me?"

"I would indeed. Another pair of these gin-things to the table, please, Zig, and if The Great Man shows up, tell him we're incognito."

"A pleasure, Alec," the bartender said. "Nice to see you two together again."

"Whatever did he mean by that?" Barbara murmured as they walked to a far corner.

"Heartfelt, in any case. Let's don't order for a moment. I need some boy-talk out of you. You're God-sent. My soul was sick and sore for poor old Ben."

"I'd say that was a compliment of a sort. Even if my shape is beginning to emulate our departed chum's. Tell Mother where it hurts."

"I got a problem, self-imposed, and this is the story of my life," Alec said. "It seems that. . . ."

". . . And I don't particularly fancy being called Dad and Pop and Foxy Grandpa," Alec said at six o'clock that evening, after Barbara had finished her taping session and they met for drinks in the English Grill.

"You went shopping for a wife and you bought a daughter," Barbara said. "It's the great American Supermarket System. Something should be done. What you want is a listener, first, an advisor, second, and you wind up as counselor in a girl's summer camp. That about right?"

"That's about it," Alec's voice was morose. "I can talk to you. Who else can I talk to?"

"We used to fight a lot. I suppose it was because I loved you desperately—and I think you loved me—and neither one of us was big enough to handle it at the time."

"Also we were terribly *busy,* darling," Alec said. "But at least when we were fighting we knew the difference between Paul Robeson and Jackie Robinson. My basic trouble in the nest is that we really haven't got any topics worthy of argument, if you except Elvis Presley."

"You poor, poor chap," Barbara said. "You have made your bed, you should pardon the expression, et cetera."

"I know it," Alec said. "And I haven't said this to anybody else. Not since Ben Lea. But I cannot be a lover *and* a worker. I cannot be a worker *and* a lover. And I am rapidly running out of gas as a lover."

"You said it to me once, and I said—"

" 'Nobody will ever get between you and that goddamned Underwood' is what you said, right?"

"Right. And I think you quoted Ben Lea as saying that your—again you should pardon the expression—your balls were all wrapped up in the space bar of that goddamned Underwood."

"Exactly. And the trouble now is that I'm running out of balls," Alec said. "Look, I have to go. I don't want to fan any ancient embers, Barbara, and I'm certainly not making any delayed-action passes, but would it bore you terribly if we had a drink now and again and talked about baseball or something? Anything to get me away from the children?"

"I have no steady fellow, and no ideas about romance," said Barbara Bayne. "I have a very decent little town house. I am mostly at home because the old night life bores me. And I need my sleep. Feel free, friend, to drop in for whisky and sympathy. But one thing, one very important thing." She held up an admonishing hand. "No hanky-panky. I am a very moral lady these days, and I do not wish to start anything serious again—not at my age, which is about the same as yours. Okay?"

"Okay," Alec said. "It's a pact. Shake."

127

The pact endured, and Alec Barr began another double life. The almost daily drop-in on Barbara Bayne became set in his schedule, as, in the old Amelia days, the stop-off-for-coffee with Dinah Lawrence had become fixed. There was no temptation toward bodily intimacy; if Barbara had any fleshly yearnings she hid them very well, and Alec was revolted at the idea of going home to Penny with the musk of another woman's passion impregnated in him. This, he thought with some amusement, was less because of morality than age, because Penny was all and more than one man could handle.

But it was quite wonderful to have an—an *equal*—to talk to again. Barbara Bayne was a news-nut, possibly worse than Alec. She even read the truss ads in the papers, and she gobbled books like peanuts. Galsworthy and Thomas Hardy were not the names of pop singers in her vocabulary, and you did not have to explain that Walter Johnson was of no blood kin to the Senator from Texas. She spoke of Fats Waller in the present tense, although God knows how long Fats had been planted, and when she casually mentioned The Duke she was not referring either to Windsor or Wayne, but only to Ellington.

They wrangled happily over words, and fought furiously for an hour over Barbara's use of the word *exploited* in connection with British colonial policy. They larded their talk with "do you remember when?" and such non sequiturs as "that was when the *Hindenburg* blew up" or "the *Morro Castle* burned" or "the Pig Woman testified" or "Capone knocked off Colosimo" without having to refer to footnotes. Gallico was their sports writer, and they rattled off a happy lexicon, including The Orchid Man without having to name Georges Carpentier. They spoke of Tiger Flowers and Earl Sande and Suzanne Lenglen and the Big Red and René Lacoste and Red Grange and the Match King and Clara Bow and Rod La Rocque and Wallace Reid. When they mentioned The Crash it was Wall Street, not the newest jet disaster.

It was all wonderful, and all disastrous, when Alec went home to what he had inadvertently—and ashamedly—referred to as the kindergarten. And, God knows, he thought, none of it is Penny's fault. She's damned close to perfect—too damned close to perfect. She never asks where I've been, what I've done, why I go out for an hour or so every day when there's no dog to walk, or what's new with the book. She's afraid to mention what's new with the book, or even speculate—at least aloud—as to why I take hunks of it with me when I do go out.

That had become ritual, too. With Barbara Bayne he could talk book-problems and receive an honest answer, even if it might be unpleasing. He formed the habit of lugging slabs of manuscript for review at first, and Barbara's criticisms were so acute that he swiftly formed the habit of also taking a notebook along to record her suggestions on the next projected scene. He found, to both his gratification and dis-

may, that fighting out a scene with Barbara Bayne—before
he wrote it—was better than six rewrites of a piece in which
he had led himself up a blind alley.

Alec Barr had come full circle in infidelity. He found
himself in the unusual position of cheating with his mind
while leaving his body faithfully at home on the connubial
couch. The schizoid life became more and more wearing,
particularly as his libido lessened and his mind flared in-
candescently.

But The Book was going great—went great, picked up mo-
mentum, and one day, miraculously ended, with the others
beckoning eagerly. In bitter self-appraisal, Alec gave a deal
of credit to Barbara Bayne, with whom he did not have to
spar or temporize as with Amelia, or completely withhold
as with his pretty Penny. There had been no real point to
discussion with Penny, because she would automatically say:
"But it's wonderful, darling, magnificent," when Alec had
already written a memo to himself saying: "This stinks. Redo
all."

How weird it all is, Alec Barr thought. I am an intellectual
adulterer who sneaks out of the house to talk baseball and
politics with an old girl friend while I've got the best-
looking, sexiest woman in town waiting sadly at the gate
for Papa's physical return to the boudoir.

Alec, as a writer of fiction, owned the appallingly uncomfortable habit of reviewing himself, and the reviews were
nearly always unfavorable. He had, he reflected, made a
proper mess of everything. He had deserted Amelia for Barbara, and had fled Barbara in relief. He had fallen in love
with Jill, and had deserted her from fear and weakness and
the desire to not face reality in the shape of divorce. He
had then been jilted by Jill and had collected the divorce
anyhow from Amelia, who had left him not because of other
women but because he was a wishful wanderer who ran
away instead of meeting facts and fighting unpleasantness.
He had then married Penny, the daughter of a woman who
loved him and whom he really should have married in the
first place, and now was cheating intellectually on Penny
with Barbara Bayne, whom he had once goaded into a final
renunciation because she interfered with the work she now
was in process of abetting.

"Christ, Barr," he said aloud as he shaved. "No wonder

everybody warns everybody about going steady with writers. They aren't really people."

And that, too, he thought, was plagiarism, because Ben Lea had said it and Marc Mantell always said it, and the only thing that made it rewarding were the *Time* and *Newsweek* covers which were written and ice-boxed for the week in which he earned his second Pulitzer Prize with the first African book of the projected saga.

The day his face bloomed on *Time,* after the awards announcements had been made, was also the day he went to see his doctor.

128

The reception of the new book had been more than heady. Alec titled it *Dark Dawning,* and the critics were generally expansive and largely laudatory. "Barr's fresh awakening" was the general theme of the critiques. "Barr's promised fulfillment at long last." The whole thing was reminiscent of the time John Marquand quit writing *Mr. Moto* and came up, to everyone's surprise, with *The Late George Apley* and *H. N. Pulham, Esq.* As in Marquand's case, the critics said that nobody really believed Alec had the serious change of pace in him, which made Alec snort. He had been preparing, he told Marc Mantell, this change of pace for the last thirty years.

Mantell made a massive deal for hard-cover, paperback, and moving picture, with forward-spread options for the next two of the serious cycle. Alec Barr found himself finally a millionaire in fact, which failed to impress him. He bought Penny a mink coat and some jewelry, but there was nothing at all he particularly wanted for himself. He had more than enough shotguns and he was not interested in Rolls-Royces or yachts. He and Penny had decided that the apartment was too cramped for their long-term needs, so he did invest a hundred thousand dollars in a cooperative in Sutton Place and gave Penny a free hand with the checkbook for its furnishing. The view of the river was soothing, and the neighborhood was quiet, apart from the tooting of the tugboats. The basic trouble was that going crosstown approximated a safari, especially in poor weather.

He liked the book, of course. It was factually full-bodied and solidly constructed, and the fictional content was honest and succinct. He was truthfully excited about the prospect of its companion pieces, but he was tired, terribly tired, and the idea of physically getting on with the new labors dismayed him. He decided he'd take Penny to Europe and possibly to Africa before he tackled Book Two.

In the meantime he wanted a complete checkup. He had been disturbed by an occasional bleeding from the anus, and a general feeling of malaise. The pains in his back had increased—not so bad by day, but nearly unbearable by night. The bleeding didn't fret him particularly, because it was a common enough symptom if one drank too much, and Alec had been punishing the bottle fairly steadily—mostly to still his seething brain at the end of a long day's session at the typewriter.

Alec detested barbers, dentists, doctors, and lawyers, not necessarily in that order, but he finally goaded himself into making an appointment with the house quack, as he called his friend Doctor Jacob Ernst. Alec was very fond of Jake Ernst, if only because Jake Ernst never really insulted his intelligence in the time-crusted tradition of TV-type doctors keeping painful truths from the patients for their own good.

Jake Ernst was a little round man, onion-bald, with a rosy plump wife, three grown children—two boys and a girl, all doctors—and a propensity for poker and horseplaying. He was famous in three countries as a diagnostician. He also drank whiskey and smoked cigarettes furiously. He was quite grossly profane.

"What the hell's wrong with you?" was his greeting. "Booze or babes or both?"

"I dunno," Alec said. "I feel generally rotten. I got back pains and bloody toilet paper and Christ knows what-all. Also I'm going up against some insurance croakers and I want a prior opinion from an old-fashioned quack with dirty fingernails and a whiskey breath."

"You came to the right store, sonny," Doctor Ernst said. "You want the full course, or just the customer's phony you'll-be-all-right-if-you-watch-the-cholesterol-count-and-take the-low-blood-pressure-pills?"

"Gimme the full treatment," Alec said. "Pretend I'm a cadaver."

"I like honest self-appraisal," Jake Ernst said. "I trust you followed my telephonic instructions about no booze, no breakfast, and didn't cheat on the specimen in the bottle?"

"I come to you pure," Alec said. "What do we do first?"

"Some blood. Some X-ray. Some barium. Some basal met. Some liver-dye retention tests. And finally you bend over for me. I want to know if I can see daylight."

"The only thing I really hate worse than humorous barbers is humorous doctors," Alec said. "Let's get on with the dissection."

At the end of the interminable morning, Alec assumed the classic position on the table, head down, rump upraised. Alec's arms were crossed beneath his chest, head turned to one side as he reared his naked backside for the doctor's prostatometer.

"Take it easy with that drilling gadget, Doc," Alec said.

"I just have to have a look. We may strike oil."

"The finger didn't bother me," Alec said grinning, "but that bloody great machine carries certain attributes of *lèse majesté*. I never did understand the fun part of pederasty."

"You have got a very tight sphincter muscle," Doctor Ernst said. "Perhaps the tightest I have ever seen."

Alec grinned painfully from his awkward position.

"I bet you say that to all your patients."

After a bit Alec said: "You see any new planets in there with that telescope?"

"No planets, but a little lump I don't like, and you *are* pretty mushy. Certainly the prostate is enlarged. I don't want to cause you any undue alarm, but I think you had better see a good urologist for some more studies. These things aren't very troublesome if you catch them early, but left alone they can be a damned nuisance. That's all from me right now. I know a good guy—Nate Einmann. I'll fix a date."

Alec got up gratefully from the table. "Brother," he said, "am I glad I am not a dame. This is the first time I have been peered into and I hope to Christ it is the last."

"Einmann will want some X rays and some more blood, and he might want to take a little tissue off you. It won't hurt, but I would like us to be pretty sure about your general condition."

Dressed once more and smoking a cigarette, Alec said:

"You can level with me, Doc. What are you really looking for? I am a real big boy. Do you see something there you don't like?"

The doctor shook his head.

"At your age, my friend, I don't like any lumps anywhere that I don't understand. That's the why of the urologist. Nothing more."

Alec raised an eyebrow. "You wouldn't be gently hinting that I might have myself a cancerous backside, I suppose?"

"I am not hinting anything. I just want to be goddam sure that you don't."

"On the off chance that I *do*," Alec replied, "what's the gen on this prostate business? Cancerwise, I mean?"

"Not as bad as you might think," the doctor said. "If you catch these things early enough you can whip out the prostate and you've got a decent expectancy of living your life fully and completely—with one minor exception. I suppose you studied enough physiology to know that when you subdivide a man from his prostate gland, his sex life goes with it. You might have your normal libido—that is to say, you will have it in your head—but you are not going to be doing any practical business down below. In effect, we take out the fun factory."

"That seems rather harsh," Alec said. "What's the actual process?"

"Well, the surgeon has to divide the nerves that lead to the penis in this particular bit of butchery," Doc Ernst answered. "These are the nerves that control the blood vessels that produce the erection. This is the price you pay for cure or at least an arrest."

"It is a very cheerful choice," Alec said, "like rather be Red than dead."

"That's about the size of it," the doctor said. "Now run along and see this colleague of mine. He will stick a slight needle which won't cause you as much embarrassment as that machine I just took out of you, up your backside, and he will check your blood levels, and throw a little X ray at you and you will be happy home in two days with a verdict. One way or the other."

"You have just made my week," Alec said. "I will keep in touch. Can I drink while I am waiting for the word?"

"Sure," the doctor said. "We are no longer worried about your liver. That's past redemption anyhow."

"It's a pity there's no such thing as a used-man market," Alec said. "I feel like trading myself in on a new model . . ."

The urologist was a lean man who reminded Alec of Marc Mantell. He had the similar hawk face, the enormous eyes behind the thick-paned glasses, and he seemed a serious man. (I'd be serious too, Alec thought, if I owned a microscope that spelled life or death on the slides. Mustn't be a great deal of fun to deliver the hard word. Have I got cancer, Doc? *Yeah.* Be a hard act to follow.)

This new medical gentleman, Doctor Nathan Einmann, was a Heidelberg-Vienna type, Jake had said. Nazis ran him through most of their better summer-outing camps—Auschwitz, Dachau, Buchenwald. Seemed to be a pretty hardy gent. The concentration-camp tattoos showed on his arms below the short-sleeved smock, and suddenly Alec remembered the Jewish tuberculosis expert at Doctor Schweitzer's hospital in Gabon, in the Congo, the one who said that being a Jew in wartime Germany was a very cheap way to see Europe.

He was not quite so coarse as his colleague, Doctor Ernst, but coarse enough. It seemed strange, Alec thought, that all of the really good medicos he had met were earthy types, who liked booze and broads and dirty jokes. It was the mealy-mouths who gave you the bum steers and sent you the outrageous bills. He liked this Einmann very much on sight. He didn't fuss.

"We are looking for a cancer," he said, after polite hellos. "I am going to run an enzyme acid phosphotase on you."

"That's nice," Alec said. "Be even nicer if I knew what it was."

"This enzyme is normal to the prostate," Doctor Einmann said. "It normally doesn't go out to blood level. In the presence of metastes—cancer—you will generally find a high level of this enzyme in the blood stream. Supposing I don't find any undue amount in the general blood level, we will all shout hurrah, because the cancer, if any, has at least not spread through your entire pelvic area."

"Then I go out and get drunk and pinch all the girls?"

Doctor Einmann smiled, and shoved a cigarette box at Alec, showing the tattoo marks on his hairy forearm.

"No. I'm a skeptic. After I've seen the X rays and am

convinced you haven't got anything in the bones—no carcinoma—and am happy with the state of your blood, I'm still not convinced. I will then chuck you in a hospital for two days and do a biopsy on your ecstasy department. It's called a prostatic punch."

"By God, you fellows do think up the nicest nomenclature," Alec grinned and lit a cigarette. *"Prostatic punch,* yet. It sounds like a lethal blow by a prize fighter or a drink that somebody's loaded when the host wasn't looking."

"It won't bother you," Doctor Einmann said. "We just stick the needle through the rectum and into the gland. Slight local anesthetic. But then we'll know if you are or if you are not."

"You guys must have had a lot of time on your hands in those concentration camps. Every one of you *summa cum laude* graduates I've met make more bad jokes than the late Al Jolson."

"One does develop some sort of a warped sense of humor under those conditions," Doctor Einmann smiled. "It is rather necessary as a portion to the maintenance of sanity. *So.* We get to work, eh?"

"Press on," Alec said. "And keep me clued on them enzymes."

"So tell me, Doctor Einmann," Alec said. "Is it is, or is it ain't?"

"I wish I could say it ain't," Einmann said. "Unfortunately, it *is.* It is not necessarily as bad as it sounds, but there it is and we have to do something about it."

"Like what?" Alec said. "I am naturally overcurious about these things as an author. I might have to write it sometime. And everybody says it's not as bad as it sounds."

"There is a variety of alternates," the doctor answered. "I still don't know really how widespread it is. We will need an exploratory to determine that. If it will cheer you up, a good fifty per cent of people with this particular thing, even if it is very widespread, have five years or more. If we can localize it, remove it, you can probably live out your life expectancy, and with any sort of luck die of a coronary before it starts to hurt too much."

"That's a charming prospect," Alec said. "Happy coronary. So give me the whole thing, the full *schmier;* what do we actually do?"

"Well," Doctor Einmann said, "about the first thing is to buy you a drink, and while you are drinking it I will tell you that most of these cases can be controlled with proper treatment and most men live reasonably normal lives. The only thing is that there are some sacrifices you will have to make. One, you will have to take female hormones. We may have to remove your testicles, but in any case you will have to give up your sex life. This is a pretty small price to pay for your life itself."

"Jesus Christ," Alec Barr said. "I suppose I will have to go back to my old joke about the colored boy with his throat cut who says, 'It only hurts when I laugh.' This means I have really completely had it in the hay?"

The doctor nodded. "You have definitely had it in the hay, my boy. I hope you have a lot of fragrant memories."

"Memories I have got," Alec said. "But there couldn't be any small chance that I could kind of keep my balls, just for, shall we say, ornamental purposes—I mean to sort of make my pants fit the way they always fit?"

'Sure," the doctor said, "for a while, anyhow. They will be like teats on a boar. Tangible but functionless. Ideally we should, I hate to use the word, castrate you, so that the female hormones won't find too much male resistance. But if you don't want an orchiectomy, we will try it with hormones alone and see how far they can push the metastes back."

"For a start," Alec said, "let me hang onto my balls, please, even if they are only window dressing, seeing as how I have grown accustomed to them after all these years. They have become sort of friendly adjuncts to my personality. Tell me, Doctor, just what *is* this female hormones jazz?"

"About the best is a thing called Diethylstilbestrol. It is a pill you take twice a day. It will stop that pain in your back almost immediately, and you will figure that it is worth the trouble because you will start to feel pretty good again pretty soon. But no action in bed." The doctor shook his head again. "No action in what you call the hay, because, my friend, if you haven't lost your libido from worrying about the disease you've got, the Diethylstilbestrol pills would drive you off sex after you have taken them for a couple of weeks. But I can assure you that in general you will soon pick up emotionally and you will get along just fine—you might even be glad to be alive."

"This I doubt," said Alec Barr. "But then I never tried being dead. Now tell me, Doctor, when you turn me into a woman, what kind of physical changes occur? Do I have to go shopping for brassières? Can I get pregnant?"

"It's not all that funny," Doctor Einmann replied. "After about six weeks you begin to find that your breasts are getting bigger, and that your nipples hurt when your shirt rubs on them. Sometimes this goes away in a few months. Sometimes it lasts for the rest of life. You skin is going to get smoother and you won't have to shave so often."

"By God," Alec said, "Mama said there would be days like this, but she never prepared me to be a eunuch. It will take a little practice. Will my voice change?"

Doctor Einmann smiled. "No, your voice won't change, but I shouldn't appear publicly in tight sports shirts after about six months. Unless you want to emulate the movie stars and find yourself a good plastic surgeon."

"And what would this plastic surgeon do?"

"Well," the doctor said, "he would give you a little mastectomy in which the fatty tissues under your bosoms are removed and the skin is sutured back flat, forming a little crescent-shaped incision which half the women you see in the better restaurants have already had performed in the interests of high style."

"Christ," Alec said, "I have been using the same tailor for twenty years, and now I have got to start going steady with Yves St. Laurent. What'll Angelo think, in Brioni's? But as long as I'm here, Doc, before I go shopping for girdles, give me all the rest of it. What happens next?"

"I don't know if you will want to hear it. Why don't you just let it ride and maybe you won't have to face it?"

"Planes are getting safer all the time," Alec said. "Let me have it all."

"All right, then here is the rest of it. I will check you every three months with the blood tests for your enzyme count and the acid phosphatase. Your enzymes by that time will have reacted to the hormones, but in about eighteen months the count will go up again because all the female hormones in the world can't fully control the cancer. We are going to have to remove your testicles at that time. The idea won't appeal to you, but the operation is easy. You can even have it done as an out-patient. Personally I recommend a week in a hospital, just to keep you from riding bicycles."

"Very funny," Alec said. "This isn't a dangerous operation then? How do we go about separating me from my crown jewels?"

"Simple," the doctor replied. "We make a small incision in the scrotum, sever the connections, take out the testes, sew up the scrotum, stick in a drain which is removed after a day, leave the catgut stitches in, and nature absorbs them. For all practical purposes you could be up and around next day. But no horseback riding for a bit."

"Sounds simple when it is happening to someone else," Alec said. "Just supposing I am very vain about the way I dress left in my trousers and don't particularly fancy a vacuum down there?"

Now Doctor Einmann raised his eyebrows. "It is not the first time I have heard the question," he said. "There are prosthetic devices to replace the testes. I had one case in which I inserted two hollow plastic balls like the ones we ordinarily use to support the rib cages of TB patients with collapsed lungs, but they got to be a bit of a nuisance."

"Nuisance?"

"Well, yes," the doctor said. "The patient came back and begged me to take them out again. It seems that the membrane which separated them had eroded and they had a tendency to *click* at the most inopportune moments. We didn't improve his appearance but he was certainly less noisy when he entered the drawing room."

"So with this done, I will live happily ever after?" Alec said.

"With luck yes . . . ten years anyhow . . ."

"Ten years. Ten years. I can do five more books in ten years. That's a fair shake. But then do I die horribly? You might as well give it all to me, as I'll undoubtedly use it in a book." Alec snapped his fingers. "I have an even better idea, Doctor, why don't you just write me the whole thing in simple language, so I can digest it at my leisure?"

"If you want it that way, I will be willing, if not delighted."

"Fine," said Alec Barr, "considering the time I will save from not screwing, I will have plenty of leisure to keep abreast of my breasts."

129

Alec read with increasing horror the document Doctor Einmann had sent him by messenger.

"We go on taking the synthetic female hormone and the blood tests. Anywhere from a few months to ten years, our patient first gets a 'urinary obstruction' in the urethra. This is characterized by frequent urination although he cannot empty his bladder. The pain is continuous and becomes more intense when he urinates. There could be visible blood in the urine, or no blood.

"Temporarily we insert a soft rubber catheter into the penis and up the urethra to the bladder. This has a clamp on the end of it. Our patient opens the clamp when he needs to urinate.

"If we decide that it is not a simple infection, our patient enters the hospital for a week to ten days. The surgeon goes into the channel of the urethra with an operating cystoscope which is called a resectoscope. Essentially, it reams out the tube.

"But in two or three months the symptoms recur and the tissue grows back and the urethra closes to the point where it is impossible to reinsert the catheter tube.

"A superpubic cystostomy is indicated. This involves a midline incision in the lower part of the abdomen just above the penis, and directly into the bladder. As soon as the incision heals sufficiently, the patient is equipped with a tube which differs from the drainage tube used in the hospital. This one has a balloon or flange on the end to hold it in the bladder. He wears a clamp on the end of the tube, and again opens it when he wants to urinate. It is possible for him to use a urinal in his accustomed manner if he wishes.

"Unfortunately the tube becomes encrusted with a stone-like material from the urine. Our patient must go to the doctor's office every two weeks and have the tube changed.

"By the time the widespread cancer gets to the lower bowel, we must concede that our patient is at the terminal point. Cancer of this type generally means that there is obstruction of the tubes from kidneys to bladder and that the patient will die of uremia in short order. Uremia is known as the old man's friend—it kills the patient and saves him from most of the terminal pain.

"A patient with cancer of the lower bowel has bowel movements with difficulty. There has been some bleeding from the rectum accompanied by mild pain and distension. At the hospital a barium enema and X rays indicate almost complete obstruction of the lower bowel.

"It is necessary to perform a colostomy. In your particular case, it will be a sigmoid colostomy, low on the left side of the abdomen because your obstruction will be low.

"But before the operation it is necessary to deflate the bowel as far as possible. The conscious patient swallows a tube as far as the upper intestine in an attempt to pull the gas out. This tube is kept in place, usually about 48 hours. Meanwhile the patient is fed intravenously.

"The incision is made low on the left side exposing the bowel. Clamps are fastened on the bowel and it is divided. The lower end is sewed off. The surgeon brings the upper end out of the abdominal wall and connects it to the skin. For two or three days a tube is left in the hole to release gas and fecal matter. Then the tube is removed and the patient wears a bag over the opening.

"After his colostomy, the patient probably takes a small enema each morning to clean out his bowel. He then fastens a bag over the opening. Some men keep this bag on with a belt device which holds the little pneumatic ring closed over the opening. Others simply glue the bag in place, using surgical adhesive directly on the skin.

"For the first two or three weeks, the patient has to change the bag several times a day, but later, once a day is sufficient. There is no constant drainage unless the patient gets diarrhea.

"Most urologists advise that by the time the cancer spreads this far the patient has only three or four months left."

130

Well, that would be about that, Alec thought. What a brilliant future the delightful doctors have mapped for me Just like old Ben; go to the bathroom in a bottle, no balls at all, a gelding in a stallion's world. Then the Big Casino. Good night Irene. So nice knowing you, Alexander Barr. Two years, ten years, who knows? My brassière will be getting tighter all the time. Alec Barr, girl author, with a sigmoid colostomy and a catheter in his bladder yet. Not to mention a superpubic cystostomy and all those other goodies. Hot diggity dog.

I often wondered how you'd take it when it really hit you. I guess you just take it like I'm taking it. *Stunned.* Making funnies to keep from screaming. And as the good doctors say, maybe I'll even get to like the hormones. Maybe, at long last, I can get to join the Girl Scouts. The hell of it is there's a good chance I'll stay alive long enough to write four or five more books. *Libido?* Forget it, Charlie. I done lost mine when I got the sad word, and they haven't even gelded me yet.

Well, Barr, he thought, we can do one of two things. We can take the whole passel of pills, and finish it for all time—but it's powerful black out there in the nowhere—or we can make the best of our bathroom bottle and our falsies in the ballses. And I think we lack the guts to quit this troubled sphere immediately, when there are quite a lot of sunsets and sunrises left to contemplate, and a lot of words unwrit. And there are, God damn it, a lot of words unwrit in me—words I *want* to write. Which brings us now to the marrow of the matter. How about Penny? How about my pretty Penny, who isn't thirty yet, and who is saddled with an old crock sweating out a sticky finish, who can't give her anything at all in bed, and who will be so all-fired cussedly cross that he'll make her absolutely miserable even if she did have any real conversation that wasn't tinctured by pity?

And she'll stick. She'll stick until Hell claims me. But it's a waste of her life and, in a way, a waste of what's left of mine. I don't want a young nurse. I don't want a full-bodied frustrated female being faithful to a feeble husband with no balls at all. Pity I do not need; loyalty I do not want at the cost of a young life which has a long time to live. The hell with it. What I want right now is a drink and nobody to talk to. Maybe I'll just go home, lie down, and think about that old elephant. Turns out we had a lot in common. Including, really, nobody to talk to.

The old bull was terribly, awfully old. He had lived too long—much too long. Quite possibly he had seen more than one century switch—the eighteenth change over to the nineteenth, the nineteenth to the twentieth. Nobody will ever know accurately just how long a wild elephant lives. In zoos his life-length is an average man's three score and ten. Twenty-one to grow up; twenty-one to fight and breed; twenty-one to teach his wisdom to the young bulls; and ten or twenty more to brood and die. In Africa you would have to follow him on his thousand aimless meanderings from Ethiopia to Rhodesia; watch him grow huge and fight and breed and finally become outcast and you would still never know if it were the same elephant if you had a hundred years to follow his plod. From the look of him, our old gentleman was at least 150 years old.

For many, many years he had been prison-pent. He had lived on this dry-river *luga* named Illaut. As long as the oldest native around the waterhole could remember, he had lived near Illaut. He came to drink daily at the waterhole a few hundred yards from the only crap game in town—the one-room Somali general store. He was so far gone in ignobility that he no longer minded drinking with goats and donkeys. He did not even try to murder people any more, because people and goats and sheep were really all he had to associate with.

The old bull was possibly fifty years past his last breeding. He was exiled from the world of other elephants. Likely one of his own sons had kicked him out. In any case his memory of women and palm toddy was dim and possibly exaggerated. The young bulls no longer came to him for counsel, although his accumulated wisdom was vast. He had long since run through his repertoire of jokes, and no longer found listeners for the chest-rumbling, trunk-probing, nostalgic tales of the good old days before the white man came with guns—the quiet days before the iron birds ripped the heavens apart with rude noise on their way to Ethiopia. Somehow the skies had been bluer in those days, and you could count on the seasons. Now the weather, like everything else, had gone bloody well mad. Three straight years of drought, for instance—and then it rained until it fair washed the country away.

He was more than a little deaf, of course, and certainly his eyesight was clouded by the years. His great ears, which once clapped like giant hands as he shook them irritably at the little hold-me-close flies, or smacked against his head in harsh anger as he lofted his trunk and screamed in a charge, now hung in pathetic tatters; now his ears swung limp and shredded and flapped only feebly. Over his entire back a green-mossy excrescence had grown. He was as barnacly as an old turtle or an ancient salt-water piling. He was wrinkled excessively, and perhaps he had lost three tons of weight from his original seven. He carried his tusks awkwardly, as if they were too ponderous for his head; too heavy to tote in comfort now that all the counterbalancing weight had left his behind. How he'd reached this great age without breaking one or both tusks in that harsh, stone-studded country, with the full thirty years of routine fights, was one of God's mysteries. But there they were, great ivory parentheses stretching low and out and upward from his pendulous nether lip. Age had made him visually ridiculous; he wore a warrior's heavy weapons on his front end, and no single hair survived on his obscenely naked tail.

There would be curious growths in his belly that old elephants frequently have, like the hair-balls one finds in the stomach of a crocodile or big catfish. Ants would have crawled up his trunk; certainly his feet would be cracked and wincingly hurtful on the lava rocks of his self-imposed prison. You could tell that from the ridged tracks of his pad-marks which covered ten miles of country outside the water area. Old gentlemen always hurt somewhere.

He swayed from side to side now and grumbled to himself, as old men will, and the burden of his complaint rode clear on the wind. The old bull had been a flashy traveling man in his time—all the way from the high blue hills of Ethiopia through Tanganyika and then into the Rhodesias, traversing the miles and miles of bloody Africa as he followed the dôm palms whose red nuts he adored—as he occasionally ravished a maize field, as he whimsically butted over a railway train or upended a water tank; or, just for the hell of it, swung his trunk like a rubbery scythe to wreck a native village. Cows had touched him tentatively with their trunks, in girlish admiration; he had smelled the blood of a close cousin as he took out his tusks from a gut-spilling belly. Sycophants had swarmed around him, young *askaris* eager for the knowledge he had amply to give; stooges to fetch and carry and, always, to heed his wit and wisdom.

But now he was very much all alone; chained by necessity to the creaking rocking chair of old age. All the cows and calves and younger bulls were long gone. They had tolerated his presence in the area, even though he had become a bore with his stories of old slave caravans and regiments of spear-hunters. The country had played out. It had rained again on the other side of the mountain, and everybody had whistled off, following the fresh green that thrust upward under the rim of the escarpment. Everybody had gone but the old bull. He was too feeble to trek with them. His head was heavy and his feet hurt.

Now he stood sadly alone, because he could not leave certain water for an uncertain excursion for food. And he was starving himself, because he had eaten the country clear. But he would not travel the usual two-day, two-hundred-mile grazing distance of a younger bull. He had grazed his land rock-hard, and his tracks were imprinted atop each other. His dung abraded on itself in piles and was scattered by the clichéd passage of his own feet. He had made tracks enough for two hundred elephants, and they were all his own.

Soon he would die. Unless the rains came almost immediately to green his prison yards, he would die, of senile decay and lack of nourishment—and most of all, of purest boredom. The boredom was the worst of all the ills, and he would be glad to see the finish of it all.

There he stood now, pathetically magnificent on the slope of a sere brown rise, the morning sun red behind him. There he stood against a cruel blue hill, his enormous curving tusks a monument to himself and to the Africa that was— the Africa that had changed, was changing, would forevermore change until nothing beloved of it was left.

"Poor old beggar," the white hunter said. "Poor, poor old boy."

We had come there to shoot an elephant, in an untouched savage land, a land untrod by tires, unseen by tourists. I did not weep when I shot the old bull twice through the heart and he crumpled to his creaking knees. In retrospect, yes, of course I would weep—but only for a testimonial to another age. When the old bull fell with a mighty crash, much of what I loved best of old Africa died with him.

131

Barbara was the only person he knew to whom he could honestly unburden himself. He had debated briefly whether to tell Marc Mantell, and decided against it. Marc Mantell saw Alec Barr as the professionally functional man—the producing machine. Their friendship was deep, much deeper than the usual relationship between author and agent. But Marc Mantell had always evinced a chilled-steel evaluation of Alec and his work, and now Alec certainly did not want that evaluation tarnished by pity. If he was lucky—he grinned sardonically—he had perhaps ten years of nothing to do of real interest but write books. He did not want those books colored by pity, excused by pity, sold in the open market under the shelter of charity. If the next book stank, Alec Barr wanted Marc Mantell to inform him that the book stank. He did not desire to have sloppy construction or tedious dialog excused by the fact that he had a bowel-bag taped to a hole in his belly, and no nuts at all to itch in the summer heat.

And so he bought Barbara Bayne a drink in Michael's Pub and said:

"Guess what?"

"What? Not another fresh set of triumphs, after making both *Time* and *Newsweek*'s cover in the same week? The Nobel boys nibbling?"

"Not yet. I just wanted to tell you that you're forever safe from any lustful urges on my part. Unrape. No seduce. It seems I have a slight case of cancer—in a very precious portion of my overworked anatomy."

"Oh, Alec! It can't be true! And if it is, why did you choose a place like this to tell me?"

"Because if I told you in a public place like this you wouldn't cry. And the last thing I want right now is tears, because it'll start me to weeping myself. Let's have another martini. If you want the grisly details later I have them all here"—he tapped his breast pocket—"and they're very thorough. That refugee doc of mine would make a marvelous medical writer for *The Reader's Digest*. Even I can understand what I've got."

"You're not going to, certainly not going to—"

"Die?" Alec barked a short laugh. "Nope. Not immediately. Probably not for years and years and bloody dreary years. I am going to learn to live with what I've got. I shall be very cheery and most brave and all that sort of rot. I shall keep the upper lip stiff, because it's the only rigid thing I'll own. I gather you get the message?"

Barbara shook her head.

"It's not fair to come at me all of a sudden. Where? How bad?"

"Where it counts. Bad enough. Loverboy Barr does not ride the range any more. In short, they're going to geld me in order to keep me alive. I shall be bombarded with female hormones, and we can go safely to the Little Girls' Room together. Do you think I'm a candidate for a B cup for a start? I know so little about buying brassières, and the doc says I'll be the best-stacked male author in show business."

"Stop it! Stop it! *Stop it!* I can't stand it if you're flip about it! For Christ's sake let's go to my house where we can both cry out loud!"

"I love you, Barbara Bayne," Alec said. "It's really what I've been wanting to do all day. It is rather horrible when it happens to you, instead of Damon Runyon . . ."

". . . And so that leaves us with a great big problem about young Penny," Alec said, stuffing the sheaf of papers back in his pocket. Barbara, pale but now unweeping, had just finished Doctor Einmann's detailed prospectus.

"I'm enormously fond of this kid," he said. "Not love, not *in* love, as I was with you, not even the same kind of love I had for Amelia. But I do love her, and I will *not* saddle her with an ailing old husband who is useless as a functional man and noncontemporaneous as a companion. I may go on for years, the quacks say. And she isn't even thirty yet. A whole life to waste if she sticks with me."

"And she *will* stick with you, of that I'm certain sure," Barbara said. "I don't know her, of course, but from everything you've said. . . . You don't want to go purest Sydney Carton on me now, with this 'far far better thing I do' bit—"

"I will tell you absolutely honestly, shamelessly, that I am being entirely selfish," Alec said. "I will *not* be hovered over as an object of pity. And I also will not be guilt-ridden, and impotently jealous, through what years I've got left in me to drink whisky and read books and write books and shoot quail. Nurse-housekeepers I do not need. I love Penny as a pet; I have loved Penny as a woman, in bed. But beyond that point we really don't have very much in common except her mother."

"You should have marr—"

"Shut up," Alec said. "I know I should have married her mother. But her mother is rich and famous now and way out of reach, and her mother doesn't really like me very much for bedding down her daughter."

Barbara got up and paced before the fireplace with what Alec used to call her Bette Davis walk.

"But you'll have to tell her, surely? I mean you can't really keep a cancer *secret.*"

"I don't have to tell her for quite a while. It's not all that desperate. But I've got to drive her off, Barbara! I've got to drive her *off!* Otherwise she'll wither and waste and wind up on the quiet cheat, and she'll hate me for making her do it. She'll hate me for being old and sick and tied to her."

Alec grinned unhappily.

"I'm selfish, like I said. I just don't want to be bored to death when I can't provide the only thing that prevents me from being bored to death. Does that make me into some kind of a terrible bastard?"

Barbara kissed him on the cheek.

"No," she said. "You're not a bastard. You're a pretty brave guy, as a matter of fact."

"Brave or not, I'm right," Alec said. "And by the time the relentless progress of my—of my indisposition—becomes common knowledge, she'll have found herself a new boy who understands *schusses* and *slaloms* and *christianas* and the music of Ahmad Jamal and Gerry Mulligan. When I go down to my death, I want to do it to the accompaniment of Joe Bushkin, Jonah Jones, and possibly Artie Shaw."

"Show business," Barbara said, but she couldn't say any more because she was crying.

132

The book was finished, the party was over, the move to the new flat made, and *Dark Dawning* was still riding high on all the better book lists. Hedda and Louella were full of the intimate details of casting the picture.

And Alec Barr was not going to bed with his wife. This puzzled the wife, who could understand a certain lack of physical interest on the part of her husband when he was correcting proofs and appearing on television shows and attending publisher's parties, but Alec's aloofness now, with the work done and the money rolling in, was quite incomprehensible to Penny Barr. Equally incomprehensible was Alec's invariable habit of lunching out almost daily, and rarely appearing back at the house until seven o'clock. Because now Alec had no stacks of fresh manuscript under his arm— manuscripts he was presumably going to show his agent or his publisher.

Penny had no conception of what she was, or had been, doing wrong. She racked her brains. She was loving, God knows, and she fetched the slippers and answered the phone and if Alec had smoked a pipe she would, unbidden, have stuffed it with tobacco. She wore her prettiest shorty nightdresses, and she never, ever appeared at breakfast with the pincurlers rampant and the face greasy. She tried and she tried and just as consistently as Alec watched *Bonanza,* she failed.

He looked at her blankly when she talked of furniture and paintings and draperies, and stared unseeingly at the products of her thrifty raids on the galleries and antique shops. When pressed he admitted the new flat was "nice," but once, when

Penny was exasperated at his vague detachment, she asked him if she should throw out the chair he was sitting on, he replied: "I think that would be very nice."

Penny tried seduction, physical and mental, overt and oblique, and failed on both counts. It appeared now that Alec was trying to find ways of going off to bed either before or after Penny's decision to seek the couch. They had slept together, in the one great bed; now Alec activated his old Amelia tactic that he thrashed and snored and ground his teeth and that for a little while, it would be better if they kept to separate rooms. Penny lay alone in the great double bed and ground *her* teeth and thrashed about, and very possibly had horrible dreams. Alec could hear her in the next room, and what she said in her sleep, after the bye-bye pills, was consistently *"Alec. Alec. Alec."*

Alec owned the countermeasure for those nightcries. He took the Scotch bottle to bed with him, and its admixture, with sodium amytal and the female hormone pills, was sufficient to stone him into slumber.

Penny was increasingly distraught. They had no conversation at all, now, beyond the polite formalities. Penny had nothing to *do*, once the house was furnished and settled. She had given up the skiing group and the week ends in Vermont. She now made fresh overtures to The Group, if not to ski, at least to lunch. And so one day when she decided against "21," against The Colony, against Laurent, against Pavillon, it was inevitable that when she went to the Absinthe House she would run into Alec Barr having lunch with Barbara Bayne.

133

There was, naturally, no scene beyond a friendly wave from opposing sides of the room. There was no real reason for Alec *not* to be having lunch in the Absinthe House, or any other place in the world, with an old female friend from another war. There was something very implicit in the eyes of her girl friends when Alec wafted a wave across the crowded room. There was everything in the eyes of her girl friends that Penny Barr had been dreading since Alec Barr had moved out of her bedroom.

"That was a very pretty woman you were lunching with," Penny said that evening over cocktails at home. "I couldn't see very well—it's pretty dark in there—but she looked like some of the old movies we see on TV—older of course—but she looked very much like Barbara Something—Wayne?"

"No," Alec said shortly. "Bayne. Barbara Bayne. A creature from my murky past. In fact, an old girl friend. She goes back to postwar, and I don't mean Korean."

"Oh." Penny stirred her martini with a finger, plucked out the olive, and laid it carefully in an ashtray.

"Well?"

"Nothing. But I just wondered—you never mentioned her. Do you see her often?"

"Quite. I don't have many people to talk to any more now that your mother's never in town. Old friends, I mean. Most of the others are dead."

Penny got up.

"I think I'd like another drink. Fix yours?"

"I'll do it. You're a little heavy with the vermouth. Here. Give me your glass."

Penny was looking, this evening, what could only be described as scrumptious. She was wearing a pair of slim black velveteen Capri slacks and a silk Pucci blouse in iridescent colors that deepened the blue of her eyes and did something extra-special to the fine flushed skin and carefully waved cloud of black hair. She wore golden sandals on her feet and perfume at her throat and behind her ears. All of the skills of the hairdresser and the bath-salts industry were helping her to gird for combat. The brassière boys were in on the act as well; her blouse was unbuttoned nearly to the navel, but the breasts rode high and firm beneath the shimmering silk of Rome.

Alec came back from the bar—in the new apartment Alec had insisted on a bar which bore a nonremarkable resemblance to the old bar in the Amelia penthouse—with the drinks.

"There you are," he said. "You were going to say?" His voice was impersonally polite.

Penny took a big gulp from the martini.

"You make me feel so—so young! Left out! I ought to ask

you what the hell you were doing with an old flame and you make me feel like it was all *my* fault that I saw you."

Alec tugged at an earlobe.

"Perhaps," he said. "It was. Or is."

"I can't help it if I'm young!" Penny tried to keep a childish wail out of her voice and only partially succeeded. "You married me knowing that I was young! It's not my fault that I'm younger than you! Or that I love a man older than me!"

"Let's for God's sake not get hysterical about a matter of time in space," Alec said. "You're young and you're beautiful and intelligent and sexy and rich. That's nothing to cry over."

Penny bit her lip.

"I have just aged a little bit," she said. "What exactly in the hell *were* you doing with an old flame, and is that what you've been doing all these months when you go out at noon and don't get back until seven? Is that why you come home tired and don't talk to me and go to bed early? Are you having a—are you back again in Barbara Bayne's bed, which is why you don't sleep in mine?"

"Not in her *bed*," Alec said. "We got over that when you were in bobby sox. Perhaps only in her brain. Barbara's brain, if you want a bum gag."

"I don't want a bum gag!" Penny pounded her knee with a clenched fist. "I want to know what's gone wrong with us —and if it's another woman, why—and what the hell's wrong with me? What has that old bag got that I haven't got?"

"Here now," Alec said. "Let's not get all emotional. Barbara Bayne has the standard complement of female machinery, and, I should imagine, most of it obsolescent. Let's not go calling names and talking dirty."

"Talking dirty used to be fun when we did it in bed. Now we don't go to bed any more, and you don't like talking dirty with your clothes on. What is so wrong with me that you've gone back to this Barbara broad?"

Alec winced.

"Not Barbara broad, please. Barbara *friend. Old* friend."

"Old friend!" Penny's voice lit to rage. "You and this God-damned patronizing business about people who happened to get born earlier than other people! It's like you were working for a secret society or a closed corporation or something! You should have—"

Alec held up his hand.

"Don't say it. Everybody tells me. I should have married your mother. If I had married your mother every time somebody suggested—"

"You *should* have married my mother! She was good enough to sleep with once! And she's certainly a member of this precious age group of yours that knows all the secrets of the universe!"

"That'll be enough of that," Alec said coolly. "I shouldn't imagine that Dinah Lawrence bared all her secret sex life to her daughter. My sleeping with your mother is purely a matter of conjecture on your part."

Now Penny pounded both knees with both fists.

"Quit talking like a lawyer! I'm your wife, remember? I'm not a—a subject for dissection! I'm not a piece of furniture! I'm a grown woman—a grown woman you used to love!"

"A woman, yes." Alec drawled. "Much woman. But grown?" He arched the left eyebrow. "I doubt the qualifying adjective."

"What are you trying to *do* to me?" Penny's voice now was very tiny. "Pull off all my wings? Take me to pieces bit by bit? What's come over you, Alec?"

"Nothing's come over me except middle age and a possible desire to talk about something that doesn't involve the discussion of powder quotient of a recent snowfall or whether cigarettes really cause cancer or the latest bulletin from Doctor Spock. I occasionally find the newspapers interesting, and there's a hell of an author around named Charles Dickens. He wrote a thing called *Oliver!* by Lionel Bart. This was just after Rex Harrison wrote *My Fair Lady*, out of Shaw by way of Pygmalion."

"You are really a cruel bastard," Penny said. "Really. You love to twist the knife, don't you?"

"As Charles Lamb said to Mary Lamb, I seem to have heard this song before," Alec said. "Another martini?"

"Why not? Why not? What can I lose with another ounce of gin?"

"Very little, I should think," Alec said, rising. "I won't be more than 'arf a mo'. Gin is mother's milk to me. That's from the original movie involving Leslie Howard and Wendy Hiller—one dead and the other well-weathered. Did I ever tell you about Bill Gargan and Howard in 'Sadie Thompson'? An old party named Maugham wrote it as a short story called 'Miss Thompson,' which very few people remember. Pretty soon they'll make a musical of it called *Adorable Whore,* with the book by Gerold Frank."

"Oh, Alec, Alec! What are you doing? You know I love you!"

Alec lit a cigarette and coughed delicately. He looked interestedly at the cigarette's glowing tip.

"I wonder if these things really *do* cause cancer," he mused. "Probably not. It's probably caused by the milk of human kindness. To answer your question, of course I know you love me, else you wouldn't have swept me off my feet and into your bed and into the J.P.'s office with the ring. And to continue, I might as well say that we've got very little in common except bed and the memories of your mother. I seem to be well past both."

"You really seem intent on taking everything away from me, to—"

"To burn as the Vikings did when they slew the horse and dog and set fire to the whole ship," Alec finished. "This started out, I believe, as a probing into why I might be having an affair with, I quote, an old bag like Barbara Bayne?"

"I didn't mean to pry. You know I've never asked you for any account of your time—"

"But?" Alec's voice was very light. "There's always that big fat *but.*"

"But you can scarcely blame a woman for wondering why her husband quits coming to her bed, leaves the house regularly, spends all the afternoon away, and doesn't say so much as 'Mantell said' when he comes home to eat dinner and then go to bed with a book. You wouldn't call it exactly standard operational procedure!"

" '*Standing* operating procedure' is the correct Naval term," Alec drawled. "The truth of the matter is that I visit Barbara Bayne for mental stimulation, something I find very little of in this house. You have a beautiful body and a kind heart and, undoubtedly, a lovely soul, my dear, but to be quite frank, you bore me stiff. As your set would say, but very stiff, like."

Penny burst into a flood of tears.

"You're horrible, horrible! And you're cutting me to bits deliberately! Why? *Why?* I've tried the best I know how to be a good wife to you, to love you, to be considerate of your work, to—"

"I expect you've tried too hard," Alec said silkily. "You

walk too softly. You never come barging into the office with the problems of the grocery boy and the milkman. You *understand* me too well. You never obtrude your fair body on me when I'm having plot trouble. You're altogether too God-damned perfect to be borne and, as I said, if you missed it the first time, I'm bored to death. *And,*" he let his voice hang:

"Barbara Bayne, old bag that she might be, doesn't bore me to death. That's why I spend a lot of time with Barbara Bayne. I couldn't expect you to believe this, but I haven't laid a glove on her since you were in rompers. I suppose it's pointless to try to convince you of that unimportant, but very actual, truth."

Rage succeeded in drying Penny's tears, and she blew her nose with a huge snort.

"I don't give a good God damn if you've fucked her flat! I just want to know what she's got that I haven't got! I want to know what she can give that I can't offer! What in the hell is so very wrong with me—your 'pretty Penny,' you always called me! I'm still pretty, see?"

Penny ripped off her blouse and broke the fastenings of her brassière in a furious gesture. She stood up, breasts erect, legs spread.

"Are hers better? Is there anything more special between her legs?" She lifted her breasts with cupped hands. "Has she got an improvement on these? Or do you want me to take up perversions with the mailman so you can watch?"

"Well, well, Gypsy Rose Lee," Alec said, and clapped a slight sarcastic applause. "I suggest you reclothe yourself. You might just catch a nasty cold. I readily agree that Barbara's physical charms are definitely inferior. And I do not fancy your taking a perverse interest in the mailman. Possibly the Bureau of Internal Revenue chap, perhaps . . ."

He stood up, massaged his back, and said wearily:

"Let's stop all this nonsense. I made a mistake. I married a daughter. I don't want to be married to a daughter. As a matter of fact, I don't want to be married to anybody. I'm not good at it—I'm not even useful at it. If you doubt that you can check with your mother, with Amelia, with a lady you don't know in London, and even with Barbara Bayne. Let's pack it in, sweetie. Let's call it a day."

Penny buried her face in her hands. He made an involuntary move toward her, as rapidly checked himself.

"It's a nice flat," he said. "And it is, oddly enough, in your name. I expect I forgot to tell you. You're my only heir. They make easy divorces in Mexico. Find yourself somebody your own age to play with and forget you ever got hooked up with an old mess named Alexander Barr. That Daddy Long-legs bit was all right for Wallace Reid, but on me it don't look good.

"And Penny?"

She looked up, her fingers still stretching to her eyes.

"I'm really not as big a bastard as I sound. It's just that" —his voice caught—"it's just that I do love you except for one small fault which is very important at my age. We have nothing at all to talk about, and for a garrulous old man that is a fate much worse than the death which lurks in every banana peel."

"Alec, I— Then it's all finished, all done, no hope—"

He held up his hand, and his voice was gentle.

"No," he said. "Wrap it up. Find yourself a nice new young fellow and have some kids and try to have some fun. I mean, you really couldn't be expected to care about either The Black Crook or Primo Carnera, could you? I'll be off now, and I'll send over for the clothes. There's a ton of money in the bank."

He looked briefly around the new furniture in the new flat and shrugged. He shook his head in his chronic weary leonine fashion.

"Like the Indian gentleman said, 'always unpacking.' I guess it's the story of my life. Cheers, baby," he said, and went out the door.

134

It was nearly midnight when Alec left the flat, twoish when he arrived at the Jersey house. The Jersey house seemed more than a refuge, and Alec silently thanked God for it, and for Luke. As long as he, Alec Barr, was going to be a battle casualty, it was nice to have the correct station for it. Hospitals depressed him, as did most doctors and especially female nurses. Luke would make a good nurse. God bless Chief Yeoman Luca Germani.

He pulled up into his back yard and saw a white Cadillac convertible nosed close to the kitchen door. The house blazed with lights. Well, well, Alec Barr thought. How the word has spread. Tea and sympathy and very possibly a jar of calf's-foot jelly for the patient. Or is Luke having a ball? Watch that word, Barr.

He walked into the house and there, in the patio room, sipping a beer, was Barbara Bayne.

"Well, how *do* you do?" Alec bowed. "What brings you to our shores at this hour? And where's Luke?"

"Off to bed. With some pills. I already filled him in on your problem. Figured it might save you some additional pain."

"Kind of you." Alec's voice was light and mocking. "I trust he took our tragedy well?"

"I don't really like to see men cry," Barbara said shortly. "Especially middle-aged ex-petty officers. I really think he'd be glad to swap places with you."

"He's a good kid— Good man, Luke. I'm lucky to have him. At least he won't give me the royal *we* like the average nurse does. The first time Luke says 'and how is our patient this morning?' or 'why aren't we eating our nice soup?' I'll skull him."

"I love your little-boy's house, Alec. Luke gave me the conducted tour. You know I never saw it?"

"I guess you didn't. We were too busy at the Ritz, or kicking over ashcans. Well, it'll come in handy. It's quiet, and it's mine. I keep running out of apartments. You can make that a pink gin, please, long as you're bartending. At least I don't have to worry about my liver. By the time this evil black flower of mine climbs that high, there won't be anything left to salvage."

"Quit being so God-damned cheerful and Noël Cowardy," Barbara said. "I saw your eyes before you had a chance to change them for my benefit. Was it awfully bad with Penny?"

"Very bad with Penny. I was brilliant. You called me a ham once. You were right. I'd have made a marvelous actor. *The Scoundrel*, as played by Alexander Barr instead of Coward. Hecht and MacArthur would have been proud of me. Incidentally, just as a matter of idle curiosity, what the devil are you doing here, anyhow, in the middle of the night?"

Barbara handed him his drink. She was fetching, he

thought, in slacks and turtleneck, although she was a little broad in the beam. . . . But then I don't think these thoughts any more, do I, Barr? Pointless when it's all in your head.

"What the devil I'm doing here is a silly question. I knew that you wouldn't waste any time destroying Penny for her—and your—own good. I figured you'd be sick and sore and mostly lonely, and just might like the society of an old bag you didn't have to be brave in front of—didn't have to put up a front for. That's all. I'll leave if you like."

"No, for God's sake, don't. It's quite wonderful of you, as a matter of fact."

"I barged in unbidden because I figured you wouldn't have guts enough to ring me up and say you had the awfuls and would I come hold your hand. So I rang up Luke, and he beamed me in. I got your number from Mantell. When do you tell *him?*"

"Not until my backside really begins to drop off. And for the same reason I wouldn't saddle myself onto you, apart from the first urge to find somebody my age—whom I love—to weep on. Mantell sells copy. I don't want him selling sympathy. I don't want Barr's sad plight to get around the publishing circles. I got books to write which have nothing whatever to do with cancer of the prostate." He grinned suddenly, almost cheerfully. "You know—books with a lot of screwing in 'em. I want the fornications to sound smirkingly authentic."

Dawn was breaking as Barbara walked over to the broad window and looked across the lake. The sky was pinkening and the deer were drinking—half a dozen does and one heavily antlered buck.

"It's really lovely here," she said. "The deer have just come down. One wonderful buck."

"I know," Alec said. "He was almost a house pet as a little fellow. But then he grew up and sprouted horns and large ideas about girls, and now he doesn't come to the house any more. That's his harem with him. We don't shoot *any* deer here now. That's why he's managed to keep his horns."

Barbara turned around to face him. She was, against the rosy light, really quite beautiful still, Alec thought, when you figured they were both about the same age—two old bags together. You wouldn't take her for a day over thirty, in the right light, unless you got close enough to peer under the pancake.

"You know," she said calmly. "We're both a lot older, and I think more practiced in humility than we were those oh so many years ago. I was so terribly in love with you, Alec. We just had too much gunpowder for each other. I think we could make it work together now—with or without the ring and the book. I'd stay if you asked me."

Alec shook his head.

"No. Absolutely no. Not that I don't appreciate what you're offering—not that I don't want us *not* to keep on being friends. What we had long ago was sex and fights and arguments without pity. I can't sign on for pity without sex. And we wouldn't fight or argue any more, out of respect for my delicate condition." He tapped his side and chest. "In the sum we'd have just what I canceled out with Penny— a great big fat nothing."

"But you wouldn't have to be concerned about me—"

Alec held up his hand.

"Cut. I wouldn't, especially, be concerned about *you*. I'd be concerned about *me*. One of the croakers said he hoped I had some fragrant memories, because Barr the Buck was no longer standing at stud. And I have got some fragrant memories—lovely memories of my beautiful Barbara and my pretty Penny. I intend to keep them intact, because they're all I've got left of that part of me."

Barbara sighed.

"I just thought I'd give it a try," she said. "I was almost certain you'd react the way you did—ornery to the end, let nobody help you, old Basic Barr the Bastard Boy."

Alec grinned at her.

"Now, that sounds more like my girl. You were born for the bed, not the bed*side,* my good wench. The Florence Nightingale cap don't fit. Make us another piece of booze, please, while I go slip into something loose. These city clothes are confining to my cancer."

He came downstairs a few minutes later wearing baggy old corduroys, scuffed loafers, and a faded flannel shirt.

"This is uniform of the day from now on," he said. "I don't figure on going to town very much, except to see my quack. There's too much in that town to remind me of the days when I was more than half a man."

"Oh, my dear, I *am* sorry, so very sorry," she said, and

brushed the back of her hand across her eyes. "I swore I wouldn't do that. I won't do it again. Promise."

Alec walked to the window. He looked over the lake a long time before he spoke.

"The deer are gone now," he said. "Please, Barbara, do please try to understand me. There was too much of an age gap between Penny and me. But it was closing—intellectually at least—and if this thing hadn't happened I'd have played Pygmalion fairly happily and built myself a woman in my own image. But the one thing vital to that was keeping Galatea happy as a physical woman while I modeled her mind. And a gelded smelly old man isn't very likely to have an attentive audience from a bursting young bride. So Penny had to go—painfully or not—and one day she may remember that bastard Barr with kindness. You have to go for the same reason—I want you to remember that bastard Barr with kindness, and also a sharply recalled honest sweaty lust. Now I think we'd better begin the going."

He walked over, pulled Barbara to her feet, and kissed her long and deeply. Then he led her gently toward the door.

"That last kiss was from the old bastard, Barr," he said. "It was still accompanied by that old black magic feeling. I don't want ever to lose it. Never. *Go*," he said, and pushed her out of the door. "For God's sake, *go!*"

Alec Barr waited for the sound of the car's motor and the squish of the wheels on gravel before he threw himself down on the divan to weep as he had not wept since he was a child.

135

Barbara drove slowly in the morning light to New York. Certainly, she thought, the spurned Penny and the rejected Barbara Bayne shared the same leaky boat. Poor Alec Barr, left with nothing, nothing at all to stand between him and that God-damned typewriter.

"Both of us just one-night stands," she said harshly aloud.

"A roll in the clover and then when it's over, tell me, honey, just what is your name?"

He was right, of course, about the Penny part. There was no point in ruining the girl's young life. But I would have signed on, she thought. I've largely had it as a functional female, and a book and a bottle is about all I'll need to see me through. But again I appreciate his point. He wouldn't be seeing *me*—broad-beamed Barbara with the wrinkles, changing his waste bottle and giving him enemas. He'd be remembering beautiful, young, funny, smart-cracking Barbara Bayne —the Barbara Bayne of the Pump Room in Chicago, the can-kicking, lovemaking, Ritz-enjoying, martini-drinking, wild-swinging Barbara Bayne of bed and unbored. He's dead right; you cannot taunt a man's inadequacies with a constant reminder of what used to be. Candy was not very useful to diabetics, and it did little good to blow cigarette smoke at a man with cancer of the lungs.

"But he's *got* to have something, *somebody,* more than Luke," she said aloud to the morning wind. "Someone who loves him and who won't constantly remind him of the fact that he—by God, I think I've got it!"

Barbara Bayne had been easing along on the Turnpike. Now she tramped the accelerator. She was in a hurry to get back to her house, to bathe and change and breakfast and dig through a phone book and to make a call.

"You may be ruinously wrong, B. B.," Barbara said aloud, and dialed a number, after waiting for the decent hour of 11 A.M. "I don't imagine I'm wildly beloved in that particular house. However . . ."

She lit a cigarette while the phone buzzed, and then said:

"Mrs. Barr? I hope I didn't disturb you. This is Barbara Bayne. And please don't hang up. It's important, and nothing to do with me."

Words came coldly from the other end.

"I understand your personal feelings about me completely," Barbara said. "But I think even curiosity might justify your giving me an hour of your time, at my house or yours."

"What could we possibly have of mutual interest to justify an hour of my time?" The voice from the other end of the line dripped icicles.

"Just one thing, a very important thing. A man named Alexander Barr."

136

Barbara dressed very carefully. She used only the faintest hint of eye-shadow, a very light lipstick, and took no pains to mask her wrinkles with pancake. She put on a dark-blue, straight up-and-down silk suit, short white gloves, and a pair of pumps with less-than-needle toes and reasonably low heels. She chose a small patent-leather handbag, braced her shoulders, took a deep breath, and went out into the street to hail a cab.

Amelia met her at the door in street attire—a Balenciaga black, pearls, and hat. The hair had been carefully done, and so had the face. She did not extend a gloved hand. She was looking, Barbara thought, quite young and very well-tended. Barbara envied her the skin. It was still as clear and rosy as a girl's.

"Will you please come in," Amelia said coldly, with no question mark at the end of the invitation. "Pardon my dressing to go out. But I *do* have an early lunch date."

"You're very kind to see me," Barbara said. "Thank you."

"This way," Amelia said. "It's more comfortable than the living room. I use it for most of my business conversations."

She led the way to Alec Barr's old office. All traces of masculinity had been removed, with the exception of the bar, Barbara noted. Gone the leather, gone the leopard, even gone the *Encyclopaedia Britannica*. Alec's office had been remade, effectively, into a woman's sitting room. The typewriter was small, pale green to match the telephone, and the slipcovers and draperies were definitely chintzy.

"Please sit down," Amelia said coldly. "What did you have in mind to tell me about my former husband?"

Barbara took a deep breath. *Bitch,* she said to herself. I will *not* lose my temper. It's not what I'm here for, with my hat in my hand. I will speak my little piece and blow.

"I came to see you because I am very fond of your husband, even though we have seen little or nothing of each other for

619

a great many years," she said evenly. "Do you mind if I smoke?"

Amelia tapped a lacquered Chinese cigarette box with a gloved hand.

"There are cigarettes there," she said. "Yes? About my husband?"

"I think you should know," Barbara said, "that he has cancer. And I think you should know where he has cancer, and what having it means to him." She lit a cigarette.

Amelia got up and walked to the far end of the room. She ran a finger over a row of books, as if searching for dust, and then opened the door to the terrace. A breeze stirred the curtains. Then she walked back to where Barbara sat, and stood squarely in front of her. Her face was very white.

"This is quite a blow for Alec," she said. "And naturally, for me. It is a horrible thing to happen to anybody, but to a man like Alec—I think we might discuss it more sensibly over a drink. It's not very much too early. What would you like?"

"I think a simple Scotch on the rocks." Barbara said with a faint smile. "It's not the kind of conversation that needs too much extra effort on the part of the bartender."

Amelia smiled as faintly back and moved over to the swing-out bar Barbara remembered from her only visit.

"Tell me."

"Your husband has a very well-developed cancer of the prostate with a considerable spread through his lower body," Barbara said. "It is not apt to be immediately fatal. But certain drastic things are involved."

"Yes?" The question came through compressed lips. "And how would you know this if you haven't seen much of my husband for so many years? Since you had an affair with him?" The last came hurtfully. "Why would he confide in *you*?"

Barbara pressed a placating palm toward Amelia.

"Please. Until I tell you the facts, there's no point in digging up dry bones. Your husband came to me because, since your divorce, we have become very good *friends*."

"I suppose his new wife vastly approved of the friendship?" Amelia's voice was harshly bitter. She took another, now-angry sip from her gin. "One big happy family?"

"Please," Barbara said again. "This is useless if we do it this way. Alec has left his wife. Alec will have nothing to do with me. Alec only came to me when he found out from the doctors because—very probably—there was nobody else he felt he could come to. His present wife—Penny—doesn't even know he has cancer. He made a point of not telling her. He frankly doesn't want her to waste her life on a long-term but inevitably terminal case."

"Very thoughtful of him, I'm sure," Amelia said. "Although I'm sure she's quite young enough to bear up under the impact of the knowledge."

"I seem to be saying nothing but 'please,'" Barbara said. "But *please*. Alec Barr has a disease which has destroyed, and which will further destroy him, as a man. All that he was as a man is finished. All Alec has left of himself is his work."

"I'm sorry," Amelia said, and got up to refill her drink. When she came back to the bar she was composed, and her face had regained color. "I'm very sorry. But I really don't know a lot about these things. Please explain. I—I didn't really mean to be rude. I know it must have taken an effort for you to have come here—"

"Thank you." Barbara lit another cigarette. "It did take a lot of effort. So I might as well give it to you short, fast, and honest. Your husband has already lost his manhood. Even the luckiest combination of treatments would mean a successful removal of his prostate, which automatically renders him impotent. That luckiest combination means a steady taking of female hormones, which would render him physically impotent even if he weren't already psychically impotent from worrying about the disease. And—"

"And?" The whites showed over Amelia's pupils. "And?"

"Eventually he will have to be castrated, and certain holes bored in him to allow him his basic physical functions. It is not a very pretty way for a man like Alec Barr to end his life—going, as he says, to the bathroom in a bottle, like Ben Lea."

Amelia clapped the heels of her hands to her eyes. She shook her head, closed her eyes, and bit her lower lip.

"But this is horrible—terrible! For a man like Alec—"

"He's taking it very bravely," Barbara said. "Much too bravely. That's not going to last forever. He's going to need a lot of future help. And he won't take any help from me. And he won't impose on his *young* wife. He literally threw her out last night."

"Why? *Why?*" Amelia's voice sharpened again. "He came to *you* with his problem—with his tragedy—and he does have a wife! Why won't he take help from her, accept help from you?"

"Alec's not much of a taker," Barbara said. "In most respects, anyhow. He might steal your brain but he won't barter the body—his *or* yours. The simple answer here is that I had no brain or long physical association to give him. Forgive me, but the only thing Alec and I ever had was a sort of brushfire, a flash flood. It only lasted weeks—and do please believe me—had nothing really to do with you."

"I believe you, honestly," Amelia said. "These things happen. But this"—she hesitated over the word—"this new *wife*. This *Penny*."

"Mind if I fix myself another drink?" Barbara asked gently.

"Please do. But this—"

"This Penny was a traffic accident as well," Barbara said, turning back from the bar. "I should imagine Alec was having a sort of male menopause—you *did* divorce him at that time, and something else happened in Africa or England, and a lot of people got themselves dead in the interval—Alec was suffering from loneliness and uncertainty and that sad old male feeling. You know, the world is passing me by. In comes a sprightly miss, pays a pretty compliment, and the father complex merges with a late-blooming libido. He was seeking to retrieve his youth. Or something. But Penny wasn't any more important to Alexander Barr than I was. One was an *early* male menopause—that's when I figured—and the other was a proper, normal one."

Barbara sat down again and pointed a forefinger at Amelia Barr.

"He never had but one woman, really, only one wife. And that was you, Amelia Barr!" Her voice rose now to actress timbre. "For better for worse, for richer for poorer, in sickness and health, all that Biblical jazz, all he ever really had for a woman was you!"

Amelia shook her head again.

"I feel like I'm having a heavy bout of sinus," she said. "It's all coming a little too fast for me. Skull full of wool, with a tight band around it. I have to get down to some brass tacks."

"I know the expression," Barbara smiled. "I'm a Southern girl myself. What sort of brass tacks?"

Amelia looked bewildered, and in the bewilderment, younger.

"What in the name of God are you, Barbara Bayne, the woman who went off with my husband, doing here playing Little Mother Comforter to a woman you never knew, don't want to know, and who quite naturally hates your guts? Why are you making the pitch, excusing Alec Barr in terms of yourself and some bobby-soxer he took up with because, I guess, he couldn't make it with her mother?"

"Because I happen to love Alec Barr," Barbara said. "And he won't have me. And he won't have Penny, and he won't have Penny's mother. He hasn't got anybody to stand by him in just about the biggest time of need a real man will ever know."

"Then who in hell *will* he have? Who'll he find to stick by him in this hour of need? Certainly not that British bitch! Who'll he *have?*"

"*You,*" Barbara said. "He'll have *you.* If you're woman enough to make a compromise for the man who never really loved anybody else but you, nothing else counts no matter what the mistakes the drivers made on the highway."

"I can't go back to Alec out of pity!"

"You can go back to him because you spent the best part of a quarter of a century with him, because you're part of him, because you love him—and"—Barbara went back to the Method School—"because he needs *you* and you need *him.* And also," she abandoned the Method and dropped her voice to a conversational tone. "You're the only crap game in town for Alec Barr. You wouldn't have stuck with him that long if you hadn't loved him. He has always come back to you for comfort. You're the only person he knows today from whom he'll accept a love without too much accent on pity. Look, girl," Barbara said softly, "a guy who hasn't got his balls any more doesn't spend the rest of his life with an old short-term lay or a new short-time bride. He spends it, as someone like the Duke of Windsor once said, with the woman he loves. And that's *you.*"

"You sound like some sort of syndicated agony columnist!" Amelia was angry again. "Who the hell are you to come telling me what to do with the rest of *my* life? I have a life too! How do you know I'm not in love? How do you know that I don't want to marry again—marry a complete man? How do you imagine that I'd be overjoyed to spend my last best years emptying bedpans and giving enemas?"

Barbara shrugged. She got up and dusted a speck of ash from her skirt.

"Thank you for letting me come here to speak my piece. I was presumptuous only in assuming that you might still care for the basic man you lived with most of your life."

"Of course I care, but—"

"Good-by," Barbara said. "Don't bother seeing me to the elevator."

137

Amelia Barr had fallen into two or three casual amorous adventures since she divorced Alec Barr. This was what she might have called "proof of the pudding"—*I am free and I can sample.* The field is there, and I am still reasonably young, reasonably pretty, reasonably sexy. What a very lousy word, *reasonably*.

The affairs were unsatisfactory. Sex didn't seem to mean that much, and Amelia didn't care for the idea of being taken surface-lightly. And face it, baby, she said to herself, if you get taken at all that is how you get taken—lightly. At *your* age. There's an awful lot of that eager young plump stuff around.

The first tragedy dwelt in the fact that there were a lot of young men who liked home comforts—and the cosy thought of a greasy bankroll to oil the home comforts—and a lot of older men around who fought awry, unwilling to make another major mistake after the initial one or two or three or four.

And the other tragedy was that Amelia Barr was not about to take on a young man to wean into inevitable infidelity—not on her time and her money—and certainly *not* willing to be fumbled by the much older gentlemen who were largely incompetent in the one department that really mattered to a grass widow who had not yet been cured of old love or found a winter replacement.

Also importantly portion to it was finance. Amelia Barr was very comfortably off, especially now, since Alec's most recent success. That cynical good-by gesture came in impeccably on the first of every month. As she waxed apace, Amelia tended to think more and more of creature indulgence. Money was real comfortable when a girl was no longer in the biddable business. A third of Alec's income, plus the ransom in the bank and in the bonds, was more than enough. She didn't really *have* to have her last mink reglazed. And she could always squirrel up enough for the occasional trip abroad.

The other portion was you got lazy. It wasn't worth the effort to give the big parties. It wasn't worth the effort to see a lot of people for lunch when the daily maid could fix you a cheese sandwich. Television owned unsuspected virtues. If you had insomnia there was always the *Late Late Show*. Most of her best girl friends were recovering from late late marriages as well, and Amelia wasn't shopping any part of adapting herself to a fresh flock of bad masculine habits.

It was a peaceful life—largely unirritated by *libido*—and she was always comforted by the presence of Francis Hopkins. Francis was having his menopause, too; once, in a fit of alcoholic frankness, he had confessed that he was going to give up boys for books. Francis regularly came around with the freshest gossip. Francis could still be depended on for the theater and the dinner and the fashion showings. Francis was perfect if you didn't want to fight off the duty-bound sixty-year fumblers, or the overeager young swains who were looking for a grubstake. Francis was always there when you needed him. And when you didn't need him you merely sent him away.

Tranquility had deeply penetrated Amelia. And now, *now,* all of a sudden now, this Barbara Bayne bitch had invaded that tranquility.

It was troublous to think again. There was one favorable thing to be said of Alec Barr; if you lived with him, at least you *thought*. Until it had all gone total sour there were jokes and confidences and plots and plans. You could *confide,* in the older days, without fear of having it hurled back at you —until something spoiled it. And I'm afraid, Amelia thought, that I know who spoiled it. No man was ever possessible, and I tried with Alec. You can't really keep a tiger tamed, if he's the kind of tiger you'd want to tame in the first place.

Amelia Barr stripped off her gloves and got out of her Balenciaga and kicked off her shoes and shrugged out of her bra and wiggled out of her girdle. She had not, of course, really been going out for lunch when Barbara Bayne came to call. All the Manhattan lady dress-up was the kind of surface crap that women indulged in when they came face to face with rival women. The entire conversation possibly would have gone better in slacks. Amelia was tired of crap—what a lovely, expressive word, *crap*.

She was also weary of the battle between men and women, women and women, men and men. Her breasts had begun to sag. Her backside had certainly begun to spread and would spread further—unless she reprised one of those horrors like the Rancho Nuyu and let people pound the meat off her. Diets were a bore, no matter how fashionable. They were really only something to talk about when you were desecrating the diet at lunch.

Most everything these days was a bore for the lonely girl who was ten pounds over the bikini mark and tending steadily toward twenty. You didn't even have the curse to worry about any more. Francis Hopkins was a bore. Most of her female friends also were bores.

What Amelia Barr wanted at this time, she thought as she added tonic to a fresh gin, was to take it easy—to take it very slow and cool with somebody she liked and could talk to and didn't have to spar with and could trust—

Out of her sight?

Amelia Barr gasped.

And love? Love without jealousy, love without pain, love without real physical possession, love without substituting a faggot or a girl martini lunch for entertainment? Just love and take off the shoes and sit before the fire *with* and just love without the urgency for sex if there was a really good picture at the neighborhood movie or something special on the TV? Just to grow older and nonguiltily fatter and sloppily more comfortable, and not have to go to the Rancho Nuyu and the hairdressers three times a week and always watch the diet—and, just maybe, to read with and talk with without the brand of sexual jealousy always burning foremost in her head?

Just plain *love,* and maybe a lot of companionship, maybe just a little bit of *us* instead of the old *you* and *me?* Maybe a little more *give* and a little less *take?*

This man is no man, but two women wanted him, no man or not. He refused them both. He refused the offer of one and he rejected the loyalty of the other. But I—*I*—can get him back. Only *I* can get him back. Because I always owned him even when he left.

"Call it habit," Amelia Barr said. "Or call it love. But this is one I think I can control."

138

Everybody, Amelia Barr thought, has to have somebody to turn to. Evidently Alec chose Barbara Bayne. Well by God I need some counsel as well, and whom have I got to turn to? Don't answer, girl, she said to herself. Who else? She picked up the phone and dialed that old—my God, *how* old familiar number.

". . . And that's the whole picture, dear heart," she said. "That's the whole tragic picture. Please come over and tell me what to do."

Francis crossed his right foot under his left instep. He had just come back from Jamaica; the tan looked very well under the white crew cut. Francis did hold together very well. He was watching his drinks and his diet, because, as he frequently said, he *hated* people who let themselves go to *pieces*. It was comparable, in a way, to stupid molestations in subway stations. You didn't really want to wind up on a police blotter, one way or the other, just because you got carried away. A men's-room scene made a very untidy site for an epitaph.

"I just say it's deplorable," he said. "*Such* a vibrant man. And precisely what *is* happening to that poor child who married him at pistol point?"

"Just this once, please, just this *once*," Amelia said. "Stop being chic. I want some help, some real honest help."

Francis tapped his teeth with two fingers. He arched hi
eyebrows. He kicked his foot.

"I'd really have to know what sort of help you wantee
before I volunteered any," he said. "What about this—thi
Penny person?"

"I gather Alec just sort of fired her, according to hi
old playmate. Didn't want to saddle the poor young thing
with an old and useless male responsibility."

"But this Barbara babe wants you to climb back into the
act? Suggests that *you* take over this old and useless re
sponsibility?"

"So she said. Like it was *my* responsibility because of aule
lang syne."

Francis watched his swinging foot with fascination. Up and
down, up and down, like a metronome.

Presently he said:

"I was thinking that what goes up must come down. Ev
erything in life is a waiting game. *Women*—all they do i
wait. They wait for the first curse so that boys aren't really
nuisances any more. They wait for serious courting and ther
they wait for marriage and they sweat out the curse if they're
playing on the side, and then they herald its absence i
they're married and pregnant. Then they wait for Papa to
come home from work. Then they wait for the dreadec
menopause to relieve them from that ancient anxiety of wait
ing for the curse, or waiting for the baby—or just from
waiting for Papa to come home—mostly smelling too swee
from some other babe's perfume. Am I right or wrong?"

Francis got up and paced the room for a moment. Ther
he came over and rested his elbows on the shining Steinway
looking over his shoulder at Amelia Barr.

"I do love you, Amelia, in my peculiar fashion. There i
no point in my amplifying what you already know. I'm a
homosexual by inclination as well as persuasion, but I an
not utterly incapable of loving a woman. And I make strong
a point here: You love me, too. And do you know precisely
why you love me?"

"Just—just because we get on together and keep each othe
company and laugh and travel and go to the theater and
have fun when we're lonesome and—"

"*And?*"

"We're both talking straight. And because you don't con

stitute a threat, a hazard, a possible heartbreak because
you're—"

"*Fag* is the accepted word. Fag. Eunuched for normal
women from my first youth. There is no such thing as what
the psychiatrists call 'penis envy' between you and me. That
right? We're just two jolly girls together?"

Amelia got up and put her arm around Francis' shoulder.
She kissed him softly on the cheek.

"It's a harsh way of putting it," she said. "But you *are*
my best friend, male or female. And that you know."

"All right then," Francis said. "A few other things we
have to face, pussycat. One is that you ain't so young no
more."

"I am not *that* old." She spread her hands, smoothed the
dress over her hips. "I'm not exactly a crone."

"You're not exactly a debutante, either." Francis made the
next words cruel. "How many men have sincerely asked you
to marry them lately—? And I don't mean *boys*. And I don't
mean half-fags looking for a meal ticket. How many men
have merely pushed you into bed—expecting you to be grass-
widow grateful—without even a slight suggestion of a lot
of nice sunny tomorrows?"

"There's no point in answering that kind of question. You
know it or you wouldn't have asked it. Grass widows are a
nickel a million. The man is doing *you* the favor. You go to
dinner, you come home, you get laid. Or you just don't go
to dinner. Not any more. Not with that man. *Boys?* You
can see the dollar signs in their eyes—the dollar signs of
my money."

Francis fell onto the circular divan and picked up his glass.

"Come here and sit by me," he said. "*Tell me.* How much
fun do you really have out of these short-term dinner-date
excursions? How many men have you met lately that you'd
really like to live with?"

Amelia shook her head.

"None. It's a relief not to be alone, that's all. No shooting
stars, no thunderstorms, no ceilings falling down. To the second question? I haven't met anybody lately that I'd want
at all."

"This is all out of character for me," Francis said, and put
a hand firmly on her knee. "I'm supposed to be a male bitch
—*I* told you to divorce him, *I* listened to all your little
moans and groans—but for once I'm not going to be a bitch,

male or female. You know that there's really no such thing as a happy ending?"

Amelia said, "Life doesn't seem to work out for the long pan shot into the sunset."

"Okay. But there is such a thing as compromise. I've been doing it—and nearly everybody like me—all my life. You know it's not much fun being a pansy, even if you go the whole way and use lipstick and start dressing the part. I know exactly what you and your girl friends and their husbands think of me, and people like me. 'Dear Francis. *So* safe. *So* nice to have a house faggot to take you to tea.'" Francis made his voice mince hurtingly.

"I know that there never was a bit of trade that didn't take me for my dough or my booze or my house-room. If they're male enough to make *me* want *them* they'll be out cheating with some waitress on *my* money, or having the women in the house to drink *my* whiskey. I know all this about me," Francis said.

"You don't have to do this to yourself," Amelia said. "I really do love you as a friend, Francis."

"Balls," Francis said. "Pardon the expression in any context. You like me, *sure*—as a convenience. But I'm very little better than a public comfort station for you and all the women like you—you disenchanted wives with bored and certainly straying husbands. But I'm not of a great deal more importance in your life than a menopause."

"You poor, poor man," Amelia said. "And all your life you've lived with this?"

"Basically, yes," Francis' voice was coldly bitter. "Since I first found out I liked wearing my mother's hats. Being a girl in trousers is not really fun, and being beaten up by strangers you pick up in parks is even less fun. Being betrayed by people you really love—and I'm referring to the few important men in my life—is even less fun than being beaten up by strangers. But what is the least fun of all is knowing that you're being used as a public toilet by *both* sexes. All your kind of people want is my *time*." Francis spat. "And all the other kind of people want is my *money*. The only difference is that at least I *give* my body to the other people, as well as my money. To you I merely lend my body as the extra man to fill in for dinner at the Hazeltines when your husband walks out on you for a broad!"

"I think we could both use another drink, dear," Amelia

said, and dropped her hand lightly on Francis' head.

"You'll never know just how bloody bad it is," Francis said, when she returned with the drinks. "Because you're a real woman—not a—not a cheap substitute for a woman, not a pasteboard imitation man—like me. You'll never know what it's like to have a man's natural equipment below the belt when all you really want to worry about is why you're late with the menstrual period. You don't know—you *can't* know —what it's really like to be held in contempt by both sexes, to belong to nobody, to get old and dried and think of *yourself* as nothing more than an unwanted old auntie who isn't sharp enough to be a convenience to normal women and isn't pretty enough to hustle the male trade! Not even in make-believe! Self-deception works only if you're still attractive enough to pick up a body in a Third Avenue bar, take it home, and delude yourself into thinking that this is *it,* this is *true,* this is *real,* before the new love beats you up and runs off with your money!"

"You're in quite a state," Amelia said sharply. *"Stop* it. It doesn't bear on what I rang you for, anyhow."

"The hell it doesn't bear on what you called me for anyhow! I've been castrated all my life, and with nobody to give me any aid or comfort! You've got an Alec Barr who's only just losing his balls, but he has his memories! Women's smiles, and friendly female pats, and tiny female gestures of love, and honest female twistings and sweatings and loud cries in bed, and all of the stinking triumph that goes with subduing a woman, of taking, holding, of *destroying,* a woman in the only place in the world, doing the only thing in the world, to the only person in the world—and that is taking a woman who loves you to bed!"

"Jesus," Amelia said. "I am really truly sorry. And to think *I* rang *you* up to talk about my problems."

"Excuse the faggified outburst," Francis said. "But I'm so old and finished and really so *done,* and I've got no backlog of any kind of love to put in the fireplace to warm my creaking bones."

He stabbed at her with a finger.

"But *you!* You've got twenty-five years of backlog! You've got a *man!* So all right, he can't do the same things he used to do! But they've dried you up, too, my girl, and that old ovarian process doesn't operate for you any more! Anything you do in bed from now on is an exaggerated remembrance

of things past. But you've still got life, and I think you still
have love, and I think you still have a man who needs you
for the rest of his life and his love! So he has trouble downstairs—many a young mother diapered a baby she adored."

Francis glided his voice into his old feline, slinking drawl.
"If he can't screw *you,* he can't screw anybody else. He won't
be catting around, scouting for new trade. He'll be as happy
at home as a man can be who hasn't got his basic implements any more. And *you,* puss, you will be entirely
secure, and you certainly won't open any old wounds, and
you certainly won't bring up any old hurts and revive any
nasty old bruises from the misty old past, for just *one*
old tired reason. One reason only." Francis paused.

"And," Amelia said, "after all this tired old rhetoric, what
reason?"

Francis' voice was deadly cold, his eyes half-closed. He
leaned back in his chair and gently bounced his foot, one-
two, up-down, two-three, down-up.

"Because you've got your man exactly where you, and all
the other ones like you, precisely where you want him!
Eyeless in Gaza! Hair shorn like Samson! Ball-less in your
own sterile Utopia! You've got him where you wanted him
when you bought him—castrated, and as a result of being
castrated, safe! Daddy will surely come home on time for
dinner. Daddy will surely not be casting goo-goo eyes at the
blonde at the party. Daddy will surely work hard and surely
make money and surely not annoy Mommie with any rude
attentions. Daddy will be exactly what Mommie ordered!
The sailor who does not go to sea, the hunter who does not
hunt, the reporter who does not go off to report. And Mommie will be deliriously happy because she will be in complete control. Daddy will surely be Mommie's baby again!"

Francis stopped and sighed.

"I'm very sorry," he said. "But you might as well face the
fact that you've achieved female perfection. You've cut your
boy off at the knees, as his mother cut her boy off at the
knees, as his grandmother made the old man smoke on the
porch—as all you God-damned women have been emascu-
lating your men since the whole dreary business started. A
woman—*my* mother—made me into a homosexual. You
made Alec Barr into a fugitive. Okay. You've got your vengeance intact. Except in this case a surgeon will remove Alec
Barr's testicles, as other doctors have already removed his

roving thoughts about the female body beautiful. You've got nothing to fear from anybody—Barbara a lunch-time chumbuddy, Penny off and away—you've got Alec Barr all to yourself. And I hope you like it. At least his presence in the lodge, for talk and whisky, will give me a little more private time to be miserable in. I can use a summer replacement!"

Francis got up.

"I love you, and I want to see you, and I also want to see Alec. You're nearly the only family I've got. We're sexless together, and from this point on we're all equal—one way or the other—Samsons without the hair. And we don't necessarily have to pull all the pillars down."

He kissed Amelia lightly.

"For Christ's sake," he said. "Get on the phone and tell the poor sad bastard to come home! You're all he's got left in the world that his pride'll let him accept!"

Francis headed toward the door, and turned.

"None of this newfound-nobility nonsense makes me unavailable for lunch," he said. "Or even a little piece of Scottish wine when the boss is buried in a book."

Amelia heard the elevator open and shut. She wept only briefly, but on this occasion she was weeping neither from rage nor for herself nor for Alec Barr.

139

Alec Barr looked at his old chief yeoman. He saw a lean, silver-haired Italian of his own age—a self-chosen bachelor —almost an ascetic apart from Saturday night. Luke had long ago adopted the country dress—mackinaw for winter, corduroys and flannels for the off season, and shorts and T shirt for summer.

I sure had him a hell of a long time, Alec thought. *Without thinking of him. Damned near as long as he had me.*

"Chief," he said. "I'm going to give you a real hard time."

"How you mean, Commander? I fouled the signals again?"

"You fouled the signals again. You remember an old naval term called *knock off?*"

Luke grinned. He walked over to Alec in the patio room and stood in front of the fireplace with his hands caught behind him in the at-ease pose, legs spraddled but the body at attention.

"I heard enough knock-offs in my time. What do I knock off now?"

"You want to go on a safari to Africa this year?"

"A safari to Africa? Boss, I'd give a ball——" Luke stopped, shocked. "I'm sorry. I didn't really mean it that way. Just a way you get talking——"

Alec nodded his head up-and-down.

"That's what I mean about knock off. You can knock off this supersensitivity about my tragic condition. You can for Christ's sake quit catfooting around the premises like you're afraid I'm fragile. You can quit minding your language. I am not repeat *NOT* a piece of delicate china. Now sit down and listen to me."

"Yes*sir*," Luke said. "But I could fix us both a drink first?"

"Allowed," Alec said. "But look." He was talking to Luke's back as Luke approached the bar.

"Point *one*," Alec said, "is that I have cancer. Point *two* is that I am through with women, as of now and in all the future, for every practical purpose. Point *three* is that one of these days I'm going to have my balls chopped off. Point *four* is that I'm going to have to wear a lot of apparatuses to let me get rid of my sordid wastes and they're going to have to drill portholes in me for this rather distressing necessity. I am going to have to have daily enemas. And point *five* is that I am going to get meaner all the time. But point *six* is that, mean as I am, I'm very possibly going to outlive you."

"I receive the message loud and clear," Luke said. "So?"

"So you're fired. New duty. Thirty days' transportation time and of course per diem. So long, Chief. It's been nice knowing you. Cut your own orders. You can include your retirement pay. It'll go on monthly at the regular rate. That's all." He flipped a casual salute.

Alec got up and walked into the yard. Luke followed him.

"You're right about the hard time, Commander," he said. "But I can't believe it. Why? I got no home but here. I got no job but you."

Alec turned to him, and his face was furious.

"By God, this is what you get for treating enlisted men like equals! Can't you see, you stupid son-of-a-bitch, that

I'm transferring you off a sad ship? You want to be a God-damned nurse to a guy with no balls and a lot of sad memories and stinking disposition? You want to get barked at and screamed at when what you've done isn't *your* fault, but only because I hate the idea of morning enemas?"

"Yes, Commander," Luke said simply and with dignity. "That's exactly what I want. I ain't leaving. I'm a plank-owner in this ship."

Tears streamed down Alec Barr's face.

"God damn you! God damn all of you! You and Barbara and everybody else! You want to work for a man who cries —a man who never cried in his life before?"

"Quit giving yourself a hard time, Commander," Luke said. "I don't know if Miss Barbara told you, but I can cry too. Except not right now. Somebody's got to be Chief of the Boat, if the commanding officer is going to burst into tears every time he thinks that he's run out of liberties. I had the clap a couple of times. After a while you didn't miss the women."

"Oh, God," Alec said, and shrugged. "So you're signing on for a new hitch?"

"I ain't planning to retire," Luke said. "I ain't got enough seniority. Also I like the duty."

"Well," Alec said. "You named your own poison. But if you think Genial John was a problem—"

"After Genial John *and* Admiral King there ain't no such thing as a problem," Luke said. "You been neglecting your drink. Is this a dry ship or not?"

"Not, definitely *not*," Alec said. "And say, Chief?"

"What say, Commander?"

"I wasn't kidding about the safari. One of the few things I can do now is hunt. Maybe we'll go later this year after I get fitted out for my traveling kit and the sutures absorb. You can shoot all the elephants and I'll watch from a safe distance. That's if you don't mind being my enema-bearer."

Luke smiled broadly now.

"Commander," he said, "I been taking a lot of crap from the brass all my life. A new variety won't be nothing very un-usual."

"I'm taking you seriously that you've signed on for the cruise," Alec said later. "We got some new articles. I'm obsolescent, if not actually obsolete. But no change, no change. No tiptoeing around the deck. No change in ordinary nomenclature—no revision of standing operating procedure. Okay? Or you're fired once again, and I was never more serious in my life."

"Aye aye. I got it. Understood and will do. But just *one* thing, Commander?"

"Shoot."

"Just kind of don't be too brave when it hurts too much. You can be brave as you want to when it hurts where it's supposed to hurt. But don't be too brave in the head. We brought a lot of nuts back from the islands who made a mistake of being too brave in the head. The head is where you can be a real coward—and," Luke grinned, "if there's nobody here but the Chief of the Boat to see it, nobody'll ever know it. You want to yell, *yell*. I'll hear you and burn the files."

Alec suddenly felt enormously better.

"We got quite a lot of work to do," he said. "We might as well start. Is there anything else on your mind before we start?"

"Long as we're leveling, Boss, I feel kind of guilty about Miss Penny. I was a little bit responsible for that—playing amateur Cupid, I guess. Where do we stand with Miss Penny now, just so I'll know? This is going to be a fairly tight operation."

"We stand now with Miss Penny exactly this way: She does not know why I raised a row and turned it into a direct order to leave me. Pray God she won't realize it until she's found herself a good new man and most of the damage I've done has been fixed up with some sort of collision-mat. I had to change her orders. Satisfactory?"

"Roger Dodger, over and out. And you were trying to do the same thing with me, Boss?"

"I suppose. But with you I had a choice, because you're such an old and ugly Wop that nobody else'd want you anyhow. With Penny there wasn't any choice."

"Boss, I wish—" Luke's face hurt.

"Skip it. I'm still a man in my *head*—and, I hope, my heart. Never fret about *that*, Buster. It's just that"—Alec smiled gently—"it's just that the sight of beautiful women is slightly disturbing to the other part of me that ain't there no more. We shall take up male companionship and possibly poker until my psychic wounds heal."

"The way we're headed," Luke said, "with any sort of luck, we can make the battleship popular again."

"I suspect you're developing a sense of humor," Alec said. "And I also suspect you'll need it if you hang out with me. Tomorrow we turn to on the new book."

"Aye, aye," Luke said. "Chow will be down as soon as I can defrost it."

140

Alec was dictating a rough outline of Book Two to Luke when the phone rang. Dictating an outline of Book Two to Luke seemed like a good way to pass the time before he started his program of female hormones. Alec had never dictated an outline of a book to Luke before. But it was one way of keeping someone in the room. And it, at least, released his thoughts.

"I think you got a real gasser in this second shot, Commander," Luke said. "That Mombasa must of been something fifty years ago. Those first settlers didn't seem to do much but drink and—"

"Go ahead and answer, Luke."

"Aye aye, Commander," Luke said, and picked up the phone.

"It's Missus Barr," he said.

"I don't want to talk to her," Alec said.

"It's not *that* Missus Barr—not Miss Penny. It's Miss Amelia. The old Missus Barr."

"Oh, Christ, what new catastrophe that we don't need? Okay, I'll talk to her. You can start transcribing the notes."

"I dig it, Boss. I'll fade."

Alec went deliberately to the bar and mixed a Scotch and water. He searched around for a packet of cigarettes and then went to the phone.

"Hello, Amelia," he said. "How are you? Is anything wrong?"

"No," the voice said. "Not with *me*. But I'd like to see *you*

—like to talk to you—like to talk to you about a lot of things."

"Anything in particular?"

"Yes. *Us.*"

"I got it. You know the news, then?"

"I know the news. And, oh, Alec—"

"I detest emotion over the telephone," Alec Barr said. "You want to talk? Do you want to come out here, or shall I come—home?"

"Would you—please? Come home?"

"I suppose so. No trouble. *Yes.* I'll come home. Thank you for calling."

He racked the receiver and yelled for Luke.

"I'm going into town for a day or so—business. Got to see the sawbones anyhow. Look after the shop, Luke. We got some books to do, and you might as well spread out all that research to a point where the papers are at least some sort of chronological. Okay?"

"Aye aye. Commander?"

"Yes?"

"Miss Amelia doing all right? No big trouble there?"

"No trouble there, Luke. Run us a taut ship."

"I'm glad, Commander," Luke said. "Anything I can do, just hit the General Quarters horn."

"You're a good lad," Alec said. "Some day you might just make Chief Warrant. Be seeing you."

Alec went upstairs to dress for the city. The old hat with the bird dung on the bill was unaccountably hanging in his closet. From ancient habit he tried it on for size, then slung it onto the bed.

"I would have made a magnificent bird commander," he said aloud. "Given the opportunity. I wonder if she still reads lying flat on her stomach?"

Luke yelled up the stairs.

"It's Mister Mantell," he said. "Business."

"I'll take it on the extension," Alec said. He inserted gold cufflinks into a city-going shirt and picked up the phone.

"Yes, Marc? I was just leaving."

"Two things, Alec. *One,* Otto Erlinger wants to do a play off the back of *Dark Dawning. Two,* distress signals from the South."

"Mother or Father? Which one is loose now? And how much does it cost?"

"Mother. And it'll cost plenty."

"So long as I am coming into town," Alec said, "I'll talk to you tomorrow. Maybe a nice drunk lunch? You pay."

"Fine. How're you keeping? Apart, I mean?"

"Never better," said Alec Barr. "Great. First class. Beautiful. Marvelous. The play idea sounds wonderful. Good-by until tomorrow."

Alec cradled the phone and shook his head. The situation seemed completely normal. First he'd see Marc, then go home. It would be nice to have Francis dropping in for drinks again. Perhaps they could all go have dinner at the Hazeltines.

About the Author

Robert Ruark was born in Wilmington, North Carolina, in 1915, and spent much of his early youth in a nearby fishing village with his grandfather, a retired sea captain. At fifteen he entered the University of North Carolina. Enough of his journalism course there rubbed off to get him a job on a small-town weekly, as editor, reporter, advertising manager, and subscription seller at ten dollars a week. Subsequently and briefly, he worked as an accountant for the WPA, as a seaman, an office boy, a copy boy, and a sports writer.

A commissioned officer in World War II, he began writing and selling articles about his wartime experiences to various national magazines, and although wounded, he returned to duty as press censor after he recovered. When the Japanese surrendered, he was hired by Scripps Howard as a reporter.

His rise was meteoric. Travel and writing filled the postwar years in which he became one of the best-known journalists and syndicated columnists in the nation. His first book, *Grenadine Etching*, appeared in 1947. It was after many trips to Africa that he wrote two tremendously successful novels with African settings, *Something of Value* and *Uhuru*, which attracted the admiration of millions of readers. In recent years Mr. Ruark lived abroad, dividing his time among Africa, Spain, and London. He was taken ill in Spain and flown to London where he died two days later on July 1, 1965, at the age of forty-nine.